Praise for the Shadow Falls series

"The Shadow Falls series . . . has everything I wish for in a YA paranormal series. A thrilling tale that moves with a great pace, where layers of secrets are revealed in a way that we are never bored. So if you didn't start this series yet, I can only encourage you to do so."

—*Bewitched Bookworms*

"There are so many books in the young adult paranormal genre these days that it's hard to choose a good one. I was so very glad to discover *Born at Midnight*. If you like P. C. and Kristin Cast or Alyson Noël, I am sure you will enjoy *Born at Midnight*!"

—*Night Owl Reviews*

"Great for fans of Vampire Academy. This book has it all, and readers won't want to put it down. Hunter packs on the twists, and then leaves you hanging with an amazing hook ending, just waiting for more."

—*RT Book Reviews*

"With intricate plotting and characters so vivid you'd swear they are real, *Born at Midnight* is an addictive treat. Funny, poignant, romantic, and downright scary in places, it hits all the right notes. Highly recommended."

—*Houston Lifestyles & Homes*

"I laughed and cried so much while reading this . . . I *loved* this book. I read it every chance I could get because I didn't want to put it down. The characters were well developed and I felt like I knew them from the beginning. The story line and mystery that went

along with it kept me glued to my couch not wanting to do anything else but find out what the heck was going on."

—*Urban Fantasy Investigations Blog*

"This has everything a YA reader would want. . . . I read it over a week ago and I am still thinking about it. I can't get it out of my head. I can't wait to read more. This series is going to be a hit!"

—*Awesome Sauce Book Club*

"The newest in the super-popular teen paranormal genre, this book is one of the best. Kylie is funny and vulnerable, struggling to deal with her real-world life and her life in a fantastical world she's not sure she wants to be a part of. Peppered throughout with humor and teen angst, *Born at Midnight* is a laugh-out-loud page-turner. This one is going on the keeper shelf next to my Armstrong and Meyer collections!"

—*Fresh Fiction*

"Seriously loved this book! This is definitely a series you will want to watch out for. C. C. Hunter has created a world of hot paranormals that I didn't want to leave."

—*Looksie Lovitz Book Blog*

"*Awake at Dawn* was an enjoyable read with a refreshing cast of teenagers with a unique take on the paranormal. . . . The ending took me totally by surprise and I am anxious to see what the next book holds!"

—*Night Owl Teen Reviews*

"Fans of the Twilight series will love this series. I cannot wait to see how this all plays out in book three."

—*Fallen Angel Reviews*

Shadow Falls:
The Next Chapter

Taken at Dusk

and

Whispers at Moonrise

c. c. hunter

 ST. MARTIN'S GRIFFIN ☙ NEW YORK

SHADOW FALLS: THE NEXT CHAPTER. TAKEN AT DUSK Copyright © 2012 by C. C. Hunter. WHISPERS AT MOONRISE Copyright © 2012 by C. C. Hunter. All rights reserved. Printed in the United States of America. For information, address St. Martin's Press, 175 Fifth Avenue, New York, N.Y. 10010.

www.stmartins.com

ISBN 978-1-250-06695-4 (trade paperback)

St. Martin's Griffin books may be purchased for educational, business, or promotional use. For information on bulk purchases, please contact Macmillan Corporate and Premium Sales Department at 1-800-221-7945, extension 5442, or write specialmarkets@macmillan.com.

First Edition: October 2014

Taken at Dusk

There's always a person in your life who you know helped make you who you are. A person who, without them, you wouldn't have taken the same journey. A person who didn't just make a difference, they were the springboard for all you've achieved. Thank you hubby, Steve Craig, for all you have done to help me become who I am. Thank you for the love, for the years, and for the endless laughter you share with me. We make a hell of a team, don't you think?

Acknowledgments

To my agent, whose support and guidance is just what this writer needs. To Rose Hilliard, an angel of an editor. To Faye Hughes, my first reader, who isn't afraid of my scary first drafts. Thanks for the help, but mostly thanks for the friendship. To Susan Muller, Teri Thackston, and Suzan Harden: thank y'all for the support, the friendship, the critiques, and a heck of a lot of laughter. You will never know how much you mean to me. To Jody Payne, a woman whose courage and strength inspires me, whose writing support and friendship is invaluable.

To Rosa Brand, aka R. M. Brand, whose brilliance as a graphic artist stuns me. Thanks for your support, for your fabulous videos, and for the newfound friendship. Thanks to Kathleen Adey for the editing and support with publicity; you make meeting my deadlines an easier task.

Chapter One

They were here. Really here.

Kylie Galen stepped out of the crowded dining hall into the bright sunlight. She looked over at the Shadow Falls office. Gone was the chatter of the other campers. Birds chirped in the distance and a rush of wind rustled the trees. Mostly she heard the sound of her own heart thudding in her chest.

Thump. Thump. Thump.

They were here.

Her pulse raced at the thought of meeting the Brightens, the couple who had adopted and raised her real father. A father she'd never known in life but had grown to love in his short visits from the afterlife.

She took one step and then another, unsure of the emotional storm brewing inside her.

Excitement.

Curiosity.

Fear. Yes, a lot of fear.

But of what?

A drip of sweat, more from nerves than Texas's mid-August heat index, rolled down her brow.

Go and uncover your past so you may discover your destiny. The death angels' mystical words replayed in her head. She took another step forward, then stopped. Even as her heart ached to solve the mystery of who her father was—of who she was and, hopefully, what she was—her instincts screamed for her to run and hide.

Was this what she feared? Learning the truth?

Before coming to Shadow Falls a few months ago, she'd been certain she was just a confused teen, that her feelings of being different were normal. Now she knew better.

She wasn't normal.

She wasn't even human. At least not all human.

And figuring out her nonhuman side was a puzzle.

A puzzle the Brightens could help her solve.

She took another step. The wind, as if it were as eager to escape as she was, whisked past. It picked up a few wayward strands of her blond hair and scattered them across her face.

She blinked, and when she opened her eyes, the brightness of the sun had evaporated. Glancing up, she saw a huge, angry-looking cloud hanging directly overhead. It cast a shadow around her and the woodsy terrain. Unsure if this was an omen or just a summer storm, she froze, her heart dancing faster. Taking a deep breath that smelled of rain, she was poised to move when a hand clasped her elbow. Memories of another hand grabbing her sent panic shooting through her veins.

She swung around.

"Whoa. You okay?" Lucas lightened his clasp around her arm.

Kylie caught her breath and stared up at the werewolf's blue eyes. "Yeah. You just . . . surprised me. You always surprise me. You need to whistle when you come up on me." She shoved down the memories of Mario and his rogue vampire grandson, Red.

"Sorry." He grinned and his thumb moved in soft little circles over the crease in her elbow. Somehow that light brush of his thumb felt . . . intimate. How did he make a simple touch feel like a sweet sin? A gust of wind, now smelling like a storm, stirred his black hair and tossed it over his brow.

He continued to stare at her, his blue eyes warming her and chasing away her darkest fears. "You don't look okay. What's wrong?" He reached up and tucked a wayward strand of hair behind her right ear.

She looked away from him to the cabin that housed the office. "My grandparents . . . the adopted parents of my real dad are here."

He must have picked up on her reluctance to be here. "I thought you wanted to meet them. That's why you asked them to come, right?"

"I do. I'm just . . ."

"Scared?" he finished for her.

She didn't like admitting it, but since werewolves could smell fear, lying was pointless. "Yeah." She looked back at Lucas and saw humor in his eyes. "What's so funny?"

"You," he said. "I'm still trying to figure you out. When you were kidnapped by a rogue vampire, you weren't this scared. In fact, you were . . . amazing."

Kylie smiled. No, Lucas had been the amazing one. He'd risked his life to save her from Mario and Red, and she'd never forget that.

"Seriously, Kylie, if this is the same couple I saw walking in here a few minutes ago, then they're old and just humans. I think you can take them with both hands tied behind your back."

"I'm not scared like that. I just . . ." She closed her eyes, unsure how to explain something she wasn't clear on herself. Then the words just came. "What am I going to say to them? 'I know you never told my father he was adopted, but he figured it out after he died. And he came to see me. Oh, yeah, he wasn't human. So could you please tell me who his real parents are? So I can figure out what I am?' "

He must have heard the angst in her voice because his smile vanished. "You'll find a way."

"Yeah." But she wasn't that confident. She started walking, feeling his presence, his warmth, as he accompanied her up the steps to the cabin. The walk was easier with him beside her.

He stopped at the door and brushed a hand down her arm. "You want me to come inside with you?"

She almost told him yes, but this was one thing she needed to do on her own.

She thought she heard voices and glanced back at the door. Well, she wouldn't exactly be alone. No doubt Holiday, the camp leader, waited for her inside, prepared to offer moral support and a calming touch. Normally, Kylie objected to her emotions being manipulated, but right now might be an exception.

"Thanks, but I'm sure Holiday is in there."

He nodded. His gaze moved to her mouth, and his lips came dangerously close to hers. But before his mouth claimed hers, that bone-cold chill that came with the dead descended on her. She pressed two fingers to his lips. Kissing was something she preferred to do without an audience—even one from the other side.

Or maybe it wasn't just the audience. Was she totally ready to give herself over to his kisses? It was a good question, and one she needed to answer, but one problem at a time. Right now she had the Brightens to worry about.

"I should go." She motioned to the door. The cold washed over her again. Okay, she had the Brightens and a ghost to worry about.

Disappointment flashed in Lucas's eyes. Then he shifted uncomfortably and looked around as if he sensed they weren't alone.

"Good luck." He hesitated and then walked away.

She watched him leave and then looked around for the spirit. Goose bumps danced up her spine. Her ability to see ghosts had been the first clue that she wasn't normal.

"Can this wait until later?" she whispered.

A cloud of condensation appeared beside the white rocking chairs on the edge of the porch. The spirit obviously lacked the power or the knowledge to complete the manifestation. But it was enough to send the chairs rocking back and forth. The creaking of wood on wood sounded haunted . . . which it was.

She waited, thinking it was the female spirit who had appeared earlier today in her mother's car as they drove past the Fallen Cemetery on their way to camp. Who was she? What did she need Kylie to do? There were never any easy answers when dealing with ghosts.

"Now's not a good time." Not that saying so would do any good. Spirits believed in the open door policy.

The smear of fog took on more form, and Kylie's chest swelled with emotion.

It wasn't the woman she'd seen earlier.

"Daniel?" Kylie reached out. The tips of her fingers entered the icy mist as it took on a more familiar form. Hot emotion—a mixture of love and regret—coursed up her arm. She yanked her hand back, but tears filled her eyes.

"Daniel?" She almost called him Daddy. But it still felt awkward. She watched as he struggled to manifest.

He'd once explained that his time to linger on earth was limited. More tears filled her eyes as she realized how limited. Her sense of loss tripled when she considered how hard this must be for him. He wanted to be here when she met his parents. And she needed him here, too—wished he'd told her more about the Brightens—and wished more than anything that he'd never died.

"No." His one word, briskly spoken, sounded urgent.

"No, what?" He didn't—or couldn't—answer. "No, I shouldn't ask them about your real parents? But I have to, Daniel, that's the only way I'll ever find the truth."

"It's not—" His voice broke.

"Not what? Not important?" She waited for his answer, but his weak apparition grew paler and his spiritual cold began to ebb. The white chairs slowed their rocking and silence rained down on her.

"It's important to me," Kylie said. "I need . . ." The Texas heat chased away the lingering chill.

He was gone. The thought hit that he might never come back. "Not fair." She swatted at the few tears she'd let fall onto her cheeks.

The need to run and hide hit again. But she'd procrastinated long enough. She grasped the doorknob, still cold from Daniel's spirit, and went to face the Brightens.

Inside, Kylie heard light murmurs coming from one of the back conference rooms. She tried to tune her ear to hear the words. Nothing.

In the last few weeks, she'd unexpectedly been gifted with sensitive hearing. But it came and went. What good was a power if one didn't know how to use it? It only added to the feeling of everything in her life being out of her control.

Biting her lip, she eased down the hall and tried to focus on her main goal: getting answers. Who were Daniel's real parents? What was she?

She heard Holiday say, "I'm sure you're going to love her."

Kylie's footsteps slowed. *Love?*

Wasn't that a little strong? They could just like her. That would be fine. Loving someone was . . . complicated. Even liking someone a whole lot came with a downside, such as a certain good-looking half-fae deciding that being close to her was too hard . . . so he left.

Yup, Derek was definitely an example of the downside of liking someone too much. And he probably was the reason she hesitated to accept Lucas's kisses.

One problem at a time. She pushed that thought away as she stepped into the open door of the conference room.

The elderly man sitting at the table rested his clasped hands on the large oak table. "What kind of trouble did she get into?"

"What do you mean?" Holiday cut her green gaze to the door, and she pushed her long red hair over her shoulder.

The old man continued, "We researched Shadow Falls on the Internet and it has a reputation for being a place for troubled teens."

Freaking great! Daniel's parents thought she was a juvenile delinquent.

"You shouldn't believe everything you read online." Only the slightest hint of annoyance sounded in Holiday's tone. "Actually, we're a school for very gifted teens who are trying to find themselves."

"Please tell me it's not drugs," said the silver-haired woman sitting beside the man. "I'm not sure I could deal with that."

"I'm not a druggie," Kylie said, sympathizing with Della, her vampire roommate, who had to deal with this suspicion from her parents. All heads turned toward Kylie, and feeling put on the spot, she held her breath.

"Oh, my," the woman said. "I didn't mean to offend."

Kylie eased into the room. "I'm not offended. I just wanted that cleared up." She met the woman's faded gray eyes and shifted her focus to the old man, searching . . . but for what? A resemblance, perhaps. Why? She knew they weren't Daniel's real parents. But they had raised him, had probably instilled in him their mannerisms and qualities.

Kylie thought of Tom Galen, her stepdad, the man who'd raised her, the man who until recently she'd believed was her real father. Though Kylie had yet to come to terms with his abandonment of his seventeen-year marriage to her mom, she couldn't deny she'd taken on some of his mannerisms. Not that she didn't see more of Daniel in herself—from her supernatural DNA to her physical features.

"We read this was a home for troubled teens." An apology rang in the old man's voice.

She recalled Daniel telling her that his adoptive parents had loved him and would have loved her if they'd known her.

Love. Emotion crowded her chest. Trying to decipher the sensation, Kylie remembered Nana—her mom's mother—and how much she'd adored her, how much she'd missed her when she died. Was it knowing the Brightens were old—that their time was short—that made Kylie want to pull back?

As if the thought of death had somehow caused it, a ghostly chill filled the room. *Daniel?* She called to him with her mind, but the coldness prickling her skin was different.

As frigid air entered Kylie's lungs, the spirit materialized behind Mrs. Brighten. While the apparition appeared feminine, her bald head reflected the light above. Raw-looking stitches ran across her bare scalp and caused Kylie to flinch.

"We're just concerned," said Mr. Brighten. "We didn't know you existed."

"I . . . understand," Kylie answered, unable to look away from the spirit that stared at the elderly couple in puzzlement.

Seeing the spirit's face again, Kylie realized it was the same woman from earlier today. Obviously, her shaved head and stitches were a clue. But a clue to what?

The spirit looked at Kylie. *"I'm so confused."*

Me too, Kylie thought, unsure if the spirit could read her mind the way the others had.

"So many people want me to tell you something."

"Who?" Realizing she'd whispered the word out loud, she bit her lip. Was it Daniel? Nana? *What do they want you to tell me?*

The spirit met Kylie's gaze as if she understood. *"Someone lives. Someone dies."*

More puzzles, Kylie thought, and looked away from the ghost. She saw Holiday glance around, sensing the spirit. Mrs. Brighten looked at the ceiling as if searching for an AC vent to blame for the chill. Luckily the spirit faded, taking the cold with her.

Pushing the ghost from her mind, Kylie looked back at the Brightens. Her gaze took in the mop of thick gray hair on the elderly man. His pale complexion told her that he'd been a redhead in his younger years.

For some reason, Kylie felt compelled to wiggle her eyebrows and check the couple's brain patterns. It was a little supernatural trick she'd only recently learned, one that mostly allowed supernaturals to recognize one another and humans. Mr. and Mrs. Brighten were human.

Normals and probably decent people. So why did Kylie feel so jittery?

She studied the couple as they studied her. She waited for them to make some declaration of how much she looked like Daniel. But it didn't come.

Instead, Mrs. Brighten said, "We're really excited to meet you."

"Me too," Kylie said. *As well as scared to death.* She sat in the chair beside Holiday, opposite the Brightens. Reaching under the table, she sought out Holiday's hand and gave it a squeeze. A welcome calm flowed from the camp leader's touch.

"Can you tell me about my father?" Kylie asked.

"Of course." Mrs. Brighten's expression softened. "He was a very charismatic child. Popular. Smart. Outgoing."

Kylie rested her free hand on the table. "Not like me, then." She bit her lip, not meaning to say it out loud.

Mrs. Brighten frowned. "I wouldn't say that. Your camp leader was just telling us how wonderful you are." She reached across the table to rest her warm hand on Kylie's. "I can't believe we have a granddaughter."

There was something about the woman's touch that stirred Kylie's emotions. Not just the heat of the woman's skin—it was the thinness, the slight tremble of the fingers, and the defined bones that time and arthritis had changed. Kylie remembered Nana— remembered how her grandmother's gentle touch had grown more fragile before she died. Without warning, grief swelled in Kylie's chest. Grief for Nana, and maybe even the forewarning of what she would feel for Daniel's parents when their time came. Considering their age, that time would come too soon.

"When did you learn Daniel was your father?" Mrs. Brighten's hand still rested on Kylie's wrist. It felt oddly comforting.

"Just recently," she said through a knot of emotion. "My parents are divorcing and the truth sort of came out." That wasn't altogether a lie.

"A divorce? You poor child."

The old man nodded in agreement, and Kylie noticed his eyes were blue—like her dad's and hers. "We're glad you chose to find us."

"So very glad." Mrs. Brighten's voice trembled. "We've never stopped missing our son. He died so young." A quiet sensation of loss, of shared grief, entered the room.

Kylie bit her tongue to keep from telling them how she'd come to love Daniel herself. From assuring them that he had loved them. So many things she longed to ask them, to tell them, but couldn't.

"We brought pictures," Mrs. Brighten said.

"Of my dad?" Kylie leaned forward.

Mrs. Brighten nodded and shifted in her chair. Moving with old bones, she pulled a brown envelope from her big white old-lady purse. Kylie's heart raced with eagerness to see the pictures of Daniel. Had he looked like her when he was young?

The woman passed the envelope to Kylie, and she opened it as quickly as she could.

Her throat tightened when she saw the first image—a young Daniel, maybe six, without his front teeth. She could remember the images of her own toothless school pictures, and she could swear the resemblance was amazing.

The photos took her through Daniel's life—from when he was a young teen with long hair and frayed jeans to when he was an adult.

In the adult photo, he was with a group of people. Kylie's throat tightened even more when she realized who was standing beside him. Her mother.

Her gaze shot up. "That's my mom."

Mrs. Brighten nodded. "Yes, we know."

"You do?" Kylie asked, confused. "I didn't think you ever met her."

"We suspected," Mr. Brighten spoke up. "After we learned about you, we suspected that she might have been the one who was in the picture."

"Oh." Kylie looked back down at the images and wondered how they could have gotten all that from one photo. Not that it matttered. "Can I keep these?"

"Of course you may," Mrs. Brighten said. "I made copies. Daniel would have wanted you to have them."

Yes, he would. Kylie recalled him trying to materialize as if he had something important to tell her. "My mom loved him," Kylie added, recalling her mom's concerns that the Brightens might resent her for not attempting to find them earlier. But they didn't seem to harbor any negative feelings.

"I'm sure she did." Mrs. Brighten leaned in and touched Kylie's hand again. Warmth and genuine emotion flowed from the touch. It almost . . . almost felt magical.

A sudden beep of Kylie's phone shattered the fragile silence. She ignored the incoming text, feeling almost mesmerized by Mrs. Brighten's eyes. Then, for reasons Kylie didn't understand, her heart opened up.

Maybe she did want them to love her. Maybe she wanted to love them as well. It didn't matter how little time they had left. Or that they weren't her biological grandparents. They had loved her father and lost him. Just as she had. It only seemed right that they love each other.

Was that what Daniel had wanted to tell her? Kylie glanced

down at the photographs one more time and then slipped them back into the envelope, knowing she would spend hours studying them later.

Kylie's phone rang. She moved to shut it off and saw Derek's name on the screen. Her heart missed a beat. Was he calling to apologize for leaving? Did she want him to apologize?

Another phone rang. This time it was Holiday's cell.

"Excuse me." Holiday rose and started to leave the room as she took the call. She came to an abrupt stop at the door. "Slow down," she said into the phone. The tightness in the camp leader's voice changed the mood in the room. Holiday swung back around and stepped closer to Kylie.

"What is it?" Kylie muttered.

Holiday pressed a hand on Kylie's shoulder, then snapped her phone shut and focused on the Brightens. "There's been an emergency. We'll have to reschedule this meeting."

"What's wrong?" Kylie asked.

Holiday didn't answer. Kylie glanced back at the Brightens' disappointed faces and she felt that same emotion weaving its way through her chest. "Can't we—"

"No," Holiday said. "I'm going to have to ask you folks to leave. *Now.*"

The camp leader's tone was punctuated by the jarring sound of the cabin's front door opening and slamming against the wall. Both of the elderly Brightens flinched and then stared at the door as the sound of thundering footsteps raced toward the conference room.

Chapter Two

Three minutes later, Kylie stood in the parking lot and watched the Brightens' silver Cadillac drive away. She turned to glare at Della and Lucas, who'd stormed into the office and interrupted her meeting with her grandparents. Perry had been with them, too, but he'd wisely disappeared. Holiday, who had followed them outside, was on the phone again.

"Would someone please tell me what's going on?" Kylie asked, feeling as if her chance to discover more about her father were disappearing along with the Cadillac. She suddenly realized she still held the brown envelope of images of Daniel, and she clutched them tighter.

"Don't get your panties in a wad. We're just watching your back." The tips of Della's canines peeked through the corners of her lips. Her dark eyes, with a slight slant, and her straight black hair hinted at her part Asian heritage.

"Watching my back for what?"

"Derek called." Holiday closed her phone and stepped into the circle. "He was worried." Her phone rang again, and after looking at the call log, she held up a finger. "Sorry. One minute."

Patience wearing thin, Kylie looked back at Della and Lucas. "What's up?"

Lucas moved in. "Burnett phoned us and asked us to make our presence known to the visitors." His gaze met hers and, as earlier, concern flickered in his blue eyes.

Burnett, a thirty-something vampire, worked for the FRU—Fallen Research Unit—a branch of the FBI whose job it was to govern the supernaturals. He was also part owner of Shadow Falls. When Burnett gave an order, he expected people to obey. And they usually did.

"Why?" Kylie asked. "I needed to ask them questions." Unexpectedly, the memory of how Mrs. Brighten's hand felt on hers flashed in her mind—gentle, fragile. Emotions came at Kylie from every direction.

"Burnett never gives his reasons," Della said. "He gives orders."

Kylie glanced at Holiday, who was still on the phone. She looked worried, and Kylie felt Holiday's emotions join the others already dancing along her spine.

"I don't understand." She fought the tightness in her throat.

Lucas stepped closer. So close that she could smell his scent—a scent that reminded her of how the dew-kissed woods smelled first thing in the morning.

His hand came up and she thought he was going to reach for her, but he lowered his hand just as quickly. She fought against disappointment.

Holiday hung up the phone. "That was Burnett." She stepped forward and rested a hand on Kylie's shoulder.

She didn't want to be calmed; she wanted answers. So she removed the camp leader's hand. "Just tell me what happened. *Please.*"

"Derek called," Holiday said. "He went to see the P.I. who helped you find your grandparents and found him unconscious in his office. Then Derek discovered the man's phone on the floor outside of his office with blood on it. Bottom line, Derek doesn't think the P.I. sent that text to you about your grandparents. He called Burnett, who's there now."

Kylie tried to understand what Holiday was saying. "But if the P.I. didn't send the text, who did?"

Holiday shrugged. "We don't know."

"Derek could be wrong," Lucas said, his lack of affection for the half-fae deepening the vibration in his voice.

Kylie ignored Lucas and his vibrations and tried to digest what Holiday was implying. "So . . . Derek and Burnett think that Mr. and Mrs. Brighten were impostors?"

Holiday nodded. "If Derek's right and the text was sent by the person who hurt the P.I., then it makes sense that these two could have been sent here for other reasons."

"But they're human," Kylie said. "I checked."

"Definitely human," Della said.

"I know," Holiday explained. "That's the reason I didn't detain or question them. The last thing I need is to bring more suspicion on Shadow Falls. We already have the locals breathing down our necks. But being human doesn't mean they aren't working for someone else. Someone supernatural."

Kylie knew by "someone," Holiday meant Mario Esparza, grandfather to the murdering rogue who'd taken a liking to her.

For a split second, Kylie got a vision of the two teenage girls she'd met in town, the two who'd died at the hands of Red, Mario Esparza's grandson. More frustration and anger wound its way into her emotional bank.

"But they brought me pictures." She held up the envelope.

Holiday took the envelope and quickly glanced through the stack of pictures. For some odd reason, Kylie wanted to jerk them back, as if Holiday's action were somehow irreverent. "There aren't any family pictures in here. You would think there would be one or two of them with their son."

Kylie took the pictures back and slipped them into the envelope, trying to wrap her head around what they were insinuating. Then her thoughts went elsewhere. "But what if they really are my grand-parents and whoever went to the P.I. is going to try to get to them?" She remembered the frailness of the elderly woman's palm on top of hers. What little life the woman had left could easily be yanked away from her.

Kylie's chest ached. Had she put Daniel's parents in danger by finding them? Had that been what Daniel had wanted to tell her? She felt Lucas's gaze on her, as if offering some small amount of comfort.

Holiday spoke up again. "I don't see any reason for someone to involve them. However, Perry is following them. If anyone tries to harm them, he'll take care of things."

"Yeah, Perry could seriously kick ass if he has to," Della said.

"And I'm sure the P.I. is working a hundred different cases," Lucas said. "The P.I. being attacked doesn't mean it's linked to Kylie. It could be one of his other cases. Private investigators piss people off all the time."

"True," Holiday said. "But Burnett was concerned enough to want the Brightens away from the camp. We need to be cautious."

Kylie's mind took a U-turn and parked on the fact that it was Perry, one of the resident shape-shifters, following the Brightens. "What was Perry when he took off after them?"

The last time she'd seen Perry in an alternate form, he'd been some kind of pterodactyl creature that looked as if it had stepped out of the Jurassic age. Of course, Kylie supposed that was better than the SUV-sized lion or the unicorn he'd turned into before that. Oh hell! If he wasn't careful, Perry could end up giving the elderly couple heart attacks.

"Don't worry," Holiday said. "Perry won't do anything ridicu-lous."

Miranda chose that moment to join the group. "Please, Perry and all things ridiculous go together like toads and warts," she said, and pushed her tricolored dyed hair over her shoulder as if to punctuate her attitude.

Miranda was one of seven witches at Shadow Falls, and she was also Kylie's other roommate. From Miranda's tone, it was clear she wasn't ready to forgive Perry for being cruel to her when he'd found out another shape-shifter had kissed her . . . especially when she'd apologized. The witch's gaze shot around the group.

"What?" Miranda asked. "Is something wrong?" Concern tightened her eyes, proving that while she might not be over being mad, neither was she over caring for the shape-shifter. "Is Perry okay? Is he?" She reached up and caught a strand of pink hair and twirled it around her finger.

"Perry's fine," Holiday and Kylie said at the same time. Then Kylie's mind returned to her concern for the Brightens—if they really were the Brightens.

She looked at Holiday. "What would anyone gain by pretending to be my grandparents?"

"Access to you," Holiday answered.

"But they seemed so genuine." And then Kylie remembered. "No. They couldn't have been impostors. I . . . saw the death angels. They sent me a message."

"Oh, crappers," Della said, and she and Miranda took a step back. While Lucas didn't flinch, his eyes widened. According to legend, death angels were supposed to be the ones who doled out punishment to keep the nonhuman species in line. Almost every supernatural knew of a friend of a friend who'd misbehaved and then gotten fried to a crisp by a vengeful death angel.

While Kylie sensed the power of these angels, she wasn't so sure their harmful reputation wasn't exaggerated. Not that she was eager to test the theory. However, considering she made her share of mistakes and hadn't been burned or turned to ash, she questioned the rumors of those who had.

"What message?" Holiday asked, her tone free of any misgiving. The camp leader, another ghost whisperer, was one of the few who didn't fear the death angels.

"Shadows . . . on the dining hall wall, then . . ."

"When we were in there?" Della asked. "And you didn't tell us?"

Kylie ignored Della. "I heard a voice in my head say to go find my destiny. Why would I get that message if they weren't my grandparents?"

"Good question," Holiday said. "But maybe they just meant this situation is what will lead you to the truth."

"She should have told us," Della muttered to Miranda.

Kylie recalled Daniel showing up, the urgency she'd heard in his tone in what little he'd communicated. Had she totally misunderstood what he'd wanted to tell her? Had he come to warn her that the couple weren't his adoptive parents? Doubt built, and she didn't know what she believed anymore.

Kylie breathed in, and another concern dove right into her worry bank. "Is the P.I. going to be okay?"

"I don't know." Holiday frowned. "Burnett said Derek was at the hospital with him now. Burnett is still investigating the crime scene."

Worry for Derek tightened Kylie's chest. She pulled her phone out of her pocket and dialed his number.

When he didn't answer, she didn't know if it was because he couldn't or if he was back to not talking to her. Back to pushing her out of his life.

Men!

Why was it that boys said girls were so hard to understand, when she hadn't known a single guy who hadn't confused her to the point of screaming?

• • •

As everyone hung out talking, Kylie snuck away and went around back to sit beside her favorite tree. She opened the envelope and slowly went through the pictures, noting all the little things about Daniel. They way his blue eyes lit up when he smiled, the way his hair flipped up just a bit on the ends when he wore it long. She saw so much of herself in him, and her heart doubled over with grief at missing him.

When she came across the picture of her mom and him, Kylie found herself smiling at the way Daniel was looking at her mom, and the way her mom was looking at him. Love. Part of Kylie wanted to call her mom right then and tell her about the photo, but considering what Holiday and the others thought, she supposed it was best to keep quiet. But hopefully not for long.

"Hey."

Lucas's voice pulled her attention up, and she smiled. "Hi."

"Mind some company?" he asked.

"I'll share my tree with you." She scooted over.

He dropped down beside her and studied her face. His shoulder, so warm, came against hers, and she savored his closeness. "You look happy and sad, and confused." He brushed a few strands of her hair from her face.

"I feel confused," she said. "They were so nice and . . . I don't know what to believe now. How could they have these pictures if they aren't really the Brightens?"

"They could have stolen them," he said.

His words hurt, but she knew he could be right. But why would anyone go that far to convince her they were Daniel's parents? What could they possibly gain by doing that?

He looked down at the pictures she held in her hand. "Can I see?"

Nodding, she passed him the stack of photos.

He slowly flipped through them. "It must be weird looking at someone's face who you look so much like and not knowing him."

She gazed up at Lucas. "But I do know him."

His brows arched up. "I mean . . . in person."

She nodded, understanding his inability to grasp the whole ghost thing, but wishing it weren't so hard for him.

"Burnett will get to the bottom of this." His gaze lowered to her mouth. For a second, she thought he was going to kiss her, but he stiffened and looked up toward the woods.

Fredericka, scowling at the two of them, walked out from behind the bushes. "The pack is looking for you."

Lucas frowned. "I'll be right there."

She didn't move. She just continued to stare. "They shouldn't have to wait on their leader."

Lucas growled, "I said I'd be right there."

Fredericka walked away, and Lucas looked down at her. "Sorry. I should go."

"Is something wrong?" Kylie asked, noting the concern filling his eyes.

"Nothing I can't handle." He pressed a quick kiss on her lips and slid the photos back into her hands.

"Are you going to be okay?" Holiday asked when Kylie walked back onto the office porch.

Kylie plopped down in one of the large white rocking chairs. The sticky heat seemed to cling to her skin. "I'll live." She set the envelope on the small patio table between the chairs and pulled her hair back and held it off the back of her neck. "Do you really think they were impostors?"

Holiday sat in the other rocker. Her red hair hung loose around her shoulders. "I don't know. But Burnett won't let it rest until he gets to the bottom of this. He feels guilty that he wasn't more on top of things and let Mario get to you. I imagine after this, he's not going to want to let you out of his sight."

"He had no way of knowing what the creep was up to," Kylie said.

"I know that. You know that. But Burnett has a tendency to be a bit harder on himself."

"Aren't all vampires?" Kylie considered Della and the emotional baggage she carted around.

"Not really," Holiday said. "You'd be amazed how many vamps refuse to take any responsibility for their actions. It's always someone else's fault."

Kylie almost asked if Holiday was referring to a certain vampire who'd broken her heart in the past. But her thoughts went back to the Brightens. "You were there. Didn't you read their emotions? Weren't they sincere? I felt somehow . . . connected to them."

Holiday tilted her head as if thinking. "They were very guarded, almost too much so, but . . . yeah, they read sincere. Especially Mrs. Brighten."

"Then how could they—"

"Reading emotions is never a hundred percent certain," Holiday said. "Emotions can be disguised, hidden, even faked."

"By humans?" Kylie asked.

"Humans are masters at it. Better than supernaturals. I've often thought that since their species lack any superpower to control their worlds, they have worked harder at controlling their emotions."

Kylie listened, while her heart chewed on concern for the Brightens.

"Narcissism, detachment, schizoid personality, sociopath—these things run rampant in the human race in varying degrees. Then you have the actors who can create an emotion within themselves by simply borrowing it from a past experience. I've attended plays and shows where the emotions flowing from the actors were as real as I've ever felt."

Kylie leaned back in her chair. "I'm part human and I can't seem to control anything."

Holiday glanced at her with empathy. "I'm sorry I had to send them away. I know you were hoping to learn something. But I couldn't risk that Derek might be right."

"I understand." And she did. She just didn't like it. "Mrs. Brighten—if she really was Mrs. Brighten—reminded me of my grandmother."

"Nana," Holiday said, and Kylie remembered that Nana's spirit had paid Holiday a visit.

"Yeah."

Holiday sighed. "I know this is difficult for you."

The camp leader's phone rang and Kylie held her breath, hoping it was news on the Brightens, Derek, or the P.I.

The camp leader glanced at the call log. "It's just my mom. I'll call her later."

Kylie pulled one knee up to her chest and wrapped her hand around her leg. The silence that followed called for the truth. "I feel as if nothing in my life makes sense anymore. Everything is changing."

Holiday wrapped her hair into a rope. "Change isn't the worst thing, Kylie. It's when things aren't changing that you have to worry."

"I disagree." Kylie dropped her chin down on her kneecap. "I mean, I know change is necessary for growth and all that stuff. But I'd like one thing in my life to feel . . . grounded. I need a touch-stone. Something that feels real."

Holiday raised her brows. "Shadow Falls is real, Kylie. It's your touchstone."

"I know. I know I belong here, it's just that I still don't know *how* I belong. And please don't tell me that I should make this my quest. Because that's been my quest since I've been here and I'm not any closer to figuring it now than I was then."

"That's not true." Holiday pulled her knees up, and in the over-size rocking chair, her petite form looked even smaller. "Look how far you've come. Like you said, you know you belong here. That's a big step. And your gifts are coming in left and right."

"Gifts that I mostly don't know how to control or when they might or might not pop in again. Not that I'm complaining." Kylie dropped her forehead on her kneecap and let go of an exaggerated sigh.

Holiday chuckled.

Kylie glanced up. "I sound pathetic, don't I."

Holiday frowned. "No. You sound frustrated. And to be honest, after what happened to you this weekend, you deserve to be frustrated. You might even deserve to be a little pathetic."

"Nobody has the right to be pathetic," Kylie said.

"I don't know about that. I think I've earned the right a few times in my life." Holiday set her rocking chair into a slow swaying motion.

Kylie stared at the camp leader, and she had a distinct feeling that there were a lot of things Holiday still hadn't told Kylie about herself.

"Did I sense a new spirit earlier?" Holiday asked.

"Yeah." Kylie leaned back in the chair. "She's still not making sense. Says she's confused." Kylie recalled the angry-looking stitches she'd seen on the woman's head. "I think she died of a brain tumor or something. She had a shaved head and scars."

"Hmm," Holiday said.

"And I think she's buried at Fallen Cemetery."

"Really? Did she tell you that?"

"No, but that's where I felt like I picked her up. Driving here this morning, my mom had just passed the cemetery when the spirit popped into the backseat."

"I guess that could be it."

"But you don't think so?" Kylie asked, unsure of Holiday's logic.

"I'm not saying it can't be that simple, but I've found the majority of spirits that come to us have . . . connections more than just our driving by a cemetery. Now, I'm not saying we don't get random ghosts sometimes, because we do. The other day, I got a dripping wet, elderly man, naked as the day he was born. He died in the shower at his nursing home. Wanted me to tell the nurse to please come get him out." Holiday shook her head.

"What did you do?" Kylie asked.

"I called the nursing home and said I was a friend of the family and had tried to call Mr. Banes in his room and he wasn't answering."

"And he went away?"

"Crossed right over."

"I hope this spirit is that easy. I could use a break." Then Kylie remembered what the spirit had said. "You know . . . the spirit said that there were people who wanted her to tell me something."

"Tell you what?"

"I asked, but . . . she said something like, some people live and some people die. It didn't make sense."

"They seldom do at first."

Kylie bit down on her lip. "Could it be my dad trying to tell me something? He tried to appear right before I saw the Brightens—or whoever they were."

Holiday stopped rocking. "What did he say?"

"He couldn't completely manifest. All I got were a few words." Kylie frowned. "Why does he have to stop coming to see me?"

Holiday's expression filled with sympathy. "Death is a new beginning, Kylie. One can't begin the new until they let go of the old. He has held on to the past for a long time. He needs to move forward. Do you understand what I'm saying?"

Kylie stopped her chair's swaying. "Understand it? Maybe. Like it? No." Sighing, she stood up. "I told Miranda and Della I'd meet them back at the cabin."

"Sure." Holiday hesitated a moment. "I thought now might be a good time to chat about your new gifts."

"What's to talk about? Just because I ran through a concrete wall?" Kylie used sarcasm to cover up her unresolved feeling.

Holiday grinned. "And you healed Sara. And Lucas."

Kylie sat back down. "We hope I healed Sara."

"From what you said, I'd be surprised if you hadn't." Holiday continued to stare. "If one of your gifts is that you're a protector, Kylie, this could only be the beginning of your talents. I'm surprised you aren't peppering me with questions."

"Maybe I'd like a few answers before I start asking more questions. And I don't even mean about what I am, but about who the Brightens are. And what my dad wanted to tell me."

Holiday's eyes filled with understanding. "It's all happening very fast, isn't it?"

"Yes, and talking about it's not going to change anything." Her chest swelled with emotion.

"It could. Sometimes things don't feel real until we talk about them. "

Kylie released a breath. "I'm not sure I want it to feel any more real right now."

"Perhaps we should take a walk up to the falls?"

"No," Kylie said, unsure she could go there and not get upset if all she got from those magical waters was a voice telling her to be patient. Hadn't she been patient long enough? "Can we just talk later?"

"Fine." Holiday started to touch her and then pulled back. "But only a temporary postponement. We really need to talk."

"Yeah, I know." Kylie popped back up and reached for the envelope.

"Can I keep these for a while?" Holiday asked.

Kylie's heart clutched. "I . . ."

"Just for a few days. I'm sure Burnett is going to want to check and see if they are originals or copies."

Kylie nodded. "They're important to me."

Holiday smiled with honest understanding. "I know."

Kylie took one step off the porch and turned back around. "You will let me know the instant you hear something from Burnett or Derek, right?"

"The instant," Holiday assured her.

Kylie started to leave and then turned back, walked over to Holiday, and hugged her. Hugged her really tight.

"Thank you," Kylie said.

"For what?" Holiday sounded confused, but it didn't stop her from hugging Kylie back.

"For being here. For being you. For putting up with me."

Holiday snickered. "You're beginning to sound melodramatic, and that's just a hair away from pathetic."

Kylie broke the embrace, smiled back at Holiday, and took off down the trail to her cabin.

She hadn't gotten halfway there when the hair on the back of her neck seemed to dance and she felt the unmistakable sense of being watched. She glanced to the woods on her left but saw nothing but trees and underbrush. She fixed her stare to the right and found the overgrown terrain to be equally empty. But she still felt it—even stronger.

Glancing up at the cloudless blue sky, she blinked. A bird soared high overhead. The broad wingspan, the hooked beak, and the white splash of coloring on his chest identified him as an eagle. She studied the creature, slowly gliding as if taking his sweet time, as if he were transfixed by . . . the view?

What view?

Did he watch her? Was the feeling she got from the bird? Was it just your average eagle? Or was it like Perry, who could change his form into anything he desired? She continued to watch him, feeling uneasy.

Without warning, the eagle changed course. His movements quickened as he charged. Close. Closer. She met his eyes. The fierceness made her shudder. Or was it his thick talons held out as if prepared to attack?

The *whoosh* of air from his wings hit her face, and she slammed her eyes shut.

Chapter Three

Kylie threw up her arm to protect her face, but she felt nothing, no claws cutting into her flesh. Not on her face or her arm.

She heard rustling at her feet, accompanied by a rattling noise. Uncovering her face, she looked down. Her breath caught. She lurched back as the eagle used his sharp beak and talons to attack the snake that lay a few inches from her feet. The rattling noise hit again. She noticed the diamondlike shapes on the back of the brown-and-tan snake, then her gaze followed the coiled reptile to the dry, tan appendage growing from its tail.

A rattlesnake.

She lunged back. The bird buried his talons into the round, thick flesh of the snake. The eagle's wings worked overtime as he carried the squirming snake a few feet off the ground. The flapping of wings, the *whoosh*ing of air, and the distinctive rattle of the reptile filled her ears. The eagle hung a few feet above the ground, his wings slapping against the air.

She stood in the middle of the path and watched as the huge bird flew away with his prey. Looking back at her feet, she saw dusty marks in the path where the snake had fought for its life and lost. Beside the marks, a pair of shoe prints pressed into the ground. Her shoes. Had the eagle not charged, would she have seen the snake? Or would she now have the rattler's venom running up her leg?

Was she just lucky, or had this meant something? She considered turning around and finding Holiday, but logic intervened. She was in the woods in the Texas Hill Country. Her father—stepfather—had warned her constantly about snakes.

Convincing herself that this was just an uncanny moment that she'd gotten to experience nature at its scariest, she took another step forward. She did glance up one more time, though. The eagle, with the snake still tightly in his clutches, circled above. She stared, her breath caught in her throat. And as crazy as it seemed, she could swear the eagle stared back.

She stood, hand shadowing her eyes, and watched him until he was a dark speck fading into the massive blue sky. A thought hit that she should be grateful to the eagle, but the cold look in the bird's eyes flashed in her mind and sent a shiver down her spine.

Moving her hand away from her brow, she started for her cabin when her gaze clashed with another cold pair of eyes. Fredericka. Kylie remembered how angry Fredericka had been when she'd caught her and Lucas behind the office. Not that they'd been doing anything but looking at pictures of Daniel and talking.

"How does it feel to be a play toy?" Fredericka's voice sounded tight with anger, the kind of anger that could bring out the claws. And the hint of orange in the girl's dark eyes said the claws were definitely an option.

Kylie inhaled and reminded herself not to show any fear. "Jealousy isn't becoming on you."

"I'm not jealous." Fredericka flashed a smug smile. "Especially now."

Now what? Kylie wanted to ask, but to do so would have given the bully credence, and Kylie refused to do that. Instead, she started walking away. She told herself to forget about Fredericka, that she had other problems to chew on right now. Kylie pulled out her phone to see if Derek had ever returned her call about the detective. He hadn't.

"Lucas's bloodline is pure, he values that," Fredericka spouted from behind Kylie. "The forefathers value that, too. They've made that clear. So when it comes time for him to seek his true mate, he won't dirty up his bloodline with the likes of you."

Nonsense, Kylie told herself, and kept walking. Fredericka was just talking nonsense. She had grandparents or pretend grandparents to worry about, so she wouldn't let this she-wolf upset her. Then the memory of the eagle filled her mind. Maybe she should worry about that, too.

Less than an hour later, still not hearing from Derek, Perry, or Burnett, Kylie sat at the kitchen table in her cabin with Miranda and Della. She'd told them about the snake and eagle and her thoughts that the incident was somehow more than it appeared.

"I would have smelled it if we had intruders," Della assured her.

"And I would have felt it if magic was being used to cover someone's tracks," Miranda said.

"See, that's why I need you guys," Kylie said. "You keep me from losing it." She leaned back in her chair, wishing their confirmation had chased away all her doubts. Then again, maybe it wasn't the doubts bothering her, but everything else on her plate.

Kylie's pet, Socks Jr.—the kitten Miranda had accidentally turned into a skunk—leapt up and landed in her lap. While Kylie still felt caught in the tailspin of the emotional storm, doing something as commonplace as their diet soda roundtable discussions brought some solace.

Miranda, up first in the discussion of their weekend woes and whines, retold everything about her witches' competition, in which she'd placed second. "I was excited that I placed so high," she said. "I thought my mom would be happy. But no." Miranda hesitated. "Second just means you're the first loser," she recounted her mother's words. The tone in Miranda's voice told Kylie how much her friend was hurting. "I wanted to impress her, and for a minute there, I thought I'd actually, finally done it. I'll never make that woman happy."

Della rolled her eyes. "Why would you want to make her happy?"

"Because she's my mom." Miranda answered with so much honesty that sadness tugged at Kylie's heart. She remembered feeling much the same way about her own mom before they found their peace.

"News flash," Della said, waving her hand. "Your mom's the biggest b . . . witch I've ever heard of. At least my parents' attitude is because they're worried I'm hurting myself by doing drugs and not because they aren't happy with me." Tears brightened Miranda's eyes and anger tightened her expression as she stared at Della.

Kylie felt tension thickening in the air. "I think what Della means is—"

"I'm sorry," Della interrupted Kylie. The smartass look on Della's face quickly faded into a frown. "That sounded mean, and I . . . Truth is if my parents knew the truth, they'd probably rather me be a drug addict than a vampire." Della studied Miranda and sighed. "It just makes me furious at your mom. I know how hard you worked to impress her. And you took friggin' second place, which is fabulous."

"Thanks," Miranda said, her anger dissolving but her eyes getting wetter.

"For what?" Della flopped back into the chair, as if aware she'd shown a softer side of her personality. Della seldom let that side show. Not that Kylie and Miranda didn't see it. Well, Kylie saw it. Miranda had a harder time seeing through Della's guarded front.

Miranda brushed her hand over her cheek again and sat up taller.

"Enough about that. I've got other news. Todd Freeman, a warlock, came over and asked if he could have my cell number. He's like the hottest guy in my old school. So at least someone noticed I did good in the competition." She grinned. "Not that I think it was my trophy he was interested in. I caught him at least three times checking out my girls."

"Jerk," Della said. "I hope the only thing you gave him was your middle finger."

"Duh, didn't you hear me? Cutest guy in school. Besides, big boobs are natural guy magnets—that's just the way it is. Why wouldn't I give my number to him?"

"Oh, I don't know. Maybe because you still want to suck face with a certain shape-shifter?"

"Please, I'm so over Perry," Miranda snapped.

Della tapped the end of her nose. "Pheromones don't lie."

"No arguing on the first day back," Kylie said. "Tomorrow you two can threaten to tear each other's limbs off, but today . . . just give me a little peace today." She picked up Socks from her lap and placed him on the table. "Besides . . . you're gonna upset Socks and then we're all gonna end up getting skunked."

Della and Miranda looked at Socks. The little skunk/cat, uncomfortable being the center of attention, scurried closer to Kylie.

"Truce?" Kylie asked, stroking the scared animal's trembling body.

Thankfully, Miranda and Della nodded.

Miranda leaned closer. "I think I've figured out how to turn our little stinker back into a kitten. But I need the first rays of sunshine to do it." She reached over to pet Socks, but he backed away from her touch and then jumped back into Kylie's lap.

"Smart skunk," Della said, grinning. "No telling what you'll accidentally turn him into next time."

Miranda frowned. "Maybe I'll turn *you* into a skunk."

"And maybe I'll rip your heart out and feed it to our resident pet."

"What happened to the truce?" Kylie whined. Socks's nose nudged deeper into her armpit.

"Fine." Miranda huffed and then looked at Della. "Your turn. Give us the lowdown on your weekend."

"You mean besides constantly being told to go pee on a stick? They tested me four times. I think one was a pregnancy test. Like I've been doing the dirty with anyone." Della picked up her cup of blood and gave it a hard look. "The only thing we did all weekend was go see a movie, some old classic my mother loved. Boring. At least I got to sleep without having to explain why I seemed so tired in the middle of the day." She exhaled rather loudly. "So that's my weekend. Nothing exciting to tell. Nothing." She stared back into her cup.

It wasn't her avoiding direct eye contact that gave it away, more like the emphasis on the second "nothing" that hinted at the truth. Miranda shot Kylie a quick look that said she'd heard it, too. The little vamp was holding back . . . as usual.

While Kylie debated the wisdom of trying to push Della into giving more, Miranda, who spoke first and seldom thought things through, knocked wisdom out the window and went for it.

"Liar," Miranda accused. "If I could hear your heartbeat right now, I bet it would prove it, too. What happened? What are you not telling us?"

Della snarled at Miranda. Kylie could feel the fragile truce shattering.

"Chan didn't show up, did he?" Miranda asked.

Kylie hadn't thought about that. "Did he show up?" Kylie seconded Miranda's question—not out of curiosity, but out of concern.

Chan, Della's cousin, was also a vampire and had helped Della through the turn. However, Chan was also under suspicion of murder by the FRU. After meeting the wild-eyed Chan when he'd broken school policy and dropped by for a visit several weeks earlier,

Kylie wasn't completely sure he wasn't guilty of the crime. Not that Kylie would tell Della that.

"No, he didn't show up," Della said. "But he e-mailed me."

Miranda made a funny noise. Kylie looked at her.

"Frog in my throat," Miranda said, and returned to glaring at Della.

When no one said anything, Della looked at Kylie. "Your turn. It's much more exciting than what happened to me."

"What do you mean by 'what happened to you'?" Kylie asked.

"I knew it!" Miranda leaned forward. "Something did happen. 'Fess up. Did it involve a boy? Tell us! Spill your guts, vamp."

Chapter Four

"No, it's my turn." Kylie, regretting her inquiry, held up her hand, hoping to prevent an out-and-out war between her two best friends. She took a deep breath. "I already told you most of it when we talked on the phone. But what I still can't get over is that I healed both Lucas and Sara. Which means another ability you can add to my hodgepodge of gifts. Any idea what it could mean? Because I'd really like to figure out what I am."

"We can't figure you out," Miranda said. "You're just a weirdo." She snickered, and even Della cut a quick smile.

Kylie frowned.

Miranda wiped the humor off her face. "Just joking. But seriously, you are . . . different. Just the fact that no one can see deep into your pattern, and that it changes, well, it's not normal." She squinted her eyes and stared at Kylie's forehead. "I've never seen a brain pattern shift like that, unless it was a shape-shifter during a shift."

Kylie bit into her lip and considered the wisdom of asking the question now needling her brain. But if she couldn't ask her two best friends, whom could she ask? "What do you know about protectors?"

Silence filled the room. Then Miranda exchanged a quick glance with Della.

"Why?" Miranda asked.

"Shit!" Della said. "Oh, my friggin' God! You're a protector? I mean, I've never met one, but from what I heard they are like . . . super, super rare."

Kylie held up her hand to stop Della from jumping to conclusions. "I don't know anything for sure, but Holiday seems to think it's possible. She said that would explain how Daniel died—because he couldn't protect himself. And it would also explain why I couldn't help myself with the vampire."

"You did help. You broke down a concrete wall," Miranda said.

"Only after I heard the rogue beating Lucas."

Miranda's eyes widened. "And you were only able to take on Selynn when you thought she'd hurt your mom. Holy shit, I'm rooming with a protector. I mean, nobody will mess with me anymore because you'll kick their ass." Her voice rose. "I'm friends with a protector. Do you know how cool that makes me?"

Miranda and Della gave each other a high five.

Kylie stared at them. "Do you know how much more uncool it makes me?"

"That doesn't make you uncool," Della said. "It makes you amazing. You wouldn't believe all I've heard about protectors. It would mean that when you get all your powers, you would be even stronger than I am." A frown appeared in her dark, slightly slanted eyes. "I don't know if I like that, but it's still amazing."

"But I don't want to be amazing. I just want to figure out what I am and then go through my hybrid supernatural life with my not-so-grand gifts. Help a ghost out here and there and, yeah, it will be neat to heal a few people. I'd be fine with that. Because . . ." Kylie hesitated, unsure about being completely honest, but then decided what the hell. "Maybe it's not so much that I don't want to be amazing, it's that I'm not so sure I can live up to . . . amazing. I'm not like you." She pointed to Della. "I'm not fearless and I'm certainly not brave. I like things easy, low or no risk."

Miranda cleared her throat as if waiting for Kylie to add her to the declaration.

"I'm not like you either," Kylie said. "I'm not—"

"Don't worry," Miranda said. "I know I'm not a kick-ass girl."

"You're still braver than I am. And you're never afraid to speak your mind. You don't care what people think. I wouldn't ever dye my hair out of fear that people wouldn't like it."

"But the day you kicked Selynn's ass, you weren't afraid," Della jumped in. "You just acted. And eventually, you'll get used to putting yourself out there. It's not a big deal."

It felt like a big deal to Kylie. "Are most protectors a certain species?" If so, she hoped this might lead her to discovering what she was.

"No," Miranda said. "They can be anything, but they're known to be good and pure. Sort of the Mother Teresa of supernaturals."

"Which I'm *so* not," Kylie said.

Della and Miranda looked at each other and then back at Kylie. "Yeah, you are," they said at the same time.

"Am not! I'm not any better of a person than you two. I mean, look what I did to Selynn and Fredericka."

"Because you were protecting someone else. And that's exactly what protectors do." Miranda shrugged as if in apology when she spotted Kylie's frown.

"But . . . I'm not a saint. The other day I practically shoved Socks off the bed for waking me up. And . . . I ran over a squirrel once."

"On purpose?" Della asked.

"No."

"Then there you go," Della said. "I'll bet you even cried and felt guilty."

Kylie's frown grew tighter.

Della arched a knowing brow. "See? That's what makes you so good. You hardly ever get mad."

"I get mad. I get furious at you guys all the time. Remember—"

"Wait, something doesn't make sense," Miranda said. "I've never heard of a protector being anything but a hundred percent super-natural."

"See? That proves it." Kylie slapped her hands on the table, wanting to believe it. "I'm not that nice of a person, and I know I'm my mother's daughter. So I'm not a protector."

"Or maybe you're just the first hybrid protector to exist," Miranda said. "I mean, usually there's only one protector born every hundred or two hundred years. But, hey, enough about that. Let's get to the good part about what happened that night." She waved her hands through the air as if to push that thought to the side.

"What good part?" Kylie asked.

Miranda's grin spread into the perfect smile—one that could be used to sell teeth-whitening strips. "Pleeeassse. You were there, in the dark, late at night, for several hours, and alone with Lucas. Who happens to be the hottest werewolf alive. I mean, I'm so not into were-wolves, but even I can see it. He's like a god. So . . ." She held out her two palms. "What happened? And don't you dare tell me nothing. Because I will totally, completely lose faith in romance if nothing happened."

Kylie opened her mouth to answer and then saw Della leaning forward, turning her head slightly, as if to listen to Kylie's heartbeat to see if she attempted to lie.

"The little witch has a point," Della said. "This might be the good part."

Kylie frowned at Della. For a girl who always kept secrets, she sure didn't give anyone else a break. Then Kylie looked at Miranda, who held her breath in anticipation of Kylie baring her soul.

"Sorry," she said. "Nothing happened."

"Ugh." Miranda dropped her arms on the table and sank into them.

Della stared, and Kylie knew the vamp was listening to her heartbeat and checking for lies again. Frankly, Kylie wasn't sure what Della would hear. It wasn't actually a lie. Nothing happened. Except . . . She'd felt so safe when Lucas had held her, except that she'd turned into Wonder Woman when she'd heard the rogue hurting Lucas. What did that mean? Kylie wasn't sure. So how could she explain it?

Miranda lifted her head off the table. "See what I mean? You're Mother Teresa. Pure. Without lust."

"No," Kylie snapped, not wanting to be viewed as a saint. "I . . . lust."

Della and Miranda shared a pensive stare. "Sorry," Della said. "When it walks like a saint, and quacks like saint—it's a quacking saint."

"He held me," Kylie said. "Held me close. And I fell asleep on his shoulder. It was nice. And kind of . . . He was hot." Though she meant temperature hot, she didn't mind if they drew their own conclusions.

"Yes!" Miranda smiled extra big again. "Did he kiss you? Like the awesome kiss he gave you at the creek when you first got here?"

"No," Kylie said.

Her two friends met each other's gazes again. "Mother Teresa," they said in unison.

"But he kissed me when I got back here," Kylie blurted out, deciding she'd rather kiss and tell than be considered a saint. "And he almost kissed me when he followed me to the office earlier."

Miranda squealed and Della laughed. "So he planted one on you, huh?"

Kylie looked at the humor on her roommates' faces and didn't find any of this so funny. "I'm so confused." She dropped her head on the table. Socks, now back up on the table, stuck his nose against her head and sniffed her scalp as if he were concerned.

"Confused about what?" Miranda asked.

Kylie lifted her head and rested her chin in her palm. "Confused about what I feel for Lucas. Confused about what I feel for Derek—other than pissed off. I'm really angry at him right now." Socks bumped against her hand, seeking some TLC. Feeling as if she could use some herself, she offered the little guy some affection.

"And you should be pissed!" Della shot Miranda an odd look. "She needs to know."

"Know what?" Watching the two of them exchanging gazes, Kylie got a bad feeling.

They didn't get a chance to answer because she heard a cracking sound and the cabin's front door swung open. Burnett walked inside, and behind him stood Holiday. Behind Holiday stood Perry.

Did they have news about the Brightens? Kylie's heart jolted.

"I told you to knock," Holiday snapped at Burnett.

"I did." He looked back at Holiday.

"Well, usually after you knock, you wait until someone tells you to enter."

Burnett shot Holiday a tight smile. "Guess you need to be more specific next time." He glanced back at Kylie, and she could see concern in his eyes.

"What's going on?" Kylie's gaze went back to Perry, who looked almost guilty. But guilty about what? Oh crap! What had happened?

"I'm sorry." Perry's eyes turned deep green.

Kylie's chest tightened. "Sorry for what?"

Perry looked at Burnett and then at Holiday.

"What happened?" Kylie asked. "Are the Brightens okay? Answer me!"

Perry just stood there looking guilt-ridden.

"I'd answer her," Della said to Perry in her snarky voice. "She might go after your ears again if you don't."

Chapter Five

"I don't know what happened." Perry moved in closer, his eyes brightening to emerald green.

"How could you not know?" Kylie looked to Burnett and then Holiday, waiting for one of them to pipe up. When they didn't, she refocused on Perry. "You were following them." Suddenly, the guilt she spotted on his face did a flying leap and landed right on Kylie's own shoulders. If something really bad had happened to them, it was her fault. She'd been the one wanting to contact them. But damn it, she'd been so sure it was the right thing to do.

"They disappeared," Perry said. "One minute they were driving down the freeway in that silver Cadillac and then, poof." He waved his hands out in front of him. "They were gone. Cadillac and everything. Gone. Poof."

Kylie's chest grew heavy. "People, human people, don't just go poof." She managed to keep her voice low, but her frustration laced the tone with sarcasm.

Then the truth hit. She only thought people didn't go poof. Not too long ago she didn't think people could turn into unicorns, or that vampires and werewolves existed. She wouldn't have thought she could use her dreams to communicate with people or that she could break down a concrete wall. So who the hell knew if people went poof or not? And if they did go poof, did that mean . . . ?

Kylie's stomach knotted. "Are they dead?"

Holiday frowned. "Let's not start assuming—"

"We don't know," Burnett interrupted. "I have agents working on finding out, though. The agency is sending me pictures of the Brightens any minute now. At least then we'll know if they were impostors."

Burnett's phone rang and he snatched it up. "What you got?" His expression hardened. "That can't be. I checked them this morning." He paused and eyed Holiday, who moved closer to Burnett's side.

Della leaned over to Kylie. "The cameras aren't working." Her sensitive hearing had obviously picked up both sides of the conversation.

Footsteps sounded on the cabin porch and Kylie looked up as Lucas stepped through the doorway. His gaze found hers, his concern for her reflecting in his eyes, and he stopped beside her. His arm brushed against hers, and she felt his warmth. The memory of his kiss flashed through her head and she felt a little guilty about sharing it with Miranda and Della.

Kylie saw Lucas glance at her two roommates and nod. It wasn't an overtly friendly nod, either. Kylie had heard that werewolves were pretty standoffish, and she supposed it was true. Other than Lucas, Kylie hadn't really befriended any of them at the camp.

"Did Burnett get the pictures of your grandparents yet?" Lucas looked down at her.

"Don't know." She found herself staring at his blue eyes. For just a second, she wished she didn't question what she felt. Wished he weren't another unanswered part of her life. It would feel so good to just give in. So, why didn't she?

"You okay?" He mouthed the words more than spoke them. She nodded but wasn't so sure how true it was.

"Then someone tampered with them!" Burnett paced across the

living room. "Have you gotten the Brightens' DMV records yet? I want to see a copy of their licenses to determine if they're who they said they were." He tightened his jaw muscles and glanced up at Kylie. Empathy for her flashed in his eyes, but it faded within a flicker of a second. Showing emotion, even a glimmer in his eyes, seemed too much for him.

Everything about the man looked hard and dark. And he seemed to like it that way. He had black hair, olive skin, and a body rippled with muscles that kept most men at a distance and most women his age wishing he'd get closer. Kylie saw Holiday studying Burnett and amended her last thought. In spite of the obvious attraction that ran deep between them, Holiday wouldn't let Burnett get close.

"I don't understand what takes them so long," Burnett snapped at the caller. "It's as simple as pulling records at the DMV. I could have done it myself by now." He released a deep, frustrated sigh. "Just send them as soon as they come in." He hung up, dropped his phone into his shirt pocket, and looked at Holiday.

His eyes tightened with frustration. "Someone tampered with our cameras. I checked this morning and everything was working. Conveniently, they went down about an hour before the Brightens arrived. I think we know what that means."

Burnett glanced at Kylie. She knew he thought the Brightens were impostors. And maybe she should be hoping he was right. Because that would mean that it wasn't Daniel's adoptive parents who'd gone poof on the highway. But Kylie wanted proof. Proof of who'd gone poof.

She pressed a hand to her forehead and fought an oncoming headache. "When do they think they'll get pictures of the Brightens?"

"Any time. If they know what's good for them." Burnett's deep voice sounded sincere.

Kylie found herself praying Daniel's parents were okay. That they weren't the couple who'd visited earlier. But even so, she wasn't sure she was emotionally off the hook. Impostors or not, she wasn't sure the elderly couple deserved to . . . She stopped herself from mentally pronouncing them dead. Poof didn't necessarily equal death.

The back of Lucas's hand brushed against the back of hers. Somehow she knew the touch was deliberate and meant to comfort her. And it did.

Burnett's phone beeped. He yanked it from his pocket, pressed a button, and stared at the screen. Glancing up, he held the phone over to Holiday. "Is that the couple that was here?"

Holiday looked at the screen and then at Kylie. "No. That's not them."

It wasn't that Kylie didn't believe her, but she had to see for herself. She stepped over, took Burnett's phone, and stared at the two images side by side. An elderly, partly balding man and an older, gray-haired woman with bright green eyes gazed back from the phone's screen.

"These are the Brightens?" she asked.

Burnett nodded. "Sent from the DMV records."

"It doesn't even look like them." Kylie couldn't deny the relief that washed over her, yet she remembered the touch of the elderly woman's hand, the grief they had seemed to share, and even the sheen of tears in the woman's eyes. Had it all been an act? Kylie looked at Holiday. "Even you said the woman seemed sincere. How could we both be wrong?"

Holiday frowned. "Like I told you, reading emotions is never a hundred percent accurate."

Kylie swallowed the disappointment at having her emotions toyed with by an elderly couple. At least when Derek or Holiday toyed with her emotions, it had always been to soothe or help her. This was different; it had been meant to deceive. And maybe more.

She fought the anger crowding the other emotions in her chest. Targeting her anger toward the elderly couple still didn't seem right.

"But I don't understand what they were going to accomplish by pretending to be my grandparents."

"Obviously, they weren't here just to pat your cheek and offer you cookies," Burnett stated. "Luckily, Derek got wind of it and whatever they were attempting got foiled."

Kylie met Burnett's gaze. "Is Mario behind this?"

"Who else could it be?"

Kylie still struggled to understand. "But why would he send an elderly couple to do this when he could have gotten someone more powerful?"

"Because he thought it would fool us. And it almost did." Burnett frowned. "From now on, we're going to have to be more careful. I'm assigning you a shadow."

"A what?" Kylie was certain she wasn't going to like this.

"A shadow," Holiday said. "Someone who stays by your side at all times."

Yup, she was right. She didn't like it.

"I'll do it," Lucas said.

"No, I'll do it," another deep voice said from the open doorway.

Derek's voice sent sharp little needles of hurt into Kylie's chest. She looked up and stared into his greenish—almost hazel—eyes.

Her heart jerked as she soaked in his image. His brown hair was a little mussed, as if he ran his hands through it one too many times. His faded T-shirt clung to his wide chest, and his favorite worn jeans hugged his waist and legs. His gaze pulled her attention up again, so much emotion reflected in those eyes. She hadn't realized how much she'd missed him until now.

Right now.

She wanted to go to him, to lean against him. To assure herself he was okay.

The warmth from Lucas's shoulder pressed closer.

She saw the slightest narrowing in Derek's eyes, as if he noted how close Lucas stood. Then Derek frowned.

A storm of emotions swirled inside Kylie. One emotion stood out more than the others. Anger. Derek had no right to be upset about how close Lucas stood to her. He'd walked away, even when she'd begged him not to leave. So why did she feel the urge to add an inch or two between her and Lucas?

"I think you've done enough by getting that P.I. involved." Lucas's blue eyes drilled into Derek.

Derek's posture instantly went defensive. "Mr. Smith isn't behind this."

"Maybe not," Lucas said, his voice tight, "but it was through him that trouble arrived."

The tension in the air thickened so much, it made breathing a chore.

Burnett looked at Lucas. "There's no reason to lay blame."

"Burnett's right," Kylie said. "Besides, I'm the one who contacted Mr. Smith." She felt Lucas tense beside her and suspected he didn't like her standing up for Derek. She wasn't sure she liked doing it, not when her anger toward Derek still bumped around her chest. Nevertheless, she wouldn't let Derek get blamed for trying to help her. She continued to stare at the half-fae, wishing she could read his thoughts—or at least his emotions—the way he could read everyone else's. "Is Mr. Smith okay?"

Derek met her gaze again. Anger flashed in the gold flecks of his eyes. She didn't know if he was reflecting her emotions or if he was angry himself. Probably both. "He's going to live." His gaze left hers, and emptiness swelled in her chest. And something told her it was a feeling she'd have to get used to because nothing had changed between them.

Nothing.

"I can shadow Kylie," Della said.

"Me too," said Miranda.

Burnett looked at the two of them. "Since you are in the cabin with her, you two will have your turns."

"She'll be safer with me," Lucas said.

"Get real!" muttered Della.

"Ditto," Miranda added, and held out her pinky as if pointing out her weapon.

Kylie looked from Miranda to Della and then on to Derek and Lucas. Unreal. They were talking about her as if she weren't even here. Still, she knew they were just trying to help, and she loved them all for it. Well, she would when she stopped feeling pissed off.

Burnett looked back at Lucas and then at Derek. "I'm concerned that both of you might be too close to this."

"Which is why we'd be good at it," Derek said.

"Which is why *I'd* be good at it," countered Lucas.

Derek shot Lucas a dirty look. "You're a real jerk, Parker."

Both guys started slinging insults.

"For cripes' sakes, guys!" Kylie snapped. "This is getting—"

"Stop it!" Burnett ordered. And just like that, Derek and Lucas both fell silent. "This is what I mean. Both of you have other agendas where Kylie is concerned."

Kylie felt her cheeks redden, more from anger than embarrassment. "Here's an idea. Maybe somebody should ask me what I think about—"

"That's ridiculous," snarled Lucas. She blinked at him for a moment until she realized he was referring to Burnett's comment, not hers.

Burnett's shoulders grew tighter and his gaze shot from Lucas to Derek. "Right now, I don't think either of you would be focusing on protecting when you're with her. I'm not saying you won't be asked to help in the future, but right now—"

"Still ridiculous." Lucas stiffened beside Kylie, and she could swear she felt his temperature go up a degree or two. "I would die before—"

"As would I," Derek barked out.

"And my job is to make sure no one dies," Brunett countered.

At least on that point, Kylie could agree with Burnett.

An hour later, after Burnett and Holiday went back to the office to assign Kylie shadows, Kylie lay shivering in her bed, staring at the ceiling, wondering when and how her life had gotten so out of control. Right after Burnett left, Lucas had been summoned again by his pack. With regret in his blue eyes, and maybe even still a little anger at her for standing up for Derek, he told her he would see her as soon as his pack business was handled. Kylie hadn't begrudged him going; she'd kind of needed to be alone. But she couldn't help remembering what Fredericka had said. *Lucas's bloodline is pure, he values that. The forefathers value that, too. They've made that clear.* Were those just words cast out to cause Kylie doubt? Or was there something going on?

Kylie closed her eyes and moaned. Socks burrowed deeper under the covers at her side, while a dead bald woman paced around the room, jabbering about how she couldn't remember shit. Kylie released a deep breath, and steam rose from her lips and slowly snaked up to the ceiling.

"Can't remember," the ghost muttered. *"Nothing but a blank."*

Little did the woman know that Kylie kind of envied her right now. She wished she could forget. Forget that look of anger she'd spotted in Derek's eyes, forget the sudden tension she'd felt in Lucas's body when she stood up for Derek. Forget that she very well might be responsible for killing an elderly couple and getting the P.I., Mr. Smith, sent to the hospital.

"What's it called when you can't remember who you are? Isn't there a word for that?" the spirit asked.

"Amnesia." Kylie considered telling Jane Doe—the spirit needed a name, and Jane Doe was as good as any—that her memory loss might be more about the eight-inch scar running across her head than your average amnesia. Then again, Kylie supposed the reason Jane couldn't remember didn't matter. The fact that she had no memory was the problem. How the hell was Kylie supposed to help a ghost who didn't even know who she was?

Kylie suspected that if she asked Holiday that question, the camp leader would say to start looking for clues in what the woman did and the way she was dressed. The jeans and T-shirt the woman wore didn't give much of a clue. As for the bald head and scar, yeah, that might be a clue. However, when Kylie first met the woman, she'd had hair and looked as if her abdomen had been ripped open. Was that a clue, too?

Heck, Kylie wasn't even sure if the woman knew she was dead. Just coming out and asking her seemed a little rude.

"I just don't get why I can't remember," Jane said.

Kylie pressed her palm to her aching temple. She was so not in the mood to deal with this right now. Not that she had a choice. So far, ghosts didn't seem to respond to rain-check requests.

"Are you listening to me?" the woman asked.

Opening her eyes, Kylie sat up a bit. Socks's fluffy black-and-white tail fell out from under the sheet. "I am, I just—"

"Does your head hurt, too?"

Kylie looked up at the woman's angry scar. "A little." She pulled up her quilt from the end of the bed to ward off the chill. "But I've just got boy troubles."

"Boy troubles?" Jane frowned. *"Be careful. Boys—and men—can really hurt you."* The words sounded heartfelt. Was this another clue?

"Did someone hurt you?" Kylie asked.

The woman stopped moving, and her brow crinkled. *"Maybe. I don't remember."*

"Think hard. I mean, you said it like you remembered something."

The sooner Kylie got the ghost to remember who she was, the sooner she could discover what she needed and help her move on.

The spirit placed her index finger on her forehead. "No. Nothing. It's empty up here." She moved her hand to the side of her scalp and traced a finger over her scar. Kylie wasn't sure if she was just discovering it or not.

"Do you remember what happened? How you got that cut on your head?" *How you died?* Holiday had explained that a lot of the time when a death had been sudden or traumatic, the spirit's ability to recall it was difficult. However, to help them cross over, the details of their deaths might be important.

"No." Jane went back to pacing. *"I hate not knowing."*

After a few more laps around the room, she stopped talking and Kylie went back to thinking about Derek, about how her heart had lurched at the sight of him. She couldn't help but wonder if that meant her feelings for Lucas were not as important as she'd originally worried they might be.

Suddenly the ghost stopped at the end of the bed and stared at Kylie. *"I gave you the message, didn't I?"*

Kylie sat up a bit. "You mentioned it, but what was it again?" Perhaps the message wasn't really a message, but a clue.

"Someone lives; someone dies." Her tone dropped to a whisper and sounded like something out of a scary movie. *"That's what they said to tell you."*

Socks, as if responding to the grim note in the spirit's voice, nestled closer.

"Do you by any chance know what that means?" Reaching under the covers, Kylie gently pushed the skunk's nose away from her ribs. Considering the little fellow was afraid of ghosts, fate had really screwed up by pairing them together.

"I . . ." The spirit rolled her eyes as if trying to think. *"They didn't say."*

"Who are 'they'?" Kylie was concerned by the mention of death, but considering she was dealing with an amnesiac ghost, she wasn't so sure how much stock she could put into the message.

Jane inched closer, moving down the side of the bed, her light green eyes filled with fear. *"You know who it's from."*

"No, I don't know."

The spirit bit down on her lip as if saying the name caused discomfort. Then she leaned down, bringing her slightly blue lips only a few inches from Kylie's face. *"The death angels."* Icy crystals floated from her lips and cascaded down onto Kylie's quilt.

Socks bolted from beneath the covers, onto the floor, and under the bed.

"The death angels?" Kylie wrapped her mind around the answer. "How do you know about them?" It suddenly dawned on her that she hadn't checked to see if the woman was a supernatural.

Staring at the spirit's forehead, Kylie tightened her brows. Nothing. Which had to mean something. Everyone had a brain pattern, didn't they? Even humans. Kylie had seen Daniel's brain pattern, and Holiday had said she'd scanned Nana for one, so Kylie knew ghosts didn't just lose them after death. So why didn't this spirit have a pattern?

Closing her eyes, Kylie squinted harder and refocused. Still nothing. The icy chill of the spirit seemed to grow colder, and it clawed at Kylie's uncovered flesh. Yanking the sheet up to her chin, she shifted back from the spirit and asked the question she hated when people asked it of her.

"What *are* you?"

Chapter Six

An hour later, Kylie paced half-moon circles in her tiny room, making almost the same path as the ghost—the ghost who'd vanished without even trying to answer Kylie's question. But the skittish spirit hadn't faded before Kylie noted the sheer panic on her face.

Not that Kylie didn't empathize with the ghost.

How many times had Kylie heard the same damn question? *What are you?* Or rather, *What the hell are you?* Frankly, she didn't like either version.

But did either question instill panic or fear?

Frustration, maybe, but fear? Okay, maybe in the beginning it had scared her, but only after she'd accepted there was a possibility she wasn't human. Should she assume the spirit suspected she wasn't human? Kylie recalled the look on the spirit's face. It was as if the question sent up a red flag or stirred up some forgotten memory. And not a good memory, either.

An eerie chill filled the air, announcing the return of the ghost, and Kylie hugged herself.

"I'm sorry," Kylie said. "I know you're confused. Believe me, I know how you feel. There's a hell of a lot I'm trying to figure out about myself, too." The cold ebbed away. So the ghost wasn't up to talking. Kylie empathized with her on that point as well.

She had almost run to Holiday with questions about the spirit's lack of a brain pattern. Then, because Kylie suspected Holiday would want to go into all the other issues they needed to discuss, she decided to postpone asking the questions. And by issues, Kylie meant her newly acquired gift of healing, knocking down concrete walls, and the possibility that she was a protector. The healing and the walls, she might be able to handle. The whole protector/Mother Teresa thing? Nope. That could go unhandled for a while longer.

And it wasn't as if she were procrastinating, as Holiday accused her of so often. She was prioritizing. Right now, her top priority was Derek and the on again/off again signals he put out. How could he want to be her shadow when two weeks ago he wouldn't even look at her? Had he experienced a change of heart? Did she want him to have experienced a change of heart?

She considered it. Remembered how close she'd felt to him when they'd snuck off and he'd kissed her senseless. She even missed how he'd made everything look like a fairy tale. What she wouldn't give to be in a fairy tale right now and not have to deal with all this mess.

But did that mean if he said he was sorry, she would forgive him? After she made a few more laps around her small room, she came to the conclusion that her heart was too damn confused to know what she wanted.

As if to drive the point deeper, she had an instant recall of how it had felt when Lucas kissed her. No fairy-tale visions, but she couldn't, wouldn't, deny that it had felt pretty awesome.

Damn!

She slung herself on the bed. She was so friggin' messed up. She gave her pillow one good punch and then screamed into the fluffy down.

One deep breath later, she popped back up. She had to do something. Even if it was the wrong thing. After slipping into her tennis shoes, she grabbed her brush. She gave her blond hair a few swipes, slipped on a clean white tank top, and bolted out of her bedroom.

Della popped up off the sofa. "Hey."

"Hey." Kylie continued moving to the door, not wanting to explain where she was going because hearing herself say it aloud might make her think twice. And she didn't want to think twice; she hadn't really thought it through once yet. But she had to do something. She was tired of being in limbo.

"Where are you going?" Della asked.

"Out." Kylie reached for the doorknob. Instead, however, she ended up grabbing Della's waist, because Della had shot across the room in a flash and now stood blocking the door.

"Excuse me." Kylie tried not to let her mood sound in her voice. As moody as Della was, she had no patience for anyone else's bad mood. And getting into a pissing contest with Della right now wasn't in Kylie's plans.

"Where are *we* going?" Della asked.

"*We* aren't going anywhere. I'm going somewhere."

"I gotta come, too."

"No, you don't."

"Yes, she does." Miranda stepped out of her bedroom. "Kylie Galen, meet your first shadow, Della Tsang."

"At your service." Della's tone dripped with sarcasm. She even gave a little bow.

"Oh, screw this!" Kylie said. "I'm not leaving the camp. I'll be fine."

Della frowned. "You're not leaving the cabin unless I come with you." Her right hand landed on her right hip as if to punctuate her tone.

Kylie inhaled and tried to calm down before this got ugly. "Look,

I want to go talk to Derek, okay? And I'm sorry, but I don't want you with me. This is private."

Della's pissed-off expression vanished into something that looked almost like empathy, and she glanced at Miranda. "You still think keeping this from her is the best thing?"

"Oh hell." Miranda plopped down on the sofa. "Maybe you're right. But don't just tell her, show her."

Kylie looked back at Miranda and instantly recalled her friends acting all secretive right before Burnett had charged into the cabin. "Keep what from me? Show me what?"

Della snatched her phone from her jeans pocket and started key-ing in something. "I got it from Chan. I wanted to tell you right away, but Miranda said with you being kidnapped and all that you had enough on your plate."

"Got what?" Kylie leaned down almost nose to nose with the vamp. Her patience had been stretched to the max.

"Jeez." Della lunged back. "Patience. You're acting like it's a full moon again." She studied Kylie. "It's not, is it?" Then Della looked back at Miranda, who was still stretched out on the sofa. "Is it time for the wolves to have PMS yet?"

Kylie considered the question, almost afraid Della might be right. Was the moon cycle making her feel out of sorts, or was it everything that had happened the last few days?

"No." Miranda popped up and moved in. "We got another week before we have to deal with lunar PMS."

Kylie frowned. She hadn't morphed into a wolf the last full moon, but it appeared she'd experienced the typical mood swings that af-fected weres right before their shift. And obviously her two room-mates still considered it a possibility that she might wind up being a werewolf. Not that Kylie thought the consideration didn't have merit. At this point, she could turn out to be just about anything.

"Somebody better start talking," Kylie said. "And fast."

"Good Lord!" Della snapped back. "I'm trying to find it. Here it is." She looked up. "You see, my cousin Chan sent me a couple of images and asked if this was one of our campers. You know he lives with that vampire commune in Pennsylvania, right?"

She held out the phone and Kylie looked at the image. "That's Derek." A few seconds passed. "What was Derek doing in Pennsylvania?" Then again, she didn't know where the FRU had sent him or where the half-fae had gone looking for his dad.

"I have a better question." Della pulled back the phone, hit another button, and then held it back out for Kylie to see. "What's Derek doing sucking face with a vampire in Pennsylvania?"

Kylie's heart jolted when she saw Derek lip-locked with a dark-haired girl. And it wasn't just their lips that were locked. The girl's legs were wrapped around his waist, while Derek's hands—obviously holding the brunette up and close—were placed on her cute little jeans-covered butt.

An ache settled in Kylie's chest. "Who . . . how . . . what?"

"I asked the who question," Della said. "Her name is Ellie Mason and she was new to their vampire commune. Chan said someone mentioned Derek was from Shadow Falls and he just wanted to see if his source was telling the truth."

Ellie? Kylie recalled Derek telling her he'd dated a vampire named Ellie. She also recalled he'd told her that he'd given Ellie blood. Odd how she hadn't even known she'd remembered it, but now it seemed carved into her memory bank. "Ellie." The word leaving her lips caused a sharp and painful yank on her heartstrings. The heartstrings must be connected to her emotions, because about a dozen different ones started flapping around her chest like wild birds going after a swarm of moths. Anger, jealousy, betrayal, distrust . . . the list went on.

"I need this." She took Della's phone and tried to push Della out of the way. Not that her effort got her anywhere. Della stood cemented in place.

"Sorry. I still can't let you go alone," Della said. "Seriously, I'm your shadow."

"Fine, come. Just don't get in my way! And stay back. Way back. I need to talk to him alone." Tears prickled Kylie's eyes.

Tears of jealousy, betrayal, and frustration.

Tears of knowing that she had no right to feel any of those emotions. She wouldn't let herself cry. But she still felt those tears. Felt them as she swallowed them down her throat and they burned her chest.

Phone gripped tight, Kylie took off through the woods toward Derek's cabin, hoping that he was there. She didn't have a clue what she'd say when she saw him. She didn't want to think; she just wanted to get there. She leapt over thornbushes, ducked under low-hanging branches, and made darn good speed. Della's footfalls sounded behind her, staying close—her friend took her job as shadow seriously.

Too seriously.

The thud of Kylie's feet hitting the earth echoed, and the smell of rain hung in the air. A summer storm brewed somewhere in the distance. But not too far, because thunder rumbled overhead.

Silence followed one particularly big boom. A flash of lightning sent sprays of sizzling silver light dancing through the leaves to the moist earth. Kylie kept running, kept hurting. She could feel the storm, the energy, the power of it, in the air. More thunder followed.

Suddenly, a loud rustle sounded off to her right, and a large deer—a buck with antlers big enough to decorate a hunter's wall—darted out and jolted to a stop in the middle of her path. Shocked, she came to an abrupt stop, too. A few more inches and she might have impaled herself on the beast's antlers. She hadn't caught her breath when a bolt of lightning shot down and struck the trunk of an old tree buried only a foot past the buck. The light still sizzled when Kylie felt Della slam into her.

"What the hell?" Della said.

The buck reared his head back, the heavy antlers dropped forward almost in a threat, and then he shot off. But not before Kylie felt the beast's cold and somehow evil gaze.

The hair on the back of her neck rose. That calculating gaze meant something. Like the look the eagle gave her earlier. She pulled oxygen into her lungs and hoped it would clear her mind and she might realize she was wrong.

She didn't want to add something else to her list of things to figure out. But the air in her lungs didn't help.

The ground still sizzled and popped as tiny sparks danced around the trunk that had taken the direct hit. The smell of burnt wood and oncoming rain flavored the air. Kylie wasn't sure if she imagined it or not, but she felt a few currents of energy sting the heels of her feet.

"That was creepy," Della said.

"Yeah."

"Damn, it almost hit you!"

"But it didn't." Kylie stared at the phone in her hand and remembered Derek.

"Damn," Della repeated. "If the deer hadn't shown up . . ."

"Doesn't matter." And Kylie wanted it to be so. She heard the sound of driving rain pelting down on the leaves above her before she felt it sting her skin. The day had almost turned to night. The storm had arrived, and it matched her mood. She curled her hand around Della's phone, protecting it from the rain, and took off again at a dead run.

In a few minutes, barely winded but wet, Kylie jogged up onto Derek's porch while Della hung back. Kylie's second step brought back a memory. She'd come here looking for Derek once before and had seen blood on his porch. She'd thought he'd been attacked and had barged in only to find him . . . in the shower.

She'd gotten an eyeful that day, and after he'd gotten dressed, they'd sat here, leaning against the cabin, and talked.

Shared.

Laughed.

She couldn't ever remember feeling closer to anyone. How could things have changed between them so quickly?

She moved to the door and knocked. The door swung open, and Chris—Derek's vampire cabin mate—stood there. "Hey." His eyes widened and lowered. "Wet T-shirt contest?" he teased.

Kylie looked down, sending heavy strands of wet hair dancing around her shoulders. Her white tank and thin bra were almost invisible. She frowned and pulled her hair in front of her breasts.

"Is Derek here?"

"Yup," he said. "If he'll come to the door is another thing. He's been brooding in his room since he got back." He looked over his shoulder and called out, "Derek, you got company."

Not wanting to stand there to be ogled by Chris, Kylie stepped back from the door and waited at the edge of the porch. Still trying to control her heartbeat, she peeled her soaked shirt from her chest and flapped the fabric back and forth, hoping it would dry.

In a few minutes, familiar footsteps moved to the door. She turned around and faced Derek and had to will herself not to run and throw herself into his arms.

She took one step toward him, then stopped herself. If he rejected her, it would hurt so damn much.

Chapter Seven

Derek ran a nervous hand through his hair. Hair that looked longer than when he left. And softer. She could remember brushing it back from his brow then, and she longed to do it again. She wanted to hit the rewind button and go back to the way things were before. When things between them had been so good. But life didn't have a rewind button.

"Hey." He tucked his hands into his jeans pockets.

"Hey." Her heart raced a little faster and hurt more at the sight of him. She tried not to notice things like the muscles in his arms or how tightly his T-shirt hugged his chest. She inhaled.

While it had stopped raining, the scent of rain still clung to her clothes and hair. It still flavored the air. But it didn't hide the scent that she recognized as Derek.

She felt the phone in her hand and looked down at it.

"Sorry about not calling you back earlier," he said, as if he thought that was why she was here. "I had cut my phone off when I was in the hospital with Brit."

She nodded, not completely sure if she believed him, and felt the rise of emotion in her throat. Her sinuses stung. But she'd be damned if she would cry. At least not now. At least not here.

"Where did you go when you left Shadow Falls?" she asked.

"Just on a job assignment for Burnett." He hesitated. "I'm not really supposed to talk about it."

That hurt. She knew he was probably telling the truth, but there had been a time she hadn't believed they kept secrets from each other.

His gaze met hers and she could see the gold flecks meshing into his green irises. She saw emotion there. Hurt, jealousy, betrayal, anger. It struck her right then that everything he felt was what she, too, was feeling.

For a flicker of a second, she told herself he didn't have a right to feel those things; but she'd never been a great liar, not even when she lied to herself. Lucas had kissed her. She had feelings for Lucas, albeit confused feelings, but she still had them for him. How could she be so mad at Derek right now and not accept that he deserved his own anger?

She blinked, and the moment grew more awkward with each beat of silence. "I came here to ask you about . . ." She held out the phone and then dropped her hand back to her side. "But I suddenly realize you don't owe me an answer. I'm sorry, I . . ." Unable to finish, she turned to go.

He caught her. No sooner had his touch warmed her skin than he jerked away. And that hurt, too. Was touching her so unpleasant that it caused him to flinch?

"Ask me about what?" He frowned. "What has you so upset?"

"It's nothing. I'm fine." She started to walk away again.

"Damn it, Kylie!" He jumped in front of her. "Don't lie to me. I feel it, remember? I feel everything you feel tenfold. You're really upset about something. You came here to say something to me, so say it."

She hesitated and then turned on Della's phone.

He watched her. "What are you—"

"You'll see." She found the picture and held it out.

His expression shot from angry to . . . something different. "Shit." He ran a palm over his face.

"It's okay," Kylie said. "I realize you don't owe me an explanation. Really, I overreacted." She tried to step around him, but he grabbed her again. This time his hand lingered for a few seconds before pulling away.

"Please don't go," he said. "Look, that's Ellie. I told you about her when we first met. I dated her for a while. We ran into each other when I was on the job for Burnett. She was . . . she was just happy to see someone she knew."

"Yeah, she looks happy," Kylie said before she could stop the words, and there was an edge of sarcasm to them.

"It looks worse than it really was," he said, but he couldn't hide the guilt that flashed in his eyes.

"You really don't have to explain," Kylie said, suddenly realizing how unfair it was to confront him about this. The last thing she'd want right now was him confronting her about Lucas. She closed the phone and tucked it in her pocket. "You don't—"

"Yes, I do have to explain," Derek snapped. He drew in a pound of oxygen and hesitated before starting again. "Look, I was going to tell you anyway."

"No, you weren't," she said, finding that impossible to believe. "Not that I blame you. We weren't really going out. You don't have to tell me anything."

"I *was* going to tell you. I don't have a choice."

She studied him, not sure what he meant, and she saw more guilt in his eyes.

"Look," he said. "Ellie's here. I brought her back to the camp."

The bolt of lightning that flashed in front of Kylie a few minutes ago had shocked her less than Derek's admission. But she was pretty damn proud of herself for not letting it show. Then again, she didn't have to let it show. He could read her, but it didn't stop her from pretending. And if she pretended long enough, she might even believe it herself.

"That's good." She forced a smile.

"I had to, Kylie. She'd run away from home and was living in some hellhole of a commune. She needed help."

"I'm glad you were there for her," she said.

"Christ, Kylie! Quit friggin' pretending like I can't read you. It's me, damn it."

"Then stop reading me." Kylie's throat knotted instantly. Tears threatened, but she held them back.

"I wish I could. It would solve all our problems. I wish to God I could stop it!" He swung an angry hand through the air.

"What do you mean?" she asked.

He shook his head. "You still don't get it, do you? Being close to you is like sticking my finger into an emotional socket. I don't know why. It wasn't like that in the beginning. I mean, I could feel you more than other people, but this last month, it increased tenfold. When I'm with you, it's like being bombarded . . . attacked with emotions. I can't think straight, I can't rationalize. And if Lucas's name came up, I could feel your emotions connected to him and . . ."

He took another breath. "Maybe what I was feeling was even more than what you were feeling, but . . . I just couldn't handle it. And it wasn't just Lucas. If you were upset at your dad, I would feel the hurt you felt and I wanted to kill the bastard. I couldn't handle it anymore."

She stepped back, hoping a few inches away from her would help him. "Why didn't you tell me?"

"I did, or I tried to. You just didn't hear me. Oh, hell, I probably didn't make it clear because I didn't understand it. I still don't . . . understand it. I just know that being close to you makes me crazy." He did another pass of his fingers through his hair. "I hoped when I got back it would have changed."

"But it hasn't?"

He shook his head. "No."

"Have you asked Holiday about it?" A breeze stirred her wet hair, but it brought with it the smell of sunshine, as if the storm had passed. If only the storm inside her had done the same.

"No. I don't want to . . ."

"Ask her for help," she finished for him. A spray of bright sunlight snuck behind a low-hanging cloud and caused her to blink.

"It's not just that. I don't want her trying to get inside my head to read my emotions. I've seen things in other people's minds that they don't want me to see. I prefer to keep mine private. It's sort of like seeing someone naked." He half smiled.

She tried to respond with a smile, but she couldn't quite do it. First, because this meant his pride was more important to him than trying to fix the problem. And second, because she couldn't help wondering how many of those naked emotions were about her and how many of them were about Ellie.

"We're really mostly just friends, now," Derek said, obviously picking up on her jealousy.

Mostly? She wondered how one defined "mostly" friends? The kiss must have happened in one of the "unmostly" moments. Then she recalled the kiss she'd shared with Lucas, and guilt ran through her for judging Derek.

She met his gaze again. "You don't have to explain it."

He studied her, and God help her, because she knew he was picking apart her emotions. Reading her jealousy, followed by her thread of guilt, and then her feelings of being unfair to him. And he was probably figuring out what had happened, too.

He frowned and stepped back as if standing too close to her caused him pain. "So you and Lucas . . . ?"

The thread she'd tried to push back suddenly tied itself in a big knot in her chest. She searched for the right way to answer, then decided to borrow his. "Mostly friends."

Hurt flashed in his eyes, and she knew he understood exactly what she meant. Though she hadn't really said it to hurt him, she tried again. "I'm still trying to sort through things," she offered, hoping to soften the blow, because damn it, she knew exactly how he felt. Unknowingly, they had done the same thing to each other.

He nodded and met her gaze. "This is killing me."

The pain in his eyes echoed his words, and the knot in her chest tightened. The tears she vowed not to cry stung her eyes again.

"Same here." Her tonsils seemed to swell in her throat. "I should go." She stepped back.

"Wait. Aren't you supposed to have a shadow with you?"

For some reason, his question reminded her of the bolt of lightning. "Della's close by."

"And listening." He frowned.

"I told her not to."

"Right." Cynicism filled his voice.

Kylie took another step back, but the question slipped out before she could stop it. "Why did you offer to shadow me if it's so hard to be close to me?"

He scrubbed his tennis shoe on the wooden planks of the porch. "Because keeping you safe is more important than anything else." He inhaled. "But maybe Burnett's right. I'm too close to this. The fact that someone wants to hurt you makes me feel crazy." He looked down and then up again. "Besides, you have . . . others who claim to feel the same way." Jealousy sounded in his voice.

She wasn't sure how to answer, so she didn't.

"You do know that Brit, the P.I., isn't behind this. I don't know how anyone got to him."

Kylie recalled that Lucas had accused the P.I. of being part of the problem. "I'm not blaming him. I'm sorry he got hurt. Is he really okay?"

Derek nodded. "Yeah."

"Does he remember anything?" she asked, hoping all this could be solved that easily.

"No. And that's strange. It's almost as if he's had his memory erased. And there aren't many people who can do that."

"Maybe it's just a concussion."

"That's what the doctor thinks and what Burnett believes, but . . ." He ran another hand through his hair. "Be careful, Kylie. I heard about what happened—about that Mario guy and his grandson." His gaze dropped. "I'm sorry I wasn't there to help you."

"You had to do what Burnett wanted," she said, even though she clearly remembered begging him not to go.

"I'm serious about you being careful. I just think there could be more to all this than meets the eye."

"More like what?" she asked.

He shook his head. "I can't explain it. I just remember fighting with that rogue at the Wild Life Park that night, and he seemed different. Eerie different."

"I got the same feeling," she confessed.

"Be careful." He reached out as if to touch her, then pulled back.

"I will." She watched him stick his hands into his pockets. Their gazes met again, and it took everything Kylie had not to insist he talk to Holiday and try to fix the problem with reading her emotions too strongly. Instead she walked away. Something told her it was the right thing.

But could someone please tell her why doing the right thing hurt so damn much?

The moment Kylie hit the edge of the woods, she started running, wanting to outrun the living, breathing ache in her chest. In a few seconds, Della was beside her.

"You okay?" Her feet thudded in rhythm with Kylie's own foot-falls.

"No," Kylie answered, and ducked beneath a tree limb.

"Where are we going?" Della asked a few minutes later when Kylie turned and headed in the opposite direction of their cabin.

"I want to run," Kylie said.

"Okay." Della stayed beside her.

They ran and ran. When Kylie spotted the fence at the end of the Shadow Falls property line, she stopped and dropped to the ground. Curling her arms around her bent legs, she rested her forehead on her knees. Her lungs worked overtime as she fed them wood-scented air that still carried the scent of rain.

Della, not even winded, sat beside her. The sounds of the forest surrounded them—a bird stirred in the trees, some unnamed creature shuffled in some underbrush not far away. But mostly Kylie heard her own heart racing, sending gushing sounds through her ears.

"Your heart's still beating fast," Della said.

"I know." Kylie kept her face down.

"He was telling the truth."

Kylie knew Della was talking about Derek. "I know."

"I tried not to listen, but it was impossible. I considered moving farther away, but then I wouldn't be doing my job as shadow."

Kylie raised her head. Her gaze went to the fence and she realized where they were. Just through the barbed wire were the dinosaur tracks. And the creek where Lucas had kissed her. She let herself think about it for a second, because thinking about Derek hurt.

Then she looked back at Della. "You listen in on my private conversations, but then you don't share."

"Share what?" Della sounded clueless.

Kylie raised an eyebrow. "What happened while you were at home? I know you were lying. So does Miranda."

"Oh, that." She pulled a long blade of grass from the ground and started tying it around her finger.

Kylie thought Della wasn't going to answer, and then . . . "I went to see Lee."

Kylie suspected that Della hadn't stopped caring for her ex. Not that Della had admitted to it. "And?"

"He's practically engaged to another girl. His parents are pushing him to make it official. They like her." The pain in Della's voice matched the pain Kylie felt for Derek.

Kylie hugged her knees. "I'm so sorry."

"Don't be," Della said. "It's for the best. He could have never accepted me being a vampire."

"Doesn't mean it doesn't hurt." And damn if Kylie didn't know that for a fact.

Della hesitated. "She's a hundred percent Asian. Not a mishmosh like me."

"He said that?" Kylie really disliked this guy.

"Not exactly, but he said his parents had pushed him to date her. And I know they didn't like me because I'm half white."

"You need to move on," Kylie said.

"I already have." Della tossed the grass back to the ground.

It was a lie, but Kylie didn't think calling Della on it would do any good. Kylie leaned back and stared up at the trees. The moisture from the recent rain soaked into her clothes, but she didn't care. The coolness felt good in the Texas heat. A blue jay flitted from one limb to another in the tree. Kylie's emotions seemed to be doing the same.

She studied the bird, so happy, so innocent and trouble-free. Della released an exaggerated breath, as if she were still thinking about Lee.

"Steve likes you," Kylie said.

"No, he doesn't."

"Yes, he does." Kylie glanced at Della. "I saw him looking for you today when we were in the dining hall. You should go for it."

"If he likes me, he'll come to me."

"I don't mean throw yourself at him. Just be nice. Make yourself more approachable."

"I'm approachable," Della said.

About as much as a rattlesnake, Kylie thought.

Della picked up another blade of grass and then lay back on the ground beside Kylie. Their shoulders almost touched. "It's not easy."

"Believe me," Kylie said. "I know."

They lay stretched out on the damp ground for several long minutes without talking. The sun leaked light through the trees and created shimmering golden shadows throughout the woods. Through the leaves, Kylie saw the sky painted in an array of stormy-looking clouds in a variety of colors. Her mind went round and round and somehow landed back on Derek.

"I can't believe he brought Ellie with him." The idea of having to see Derek with Ellie made Kylie's chest tighten.

"Yeah, that'll be tough. I mean, if I had to see Lee with his girlfriend, I'd end up killing someone."

"No, you wouldn't." Kylie sat up, pulled her hair over one shoulder, and removed a few clinging twigs. "You'd do exactly what I'm going to do."

"What's that?" Della sat up.

"Pretend it doesn't hurt, and hope like hell that one day it doesn't anymore."

"Nope. I'd rather kill someone." Della stood and dusted off the wet grass that clung to her backside. Then she looked down at Kylie. "So does this mean you're actually going to give Lucas a real chance?"

Kylie stood up and gave her own butt a few swipes to dislodge most of the grass. "Maybe. If it's what he wants, too."

"If? Didn't you hear him getting pissy with Burnett about shadowing you? He's got it bad for you. I mean, I know you're hurting over Derek, but he doesn't deserve you angsting over him. You have an opportunity with Lucas. Go for it."

She hesitated to say anything, but it spilled out. "Fredericka said something that made it sound like his pack doesn't want us seeing each other."

"Don't listen to anything that b with an itch says. She'll say anything to come between you and Lucas."

Kylie nodded, knowing that Della was right. Or at least she hoped she was.

The bird in the tree called out. Kylie looked up and wondered if that was a mating call. Did birds experience romance? Did they ever suffer from broken hearts? She had to admit it looked awfully lonely up in the tree alone. Almost as lonely as it was where she stood.

"Let's make a deal," Della said. "You give Lucas a chance and I'll give Steve a chance."

Kylie smiled. "Are you that worried about me, or do you just need an excuse to go after the good-looking shape-shifter?"

"Maybe both." Della grinned. "We got a deal?"

Kylie considered it, and mentally she stopped trying to hang on, stopped trying to fix something that didn't seem fixable, and opened herself up to other possibilities. "Yeah."

Della started walking, and Kylie took a step. Then the cold grabbed her. She turned and watched Jane Doe's spirit materialize in the beam of sunlight.

The woman met Kylie's gaze. *"Do you know?"*

"Know what?" Kylie asked.

Della turned around. "What?" She stared at Kylie for a second and then said, "Oh shit. Not again." She backed up. "I'm not freaking out. I'm not. Really, I'm not freaking out."

Kylie held up a hand to silence Della and stared at the spirit as she edged closer.

"Do you know what I am?" Jane spoke in a hushed tone that

seemed to whisper through the trees. The blue jay in the tree chirped extra loud.

"No," Kylie said. "I don't." Then the bird chirped oddly and fell from the tree and landed with a lifeless thud at the spirit's feet.

Chapter Eight

"What was that?" Della demanded.

Kylie stared at the bird. It didn't move. Didn't make a noise. Was it . . . ? Her heart squeezed.

"Screw this! It's raining dead birds. *Now* I'm freaking out. Can we leave, *please*?"

The spirit looked from the blue jay to Kylie. *"Is it dead?"* She knelt and stared at it. When she looked up, she had tears in her eyes. *"It's dead. Just like me. Just like the death angels warned. Someone lives and someone dies."*

"No one is going to die."

Kylie picked up the limp bird. Its neck flopped to one side. She remembered seeing the bird so full of life just moments before. What happened? She looked back at the spirit. "Did you kill it?"

"No, I didn't kill it," Della said. "Wait, you aren't talking to me, are you? Is this a death angel or just a ghost?"

"No." Jane looked around as if she were as frightened as Della. She moved closer. *"The others did. They're not nice."*

Kylie shivered from the ghostly cold. "What others?"

"Shh." The spirit lifted her finger to her lips. *"They're coming."* She faded away.

Della stood back and continued to stare. Kylie cupped her hands around the blue jay. She'd healed Sara. Was it possible that she might be able to . . . ?

Kylie closed her eyes and tried to think healing thoughts.

The bird started quivering. Kylie opened her hands and its wings spread. Its feathers, a bright royal blue and white, caught a spray of sunshine and shimmered in the light, then the bird lunged to its feet and flew away. Kylie watched it disappear into the tops of the trees, her emotions ambivalent. On the one hand, she'd given something life, and that was cool. On the other . . . Well, it was just too freaky.

"Did you do what I think you did?" Della asked. "Did you just bring that dead bird back to life?"

Kylie looked up. "I'm not sure." Suddenly silence filled the forest. The spirit's words echoed in Kylie's head. *They're coming*.

The lack of noise seemed ominous.

She looked at Della. "Can you sense anyone here?"

Della sniffed the air. "No. But it's too damn quiet."

"We should go," Kylie whispered.

"You don't have to ask me twice." Della tore out.

Kylie was right behind her, hoping to outrun the silence, the feeling of danger, and another startling realization about her powers.

"You sure it was dead?" Holiday asked.

"I didn't listen to its heartbeat." Kylie paced the small office. "But do birds regularly fall out of trees unconscious?"

Holiday bit back a smile. "I don't think so."

For some reason, this news didn't seem near as startling to her camp leader as it did to Kylie.

Kylie, still winded from her run, had left the woods and come straight to find Holiday. Della, who took the job of shadowing seriously, waited outside.

"The ghost was there. Do you think her presence did this? Maybe it had nothing to do with me. The bird came back to life when she left. So maybe it was just her."

"It could be. However, I've never heard of a ghost's presence killing wildlife, even temporarily. Maybe the bird was just stunned. Maybe all this is a clue."

"To what?" Kylie asked, frustrated.

"Her identity, maybe."

Kylie stopped in front of the desk. "How is a bird dying going to tell me who she is?"

"Sometimes the spirits have crazy ways of communicating."

Kylie rolled a few things around her already confused mind, and then she remembered. "Jane Doe has no brain pattern. Nothing. It's blank."

"Blank?" This time Holiday appeared genuinely puzzled.

"Yeah. I kept trying to refocus, thinking I was . . . just not seeing it right. Because I thought we all had brain patterns, like fingerprints." Kylie dropped in the chair across from the camp leader.

"I've never seen one that's blank, but . . ."

"I think she's supernatural." Kylie chewed on the side of her lip.

"Why would you think that?"

"Because she knew about the death angels."

Holiday appeared to consider it. "She probably heard you talking about them."

"Maybe. But . . . she's really scared of something."

"Dying can be scary if you're not ready."

"I think it's more," Kylie said.

"More like what?"

"I don't know yet. But it's . . . something."

"Wait." Holiday pressed a hand on the desk. "Didn't you tell me she had some kind of brain operation?"

"Yes." Kylie touched her temple. "She has stitches and her head is shaved."

"It's probably a tumor. I've never seen anyone with one, but I've heard tumors can make one's brain pattern do strange things."

"But can a tumor make it disappear?" Kylie asked. "And what about her getting freaked out when I asked her what she was? I really think she's supernatural."

"I'm not saying she isn't one of us, but . . . rarely do we supernaturals hang around long after we pass. In all my years of dealing with ghosts, I've only had three supernaturals."

"But my dad hung around."

"But he had a very big reason to hang on. To check in on you."

Kylie pulled her leg up in the chair and hugged her shin. Her mind zipped from the ghost to her dad to the ghost again. "I don't know . . . There's something about her that's . . . different. Remember, she told me she had messages from others."

"That's not unusual. I often get spirits who tell me something for someone else." Holiday rolled a pencil between her hands.

"But from the death angels?" Kylie asked.

"No, but like I said, she could have heard you mention the death angels and simply be confusing things. Has she mentioned the message again?"

"Yeah. Every time, like it's important." Kylie frowned. "She keeps saying that someone lives and someone dies. And I don't like the die part." She hugged her knee tighter.

"Me either," Holiday said. "But as you've learned, ghosts aren't the best communicators. So don't panic. Just keep asking questions and watching for clues."

"Is it possible that the only reason she's here is to give me this message?"

"Rarely. She's probably here for something else."

Kylie frowned. "Then how the heck am I going to help her if she doesn't even remember who she is?"

Holiday dropped her chin in the palm of her hand. "I think this might be a difficult one."

"As if any that I've had have been easy." Kylie tightened her hold on her leg. "There's one thing I want to check out."

"What's that?"

"Fallen Cemetery. I know you said she could have come from anywhere, but I still find it odd that this is where she popped into my mom's car."

Holiday pinched her brows together. "I'm not going to tell you not to go, but cemeteries aren't the best place for a ghost whisperer. By now you should be able to see more than just one ghost, and a lot of ghosts hang around the cemeteries for a long time."

Kylie remembered. "At Nana's funeral I got a terrible headache."

"That was probably them trying to get through to you. And that was before you could see them. Sometimes they can come at you all at once and it gets . . . difficult."

"But if that's the only lead I have, I have to try."

"You don't have to," Holiday argued. "In the beginning, I wouldn't have ever refused to help a spirit. But I learned that sometimes you have to say no for your own sanity."

"But they'll just keep coming back."

Holiday tilted her head a bit. "Don't you remember us talking about how to shut them out?"

Kylie frowned. "I remember, but I haven't mastered that so well."

"We could go over it again, but . . ." Holiday looked at her watch. "I have an appointment—"

"I want to help her. There's something about her." Kylie might not have amnesia, but there was so much about her life she didn't know, things she wanted to know.

Holiday nodded. "I understand. And I'll support whatever you feel is right. But just make sure you check with me before going, and . . . as Burnett said earlier, you're not to go anywhere without a shadow."

"I'm not too keen on the whole shadow thing," she said.

"Just until we see how things go."

Kylie bit down on her lip, remembering the other things she needed to discuss with Holiday. The whole healing and protector issues. Not to mention the questions she had about her sudden overpowering effect on Derek's emotions.

Then there was . . . She would never get rid of the shadows if she confessed her other concerns. But to not discuss them was stupid. And Kylie wasn't stupid. "Are our security cameras set for . . . shape-shifters?"

Holiday leaned forward. "I'm sure they are. Why?"

"It's probably nothing, but a couple of things happened. They could be nothing, but they didn't feel like nothing."

Holiday stopped rolling the pencil in her hands. "What kind of things?"

"When I left to go back to the cabins, I came across a rattlesnake, but I didn't see it until an eagle swooped down and snatched it up. It was freaky."

"Did it go after you?" Concern darkened her green eyes.

"No, it never got the chance. But the whole thing was just strange."

"Strange like how?"

"The eagle just swooped down." Kylie suddenly felt as if she were overreacting.

Holiday added, "Rattlesnakes are prevalent this time of year, and I admit seeing an eagle swoop down might be—"

Kylie didn't wait for Holiday to continue. "And then when I went to . . . run in the woods, a deer—a big buck—came hurtling onto my path. I stopped and, not a split second later, lightning struck right past the deer. If the deer hadn't stopped me, I might have been hit."

Holiday frowned. "I don't like the sound of this."

"And the deer and the eagle, they . . . looked right at me as if they were trying to tell me something."

Holiday's brow wrinkled. "You think you can communicate with animals?"

"No. I don't think that. They looked evil."

Holiday tilted her head to the side. "The deer and the eagle appeared evil?" When Kylie nodded, Holiday looked even more perplexed and worried. "With two of these strange things happening, I can't believe they are accidents. However, if I'm understanding you, both the eagle and the deer saved you from getting hurt. How could they have been evil? If anything, they were protecting you."

Kylie pulled a handful of hair over her shoulder and twisted it. "I know it doesn't make sense, but it felt that way."

Holiday set the pencil on her desk and reached for her phone. "We'd better let Burnett . . . Wait." She put down her phone. "Burnett left to have a meeting with the FRU. I don't want to disturb him now, but I'll tell him about this as soon as he gets back."

Kylie heard the front door of the cabin open.

Holiday looked at her watch and frowned. "I have another meeting, but we need to talk more about this. Can you wait until I finish so we can continue this?"

"I can come back later," Kylie said, not really wanting to hang out at the office. It would make her feel like a kid sent to the principal's office. "Oh, does Burnett still need the pictures of my dad? If not, I'd like to have them back."

"He's having them tested to see if they are originals or copies. It shouldn't be more than a few days."

"Hi," came an unfamiliar female voice from behind Kylie. "I'm sorry. I didn't know you had someone in here. I can wait in the—"

"It's fine," Holiday said.

Kylie's heart did a little tumble when she recognized the brunette as the one who'd been plastered to Derek in the picture on Della's phone.

"Kylie," Holiday said, "this is Ellie Mason. She's signing up for Shadow Falls."

Showtime, Kylie thought. Time to pretend it didn't hurt. She forced a smile. "Hi."

"Are you Kylie Galen?"

Kylie nodded, unsure what to expect.

"Derek told me about you." She smiled, then tightened her brows to check out Kylie's brain pattern. "Wow. You do have an odd pattern." She made a funny face as if embarrassed.

"Yeah," Kylie said. "Everyone tells me that." Her forced smile melted.

"I'm sorry," Ellie said. "I didn't mean to be rude. Derek has nothing but great things to say about you."

"Don't believe everything he says." Kylie attempted to soften her tone because she felt like a bitch for not liking her. But how could she like Ellie when all Kylie could think about was how Ellie was most likely one of the four girls Derek had slept with? Then she wondered if a kiss was all they'd shared in Pennsylvania.

"I always believe Derek. Especially about people." Ellie took another step inside.

Kylie hated to admit it, but Ellie was pretty. Blue eyes, thick brown hair, and dimples.

Ellie's sincere smile widened. "Derek doesn't tend to exaggerate. And being half-fae, he's a good judge of character. If he likes someone, they deserve it."

Kylie wished she could have disagreed. Not so much because she didn't want to be considered deserving. But because Derek obviously cared for Ellie enough to bring her back here, which meant Ellie was a deserving person.

The being-a-bitch feeling hit again, and Kylie tried to push it back.

"Maybe I caught him on an off day." She attempted to put some teasing in her voice and stood up. "I should go."

"Kylie, why don't I drop by your cabin in about half an hour?" Holiday asked, concern deepening her tone.

Kylie nodded.

"And be careful," Holiday said.

"I will." Kylie stopped when she neared Ellie. "Welcome to Shadow Falls." And she tried to mean it.

"Thank you," Ellie said.

"Is my vampire hearing off? Did you actually say, 'Welcome to Shadow Falls'?" Della asked sarcastically when Kylie got outside. "I would have bitch-slapped her."

"No, you wouldn't have." Kylie noticed the stormy weather had passed.

"Maybe not, but I would have wanted to." Concern shaded Della's eyes.

"And you think I didn't?" Insecurities rained down on Kylie. "She's pretty, isn't she?"

"No," Della said, but Kylie knew it was a lie. Ellie was pretty and nice and she'd probably had sex with Derek.

Kylie's chest swelled with unwanted jealousy, and her mind created an image of Ellie and Derek together. Of them kissing . . . of them . . .

She started walking toward her cabin. Walking fast. Della stayed with her, but somehow she must have sensed Kylie's mood, because she didn't say anything else.

Kylie got to their cabin without speaking, but once she stepped up onto the porch, she faced Della. "Do you think they had sex?"

"I . . ." Della made an odd face.

"I know I shouldn't care. But I guess I do. And damn it, why does it seem that it all goes back to sex? I'm beginning to hate sex and I haven't had it yet. I've got these images flashing in my head. It's like a porn movie and I just keep seeing them—"

Della pressed her hand over Kylie's mouth and shifted her gaze to a point over Kylie's shoulder.

Kylie reached up and peeled Della's hand from her lips. "Is someone standing behind me?" She prayed the answer was no.

Della's sassy smile told Kylie her prayer hadn't been answered.

Swallowing a lump of embarrassment, she tried to imagine the worst person possible standing behind her. Ellie? Derek? No. She met Della's eyes again and mouthed the word *Lucas*.

Please. Please. Please don't let it be Lucas.

Della nodded. Kylie bit back a moan. Not quite ready to face him, she stared out at the woods. Through a maze of trees, she saw the sun slip lower in the horizon. She wished she could follow it and disappear.

"Can you give us a minute?" Lucas's voice came right over her shoulder.

Knowing it was inevitable, Kylie turned. Her face burned when she recalled what she'd said about a porn movie and her whole "I hate sex" conversation. Great!

"Can't," Della answered. "I'm her shadow."

"Well, I'm taking over," he said, almost growling.

"It's okay," Kylie said to Della.

Della frowned. "If something happens to her on my shift, I swear I'll be all over your wolf ass."

"Nothing's going to happen." His blue eyes grew darker, and around the edges, Kylie saw flecks of burnt orange, which meant anger.

Kylie couldn't help wondering if that was targeted at Della or—

"Fine." Della stormed inside. But not without slamming the door so hard, the porch shook.

Kylie met Lucas's gaze. He still looked half-pissed.

"Let's take a walk," he said.

Kylie recalled how he'd stiffened earlier when she'd taken up for Derek. Was he angry at her, too? The thought of hurting him when he'd risked his life to save her made her stomach clutch. He didn't deserve that, not that she'd meant to hurt him. But neither did Derek deserve to be blamed for trying to help her.

He started off the porch and looked back.

His eyes were a brighter orange now. Kylie remembered a time she would have freaked out at seeing an angry werewolf. Heck, she remembered a time when she hadn't believed werewolves existed, angry or not.

"You coming?" Lucas asked.

Chapter Nine

She could say no, but she didn't want to. She followed him. The sun hung low, but its light clung to the sky. However, once they moved into the woods and under the umbrella of the trees, the remnants of daylight faded into dusk. They walked without talking.

She remembered the dead bird and the ghost's announcement that someone else was out there. Fear brushed against Kylie's neck. Almost as if she could feel the hot breath of something evil on her nape, she reached up and tried to brush away the sensation. Everything seemed to grow darker.

"Should we be going into the woods?" She heard a rustle and looked to her left. And she walked right into Lucas's back, unaware that he'd stopped. He turned and she saw him lift up his face as if to sniff the air.

"You're scared of me?" he asked.

Even through the dimness she could see anger in his expression.

"No. I'm scared of . . . other things." She didn't know what to call them.

"Scared Derek will hear you went off with me?" His tone came with accusation.

"No."

He swung back around and commenced walking again. She matched his steps. He stopped abruptly and faced her again.

"I said I'd be patient and I will, but I won't be made a fool of."

"I didn't make a fool of you," she insisted.

"You stood up for Derek."

"I just stated the facts. You were wrong to blame Derek." Her throat tightened again. She'd been fighting tears all day, and this time when they crawled up her throat, she was helpless.

She turned away, hoping to stop them before he saw. But when she reached up to swipe away the first tear, he caught her hand. How he could have moved in front of her without making a sound was unnerving.

He let go of a deep breath. "I didn't mean to upset you, it's just . . ."

She tried to tell him it wasn't him making her cry, but the concern in his tone had the knot in her throat doubling in size. The next thing she knew she was against his chest, her tears and almost silent sobs being absorbed by his pale blue T-shirt and his extra warm chest.

His arms were around her and she felt his cheek resting on top of her head. She felt safe. Safe and something else. She felt cherished. The way his arms held her, the way every inch of him embraced her—she wanted to stay here. Savor it.

"I'm sorry," she muttered, her face still buried against him. "I shouldn't be sliming up your shirt."

"Is it over?" His words tickled the top of her head.

"Is what over? My crying?" She wasn't ready to give up the wall of muscle or having his arms around her. Nor was she ready to let him see her all red and splotchy.

"No. You and Derek." His tone deepened, and she sensed it was hard for him to even ask the question.

"Yeah." She nodded her head against him.

His arms tightened around her. She almost sighed because it felt so good.

"Then you're welcome to slime my shirt," he said, and the undercurrent of anger vanished. "I don't have a lot of rules, but that's one of them. Only uncommitted girls can slime my shirt."

She chuckled.

"Is that a smile I feel against my chest?" His words stirred her hair.

"A slimy one." She snaked her hand up between their bodies to clear her face before looking up.

"I'll bet it's still beautiful."

He inched back, and in the dark woodsy light, she felt his eyes on her.

"You might lose the bet." She wanted to cover her face but would feel silly doing it.

"You're right, I would have lost." He laughed. "You don't cry pretty."

She thumped his solid chest with her palm. He laughed again.

"Come on." He fitted his hand in hers and started walking again, deeper into the woods. With the night sounds around them, she tuned her ears and waited for it to go silent—for something bad to suddenly appear.

She gave his hand a slight pull. "Let's go back the other way."

He turned and studied her. "What are you afraid of?"

"If we walk out of the woods, I'll tell you." She tried to make light of the dread gnawing at her gut.

A frown pulled at his brows. "I wouldn't let anything hurt you."

"I know, but I'd feel better if we went that way." She nodded back to the clearing.

"Fine." He began walking in that direction. "But start talking. Why are you afraid? Is it still the elderly couple?"

"No." She wished she could see the clearing of the woods ahead, but the night seemed to close in on her.

Suddenly, something dark *whoosh*ed down from a tree. She lurched back and pulled him with her. Her heart shot up in her throat. She tightened her hand in his, and with everything she had, she started to run. He ran with her, two people moving in one solid, fluid motion, his palm clutched tightly in hers.

Once they reached the clearing, Kylie stopped, bent over, and hungrily sucked oxygen into her lungs.

Finally rising, she looked at him. Out from under the thicket of the trees, night hadn't completely fallen and she could make out his features.

He stood there, watching her. He didn't gasp for air or hold his stomach the way she did. Damn it! He didn't even look winded.

Curiosity filled his eyes. "It was just an eagle."

"It was?" She looked up at the sky, which was painted with only a few lingering colors of sunset, and prayed the bird hadn't followed. Thankfully, only the first few stars of the night twinkled back at her. No eagle. At least she didn't see it.

"Did it follow us?" she asked, remembering he could see better than she could.

"No." He studied her. "Something happened, didn't it."

"Yes. Maybe. Just weird stuff." She realized she still held his hand, and while it was balmy outside, his hand felt nice. It warmed her palm in a good way, like a cup of hot chocolate, a comforting feeling. While his touch didn't hold the magic of the fae to calm one's fear, it did calm her.

"Come on." He went back to running. Fast. Then faster.

Every time she'd push herself to meet his speed, he'd increase it. Then he'd glance at her as if to make sure she wasn't having to work too hard. She got the feeling he was testing her, wanting to see just how fast she could run.

"Where are we going?" she asked, barely able to speak.

"To the creek." His voice sounded even.

His pace kept getting faster. Wanting to impress him, forgetting all about the eagle, she pushed herself to keep going. Finally, he stopped. Not prepared for the halt, she continued forward. She felt the tug on her arm where she still held his hand, and then suddenly his arm swooped around her waist.

Out of energy and off balance, she fell into him and they both went down. Not hard, or at least not for her, because she landed on top of him.

"You okay?" Her heart still pumped, her chest moving up and down as she gasped for air. As her lungs expanded again, she became aware of the intimate way her body rested against his.

He laughed. "Me okay? You're the one who can't breathe." He wrapped his arms around her. His hands rested on the small of her back.

"I can . . . breathe." She laughed. Warm contentment filled her, and she realized she liked being with him. Liked being this close. Maybe too much.

She could feel every inch of his body under hers, and it made her even more breathless. She rolled off of him. The earth and grass beneath her back felt cool, especially considering how warm he had been. The sounds of the night, crickets and a few birds, sang around them. She stared through a curtain of her hair at the midnight blue sky and focused on a star flickering its brightness down from the heavens.

"I'm impressed. I didn't know you could run like that." He rolled to his side, propped up on his elbow, and brushed her hair from her face.

"Yeah." One word was all she could manage. She blinked and stared up at his face. Even in the night, she could see and appreciate the angles and lines of his features. He was so masculine. Always had been, even when he'd been seven. But now, with the light shadow of a beard, he was downright stunning.

The temptation to touch his cheek, to run the tips of her fingers over the stubble, tiptoed through her mind.

She inhaled, her lungs still thirsty for oxygen. Suddenly the sound of water trickling nearby filled her senses. "Are we . . . ?" She raised her head and realized they'd arrived at the creek, the spot she'd brought her mother the day she'd asked about Daniel.

Sadness whispered through her when she remembered she might not see her dad again. She pushed that back and tried not to let the happiness of this moment melt away.

"We made good time." She realized how far they had run.

"How long have you known you could run like that?" he asked.

"Only since I've been here. But I'm getting faster."

He picked up a thick lock of her hair and watched it slide off his palm. His face was only a few inches from hers. She saw him tighten his brows to check out her pattern.

"It's still a mystery," she said.

He met her eyes. "You don't even suspect what you are?"

She frowned. "I wish."

He pulled a long blade of grass from the ground and twirled it in his fingers. Then he looked over his shoulder at the moon, only half-full. "When I was a kid and lived next door to you, when I'd shift, I'd jump the fence into your backyard and watch you through your bedroom window, waiting and hoping I'd see you turn."

"You peeped into my window?"

He smiled. "It's not like you were naked or anything. You mostly wore that Little Mermaid nightshirt." A laugh spilled out of his throat. "You looked like an angel. Sometimes I would stay there half the night thinking you still might turn."

She studied his eyes. "Did you think I was a werewolf?"

"I hoped." He touched the tip of her nose with the grass. Then he slid it over her lips. It tickled and yet somehow felt seductive.

He continued staring as if remembering. "I wanted to run in the woods with you. To show you how fast I could go. To take you to my favorite watering hole so we could chase each other in the spring and play in the moonlight."

"Do you still hope I'm a werewolf?"

He hesitated. "Yeah. I probably shouldn't tell you that, but yeah, I do. It would make everything easier."

"Make what easier?" She thought about what Fredericka had said.

"Everything." He brought the blade of grass back over her lips. "I wouldn't have to be away from you when I shift. We could hunt together. You would be with me when I'm leading the pack."

The thought of hunting and killing wild animals didn't sit well with her, even being with the group of weres that included Fredericka didn't hold a lot of appeal, but she tried not to let it show.

"We'd make a great team."

"And what if I'm not a werewolf?"

He smiled, but for just a second she thought she saw disappointment in his eyes.

"We still make a good team," he said.

"Does everyone feel that way?" she asked, not wanting to mention Fredericka.

"What do you mean?"

"The last couple of times we've been together, someone from the pack sent for you as if they didn't want you with me."

"It's nothing," he said.

"You sure?"

He tickled her cheek with the grass. "Trust me."

"I do trust you."

"You haven't told me what you're afraid of."

She bit down on her lip. He swiped the blade of grass over her mouth.

"Start talking."

She told him about the eagle and the snake and then about the huge buck and the lightning.

He frowned. "Do you think Derek is doing this? He communicates with animals."

"No. Derek wouldn't do that."

"You say that like you trust him." Lucas's tone deepened.

"I do. Please don't take it the wrong way. It's over with us, but I know he wouldn't try to hurt or even scare me. He cares about me."

"And you him?" His eyes went from blue to almost orange.

"Yes. But it's still over." She could tell he didn't like hearing her say that, but he seemed to understand. For a flicker of a second, she wondered how long it would be before she could understand it herself.

He stared back up at the moon. "If it's not him, then who?"

"I think Holiday and Burnett believe Mario and Red are behind it. And they sent the impostors posing as my grandparents. But then Della said that they're vampires, not shape-shifters, so they couldn't be doing it themselves."

"Maybe Mario has a shifter working for him. Though it's uncommon that two species work together like that." He brushed a strand of hair behind her ear. "I won't let that creep lay another finger on you."

She knew he really didn't have the ability to keep that promise, but she liked hearing it.

Then, because it felt good talking about it, she told him about the ghost and the bird falling from the tree.

He looked concerned. "Do you think she's a death angel?" He was obviously more disturbed by the ghost than the fact that Kylie had brought a dead bird back to life.

"No, but I think she's a supernatural."

"Did you check her pattern?"

"That's part of the problem. She doesn't have one."

"Everyone has a pattern," he said.

"But she doesn't. Before she disappeared, she told me the others were out there."

"What others? Like more ghosts?" Lucas looked around.

"I don't think she meant ghosts. She made it sound like they were evil."

"And ghosts aren't evil?" he asked in disbelief.

"Not really. At least none of them that I've met."

He shook his head. "I can't imagine dealing with them."

She hesitated before answering. "It was hard in the beginning. It's still freaky, but not as bad." She met his eyes. "Besides, I can't imagine shifting into a wolf."

He smiled. "It's a piece of cake. I hope you figure that out for yourself, too."

She chewed on the fact that he really wanted her to be werewolf. No disrespect intended, but she wasn't so sure she shared his hope.

"I heard you experienced some of the mood swings last month." His gaze lowered to her breasts. "You also underwent some hormonal changes like female weres do."

Yeah, she'd grown an inch, a cup, and a shoe size—not so strange until you realized it happened overnight. Not that she really liked being reminded of it. Her face heated.

She pushed back the embarrassment. "True, but there's just as much evidence that I'm not a were. According to Holiday, weres are seldom ghost whisperers. They start turning when they're very young and they don't have the ability to dreamscape."

A light smile appeared in his eyes and, blast it, she knew exactly what he was thinking about, too. The dream. The one of them swimming, practically naked and . . .

"Guess we'll have to see in a couple of weeks when the moon is full."

He ran the blade of grass over her lips again and then down past her chin.

Her breath almost caught when it glided across the swell of her breasts above the cut of the tank top. It was just a piece of grass, but it could have been his finger for the sweet sensation pouring into her chest.

He leaned down, his lips inches from hers. "I have a request."

"What's . . . that?" She was barely able to think, much less speak.

He swept the blade of grass up and swirled it around her forehead. "When you close your eyes and get images flashing in your mind . . ."

His words reminded her of what he'd heard her say to Della about the porn movie. Her face grew hot again.

"I want that movie playing in your mind to be of us. Only us."

She felt the warmth of his mouth, then in a flash he pounced over her. He landed in a crouch, then slowly rose, a low growl rumbling from his throat as he stared out at the line of trees.

She scrambled to her feet. "What is it?"

He looked back at her. His eyes glowed that bright burnt orange color. "Someone's coming."

Chapter Ten

Kylie's heart started to pound. "Should we run?"

"No." Lucas's defensive posture relaxed. "It's just—"

"Me," another deep male voice said.

Kylie recognized the voice before she saw Burnett standing behind her. Even in the darkness, she was close enough to recognize the look of discontent on his face. His eyes weren't glowing, so it wasn't about danger, but everything in his expression said he wasn't happy. And he was looking right at her.

What could he be so upset about?

He stepped closer, his presence larger than life. "Holiday is—"

All it took was his two words and Kylie had her answer. "Crap! Holiday was supposed to come by my cabin. I'm sorry."

"Yeah," he said. "And she really got worried when we couldn't find Della, who was supposed to be your shadow." He turned his focus on Lucas, and his grimace deepened.

"Where's Della?" Kylie asked. "Is she okay?"

"She's fine. She and Miranda had gone for a swim. But none of this would have happened if someone hadn't insisted she be relieved of her shadow duties."

"That's my fault," Kylie insisted.

"It's not anyone's fault." Lucas stiffened his shoulders. "I wouldn't have let anything happen to Kylie."

"That's not the point," Burnett growled into the night. "Considering your affiliation with the FRU, you of all people should understand the importance of following protocol. I assigned Della as Kylie's shadow, and it's not your place to change my orders. And by changing them, you caused this situation."

"I wouldn't have had to change it if you'd assigned her to me in the beginning as I asked. And considering my affiliation, you should trust me to protect her."

Kylie looked from Burnett to Lucas and then back again. "I'm the one who forgot about Holiday. If anyone is to blame—"

"I came looking for you," Lucas snapped, as if refusing to let her take any blame. He stared back at Burnett. Lucas's eyes started to change colors.

An owl called out in the woods. The half-moon seemed to grow brighter as the two of them, vampire and werewolf, stood staring at each other.

Burnett was the first to blink, not that it came off as weakness, but rather a sign of reasoning. "Trust is earned. Your overconfidence will not serve you well in the FRU."

"My overconfidence only comes second to yours," Lucas said. "And I think it's part of the reason the FRU is interested in me."

"Perhaps. But there is a fine line between indomitable and supercilious. And the latter character trait is nothing the FRU accepts." Burnett pulled his cell phone out of his pocket and hit a button.

Kylie saw Lucas's jaw tighten, and she knew how hard it was for him to be reprimanded by Burnett, especially in front of her.

Lucas looked away, but not before Kylie saw his eyes glittering with anger. But then he said, "I apologize if I caused a problem." He might be angry, but he was willing to concede.

Burnett nodded and spoke into the phone. "Holiday, I have her.

She's fine. . . . Yes. I will." He hung up and refocused on Lucas. "I'll meet you back in the office in a bit. I need to speak with Kylie."

Lucas met her eyes, as if asking if she was okay with his going.

She nodded. "I'll see you later."

He took off and in seconds was nothing more than a speck shifting between the moonlit trees in the woods. Burnett watched him disappear and then he looked back to her.

Kylie spoke before Burnett. "I should have remembered Holiday was coming."

"True. But Lucas shouldn't have requested you leave your shadow without conferring with me."

"He's not supercilious like you said." She frowned.

"Yes, he is." Burnett chuckled. "But so was I when I was his age. He'll grow out of it. I did."

Kylie didn't like Burnett's answer, but she felt better knowing he wasn't holding a grudge against Lucas.

When Burnett didn't automatically go into what it was he wanted to talk with her about, she asked her own question. "Any more news on the people who were pretending to be my grandparents?"

"No, but the car they were driving was found. It was listed as stolen. We're checking for fingerprints."

Kylie nodded and looked back up at the moon as a lacy cloud passed over it, making the night appear darker. When she looked back, Burnett stared and his brow twitched as if he were checking her pattern. Puzzlement filled his eyes.

She should be used to it, but at times she wanted to wear a shield over her forehead.

"Is Holiday mad at me?" Kylie asked.

"More worried than angry. She saves all her hostile emotions to use on me." He shot her a tiny smile.

"But you're still here. That has to mean something."

"It means I'm a glutton for punishment." He hesitated, and while his words came out with humor, his eyes didn't express the same emotion.

"No, I meant the fact that she accepted you being a shareholder of Shadow Falls has to mean something."

He frowned. "She needed my money."

Kylie had to bite her lip not to tell him about the other investor. "You really like her, don't you?" Her heart ached for him. Not that he wanted sympathy. And maybe that's why she felt it. When someone this strong and prideful had a heartache, it made an impression.

"That's not important."

Yes, it is. Kylie saw rejection pass across Burnett's eyes. Somehow, some way, she was going to get Holiday to stop being so stubborn and give the man a chance. It just didn't make sense why she was so hesitant. If he was ugly or obnoxious, Kylie would understand. But Burnett was none of those. And he cared so much about Holiday that Kylie could almost feel it.

"I wouldn't say it wasn't important," Kylie added.

He shrugged. "Tell me about the snake and the deer incident."

Kylie told both stories for what felt like the hundredth time. At least now she could tell it without hyperventilating. When she finished, Burnett just stood there, his dark brow pinched and his lips tight.

"You think I'm overreacting, don't you."

His frown deepened. "No. I agree with Holiday. With two of these instances happening, it can't be a coincidence."

"So the security system isn't working?" she asked.

"No, it's working."

"Then how could—"

"That's what we don't know. A shifter has infiltrated the camp, specifically to target you. And I don't like it one damn bit!"

Kylie felt her stomach drop. He wasn't the only one.

• • • •

That night, the dream came on slow. But this one was different from the others. Kylie wasn't moving, she'd just woken up here. She saw Lucas standing by the lake where they'd run to earlier, and just like that, those differences didn't matter. Before she'd gone to bed, he'd tapped on her window. When she opened it, he'd pulled himself up and kissed her quickly on the lips.

"Good night," he'd said, and dropped back to the ground.

She'd grinned as she watched him leave. And she'd gone to bed wishing he hadn't run off so quickly.

Suddenly, the dream became her reality, grounded into the world of the mind where everything felt so real. She stood behind him and enjoyed being this close. Reaching out, she touched his arm and he turned around—not surprised that she was there, but happy to see her. For a second, something didn't feel right, but when he pulled her against him, she nudged away the feeling.

"Have you always been this beautiful, Kylie Galen?" Lucas's hands fell to her waist.

She grinned. "Why don't you tell me? You peeked into my windows when I was five."

"Shame on me." He leaned in closer. Uncertainty nagged at her. There was something off, but she couldn't put her finger on it.

She smiled up at him.

"Tell me what makes you happy," he said.

His statement stirred confusion. "What do you mean?"

"Do you want a mansion? A new car? Do you want to go to Mexico and drink beer on the beach? I can give you that and more."

She shook her head. "I don't want any of that."

"Then what?"

These questions weren't like Lucas, but she felt compelled to answer. "I want everyone to get along. Miranda and Della fought again last night. I want my dad to be able to visit me again. I want the Brightens to be okay. I want to know what I am. And I want to take care of whatever problem it is that this new ghost has."

"I can give you most of that. Just say yes."

"Yes to what?" And that's when it hit her. That's when she realized what was wrong. Lucas wasn't hot.

"You're cold." She took a quick step back, moving out of his arms. "What's going on?"

"I wanted to see you. I knew you would leave if . . ." Suddenly, it wasn't Lucas standing there. It was Red, the rogue vampire who was Mario's grandson, the one who'd killed the girls. The one who'd kidnapped her and beat up Lucas. She started to scream, then realized that this was just a dream and she had the ability to wake up.

"My grandfather and his friends don't think you can be convinced to work with us. I only want to help . . ." His last words faded as Kylie shot up on the bed, gasping for breath. She recalled how her senses had told her in the beginning of the dream that something wasn't right. If she'd only listened to her instincts, this wouldn't have happened. Then she remembered how Holiday had said she could temporarily shut them off. When she was able to think straight, Kylie leaned back on her pillow and did the visualization.

The last thing she wanted was to see him in her dreams.

Or her reality.

The next morning, Kylie felt tiny little skunk paws walking up her chest and then felt a wet pointed nose bump her chin as if summoning her awake.

She lay there for a few seconds, not moving and not opening her eyes, trying to decide why something felt wrong. Her first thought went back to the dream she'd had with Red, but no, this wasn't about that. Then bright light leaked into the corners of her closed eyes. She opened her eyes.

Sitting up cautiously, giving Socks his obligatory morning pat, she looked around. The sun streamed through the blinds and cast horizontal shadows on the floor.

What time was it? She swept her hair from her face.

Her gaze shot to the clock. Seven. Was that what didn't feel right . . . that she hadn't been nudged awake by an impatient spirit? Was her Jane Doe ghost not a morning ghost? Then again, maybe amnesia prevented someone from judging time.

Not that Kylie was complaining. Her last spirit had rarely let Kylie sleep a minute past dawn.

Seeing her phone, Kylie remembered Holiday and snatched up the cell, hoping to find Holiday had called or texted her. Before Kylie and Burnett had gotten back to the office, Holiday had called Burnett and asked if he could take over the camp for a day or so because she had a family emergency and had to leave. The only thing Holiday had told Burnett was that she had to deal with this.

Burnett had been worried, too. Kylie had heard the frustration in his voice when he spoke with Holiday and she wouldn't elaborate on the type of emergency.

Kylie had phoned and texted Holiday but hadn't gotten an answer before she'd gone to bed.

Checking her call log, she found two texts. One from Sara, her old best friend whom Kylie had probably just healed of cancer—please let that be so—and then one from Holiday.

Kylie breathed a sigh of relief as she read Sara's message that she was feeling great, then quickly read Holiday's. It was short and simple. *All is ok. B back soon.*

Wanting more reassurance, Kylie dialed the camp leader's number.

"Hey," Holiday answered. "Is everything okay?"

Kylie almost told her about the dream with the rogue vampire, but her gut said Holiday had something else on her plate. Besides, Holiday had already told her how to deal with this, and if Kylie had listened to her instincts, this wouldn't have happened. "Yeah, just worried about you. Are you back at camp yet?"

"Not yet. I should be there this afternoon." She grew quiet. "I'm sorry I had to bail before we talked. Are you dealing with everything okay? Nothing else has happened, has it?"

"No, I'm fine. We were just concerned about you."

"We?"

"Burnett and me," she said, remembering her promise to herself to play matchmaker. "What happened?" Kylie asked hesitantly, not wanting to overstep her bounds. But her relationship with Holiday felt like more than just camp leader and camper. She truly cared about her.

Holiday was quiet for a moment. "My great-aunt passed away."

"Oh, Holiday, I'm so sorry. Can I do anything?" A cold entered the room. Kylie ignored it and focused on the phone conversation. She'd deal with Jane Doe in a few minutes.

"No. I'm fine," Holiday said. "It was her time. But she didn't get her estate in order and now . . ."

Kylie felt her mattress dip down. She glanced up, and sitting on the foot of her bed was an older woman wearing a yellow housedress and a beautiful pale blue tear-shaped crystal necklace.

"The will is taped to the bottom left drawer of my dresser. But I want her to take all my crystal pieces. Don't let Marty take them, and she'll try. She's a sneaky little twit."

Kylie studied the woman's gray hair hanging down around her shoulders and then noted her eyes were a bright green that looked vaguely familiar.

Kylie's hold on the phone tightened and she shivered. Holiday had told her that she would eventually be able to see more than one ghost at a time. It looked as if that time had arrived. But could she handle it?

"Tell her," the ghost said, and that's when Kylie knew why the eyes were so familiar. She tightened her brows and checked the woman's pattern.

Holiday started talking. "Dealing with the estate is going to be such a—"

"Uh, Holiday . . . ?" Kylie said. "What does your great-aunt look like?"

"Why?"

"Because I think she's sitting on the end of my bed. If it's her, the will is taped to the bottom left drawer of her dresser."

The ghost started floating up to the ceiling as if something were pulling her away.

"Long gray hair," Holiday answered. "And green eyes."

"It's her," Kylie answered, now looking at the spirit floating near the ceiling. "So you'd better check out her dresser."

The ghost smiled. *"Thank you."*

"Thanks, Kylie," Holiday said.

Kylie felt another chill and pulled the covers up a bit. "No problem."

The ghost started to fade into the ceiling, then stopped and slid back down. *"Almost forgot. They wanted me to tell you something. Someone lives and someone . . ."* She vanished, leaving the sentence unfinished.

But Kylie knew what she meant.

"Dies," Kylie said, and closed her eyes. *Someone lives and someone dies.* The message wasn't just the mutterings of a crazy amnesia ghost. But how could Kylie make things right if she didn't know what to do?

Chapter Eleven

Dressed and still fighting the feeling that something wasn't right, Kylie stepped out of her room an hour later. Either Miranda and Della had already left, or they were still asleep. Either way, Kylie was happy not to have to face them. First, she hoped to find Helen, the half-fae who also had the gift of healing. Kylie wasn't sure if the "someone will live and someone will die" message meant she could prevent a death, but she had to try. Then she planned to talk with Burnett and tell him what she knew about Holiday. Not that Kylie was doing it behind the camp leader's back.

Before they'd hung up, she had asked if she could share their conversation with Burnett. When Holiday had wavered, Kylie asked her how she'd feel if Burnett disappeared on "an emergency" and didn't explain himself.

"Fine," Holiday said.

Although she hadn't sounded happy about it.

A few minutes later, Kylie started out of the cabin, tripped, and landed half on and half off the huge black Lab that was curled up on the welcome rug in front of the door.

"What the heck?" Stunned, she scrambled to get up and, in the process, stepped on the canine's tail. The dog yelped as if in pain, and guilt filled Kylie's lungs. "Sorry."

Was the animal hurt? Once an injured dog had shown up at her doorstep when she'd been a kid. Her mom had her dad take it to the vet and they'd ended up having to put it down.

Kylie had cried and blamed her mom for killing the dog. With the emotional footprints of that memory tugging at her heartstrings, Kylie crouched down.

"Sorry," she told the dog again, and let it sniff her hand before she gave it a gentle pat. "Are you hurt? You get hit by a car or something?"

"No. You stepped on my tail, and of course it hurt," the dog said.

Kylie, still down on her haunches, fell back on her butt and glared at the talking canine.

"What?" the dog asked.

"Don't do that!"

"Do what?"

"Talk!"

Okay, the sparkles now popping all over the place and the changing eye color told her it was Perry, but seeing a dog talk still freaked her out.

She jumped to her feet and continued to scowl at the animal. Basically, she needed a kick-dog to target her frustration, and she'd just found one. A black Lab that at this moment was changing forms.

She waited until Perry was transformed. "Why the hell is your canine butt sleeping on my porch?"

"I was afraid Miranda would come out, and if she knew it was me, she'd wiggle her little pinky at me and give me zits or something."

"Okay." She tightened her gaze. "But that doesn't explain what you're doing on my porch."

"Duh, I was waiting for you," he said matter-of-factly. "I'm your shadow for the day."

"Oh, crap. I forgot about . . . that." She took a deep breath and tried to resign herself to having a tag-along following her around like a . . . lost puppy.

He studied her with his gold eyes. "You're mad at me, aren't you."

"No," she said, biting back her frustration. "You're right. Miranda would have zapped you with zits or something. But you just blow my mind when you're an animal and you talk." She put a hand on each side of her head. "It hurts my brain."

"No, I meant mad about the shit that happened yesterday."

Kylie just stared at him. "You're gonna have to be more specific. Because a lot of shit happened yesterday."

He grinned, but the smile faded quickly. "I mean how I lost track of the old couple who were pretending to be your grandparents." A sincere apology filled his eyes. "I failed."

"That wasn't your fault."

"Yes, it was. Who else are you going to blame it on? I was the one supposed to follow them."

"How about we not blame it on anyone?" She started walking down the path toward the office.

He fell into step beside her. "Sounds good."

They walked a few minutes in silence. Kylie noticed the sky was painted with clouds, the big white fluffy kind, and tried not to think about the elderly couple Perry had followed or exactly what it meant when they went poof.

"Do you think they're dead?" she asked.

"Who's dead?"

"The elderly couple."

His features tightened. "I really don't know. I've never seen humans disappear like that."

They both got quiet again. The morning temperature hadn't risen to the uncomfortable level yet, but she could feel it climbing.

Perry tossed his own question next. "Do you think Miranda is ever going to accept my apology?"

Kylie looked at him. "Did you apologize?"

He looked honestly perplexed. "I spoke to her. That's the same thing."

Kylie shook her head. "Oh no, it's not. Speaking to someone is not an apology, Perry. What you did—kissing her like that, then blowing her off—that was mean."

He frowned and kicked a rock. "She kissed Kevin. I was mad."

"I get that," Kylie said, and remembered seeing the picture of Derek kissing Ellie. "And I know it hurts, but it was really Kevin who kissed her. But even still, two wrongs don't make a right."

She caught him checking out her brain pattern, and she frowned. He continued walking but shifted his gaze to the ground. They didn't talk for a bit, and then Kylie just blurted it out. "Everyone says my pattern moves around like a shape-shifter now. Is it true?"

"Yeah," he said. "But ours only move when we're shifting."

She stopped walking and faced him. "Is there anything else about my pattern that looks like a shape-shifter? I mean, do you see any sign that I might be one?"

He smiled. "You want to be a shape-shifter?"

"No." *Hell, no!* "I mean, not necessarily. I just want to figure out what I am." She bit down on her lip and decided to plunge right into the subject. "How old were you when you started shifting?"

"Oh, I was really young, too young. Five years younger than most shifters. Like barely two years old. Try handling a terrible two tantrum with a shape-shifter. Blew my parents' minds. And their marriage."

Kylie heard the tiniest bit of hurt in his voice. "They split up?"

"Yeah."

"I'm sorry."

"Hey . . . it wasn't my problem."

Oh, yeah, it was. Even his eyes had grown a lonely shade of muted brown. "Who did you live with, your mom or your dad?"

He didn't answer for a minute. "Neither."

She hesitated to ask, but somehow she almost sensed he wanted her to. "Why?"

"Supposedly, I was that hard to handle."

"Where did you go?"

"The FRU has a foster care program. You know, for unwanted strays. I stayed here for a while, and then there for a while."

Kylie felt she understood Perry better than she ever had. And she almost forgave him for being the smartass that he was sometimes.

"Was it terrible?" she asked, and suddenly she knew that she'd lost all her whining rights about how bad her own life had been.

"Nah," he said. "I'm a shape-shifter, I learned to fit in . . . at most places. Of course, I wasn't invited back to some of them." He laughed, but as Kylie had already suspected, Perry hid a lot of pain behind his humor.

She also got a feeling there was a lot he wasn't saying. Not that she blamed him. But damn, she couldn't imagine how it must have been being passed from home to home.

"You know," he said as if he suddenly wanted to change the subject, "some shifters don't start until they're in their teens. Maybe you're one of them."

"Maybe," she said. "But I'd only be half. Do half-breed shifters ever have different gifts? Like healing and stuff?"

"Not that I've heard. I have some cousins who are half-breeds and they're limited on what they can shift into. One can only shift into a bird. I used to turn into a cat and chase him around, and one time—"

"Please don't tell me you ate him," Kylie said.

"I just tortured him a little," he said with a grin. "Hey, when he shifted back, he was fine." He inhaled and almost seemed to get lost in a memory. "You know, I should probably try to find some of my cousins."

Kylie wondered if he ever thought about finding his parents, but not wanting to pry too much, she didn't ask. "Oh yeah," she said, grinning, trying to keep it light. "I'll bet they would love to see you coming."

A few minutes later, they'd reached the end of the path where the cabins that housed the office and the dining hall were located. She glanced around to see if she could spot Helen, the shy half-fae who had checked Kylie for a brain tumor, but Kylie didn't see her.

Because Helen was also a healer, Kylie figured she would be the person to ask about the gift. Questions like "Have you ever brought something back to life?" But Helen wasn't one of the teens hanging out front of the dining hall. However, Kylie did see Burnett walk into the office and she remembered she had things to talk to him about, too.

She turned to Perry. "I need to chat with Burnett for a bit. I'll see you in few—"

"No, you won't," Perry said. "Where you go, I go. It's questionable if you can pee today." He grinned. "And I've got Burnett's permission to morph into a giant anteater and kick ass and ask questions later if anyone tries to take over my job."

Kylie rolled her eyes, knowing Burnett had been talking about Lucas. And thinking of Lucas, she looked around a second time, but he wasn't in the crowd either.

Looking back at Perry, she added, "Yeah, but I'm going to see Burnett. I don't think you have to be there then."

He tightened his shoulders. "Where you go, I go. Until Burnett dismisses me."

"Oh, hell. Come on."

· · ·

Breakfast started out awkward. As had walking into Holiday's office, Perry in tow, and seeing Burnett sitting at Holiday's desk for the second time. Thankfully, Burnett dismissed Perry for their chat. Kylie asked for any update on the elderly couple who had pretended to be her grandparents and was told that nothing had come through yet.

She almost told Burnett about the dream with Red but at the last moment decided she wanted to be able to handle one thing on her own. And this was it. If it happened again, she'd talk to Holiday, but for now, she was flying solo on this mission. As crazy as it sounded, it felt kind of good, too. She wanted to believe she could take care of herself.

When she'd told Burnett about Holiday's aunt passing away, he'd looked shocked and . . . something else. It took her a second, but she'd recognized the emotion in his eyes. Hurt.

"Why would she not tell me this?" he had asked.

"I'm sure she's just dealing with it in her own way," Kylie had tried to assure him, but she could tell her efforts were futile. And as she'd turned to leave, she didn't know what compelled her to do it, but she'd looked back over her shoulder and said, "Be patient with her. She's worth it."

Now, in the dining hall, Perry still in tow, Kylie stared at her breakfast of bacon, eggs, and toast. For a change, the eggs weren't runny and the bacon wasn't raw or burned. But she'd eaten only a few bites, and after being painfully aware that everyone was staring at her forehead again, she decided she must have left her appetite at the cabin.

A symphony of noise—people jabbering, forks clinking, and trays being dropped onto the tables—bounced around the large cabin. Both Miranda and Della were missing in action, and Kylie hadn't spotted Helen or Lucas either.

Unfortunately, she had spotted Derek and Ellie.

They sat together at a table toward the back. It was only right that Derek sit with her, considering she was the new kid at camp. Last night, staring at the ceiling for a good two hours, Kylie had resigned herself *not* to hate Ellie or Derek, but to accept things—even if it meant seeing them come together as a couple—and move on.

Kylie had also resigned herself to making good on that promise to Della and give Lucas a chance. However, even after all that resigning she'd done, seeing Derek and Ellie whispering to each other stung like a fire ant bite between the toes.

Time, Kylie told herself. In time, it wouldn't hurt. "I need a fast-forward button," she muttered.

"A what?" Perry asked.

"Nothing," Kylie said. "Just muttering to myself." She looked up and caught another three or four people twitching their brows at her. She turned and looked at Perry. "What's it doing now?"

"What's what doing?"

"My friggin' pattern. Everyone's staring again."

Perry twitched. "Oh, shit! It's doing that shifting thing again. Only faster."

Kylie closed her eyes. "I'm so tired of being everyone's entertainment, of being the freak on display."

"You're not a freak," Perry said, sounding concerned. "You're just different." He gave her a nudge with his elbow. "But everyone likes you anyway."

Opening her eyes, she muttered, "Thanks."

"Are you going to eat that piece of bacon?" Perry asked.

"No." She pushed her tray over to him. Miranda came strolling by with her breakfast tray in her hands. Stopping, about to plop down beside Kylie, she spotted Perry.

She froze. "What is *he* doing here?" she asked as if Perry couldn't hear her.

"Eating breakfast," Kylie said, hoping to deter Perry from saying something smartass. Seeing him open his mouth, she gave him a good kick under the table. He flinched but closed his mouth.

"Well, I'll just join my sister witches today and let you enjoy each other's company." Miranda turned to leave.

Kylie grabbed Miranda by the arm, bringing her to a sudden halt that almost had Miranda's eggs taking a flying leap off her tray.

"Sit down. Please," Kylie begged. When Miranda looked about to argue, she added, "I could use the support." She cut her eyes toward Derek and Ellie. And it was true, she could use the support, but neither could she deny that she wanted to get Miranda over her repugnance of Perry. He really wasn't a bad guy.

Miranda relented and dropped down on the bench seat. Kylie mouthed, "Thank you," and then asked, "Where's Della?"

"Off drinking blood with the other vamps," Miranda answered just as she shoved a piece of toast into her mouth.

Kylie grabbed her milk and took a long sip while searching for a topic of conversation that would get Miranda and Perry talking.

"So," Kylie said, dropping the half-empty milk carton. "Does anyone know if Holiday has hired any teachers yet for the school year?"

Perry, as if he'd figured out what Kylie was up to, jumped into the conversation. "When I was at the office last night with Burnett, he got a call from some fae dude that Holiday had supposedly hired. I think he's supposed to show up and move into his cabin next week."

Miranda, as if she'd figured out what Kylie was up to, too, started forking eggs into her mouth.

Kylie and Perry chatted a few minutes about the fae teacher and how it would be odd to actually go to real classes at the camp in the fall. Miranda continued to shove food in her mouth as if needing an excuse not to talk.

Accepting that her last subject had proved to be a failure, Kylie reached for her milk again and went back to brainstorming topics. Finally putting her milk down, she looked at Miranda and said the first thing that came to her mind. "Did you know that Perry nearly ate his cousin when he was two?"

Chapter Twelve

Kylie watched as Miranda dropped her fork to clatter against the tray, leaned forward, and for the first time made eye contact with Perry.

"What?"

Perry smiled. Just having Miranda's gaze on him made the boy's face glow and his eyes turn a nice shade of blue. For just a second, Kylie wondered what his real eye color was.

"I didn't almost eat him," he said. "I just chewed on him a little and spit him out. I was a cat and he was a bird. And he was older than me and always stealing my animal crackers."

Perry continued talking and Miranda continued listening and their eyes met and they both appeared almost mesmerized. Kylie, mentally giving herself high fives, leaned back a bit to make sure not to block the two lovebirds' views of each other. Then Miranda's phone rang. She broke eye contact with Perry and snatched up her phone, which sat beside her food tray.

Checking caller ID, she let out an excited squeal. "It's Todd Freeman. Oh, my God, he's actually calling me!" Miranda's grin brightened her eyes, and she did a little butt-wiggling dance on the bench.

It took Kylie a half second to remember that Todd Freeman was the warlock, aka the best-looking boy in Miranda's old school, who had asked for Miranda's number at the witch competition. It took Kylie the other half of a second to realize this might not be a good thing. Not for Perry, at least.

Miranda's gaze shot back to the blond shape-shifter, and for a flicker of a second, she looked guilty. It wasn't much, but it offered Kylie a bit of hope.

"Excuse me," Miranda said, and then stood up, phone in hand, and zipped out of the dining hall.

Perry watched Miranda go and then looked at Kylie. His eyes were now a bright green color and they were slightly pinched, giving off a hint of anger. And that contented glow on his cheeks from a few seconds ago was gone. Vanished.

"Should I ask who the hell Todd Freeman is, or do I friggin' not want to know?"

Kylie's mind raced as she tried to find the words to answer. "He's just . . ." Just when she thought she knew what to say, something that would soothe him and hopefully not make him angry, she spotted Derek and Ellie walking out of the dining hall. Derek's hand rested against Ellie's lower back. An innocent enough touch, but it didn't look so innocent to Kylie.

"He's just who?" Perry bit out.

Kylie looked back at Perry. Why, Kylie wondered, was she so involved in trying to fix everyone else's love life when she couldn't even fix her own?

"I don't know what to tell you, Perry. Life's hard. Love's harder."

Thirty minutes after breakfast, Kylie—with Perry still dogging her steps—stood in front of the dining hall again, looking for Helen. Kylie suspected Helen would be among the noisy crowd waiting for the names to be called for Meet Your Campmates hour.

She wasn't.

Lucas walked up, trailed by Fredericka. "Hey." He came close enough that his shoulder brushed against hers. His warmth reminded Kylie of the dream last night when he hadn't been warm. She so preferred him warm. She preferred him to be himself and not some psychotic killer vampire.

"Hey," she said, and tried not to look at Fredericka, who ambled slowly past.

"Everything okay?" Lucas asked, and then frowned at Perry, who stood on the other side of her, not that it affected Perry. He just nodded.

Fredericka kept slowing down, and unable to stop herself, Kylie glanced up. The she-wolf shot Kylie a sassy smile, no doubt wanting to rub it in that she'd been with Lucas.

Lucas dipped his head down a bit. "Sorry I missed breakfast. I had some pack business I had to take care of."

Pack business? Kylie couldn't help but wonder if the pack business wasn't all about them keeping her and Lucas apart. Frustration swelled in her chest. It was bad enough to have Fredericka plotting against her, but to think the whole pack was also against her was too much. She looked at Lucas. "I . . . have to go."

"You okay?" He leaned in, concern filling his blue eyes. She wasn't sure if he'd picked up on her flicker of fear from last's night dream or if it was her jealousy for the little she-wolf who followed him around like a lost puppy.

"Yeah," she lied, and started walking.

"Where are we going?" Perry asked, his footsteps matching hers.

"To find Helen," Kylie answered, and stared straight ahead, even as she felt Lucas staring after her. She might not be able to solve her romantic issues, but perhaps Helen could shed some light on the whole healing process and the fact that Kylie had brought a dead bird back to life. With Holiday gone, she needed all the help she could get. A

blue jay swooped past and hovered right in front of her for a millisec-
ond before flying away. Could things get any crazier?

Kylie shook her head. Oh hell, what was she thinking? She was
at Shadow Falls; things could always get crazier.

As Kylie drew closer to Helen's cabin, she turned to Perry and looked
him right in the eyes. "I want to talk to Helen alone."

"No can do," Perry said.

She frowned. "Perry, I'm serious."

"So am I," he said without a touch of sarcasm or humor, and for
Perry, that was a rarity. "Look, I know you don't want me hanging
around, but Burnett told me what happened with the eagle and snake
and then the deer. And on top of not wanting you to get hurt by an
evil being of my own kind, I can't mess up again. I've already screwed
up by losing that old couple, and I'm not screwing up again. So you'll
just have to suck it up."

Kylie frowned, but she did understand. Who wanted to screw
up? And as much as she didn't want to accept that she was in danger,
she couldn't argue with the probability that Burnett was right. She
didn't want to be hurt by an evil being of Perry's kind, either.

She looked Perry right in his yellow eyes and spotted a touch of
insecurity. She felt bad.

"It's just that I need to ask Helen some questions and I'm not sure
she'll feel comfortable answering with you here."

"How about I transform into something else and hang back?"

Kylie suddenly got an idea. She didn't know if it would work,
because she didn't know how the whole transforming thing worked,
but it was worth a shot. "How about you change into a male white
cat with bright blue eyes."

"The last time I made myself a cat, you got pissed, bruised my
ears, and threatened to neuter me."

"Well, don't start playing Peeping Tom in my cabin windows and you won't be in any danger. Just make sure you're white with blue eyes. Oh . . . and you have to be male."

"Like I would ever become a female," he said.

"Then do it already," she said.

"Fine." He waved his hand up and the sparkles started appearing. In just a few seconds, Perry disappeared and a long-haired white cat with a cute piggish little face and beautiful blue eyes stood in his place, swishing its tail back and forth.

The animal was so adorable, she had to stop herself from picking up the little fellow and snuggling with him. "Very cute," Kylie said.

The kitty, aka, Perry, cocked its head to the side as if puzzled. He reached up with his paw and gave his right ear a good scratch.

It worked. Kylie remembered her reasoning for insisting on the specific animal and smiled.

"I can't hear!" Perry said. "How did you do this?"

Kylie had to bite her bottom lip not to smile. "I didn't do it. Most male white cats with blue eyes can't hear." She said the words slowly so he might be able to read her lips. "You can watch." She pointed to her eye. "But you can't hear."

"That was sneaky," Perry said, obviously able to read lips.

Kylie smiled. "No, it was genius. Now stay back."

"But stay where I can see you."

"Fine." She took off to Helen's cabin and kept an eye out for any unwanted shape-shifters.

Helen answered the knock almost immediately. "Hey, you came to see me." She hugged Kylie so tight and had such a big smile on her face that Kylie felt a tad guilty for not visiting sooner. Helen was . . . well, a little quiet and didn't have a lot of friends.

However, some of the guilt faded when she remembered she had asked Helen to come over to the cabin half a dozen times. The half-fae had declined each and every time because she spent all her free time with Jonathon, her newfound love.

"Come on in," Helen said.

Kylie started to step inside and remembered Perry. "I can't."

"Why?" Helen asked, and ran a hand through her sandy brown hair.

"I've got a shadow."

"Oh, yeah." Helen's hazel eyes widened with concern. "Jonathon was telling me what happened. They think some shape-shifters broke through the security. Are you okay? I mean, after your weekend and now this." Helen stepped out and closed her cabin door. She moved over to the edge of the porch and sat on the whitewashed wooden planks.

"Yeah, I'm fine." Kylie answered, which was a bit of a lie, but she didn't need to dump her problems on Helen.

"Did you actually see the intruder?" Helen asked.

Kylie dropped down beside the girl. Their feet dangled off the edge of the porch. "It was an eagle and a snake and then a deer. And we're not even sure that it's anything. It might not even have been shape-shifters." Or at least, Kylie had been telling herself that. And since nothing else had happened today, it was getting easier to believe it—as long as she didn't remember the evil look she'd seen in the eagle's and deer's eyes.

Kylie suddenly became aware of two birds soaring overhead. A shimmer of fear ran down her back, and she looked out toward the patch of trees to see if she could spot Perry.

He didn't seem too worried. He'd found a patch of sunlight spilling through the trees and had stretched out, as if to soak in the warmth. "Who's your shadow?" Helen asked, following Kylie's gaze but obviously not noticing the cat.

"It's Perry. I had him turn himself into a male white cat with blue eyes."

Helen arched a brow with understanding. "So he couldn't hear us. Good one." She brushed an ant off her knee.

They sat there for a few seconds in silence, both of them gently pumping their legs back and forth.

Finally, Kylie spoke. "I was hoping you wouldn't mind answering a few questions about healing?"

"That's right, I heard you healed your friend," Helen said. "And then Lucas, too. Pretty cool."

Kylie bit down on her lip. "Yeah. It's cool. I mean, I'm still trying to wrap my head around it, but I like knowing I did it. That's what I wanted to ask you about. I really don't know how it works."

Suddenly, a thousand questions started running rampant in her head. Could she heal anyone? Could she go to the hospital and just heal everyone?

"Holiday hasn't talked to you about it?" Helen pulled one leg up.

"She tried. I just wasn't ready to hear about it. And then she had to leave. Her aunt died, but she's supposed to be back this afternoon."

"That's sad," Helen said with sincerity, then she added, "Holiday said that we two were going to start meeting with her on occasion to discuss healing as a group. I've read up on a lot of it, but I've barely made a dent in all there is to know about the gift."

"There are books on supernatural healing?" Kylie asked, surprised.

"Yeah, there's a whole library on all different supernatural subjects."

"Really? I never heard about them."

"Oh, yeah. There are tons of books on just about every subject."

Every subject? If that was the case, Kylie couldn't help wondering if there might be some information somewhere about anomalies like herself. "Who . . . ? I mean, where do you get them?"

"From the FRU library. If you can call it a library. More like a vault with books. It took almost a month before I was approved to check out the books I got. Burnett finally went in and got me approved."

"Why would they not want you to read up on healing or . . . any subject concerning supernaturals?"

"Beats me."

Kylie chewed on that for a few minutes and then asked, "So what did you learn about healing?"

"A lot of it's about the homeopathic. But some of it covers the basics like the different kinds of healers."

"There are different kinds?"

Helen nodded. "And different levels."

"Is any of this based on what type of species you are?"

"Yeah, some. The gift is most common to fairies and witches. But it's found in all sorts of half-breeds, too. I even read one book that said some half-breeds can have more healing powers than full-bloods."

Kylie tried to absorb everything Helen was saying. "What are the different kinds?"

"Well, some of us can just ease pain, but not really heal. Some witches can cure things by mixing up brews and performing certain rituals. Then there are those who heal internal diseases like cancer through touch. And then there's a few of those who are like you."

"Like me how?" Kylie asked, confused.

"Who can heal internal issues, like cancer, as well as physical injuries, like you did with your friend Sara's cancer and Lucas's injuries."

"You can't heal physical injuries?" Kylie asked.

"No. I wish. Jonathon fell a while back and cut his hand. I tried several times to heal it, and got nothing."

Kylie tried to absorb the new information. But mostly what she absorbed was the fact that once again, she was an anomaly. For once, couldn't she fit nice and neatly into a niche?

"You look worried," Helen said, looking at her.

"A little," Kylie admitted. "I'm still overwhelmed, I guess."

"Hey, just be glad you're not like the real freaky type."

"What type is that?"

"The kind that can raise the dead. And every time they do it, they give up a piece of their soul in the bargain. That would be off-the-chart weird, don't you think?"

A chill of fear settled around Kylie's heart. "Yeah. That would be super weird."

Kylie got a text from Holiday on her walk back to her cabin. *Problems. Can't make it bk til tomorrow. U ok?*

Am I okay? Kylie nearly laughed out loud. Hell, no, she wasn't okay! She'd given away a piece of her soul to a blue jay and didn't know what it meant.

As soon as Perry's shadow duties ended and he was replaced by Della, Kylie snatched her phone and started out of her cabin, feeling desperate. Holiday wasn't here, but Burnett was. He might not have any answers, but at least she could personally tell him she wanted a library card to the FRU's source of books. If there was even the slightest chance that their library held something that would help her figure out what she was, then Kylie would keep her nose in a book for years.

"Where are we going?" Della asked, following Kylie out.

"To talk to Burnett about my problem."

"What problem?"

"You got a problem?" Miranda asked as she, too, joined them on the cabin porch.

"It's just crazy shit," Kylie said, unsure she wanted to explain it, and started walking.

"What kind of crazy shit?" Miranda asked. "Does it have anything to do with Perry being in love with you?"

"What?" Kylie spouted out, low on patience.

"I saw the way he was hanging around all day."

"Please! He was hanging around me because he was shadowing me." She met Miranda's gaze head-on. "Okay, look. I'm gonna say this once. Perry's in love with you. But if you don't stop playing hard to get, you're gonna lose your shot with him."

"Amen, sister!" Della said.

Miranda's face tightened and she glared first at Della and then at Kylie. "Since when are you two taking his side?"

Kylie closed her eyes in frustration. "Fine, he was wrong when he did that, but you admitted that you were a little wrong in kissing Kevin, too. It's time to get past it or get over him."

"You make it sound easy." Hurt hummed in Miranda's tone.

"It is easy," Della said. "Just kiss and make up."

Miranda ignored Della and stared at Kylie. "Like you don't have issues with Derek." She turned to Della. "And you with Lee."

"That's different!" Della snapped, her eyes growing bright as she immediately took the offensive.

No, it wasn't different, Kylie realized. "Look. Truth is, all three of us are in the same boat. The sucky romance boat. And Della and I made a pact yesterday." She glanced at Della, hoping she didn't look upset that she was sharing this with Miranda. But hey, they were a threesome, right?

Thankfully, the vamp didn't look pissed, and Kylie continued, "We're moving on. I'm gonna get past the whole Ellie and Derek thing and give Lucas a chance. Della's going to try to be nicer to Steve and see what happens. You want to join the pact?"

Miranda frowned. "But Todd Freeman called me this morning. He said he may come up here this weekend for a visit."

"Who's Todd?" Della asked.

"The cute warlock from her old school," Kylie answered, and glanced back at Miranda. "Look, if you don't want to forgive Perry, or can't forgive him, then that's one thing. But you can't stay on the fence."

"Yeah. Shit or get off the pot." Della snickered.

"I'm not on the fence," Miranda insisted. "Or a pot."

"Yes, you are," Kylie countered. "You still care or you wouldn't be jealous." So what did that say about her and Derek? Kylie pushed that question aside.

"But what if I blow Todd off and then Perry goes back to being an ass?"

"There are no guarantees," Kylie countered. "Not with love or with life. But we can't go through life never taking a risk. And that's what we are all agreeing to do. Put our hearts out there. Take a chance with a boy. We might end up hurt, but we might not."

Miranda stood there, her expression pinched as if considering the offer. "Okay, how about I make a pact to talk to Perry and try to figure it out?"

"Talking's a good start," Kylie said.

"Making out would be better." Della grinned.

Kylie started back walking. Miranda and Della followed.

"So what's the crazy shit problem you need to discuss with Burnett?" Miranda asked.

Kylie sighed. "I gave away a piece of my soul and I think I want it back."

Chapter Thirteen

"What's wrong?" Burnett called out from Holiday's office a couple of minutes later when Kylie stepped inside the camp's main offices.

The camp leader had set up an office for Burnett in the back of the cabin, but he apparently preferred using Holiday's office in her absence. Not that Kylie blamed him.

Holiday's office was small but nice. A tan sofa stood against one wall, leaving only enough room for a desk and a couple of file cabinets. Not that Holiday hadn't added her own mark to the tiny space. Plants, different kinds of ferns, and even some herbs were stationed at every corner. The air even smelled like Holiday—a light floral aroma. And on top of the large metal file cabinet were several different-colored crystals. The light from the front window streamed into the room and got pulled into the crystals, reflecting rainbow colors on the walls.

Burnett quickly closed a few files that were on the desk and then leaned back in Holiday's chair. Kylie couldn't help wondering if Burnett wasn't using her office simply because Holiday's presence was so alive in the room.

"What's wrong?" he asked again.

She just blurted it out. "Do you know anything about healing powers?" She dropped into the chair across from the desk.

"Not a lot, but some."

"If I bring something back to life, do I lose a piece of my soul?"

His brow creased deeper. "What happened? Did someone get hurt? Did you have to—"

"Not someone," Kylie answered. "A bird."

"Oh. Holiday told me about that," Burnett answered. He leaned forward. "However, she said you weren't sure it was dead."

"It looked dead," Kylie said. "And I just want to know, did I lose a piece of my soul when I brought it back to life? And what does that mean?"

Burnett folded his arms on the desktop. "I'm not nearly as up on this as I'm sure Holiday is, but she wasn't concerned. So I don't think you have anything to worry about."

Not happy with his answer, Kylie remembered the second thing she wanted to discuss. "I want a library card."

"A what?" he asked.

"I want to be able to read the books that the FRU have in their library."

He frowned. "It's not a library, or not a normal library. Before you are allowed a book, it has to be cleared."

"Why?"

"Because a lot of items in the collection are FRU documents."

"What is the FRU hiding?"

He looked almost annoyed at her question. "We're not hiding anything. But we can't let normals get their hands on the books."

She pressed a finger to her forehead. "Do I look normal to you?"

"We still have to be careful."

"So you're telling me I can't check out the books."

His frown deepened. "I will see about getting you a few books on healing," he added, as if wanting to console her.

"What other kind of books do you have?" she asked.

"It's not a library, Kylie," he said with some firmness, and then settled back and didn't speak. Finally the awkward silence brought Kylie to another question. "Any more news on the elderly couple who pretended to be my grandparents?"

His guarded expression slipped away. "I just got a call. The fingerprints we were able to pull belong to the owners of the car. I'm afraid it's not going to help us. I'm sorry. But I can return these." He handed her the brown envelope that held her father's pictures. "You really resemble your father."

The genuine concern in his eyes and his tone should have made her feel better, but it just validated her suspicions that he hadn't been completely honest about the whole FRU and the library. What was the FRU hiding?

Kylie took the envelope. "Thank you," she said. While she wasn't going to start mistrusting Burnett, she would proceed with caution when dealing with him.

Kylie started to leave when Burnett looked at the door and said, "Come in."

Lucas walked in. He met Burnett's gaze head-on. "I'd like permission to walk Kylie back to her cabin."

"That's up to her," Burnett said.

"Without her shadow," Lucas said.

Kylie could see it cost Lucas a chunk of pride to ask permission. She recalled something Della said about werewolves hating to be submissive. And asking permission was a submissive gesture.

However, from the look on Burnett's face, Lucas's request had won him some respect and hopefully a few minutes to be with her. Burnett looked at Kylie as if to make sure it was okay, and she nodded.

"Just back to the cabin. And stay on the path." Burnett looked toward the window. "Della takes over again when she gets to the cabin. You got that, Della?"

"Yes," came her answer, and Kylie rolled her eyes a bit, wondering if Della was always listening in.

• • •

Della and Miranda were gone when Kylie and Lucas walked out of the office. The afternoon air was warm but tolerable. A few campers hung around the front of the lunchroom. Kylie saw Will, another werewolf, standing to one side, watching them. She also saw Lucas shoot him a frown.

"Come on." Lucas started walking toward the path.

Only after they made the first turn and were out of view did Lucas reach for her hand. Right then, Kylie suspected that Fredericka wasn't just blowing smoke about the pack's disapproval of her.

She started to ask, but Lucas spoke first. "Are you okay?" He stopped and turned to face her. His blue eyes studied her with intensity. "For a second, you were scared of me this morning, and then you just ran off with Perry as if you were mad."

She hesitated to tell him, but she wanted Lucas to be honest with her, so she needed to be honest with him. "It wasn't you I was afraid of. Last night I was pulled into a dreamscape. I wasn't sure what was happening, but you were there."

"No, I wasn't," he said.

"I know it wasn't you now. It was Red, Mario's grandson. He appeared as you in the beginning."

Lucas stood there as if contemplating. "He's vampire. They don't dreamscape."

"Well, he did. I don't know how, but he did."

"Maybe it was a regular dream."

She shook her head. "I know the difference now."

"Did you tell Burnett?"

"No," she said. "I . . . handled it myself. I know how to shut it off. If it happens again, I'll tell him. Or I'll tell Holiday."

He frowned. "What did the freak do in the dream? He didn't . . ."

She understood what he was asking. "He only put his hands on my waist. Then I realized he wasn't hot like you are." For the first time, she wondered why Red hadn't tried to do more. Then again, she should just be happy he hadn't. The thought of kissing him was too much.

Lucas pulled her against him. "I really want to catch that slimy vamp." He wrapped his arms around her. She stood there for a few seconds, her cheek pressed against his chest, absorbing his embrace. Finally, she lifted her face and looked at him.

He pressed his lips against hers. It wasn't the really hot kind of kiss, but it was nice. Nice enough that she let her feelings about how he was always followed by Fredericka slide away.

"So you're not mad at me?" he asked.

"A little," she admitted.

He looked perplexed. "About what?"

She didn't have a clue how to say it but then just blurted it out. "Every time I see you walk up, Fredericka is with you."

He pressed his forehead to hers. "I've told you nothing is happening there."

"I know, and I believe you, but she's so . . . smug."

He half grinned. "She's a werewolf; smugness is instinctual."

"I don't care. I don't like it."

His half smile faded. "She's part of my pack. I can't kick her out without just cause and major consequences for her."

The fact that he cared about Fredericka stung, but then she realized she wouldn't want bad things to happen to Derek. But it wasn't just Fredericka causing this problem.

"Your pack doesn't want you with me, do they."

He looked a little shocked. She almost repeated what Fredericka told her, but she didn't want to come off like a jealous girlfriend.

"It's stupid," he said. "It doesn't matter what they want."

"Doesn't it?"

"No, it doesn't," he said with firmness. "I refuse to let anyone dictate who I like or see. Besides, you might end up being one of us."

"And if I'm not?"

"It still doesn't matter," he said, but the conviction in his voice had lessened.

"What will happen?" she asked.

"Nothing. Because I won't let it happen." He touched her cheek. "This is my issue. Let me deal with it."

Thirty minutes later, Kylie walked into her chilly bedroom—yep, she had a ghostly visitor, but Kylie was determined to ignore her. She had to mull over her conversation and suspicions concerning Burnett and her conversation with Lucas. His pack's attitude was his issue, but it involved her. She also wanted to spend some time looking at her dad's face. As crazy as it sounded, she hoped staring at the pictures would somehow bring him closer to her.

"Someone lives and someone dies."

Kylie frowned. Okay, ignoring the spirit was probably going to be harder than she thought, especially since the so-called message the ghost was delivering was supposedly something the death angels had sent Kylie.

Ditto for Holiday's aunt, when she dropped in the day before.

"Who lives and who dies?" Kylie turned around to see the ghost woman hovering behind her. She had hair again, long dark hair that hung around her shoulders.

"They didn't say. But they did say that it isn't your fault."

"What's not my fault?" Kylie demanded.

The spirit shrugged. *"They never explain anything. They just tell me to give you the message."* She nipped at her bottom lip. *"They scare me."*

Kylie dropped onto the bed, and that's when she noticed something else about the ghost. She was pregnant. The pink maternity shirt clung to her round belly.

Suppressing her frustration, Kylie motioned to the woman's baby bulge. "You're pregnant."

She glanced down and dropped her hands around her middle. *"How did that happen?"*

Kylie shook her head. "If I was at home, I could give you a pamphlet to explain it step by step. A sperm meets an egg and so on. My mom gives me one of those every few months. But basically, it means you had sex with someone."

The spirit's expression grew puzzled. *"Sex?"*

"Please tell me you know what that is, because I'm too young to have to give you the whole sex talk. I haven't even heard it yet. I've just read the pamphlets."

"I know what sex is. I'm just . . . Who did I have sex with?" she asked. *"I can't remember."*

"I wouldn't know that."

The spirit moved closer, and so did her chill. She dropped down on the bed beside Kylie, her palms still stretched across her belly. Closing her eyes, she sat there in silence. Kylie sensed she was searching her mind, trying to remember.

Kylie pulled a throw over her shoulders to ward off the chill. After several silence-filled minutes, the ghost opened her eyes but continued to stare down at her round middle. Her hands started moving tenderly over the child she carried within, as if to show it affection.

Kylie had never seen so much love shown in a simple touch. For a crazy second, she wondered what it would feel like to carry a child inside her own belly.

When the spirit looked up, she had tears in her eyes. *"I think my baby died."*

The grief on the spirit's face and in her voice brought a lump to Kylie's throat. "I'm sorry."

Then the spirit pulled her hands away from her belly, and both her palms were bloody. Kylie's breath caught when she saw the spirit's rounded abdomen was gone and the front of her dress was drenched in blood. *"No."* The deep, painful sob of the spirit filled the tiny room and seemed to bounce around from wall to wall.

Kylie opened her mouth to say something, to ask the spirit if she could remember what happened, to offer more apologies and sympathy. But before she could say anything, the woman disappeared.

The spirit's cold vanished but left a wave of icy sadness and grief so intense that it filled Kylie's chest with pain. And it wasn't just any pain. It was the grief of a mother losing a child. Kylie reached for her pillow and hugged it.

After a few minutes, Kylie pulled the pictures out of the envelope and flipped through them slowly. When she came to the one of her mom and Daniel in a group of other people, Kylie reached for her phone.

"Hi, sweetie." Just hearing her mom's voice brought back some of the empathy Kylie felt for the spirit.

"Hey, Mom."

Odd, how not so long ago, Kylie felt certain her mom didn't love her, didn't even want her. Now, there wasn't a doubt of her mom's devotion to her. Deep down, Kylie wondered if this was a part of growing up. The part where teens stopped seeing their parents as instruments out to destroy their lives and started seeing them as people.

Not perfect, of course. Kylie knew her mom still had flaws—lots of them—but none of them involved her love for Kylie. And none of them prevented Kylie from loving her.

"I'm glad you called," her mom said. "I've missed hearing your voice."

"Me too," Kylie managed to say without choking up, and she wished her mom were here to hug her. She wished she could tell her mom about the pictures, but then she'd have to explain about the Brightens, and she didn't think that whole mess was explainable. Not yet, anyway.

"I was going to call you tonight if I didn't hear from you," her mom said.

"I'm sorry, I've been going a little crazy since I've been back."

"I figured as much. Sara called and said she'd tried to call you and you hadn't returned her call. She sounded so good. She told me it was like a miracle—her cancer up and disappeared."

"I'm sure it was one of the treatments they did on her," Kylie said, biting down on her bottom lip and wondering how she was going to handle the whole Sara issue. Kylie hadn't returned Sara's call because she'd wanted to ask Holiday first. Poor Holiday. When she did return, Kylie had a list of things they needed to discuss.

"I guess," her mom said. "But I would like to believe in miracles."

"Then you should believe," Kylie said, now unsure what to say to her mom about it. Because more than ever, Kylie knew miracles did exist. The fact that she had been the one performing the miracle still had her feeling out of sorts.

"Are you okay?" her mom asked, as if picking up on Kylie's mood.

"I'm fine."

"No, you're not," her mom said. "I hear it in your voice. What's wrong, baby?"

"Just . . . boy trouble," she said.

"What kind of trouble?" her mom asked, the tension in her voice indicating that she worried Kylie's problem concerned sex.

"It's nothing." Searching for a change of subject, Kylie tossed out, "How was work today?"

"It was strange," her mom said. "I got a new client."

"Why is that strange?" Kylie asked. Her mom worked in advertising and she was always getting new clients.

"*He's* strange."

"Strange in what way?" Kylie asked, glad the subject had taken a turn.

"He seemed more interested in me than . . . the campaign." Her mom giggled.

Kylie frowned. "Define 'interested.'"

"Oh, I don't know. It's just the way he acted," her mom said, as if she were trying to make light of the subject. "We're supposed to do lunch tomorrow and discuss his ideas for the special promotion on his new line of vitamins."

"Is it a work lunch or a . . . date lunch?"

"Don't be silly," her mom said. "It's work."

"Are you sure?" Kylie asked. "I mean, if he seemed interested in you . . ."

"I think it's work," she said, no longer sounding so sure. "But . . . if it were a date lunch, how would you feel about it?"

Kylie took a deep breath. An image of her stepfather filled her head. She recalled him sitting on the edge of her bed only a few weeks ago, crying when he told Kylie he'd made a terrible mistake. She knew he wanted to reconcile with her mom, and while Kylie wasn't sure he deserved a second chance after cheating on her, she couldn't deny wanting at least one thing in her world to go back to the way it had been.

"You're not answering," her mom said.

Kylie swallowed a big lump of indecision and stared down at the image of her mom and Daniel. Was it fair of her to want her mom to forgive her stepfather just to bring a sense of normalcy back into Kylie's life, especially when she sensed the man her mom really loved was dead? The question bounced around her head, and Kylie decided to be honest.

"That's because I don't know what to say. I guess part of me was thinking you and Dad might work things out. Don't you love him anymore? Or did you ever really love him?"

It was her mom's time to get quiet. "I loved him. I probably still love him," she finally confessed. "But I'm not sure I can forgive him. Or trust him. And ever since we talked about Daniel, I just . . . I'm not sure that marrying Tom wasn't a mistake. And if that's true, then us getting back together would also be a mistake. But I shouldn't be talking to you about this, Kylie."

"Why not?"

"Because, my darling, you shouldn't have to worry about this."

"You're my mom. I have a right to worry." And Kylie realized she did worry about her mom being alone and being lonely. But did that mean she wanted her mom to start dating? To completely rule out getting back with the man Kylie had loved and considered her real dad all her life?

"No," her mom said. "You've got that backwards. Moms have a right to worry about their kids, not the other way around."

"Then we'll just have to agree to disagree," Kylie said.

"You are way too stubborn, you know that?"

"And I wonder where I got it from," Kylie answered with a chuckle. Kylie's mom's phone beeped with an incoming call. "I'll let you go," Kylie said. "But Mom . . ."

"Yes?"

"Enjoy the lunch. Just be careful. And don't go falling in love or anything. Oh, and no kissing on the first date. That was your rule, remember?"

Her mom chuckled. "I'm sure it's just a business lunch. I'll talk to you tomorrow."

When Kylie hung up she heard a tap at her window. She looked over, expecting Lucas, but instead the blue jay perched on her windowsill. It flapped its wings, hovered right outside her window for a second, and then flew away.

Great. Now she was being stalked by the blue jay she'd brought back to life. What did that mean?

• • •

The melancholy from the ghost and the mixed feelings about her mom—as well as the possibility that she'd given a piece of her soul to the blue jay—hadn't completely faded an hour later when Miranda and Della stormed into her room.

"Get ready," Della said.

"Ready for what?" Kylie asked, lying on the bed, still hugging her pillow and staring holes into the ceiling.

"Burnett agreed to let us have a party tonight," Miranda said. "This is our chance to work on our pact. Steve will be there, so will Lucas and even Perry. We're ordering pizza and playing music. Maybe even dancing. I think I'll wear the new jeans I bought last weekend."

"You didn't tell us you got to go shopping," Della said.

"Yeah, and I also got this brand-new jeans skirt." Miranda looked at Della. "It would look fabulous on you. Why don't you borrow it?"

"Really?" Della said. "You'd loan me your new skirt?"

"Of course. I like you most of the time," Miranda said, and nudged her with her elbow.

Kylie's lips were poised to say, "You two go without me," but she spotted a hint of excitement in Della's eyes. Kylie remembered that since the vamp was assigned as her shadow, if she didn't go, Della didn't go, either.

So Kylie stood up and went to her closet. "I say we get all dressed up and impress the socks off those guys."

Thirty minutes later, the three of them, dressed to kill, walked into the dining hall. Miranda had loaned Della her new jeans skirt, and it looked really good on her, especially paired with the spaghetti-strap top with art deco black-and-red print with flared tiers of fabric hanging down the front. Miranda wore her new jeans with a low-cut pink lacy tank top that showcased her girls. When Kylie had packed to return to camp, she'd brought some more clothes. Her black knit dress wasn't fancy, but it still fit well, especially with her recent growth spurt. The hem of the dress now came a tad higher, and the scooped bustline fit tighter. While she had been faking her enthusiasm in the beginning, somehow getting dressed up had her looking forward to the evening.

The music was already playing and boxes of pizza were stacked on one of the tables that had been pushed against the walls, making room for dancing. Most of the campers were already there, mingling and talking. The smell of pepperoni and zesty tomato sauce filled the air. Then Chris walked in from the kitchen carrying a large pitcher and a bunch of cups.

"Man, that smells good." Della lifted her face into the air, and Kylie caught the wild berry scent of blood. And though she didn't like admitting it, her mouth watered more from that aroma than from the pizza.

Not that she would indulge in it, or had indulged in it since she'd tasted blood at the vampire ceremony. If Kylie ended up being vampire, she'd deal with it. But until then, the idea of drinking blood, even when it tasted like ambrosia, was not her cup of tea.

Miranda must have pushed the door closed a little hard because it slammed shut and the crowd looked up. Kylie felt everyone's eyes on her, or on her forehead, checking to see what her forever changing brain pattern was doing now.

But then she noticed one pair of blue eyes, and they weren't looking at her forehead. They were looking at her.

She knew Lucas liked her dress. Or at least he liked her in it. And wasn't that what she wanted?

The desire to do another visual sweep of the room to see if Derek was there hit strong. She fought it. Tonight was about Lucas. And from the way he stared at her, she had a feeling he wouldn't mind.

Chapter Fourteen

Lucas didn't smile. Well, not with his lips, anyway. His eyes, however, did smile, and their warmth washed over Kylie as he started moving her way. He took slow, even steps, as though he had all the time in the world, but what mattered was that he was coming. When she first saw all the weres clustered together, she worried he might not want to leave them. Somehow Kylie sensed he did it purposely to send a message to her and to his pack. And suddenly she was glad Miranda and Della had pressed her to come to the dance.

Lucas had gotten about halfway across the room when she felt another pair of eyes on her. Pulling her gaze away from Lucas, she spotted Fredericka. Refusing to let the were bully intimidate her or ruin her good mood, Kylie ignored her and refocused on Lucas. He looked good tonight, too. He wore jeans that fit just right and an aqua blue shirt spread across his chest. The color made his blue eyes appear bluer.

When he stopped beside her, his natural scent filled the air and she could feel her pulse flutter from his nearness. He didn't tell her she looked beautiful; he didn't even touch her. But his eyes did both.

"Hey," he said.

She smiled. "Hey."

His gaze moved to Della. "Burnett said I could take over shadowing."

Della nodded.

"Want to get something to drink?" Lucas asked Kylie, and motioned toward the back where the sodas were waiting and the people weren't. Lucas wasn't much with crowds. Tonight, she felt the same way.

She nodded and turned to her two roommates. "I'll see you." Then she leaned in toward them. "Remember the pact."

Miranda smiled and wiggled her eyebrows in excitement. Della, who Kylie knew struggled with the whole romance issue, frowned.

"Yeah, yeah," Della said. "But I'm not making a fool out of myself."

"Just be more approachable," Kylie whispered, and then turned back to Lucas. They moved together across the room, and Kylie could feel people staring at them. She forced herself to ignore them.

Lucas moved in a step closer to her. "What's going on with those two?" he asked, obviously having overheard Kylie's conversation with Della and Miranda.

"Nothing really," Kylie answered.

He grabbed them each a drink and then pushed two folding metal chairs against the wall. When she sat down, he edged his chair closer and sat beside her. His jeans-covered thigh pressed against her bare leg. She could feel his warmth through the cotton material, and it sent a fluttery feeling to her stomach.

He leaned in so his voice could be heard over the music. "I'm glad you came tonight."

"Me too," she said.

"You're not mad at me anymore?" The back of his hand shifted against her forearm and she felt his fingers glide gently up past her elbow.

"I think I'm over it." She smiled.

"Good." His gaze swept over her. "You make my blood race," he said, so low that she could hardly hear him.

She smiled. "Really?"

"Feel for yourself." He took her hand and placed it on the back of his wrist. The flutter—more like a vibration, really—was so rapid that it almost felt electric. Her first instinct was to jerk away, but his steady, tender gaze kept her fingers against his warm skin. And after a second, it wasn't actually scary.

"Is this a werewolf thing?" she asked.

He leaned a bit closer until she felt the warmth of his breath against her ear. "Yeah."

She shivered a little. "So I really didn't cause it?" she asked, feeling a bit disappointed.

A light smile tilted his lips. "Oh, it's all your fault. It only happens when I'm . . . captivated by something or someone."

She returned his smile. "Then I'm glad I captivated you."

The smile in his eyes suddenly vanished, and she could swear she heard a light growl rumble from his throat.

She barely had a chance to wonder what could be wrong when Perry stopped right in front of them.

He nodded at Lucas as if making a point that he wasn't the least bit afraid of him. "You want to dance?" he asked Kylie.

She was so surprised, she wondered if she'd misunderstood his question. Then she felt Lucas tense beside her. "Uh, not now," she said, trying to keep her tone light. "But thanks for asking."

Perry disappeared into a group of campers. When she looked back at Lucas, he scowled into the cluster of people. "Am I going to have to teach a smartass shape-shifter a lesson?"

"No."

"I can't believe he actually hit on you when—"

"He wasn't hitting on me." Kylie looked back at the crowd and found Perry standing away from the others, watching Miranda, who was surrounded by a group of boys. For a second, Kylie felt bad. Perry had probably wanted to ask her something about Miranda and she'd brushed him off.

"I don't buy it," Lucas said, his tone deep.

"He only has eyes for Miranda," she said. "Look at him, he's green with jealousy." And literally, his eyes had changed color to a bright green.

"Yeah, right."

"It's true. Believe me; he's not into me."

He dipped his head closer. "And you're not into him?"

She grinned. "Are you jealous?"

"No." He sat up straighter. "I'm just . . . possessive," he said as if the two traits were somehow different. "And you didn't answer my question."

"I'm not into Perry," she assured him. "We're just friends."

"Fair enough. So, who are you into?" he asked, and those blue eyes captured hers.

"I'm sort of falling for a jealous werewolf at the moment."

He grinned and quickly brushed the back of his hand against her forearm. "Well, don't tell me his name, because I'm likely to whip his jealous ass."

They both laughed and then sat and stared at each other until it got awkward. Not awkward because looking at him felt strange, but it just seemed as if one of them should lean in and finish the moment with a kiss. But neither of them seemed to want to take the initiative. Kylie suspected his reason was the same as hers. Too much of a crowd. She just hoped it wasn't because of his pack.

"I've been meaning to ask, did you get the answers from Holiday about the whole bird thing?"

Remembering the bird's little visit this afternoon, she felt frustration tickle her mind. "No."

She took a sip of soda, focusing on the music, and tried to push all the negative stuff back. Unfortunately, it kept coming at her. "Did you know the FRU has a library of books on everything super-natural?"

"Yeah, I heard about it. Why?"

"Do you know why they don't let us read them?"

"I think some of them contain government documents."

"But why would they need to hide anything?" she asked.

He shrugged. "The same reason the U.S. government hides things. Some things might skirt the ethics line, or if certain information got into the hands of the wrong people, it could be detrimental."

The music changed to a slow song. Kylie looked up and saw several couples moving to the center of the dining hall to dance. Helen and Jonathon, holding hands, were among the first to make their way to the empty floor space. They wrapped their arms around each other and started swaying to the music. They didn't even appear to be dancing, just holding each other and occasionally doing a small side step. Not that it looked dorky; it sort of looked sweet.

A few other couples moved to the dance floor and started to sway to the beat of the music. The lyrics of the song spoke of love, being close, and kisses. Someone turned down the lights, and since Kylie didn't think the lights had a dimmer switch, she suspected it had been one of the witches using a touch of magic.

Maybe they'd even added a bit of romance potion to the air, because Kylie felt it. Suddenly, she wanted to be out on the dance floor, too. She wanted to feel Lucus's hands on her waist while she rested her cheek on his shoulder.

She glanced at Lucas, leaned in, and asked, "Do you want to dance?"

He made a funny face as if she'd asked him to stand on his head or something. "I . . . no. Sorry."

"I guess that might upset the guards too much, huh?" She looked over at the pack of weres watching them.

"It's not that." Lucas released a deep breath. "Come on." He took the plastic cup that held soda from her hand and set it on the floor beside their chairs. He caught her fingers and pulled her up. For a second, she thought he meant to take her out on the dance floor, but instead he headed to the front of the dining hall.

"Where are we going?"

"Outside."

He pulled her through the crowd so fast, Kylie didn't have time to ask his reasons. When he stopped, they stood outdoors and off to the side of the dining hall.

Alone.

The music, while only a distant humming, could still be heard, and it seemed to play along with the night sounds. Crickets and a few birds sang along with the lyrics.

"Isn't this better?" He took her hands and placed them around his neck and then set his hands around her waist as if to dance.

"So the pack won't see us?" she asked, insecure.

"No," he insisted. "Did you see one were out on that dance floor?"

She had to think, but then she shook her head. "No."

"We don't like drawing attention to ourselves in public."

The air was warm, but not as warm as Lucas's hand pressed against her hip. Kylie glanced up and saw a half-moon offering the night a minimum of light. Not that it was all that dark outside; the stars appeared to be working overtime. No clouds hung in the heavens, so the sky seemed sprayed with stars. She could hardly find a piece of sky that didn't have a tiny diamond shape twinkling and adding a silver glow to the night. Slowly, he started moving to the distant music.

"But in private, that's another matter." He didn't just sway but danced. And he obviously knew how, because his steps encouraged her feet to follow the same pattern his were making.

With scents of pizza and blood no longer perfuming the air,

Lucas's own scent stood out and mingled with the woodsy scent of the night air.

She looked up at him again. "Who taught you to dance?"

"My grandmother. She told me it was the way to a woman's heart," he said, his voice a light whisper against her ear. His head dipped down and his lips brushed against her cheek. "I personally believe when two people get this close, it should be in private."

His words made her realize how close they were standing to each other. She gazed again into his eyes, and his mouth met hers. They danced and kissed for what seemed like forever. Not that she was complaining. She felt as if they were floating, lost in a moment. His kiss didn't push for more than she was ready to give. It was just a soft meshing of his mouth on hers, with an occasional slip of his tongue across her bottom lip.

The kiss finally ended. She placed her hand on his warm chest right beside where her head rested and listened to his heartbeat, which was very fast.

"Is your blood still rushing?" She raised her head, rested her chin on his chest, and smiled up at him.

"More than before." His tone rang deeper than it had been. He adjusted his hands on her waist and she could feel the racing of his pulse where his wrist touched the bottom of her rib cage.

"Feel it?" he asked.

"Yeah." Leaning her head back on his chest, she decided she could stay there forever with his breath stirring against her hair. Closing her eyes, she enjoyed the closeness and the sensation of being held, of being cherished.

With her ear again pressed to his chest, she heard a soft humming, almost a purring. The sound filled her head and she felt as if it pulsated inside her. She sensed he'd pulled her closer, his nearness warmed her inside and out, and the floating sensation returned even stronger this time. Leaning into him a bit more, she longed to be closer still.

His fingers pressed against her waist, making tiny little shifts up and down. The light touch tickled and caused a fluttering sensation deep in her belly. Then his hands glided up her sides, almost to her breasts. The slightest warning whispered in her head, but she pushed it back. This felt too good to—

He inhaled, sharply, and she thought she heard him swear, then he yanked his hands from her and stepped away.

Without his support, she almost felt dizzy. She gazed up at him confused. "What . . . ?"

"We should . . . we should go inside."

When she met his eyes, they glowed a brighter blue. "Is something wrong?" she asked.

"No. It's . . . just safer inside."

"Safer from what?" She looked around, thinking he'd seen something. Had the eagle or deer returned? It could even be the blue jay, back to—

"From me," he said, and shoved his hands into his pockets. "I'm low on willpower tonight, Kylie. About a week and a half before the change, I tend to run more on instinct than logic. And right now, my instinct says to pull you in the woods, find a soft spot of grass, and have my way with you."

She moved in and placed a hand on his chest. "I know you well enough to know that you would never force me to do something I didn't want to do."

He pulled her palm from his chest and held her hand gently in his. "I would never force you, Kylie. Never. But I'm not above trying to persuade you. And . . ." He tilted her head back with his other hand as if to make sure she knew he was serious. "Werewolves have a knack for persuading. And that's not how I want this to happen."

She blinked and tried to understand what he was saying. Her insides still felt like liquid, and she missed his warmth against her. She tried to move closer to regain what she missed, but he took another step back.

He pulled her hand to his lips, and after placing a quick kiss to her knuckles, he tightened his grip and gave her a tug back toward the dining hall.

She took a few steps. Then, still trying to process what he'd said, she put on her mental brakes. "What do you mean by a 'knack for persuading'?"

Chapter Fifteen

Lucas didn't answer. Instead he just tugged on her arm, and she let him pull her back inside the dining hall. But the more she thought about what he'd said, the more she wanted answers. For a minute back there, she'd felt almost drunk with . . . passion. Did werewolves, like faes, have the ability to manipulate a girl's feelings so she would . . . give him anything he wanted?

Kylie stared up at Lucas, who was holding her hand and leading her back to the place where they'd sat earlier. Mentally, she sorted through her emotions.

She wasn't angry at Lucas; she didn't even regret their slow dance in the moonlight. On the contrary, she'd loved every second of it. So, what was the problem?

A tiny internal voice answered the question. The problem was she didn't want to think that someone other than herself could persuade her to do something that she might not have done otherwise.

And yet, another little voice whispered, wasn't that what passion and seduction were about? All the magazines talked about how women wanted to be seduced. So was it a bad thing?

Okay, so she was confused. She looked at her hand where Lucas's fingers locked with hers and tugged her along. She followed him through a small crowd of campers to get their seats. Finally settled in their chairs again, she wondered when any of this was going to get any easier.

"You want something else to drink?" he asked, having to raise his voice for her to hear him over the music and the crowd of voices.

"I'm fine."

"Pizza?" he asked.

"Not now." She almost asked for an explanation about what he'd said earlier. Then she realized that the noise and the crowd would make having a lengthy and private conversation impossible. She glanced at Lucas and found him studying her, staring deep into her eyes—almost as if he were trying to read her thoughts.

He leaned in and rested his forehead against hers. "Are you upset with me?"

"No," she said honestly, and meant it. It wasn't anger she felt, just uncertainty, confusion. Because even if Lucas had the ability to seduce her to do certain things, he hadn't done it.

Blinking and offering him a smile, she decided tonight, at least at the party, might not be the time to talk about this. However, before she did any more moonlight dancing or make-out sessions by the creek, she needed answers.

She recalled Holiday's words weeks earlier when they were talking about boys and sex: *What I'm asking is that when you decide to do something, that it's something you've thought about and decided to do. Not a spur-of-the-moment decision that you might regret later.*

Did Holiday's words of wisdom have more meaning to them than Kylie had guessed?

An hour later, they'd indulged in pizza and drunk enough diet soda to drown an Italian fish. The number of couples dancing had dwindled; now, almost everyone was eating and mingling. Even the lights had been brightened. When people started stopping by to chat, Kylie had expected Lucas to disappear, but he hung in there and was even very friendly, which was so out of character for a werewolf. He was doing this for her, and she appreciated his effort.

Both Della and Miranda had stopped by and said hello as they got drinks and pizza. Kylie wanted to ask them if all "pact" things were going well, but she couldn't find a way to do it without being overheard, so she decided to wait until later to get an update.

As soon as the pizza disappeared, someone lowered the lights again and several couples started making their way back to the makeshift dance floor. As Kylie's vision adapted to the change of light, her eyes lit on Della being led to the dance floor by . . . Chris.

Kylie immediately did a sweep of the room for Steve, and she was pretty sure he was the guy in the black T-shirt, standing in the shadowy corner talking to a couple of girls, one of whom was Fredericka. The other looked like . . . Ellie.

Kylie's gaze moved around the room for one quick second, searching for a certain fae. She didn't find him and wondered if he hadn't come because he knew she'd be here.

I'm not thinking about Derek. She closed her eyes and repeated those words to herself as if they were her new mantra.

When she looked back up to find Della, Kylie spotted Miranda moving on the dance floor with Clark. Kylie didn't know Clark that well, except that he was a warlock and known to be a bit of a troublemaker.

What were Miranda and Della doing? What happened to their pact? Why weren't they going after the right guys?

"Something wrong?" Lucas asked.

She glanced over at him and realized she was frowning. "Not really. It's just . . ." She looked back at the crowd, stalling, trying to figure out how much she could tell him. Before she could come up with an appropriate answer, she spotted Perry. Perry, who looked angry enough to chew nails and spit out staples. His gaze met hers, and then he started walking to the door.

"Give me just a minute, please," she told Lucas, and shot up and took off after Perry.

By the time Kylie got outside, Perry was nowhere around. Then she saw him. Well, it had to be him. One of those big prehistoric-looking birds stood in front of the main office.

"Perry!" she called out, and ran to catch him.

His wings, a span of about five feet, were spread open, and he appeared ready to take flight.

"Don't just run away," Kylie snapped.

"I'm not running. I'm flying. And for a damn good reason. If I have to stand there and watch her flirting with all those guys, I'm gonna end up hurting someone."

Kylie watched the bird's beak move up and down as it talked. "First, turn yourself back into human form before you speak to me. Second, you don't have to just stand there. Go ask her to dance."

Diamond-shaped sparkles started appearing around the bird. From where Kylie was standing only a foot from him, the air seemed to get thin. She wasn't exactly sure what happened when Perry shifted, but it had to do some weird stuff to the ozone.

One of the sparkles floated up; on its descent, it brushed against her arm and popped like the blow bubbles she'd played with as child. But instead of a tickling sensation, Kylie felt a jolt of electricity run up her arm.

Suddenly Perry stood there instead of the pterodactyl. His eyes were red, angry. "Ask her to dance so she can reject me in front of everyone? Do I look like an idiot to you?"

"No, right now you look like a coward afraid to take a chance on what you want."

"I'm not a coward!" he growled. "I have more power in my pinky finger than ten of you supernaturals."

"Then prove it by standing up for yourself." He didn't looked convinced, so Kylie added, "I have a feeling she won't reject you."

He just stared at her, disbelief shining in his eyes as they changed from red back to his normal blue.

"Trust me," Kylie added.

She could see he wanted to give in. But then he waved a hand back toward the door. "She's already dancing with someone else."

"Then cut in." Kylie frowned when she saw Lucas standing in the shadows. Then she remembered he was her shadow. He had to follow her.

"Cut in?" Perry asked, as if he weren't familiar with the term.

"Go tap on the guy's shoulder and just say you want to cut in."

"And he'll just step aside and let me dance with her? Where the hell did you get that idea?"

"It's not an idea. It's proper dancing etiquette. When someone wants to dance with someone who's already dancing, you're supposed to tap on the guy's shoulder and just say you're cutting in."

Perry frowned. "And what happens if he says no?"

"He's not supposed to say no."

Perry rolled his eyes. "In the human world, maybe, but—"

"Oh, for Christ's sake." She held up her hands in frustration. "Just try it."

"Fine," he said. "But if he gives me any shit, I might end up hurting him." His eyes turned red again. Blood red.

"No, you can't hurt—"

Before she could finish, Perry shot back inside. She took off after him. Oh, friggin' great. Maybe this hadn't been the best idea.

Lucas called to her, but she didn't slow down.

Kylie had barely made it back inside when she heard the commotion. She took off toward the dance floor.

"I said I'm cutting in!" Perry's voice rose over the music and chatter of the other campers.

Kylie tried elbowing her way through, hoping to get to them in time to prevent things from escalating, but a crowd had already started to circle and her elbows must not have been sharp enough because everyone just grunted and ignored her.

"And I said go to hell!" a voice, obviously Clark's, answered back.

"What about what I want?" Miranda said.

Kylie stood on her tiptoes to get a better view but still couldn't see anything.

The sound of a scuffle filled the room. Most of the female campers started squealing, while the males just started cheering the fight on.

"Stop it!" Kylie yelled, and started jumping up and down, hoping to see what was happening.

"Watch out!" someone screamed, and like a wave, everyone dropped to the ground as a fireball the size of a volleyball shot through the air.

"Crap!" Kylie yelled, and took advantage of everyone's position to move in. By the time she'd stepped over two or three people, apologizing when she felt fingers or feet beneath her step, she spotted Miranda giving Clark hell.

"I said I wanted to dance with him!" Miranda yelled.

Perry stood there watching, listening to Miranda with a big smile on his face.

Miranda continued her rant, and Kylie couldn't make it out because of everyone else's chatter, but she could see Clark's face turning angry red. Miranda poked him in the chest. Clark retaliated by shoving Miranda back and calling her a name.

Miranda hadn't caught her balance when diamond sparkles started popping off like fireworks. A huge green dragon the size of an eighteen-wheeler appeared where Perry had just stood. Smoke billowed up from the dragon's long, bumpy snout. Most of the campers started running like cockroaches in a Raid commercial.

Well, everyone but Kylie, Miranda, and Clark. Kylie moved in and grabbed Miranda's arm, hoping to get her out of the way of danger. But the little witch slipped out of Kylie's hold and stood there staring up at the dragon with what looked like admiration.

"Oh my, he's beautiful," Miranda muttered.

Kylie gazed up at the huge green beast, and while she couldn't agree with Miranda, she decided to forgo speaking her mind. Especially when Perry swiped his fifteen-foot tail around the room, knocking down several of the daring onlookers and tossing a few others across the room. The building shook again, and then everyone left standing moved back.

Della swooped in and screamed at Kylie and Miranda to get back. Miranda ignored Della, too. And until Kylie could get Miranda out of harm's way, she wasn't leaving.

"He won't hurt me," Miranda snapped, and then she turned her angry eyes on Clark. She started wiggling her pinky and chanting.

Unfortunately, right then Burnett swooped in, landing directly in front of Clark. He looked mad enough to kill innocent puppies. He opened his mouth, no doubt to give them all hell, but before he spoke a swirl of rainbow colors started swirling around him like ribbons. Then the hard-as-nails vampire vanished into the smoke-filled air and standing in his place was a very pissed-off kangaroo.

"Oh, shit!" Kylie said.

"Oh, shit!" screamed Miranda.

Burnett, now a very unhappy kangaroo, started hopping around like a marsupial on speed. Miranda, shaking and dancing from one foot to the other, had her pinky in the air, muttering out chants so fast that Kylie couldn't catch one word.

Perry, aka the large, out-of-control dragon, took a step toward Clark.

Clark, looking about ready to crap his pants, started tossing more fireballs. One missed and hit the dining hall wall. One slammed into the trash can containing the pizza boxes, which immediately burst into flames. Another went sailing through the air, heading right for . . . Miranda.

Kylie felt her blood fizz and rush to her brain. Without thinking, without even realizing what she planned to do, she jumped into the fireball's path, caught it, and tossed it to the other side of the room.

Perry released an ominous sound, half roar, half cry. Smoke shot out of his nostrils. Clark tossed another fireball. Before Kylie could stop this one, it hit Perry—in dragon form—and singed the green scales on his side.

The smell of burned dragon, along with burning pizza boxes, scented the air. Smoke rose to the ceiling.

Perry reared his head back and roared so loudly that it shook the whole dining hall to its rafters. It wasn't so much a cry of pain as a cry of warning and of complete and utter fury.

Lucas suddenly appeared beside Kylie and caught her hand in his. He looked at her palm. Then, appearing perplexed, he grabbed her by the elbow and started yanking her away. She pulled free and leapt over some turned-over chairs to grab Miranda.

Just as Clark tossed another fireball, Della swooped back in and was hit by a cylindrical flame in the hip. It knocked the little vampire back a good five feet, and she landed in a dead heap on the floor.

Kylie screamed, Miranda chanted louder, Perry snorted more fire, and Kylie bolted back over the chairs to get to Della.

Before Kylie got to her side, Della popped back up, apparently unharmed. But Kylie had never seen her so pissed. Her eyes glowed bright green, her fangs extended past her bottom lip, and if looks could kill, Clark was worm bait. Growling with raw anger, Della shot across the room after Clark. Burnett, in all his kangaroo glory, jumped in front of Della, blocking and preventing her attack.

Perry let loose a breath of fire that shot clear across the room and left black marks on the log walls and the ceiling.

Miranda, pinky still in the air, chanted louder. Then another swirl of rainbow colors flew across the room, and Burnett zapped back to vampire form. Not a happy vampire, either.

With eyes glowing neon red, he let loose a scream that matched Perry's dragon roar. "Everyone stop! Right now!"

The commotion stopped. Even the crowd standing at the front of the building ceased jabbering. Silence reigned.

Burnett looked first at Clark. "Throw another fireball and you'll be expelled from Shadow Falls until the day I die. And I plan to live a very long time." He turned his gaze to Lucas. "Can you please put the garbage fire out before this whole place goes up in flames?" Whirling, he faced a very angry Della. "As much as I'd love to let you rip this guy's head off"—Burnett glared at Clark—"I think Holiday would disapprove. So, go cool off somewhere." He pointed toward the door.

Before he lowered his hand, Della was gone, leaving only an angry blur in the air.

Taking a deep breath, Burnett aimed his angry gaze at the dragon. "Change back this instant!"

Perry let out one roar of protest, but then the sparkles started floating down from the ceiling to the floor. Kylie noted that everyone else knew to avoid the little bubbles of electricity. Funny how people didn't warn her about these things.

A second after it stopped raining charged, diamond-shaped bubbles, the dragon disappeared and Perry stood before Burnett. He didn't look any less angry than Burnett. Then, proving Kylie's assumption, he took a flying leap over Burnett and landed on top of Clark. Fists started swinging.

Burnett reached effortlessly into the scuffle and yanked Perry up by the collar of his shirt and held him a good five inches off the concrete floor. "No more fighting." He dropped Perry on his feet.

Perry glared at Clark and then looked at Burnett. "He pushed Miranda," Perry said, fury in his tone. "You never, ever hurt a female. You taught me that when I was six."

Six? Kylie looked from Burnett to Perry. Did that mean Burnett knew—?

"I know," Burnett said. "And I'll take that up with him later. But you have to learn to deal with things without shifting, or you'll never be able to coexist with humans."

"He was throwing fireballs!" Miranda piped in. "It's logical that Perry would shift into something that could deal with it."

Kylie saw Perry cut his gaze to Miranda. The anger in his eyes faded and he stared at her in something like astonishment. Something told Kylie that Perry wasn't accustomed to people standing up for him. Right then, her heart broke a little bit more for the shapeshifter who'd been abandoned by both his parents.

Burnett let go of a deep breath and his angry gaze went back to Clark. "Go to your cabin. I'll be there shortly to dish out your punishment."

Clark took off, but not without sneering at Miranda. For a second, Kylie thought Perry was going to attack again. So did Burnett, for he reached out and latched on to Perry. "Don't you dare shift."

Again, Kylie noted the familiarity with which Burnett treated Perry. Obviously, Perry's stint with the FRU foster program had brought him into contact with Burnett. And somehow she sensed that Burnett had taken the orphaned shape-shifter under his wing. It weakened Kylie's earlier misgiving about Burnett and the FRU library. Not that she was completely over it, but everything in her said Burnett wasn't the enemy.

Lucas returned, bringing with him a scent of smoke, and stood by Kylie's side. She looked over at the trash can that minutes ago had been shooting flames up to the ceiling. It had been extinguished, and now only a few wisps of smoke floated up from the rim of the can.

Lucas reached for Kylie's hand again, opened her palm, and studied it. Then he leaned down and whispered in her ear, "Are you really okay?"

"Yes," she said, perplexed by his question.

He stared at her hand again and tenderly ran his finger across her palm. "It should have burned you."

She remembered catching one of the fireballs aimed at Miranda. "Well, it didn't." Then she recalled how she'd felt as if her blood had turned into soda and she'd felt it fizz into her brain.

His look of awe changed into a tight frown. "Nevertheless, the next time I try to remove you from a dangerous situation, don't fight me."

She frowned right back at him. "I wasn't fighting you. I just wasn't leaving Miranda or Della."

He shook his head as if she exasperated him. "You really are a protector, aren't you?"

"Maybe I'm just a good friend." For some crazy reason, she sensed he preferred she not be a protector. Why? Did her being a protector mean she had less a chance of being a werewolf?

Burnett looked back at the crowd of campers watching them. "You guys go back to your cabins. Party's over."

As soon as they left, he fixed his gaze on Miranda. "You so much as twitch that finger at me again and I'll . . ."

"Della says she'll rip it off," Miranda said, and giggled, not the least bit intimidated by Burnett. Burnett let go of a growl, not appreciating Miranda's candor.

"She didn't mean to turn you," Kylie and Perry said at the same time.

"It was Clark she was aiming at," Perry added, frowning at Burnett.

"I don't care," Burnett said. "It will never happen again. You understand that?" He glared harder at Miranda.

Miranda nodded. "Understood. I'm sorry."

Kylie could tell she had to work to look reprimanded, but the apology rang sincere. And that was when Kylie knew all the campers had accepted Burnett as one of the leaders. He might not have Holiday's easy, somewhat loving method of connecting with the campers, but he made up for it in other ways.

Burnett folded his arms over his chest. "Now, all of you go back to your cabins."

They all turned to leave. Lucas slipped his hand in Kylie's, letting her know he'd be walking with her.

But then Burnett added, "Everyone but Kylie."

Oh joy. What now? Kylie stopped moving and turned around to face Burnett.

Chapter Sixteen

As soon as the sound of the heavy wooden front door closing echoed in the empty, still smoky dining hall, Kylie decided to confess and get it over with.

"I know, it's my fault. I apologize. I thought I was helping."

Burnett, arms still crossed over his chest, stared down at her. "What's your fault?"

"This," she said, suddenly wishing she hadn't been so gung ho to take the blame. Then again, accepting responsibility was right.

Burnett stared down at her as the seconds passed, which only intensified Kylie's growing need to fill the silence. "Okay, look," she said. "I'm the one who told Perry to cut in on Miranda and Clark."

He nodded. "Yeah, I heard that. I was in the office."

Kylie frowned, wondering if he'd also eavesdropped on her conversation with Lucas.

He dropped his arms to his sides, making him appear less intimidating. "But that doesn't make it your fault."

"So you didn't have me hang back to read me the riot act about starting this mess?"

"No." He reached down and snatched two chairs upright and motioned for her to sit down.

"Am I in trouble for something else?" she asked as she sat down.

He flipped the chair around and straddled it. "No. I just wanted to talk to you." His palms curled around the back of the chair. "Is your hand okay?"

She held out her palm for him to see. "Yeah."

He looked down at her hand, then up at her face again. "Holiday called and was worried about you."

"Why?"

He seemed to struggle to find the right words. "I told her what you'd asked about the bird."

"What did she say?" Kylie leaned in a bit, ready to get at least one answer to her long list of questions.

"She said you shouldn't be worried. If you did bring the bird back to life, it would only cost a very, very small piece of your soul."

"But I did give some of it away?"

"Possibly," Burnett said.

Kylie hesitated to ask, but she needed to know, so she just did it. "Did she say anything about the bird stalking me?"

"Stalking you?"

"Yeah, it was flying around me today, but I wasn't so sure it wasn't just some fluke. But then it came to my window earlier today and tapped on it."

Burnett's eyes widened a little in surprise, and then his inscrutable expression slammed down again. "Are you sure it's the same bird?"

"No, but it's too much of a coincidence not to be, don't you think?"

"Perhaps," he said. "Did you feel any kind of threat from the bird? Like you did with the eagle and the deer?"

"No, nothing. It was all peaceful and serene."

"Good." He stared down at his hands as if he had something else to say and it wasn't going to be easy. "Look, about the FRU library . . ."

"What about it?" she asked, immediately feeling nervous.

"I don't want you to think I was lying earlier. I wasn't. However, considering that I work for the FRU, I'm only allowed to say so much."

"So you did lie to me?" she asked.

"No." He tightened his lips as if frustrated. "I told you as much as I could. The truth is that there are some books there I'm not allowed to see."

She felt suddenly cold, the kind of a chill that came from being afraid of where their conversation was headed. Of being afraid to discover the truth about herself.

"There are books about . . . others like me, aren't there?" she asked. "Others who don't know what they are."

He hesitated again and laced his fingers together in a tight ball. "I don't even know what all is there, but if they were there, I doubt very seriously that I could obtain permission to allow you to read them."

"Why?"

"The FRU considers ninety percent of what they have collected as classified."

Frustration built in her chest. "What's the big secret? I mean, the key to understanding what I am could be in that library. And you're locking me out—it's so frustrating. It's like you're deliberately trying to keep me in the dark about my powers, my identity."

"You're not being kept in the dark, and the key to understanding what you are is much more likely to be elsewhere—here in the outside world—than in that library. There's a lot of classified information at stake, but there's nothing we're trying to hide from you."

"It sure as hell feels that way," she said. "Tell me the truth, please. Do you know what I am?"

"No," he said again, and her instincts told her he wasn't lying. "Look," he said. "The only reason I brought this up is that I don't want you to stop trusting me. I'm as perplexed by you as . . . well, as you are."

Kylie slumped in her chair, resigned to the fact that he wouldn't, and maybe even couldn't, give her anything more. "Fine."

He nodded and then looked around the dining hall. "You think we might convince everyone not to tell Holiday about this disaster?"

Kylie looked up at the singed wood, which had been marked by the dragon's breath and Clark's fireballs. "It might be difficult."

He looked around and frowned. "I guess so. But damn, I wanted to prove to her that I could run the show without screwing up."

"You didn't screw up," Kylie said. "All's well that ends well. No one's hurt."

He let out a deep gulp of air. "I got myself turned into a kangaroo."

Kylie couldn't help but snicker. Then Burnett laughed. Kylie couldn't swear by it, but she thought it was the first time she'd ever heard him do that. "Holiday is going to enjoy that one, isn't she?"

Kylie continued to grin. "Oh, yeah. Can I be the one to tell her?"

"Afraid not." Then he flashed her what she could have sworn was a smile. "If it involves making her laugh, I'll keep that pleasure for myself."

She studied him for a few moments, again feeling his devotion to Holiday. Thinking of devotion and Burnett, she decided to ask another question that had been pulling at her mind. "You and Perry have a history, right?"

He paused for a second and then said, "Sort of. Why?"

"The way you two relate to each other."

He nodded but didn't offer any details.

"It was through the foster program, right?" she asked. "Were you like a caseworker or something there at one time?"

Burnett's expression stayed stoic. "He told you about the foster program?"

"Yeah."

Burnett nodded. "Yes. We crossed paths through the program."

He didn't seem eager to share anything else about his past, so Kylie decided to drop it, or at least drop part of it. "Perry's not going to get in too much trouble for this, is he?" She frowned. "I mean, I was the one that sort of caused it. He was leaving and I stopped him."

Burnett arched a brow. "Truth be told, he behaved extremely well . . . considering." He looked around again. "You wouldn't believe the kind of messes I've had to clean up because of him."

Kylie imagined Burnett coming to the aid of a younger Perry—a Perry who had no one because his parents abandoned him. Her doubts about Burnett and trusting him practically vanished. Without thinking, she said, "You know, you aren't near as badass as you pretend to be."

Burnett frowned as if he didn't like being considered anything but bad. "I wouldn't bet on it," he said. "Just ask Holiday." He stood up. "Come on, I'll walk you to your cabin. I need to go deal with Clark before it gets any later."

"You don't need to walk me. I think I can manage."

"Nope. You're still under shadow guard."

As they walked out of the dining hall, Kylie welcomed the night air without the scent of smoke. The memory of her dance with Lucas tickled her mind, but she pushed it back, not wanting to think about that with present company. Especially when she half feared that Burnett might have been privy to their entire conversation.

They started down the path to her cabin. A few night creatures rustled the underbrush along their way. Burnett cut his gaze from one side to the other, always aware, always on guard.

"You haven't experienced any more threats, have you?" he asked.

"No."

"It always amazes me what just having a shadow with you can prevent."

Kylie looked up at him through the darkness. "Do you think that's the only reason it hasn't happened again? That someone, more than likely Mario or his grandson, is still waiting to get me alone?" She considered telling him about the dream but didn't see how it would help.

"I think we can't be too careful."

Kylie felt a familiar chill slide past her, slowly, and she knew they had company. She gazed around to see if the spirit had materialized yet, but she saw nothing.

But the sense of grief that seemed to seep into her pores told her it was Jane Doe. Kylie's mind shot back to the spirit and the loss of her child. A need to help the spirit tightened her chest. If Holiday were here, she'd talk to her about it. But she didn't think Burnett would be helpful where ghosts were concerned. Especially when it involved a pregnant ghost.

"Who's shadowing me in the morning?" she asked.

"I believe it's Della," Burnett said, and looked around almost as if he felt the ghostly presence.

"Would you mind if we go to the cemetery in Fallen tomorrow?"

Burnett stopped walking. "Why would you want to go there?"

Kylie rubbed her arms to try to chase away the chill. "It has to do with my latest ghost."

"Which is a good reason not to go," he said.

Kylie frowned at the thought that she and Holiday were the only ones who weren't antighost. "The spirit can't remember who she is, and because the first time she appeared to me was when my mom and I were driving past the cemetery, I think she might be buried there. I asked Holiday about going and she said it would be okay as long as I had someone with me and if you guys knew where I was."

His expression didn't change, but something about the way he held his shoulders told her he'd given in. "Let me check with Holiday. If she says it's okay, I'll . . . I'll go with you."

"You shouldn't have to go. I'm sure Della and I would—"

"No." From his tone she knew he wouldn't budge. "Until we

know the threat against you is over, you won't leave the camp without me." His stern gaze punctuated his words, and then he continued, "I'm serious about this, Kylie. I don't want to scare you, but if this is Mario or Red, they won't give up. They're waiting for a time that you are at your most vulnerable to attack again. And next time you may not be so lucky."

Kylie, with a cloud of the spirit's cold following her, walked into the cabin a few minutes later. Della and Miranda were sitting at the kitchen table, chatting.

Miranda popped up. "Did you see Perry? Was he not totally off-the-chart awesome? He even fought for me when he was in human form."

"Yeah, I saw that," Kylie said, hanging back a bit, not wanting to ruin the moment by having them sense the spirit. Kylie looked at Della, whose eyes still glowed with anger.

"Is Burnett sending Clark packing?" Della asked. "Because if he doesn't, I'm gonna have to teach that warlock a lesson he'll never forget."

Kylie recalled Della taking a hit with the fireball, and she knew that for a vamp that was probably embarrassing—especially when Kylie had somehow managed to catch one and toss it aside. "I know Burnett is going to see him now, but I don't know what he plans on doing about it."

"He burned Miranda's new skirt!" Della held up the skirt, which had been scorched.

Miranda waved a hand. "I told you it's not a big deal."

"It is a big deal," Della retorted. "If Kylie hadn't been there, he could have hurt you."

"What about you?" Kylie asked, looking at Della. "Did you get burned by the fireball?"

"A bit, but I've already healed." Della's gaze went to Kylie's hand. "You must heal fast, too. "

"Yeah." Kylie decided not to tell them that she'd never been burned by Clark's fireball. Or at least she hadn't gotten the sensation that she'd been burned. She recalled Lucas's remark *You really are a protector.* And again, she wondered why he'd sounded almost unhappy about the possibility.

The spirit's cold drew closer, and Kylie ran her hand over her forearms where goose bumps chased goose bumps over her bare skin. She leaned back against the edge of the sofa.

"How pissed is Burnett at me for turning him into a kangaroo?" Miranda asked.

Kylie grinned. "I think he's over it."

"I'd still avoid him for a few days if I were you," Della suggested. "I mean, did you see how mad he was when you turned him back?" She grinned. "Though not as mad as I'd have been. I swear, if it'd been me, I'd have hopped all over your ass, right after I'd kangaroo-punched Clark out. But damn, it was funny seeing Burnett hopping mad."

"I didn't mean to do it," Miranda said. "I wasn't even going for a kangaroo."

"What were you going for?" Kylie asked.

"A cockatoo. I guess I said it wrong." She pursed her lips as if thinking. "But hey, at least I figured out how to turn him back. I should get some credit for that."

"Credit?" Della snickered. "If you hadn't been able to change him back, I have a feeling you'd be kangaroo food right about now."

Miranda sighed.

Kylie decided to change the subject and looked at Della. "So what happened with the pact?"

Della frowned. "Let's just say it didn't work out as well for us. But forget about us. How did things go with Lucas? I saw you two went outside for a while."

Kylie bit down on her lip, unsure how much she wanted to share. "It went good."

"How good?" asked Miranda, never one to appreciate privacy. The little witch even rubbed her hands together in giddy anticipation.

"Really good," Kylie answered, remembering how it had felt to dance with Lucas—to kiss him as if they had all night. The memory chased away some of the ghostly chill prickling her bare arms. Kylie glanced around again to make sure Jane Doe hadn't manifested.

"Good as in first base? Second base?" Miranda's hazel eyes got big. "Or are we talking third?"

"We just kissed." Remembering their accusation that she was up for sainthood, Kylie added, "And slow danced in the moonlight. It was very romantic."

"Romantic or sexy?" Della asked. "There's a difference, you know."

Kylie frowned. "No, there's not."

"Oh yes, there is," Della smarted off. "Romantic is . . . 'Oh, he's so sweet,' and sexy is . . . 'He's so hot, my panties might just catch fire.' So which was it? Romantic or sexy?"

"Panties catch fire?" Kylie rolled her eyes.

"It's just an expression, but you know what I mean," Della insisted. "So which was it? Romantic?" She held out one hand. "Or sexy?" She held out the other.

Kylie considered the question and then admitted the truth. "It was both."

Miranda squealed. "Was it as hot as the kiss at the creek he gave you?"

Kylie remembered being at the creek with Lucas over a month ago. She'd fallen on top of him and they had kissed. Kissed deeply while the cold, crisp water ran over them and Lucas's hot body pressed against hers. And she decided Della might have a point about the difference between sexy and romantic. The kiss at the creek had been sexy. Tonight had been . . . well, more romantic, but still sexy.

"You know, you guys have to start having your own romantic escapades. I'm tired of being the only one sharing this stuff."

"We're working on it," Miranda said, and shrugged. "So? Give us more details. Was tonight as hot as the famous creek kiss?"

Socks waddled out of her bedroom and came and bumped his pointed nose against her ankle. "Not quite as hot," Kylie said, reaching down to pick him up. She pulled the little skunk close and nuzzled his nose. "But almost."

Remembering just how "almost as hot" tonight had been, Kylie looked at her two best friends and wondered if they might know the answer to the question she planned on asking Lucas later. "How much do you guys know about werewolves and their powers?"

"I know they're not nearly as powerful as vampires," Della piped up.

"I'm not talking physical strength. Other kinds of power."

"What other kinds of power?" asked Della.

Kylie tried to figure out how to put it. "The power to persuade a girl to do things?"

"Things? What kind of things?" Della glanced at Miranda, whose eyes grew round. "Do you mean . . . ?" They both turned back to Kylie.

"Okay, spill it," Della said. "Just what the hell happened out in the moonlight?"

"Yeah," Miranda added. "And don't leave out a single juicy detail."

Chapter Seventeen

Kylie felt her cheeks begin to redden. "Okay, it's not what you think. . . ."

Even as she said the words, she knew she was lying.

"Okay, fine," she said. "It's exactly what you think."

Miranda's mouth dropped open. "You mean . . . Did you—"

"No." Kylie slapped her hand against her chest. "God, no. I mean, like I told you, we just danced and kissed. But . . ."

"But what?" Della demanded.

"Yeah," Miranda said. "But what?"

Kylie took a deep breath. "But . . . he said something that made me think that maybe he had the ability to convince me to, you know." She blushed again.

"Do the horizontal bop?" Della offered. "Do the Humpty dance? Knock boots?"

Kylie rolled her eyes. "Where do you come up with that stuff?"

Della grinned. "I get around."

Miranda giggled.

"Uh-huh." Kylie felt her cheeks grow even hotter. "Anyway, yeah, that's what I mean," she added before the smart-mouthed vamp could come up with some more half-vulgar, half-hilarious terms for sex. "I just want to know if werewolves have any special powers, okay?"

Della leaned back in her chair. "Maybe he just means he'll seduce you by kissing you. Let's face it, he's pretty hot and you said his kisses were out of this world. Hey, he makes my knees weak, and I'm vampire with a natural dislike for weres."

"He is hot," Miranda added.

Kylie tried not to think about her two roommates weak-kneed for Lucas.

"Then you don't believe that power really exists?" she asked instead.

"Yeah, it exists," Miranda said, and her brow pinched as if she were thinking. "I've heard something about it. Nothing specific, but just a few mumblings."

"What have you heard?" Della and Kylie asked at the same time. Kylie put Socks down, moved to the table, and dropped onto a kitchen chair. For some reason, the ghost had decided to move on, which didn't bother her at all. She could use some downtime.

Especially right now.

"I can't remember the details," Miranda said. "Just that it's a little dangerous to date a were. It has something to do with animal pheromones. They're basically animals, and all animals have a natural way of attracting the opposite sex."

"Attracting like how?" Kylie asked.

"Well," Miranda said, "lizards have a brightly colored balloony thing that they blow out from their throats and supposedly girl lizards find that all kinds of sexy."

Kylie shook her head. "Lucas doesn't have a balloon in his throat."

"Hey," Della added. "Have you ever seen those blackbirds—grackles, I think they're called—do the mating dance? They jump around on one foot and ruffle their feathers out. The females supposedly get horny just seeing the male birds do it. I mean, the guy with the better feathers always wins. Or is it the bigger feathers?"

Miranda snickered. "And I heard some male baboons have brightly colored buttocks and they go around mooning the females. Supposedly it's a huge turn-on."

While Kylie was serious about finding answers, she couldn't help but laugh. "I don't think Lucas has colored buttocks, either. Not that I've seen them." She laughed harder.

Before their conversation was over, Della was on the computer looking up strange mating behaviors that included everything from exploding testicles to slinging poop with a tail, and they laughed themselves silly until way past midnight. It was, Kylie decided as she finally slipped into bed, just the type of evening she needed.

Although she still didn't have the answer to her original question: Just what kind of power did Lucas really have?

And could she trust him not to misuse it? Her gut said she could. But was her gut being persuaded by outside influences?

The floating sensation filled Kylie's head several hours after she went to bed that night. Mental alarms went off. Was this Red again? Then she realized the difference: she was floating, which meant she was the one moving.

She considered trying to stop it, but she was too tired, so she just let herself go. Let herself float and zip through the air—moving through clouds of sleep.

The sense of freedom was exhilarating. She didn't have a clue where she was going, and she didn't care. Obviously, her subconscious had a plan. But what?

And then she saw him. He looked so good, lying in his bed, that her breath caught and she put on her flying brakes. He was shirtless, too. The covers came low on his waist, several inches past his belly button. Her gaze moved up and then down his bare torso. There was a lot of skin to appreciate.

Then she studied his face. So peaceful in his slumber. His eyelashes rested against his cheeks. His hair rested against his brow in a ruffled mess, as if he'd run his fingers through it too many times. Her heart spasmed and then she felt herself moving closer, into the room, into the bed, into his . . . head.

No! She stopped herself at the last moment.

She'd vowed to get over Derek. To move past him. Unfortunately, her subconscious hadn't gotten that message. Then, as if gravity, or maybe her own will, started pulling her backward, she let herself sail through the clouds, back through the universe of sleep.

She woke up with a start, as if she'd been slammed back into her body. Catching her breath, she reached for her pillow and hugged it tightly to her chest. The vision of Derek asleep filled her head. *No! No! Don't think about Derek. Think about Lucas.*

Lucas, who'd danced with her in the moonlight. Lucas, who'd kissed her so sweetly. Lucas, whose blood raced every time she was with him.

Closing her eyes, she lost herself again in the oblivion of sleep. The sweet nothingness of slumber. The next thing she knew, she stood in a room of clouds, in front of Lucas. Thoughts of Red hit, but Lucas spoke. "It's me. Feel me. I'm hot." He reached out and took her hand in his. His touch sent warmth through her palm and her heart.

She remembered telling herself to think about Lucas, and she wondered if she was learning to control her dreamscapes. A little thrill ran through her as the sensation of accomplishment filled her chest. With so many unknowns and out-of-control issues happening, it felt great to think she'd mastered something.

He smiled up at her with his sleepy blue eyes. "I was beginning to think you would never visit me in my dreams again."

Suddenly, the clouds evaporated like unwanted fog and they

were back outside where they'd danced earlier that evening. The moon and stars cast lovely shadows around them. Only this time, the night played the music. Crickets and an occasional bird harmonized with the sound of a light breeze stirring through the leaves of shrubbery and the rustle of live oak trees.

"Shall we dance?" He held out his hand.

She started to place her hand in his palm when she realized he didn't have on a shirt. Instead of jeans, he had on a long, loose-fitting pair of boxers. The kind boys slept in—if they didn't sleep nude. The kind the movie stars often wore in those sexy photos.

She swallowed a nervous tickle. He looked really good. Warm and so touchable. And almost naked. As if nothing more than a flick of his thumb could leave him completely bare.

"Uh . . ." She waved her hand up and down. "Shouldn't you get dressed?"

He grinned and then laughed outright—something he didn't do often. "This is your dream, Kylie. You dressed me for the occasion. You're in charge of what I wear. So, the better question is . . . is this how you want me to be dressed?"

She felt her face heat up and wished she could deny it, but Holiday had told her as much during their discussions of dreamscaping. She controlled everything, from the person she visited to what happened during her visit. So what did it mean that she had visited Derek first?

And why had she wanted Lucas half-dressed?

Okay, that was a stupid question.

"Oh . . ." She let her voice fade away, not really sure what else to say. That's when she noticed what she was wearing. The same short pajama set she'd worn to bed—they consisted of a pale blue body-hugging tank top and a pair of tight dark blue boy shorts. A bathing suit would have shown more skin, but she still felt slightly naked.

She wasn't sure how she could change the clothes they were

wearing, but she closed her eyes and concentrated for a couple of seconds. When she opened her eyes again, she saw she was back in her black party dress—much more appropriate. Lucas wore jeans and a white T-shirt with a big yellow smiley face on it.

He looked down at his shirt and then back up at her with a funny frown. "Seriously? This is what you chose?"

"I'm new at this," she said, defending herself. "But it's not that bad."

"A smiley face?" He chuckled again. "Just remind me to never let you buy me clothes."

She laughed, and then he held out his hand again. "Are we here to dance?"

This time, she took it and let him pull her against him.

When his warm arms went around her and his chest melted against hers, it reminded her how it felt to slip into a warm bed on a cold night. She sighed at how comforting it felt to be held by him again. When she rested her cheek on his chest, his hand moved around her waist and his almost electric pulse fluttered against her lower back. That flutter seemed to move inside her and caused her blood to pulse.

She recalled the question she needed to ask him and lifted her head and rested her chin against his chest. He looked down and met her gaze. His blue eyes were hooded with something that looked like passion, and she wondered if her own eyes showed the same emotion.

"Can I ask you something?"

"It's your dream," he whispered. "We can do *anything* you want." There was an emphasis on the word *anything* that caused a ripple of nervousness to move through her.

Anything.

Taking a deep breath, she stopped dancing and slid her hand up his chest to where she felt his heart pumping.

"Tonight, you mentioned that you were good at . . . the art of persuasion."

His lips curled into a smile. "Yeah, I remember that." His voice had a teasing, sensual quality that made her want to shiver and press herself closer to him.

"What . . . what did you mean by that?"

His smile turned ultrasexy. "I'd rather show you."

She nipped at her bottom lip, considering his offer. She was tempted—Lord, how she was tempted. And what would be the harm in saying yes, just this one time? After all, this was just a dream. Anything that happened here would have no effect on her real life. Right?

"Relax, Kylie," he said. "It's just a dream." His words echoed her own thoughts. Then his warm lips brushed against her brow and the ripple of unease increased.

"Maybe it's just a dream," she said. "But it feels real and I'm . . . I prefer you just answered my question the old-fashioned way."

He nodded. For a second, he appeared not to want to continue, but then he said, "It's not like a trick or anything. It's part of what I am. It's instinctual."

"What's instinctual?"

"When a were is with a potential mate, our bodies react in certain ways." He paused as if he knew his explanation wouldn't be enough. "Last night, when you had your head on my chest, you heard the sound . . . the low growl."

"Like a purring or humming," she said, remembering being lulled by the soft noise.

He nodded. "Well, that reverberation is supposed to be somewhat hypnotic. It encourages our potential mate to want to be closer."

Close and naked, Kylie thought, but didn't say it. "It makes one dizzy, too," she said, remembering how she'd felt last night.

He caught her face in his hands. "I guess maybe a little." He brushed his thumb over her cheek. "But it's not a ploy to trick girls into bed. It's just a natural thing male weres do. If that's what you're worried about."

"I'm not exactly worried," she said. And she wasn't. Because as potentially dangerous as the werewolf's purr could be, she didn't think she had to worry about Lucas misusing it. Last night, he'd had a chance to let things escalate between them and he'd put a stop to it.

"Like I told you," she said. "I trust you." And she still did.

He studied her face. "But?"

Okay, there was a but. She hesitated to find the right words. "But knowledge is power. I like knowing what I'm dealing with. And I like being the one in the driver's seat, if you know what I mean."

He frowned slightly as if he didn't like her answer. "It's not like entrapment. A female has to be close, really close, to a male were before she's even aware of it."

Kylie smiled. "So I guess I need to be careful how close I get to you."

"Or not." He leaned in and kissed her softly on the lips. "I really, really like you, Kylie Galen."

"And I you, Lucas Parker." She raised herself up on her tiptoes to press a quick kiss to his lips.

His eyes met hers and he let go of a deep breath. "Okay."

"Okay, what?" she asked, sensing his remark meant something.

"Okay, I'll be a bit more patient. Okay, I'm happy with this. With just being this close to you." He picked her up and twirled her around.

She grinned when he set her back on her feet. "Thanks," she said, and touched his lips with her fingertips.

He caught her hand. "We just have to be a little careful when we're not dreaming."

"Careful about what?"

"Like I told you last night. The closer to the full moon, the more I run on instinct. And sometimes, my instincts are short on patience."

She didn't like the sound of that. "Do you mean we can't see each other when it's time for your change?"

"I didn't say that." He frowned. "We can see each other. But we shouldn't . . . dance in the moonlight for too long. Or roll around on the ground by the creek." He grinned. "Or go skinny-dipping at the swimming hole." His tone seemed to deepen.

"That was just a dream." She felt her face flush.

"A good one, too." He smiled. Then he breathed in as if to sober his thoughts. "But basically, we'll be fine as long as we don't play too close to the fire until after the change." He ran his hand through the curtain of her hair and brought a handful of it to his nose. "Unless you change your mind. You do know that what happens in dreams isn't really real, right? I mean, we could—"

Suddenly, she felt something yanking her from behind and pulling her away from Lucas. Pulling her to someplace she didn't want to go.

Lucas yelled out her name. But a cloud appeared between them. She realized that two men dressed in white lab coats had her in their grips. One on each arm, holding her so tightly that she couldn't get away. The camp had dissolved. Now she was in a building of some kind, and the two men pulled her down a dark, dismal hall. She screamed and tried to pull away, but she was helpless.

Her heart thumped in her chest, and she tasted fear on her tongue. Nothing made sense. Then she remembered—this was a dream. All she had to do was wake up.

She slammed her eyes shut. Tight. Then tighter.

Wake up. Wake up. Wake up.

Suddenly, a bright light shone in her eyes. Everything had changed again. The men who had dragged her away were gone. She felt disoriented, lost, alone. Empty. She felt empty. What was happening to her?

The light shifted from one eye to the other, and she saw a man's face inches from her nose. She realized she was lying in a bed. Not her bed, though. Not the twin one at camp or her full-size mattress at home. This bed felt different. She tried to move but felt numb. No, not numb—she felt paralyzed.

"Is she okay?" a female voice asked. Kylie cut her eyes to the side to see her new captor, but she was out of vision range, and Kylie was unable to turn her neck. Panic started to tighten her throat again.

"She should be," said the man, shining the flashlight into her eyes. Kylie blinked and when she opened her eyes, she saw his pattern. He was vampire.

Then he turned her chin in his large hands and ran his finger over her head. Oddly enough, Kylie realized he touched her bare scalp. She was missing her hair.

Missing her hair?

She blinked again and remembered her ghost, Jane Doe. Was that what was happening? Was this a vision sent to her by the amnesiac ghost—one of those crazy ones where Kylie actually became the spirit? Fear swelled in her chest. She cut her eyes to the side and stared at the man's eyes until she saw her own reflection. Or saw the ghost's reflection.

It should have calmed her, but the panic built higher. She wanted out of here. She hadn't wanted to be here to start with. She'd already lost everything that mattered. Thoughts, feelings, and emotions collided in her chest and she wasn't sure which ones were her own and which ones belonged to her spirit.

"Wake up. Kylie, wake up!" Kylie could hear voices coming from somewhere far away. But then the voices faded and she felt the vampire's hand on her head again.

"She's healing nicely," he said. "Maybe she'll just take a while longer to come around. Let's do another MRI scan on her." The man stood up and twitched his brows at her. "Then again, it could be more. Her pattern still hasn't emerged." He frowned. "I don't understand that. Something isn't right."

"What do I tell her husband? He woke up several hours ago and is asking for her," the female voice said. Kylie had yet to see the owner of that voice.

Help me! Kylie screamed in her head, because she couldn't make her throat work.

"Tell him she's doing fine. But we're keeping her for observation. Release him if he's ready to go."

"Do you think she's going to live?" asked the woman again.

"I don't know." He slipped his flashlight into his coat pocket. "But I guess it's inevitable that we will lose a few subjects. We just have to remember it's for a good cause."

"I guess," said the female voice.

"Get me the results of the test. However, if she hasn't awakened by tonight, go ahead and extinguish her."

Extinguish her?

Kylie's fear ratcheted up a notch.

Noooooooooooooo!

Chapter Eighteen

"Damn it! She's not breathing!" a familiar male voice boomed in Kylie's ears, and she wanted more than anything to answer him. She tried to move but couldn't. She still felt paralyzed.

Help me. Please . . .

"She did this once before." That was Della talking now, but panic filled her voice. Della never showed panic or fear. To the contrary, the vampire was fearless.

"Kylie, wake up!" the deep male voice said, and this time Kylie recognized it as belonging to Lucas.

Suddenly, Kylie's lungs opened up and demanded air. She opened her mouth and gasped and started coughing as if her lungs wanted to reject the oxygen. Rolling over on her side, she continued to cough, certain she was going to blow a lung. Finally, she opened her eyes and realized she was on the kitchen floor in her cabin.

After a few more seconds passed, the coughing stopped and she focused on breathing. Someone grabbed her and pulled her up into their lap and held her. Heat surrounded her. He was hot. So hot. And she was cold. So damn cold.

She focused on the face of the person cradling her so tenderly. So close. So warm. And his eyes were so blue. Lucas.

Then his face faded and she saw a strange woman's face moving close. The feel of Lucas's arms around her seemed like a memory that time was pulling away a little bit each moment.

"She stopped breathing again!" Lucas shouted, and he started rocking her. "What do I do? Someone tell me what to do!"

"Holiday says she'll be okay."

Kylie recognized Burnett's voice, but it seemed to be coming from somewhere else, from someplace far, far away.

"Holiday thinks she's probably having a vision. That sometime . . ." His voice faded into the background.

The vision yanked Kylie back completely, and she watched in horror as a group of women brought something up to her face. Only it wasn't her. She was experiencing Jane Doe's life, but it felt as real as if it were happening to her.

She felt a thick, nubby towel being forced against her mouth. She gasped, tried to move, but couldn't. She—Jane Doe—was paralyzed, and someone was smothering her.

The unfairness of it stung her throat as her lungs begged for air. Everything went black and then she saw the spirit standing over her. She leaned down, her blue lips frosted over. *"They killed me. They really killed me,"* she said. *"You must breathe, though. You must live."*

Kylie's lungs screamed for oxygen, but she felt unable to gasp for the air she needed. Then she became aware that she was back in her kitchen.

Kylie heard Miranda chanting in the distance. She heard Della muttering that Lucas should give Kylie CPR. And Burnett kept asking questions to Holiday over the phone.

"Breathe, damn it!" Lucas yelled.

She pressed her forehead tight against Lucas's bare chest and pulled big swallows of oxygen into her throat. Tears filled her eyes, and she cried for the life that had been so brutally taken. Cried for the woman whose name she didn't know. Cried for the woman who, in addition to losing her life, had lost her child. How unfair was that?

"She's breathing again," Lucas said, cradling her tighter in his arms. "And she's crying." He dipped his head. "Shh," he whispered for her ears only. And then he said to the others, "I'm taking her to her bed. She's so cold."

Kylie felt herself being lifted in his arms. She vaguely recalled that he'd been the one to carry her to the bed that night weeks ago when she'd had the vision of Daniel, and for some reason, it felt right him being here now. It felt right when he lowered her on the bed and then crawled in beside her and held her against his chest, with his arms around her. And being so tired, too emotionally spent to talk to anyone, it especially felt right when she fell asleep with her head pillowed on his warm chest.

Unfortunately, when Kylie stirred awake a short while later, still curled up in Lucas's arms, Burnett, Miranda, Della, and Lucas all stared at her in shock and concern, and it felt a bit like getting caught French kissing a boy in public. It didn't feel so right.

She pushed off his chest, brushed her hair from her face, and gazed at all her onlookers, who stared at her as if her head might start spinning or something. Didn't they know their own abilities and powers were just as weird to those who didn't have them?

The words *You okay?* and a couple different variations of the same question came from all four people.

She nodded. "I'm fine."

"She's awake and says she's fine," Burnett said into his cell phone, which he held to his ear. "Yeah, I'll have her call you as soon as she's able."

Kylie recalled hearing Burnett talking to Holiday. "I'm sorry," she said. She wasn't sure why she felt the need to apologize. What happened wasn't her fault. Though she still wasn't sure exactly what had happened, beyond her getting caught in a vision about Jane Doe's death. Still, she supposed it was a good idea to apologize for causing a scene in the middle of the night.

She looked at Burnett. "How did . . . Why are you . . . ?" Embarrassment fluttered in her stomach. "Was I screaming so loud it woke the whole camp or something?"

"No. You hardly screamed at all this time," Della said. "I woke up when you were walking around the kitchen, muttering and, well, screaming just a bit. When I went to see if you were okay, you were, like, totally out of it. I mean, the lights were on but nobody was home kind of thing. You weren't here."

"Yeah," Miranda said, moving in. "And I woke up when Lucas was trying to bust down our door saying he had to check on you." Miranda looked at Lucas. "How did you know she was having another one of her dreams?"

Lucas didn't answer, and Kylie recalled that she'd been dreamscaping with him when the vision had started. Had he seen it, too? He must have if he ran here.

"I . . . uh . . ."

Kylie figured he didn't tell them they were dreamscaping because he knew she probably wouldn't want him to share that with everyone.

"It wasn't a dream," Kylie answered, hoping to shift the question from Lucas. "It was a vision."

"That's what Holiday says, too," Burnett said, sitting in a chair beside the bed. When Kylie glanced at him, he added, "I was walking the camp when I heard the commotion and I came running."

Kylie nodded and glanced at the clock on her bedside table. It was almost three in the morning. "You guys should all be in bed asleep. You should go."

"Are you sure you're okay?" Burnett asked.

"I'm fine," Kylie said, and she was fine. At least she thought she was, but she needed to figure out what the vision meant without an audience.

"Holiday wants you to call her," Burnett said.

"I will," Kylie said, and the words scratched her raw throat.

Burnett nodded and waved for Lucas to follow him out. But Lucas stayed sitting on the corner of her bed. "I want to talk with her just a second," he said.

Burnett looked at Kylie, and when she nodded, he started out. "Keep it short."

"Do you need us?" Miranda asked, and stifled a yawn.

"No, you two go to bed. I'm okay. Thanks." Kylie watched both Miranda and Della walk out, and then she looked at Lucas. He was frowning, his brow crinkled and his blue eyes filled with all sorts of concern.

He leaned in a bit and spoke low. "Are you sure you're okay? That was freaky."

"You saw it, too?" she asked.

"I saw you being pulled away by two guys. But then all of a sudden it wasn't you. It was some other woman. And then it was like you disappeared in a cloud. I woke up, scared shitless, and I ran over here to make sure you were okay. When I got on your front porch, I heard you walking around and I guess I lost it." Fear flashed across his face. "Does this ghost vision stuff happen all the time?"

She wondered if he knew she was equally frightened of him turning into a wolf. "No. Not all the time."

"What is it? Why does it happen?"

Kylie hesitated. "It's the spirits' way of showing me what happened to them."

"The spirits who are haunting you?" He looked mortified and even glanced around as if thinking they were there.

"Yeah. But you can relax. She's not here now." She settled back against the pillows. And then, "It's not as bad as it seems." She recalled how helpless she'd felt in the vision. She recalled the horrifying sensation of being smothered to death, and her heart hurt for the ghost. Okay, maybe it was as bad as it seemed, but if it helped the spirit pass on, then Kylie would do it.

Kylie's phone rang. It startled her until she remembered she was supposed to call Holiday. "I should . . . It's probably Holiday," she said.

He leaned down and pressed a quick kiss on her cheek. "Call me if you need me."

She watched Lucas go and reached for the phone. She didn't check the caller ID. She just assumed it was Holiday. Who else would be calling her at three in the morning? But she assumed wrong.

"Are you okay?" Derek's voice filled the line, and the image of him shirtless in his bed, with the covers pulled to his waist, filled her head.

Her cheeks flushed. "I'm fine. How did you . . . know?"

"You came to me," he said. "In a dream."

"I did?" she asked, and bit down on her lip and stared at her lap. Had she returned to Derek and not known it? She saw Socks crawl out from under the bed and leap up to be with her. No doubt he'd been scared of Lucas.

"You were here for only a second and then you left."

She felt a little better. "Oh yeah. I realized what was happening. I didn't mean to disturb you."

"I wouldn't have been disturbed," he said, sounding disappointed. "I thought maybe you'd come to me because you needed something."

"No. I'm still learning how the dreamscaping works. I woke up . . . there."

He paused. "So you don't need me?"

"No. I'm fine." She closed her eyes and tried not to let the caring sound of his voice lure her into wanting things she couldn't have. He was with Ellie now. Or maybe not with Ellie. It didn't matter. What did matter was that he'd ended their relationship. He hadn't even wanted to try to fix whatever it was that made it hard for him to be with her.

And she'd moved on. She was with Lucas—maybe not actually going out, but practically. And he'd been here for her. He wanted to be here for her.

"Okay, I just . . . wanted to check on you. I do care about you, Kylie." His voice dropped, and for a moment he sounded like the old Derek. The Derek who'd cared about her. The Derek who'd have done anything to make her happy. "You know that, don't you?"

She swallowed before answering. "Yeah," she said honestly. "I care about you, too." And then she forced herself to ask, "How's Ellie doing?"

He was quiet for a second, as if he knew what she was doing. Reminding him that they were just friends. "She's good. Adapting."

"Good," Kylie said. "I met her briefly the other day. She seems nice." *And very pretty.* She bit down on her lip.

"She is nice," he said.

"Yeah. Well, I'm happy for you." Kylie wasn't sure how true it was, but she wanted it to be true, and for that reason it didn't feel like that big of a lie.

"I told you we're not really together," he said, sounding frustrated.

"Yeah," she said, and when he didn't say anything else, she decided to do the right thing. "I need to go. I'm supposed to call Holiday."

"Okay," he said.

She disconnected the call and pushed away the melancholy. She did need to call Holiday, and then she had to figure out what the ghost had meant her to learn from the vision.

Even though she was sleep-deprived, Kylie called her mom first thing the next morning. She had to know what happened.

"So?" Kylie dropped back on the bed.

"So, what?" Her mom sounded as if she were still sleeping.

"Was it a business lunch or a date lunch?"

"Oh. It was . . ." Her mom's pause told Kylie more than her mom probably wanted to share. "It was fun."

"How fun?" Kylie tried not to let her emotions leak into her voice as she knotted a handful of sheet in her hand.

"Just fun. I enjoyed myself, that's all. I don't mean . . . It's not as if . . . Look, baby, we had a good time, but I'm not sure anything will come of it."

"He didn't ask you out again?" Kylie petted Socks, who had jumped up to get some attention.

"He said he'd call. But you know men always say that. And they never do."

Kylie tightened her hold on her phone. "If he calls, will you go out with him?"

"I don't know," her mom said. "Oh, someone's knocking on the front door. I'd better run." The line went dead.

Kylie sighed. She had a sneaking suspicion nobody was at the door. Her mom just didn't want to talk about it. Not that she could blame her.

Seconds ticked by, but Kylie didn't move. She just lay there, stretched out on her twin mattress, staring up at the ceiling. Ambivalence filled her chest. Did this mean her mom and her stepdad would never get back together?

A quick shower later, Kylie walked out of the bathroom with a towel around her to find Miranda standing attentively in the hall, as if waiting on her.

"What's up?" Kylie asked.

"I'm your shadow," Miranda announced proudly.

"I thought Della—"

"You don't think I can protect you?" She held out her pinky. "I have powers, girlie."

Actually, Kylie had doubts about Miranda's protecting abilities, but she wouldn't dare say that. "No, I just remember Burnett saying it was Della this morning."

"She went to her sunrise ceremony and I'm supposed to get you to the office, where Della will meet us in about five minutes. So let's go."

Kylie looked down at her towel. "Can I get dressed first?"

"Someone's not a morning person this fine day." Miranda made a funny face, and Kylie took off to her room to get dressed.

A few minutes later, they walked out the cabin door. Miranda turned back to the door, waved her arms around, and began to chant. The last time Miranda did that, she felt unwanted visitors; it turned out Mario and Red had been hanging out, watching Kylie.

"What are you doing?" Kylie asked. "Do you sense someone's here again?"

Miranda frowned. "A little." She pinched her right thumb and forefinger together.

"A little?" Annoyance snaked through Kylie. "How can you sense someone here just a little? I mean, they're either here or not, right?"

"Don't wig out on me," Miranda said. "I just got a feeling and I thought it couldn't hurt to do a protection spell."

"Have you told Burnett?" Kylie asked.

"I was going to but I'm kind of scared to talk to him alone after . . ." She flushed. "You know."

The memory of a marsupial Burnett hopping around the dining hall, dodging Clark's fireballs and Perry's dragon breath, flashed across Kylie's mind. Hence, part of the reason Kylie doubted Miranda's ability to protect her.

"Anyway," Miranda went on, "you said Holiday would be back today. So I figure I'll just tell her then."

Kylie rolled her eyes and wanted to point out that if Miranda was right and there were intruders, Burnett needed to know ASAP, but she bit her tongue. A few hours probably wouldn't matter all that much. Besides, Miranda had a point; she was in a bad mood this morning, and it wasn't fair to take it out on Miranda.

As for why Kylie was in a bad mood, well, she figured her bad mood probably hinged on the fact that she was running on only a few hours' sleep. She and Holiday had spent almost an hour on the phone talking last night. They'd discussed everything from Holiday's aunt's passing to Kylie's vision and what it could and couldn't mean. When Kylie asked her about the healing powers and the whole "giving up a piece of her soul" issue, Holiday suggested they wait until they could talk about it when she got back today.

Kylie had almost told Holiday about her misgivings with Burnett over the FRU library card issue but decided to wait and discuss that in person, too.

Miranda did one more wave over the door, pulling Kylie back to the present.

"Do you mind if I tell Burnett?" Kylie asked Miranda.

Miranda made a face but then said, "Fine. But I'm telling you, it's just a feeling. It's not nearly as strong as the last time I had one. It might not be anything."

"Or it could be something," Kylie said. And since that something probably had to do with her, it made her a wee bit nervous. And face it, she had enough to be nervous about.

Kylie stood in front of the heavy, creaky-looking rusted gates of the Fallen Cemetery. Burnett stood to her right—and Della held her spot to her left. Neither vampire looked especially happy to be there.

She couldn't blame them. She wasn't all that thrilled about it herself. But after experiencing the vision sent by Jane Doe, Kylie was more eager than ever to get this spirit sent on her way.

"You sure you want to do this?" Della asked, her voice laced with fear.

Kylie nodded, but in truth she wasn't sure about anything anymore. She took a look around. If Hollywood ever needed a set for a horror film, this was it. As if to prove her point, a gust of wind picked up and the gate swayed and creaked. The eerie sound filled the air.

Air that should have brought with it a sunny mood to match the morning. Above them, blue, cloudless skies promised a picture-perfect day filled with cheer. A vibrant sun beamed down and set the last of the night's dew in a sparkle. And yet nothing felt sunny, vibrant, or cheery.

To the contrary, it felt cold—so cold that Kylie's skin crawled with goose bumps. Della let go of a deep breath and steam billowed from her lips.

"I used to hang out in cemeteries sometimes," Della said. "They never felt like this." She hugged herself against the chill.

"The dead don't disturb humans nearly as much as they do supernaturals," Burnett said. Even his voice sounded hesitant. He looked at Kylie. "If you're at all worried about doing this, just say the word and wait until Holiday is here."

Kylie considered it and then remembered the pain, grief, and confusion the ghost had felt. Jane Doe needed answers as much as Kylie did.

"No. I'm fine."

"You're lying," Della said.

"I know." Kylie looked at her and then over to Burnett. "You guys don't have to come inside."

"We don't?" Hope filled Della's voice.

"The hell we don't," Burnett snapped, and took a step forward. "If you're determined to do this, let's get it over with."

Chapter Nineteen

As soon as they crossed into the grounds of the Fallen Cemetery, a big gust of wind slammed the gate shut behind them.

Kylie started. Della jumped and growled, exposing her elongated canines. Burnett didn't move, but his eyes glowed a bright yellow.

"Don't worry," he muttered. "I can knock the gate down if I have to."

Della looked at Kylie. "I do not see why you feel compelled to do this."

Kylie looked from Della to Burnett. "Can I have some space? I need it to communicate with them."

She hated having to lie, but she hoped the offer of space would alleviate the hardship of their having to accompany her into the grave-yard. She knew they didn't want to be here. It seemed crazy, but supernaturals hated all things related to ghosts. At least maybe the coldness she always felt when a ghost was present wouldn't bite into them the way she knew it would take a chomp out of her.

"Yes, go ahead, but don't go so far that we can't see you," said Burnett.

Considering that Kylie had yet to tell Burnett about Miranda's "little feeling," she didn't mind him keeping a close visual on her.

Not that right now she worried about Mario and his grandson. Right now, it was the whispered voices Kylie heard that concerned her.

Looking at the graveled paths between row after row of graves, she let her eyes shift from tombstone to tombstone, hoping one of them would call out to her. Some graves had small concrete or marble markers with just names and dates inscribed on them. Others were ornate statues. Some looked new; others were painted with mold and time. Some had vines clinging to the arms and legs of angel and saintlike figures, as if trying to claim them from deep beneath the earth where only the dead lived.

She couldn't see any of the ghosts yet, but she could hear them. They all talked at once. Chattering. Like two or three radios left on at the same time, but with tons of static. If they were speaking to one another or to her, she wasn't sure.

Some of the voices felt as if they were a block away, others felt as if their owners stood so close that Kylie could touch them if she moved her hand. Not that she wanted to touch them. Their cold already surrounded her, reaching for her like hands trying to warm themselves against a fire.

Kylie realized in a way that was what she was to them. She was like a fire, something that drew them. She was life. Probably the only life that they had been able to feel in a long time. Or maybe the only life that could feel them.

Footsteps sounded and Kylie looked to her right down the opposite path. An old man, his cane in his hand, shuffled between the row of grave sites. For a second, Kylie didn't know to which world he belonged.

But then she noticed Burnett and Della twitching their brows at him. Kylie did the same and was not surprised when his brain pattern revealed he was human. All of a sudden, an elderly woman of the same age appeared behind him. Her gray hair was long and thin and hung without luster at her shoulders. She wore one of those housedresses Kylie's grandmother had always worn. This one was a blue paisley print. On her feet were a pair of baby blue slippers.

It took only a second for Kylie to realize that she was not of this world.

"You're not taking your meds like you should be, are you?" she said to the old man. *"I can tell because your ankles are swollen. You're supposed to take the little red pills twice a day, not the blue ones. What are you trying to do? Kill yourself? You promised me you'd take care of yourself. Why won't you ever listen to me?"*

Then the woman shifted her gaze and stared right at Kylie. Her aged gray eyes widened, then she vanished. Kylie hadn't taken her next breath when the woman materialized inches from her. Her skin was a dead gray color that matched her eyes. Her hair, only a slightly different shade of gray, got caught in the wind, and it swept up and floated almost motionlessly in the air around her head.

"Mother of God, you can see me," the elderly woman said.

The spirit's nearness brought more chills running down Kylie's spine. But the drop in temperature wasn't nearly as disturbing as the sudden silence.

The chattering of spirits had stopped. The only noise in the cemetery was the sound of the old man's footsteps. His shoes scrubbed against the gravel with his faltered steps while his cane tapped down on the earth, searching for a steady spot to rest his thick stick to support himself.

Tap, tap. Shuffle. Tap, tap. Shuffle. Tap. Shuffle.

Kylie sensed more than heard Burnett and Della move back. She'd asked for this space, but now she regretted it. Maybe she didn't want to be alone. But did she regret it enough to admit her fear? She knew someone like Burnett respected courage, and Kylie didn't want to come up short.

"Answer me, girl! You can see me, right?" The old woman waved a hand in front of Kylie's face.

She held her breath. The silence seemed to grow louder. The lack of chatter meant something. It meant the spirits were listening. Waiting for her to answer. Waiting to see if she admitted to being able to see one of their own.

Suddenly the air she pulled into her lungs grew so cold that it hurt. They, the silent spirits, were moving in. She couldn't see them, couldn't even hear them, but she could feel them. The cold increased tenfold.

Fear turned her stomach hard. She felt the thinnest layer of ice form on her lips. For a second, she questioned the wisdom of being here. Could she pretend she hadn't heard the woman? Was it too late to look away from the desperation of the elderly spirit?

"Tell him he needs to take two of the little red pills."

Kylie still didn't speak. Frost formed on the tips of her eyelashes, blurring her vision.

"He's going to get to meet our first great-grandchild. For years, all he's talked about was living until he saw his third generation make it into the world. But if he doesn't start taking his pills right, he'll never make it."

Suddenly, the other spirits started materializing around her. Ten, then twenty. Then more. And when they slowly inched closer, Kylie's heart raced with panic. She considered running, but could she outrun them?

"Can she hear us?" asked an older-sounding male spirit.

"Can she see us?" added a younger female spirit, crowding closer.

"Y'all are being silly," came another male spirit's voice. *"The living can't see us no more."*

"But this one can," argued the younger female spirit. *"Look at her."*

The spirits started to move closer.

"Do you think she can help us?" a female asked.

"Maybe," someone else said.

The older male spirit peered into Kylie's face. *"What is she?"*

The spirits crushed closer. A barrage of new questions started spilling out of their mouths, each talking so rapidly that it was hard to distinguish one voice from the other. The sound was so loud, Kylie fought the need to cover her ears. She couldn't remember what Holiday had said about the rules of shutting out the voices. Was it too late to attempt to shut them out?

"You looking for a particular plot?" The words seeped into Kylie's hearing and bounced around her panicked brain. It took a minute to realize that this male voice was different from the rest. The words were not from the dead, but from the living.

Kylie managed to look over and saw the old man walking toward her between two large tombstones. His cane pushed holes through the green grass into the moist dirt. Each time he pulled the tip of the walking stick from the ground, it created a squishing sound that seemed too loud.

Remembering she wasn't completely alone, Kylie glanced around and spotted Burnett standing at the end of the row, watching, ready to pounce in case the elderly gentleman posed any danger.

Little did Burnett know it wasn't him she feared, but all the others he could not see. The old man continued toward her. His presence brought a wave of calm that lessened the chaos sizzling in her blood. The closer he came, the farther back the spirits moved.

Kylie touched the tip of her tongue to the melting frost across her bottom lip and blinked away the shiny crystals of ice from her lashes.

"You look lost," he said again, coming to a stop a few feet away from her.

Thankful his presence had brought her some reprieve, she tried to smile, but the gesture seemed to fail.

"Cat got your tongue, child?" he asked.

"No," Kylie answered. Realizing she hadn't answered his initial question, she searched for a believable-sounding lie. "Yes, I'm looking . . . for my aunt's grave."

"What's her name? I should be able to point you in the right direction. Lord knows I've walked these grounds enough. I'm here daily, visiting my Ima."

"I'm Ima," said the man's dead wife, and she came closer and peered into Kylie's face.

Kylie hesitated and then glanced to her right and read the tombstone. "Lolita Cannon. That's my aunt's name." She still didn't know if she should acknowledge the dead man's wife or not. Kylie's heart beat around in her chest with indecision. But if she didn't tell the man about his medicine, he could—

"Why, I think that grave is right around here somewhere." He turned and started looking, pointing his cane at the markers as he read.

"Are you sure she can see and hear us?" Another spirit appeared. Kylie glanced at the newcomer briefly, trying not to give away that she could see anyone. This spirit was another woman, younger, late twenties, wearing a dress that looked like something popular in the 1970s.

"I'm pretty sure," answered Ima, and then she leaned so close that her icy presence burned Kylie's arm. *"Tell him about his medicines,"* she pleaded. *"If not, he's gonna pass without ever seeing his third generation."*

"Here, right here." The old man pointed with his cane and waved for Kylie to follow him.

"Thank you," Kylie said, stopping at his side and still wavering on what to do.

"It's a nice marker," the old man said, and had to use his cane to get his balance. "Well, I should be going. Enjoy your time with her." He started to take a step and then paused. "You know, I somehow feel my Ima can hear me, so go ahead and talk to your aunt if you have anything you want to say to her."

The man's wife held up her hands as if frustrated. *"I can hear ya, old man. But it's you that don't listen to a word I say. Don't know why it surprises me."* The woman looked back at Kylie again. *"The ol' fart never listened to me when I was alive. And he's talked to me more since I've been dead than when I was alive. But I love the ol' coot. And you gotta help me help him. Please, missy. I don't know what you are, or how come you can see me, but I'm begging ya."*

Kylie watched the old man take a few steps away from her. If she told him, she knew the barrage of spirits would return, but if she didn't . . . Kylie wouldn't be able to live with herself if something happened to the old guy. "Wait, sir. I . . ."

He turned around.

Crap! How was she going to tell him? "I . . . I couldn't help but notice you're a little shaky. You know, this happened to my aunt and it was caused by a mix-up in her meds. She was taking the wrong pills twice a day. The blue ones instead of the red ones."

The man's dead wife let out a victory yelp. The younger woman beside her stared at Kylie with complete awe. *"She can hear us. Jiminy Cricket. She can. My name's Catherine. What's your name?"*

The same look of amazement flooding across the younger ghost's face now filled the old man's expression. "Why, child, I . . . I swear you might have . . . I mean, Ima was always telling me to be careful. And I have been feeling not so good lately. I think I'll go home and check my prescription." Then he turned and headed toward the gate.

Kylie forced a smile, even though the chatter was now louder than ever since all the spirits knew the truth. Knew she could hear them. Knew she could help them. But could she? So far all the spirits came to her for help, but could she help those she accidentally came into contact with?

Just as the old man turned to leave, another wave of cold landed beside her. Jane Doe's ghost materialized. She looked at Kylie as if confused. *"What are you doing here?"*

"Isn't this where you are buried?" Kylie asked, struggling to ignore the cold and the noise.

"You say something?" The old man turned back around. His words were almost lost in the loud chattering again.

"Just to myself," Kylie answered, and prayed he'd turn around before she . . . A wave of dizziness almost overtook her. She struggled to remain standing.

The spirits had moved in again, surrounded her, all talking at once. Wanting her to do something for them. Asking her questions. Her gaze flipped from one dead face to another. Her heart felt heavy with sadness for them. It made her realize how insignificant she was—one person and so many souls needing something.

The wave of dizziness crashed over her again, only harder this time. Her head started pounding—pain exploded behind her eyes. Hugging herself against the cold, she lowered herself onto the green grass, wrapped her arms around her shins, and dropped her forehead on top of her knees.

"I can't do this," she muttered.

"Move back," Jane Doe said. *"You are hurting her."*

Kylie felt some of the cold begin to ebb, the pain behind her eyelids lessened, and she could only assume the ghost had been talking to the other spirits. The noise level lowered almost to the point where it didn't hurt to listen anymore.

"Are you okay?" Burnett's deep, concerned voice came at her ear.

Kylie raised her head and saw the only spirits remaining were Jane Doe, the old man's wife, and the other younger spirit.

Kylie looked at Burnett. "Yeah. I'm fine. Or getting better," she said.

Burnett nodded and then backed away. Kylie stared at Jane Doe and waited a few more seconds before she asked, "Isn't this where you're buried?"

Jane's brow wrinkled in that confused way of hers. *"I . . . don't know."*

"Oh, phooey!" said the younger woman who'd said her name was Catherine. *"Of course you're buried here. Your grave and marker are right over there. You were put in the ground by the Texas prison system. You'd been given life for killing your own baby."*

Chapter Twenty

Shock filled Kylie's chest. Jane had killed her baby? Was that why Jane had amnesia? The horror of what she'd done had been too much for her to bear?

Jane swerved toward Catherine and held both her fists up in front of her face, her body tight with fury. *"How many times do I have to tell you that I'm not Berta! I did not kill my own child. I would never kill my baby. I loved my baby."*

Catherine looked at Kylie. *"She's confused. I think they gave her a lobotomy. Probably trying to fix her."*

"I'm not Berta!" Jane Doe's scream rang so loud, Kylie flinched. *"And I'm sick to death of hearing you call me that."*

"Then what's your name?" Catherine spouted back.

Jane got tears in her eyes. *"I don't know. I don't know who I am, I don't know what I am, but I know who I'm not. And I'm not Berta Littlemon. I think my baby died, but I didn't kill it. I was somebody's wife. Now I'm just lost. And empty. And dead."* She turned and looked at Kylie as if remembering the vision. *"Somebody killed me."* Tears slipped down the woman's cheek and then she disappeared.

Kylie's chest filled with empathy. She got back to her feet, and while she felt inclined to believe Jane Doe, she'd come here to find answers. And to find them, she had to ask questions. "Why do you think she's Berta Littlemon?"

"*I don't think, I know,*" Catherine said. Then she smiled. "*And I'll tell you all I know if you'll do me a favor.*"

Kylie still stood by the grave of Berta Littlemon when Burnett walked over to join her about thirty minutes later. This time, he didn't inquire if she was okay. But then, he didn't have to ask. Kylie sensed he could guess she wasn't okay by the look of dismay on her face. Placing his hand lightly on her shoulder, he asked, "Was this . . . helpful?"

"I don't know," Kylie said, confused and disturbed by what she'd learned from Catherine O'Connell. Sure, she'd gotten some information, but mostly all the trip to the Fallen Cemetery had accomplished was to underscore how little she knew about Jane Doe and how impossible it would be to help her.

"Are you ready to go?" he asked.

She nodded and they started walking toward the gate where Della stood, looking as ill at ease as she had the moment they'd first arrived. The crowd of spirits followed them, moving close but not crowding her.

"*Will you come back?*" whispered an older-sounding male spirit.

"*Please, say you'll come,*" begged a younger female spirit.

"*It's not fair,*" wailed another female. "*Why does she have to leave now? I didn't get a chance to talk to her!*"

Then all of the spirits began to talk at once, making it hard to understand them and bringing Kylie's headache back in full force. Through the crowd of voices, she was dimly aware of Ima, the old man's wife, walking from one small group of spirits to another and whispering something to them.

Kylie stopped and massaged her temples. "I'm sorry," she said, and she truly was.

Right now, all she wanted to do was run from them, run into the sunlight, ignore the shadows and pretend that they didn't exist. But even as she wanted to run away, she knew she couldn't. How could she when she felt their pain, their heartbreak, as intensely as she did her own? How could she when she knew they all had some kind of unfinished business they wanted resolved and she was their only chance to make that happen?

Still, she had to establish some boundaries or else she'd likely lose her mind the way Jane Doe obviously had.

And then Kylie wouldn't be able to help any of them.

"I have to leave now," she said. "You can't come with me. You need to stay here. But . . . I will come back. I promise." It was a promise she intended to keep, but not one she looked forward to.

"I'm not coming back," Della said, and walked toward the car.

Burnett shot Kylie a worried look and she shook her head, indicating that she was fine. When they stepped out of the cemetery property and the spirits didn't follow, Kylie sighed with relief. She'd never appreciated the blast of Texas heat that swamped her as much as she did right now.

She glanced behind her at the cemetery. The spirits were still there, staring at her wordlessly. She wondered if her promise had been enough to convince them to stay behind, rather than follow her. Or if it had more to do with whatever message Ima had been whispering to them. Kylie felt a shiver move down her spine. She ignored it and walked with Burnett and Della to the car.

The drive back to Shadow Falls was short. They didn't speak. After Burnett parked, Kylie and Della crawled out of his black Mustang. Kylie locked her gaze with Burnett and asked if she could be relieved from camp activities for the rest of the day.

He hesitated and she was frightened he was going to say no, but then he frowned and asked, "Would Holiday say yes?"

Kylie nodded. "Yes," she answered with honesty. Helping ghosts was part of her job as a supernatural. Holiday would understand that, and the toll it took on her. The camp leader was probably the only one who would understand.

Burnett still paused. "Are you okay? Do you need to talk or anything?"

"No," Kylie said.

The relief showing in his face was almost comical. Obviously the idea of having to offer advice or commiserate about spirits didn't appeal to him. Kylie might have teased him about it if she weren't so wrapped up in what she'd learned. "I just want to do some stuff on my computer and check some of the facts I learned."

"Okay," he said, and motioned Della to follow her.

"Please don't ever ask me to go back there again," Della said as they walked away. "That was super weird."

"I'm sorry," Kylie said.

"Did you learn what you needed to know?"

"Not really."

"Didn't they answer your questions? I heard you talking to them."

"It's not that easy."

For a second, Della looked ready to ask more questions; then she lapsed into silence.

Good thing, too. Kylie wasn't feeling up to explaining how communicating with the dead worked. Right now, she needed to focus on what she'd learned from her trip. She hadn't even begun to mull everything over and decide what she believed and didn't believe.

Was Jane, or was she not, a child murderer and all-around evil person? Anxious to prove Catherine O'Connell wrong, Kylie hurried her steps.

She cut through the first bend in the path, where the trees hung over, creating shade. She breathed in the scents of summer, the greenness of the forest, the heady aroma of dry earth. She had almost managed to calm her chaotic mind when the blue bird swooped down and landed right in her path. The blue jay cocked its head and chirped cheerfully as if performing just for her.

"Shoo!" Della said. But the bird, intent on watching Kylie, ignored Della.

"Shit!" Della belted out. "Is that the evil shifter?" When she started to bolt forward—to do God only knew what to the bird—Kylie caught her by her arm.

"Stop. It's just a bird."

Della's eyes widened. "Is that the same bird you . . . brought back to life?"

"I don't know," Kylie said, but she knew it was a lie.

Della waved her arms, trying to scare the bird away. "This is freaky." The bird continued to sing.

"Get out of here before I break your neck!" Della bellowed.

"Just leave it alone." Truth was, the bird scared the crap out of Kylie, too, but it didn't deserve to die. Or to die again.

Besides, Kylie wasn't up to giving it another piece of her soul by bringing it back to life.

The bird finally finished its song, then flapped its wings and rose to hover in front of Kylie's face. A spray of sunshine came through the trees and made the creature's royal blue feathers glow. Then, letting out one more bit of song, it flew away. Kylie took off in a run and didn't slow down until she got to her cabin. Della followed at the same pace. Maybe after Kylie researched Berta Littlemon, she'd research blue jay stalking. Though she doubted Google would have anything on that.

"So you actually spoke to the spirits?" Jonathon asked. The vamp had taken over shadow duty for Della right after they'd arrived back at the cabin. Of course, first Della had given him the blow-by-blow account of what had happened at the cemetery. Kylie looked back at Jonathon, reclining on her sofa.

"Can I do this computer stuff right now, instead of chatting about the ghosts?" She'd been proud of herself. Instead of giving in to the desire to go straight to bed, pull the covers over her head, and have a good long cry, she'd booted up her computer.

Her screen brought up Google, and she typed in the name "Berta Littlemon." As the computer chewed on that information, Kylie looked back at Jonathon again. "I just need to get this done."

"Whatever." His tone told her he thought she was rude.

And maybe she was, but with a possible child-murdering ghost on her hands and a blue jay stalking her, she didn't have time to be polite. "Sorry," she still muttered.

Kylie read the list of Web sites that Google spilled onto her screen: *Famous female murderers in Texas, Mamas who murder, Mean women in the past.* Kylie's heart started to ache. She clicked on the first Web site and prepared herself to be disgusted.

She wasn't disappointed. The only thing she didn't find was a decent picture of Berta Littlemon that was clear enough to identify her.

"Some shadow you are, vampire."

Kylie swung around and found Lucas standing in the doorway, staring at Jonathon sleeping on the sofa.

Jonathon didn't move. He didn't even open his eyes when he spoke. "I heard you a block away. Smelled your wolf ass two blocks away."

Lucas growled.

Kylie rolled her eyes. Ah, the love between vamps and weres was never lost. For a crazy moment, she recalled Lucas's desire that she turn out to be a were. And she wondered what would happen if and when he discovered he was wrong. What would happen if she discovered she was vampire? Would Lucas still care about her? She so wanted to believe that it wouldn't matter to him, that he was above that type of prejudice.

But the truth was, she knew it probably would matter.

And that scared her more than stalking blue jays and amnesiac ghosts who possibly killed their own babies.

Lucas shifted his focus from Jonathon to her. "Are you okay?"

Kylie took a deep breath. She'd felt that hiding her weakness from Burnett had been a necessity. Nor had she felt comfortable sharing anything with Della or Jonathon, but one look at Lucas's caring blue eyes and she felt her throat tighten with the need for a little TLC.

He must have sensed her stress, or maybe it was the tears prickling her eyes, because he moved to her, grabbed her hand, and started walking her into her bedroom.

"I'm supposed to keep an eye on her," Jonathon called out from his still reclined position on the sofa.

"Why don't you just check out the back of your eyelids like you were doing when I came in," Lucas countered, and slammed her bedroom door shut. The cabin shook from the force.

Once they were alone, Lucas's gaze went back to her. "What happened?" He moved in, cupped his hand around her neck, and pulled her against him.

She rested her forehead on his warm chest and fought the need to cry. The need for TLC was one thing, but tears were too much.

"It was awful," she said, and swallowed hard.

"What was awful?" he asked.

"They were everywhere. And then—"

"Who were everywhere?" His hand moved to her back, consoling and offering just the comforting touch she needed.

Her heart hurt with the need to have someone help her understand the experience. She lifted her head and looked at him, but she didn't pull away. "The spirits. But that wasn't the worst part. I—"

He let go of another frustrated growl, cutting her off. Then he studied her for a second as if weighing his words with care. "Didn't you expect them to be everywhere at a cemetery, Kylie? After what happened in that vision, why you would even go there is beyond me."

Okay, so Lucas was like the others; he didn't understand what she did. She couldn't really blame him, though. Just as Della had pointed out this morning, ghost whispering pretty much made her a freak. Still, it hurt.

She wanted him to understand, to be able to sense how important this was to her. But he couldn't. He wasn't . . . fae. He wasn't Derek. Not wanting to go there, she pushed that thought away, far away.

"I had to," she said, though she didn't think it would make a difference to Lucas. "That's what I'm supposed to do. That's why they come to me for help."

He frowned. "But at what cost? I don't like seeing you upset like this. I sure as hell don't like thinking you're putting yourself in danger to help someone who's already dead. For all we know, they're dead because they did something stupid and now they're gonna try to make you do something stupid and you could end up getting hurt as a result."

His tone, his expression, and even his body posture told Kylie that telling him that her ghost very well may be a murderer of small children might not be a brilliant idea. So she resigned herself to her current reality. She'd just have to bundle up the rest of the story until Holiday arrived. Which Kylie hoped would be soon.

"Damn, I hate seeing you upset," he muttered through gritted teeth, and then tugged her closer.

She bit down on her lip, remembering how it had felt when it had been coated with ice. "It was a little scary, but nothing happened."

He lifted her chin and gazed into her eyes. "You sure?"

Not wanting to lie to him, she rose up on tiptoes and kissed him. He tasted so good—a little like toothpaste and a bit like chocolate. She'd always been fond of chocolate mint, so she opened her mouth wider and he accepted the invitation and the kiss went from sweet to passionate in a heartbeat.

When his tongue slipped inside her mouth, she melted against him even closer, and any remnants of worry in her heart faded. All Kylie could think about was the wonder of this moment. The wonder of passion.

She loved having him this close to her. The silky feel of his mouth against hers was so perfect. The slight stubble on his cheeks tickled her, and his hard chest pressed against hers as though it were made to fit. She savored the tight feel of his strong hands on her waist. A voice deep within said she could deal with anything, stalking blue jays, a barrage of ghosts, even the amnesiac spirit of a child murderer. She could take it all on as long as she had Lucas's arms and kisses waiting for her when it was over. She could survive as long as she had the wonderment of his closeness to help her cope.

"Someone lives and someone dies."

The voice came at the same time as the chill crawling up and then down her spine. Kylie pulled away from the hot kiss and buried her face on Lucas's warm chest, not wanting to feel this cold. Not now. Not so soon after the visit to the cemetery and the haunting memory of all those lost souls who needed her help. Not when she'd just read the terrible things this woman had done.

"They keep insisting that I tell you," Jane, aka Berta, said.

Who dies? Kylie asked the question in her mind.

"Maybe they meant me," the spirit said, sounding confused again.

Somehow Kylie knew that wasn't right. *Someone lives and someone dies.* The words flowed again through her head. Perhaps there was one thing Lucas's kisses couldn't fix. The idea of losing someone she cared about was too much to bear.

Lifting her cheek from Lucas's warm chest, she opened her eyes and tried to focus on Jane Doe.

Staring at the spirit's face, Kylie recalled bits of the story she'd read about Berta Littlemon. She hadn't killed just her own child, but that of a neighbor, too.

The spirit gazed back at Kylie without reservation. No worries.

No shame. Had the woman forgotten about what happened at the cemetery, that Catherine had ratted her out—that Kylie now knew everything?

But even now, as Kylie looked deep into the spirit's eyes, she didn't see the soul of a killer. She saw the soul of a woman who was lost, forgotten, and needed her help.

What, if anything, did this mean? Kylie wondered.

Chapter Twenty-one

An hour later, Lucas left to go to a hiking class and Kylie continued her online research. She'd read most of the articles on the Web sites containing information about Berta Littlemon. She'd also done a quick search on Catherine O'Connell, the woman who'd ratted on Jane. Not just because Kylie intended to keep her promise to her—a deal was a deal—but because she wanted to know if the woman was honest.

Kylie's quick search on the information Catherine had given her proved to be true. But did that also mean she was right about Jane Doe?

So far, she'd found one other site that had a picture of Berta Littlemon, but it too had been so fuzzy that Kylie couldn't swear it was her Jane Doe. Sure, she had brown hair and it appeared to have been long at one time, and the facial features were similar, but . . . there was still hope.

A lot more hope when Kylie vaguely remembered something that Holiday had told her about spirits who were overall bad.

Almost as if thinking the woman's name had worked magic, Kylie heard Holiday's voice.

"Can I come in?"

Kylie saw Jonathon jerk from a dead sleep, then she bolted from her chair, ran across the living room, and threw her arms around Holiday.

"I'm so glad you're home," Kylie said, releasing the camp leader only after a good long hug. She'd missed talking with Holiday, missed having her around. But Kylie probably missed Holiday's hugs most of all. "I have so many things to ask you, to tell you." She was about to dump her emotional trauma on the woman when Kylie suddenly remembered the reason Holiday had been away. Her aunt had died. And the death had rocked Holiday's world to its core.

Maybe, Kylie realized, Holiday already had enough on her plate and didn't need Kylie to add more.

Kylie paused a moment to catch her breath. "Are you okay? I'm so sorry about your aunt. Did you get things settled?"

"I'm fine." Holiday gripped Kylie's shoulders as if she understood Kylie's thoughts. "And yes, I think I managed to get everything in order. The important question is if you're okay. Are you?"

Jonathon sat up on the sofa, looking half-asleep. Holiday must not have seen him earlier because she jumped a little at the sound of him shifting.

"Oh, Jonathon. You startled me." Holiday stared at the sleepy vampire.

"Do I need to stay here now that you're here?" he asked.

Holiday looked at her watch. "I should be here for an hour, and Della will be back before that, so if you want to go, you can." They watched Jonathon leave, then Holiday draped an arm around Kylie's shoulder. "Now, tell me what's going on with you."

Kylie met her gaze. "Are you sure you can handle this?"

"Is it that bad?" Holiday's brows creased with worry.

"No. Well, yeah, it is, but I mean, can you handle my problems right now with your own?" Kylie looked at Holiday with empathy. "I know what it feels like to lose someone. When my grandmother died, I could hardly breathe."

Holiday smiled. "I'm fine. I'm still grieving a bit," she added honestly. "But let's just say I'm using the Kylie Galen method of dealing with my problems."

"Which is what?" Kylie asked, puzzled.

Holiday grinned. "Concentrating on everyone else's problems, so I don't have time to think about mine." She looked Kylie right in the eye. "Seriously, I'm fine. Now, tell me what you learned at the cemetery. And then we have a lot of things to discuss."

Kylie started walking over to the kitchen table and then remembered the imminent question she'd wanted to ask Holiday. She swung back around.

"One thing first. Didn't you tell me one time that really bad souls don't hang around, that hell claims them pretty quickly?"

"In most cases, that's right. But there are some that . . ." Worry pinched Holiday's brows together. "Why?"

Kylie frowned, and just like that, all the frustration from earlier landed on her shoulders with a big thump. "Why does everything have to have exceptions? It would be so nice to ask a question and get a definite yes or no. It's either black or white." She dropped into a kitchen chair. "Life would be so much easier."

"Easier, yes. But realistic . . . no. Few things are ever black or white." Holiday tilted her head to one side and studied Kylie for a moment, then frowned. "Please tell me you haven't gotten mixed up with a hell-bound spirit."

Fifteen minutes later, Kylie sat beside Holiday as she read the different articles about Berta Littlemon on the computer screen.

"That's it. I can't read any more!" Holiday reached over and turned off the computer. "You shouldn't even being reading this. You are not to deal with this spirit anymore." Something about Holiday's tone, so maternal, so un-negotiating, sent up warning flags all over the place.

"We don't know it's even her," Kylie said. "I can't just assume she—"

"Yes, you can! You said the other ghost told you that your Jane Doe rose from the grave of Berta Littlemon. That's good enough for me."

Kylie frowned. "Yeah, but maybe she's lying. And you saw the pictures of Berta. They are fuzzy. I mean, yes, they sort of resemble my Jane Doe, but they're not clear enough for me to be sure."

"Okay, but why would the ghost lie?"

Kylie shrugged. "Because if she didn't have information that sounded useful, she might have been afraid I wouldn't have agreed to help her."

"Wait—help who? The old man's wife?"

Kylie realized she'd obviously left out that part of the story when she'd explained everything to Holiday. "No, the other ghost. Catherine O'Connell. I agreed to help her if she'd tell me what she knows about Jane Doe."

"No," Holiday said, and put her palms over her face.

"No, what?"

Holiday moved her hands. "You never make a deal with a spirit, Kylie. Never!"

"Why?" Kylie asked.

"Because it can be as bad as making a deal with the devil. What they want is sometimes impossible, and they can be relentless about making us pay up. If they think you haven't delivered on your promise, things can get ugly."

Kylie felt her throat tighten. She had looked forward to Holiday's return so much, and now it seemed all Kylie was going to get were reprimands. "I didn't know," she muttered.

Holiday released a deep sigh. "I'm sorry," she said, and dropped her hands on top of Kylie's. "I didn't mean to snap at you. This is my fault. All of it. I knew that your going to the cemetery was a bad idea. I should have vetoed it right off the bat."

Kylie swallowed the tightness down her throat, which had seemed to lessen somewhat with Holiday's touch. "It wasn't a bad idea. And maybe I shouldn't have made a deal with Catherine, but even that doesn't seem so bad. I mean, what she wants is doable and for a good cause."

Holiday shook her head, still looking too unrelenting. "It's still not a good idea to make a deal with a spirit."

"Yeah, but all she wants is for me to send some family history stuff to her kids. She's Jewish and she lied to them and her own husband all her life because back then, being a Jew wasn't so cool. Her parents died in the concentration camps and her grandparents managed to bring her to the U.S. She changed her name. And now, it feels like a lie."

Holiday shook her head. "Kylie, I'm sorry, but I can't let you do this."

"No." Kylie stood up, and although she kept her voice low, even she heard the determination in her tone. "I'm sorry, but I'm not going to stop any of this because you're afraid I'm in over my head. Because you don't think I can handle it. I'm helping Jane Doe, and I'm sorry, but I don't believe she's this murderer, and I'm also going to help Catherine O'Connell. It's the right thing to do."

Holiday closed her eyes in frustration. "Kylie, you don't understand how dangerous this could be for you. There are things about dealing with evil spirits that . . . that will put you at risk. There is so much you still don't know."

Kylie shook her head. "Then explain it to me. But I'm telling you, Holiday, I don't think she's evil. How many times have you told me to follow my heart—that if I do that, I'll figure out the right thing to do? Well, my heart is telling me to do this, and I'm doing it."

When Holiday opened her mouth, presumably to argue again, Kylie added, "Besides, I wasn't asking you for permission. I was asking for advice."

Chapter Twenty-two

As soon as she'd let the words out of her mouth, Kylie wished she could get them back. Not because she hadn't meant them. She did. She just regretted the way she'd said them.

Holiday sat there for a long moment, staring at Kylie as if she were thinking about what to say. Kylie returned her gaze with an equal amount of vigor. Regretting her tone didn't mean she was going to back down on this. She couldn't. Maybe it was because she emphathized with Jane Doe and her identity crisis, but it felt like more. Kylie knew she had to help the amnesiac ghost. And she would help her, with or without Holiday's blessing.

"Good Lord, when did I become my mom and you become a younger version of myself?" Holiday asked, and smiled.

Kylie saw and heard the lessening of resolve in the camp leader's voice and posture. Then the tension in Kylie's shoulders dissolved and a wave of relief filled her chest. Tears stung her eyes. "I don't know."

"Okay," Holiday said. "Sit down and let's figure out how we're going to work this so I can live with it and you can, too."

Kylie gave Holliday a quick hug of thanks and then settled in to talk. They discussed how Kylie was to go to the library to e-mail the family of Catherine O'Connell. Then Holiday went over and over and over how Kylie could shut out an unwanted ghost . . . or unwanted groups of ghosts. And then she made Kylie promise that if she did discover that Jane Doe was a child murderer, she would immediately pull back.

Kylie hesitated to give her word about the last one, but after searching her heart, she realized she didn't believe Jane was a murderer, and so she promised.

When Kylie asked Holiday for an explanation of how evil spirits could hurt her, the camp leader hesitated. Kylie quickly added, "It's not for Jane Doe, but in case I ever run into any." When Holiday still didn't start talking, Kylie added, "Keeping me ignorant is not a good way of protecting me. Don't you think I need to know?"

Holiday released a deep breath and nodded. "It's as much about protecting you as it is about . . . It's about knowing you're capable of handling this."

"I'm capable," Kylie said. "It can't be much worse than . . ." She pointed to the computer, where the story of Berta Littlemon had been posted a short time ago.

Holiday nodded. "You're right about that. But before I tell you, let me say again that most evil spirits don't hang around. They are yanked away quickly, but it has and it will happen."

"What do they do?" Kylie asked.

"You've had visions from the other ghosts, so you know how real they feel. Well, these evil spirits can make you relive some of their lives, and believe me, it can rip your heart out. Being that close to evil isn't something you can forget easily."

The way Holiday said it, Kylie knew the camp leader had suffered through it herself. The thought that Kylie, too, might have to deal with it one day sent a sharp shiver racing down her spine.

"They mess with your head, Kylie. They . . ." She inhaled again. "To put it bluntly, they mentally rape you, try to break your spirit, and if you show the least bit of weakness, they can possess you. It's also believed, mostly with bad supernatural spirits, that they can take you with them to hell when they go. Legend says that they think if they can bring something good with them, they stand a chance of alleviating their own punishment."

"So how do I avoid meeting one?" Kylie asked, certain only that she didn't want to experience any of the things Holliday had just described.

"That's the thing. They are just like other ghosts. Some you might just stumble across, shortly after their demise. Others, if their powers are strong enough, will seek you out for a purpose."

Holiday must have sensed Kylie's fear, because she dropped her hand on top of Kylie's again. "If you ever find yourself in their presence, you have to remain strong."

"How?" Kylie asked, feeling her fear ebb with Holiday's calming touch.

"It's the same as shutting out the ghosts. Mentally, you need to put yourself in a different place, a place where you feel love and good things, where you experience life at its best. And hold tight to your faith, because they will try to convince you that all things good are frivolous, that they don't matter."

"Oh my gosh, you're back!" Miranda screamed at the doorway, and came rushing inside the cabin. The moment her vibrant spirit entered the room, it chased away the dismal cloud of emotion hovering over Kylie.

Miranda embraced Holiday, nearly turning over the chair in the process. "I'm so glad you're back. We need you here. I mean . . . Burnett's okay, but . . . he's not you."

Holiday arched a brow. "I hear he wasn't even himself for a while there."

Miranda frowned. "He told you about the whole kangaroo thing, didn't he."

"Yeah," Holiday said, and her brows tightened. "And I must say,

I'm very disappointed with you, Miranda." She reached out and gripped Miranda's hand. "The next time you turn him into anything, do it when I'm here to enjoy it."

They all started laughing.

It was thirty minutes before Kylie and Holiday were able to pull away from Miranda to continue their private conversation. Especially when Miranda told Holiday about her sort of/kind of feeling that they had another mystical stalker in the camp. Kylie wondered if the stalker wasn't her little blue jay friend.

Now, Kylie and Holiday sat out on the front porch. The five o'clock sun, touched with a bit more golden hue, brushed against their faces. Kylie dangled her legs off its edge. Holiday did the same.

Kylie, barefoot, swayed her feet back and forth, and the longer blades of grass tickled the bottoms of her feet. Her mind went to the things she needed to talk to Holiday about.

"Did Burnett tell you about my asking about the FRU library?"

Holiday frowned.

Not a good sign.

"Yeah, he mentioned it."

"Why would they not let me see information about other supernaturals like myself if they had that information on file?" Frustration sounded in Kylie's tone. She hoped Holiday knew it wasn't targeted at her.

"I don't know," Holiday said, and Kylie believed her. "But I do know that the FRU is like any other government organization: they have skeletons in their own closet. Why, years ago, before I was born, most supernaturals considered all werewolves basically animals. They used to hurt them."

"Why?" Kylie asked, completely insulted on behalf of Lucas and the rest of his kind.

"Ignorance. Stupidity. Take your pick. It's the same thing that happened to a lot of minority groups. Supernaturals can act a lot more like humans than you'd think."

Holiday reached for Kylie's right hand and opened her palm. "I heard you caught a fireball that would have hit Miranda."

Kylie nodded and then asked the question she'd been wanting to ask since the night of the party. "Do you think this proves I'm a protector?"

Holiday shrugged as if she didn't think Kylie would like the answer. "Probably."

Holiday was right. She didn't like the answer. Especially when it just brought on more questions. "What does it really mean to be a protector? I've heard some of it. But . . . okay, here's the thing. Miranda said that every protector she's ever heard of had been a full-blooded paranormal. And I'm not."

"I know." Holiday looked as confused as Kylie felt.

"What could that mean?"

"I don't know, but I could guess it means what I've known all along. Kylie Galen is special." She held up her hand. "I know you don't like hearing that, Kylie, but I think you better start getting used to the idea."

Fear, insecurity, and probably a dozen other negative emotions all washed over her. "What if I don't measure up?" she asked in a low whisper. "What if I'm too afraid to do what I have to do and I turn out to be one lousy protector?"

Holiday pulled one leg up on the porch, rested her chin on her knee, and gazed at Kylie as if she'd said something really stupid, like calling the earth square. "Were you scared when you caught that fireball?"

"No, but I didn't have time to be scared. If I'd known I was going to catch the fireball and had time to think about it, I'd probably have needed to carry an extra pair of panties with me, because I'd have probably pissed myself."

Holiday smiled. "Maybe, but you'd have still done it."

"I wouldn't be so sure about that," Kylie said.

"Please. Look at this whole Berta Littlemon/Catherine O'Connell issue. I'm scared for you to continue investigating this. I told you it's dangerous, but you refuse to drop it. You put the welfare of others before yourself."

Kylie hadn't looked at it like that, and she guessed Holiday had a point, but . . . "I'm not a saint," she insisted. "I sin all the time."

Holiday lifted one eyebrow. "Say what?"

Kylie stared down at her toes for a second. Her pink nail polish was chipping, and so was her courage. Then she looked back up at Holiday's eyes and decided to confess. "Miranda said that protectors are like saints. Not only am I not a saint, I don't even want to be a saint. I want to live a normal life. I want to have fun." She thought of how it felt to kiss Lucas and blushed. "Maybe even sin a little."

Holiday started to grin.

Kylie frowned. "You know what I mean. I want to live my life like every other sixteen-year-old girl. I want to tell dirty jokes with my friends, maybe drink some cool alcohol drink every now and then— that doesn't taste like dog piss—and get tipsy. Not that I'll drive afterward or anything."

Holiday chuckled and Kylie expected the fae had probably picked up on Kylie's emotions and knew what else she wanted to do.

And with whom she wanted to do it.

"Being a protector doesn't make you a saint," Holiday said. "It makes you a caring person. You don't have to give up boys."

Kylie felt her face burn a little hotter. She put her palms down behind her and leaned back. "Well, that's the best news I've had all day."

Holiday laughed again. "How are things going in the 'boy' department?"

"Better. Not perfect," Kylie answered, and she thought about Lucas's reaction to the ghosts and the whole issue with his pack.

"Better is good," Holiday said. "Derek has already called me since I've been back, asking me how you were. He said he heard about what happened at the cemetery. Have you seen him?"

"Not much." Kylie swallowed. She didn't want to talk about him, because then she'd be tempted to ask about the reason for Derek's sudden overcharged reaction to her emotions. If anyone would know that answer, it would be Holiday. But frankly, Kylie didn't think she should care. Not when Derek didn't care enough to put his pride aside and ask for the guidance himself.

The next hour rolled past and they just sat there on the porch, enjoying the breeze that wasn't exactly cool, but not terribly hot either, and they talked about everything but Lucas and Derek. Kylie asked if Burnett had told her anything about the Brightens that he hadn't shared with her.

Holiday assured her that Burnett wasn't keeping anything from her.

"Have you spoken with your stepdad?" Holiday asked a few minutes later.

"Not since I've been back," Kylie confessed. "But I have an e-mail from him and I'll bet he's planning on coming for Parents Day."

"But you don't want him to come?"

"I don't know," Kylie admitted. "I was almost ready to forgive him. But when he tried to use me to get to my mom by saying, 'Kylie would love for us all to go out for lunch,' that's when I remembered how mad I still was at him for leaving us."

"So you haven't forgiven him yet?"

"Maybe I've forgiven him, but I just haven't forgotten."

"Thing is, those two sort of go hand in hand. Not that you'll ever really forget, but you accept that it happened and move on. You accept that all people make mistakes. No one is perfect."

"And what if you can't?" Kylie watched a bee buzz past her. "What if I can't ever really forgive him?"

"Then you let go," she said.

Kylie remembered how she'd hugged her father when he'd come to see her and told her he was sorry. While it had been hard, even painful, hugging him had felt right. She wasn't ready to let go of what they'd had. It would hurt too much.

Even more than accepting the truth.

She couldn't help wondering if that was how one made the decision to forgive or not. If letting go hurt more than accepting someone's mistakes. She could only hope that in time, accepting would come easier for her.

"Are you going to e-mail and tell him to come up for Parents Day?"

"Probably. But he and Mom will have to take shifts again. I don't think they can be in the same room together. Maybe not even on the same block."

"That could change," Holiday said, and brushed an insect away.

Kylie decided to tell Holiday her fear about her mom. "I think my mom is ready to start dating."

"Yikes! I remember when my parents did that. Talk about awkward."

"Yeah. She's ready, but I'm not sure I am." Kylie bit down on her lip. "I guess down deep I was always hoping they would get back together. And I could have one thing that was like it used to be. A little bit of normal would be good, ya know?"

"Yeah, but normal is overrated, too." She grinned. "So tell me about this blue jay."

Kylie wrapped her arms around her legs tight and told her the story. Then she decided to ask the big question. "How much of my soul did I give away?"

"If you gave any of it away, it was very, very little. You won't even miss it."

"But what happens when I give it away? Do I die earlier? Am I more likely to go to hell? What's the price of a piece of my soul?"

Holiday shrugged. "Well, if you do indeed have the ability to raise the dead, the price varies. If it's ordained by the gods, then its cost to you is nothing. It even adds to your soul."

"How do you know if it's ordained?" Kylie asked.

"You'll just know. The powers that be will make it very clear."

Kylie shivered a bit at the mention of the powers that be. She hesitated to ask her next question, but as she'd told Holiday earlier, ignorance was a lousy form of protection. "And if it's not ordained?"

"Then the price is based on the quality of life that the person goes on to live. If they live a good life, the price is very low. Practically moot. If they abuse life, or the lives of others, then it can nip at your soul. Their sins, in a small way, become your sins. I'm not sure how accountable one is held for these sins, but I've heard emotionally it can leave you feeling empty. And yes, the less soul you have, the shorter the life you usually live."

Kylie frowned. "Kind of makes you not want to bring anyone back."

"Well, I'm sure it was designed that way so it gives people pause. As hard as it is, death is a part of life. But we're probably discussing this for nothing, Kylie. Just because you think you might have brought a bird back to life doesn't mean you have this gift."

Kylie wanted to believe what Holiday was saying was true, but she wasn't sure she did. "Does healing someone take a part of my soul? I mean, if bringing someone to life does, it makes sense that healing them might, too."

"Not like it does raising the dead," Holiday said. "It does drain you, though."

Kylie remembered how tired she'd felt after healing Sara and then Lucas.

"I'd like for you and Helen to work together on this," Holiday said. "Maybe even meet regularly like a species group."

Kylie raised an eyebrow and suspected she knew what Holiday was up to. "Because I don't belong to a group, right? That's why you're doing this?"

Holiday rolled her eyes. "You belong here at Shadow Falls. Just because you don't belong to a certain group doesn't mean anything."

Kylie nodded. "I like Helen."

After a few minutes of just listening to nature, she told Holiday all about the blue jay's little dog-and-pony shows. Holiday didn't have an explanation for the bird's pop-in visits, except to say that maybe the bird was only a fledgling and it sort of imprinted on her, meaning it thought Kylie was his mother.

"God, I hope not. Because I'm not chewing up worms and barfing into its mouth. I mean, I know that's what mama birds do."

Holiday laughed.

Kylie looked at her friend and counselor, and the most important question of all popped out. "Does any of this give you any clue as to what I am?"

Holiday frowned. "I wish it did."

"What if I never find out? What if I go through my life never knowing?"

"That's not likely," Holiday said. "Almost every week, we discover something else about you. Sooner or later, something is going to point you in the right direction."

Kylie looked down and watched an ant move across the porch. "I think Lucas wants me to be werewolf."

"Yes, but what Lucas wants isn't important."

Something told Kylie that Holiday understood the reason Lucas wanted this. She almost asked, but she wasn't sure she was ready to talk about it.

"You will be what you are, and whatever it is, you will be fine. Everyone has to accept that and love you for who you are; it doesn't really matter where your heritage comes from."

For some reason, Kylie remembered Derek saying pretty much the same thing.

Holiday's phone rang. She looked at the number and then glanced at Kylie.

"Who is it?" Kylie asked, sensing it was about her.

"Derek again."

Kylie sighed. Why did just hearing his name still sting?

Chapter Twenty-three

Kylie nibbled, without appetite, at her hamburger and fries at dinner that night while sitting between Della and Miranda at the dining hall. When asked, Miranda confessed she hadn't yet spoken to Perry about the dance/dragon thing from last night.

Miranda said that she'd gotten another phone call from the cute warlock back home and he'd arranged to pick her up Friday evening and take her out to dinner. "What am I going to say to Perry?" she asked. "'Hey, I'd like to just talk to you to see if we might have a chance, but first I'd like to go out on a date with another guy and see if I like him better'?"

Both Kylie and Della agreed it would be a difficult conversation. But they suggested Miranda at least thank Perry for standing up for her against Clark.

In truth, Kylie hoped Miranda would talk to Perry and cancel her date with the cute warlock. Kylie had nothing against cute warlocks, but Perry was one of their own.

Kylie placed a greasy fry in her mouth and tried to pretend she was hungry. When she glanced up, she noticed Lucas sitting with his pack of weres; their eyes met across the rows of hungry teens munching on burgers. He smiled, and Kylie returned the smile. He'd asked her to sit with him at the weres' table. She would have, even knowing it would be uncomfortable sitting with a group of his friends who didn't want him to see her. She would have done it because if Lucas could stand up to them, then so would she. But Della was her shadow, and Kylie knew the little vamp would have had a fit if she'd asked her to sit with the were group. So Kylie had refrained.

Lucas picked up a fry, and as he popped it into his mouth, he winked at her. The small gesture might not have meant anything coming from a different guy, but for Lucas to show anything in the way of public affection was a big deal. She grinned big and winked back. She did it even when she noticed Fredericka sitting two people away from Lucas and snarling as though she wanted to rip out Kylie's throat.

The she-wolf could probably do it, too.

Somebody must have said something funny a few tables over because laughter filled the large room. The smell of burgers mingled with the faint smell of singed wood. Thanks to Burnett, the physical reminders of the big fight were all gone, but the memory still lingered. Everyone at the camp seemed extra cheery tonight, no doubt celebrating Holiday's return. If the camp leader doubted how appreciated she was, the number of squeals, accompanied by "You're back!" and unexpected hugs (even from a few vamps and weres, which were not common) should have done her ego good.

For a moment, Kylie worried it might make Burnett feel like a second fiddle. But more than once Kylie caught the vampire watching the emotional greetings with so much pride in his eyes that it was like watching a romance movie. Kylie could almost hear the sappy music playing in the background. She wished she had a camera so she could show Holiday how Burnett looked at her when she wasn't aware.

The door to the dining room swished open. Derek and Ellie walked in side by side, though they weren't holding hands. Derek immediately started moving his gaze around the room, and Kylie knew he'd been looking for her when his gaze landed on hers. She couldn't help but wonder what he'd wanted to talk to Holiday about. Was it her again? And why? Shouldn't he be giving Ellie his attention?

He nodded slightly. She nodded back and forced herself to eat another bite of her hamburger. It tasted like dead meat. Which it was, but the thought made it even more unappetizing.

When the lump of food took two swallows to get down her throat, she pushed her plate aside. She was so done.

Staring at her glass of tea, she wiped away a trail of condensation and searched for a plausible excuse to escape from the dining hall. Escape before she had to watch Derek and Ellie whispering back and forth and sharing fries or something—not that she cared, of course. At least that's what she told herself. And she would continue to tell herself that until it was true. It would happen, too. How could it not when she enjoyed Lucas's company so much? Enjoyed his kisses. Enjoyed being the girl he would actually wink at with dozens of people around to witness.

Kylie's phone rang, giving her the excuse she needed to skip out. Not even checking to see who it was, she leaned over and whispered to Della that she had to take the call. Della, who'd been interested only in the rare meat on her bun and had already wolfed that down, grabbed her real meal—a tall glass of B positive blood—and followed her out.

Kylie hadn't cleared the dining room door when she looked to see the name on her phone. Oh, crappers! It was Sara, her friend from home.

Sara, whose previous call and texts Kylie hadn't answered.

For a damn good reason, too. Kylie knew Sara wanted to talk about her suspicion that Kylie had done something to make her cancer jump ship.

Problem was, Sara's suspicion was right on target.

A targeted subject that Kylie had neglected to discuss with Holiday.

So what had compelled Kylie to answer this call without checking her caller ID first?

Oh yeah, so she'd have a reason to escape from the dining hall. Putting the phone to her ear, she hit the answer button.

"Hey, Sara," Kylie said, and decided to wing it. Not that it was altogether a good idea. She'd never been a good winger.

"Hi," Sara said.

"What's up?" Kylie asked.

"I'll tell you what's up. I've just managed to baffle every cancer specialist in Texas. I still have to finish my chemo, and do one bout of radiation, but they did tons of CT scans and there's not one tumor in this body! Can you believe it? I'm not gonna die, Kylie!"

There was so much excitement, bounciness, and pure hope in Sara's voice that Kylie's breath caught in her throat and tears filled her eyes. It reminded Kylie of the old Sara. Not the sex-crazed, alcohol-loving party girl who'd replaced her, but the one Kylie had been best friends with since elementary school.

And until this second, Kylie hadn't realized how much she'd missed the old Sara, either. "That's friggin' fabulous, girl!"

"Like you didn't know already," she said.

Think. Think. Think. "I don't know what you mean," Kylie said, deciding to play ignorant. What was the saying? Ignorance is bliss? She could really use a little bliss right now.

Della looked at Kylie and rolled her eyes. Kylie frowned, not so much because Della was listening in—she would have told Della about it anyway—but because Della then mouthed the word *liar*.

"Right," Sara said. "But that's not important. We can talk about that Sunday." She let a long pause linger on the phone, as if it were supposed to mean something. "Come on. Don't you wanna know why we can talk about it on Sunday?" Sara finally asked.

"Because you're not going to church and are going to call me?" Kylie answered, throwing out the first thing that came to her mind, but her gut knotted with a strange suspicion. But a suspicion of what? How bad could it be?

"Because I'm coming to see you on Sunday," Sara said, sounding really happy about it, too.

Okay, having Sara visit Shadow Falls could be phenomenally bad. But maybe that wasn't even what she meant. "Uh, I'm not at home, Sara. I'm at camp," Kylie said. "Remember?" *Please let it be that simple.*

"Of course I remember, silly! I'm coming up there with your mom. I just got off the phone with her."

Kylie's heart, poised to make the leap, did a nosedive right into her stomach. The thought of Sara coming to Shadow Falls sent a wave of shock to her brain.

Sara was from Kylie's old life.

Everything at Shadow Falls was part of her new life.

Old life and new life didn't go together. They were like peanut butter and hot dogs. The two were fine separately, but they should never meet.

Never.

Ever.

"Uh, Sara. You . . . you . . ." She swallowed hard. "You can't just visit Shadow Falls. I mean, you have to . . . have to get permission from the camp leaders, and they are very funny about—"

"Duh, your mom told me that. So I took the bull by the horns and called and spoke with a Mr. Burnett James about twenty minutes ago. He said it would be fine for me to ride up with your mom. I can't wait to see you, Kylie. And I can't wait to meet all those hot guys you told me about. We're going to have such fun. Oh, and what was the name of that really bitchy girl you told me about? DeAnn, no, wait, it was Della. We can tag team her ass."

Della's eyes widened. *Bitchy,* she mouthed.

Kylie's hand wrapped around the phone and started to shake. "Ugh. I never said she was bitchy, I said she was blunt."

"Same thing," Sara said. "And the other one with the weird hair? Tell me, are they the ones who taught you how to heal people?"

"I'm sorry." Kylie's heart started to jump beats. "I have to go. Someone just . . . someone just called me." She punched Della in the arm.

"Hey, Kylie!" Della yelled out, and grinned as if she enjoyed playing a part in the shenanigans. Or not. "Oh, you're on the phone. We can talk later. I wouldn't want to be a bitch or anything," she said in her snarkiest voice.

"I'll call you later," Kylie told Sara. "Yeah . . . later. Sorry." She started to hang up and then said, "But I'm happy about you being okay, Sara. Really happy."

Kylie snapped her phone closed and then looked at Della. Della, who seemed to be immensely enjoying Kylie's discomfort. Della, who looked part pissed off and part amused.

"So," Della said. "We finally get to meet Miss Sara, huh? Your oldest and best friend, who has always sounded like a self-centered bitch, if you ask me. You totally upgraded when you came here. Personally, I'd have let her die. But on second thought . . ." Della flashed her fangs. "Hmm, what type of blood does she have? Think I could talk her into donating a pint or two, maybe more? Tag team my ass!"

"Kill me," Kylie said, and brushed her hair back to expose her neck vein. "Just kill me now and get it over with!"

"So we get to meet Sara. Cool," Miranda said later that night as they sat around the kitchen table.

"Not cool," Kylie said, seriously unhappy about it, and gave a demanding Socks a scratch behind his ear.

"Why not cool?" Miranda asked.

"She doesn't want us to meet her," Della said. "We might find out what the real Kylie Galen is like."

Kylie scowled at Della, and yeah, she could pull off a pretty mean scowl, thanks to living with Della. "It's not that at all. If anything, you guys know the real me. It's just . . . over-the-top weird to have her coming here."

"Why?" Miranda asked. "We've met your mom."

"And your philandering dad," Della added.

"That's different," Kylie said, and frowned at the philandering comment. Though she didn't know why she was offended, because it was true.

"How's it different?" Miranda asked. Before Kylie could answer, Miranda added, "Hey, I hope you two get a chance to meet Todd on Friday night. Will you guys wait with me in the parking lot when he comes to pick me up?"

Both Della and Kylie frowned, but they nodded.

"It's different for you," Kylie said to Miranda, still stuck on Sara coming to visit on Parents Day. "You've known you were supernatural all your life. You don't have a presupernatural life." Socks, still on the tabletop, jumped down to the floor with a catlike elegance. "It's like I was a different person back then. And yeah, you met my parents, but it's almost as if they don't count—not the way your friends count."

"I'm sorry, but I don't understand," Miranda said.

"I do," said Della. And she said it as though she hated to admit it. "Kylie's right. It's different when you had a different life. I tried to imagine how it would be for you guys to meet Lee, or one of my old girlfriends. It would be freaky." She met Kylie's eyes. "I'm sorry I gave you a hard time about this."

"Wow," Miranda said. "You'd better be careful, Della. In the last few days, I think you've used up your vampire quota of apologies for the next ten years."

"Kiss my apologetic ass!" Della snapped.

Later that night, Kylie woke up to the mist forming around her. She didn't know where she was, but for some reason she wasn't afraid. Her gaze stayed on the soft, moist mist. She looked at the trees; the leaves, even in the dark, were a perfect shade of verdant green. Beautiful sprays of moonlight spilled through limbs that seemed to reach up into the heavens with pride. Perfect. Fairy-tale perfect. Even the sounds of the forest at night were like a symphony. She heard the water, like a babbling brook, a peaceful, beautiful sound playing in the background.

She immediately thought of Derek and that crazy thing he did when he was really close to her. How he made everything look like a fairy-tale picture, one meant to capture your imagination—one meant to fill you with awe, like the pages of a children's book.

"Hey . . ." His voice pulled her away from the few stars she saw twinkling above the trees.

He sat beside her on a large rock. Not so close that she would have felt awkward, but near enough that the moonlight allowed her to see him. Then she realized this wasn't just any rock; it was their rock. The spot he'd taken her to after she'd first arrived at Shadow Falls.

She'd done it again.

She'd brought him here through the dreamscape, and that was so wrong.

"I'm sorry," she blurted out. "I didn't mean to do this." She closed her eyes and concentrated on moving back, away from the dream. She concentrated really hard, waited for the floating-flying sensation, but it didn't happen. At least she didn't think it did.

She opened her eyes just a crack. Enough to see if she'd moved.

Nope, she was still sitting on the rock. Derek was still looking at her. Why couldn't she fly away from the dream? She jerked her eyes open all the way.

"I'm sorry," she said again. "I didn't mean to do this. Just a minute and you can go right back to sleep."

She slammed her eyes shut again and tried really, really hard to concentrate. *Back. Go back to sleep. Now!*

"Kylie?" His voice tickled her ears as she tried to fix what she'd done. "Kylie."

She tried to ignore him and concentrate.

"Kylie, you're not doing this. I am. I'm the one dreamscaping."

Kylie jerked open her eyes and her vision filled with him sitting there, looking so real. She recalled how the dreamscape had felt different when Red had come into her dreams. She hadn't been able to fly away, she'd had to wake herself up. So that's what she needed to do. Just wake herself up. She didn't do it.

"You can dreamscape?"

He nodded. "Yeah."

The first thing she did was make sure she had clothes on. Hey . . . she knew her own tendencies with dreams, and from what she'd heard, boys were even worse.

She had on her pink nightshirt. Nothing sexy or showy. Good thing. A fluttering of relief waved through her that he didn't intend for this to be that kind of dream. Then she couldn't help but wonder if it was because he didn't feel that way about her anymore. He had Ellie.

"Why didn't you tell me you could dreamscape?" she asked, not wanting to think too much about him and Ellie.

He hesitated. "I sort of figured out how to turn it off before I ever got to Shadow Falls. I was constantly trying to visit my dad to communicate with him, even when I didn't want to have anything more to do with him."

Kylie knew all about unwanted dreamscapes. Then she remembered

Derek's pain at dealing with his dad, the man who had abandoned him when he was really young. "Do you communicate with him now?" she asked, remembering he'd said he was going to look for his dad when he'd left Shadow Falls. When he'd come back with Ellie, she hadn't thought about Derek's problems, only about feeling betrayed by him. A touch of shame filtered into her chest at her selfishness.

"Not really. But I now know how to work the dreamscape, so I . . ."

"You what?" Kylie asked.

"Started using it again. But that's not important. Look, the other night when you came to me in the dream."

"I'm sorry about that," she said. "I'm just now learning how to control them. But as soon as I realized what I had done, that I had gone to your bedroom, I left."

His frown tightened. "I know. But before you took off, in that second that I saw you, it dawned on me that I didn't feel it here."

"Didn't feel what?" she asked, obviously still half-asleep.

"I didn't feel the surge of your emotions." He smiled. "When we dreamscape, I can talk to you, be this close to you without it making me crazy."

Kylie felt so many mixed emotions sitting on the rock, staring at his smile. She took a deep breath. "I'm not sure this is a good thing."

"Why not? I just want to talk. To see how you're doing. Is that a crime? I thought you said you cared about me? That you wanted to be my friend?"

"Okay, let me put it another way. I don't think Ellie will think this is such a good idea."

He frowned. "I keep telling you that it's not like that with us now. Ellie and I are just friends."

"Really?" Kylie let sarcasm leak into her tone. "Because it's hard to believe after the picture I saw of you two making out."

He hesitated and then said, "Fine, you're right. When I first ran into Ellie, she was so happy to see me and I was hurting. Lucas was back and you cared about him. I was just as confused as Ellie was. We kissed and . . . Look, the important thing is that we both realized it was wrong."

It was that little pause that caught her attention the most. "You kissed and then did what?" Kylie asked.

Obviously in the dream world, she felt braver, able to ask questions she might not ask in real life. "Just exactly what happened between you and Ellie in Pennsylvania?"

Chapter Twenty-four

"Is it important?" Derek asked.

"You had sex with her, didn't you." Somehow Kylie had known this all along. It sucked being right, too.

Guilt filled his eyes. "It didn't mean anything."

She shook her head. "How can it not have meant anything? It's the ultimate form of intimacy between two people."

"Not always," he said. "Sometimes it's just two people searching for something. And a lot of times, they don't find it. We didn't find it, Kylie. Ellie knew it. I knew it. And the romantic relationship is completely over. It was a mistake and we both knew it."

"But you brought her back with you."

He flinched. "She's not a bad person, I couldn't leave her there at the commune. It was awful. She'd have been in a gang in a matter of weeks."

Kylie pulled her legs closer to her chest and tried to sort through the emotions bouncing through her. She felt hurt. She felt justified in her feelings of jealousy. And she felt . . . relieved. The last one didn't make sense, though. Why would she feel relieved that Derek and Ellie had sex?

Then the truth hit. She felt relieved because now there was no reason for her to experience guilt over being with Lucas. Not that the truth still didn't hurt. And if she was completely honest with herself, she still felt a tiny wave of jealousy. But she pushed it away, because now, more than ever, she could accept it. She was Derek's friend. Just his friend.

"We're just friends," she said.

He looked at her. "Yeah," he said, but something about that one word didn't seem as honest as his earlier words.

"All I want to do is talk. To make sure you're okay. Give me ten minutes." He studied her frown. "Five. Hell, give me three minutes, Kylie. Is that too much for a friend to ask?"

She looked at the stream and then up at him. "Three minutes. Then this ends."

"Deal." He looked at his watch, and then, as if competing with the clock, he started talking. "How are you? What happened at the cemetery? I heard about it."

She gave him the really short version. Namely, that she thought the ghost was buried there. And she'd discovered her spirit might be a child killer.

He didn't flinch like the rest of them. "What are you going to do?" he asked instead. "How are you going to get to the truth?"

"I'm waiting for the ghost to come back. She hasn't visited me since then."

"She will," he said. "And don't worry too much. I'm sure you'll figure everything out. You always do."

Kylie gazed up into his gold-flecked green eyes. "How do you know I'm worried?"

"Duh, I can feel it."

"I thought you couldn't feel my emotions here?"

"I can feel them, but they're just at a lower voltage. Normal range."

Normal. That word seemed to be popping into Kylie's mind a lot.

She nodded. "Did you ever find your dad?" When he looked upset by her question, she added, "You told me when you left that you were going to try to find him."

He nodded and then swallowed. "I found him."

She felt his mixed emotions as if they were her own. "It didn't go well?"

"I don't know. I thought I'd see him and it would make it right. It's still not right. I still don't know if I want anything to do with him. I'm pretty sure I don't."

"Why? What happened?" Kylie asked.

"He offered me a hundred different reasons why he had to leave me and Mom. His life was a lie trying to live in the human world with my mom. He told me it hurt too much trying to stay in touch. He said he'd like to get to know me again. He said a lot of things. And not one of them meant a hill of beans to me. Maybe it will in time. I don't know. But right now, it just feels totally awkward."

"I understand awkward," she said, and offered him a bit of a smile. "Sara is supposed to be coming with my mom on Parents Day."

He reached for her and then pulled back. "I'm sure it'll be okay."

There was a moment of silence, then Derek started talking. "So, with your ghost . . . have you figured out what to do? I mean, how can you find out who she is?"

"I don't know for sure. But my gut says that she's remembering more and more each time I see her."

He pondered her words and then said, "You know, I remember reading something years ago about how an old state cemetery was dug up and they found that about five percent of all the caskets had two bodies in them."

"Two bodies?"

"Yeah. The state was burying some of the really poor, homeless folks in with other caskets. Just slipping them in so they didn't have to pay for their own burial."

Kylie thought about it for a second, and it made perfect sense. Catherine O'Connell said she saw Jane Doe rise from the grave of Berta Littlemon. However, if Berta Littlemon was in there, too—and the legends about such things were correct—she would have already been snatched into hell. That meant only one spirit would have risen from the grave.

"I think you might have just solved my problem," she told Derek. "Thank you!" If things had been different between them, she would have hugged him.

He grinned. "You're welcome."

She suddenly realized that they had probably been talking way longer than his negotiated three minutes. She glanced down at his watch.

"Oh, one more thing," he said. "After we talked the other day about Red being strange, I did some checking. You know, just to see what I could find out. Contrary to the weird vibe we both got, he is vampire, or at least that's what everyone thinks. The only other thing I found was . . . about his parents."

"What about them?" she asked.

"Supposedly, his mom was murdered in front of him when he was like seven. The case never was solved. It looked as if even the FRU looked into the case, but never found who did it. Then his dad disappeared less than a year later. That's when he went to live with his grandfather."

Kylie frowned. "Damn, I could almost feel sorry for him."

Derek shrugged. "Unfortunately, most people who commit violent crimes were at one time victims themselves. But one wrong doesn't make a right. And we know he killed those two girls."

"I know." When she looked up and found herself gazing into Derek's eyes again, she said, "I guess I should—"

"Go. I know," he said, and his expression turned sad. "I miss you, Kylie. Can we . . . do this again?"

She almost said yes but realized it probably wasn't a good idea for either one of them. "I don't know," she said. "I've got a lot to figure out."

"Between you and Lucas?" he asked.

"Yes," she said honestly. She wouldn't feel guilty about her feelings anymore. She didn't know what she might have with Lucas. But for the first time since she'd recognized those growing feelings, she didn't feel at fault about them. And there was something between them. But with his pack trying to break them up, and his dislike of her involvement with the ghosts, she just wasn't sure where it was going to lead.

"Okay," he said. "But if you need me . . . or just want to talk . . . you know where I am."

Kylie nodded, and then the next thing she knew, she was awake, staring at her bedroom ceiling. "I miss you, too," she whispered, and then rolled over and hugged her pillow.

Perry met Kylie at the front door the next morning when she stepped out of the cabin.

"Hey," she said, and forced a smile. She wasn't exactly depressed about knowing the truth about Derek and Ellie, but there was an underlying sadness to her mood today.

It reminded Kylie of how she always felt the last day of school before summer vacation. She wanted summer to be here, knew there was no changing it, but a part of her wanted to hold on to life the way it was. She supposed she just wasn't a big fan of change.

Perry, his eyes a bright blue, grinned. "Hey." He looked back at the door, and Kylie knew why.

"Miranda already left," she told him.

"Why?"

Because she didn't want to see you because she's afraid of what you'll say when she tells you she's got a date Friday night with a hot warlock.

"I don't have a clue." *And I'm really glad you're not a vampire who can read my heartbeat and tell when I'm flat-out lying.*

His eyes went from blue to a sad brown. "I thought . . . I guess I just hoped that . . ."

"I know," Kylie said, and bumped him with her shoulder. "And while I can't say anything, all I can tell you is that hope is eternal."

"So I still have a chance?" he asked.

"A little one," she said, not wanting to give him false hope.

They started heading down the trail. "I want to see if Holiday and Burnett are in the office. I need to talk with them before breakfast."

"Just lead the way," Perry said, bowing at the waist. "I'm your personal shadow servant."

Kylie grinned. As they walked, she wondered if someday she could hang out with Derek like this and it would feel this right. Feel completely platonic, with no hint of regret about what could have been. She really hoped so. Although her heart said he would have made an awesome boyfriend, he would also make a hell of a good friend. And she hoped they could get there.

Holiday and Burnett weren't in the office, so Kylie couldn't tell them about Derek's theory that there could have been two bodies in Berta Littlemon's grave.

Or ask Burnett what he'd been smoking when he'd given Sara permission to visit Shadow Falls.

At breakfast, Lucas joined her and Perry at their table. Kylie spotted Miranda eating with the witches, and Della had a vampire thing that morning. So Kylie sat between Lucas and Perry, and much to her surprise, they both behaved. Well, Perry behaved.

Lucas slipped his hand under the table and touched the side of her leg. Then he leaned in and whispered, "Want to go dancing in the moonlight again tonight?"

She couldn't be sure, but she could swear the brush of his lips against her temple had almost been a kiss. She nudged him with her elbow, and as she forked a mouthful of eggs on her utensil, she whispered back, "Careful. People are going to actually know you have a thing for me."

"Good," he said. "Maybe it's time we make it official."

Her heart stopped. The eggs dropped from the prongs of her fork and landed with a splat on her plate.

She turned and looked into his blue eyes. "Are you asking me to go out with you?"

"Are you saying yes?" Hope danced in his eyes.

"What about your pack?"

"I told you I don't care what they say."

Joy danced in her heart. "Well, I think I should hear the question first."

"Okay . . . Will you, Kylie Galen, go out with me?"

Yes. Yes. Yes. The word sat on the tip of her tongue, waiting to be released. She smiled, poised to say it, and—

"Can I borrow Lucas for a minute?" Burnett's deep voice shattered the moment. He stood behind them, six feet plus of solid vampire.

Lucas looked up at Burnett. "Is something wrong?"

"I need a word with you."

Lucas got up and left. Kylie watched them leave, so in shock from Lucas asking her to go out that she completely forgot to give Burnett a large ration of shit for agreeing to let Sara come to the camp.

A bit later, Kylie stood beside Perry while Chris announced names for the Meet Your Campmates hour. Lucas still hadn't come back from his talk with Burnett, and that worried her.

Looking up at Perry, Kylie asked, "How are we going to do this?"

He stared over at Miranda. "I pulled my name from the list."

"So we don't have to stay?" Kylie asked.

"I pulled my name. Not yours. I figured I could just tag along with you on your hour."

"Isn't that against the rules?"

"I'm sure Burnett wouldn't mind."

"Speaking of Burnett," Kylie said. "I didn't know you two knew each other."

"He told you?" Perry seemed surprised.

"No. Well, he sort of did when I asked him about it. But during the whole dragon thing, you said something about him telling you something when you were six."

"Oh," Perry said. "And what did Burnett say?"

"Just that he knew you from before. Was he like your foster contact person or something?"

"Yeah, sort of."

"And Kylie Galen . . ." Chris's voice rose, and so did Kylie's attention. She glanced to the front where Chris stood pulling names out of a hat. Yes, a real-life magician type of hat, too.

Obviously, Chris had decided to jazz up his few minutes in the limelight. "You are spending an hour with . . . Ellie Mason."

"Oh, hell!" All her unresolved feeling about Derek and Ellie came bubbling to the surface.

"Oh, boy," Perry countered. "This should be loads of fun!"

Which only went to show how she and Perry had different definitions of fun.

A minute later, Kylie, Ellie, and Perry took off walking along one of the trails. For the longest time, none of them spoke.

"Where are we going?" Ellie broke the unspoken code of silence.

"Down by the creek bed," Kylie said.

"Okay," Ellie said.

They continued for another ten minutes, walking fast, supernatural fast. No one complained. At least not about the speed.

Ellie piped up again. "I'm new here, but I thought the objective of campmate hour was to talk—to get to know each other."

"So talk," Kylie snapped, and dodged a few limbs that seemed to try to reach out and grab her. She also dodged logic that said she should fake a huge migraine and send the little sex kitten on her way back to camp.

"Okay . . . My name is Ellie Mason and I have a feeling you don't like me."

Kylie stopped and swerved around—she had the script down in her head for faking a sick headache. She wouldn't even have to fake it because now her head was actually throbbing. But when she opened her mouth, her words had nothing to do with migraines.

"Okay, let's get something out in the open. I know you had sex with Derek." Her voice seemed to bounce from tree to tree.

"Damn!" Perry said, and grinned. "This is gonna be better than I thought."

Chapter Twenty-five

Kylie glared at the shape-shifter.

Perry's smile vanished.

Kylie arched a brow. "Do it."

He frowned. "Not the deaf cat again," he pleaded. "I can't hear. My equilibrium is thrown off. It's like I'm in a vacuum."

She didn't look away until the sparkles started popping off like fireworks. Then she turned and faced Ellie, who stared wide-eyed at the cascading sparkles around Perry.

"Holy shit! I've never seen a shape-shifter transform before. I mean, I heard about what happens when they shift, but that is so cool."

"Did you hear what I said?" Kylie crossed her arms over her chest as fury built in the pit of her stomach.

"Did you see him change?" Ellie asked.

Kylie tapped her tennis shoe in the moist, rocky soil. "I said I know you had sex with Derek."

Ellie continued to stare at Perry, who was now a white, blue-eyed feline. There was a sudden silence in the woods. Kylie ignored it and focused on Ellie.

"Yeah, I heard you," Ellie said, still not looking at her. "And I'm purposely stalling, so I can figure out how to answer you." The dark-haired vamp released a deep breath and looked at Kylie. "Derek told you?"

Kylie nodded.

Ellie shook her head. "Just like Derek. He's one of those nice guys who think the truth is the best policy."

"You would have lied to me?" Kylie asked, searching for a reason to really dislike the girl. As if having sex with Derek weren't enough of a reason. But then again, Kylie and Derek hadn't had a commitment; they hadn't even gone out on an official date. And Derek and Ellie shared a past.

"Yup. I'd have lied," Ellie said. "Not for spite or anything. Just because . . . well, what happened between me and Derek didn't mean crap, so what would be the point of letting that cause a bunch of shit?"

Kylie frowned. "If it didn't mean crap, then why did you do it?"

She shrugged. "Because I wanted it to mean something."

"That doesn't make sense," Kylie accused.

Ellie frowned. "Okay, look. I like Derek. A lot. I mean, he's hot, he's sweet, and so damn great. But . . . there are just no sparks. Like before when we were dating. We had a lot of sparkless sex. I'm sure you've dealt with that, right?"

Kylie didn't correct her. Admitting she was a virgin to a stranger didn't sit well with her.

"So when he appears at this party, I'm feeling a tiny bit scared, slightly vulnerable, and he shows up like a knight in shining armor. And he looks hot, and I think maybe this time there'd be sparks." She shook her head. "But no sparks."

Kylie felt the air grow cold around them. Dead cold. *Please not now,* she said in her head.

"If he told you about the sex," Ellie continued, "then he also told you that as soon as it was over, we both were like . . . 'God, that was a mistake.' And five minutes later, he's telling me about some girl he met named Kylie."

Kylie stared down at the ground, and she could swear it had just shifted beneath her feet. She glanced over at Perry, who sat on a tree limb, swatting at a butterfly.

"You do know he really cares about you, right?" Ellie asked.

The ghost materialized right in front of Kylie, and she looked panicked, scared.

Please . . . not now!

Kylie ignored the spirit and studied Ellie. Suddenly the whole conversation seemed silly and totally unnecessary. She had no right to be upset that Derek and Ellie had sex. None. Zilch. Zero.

"I'm sorry," Kylie said. "I shouldn't have—"

"Yeah, you should have. If some chick had sex with a guy I liked, I'd be pissed, too. It's cool that you just spoke your mind. I respect that."

"No," Kylie said. "I mean, it's not like . . . that with me and Derek. Yeah, Derek and I were almost something, but then . . ." *He just ended it.* She stopped herself. She didn't want to go into that. "It's over."

"Right. Over." Ellie rolled her eyes. "Seriously? Every time we walk into a crowd of people, do you know what he does? He looks for you." She chuckled. "Which is silly. And so I asked him about it. I go, 'You say you can feel her a mile away, so you know she's not here, so why do you look for her if you already know?'" Ellie grinned. "You know what he said to me? He said, 'Hope lives eternal.'"

Kylie recognized the words she'd offered Perry a little while ago.

"The guy's got it bad for you," Ellie said.

Kylie shook her head again. "No, it's over. He ended it. I'm going out with someone else now."

"You are?" Shock widened Ellie's blue eyes. "Does Derek know?"

"No. I mean, I'm going to be going out with someone else." Feeling like a dork, she added, "Lucas asked me to go out at breakfast. But I didn't get a chance to say yes."

Ellie raised her eyebrows in suspicion. "So, you didn't say yes."

Kylie frowned, and the dead cold seemed to crawl against her skin. "We were interrupted."

"How long does it take to say yes?" Ellie wrapped her arms around herself as if to fight off the cold and looked around as if confused by the sudden change in temperature.

"What's your point?" Kylie asked, feeling frustrated but not sure if it stemmed from the ghost or from Ellie. Then Kylie saw the ghost pacing back and forth, staring at her as if she needed to tell her something. Something urgent.

Ellie did her shrug thing again. "I'm just saying it sounds like you hesitated. And maybe there's a reason for that. Maybe the reason is—"

"There's no reason. I didn't hesitate."

Jane Doe stopped pacing and stared Kylie dead in the eyes. *"You should run!"*

"You sure?" Ellie asked.

"I'm sure," Kylie said, and she was. Wasn't she? She'd been going to tell him yes before Burnett came over. She would tell Lucas yes the next time she saw him.

"Run!" the ghost screamed.

"Why?" Kylie asked the spirit, and glanced at Perry still in the tree, slowly sneaking up on the butterfly.

"Why what?" Ellie asked.

"Run!" The spirit screamed the word so loud, Kylie thought her eardrums would rupture. She looked up and saw the eagle coming at her full blast with his talons out.

She ducked, barely dodging the bird's sharp claws. Right then, the ground under her feet started moving. Seriously moving. A loud rumble seemed to explode from below her.

"Run!" Kylie screamed at Ellie.

The vamp, her eyes glowing a bright yellow, stared at the ground. "What the hell?"

"Run!" Kylie screamed, and grabbed Ellie's arm and took off, dragging her with her. They had gotten less than a foot when the earth where they'd just stood dropped into a big, dark hole. A hole that kept growing wider, moving closer. Kylie got about another ten feet when she remembered.

Perry. He was stuck in a tree and wouldn't be able to hear what was happening below him.

She swung around. Just as she suspected, he was still in the tree. Still staring at the butterfly.

"We should keep going!" yelled Ellie.

The hole in the ground kept expanding as if someone sucked the earth from below. It got almost to the tree. Almost to Perry. He still hadn't seen it.

And it was her fault. All her fault.

"Perry, run!" she screamed with everything she had.

But Perry couldn't hear.

My equilibrium is thrown off. It's like I'm in a vacuum. His words raked across her mind like cut glass.

She saw the hole begin to pull on the roots of the tree.

She saw Perry the feline lose his footing.

He fought to stay in the tree. She watched in horror as he wrapped his feline limbs around the branch, his claws digging into the bark as he clung for life. But the dark hole, like a monster who didn't give up, sucked the tree down, taking the small, blue-eyed kitten into the dark oblivion.

Someone lives and someone dies.

"No!" Kylie screamed, and bolted forward, taking a flying leap into the dark hole.

Chapter Twenty-six

The darkness surrounded Kylie the second her foot left solid earth, and she tumbled down the pit. She heard screams, tortured screams, coming from below. Or were they just inside her head? It was hard to tell. Then she was struck by a cold so intense that it almost stole her breath. She instantly knew the sounds were coming from hell. Was Holiday right? Had she spent too much time with pure evil and now she was paying the price?

And because of her, so was Perry?

Suddenly, painful little sparks hit her body from beneath her, jolts of what felt like electricity. It took two or three strikes before she realized what it meant.

Perry. Perry was shifting.

Then she slammed against . . . something half-soft, half-prickly. With a lot of feathers.

She bounced off it, flipped over, and screamed as she continued her descent, falling faster now into oblivion and going headfirst.

Huge, leathery-feeling handcuffs latched on to her right arm and yanked her upward. Her arm felt pulled out of its socket. She muttered a curse at the sharp pain.

"I got you . . ." Perry's voice reverberated through the hole.

It was meant to reassure her, but it didn't. What if he lost his grip on her arm? What if whatever it was that waited for them below suddenly decided to come up for a visit?

"Kylie!"

She jerked her head up to the entrance to the large sinkhole. Bright light spilled in from the opening, making it hard to see. Then she saw a body falling.

No, not just a body. It was Ellie.

"Shit!" Perry screamed, flapping his large bird wings as fast as he could. "I can't catch her. I can't."

An eerie sense of calm settled over Kylie. She reached out with her free hand just as gravity brought Ellie's body past them and latched on to the vampire's forearm. Kylie's hold was weak, though, and her palm started to slip. She tried to tighten her grip, lost it, and finally caught the girl by her wrist.

Ellie screamed and started to fight. Her eyes glowed a bright red in the darkness.

"It's me," Kylie said.

"Everyone, hang on!" Perry's voice bounced off the earthen walls of the pit.

Ellie struggled again, and Kylie pulled her closer. "I've got you."

And she did. Kylie put every ounce of thought and strength into not letting go of Ellie's wrist.

The sound of air *whoosh*ing and huge bird wings flapping filled the darkness, and in a few seconds, Perry lifted all three of them out of the hole. Once they were back in the light, he flew them about a hundred feet up the path before he descended and dropped them carefully on the solid earth.

He landed beside them, talons hitting the earth with a thud. As Kylie suspected, he'd shifted into a prehistoric-looking bird with dark gray feathers. He was about the size of a small plane. Then the rumble beneath the ground started again.

"Run!" he ordered.

He didn't have to tell them twice. Kylie and Ellie took off, flying through the woods, dodging trees, ducking under limbs, and leaping over thick bunches of thornbushes.

Kylie kept glancing up to make sure Perry was okay. He was still following them, gliding easily over the tips of the trees, making sure they were safe.

Once they were out of the trees, Kylie dropped to the ground and gasped for air, her pulse racing. She could hear her blood gushing in her veins. Ellie dropped down beside her, breathing not quite as hard, but still a little shaky.

Perry landed beside them and transformed himself back into human form.

"What the freaking hell were you doing?" he screamed at Kylie, his eyes blood red with fury.

She swallowed another gulp of air. "Trying to save you."

"I didn't need saving!" He flapped his arms up and down almost as if he'd forgotten he was no longer a bird. He turned his anger on Ellie. "And you? What the hell is your excuse?"

She coughed and then said, "I . . . figured if I came back alive and you two didn't, the rest of your group would probably kill me. I didn't have a choice but to go in after you."

Suddenly Burnett, eyes in full protective mode and his fangs exposed, flashed onto the scene. "What happened?" he asked, his voice little more than a deep growl. "It sounded like an explosion."

"Earthquake, maybe," Perry said. "The ground just sank below us."

"But that's—" Burnett shook his head. "Is everyone okay?"

They all nodded. Burnett's gaze locked on Kylie. "You're bleeding. Go to the office and let Holiday check you all out." Kylie looked down at her arm. Ellie's nails must have scratched her when she caught her.

Burnett continued, "I'll check to see how bad the, uh, earthquake is." He turned to go.

"Wait!" Kylie called out, and Burnett returned in a blur of motion.

"What?" he asked, impatience clear in his voice.

"It wasn't an earthquake," she said. With clarity, she recalled seeing the eagle coming straight at her in full-scale attack mode. Now she understood his intention had been to make her run, but it didn't change the fact that it had been evil. She'd seen the darkness in his eyes. "The eagle was there."

And so was Jane Doe, although Kylie saw no reason to mention that.

At least not yet.

Burnett let loose another growl. "Go to the office. I'll see if I can get to the bottom of this."

As Kylie, Ellie, and Perry moved toward the office, Kylie looked at Ellie. "Thanks for going in to try and save us."

Ellie shrugged. "Don't give me too much credit. I really didn't know what would happen to me if I was the only one to survive." She chuckled. "Now that it's over with, that was fun."

"No, it wasn't," Kylie said, remembering how she felt when she saw Perry fall into the hole.

They took a few more steps, and Ellie's gaze, bright probably because of the blood, shot to Kylie's arm where the scratches ran down her arm, and she added, "I'm sorry. I'll bet I did that when I was fighting you. Thanks for saving me. I don't know what would have happened if you hadn't caught me. I couldn't seem to get into flying mode. I owe you. You name it and I'll do it, no questions asked."

"No need. You're welcome," Kylie said.

"And what about me?" Perry asked.

Kylie and Ellie looked at Perry and spoke at the same time. "Thanks."

"Can I name it and you'll do it?" Perry wiggled his brows, his tone filled with humor once again.

"No," Ellie and Kylie said at the same time.

"I know, how about instead you two just tell Miranda how I was your hero."

"I can do that," Ellie said. "Who's Miranda?"

"My girlfriend," Perry said, and he looked at Kylie. "Well, she will be as soon as I convince her."

They took a few more steps and Ellie said, "I'm sorry I slept with Derek."

"Forget it," Kylie said, because she planned on forgetting it herself.

The next couple of hours were a blur of interrogations by Burnett, who questioned all three of them, separately, several times. Kylie realized he wasn't doing it because he thought anyone would lie about what happened. He just didn't want something one person said to influence the memory of the other. Kylie didn't care about that. What she wanted to know was what had happened. Had they really gotten sucked down into a pit that led straight to hell? If so, why? Was it because of Jane Doe? Or was this something conjured up by Mario and his pals to torment her?

More important, would it happen again?

Unfortunately, Burnett had questions of his own and no answers. Holiday was just as clueless. But the look of fear on the camp leaders' faces scared Kylie more than anything else.

The moment the interview was over and Kylie stepped out of Burnett's office, Lucas met her at the door and pulled her into another room. He didn't say a word; he just pulled her against his warm—so warm—chest and held her.

"I was running errands for Burnett." His cheek pressed against the top of her head. "I just got back."

After a good long hug, he set her back and asked, "What happened *this time*?"

It was the last two words that hinted at Lucas's true feelings. Kylie frowned. "You sound like you think this was all my fault."

He shook his head. "I don't think that. But damn it, I'd like to go at least a couple of days where I didn't think I almost lost you."

She smiled. "You didn't almost lose me." And then she gave him the quick version about the sinkhole opening up and their mad tumble down it.

He stared into her eyes. "Were there spirits involved?"

"No. Well, one was there, but . . ."

"But what?" he snapped. He shook his head and growled. "You've got to stop letting them hurt you, Kylie."

"They don't hurt me."

"Bullshit!" His blue eyes turned an anger-filled orange. "I saw part of your vision, remember? I had to stand there and feel completely helpless while those people dragged you away. Do you have any idea how that made me feel?"

Kylie knew Lucas's emotion stemmed partly from his werewolf instincts. Weres were known to have an intense need to protect those they cared about. And she liked knowing he cared about her.

But she had to make him understand that dealing with ghosts was as important to her as shifting into a wolf was to him. It was her destiny, her path.

Kylie put her hand on his chest. "The spirit didn't do this," she said. "It was probably Mario and his grandson again and their shape-shifter buddy. If anything, the spirit probably saved my life."

Okay, so she was guessing that was what had happened. But it made more sense to her than it did that Jane was somehow evil.

He inhaled. "Damn it. What's with that guy? Doesn't he know when to quit?"

"Obviously not."

Lucas pulled her against him again. "The timing of this sucks."

"What timing?" Kylie asked.

"I have to go away for a few days." He touched her face. "If it wasn't an emergency, I wouldn't go."

"What happened?" Even as she asked the question, Kylie worried he wouldn't tell her. Werewolves were also known to keep things to themselves.

"I told you about my half-sister. She was supposed to come here for school when the summer camp ended."

"Yeah?" Kylie said, thrilled he trusted her enough to share.

"Well, now my dad has her with his pack and is refusing to let her come. I'm going to have to go there and change his mind."

"I thought you didn't get along with your dad."

"I don't. But I don't have a choice. I shouldn't be gone more than a few days at most, though. I'm going to have Will keep an eye on you."

Kylie remembered Lucas introducing her to Will, another were-wolf, a while back. But as with most of the weres, she hardly knew him and didn't particularly like the idea of having a stranger "keep an eye on her."

"I'll be fine," she told him. "Burnett has assigned me shadows. I don't need—"

"It'll make me feel better. Knowing one of my own kind has your back."

Kylie didn't like being reminded that Lucas trusted his own kind more than he did the others. But she had too much stuff to worry about without taking on another problem to chew on her sanity.

"When are you leaving?" she asked.

"Now. I should be back by Saturday, or Sunday at the latest." He kissed her again. The kiss went on longer than a typical good-bye kiss, and it involved a lot of passion.

When he pulled away, she heard the slight humming sound rumbling from his chest.

She grinned with a hint of warning. "You're humming again."

He arched a brow. "You bring out the wolf in me." Leaning down, he gave her another quick kiss.

Seconds after he'd left, Kylie realized he hadn't said anything about asking her out this morning.

Was he having second thoughts? Closing her eyes, she pushed that worry into the mental closet with all her other worries.

Holiday walked into the room and hugged her. "I think we need a trip to the falls, don't you? How about I set it up with Burnett and tomorrow we make it a date?"

"That would be good," Kylie said. "Really good."

The next day, Kylie and Holiday ran through the cascading water of the falls and dropped down on the rocky bank. Tiny pinpoints of water spilled over from the rush of the falls and splattered against Kylie's face. Her hair, already soaked from the walk through the sheet of water, hung around her shoulders and dripped down onto her legs.

She didn't care. The serene atmosphere seeped into her pores, and for the first time in over a week, she felt at peace. She knew this didn't mean her problems were solved. They were far from it. But for right now, for this moment in time, she felt everything in her world was going to be okay.

Burnett, unhappy about their being here, stood guard outside. He'd been extra concerned about them coming out here because of yesterday's incident. That's how they were referring to the giant hole that nearly swallowed up Perry, Kylie, and Ellie: as the "incident."

The geologist they'd called in to look at the pit was calling it a freak of nature, a sinkhole. Kylie knew better, as did most of the campers at Shadow Falls. Amazingly, the size of the hole had shrunk before the scientist arrived. Magic, bad magic, was involved. This much Kylie knew, and Miranda had confirmed it, too.

Because of the weather and the thicket of trees, the security alarm hadn't picked up on any intruders. Burnett had been over-the-top pissed about that, too. Not at anyone in particular, but at the situation in general. She'd heard him on the phone with the FRU, telling them he needed a better security system ASAP.

But since whatever happened apparently came from underground, Kylie didn't know if a system existed that would detect underground intruders.

Powerful underground intruders who, for reasons Kylie didn't understand, wanted her dead.

Kylie breathed in the serenity of the falls. Amazing. Even the thought of being on someone's hit list couldn't ruin her peaceful mood.

Leaning back on her hands, she studied Holiday, who was doing the same. "You know, we should bring all the campers up here."

Holiday opened her eyes. "I wish it was that easy."

"What do you mean?"

"You don't bring someone to the falls, Kylie. They have to be called. Remember?"

Kylie did remember and was suddenly curious. "So why does the falls call some people and not others?"

"Don't know," Holiday said. "But it's said that they call less than half of one percent of all supernaturals."

"Are all of the ones called ghost whisperers?"

"All of the ones that I know of are. There are legends of the falls that go back thousands of years. The Native Americans called it sacred grounds and decreed that only the chosen could enter."

"Burnett entered," Kylie said.

"I know, and that shocks me."

"Because you don't think he's chosen?" Kylie asked.

"No, because he can't see spirits."

"You should have seen him watching you when everyone was greeting you at dinner the other night," Kylie said, acting on impulse. "I think he loves you, Holiday."

Holiday arched a brow. "Still trying to play matchmaker, huh?"

"Maybe I'm just trying to help out a couple of friends."

"Or maybe you're concentrating on someone else's problems so you don't have to think about your own."

"Perhaps," Kylie said with a shrug, "but right now my problems don't seem very bad." She gazed at the rock ceiling, marveling at the beauty of the rock's patterns.

Holiday chuckled. "It's amazing what happens in here, isn't it?" She inhaled. "I wish I could bottle it up and keep it in my purse to take a shot of when I needed it."

"Too bad we can't live in here," Kylie said.

"Have you seen the ghost since the incident?" Holiday stretched out her feet.

Kylie nodded. "She woke me up last night. I did what you said and asked if there was another body in the casket with her."

"What did she say?"

"Nothing. But she got that look again."

"What look?" Holiday asked.

"Like I'd jogged her memory or something. Whenever that happens, she disappears on me."

"Maybe she doesn't want to remember," Holiday said. Kylie heard the implication in the camp leader's voice: that Jane Doe didn't want to remember because she'd murdered innocent children.

"I think she's scared to remember," Kylie said, "but not for the reasons you believe."

"Then why is she so scared?"

Kylie hesitated. "Maybe it's the same reason I'm scared."

Holiday glanced over at her. "What are you scared of?"

"Of discovering the truth. Discovering what I am."

"Why?" Holiday asked as if confused.

"Because it's the unknown. Because it's been kept a secret from me all this time. Because it will probably change my life forever."

Kylie sat up straighter. "It's not that I don't want to know the truth. I do. I want to know it so bad I can taste it. Sometimes it's all I can think about. But I'm still scared. The day the Brightens, or the people we thought were the Brightens, came here, I was so scared my insides shook. I almost ran away. If Lucas hadn't come along, I probably would have."

Kylie swallowed hard. And that's when she decided to ask the question she'd longed to ask Holiday and hadn't had a chance to. "Have you seen any new spirits? Do you know if the elderly couple that came here that day died?"

"Their spirits haven't come to me, if that's what you're asking," Holiday answered.

Kylie bit down on her lip. "I can still remember how the old lady's hand felt on mine. For some reason, I don't think they were here to hurt me."

"Why else would they have been here, then?"

"I don't know." Kylie closed her eyes. "But just like I know that Jane Doe isn't a murderer, I kind of know that they weren't bad."

Holiday sat up and pulled her knees to her chest. "Maybe this is just your way of refusing to see the bad in people."

Kylie considered the theory for a second. Then she recalled the two times she'd seen the eagle and then the deer. She wasn't blind to evil. She could recognize it when she saw it, and it wasn't there with the faux Brightens. "Nope," she said. "That's not it."

Kylie's mind went back to Jane Doe. "Last night I remembered parts of the vision, and I recalled what the nurse told the doctor. That her husband—Jane Doe's husband—had just woken up and was asking about her."

"And you think that means something?" Holiday asked.

"Berta Littlemon was never married. And the vision makes me believe Jane Doe's husband had the same type of operation she had."

Holiday hesitated and then said, "Sometimes visions are hard to decipher."

"But all the other times I've had this type of vision, where I'm actually the person, they weren't puzzles that I had to piece together in order to figure out what they meant. They were scenes that actually took place."

"But the visions are from their perspective. And if Jane Doe is crazy, then . . ."

Kylie shook her head. "I don't think she's crazy. Or evil."

"I hope you're right," Holiday said.

"Me too."

They sat in silence for a long moment or two, just listening to the rush of water and the sound of calm. Kylie looked at Holiday again and felt the slightest bit of worry whisper across her mind. "What am I going to say to Sara when she comes here on Sunday?"

"You don't tell her anything, except how happy you are that she's well."

"It's going to be so weird having her here. She's from my old world, and my old world shouldn't be in my new world. It's like running into your Sunday school teacher at a kegger."

Holiday chuckled. "Or your gynecologist at the grocery store. I did that once. It was so weird." She reached over and rested her hand on Kylie's.

Normally, Holiday's touch brought nothing but calm, but not this time. This time, everything went black.

Chapter Twenty-seven

For a second, it felt as if someone had turned the lights off. Kylie could feel Holiday's hand on hers, but the cave was pitch black.

Then the lights came back on. Kylie looked around, feeling confused. They were no longer in the falls. Instead, she sat in an uncomfortable folding metal chair outside in a clearing under some kind of dark-colored awning. The wind smelled like rain. It was a cloudy day, and she felt sad. So much sadness.

What happened to the serenity of the falls? What the heck had just happened?

It took her a second to realize this was a vision. She wasn't sure what she was supposed to see this time, but she didn't care. She didn't want to see it.

Kylie tried to pull herself out of it. She wanted to be back, back where everything felt right, where calm was all around her, where the sound of water soothed her mind.

When that didn't work, she tried to figure out where she was. Her breath caught when she saw a casket sitting in front of the enclosure. Quiet tears filled her eyes, and she knew someone she cared about lay in that box.

"No," she whispered. "Please, no."

Someone touched her hand. Kylie recognized Holiday's touch before she looked over to see the camp leader sitting next to her. She wore somber black clothes, no makeup, and unshed tears made her sad green eyes look brighter than usual.

Then someone started talking from up near the casket. Kylie looked up, and Chris, the lead vampire, the one who did the Meet Your Campmates hour, stood beside the coffin. "We lost one of our own today. It's our custom when a vampire dies that . . ."

"No," Kylie whispered again, and suddenly she realized she was standing up, back in the falls. The sadness filling her chest now came with a less painful emotion, one that made it easier to breathe, but it still hurt.

She looked at Holiday, who sat on the rock, her arms holding her knees tight to her chest. The tears in her eyes told Kylie that Holiday hadn't just been in Kylie's vision. She'd actually experienced it herself.

Someone lives and someone dies. The words seemed to flow from the rock themselves and bounce around the stone walls.

Kylie looked at Holiday. "What does this mean?"

Holiday blinked and Kylie saw her attempt to put on a brave face. "Whatever happens, we'll be okay."

"*We* will," Kylie said, fighting the calmer feeling and letting the feeling of grief take the lead. "But someone here isn't going to be okay. We have to do something to save her. Or him."

It's our custom when a vampire dies that . . .

Chris's words tore at her heart. *When a vampire dies . . .* Oh, God. Please say it's not Della, or Burnett.

Holiday shook her head. "There's nothing to be done, Kylie." She inhaled. "Can't you feel it? Acceptance." Tears filled her eyes again. "It breaks my heart, but that's what they are telling us. Someone we love will die, and we have to accept it."

"But I don't want to accept it." Kylie turned and walked through the wall of water to the sunlight.

The instant her gaze landed on Burnett, all the calm from the falls shattered around her. The acceptance she'd felt earlier was little more than a vague memory.

Please not Burnett. Please not Della. Please not Burnett.

She repeated the mantra over and over in her mind, as though wishing would make it so. She wanted to run to him, to grab him by his hands and make him swear to her that he would be careful, that he wouldn't take any unnecessary risks.

But even as she thought those thoughts, she knew in her heart that nothing, and no one, would stop Burnett from being himself. And that meant him taking risks.

Kylie felt Holiday come to a stop beside her. Kylie glanced at the camp leader. Her gaze was locked on Burnett, and Kylie knew she'd been having the same thoughts about his safety that Kylie had.

Someone lives and someone dies. The words repeated themselves in her head.

"Are you guys ready?" Miranda called out on Friday evening from the living room.

Kylie sighed. Miranda was nervous. Tonight was her big date with Todd, the cute warlock, and Kylie and Della were going to go wait with her at the main gate.

"Just about." Kylie grabbed her hairbrush and gave her hair a few strokes, not really caring if her hair looked as though a bird had taken up residence there.

The last few days had passed by her in a haze. Accepting that someone was trying to kill her was bad, but trying to accept that someone she cared about, a vampire, was about to die was impossible.

She and Holiday had butted heads about trying to stop the vision they'd shared from becoming a reality. What if it was Della? Didn't Holiday care that it could be Burnett? Kylie had mentally gone through a list of all the vampires at camp. Some of them she didn't know all that well, but they didn't deserve to die. Kylie had come within a breath of telling Della about the vision, but just as she was about to say it, a wave of knowing passed over her. She couldn't tell.

For reasons Kylie didn't understand, she simply knew it would be wrong.

Holiday kept pointing out that Kylie was forgetting the message came with two parts. Someone lives. But what about the someone who dies? "You can't change Fate," Holiday had insisted.

Kylie still wanted to kick Fate's ass. The acceptance that had filled Kylie at the falls occasionally returned and tried to numb the ache. It helped, but not completely.

"I'm waiting," yelled Miranda again.

So am I. Kylie looked at the ghost sitting on the edge of the bed.

"One more minute," Kylie answered Miranda. The ghost was pregnant again, and she just sat there, holding her round belly as if to protect it.

"We have to talk, you know," Kylie whispered.

The spirit didn't answer.

"If you want me to help you, we have to talk."

She still didn't speak.

"I know the other ghosts think you did horrible things, but I don't really believe it. I'm trying to prove it, but I don't know if I can do it alone. I need your help."

More silence met Kylie's pleas. Then she heard Miranda calling again.

Kylie looked at the ghost. "I have to go now." She reached for her door and inhaled, knowing she needed to put on a front for Miranda, who was excited about her date with Todd. Never mind that the girl had asked Kylie at least ten times to tell her the story about how Perry had saved both her and Ellie from the sinkhole.

Miranda needed to make up her mind. But people who lived in glass houses shouldn't throw rocks. And she'd spent a lot of time in that particular glass house herself, trying to decide between Derek and Lucas.

Not anymore.

And she meant it, too. She did.

She missed Lucas. And when he came back, she was telling him straight out that she wanted to go out with him.

Last night, she'd even tried to find him in her dreams. Had Lucas been awake at the time, or could the pack somehow stop her from reaching him? She didn't know. So this morning, she'd found another way to contact him. Through that all-powerful thing called a cell phone.

He couldn't talk about what was happening there. She couldn't tell him about the issues with Fate. And telling him yes to going out with him just seemed like something she wanted to do in person. But they talked for about twenty minute about other things, like the vacations they'd had as children.

He'd visited about every foreign country Kylie had ever heard of and some that she hadn't. But he hadn't ever been to Disney World or to a real amusement park, for that matter, and she'd told him all about them. They'd decided to make that their first real date.

Just as soon as Kylie was removed from someone's hit list and free of her mandatory shadow.

Walking out of her bedroom, Kylie found Miranda pacing by the door. She looked pretty; she wore her hair swept up, with only a few soft blond strands falling around her neck. The different colors in her hair hardly showed when she wore it up.

She wore a sleeveless yellow sundress that had a few ruffles around the bottom and a pair of matching yellow sandals. The outfit was very feminine without looking too cute, sexy without looking slutty, and dressy without looking overdressed. For just a second, Kylie envied Miranda and her evening out. She wished Lucas were here and they could go somewhere away from the camp.

Somewhere she could forget about Fate snatching away one of her own.

Della stood up from the computer desk. Kylie's heart knotted at the mere possibility that it was her in that casket, and then she remembered bits and pieces of the conversation she'd had with Holiday this morning.

"Everyone is going to die sometime, Kylie."

Kylie could tell that Holiday tried to be brave for her. But if the camp leader's eyes were any indication, she'd cried as much as Kylie had and hadn't slept any more than Kylie, either.

"Fine," Kylie had retaliated. "But why tell us this? Why, if we can't prevent it, just to torture us with knowing it beforehand?"

"For some reason, they thought we needed to be warned."

"Well, they thought wrong!"

"They are seldom wrong, Kylie."

"Well, there's always a first time, isn't there!"

"Earth to Kylie!" Della yelled, bringing Kylie back to the present. "What is it with you? Did your little trip to hell mess up your mind?" Della grinned.

"What are you talking about?" Kylie asked.

"You keep staring at me and going blank. You've done it for almost two days now, and it's freaking me out a bit."

"I'm sorry."

"It's probably because she misses her hunky werewolf." Miranda placed a hand over her heart. "She's heartsick. Her aura is all grayish. She's gone without his kisses for almost two days." Then Miranda opened the front door and waved them out.

"Poor little thing," Della said.

Kylie rolled her eyes and followed them out. Good thing she liked her roommates, or she might really be pissed.

They hadn't stepped off the porch when Ellie, with a couple of other vampires, walked past.

Ellie shot over to Kylie. "How are your scratches?"

"Gone." Kylie held out her arm.

"Good." Just a bit of awkwardness moved in, and Ellie apparently noticed. "I'll see you."

"Yeah," Kylie said, and Ellie turned to go. It dawned on Kylie that in the vision, the person in the casket could have been Ellie. "Ellie?"

She swung around, and Kylie didn't know what she wanted to say; she just didn't want Ellie to leave thinking she'd been rude. "Thanks," Kylie blurted out.

Ellie looked puzzled. "For what?"

"For . . . being considerate enough to ask about my arm." *Okay, that sounded so lame.*

"Oh. You're welcome." Ellie walked backward, waved, then swung around and ran to catch up with her group.

"What was that all about?" Della asked when Ellie was out of hearing range and they were down the porch steps.

"Yeah," Miranda said. "I mean, if I'd found out someone had boinked my boyfriend, I wouldn't be so nice."

"Derek wasn't my boyfriend," Kylie said.

"Yeah, and bears don't do it in the woods, either," Della said.

Kylie held up her hands. "Stop it, okay? I don't care what happened between Ellie and Derek."

Della mouthed the word *liar* and then said, "Truth is, I don't like the chick. I hate the way she's so friendly and nice. Gives my kind a bad name."

Kylie frowned at Della. "Don't mistreat her because of this. I'm serious, Della. She didn't know about me when it happened."

"Okay," Della said. "That means she's not devious. But it still makes her a slut."

Miranda laughed and Kylie moaned. "I don't think she's like

that." Kylie hesitated and then added, "She jumped in the sinkhole, willing to risk her life to save Perry and me."

"Yeah, she did do that," Miranda said. "But it doesn't change the fact that—"

"Damn it! Can we just *not* talk about it," Kylie said.

"Man," Miranda said. "It must be time for your lunar PMS, because Della's right. You haven't been yourself lately. You're like majorly grumpy."

Kylie wished Miranda were right. That her mood hinged on nothing more than her being a werewolf, instead of her other long list of problems.

And if she ended up being a were, Lucas would be happy. Really happy.

"Shit!" Miranda muttered thirty minutes later.

They were still waiting for Todd, who'd gotten lost and had called Miranda and told her he was three minutes away.

"Shit what?" Della asked, but then said, "Oh, shit."

"What?" Kylie asked, obviously the only one in the dark.

Then she saw it, or rather him, and she completely agreed with the assessment. "Oh, shit."

"Hey," Perry said as he moved in. Kylie couldn't help noticing that he'd gotten his hair cut and wore a tighter-fitting shirt and jeans. Something about his haircut made him appear older, more of a man than a young teen. The way his shirt hugged his upper torso accented his broad shoulders. His eyes were blue, and the way they twinkled when he looked at Miranda had Kylie's heart melting. Confidence seemed to ooze from his smile. Even his body posture spoke of a coolness she'd never seen him exude. For the first time, Kylie spotted what it was that Miranda found so attractive about Perry.

"Looking hot," Della said, obviously noticing the same thing.

"Why, thank you." His blue eyes sparkled as he shifted his gaze back to Miranda. "But I'm not the only one looking good tonight. Really good."

"Thanks." Miranda looked at Kylie as if begging her to do something.

Kylie glanced at Della, who just grinned.

"Uh, Perry . . ." Kylie started talking, not sure how she would fix this. "We were just sort of talking, privately, about—"

"About Miranda's date," Perry said.

"Oh, shit," Della said again.

Ditto, Kylie wanted to say.

Perry focused on Miranda. "I know about your date."

Miranda shot Kylie a look as if accusing her of spilling the beans.

Kylie shook her head no and refocused on Perry. His eyes changed from blue to bright green, but if Perry was about to wig out on them and change into some kind of warlock-eating monster, he gave no other indication. "I just wanted to tell you that while I don't like it, I'm hoping you'll give me the same chance you're giving this asswad . . . I mean, this guy."

Della chuckled.

"Go out with me tomorrow night," Perry went on. "Let me prove to you that I'm the guy you want."

Miranda opened her mouth to say something, but nothing came out. Kylie couldn't talk either, because she felt a lump in her throat—a lump of emotion and pride for Perry.

"I . . . I guess I could go out tomorrow night." Miranda sounded shocked and a little swept off her feet.

Then, from the corner of her eyes, Kylie saw something move at the office window. When she looked back, she spotted Burnett and Holiday standing there high-fiving each other. No doubt Burnett was listening to the conversation and sharing the details with Holiday.

Kylie should have guessed someone had helped out Perry. She was a little embarrassed she hadn't tried this herself. He so deserved his shot with Miranda.

Perry nodded, stepped closer, and then pressed a quick kiss on Miranda's cheek. It had to be the most romantic thing Kylie had ever seen.

If only the tan truck, with a personalized license plate that read TODD, hadn't pulled up right then.

"Oh, shit," Della said again.

Ditto.

Chapter Twenty-eight

Todd, a fairly hot-looking guy with sandy-colored hair, jumped out of his truck and frowned. He obviously didn't miss that Perry stood touch-me close to Miranda. From the look on Todd's face, he hadn't missed the kiss, either.

"Someone trying to steal my date?" Todd's words could have been meant in humor, but his tone told another story. He strode forward and dropped a possessive arm around Miranda's shoulders.

Kylie saw Perry's entire body stiffen. His eyes turned a bright red.

Todd, still studying Perry, tightened his brows to check out Perry's pattern.

The teen's jaw dropped a little when he realized exactly what Perry was. Kylie waited for the puddle to appear around the guy's feet.

The office door opened and shut behind them.

"Uh, Perry? Can I see you a minute?" Burnett called.

Kylie moved in close to Perry. "Don't screw it up, now," she whispered.

Perry, anger oozing from his pores, continued to stare at Todd. Kylie could feel the electricity start to buzz and hum around the shape-shifter.

"Don't do it," Kylie repeated in a whisper.

Perry looked back at Burnett, then at Kylie, and then back at Miranda. "I'll see you tomorrow night," he said, but his tone was so tight, Kylie knew what it cost him to keep his composure.

Then he turned around, transformed himself into his favorite bird, and flew up, making tight circles around them.

Della leaned over to Kylie. "He's going to crap on Todd's car, just watch!"

Kylie did watch and hoped Della was wrong. Okay, it would have been really funny, because as big of a bird as Perry was, that would have been a lot of crap, but Kylie didn't think it would impress Miranda. And that, she realized, was what this had been all about.

Still, Kylie didn't relax until Perry changed directions and flew back toward the woods.

"Hey, I know. Why don't we go to the swimming hole tonight?" Della suggested fifteen minutes later on the walk back to their cabin. "A bunch of campers have attached a swing to one of the higher cliffs so we can jump into the water. I'm dying to try it."

It was the word *dying* that had Kylie catching her breath. She'd mostly blocked Jane Doe's warning from her mind and had no idea why she suddenly felt so overwhelmed by emotion. "No." She blurted out the answer so fast that Della made a face.

"Why?"

Because you could die. "Because . . ." Kylie struggled to explain the situation until she remembered she had a real reason. "Because Holiday is bringing Burnett's computer over for me to use."

"Why would you need his computer when we have one?"

"To send an e-mail to . . . It's a ghost thing. I'm sending an e-mail to a deceased woman's family, trying to clear up their heritage, and Burnett has an untraceable e-mail address," Kylie said.

"Oh." Della fell silent. Funny how mentioning the word *ghost* was a conversation killer.

"So, what time is she showing up?" she asked finally. "I might run to the swimming hole while she's with you."

And you could get killed. Nope. Not happening. "But you're my shadow."

"Holiday let Jonathon leave early when she was there."

"But that was before the sinkhole." Her explanation sounded convincing, and the knot in Kylie's stomach relaxed. She might not be able to tell Della about Fate's premonition or whatever it was Holiday called it, but it wouldn't stop her from watching out for Della.

"Okay," Della said, but she didn't look happy about it. Which was fine with Kylie. An unhappy but alive Della was better than the alternative.

A group of campers rounded the corner and walked past them. Kylie felt the cold stare practically slap her, and when she recognized one of the girls as a werewolf, she figured she knew whose cold stare gave her shivers.

Another glance at the group confirmed her suspicions.

Fredericka.

Kylie kept walking past them, hoping to ignore—

"Hey, blondie," Fredericka called out.

Closing her eyes for a second, Kylie willed herself patience. When she turned, she found herself staring Fredericka right in the eyes. The were had silently moved in and stood so close that Kylie could count Fredericka's eyelashes. The were smirked in an unappealing way. And that's when Kylie had an epiphany.

She wasn't afraid.

Fredericka with her I'll-rip-you-to-shreds attitude didn't scare her anymore. She annoyed Kylie to no end, made her feel something akin to jealousy—although she trusted Lucas not to cheat—but nope, there wasn't an ounce of fear.

"What do you need?" Kylie put her hand out to stop Della from getting between them. Della, probably livid at being held back, growled and exposed her canines. Fredericka's eyes turned a bright pissed-off orange.

"I thought you'd like to know that Lucas phoned me and told me he's not returning until late tomorrow night," the were said in a sickly sweet voice. "He's having issues with his dad. Sad stuff. Poor guy. He needed someone to talk to."

Kylie knew the only reason Fredericka told her this was to annoy her.

And it worked.

But Kylie's pride had her smiling and pretending everything was great. But darn if there wasn't a part of her that didn't want to kick Fredericka's ass and worry about the consequences later.

"Thanks for letting me know. I'll look for his call in a bit." She smiled extra sweetly right back at Fredericka and walked away.

Fredericka caught her by the arm. Her fingers dug into Kylie's elbow. Kylie almost attempted to pull away. Then she remembered that if everyone was right about her being a protector, she wouldn't have the power to take on the were.

The only way Kylie could take on Fredericka was if she tried to hurt someone Kylie cared about.

And considering that other person was Della, and there might be a death cloud hanging around her and every other vampire at Shadow Falls, Kylie wasn't about to let Della get involved.

Kylie would have to use her wits to get out of this. Did she have enough?

"Do you want to let go of my arm?" Kylie pretended like it didn't feel as if her bones were about to be crushed under the were's grasp.

"Not really," Fredericka growled.

"Okay, but don't say I didn't warn you. Because I've got this spirit hanging around and she's been in a piss-poor mood for about thirty years." It was a lie. Pure lie. But Kylie wasn't above using what she could. "Ever since she was killed by a rogue werewolf, she's been aching—"

Fredericka's hand dropped. "Go to hell."

Kylie smiled. "Thanks for the invite, but I almost went there yesterday and didn't like it all that much." Kylie then wrinkled her nose. "Is that skunk I smell?"

Fredericka's eyes turned burnt orange and Kylie knew she'd pushed too far. The were's hand clamped down on Kylie's elbow and tightened. Someone darted out of the woods. From the corner of Kylie's eyes, she saw it was Will, Lucas's friend.

He cleared his throat, and the she-wolf didn't even look at him. She just dropped her hold on Kylie and took off with a tail-tucked-between-her-legs kind of look.

Kylie didn't like realizing that Will had been hounding her footsteps, unseen. The fact that neither Kylie nor Della had sensed he'd been hounding them told her he was good at it, too.

Della glared at him, but Kylie did the right thing. "Thanks."

"No problem." He disappeared back into the woods.

"What the hell did you say 'thank you'? We didn't need him intervening. I could have opened a can of whoop ass on that she-wolf and she'd have been whimpering like a hungry pup."

And she might have killed you.

They had gotten only a few feet away when Kylie remembered what Fredericka said about Lucas calling her. Pausing, she pulled out her phone to see if she'd missed his call.

Nope.

The were could have been lying. How could Kylie ever know? Then . . . duh, the obvious hit. Della, like the rest of her kind, was a walking, talking lie detector. She could hear heartbeats and pulse rates and knew when someone was telling a lie.

Kylie looked at Della. "Was Fredericka telling the truth about Lucas calling her?"

Della made a face. "Is lying wrong if you know it's what the person wants to hear?"

"Just tell me!"

Della mouthed the word *sorry*. "She was telling the truth."

After Kylie arrived back at the cabin, Holiday came over with Burnett's laptop and they sent an e-mail to Catherine O'Connell's family. They'd concocted a story about being an old friend of Catherine's and thought her family should know that she had wanted to tell them something right before she'd passed away. It sounded good. Convincing, even. And then they did a cut and paste of all the family tree information that came with photos.

Hopefully, it would do the trick. Not that Kylie suspected she'd ever know for sure. But she felt good about keeping her part of the bargain. Never mind that the information Kylie got from her about Berta Littlemon had yet to give her any answers. And Kylie hoped it didn't. The last thing she wanted to discover was that she was wrong about Jane Doe.

While Holiday and Della chatted at the table, Kylie sent her stepfather an e-mail and told him the shift schedule if he wanted to come on Sunday to Parents Day. She hoped he'd e-mail back and say he couldn't make it so she wouldn't have to deal with Sara and her stepdad on the same day. His e-mail came back superfast. He said he looked forward to seeing her on Sunday.

"Crap," Kylie muttered.

Holiday glanced over at her. "Bad news?"

"No, everything is just friggin' fabulous," Kylie said, and dropped her head on the desk. She didn't know if she would survive.

"Are you okay?" Holiday asked when Kylie walked her outside a few minutes later.

"As good as can be expected, I guess," Kylie lied. Holiday nodded and they said their good-nights.

When Kylie got back inside the cabin, Della was answering e-mails and Kylie sat at the kitchen table. She longed to call it a night, but she wanted to be here when Miranda got back from her date with Todd.

Kylie looked at the clock on the wall. That could be several more hours from now, though. Hours that Kylie had to fret over her own problems.

Della swung around. "That's not good. Or maybe it is."

"What?" Kylie asked.

Della pointed to the door and Miranda walked in. Her face was unreadable. She moved over to the table and dropped into a chair with as much drama as she could muster.

"And?" Kylie asked, and spotted hope in Della's eyes. Kylie knew that Della hoped the same thing Kylie did.

Hoped that the date was a complete bust and Perry still had a shot.

Miranda merely shrugged.

"Don't do this!" Della snapped. "Spill it or I'll reach down your throat for the answer myself."

Miranda spoke up. "He was . . . nice. Dinner was nice. Holding his hand was nice."

"Did he kiss you?" Kylie asked, unsure how Miranda defined "nice." If Kylie worked hard enough, she could believe "nice" meant it wasn't anything special.

Miranda nodded. "The kiss was . . ."

"Let me guess," Della said. "It was nice."

"Right," Miranda said.

Della slapped her hand on the table. " 'Nice' is just another way of saying 'friggin' boring'!"

Miranda frowned. "That's exactly what I thought."

Kylie and Della both squealed with excitement.

"What?" Miranda asked. "You're happy my date wasn't exciting?"

"No," Kylie said. "Let's just say we're more excited about tomorrow night's date."

A bright smile lit up Miranda's face. "Me too. Can you believe Perry did that? I mean, he was so . . ."

"Romantic," Kylie said.

"Hot," Della added.

"Sweet," Miranda whispered. "I couldn't stop thinking about him all night."

And that was the best news Kylie had gotten all day.

That night, Kylie stared at the ceiling forever, craving sleep that didn't come. One hour passed. Then two.

Her mind started naming off her problems. She still didn't know what she was. She couldn't stop Fate from taking someone she cared about. She had someone wanting her dead, probably the rogue underground paranormal gang headed by Mario, who still hadn't forgiven her for not wanting to marry his murdering grandson. Lucas was calling and chatting with Fredericka. Sara was coming to visit on Sunday with Kylie's mom. And her stepdad was going to drop by, too. Kylie still hadn't solved her amnesia spirit's issues, and she wasn't even a hundred percent sure the woman wasn't a killer.

Kylie's sleep-deprived brain chewed on each and every issue and didn't spit out any answers. She'd just fallen asleep when she heard a light *tap-tap* on her bedroom window.

At first, she thought she'd imagined it. Then she thought it was the blue jay again. "I'm not your mama," Kylie muttered.

The tapping stopped.

Kylie lay there, listening. The silence suddenly seemed ominous. She took in a shallow breath, and the sound seemed abnormally loud. The window was locked, right?

She recalled opening it the day before, hoping to invite in a breeze. And no, she couldn't recall locking it afterward.

But hey . . . considering the types of intruders Kylie feared the most, the kind that could create sinkholes and materialize out of thin air, what was the chance a locked window would stop them?

So why, Kylie wondered, did the distinct sound of someone lifting her window send sharp jolts of fear straight to her heart?

Chapter Twenty-nine

Kylie bounced out of bed, and her heart leapt with her. Her gaze shot to the window, where she saw two hands gripping the windowsill.

A scream rose in her throat, but then Della's voice echoed outside the window. "Try to crawl in the window and I'm gonna crawl up your ass! And the position is just about right for me to do it."

The hands disappeared. Someone hit the ground.

Kylie ran to the window to make sure Della didn't engage in a fatal fight. Della, in her loose-fitting blue cotton Mickey Mouse pajamas, had her hands on her hips, standing over someone laid out on the lawn. Her eyes were a bright green.

"Shit!" Ellie said, her own eyes glowing. "I just wanted to talk to Kylie." She looked over at the window to Kylie and grabbed her baseball hat that read, LITTLE VAMP.

"See that?" Della pointed toward the front porch. "It's called a door. And most people use them."

"I didn't want to wake anyone else."

"Then you wait until a decent hour!" Della countered.

Kylie didn't know what Ellie wanted to discuss, but if it had anything to do with Derek, Kylie was willing to hear her out.

"It's okay," Kylie said. "Come on in."

"Oh, right. Reward bad behavior!" Della looked disgusted, but Kylie couldn't help it.

Ellie smirked at Della, then stood and started to climb in the window again.

Della yanked her back. "Use the freaking door!"

When Kylie walked out of her bedroom, Della was gone and Ellie sat on the sofa.

"What's up?" She went over and sat in the chair next to her.

She looked up. "I don't know, I just wanted to talk."

"About what?" Kylie asked.

Ellie pulled one leg up to her chest. "A couple of things. Derek said you might be a good person to talk to about my issues."

Kylie chest tightened. "If this is about you and Derek—"

"No." She rolled her eyes. "I wasn't lying when I said there was nothing between us . . . romantically. I like Derek as a friend. A good friend, but that's all. And that's some of what I wanted to talk about."

"I'm not following you," Kylie said.

"I'm worried about Derek. He's really upset about you two, and I sort of feel it's my fault. And when something's your fault, you feel responsible for fixing it."

Kylie frowned. "It's not your fault. Things weren't going right when he left."

"Yeah, he said that . . . but still . . ."

"It's not your fault." Kylie cupped her knees in her palms. Did Derek really regret everything? The question hung somewhere between her head and her heart. "What's the other thing you needed to talk about?" she asked, not wanting to discuss Derek. She wasn't ready to delve into that Pandora box of emotions. The past was the past.

Ellie shrugged and adjusted her cap again. "I just don't think I belong here. I feel bad that Holiday worked so hard to get me accepted, but . . . I think it's best I go."

Kylie leaned forward. "You want to leave Shadow Falls?"

"Yeah." She frowned. "All of it just doesn't feel right."

Her words didn't make sense, so Kylie just shook her head. "All of what?"

She glanced at Della's bedroom door and scooted over to the end of the sofa, closer to Kylie, and lowered her voice. "The whole supernatural world. Derek said you would probably understand because you felt the same way for a while. I mean, don't you miss it? Don't you miss being normal? Just hanging with your old friends? I want that back. I miss . . . Before I worried about what I wanted to take in college. Now I worry about where I'm going to get my next pint of blood."

"You can't leave, Ellie. I'm not mad at you, if that's what this is about. I mean, at first I was hurt, but . . ."

"It's not that. Really," Ellie said. "Even my own kind here aren't exactly welcoming," she whispered. "But that's not even it. Nothing about being this"—she waved a hand up and down her body—"feels right. I miss . . . being human. I miss my mom, who died a couple of years ago." Her voice shook with emotion. "Maybe if I just lived among humans, I would feel better."

A wave of empathy for Ellie washed over Kylie. Damn if she didn't know exactly how the girl felt. "It's hard," Kylie said. "But you can't leave here. Holiday says that most of the young vampires end up joining gangs just to survive." A question slammed into Kylie's mind. Was Ellie the vampire who was going to die? Was she going to leave Shadow Falls and get mixed up in something terrible?

The question caused Kylie to catch her breath.

Della's bedroom door opened and she flashed across the room and stopped right in front of them, her hair a little in disarray. Kylie got an image of her burying her head under a pillow, trying not to listen. Not that her plan worked.

Both Kylie and Ellie looked at Della.

Ellie scowled. "You've been listening, haven't you? Can't a person have—"

"Yeah, nitwit. I tried not to, but I've been listening," she said in her best smartass tone. "But Kylie's right. You can't leave. Nothing is easy about being us, or trying to fit into a new family of vampires, but it gets easier."

"How?" Ellie asked.

Miranda's door swung open. "You make friends," she said, and stumbled into the room, looking half-asleep.

"Does everyone listen in to everyone else's conversations in this cabin?" Ellie asked, sounding annoyed.

"Pretty much." Miranda came over and dropped on the sofa beside Ellie. "Friends don't keep very many secrets."

"But you guys aren't my friends."

"We could be," Kylie said, and Della and Miranda nodded.

Ellie's gaze widened and she looked away, but not before Kylie saw emotion in her eyes. The warm sensation filling Kylie's chest reminded her of the feeling she got at the falls, and she knew it had been the right thing to say. Then for some crazy reason, she saw a flash of the funeral vision in her mind.

Was that a sign? Did that mean Ellie really was the person in the casket? And had this changed the outcome?

Saturday was about two things. Well, three if you counted Miranda's unending attempt to change Socks back to feline form. The other two things were: emotionally getting ready for Parents Day and getting Miranda ready for her date with Perry.

Holiday had stopped by with a plan for tomorrow. Instead of locking Socks in her closet during Parents Day, she thought it would be a good idea to cart the little stinker over to her cabin for the day. That way, Kylie, Della, and Miranda could bring Kylie's mom and

Sara back to the cabin and hang out, making it hard for Sara to ask too many questions about the whole healing process.

Since Kylie pretty much decided that no amount of effort would prepare her emotionally for seeing Sara here at camp, or for having to face her stepdad again, she put all that out of her mind and focused her energy into getting Miranda ready for her date.

When Miranda, a nervous witch, vetoed everything in her own closet, Della and Kylie gave her carte blanche with their own. Ellie even came over for an hour to help get Miranda ready. It was a little awkward, but . . . Derek was right; Ellie really was a nice person. Besides, Kylie hadn't been able to forget the feeling she'd gotten last night, a sense that Ellie had been the one in the casket in that vision. And maybe, just perhaps, befriending Ellie had saved her life.

After trying on about six outfits, Miranda chose Kylie's LBD, little black dress.

At seven o'clock, Perry showed up on their doorstep, looking as much of a hottie as he had the night before. Burnett had loaned him his Mustang, and supposedly, Perry had a night planned that would knock Miranda's socks off.

When Miranda showed up a little past midnight, she had indeed lost her socks. And her shoes. Of course, she didn't need them because she practically floated through the door.

When Kylie and Della demanded details, Miranda said only, "It was a hell of a lot better than nice." Then she floated into her bedroom and went to bed.

Having done a little celebratory dance with Della, Kylie went to bed and waited to see if Lucas would call her. She almost called him but decided against it. She'd called him last time. It was time he made the next move. As she might have guessed, though, her phone never rang. But the ghost dropped by for another cold, silent visit.

Kylie begged her to talk, and she finally spoke, but not anything helpful. *It's not your fault. That's what they wanted me to tell you.*

"What's not my fault?" she spouted out. The spirit faded, and the cold ache in the room swelled in Kylie chest and reminded her that she was no closer to solving Jane's problems than she was to solving her own.

Sunday morning, when Kylie, with Della in tow, got back to her cabin after breakfast, Lucas sat on the front porch. The moment his gaze touched hers, her heart started racing. He looked good. Was it her imagination that he looked more masculine and somehow buffer, or was it because of the approaching full moon?

He smiled at her, and she smiled back, feeling herself melt a little inside. She wanted to run into his arms and kiss him. But she knew he wouldn't like that in front of Della.

Then all those warm, gooey feelings faded when she wondered if he'd already visited Fredericka. But damn it, jealousy was such an ugly emotion.

"Don't even ask," Della said as she stepped on the porch. "I'll go inside and let you two make out." She opened the door and looked back over her shoulder. "But if you take her off this porch, I'll hunt you down."

"I won't." He nodded his thanks.

The moment the door closed, Lucas pulled Kylie into his arms. "I missed you," he whispered, and his lips melted against hers.

His kiss was light but still passionate. He held her close and she felt the subtle differences in him that she'd noted earlier—all muscle, all male. Hard in all the places she was soft.

When the kiss ended, she ran her fingers over his shoulders. "Do you get . . . buffer the closer we get to a full moon?"

He smiled and pressed his forehead against hers. "Yes. It's my body's way of preparing for the shift." He swung around and leaned against the front of the cabin. Then he pulled her against him and slid his hand down to rest on her waist.

"Did you miss me?" he asked.

"Of course." She smiled at him, breathing in his scent and loving being close.

"No new ghost disasters since I left?" He arched one dark brow.

"No," she said. "No disasters. Except, I was sort of hoping you'd call me back. It's been two days."

"I'm sorry. My dad was being an ass and I had to stay longer than I'd anticipated. Didn't Fredericka tell you?"

Kylie's annoyance peaked. "Yeah, but it would have been nice if you'd called me yourself."

His gaze tightened as if he were trying to read her. "It's not like . . . The only reason I called her was because Clara wanted to talk to her."

"Clara?" Kylie asked.

"My half-sister. She and Fredericka got to know each other when she went back with me before."

Great! Lucas's sister was friends with Fredericka. Kylie's jealousy inched up another notch.

He stared into her eyes. "I heard Will had to calm down Fredericka. I'll talk to her about it."

Kylie instantly realized she didn't want him talking to Fredericka. She bit down on her lip. Could she tell Lucas he couldn't be friends with Fredericka when she wouldn't want him telling her whom she could, and couldn't, be friends with?

No. She couldn't. So she just said, "Don't worry. I handled it." She stared at his chest for a second, trying to get her wayward jealousy under control.

He tilted her chin up and his blue eyes gazed into hers. "You okay?"

"Yeah," she lied. "Just . . . a little worried about later. Seeing my stepdad and then Sara showing up."

"Can I do anything to help? All you have to do is ask."

Her heart tightened at his concerned tone. Lucas cared about her. She knew that. She believed it. Which meant she couldn't let Fredericka come between them. She just couldn't.

"You just did by being here." She gave him a long hug.

It wasn't until he left that she realized neither of them had said anything about him asking her out.

Kylie and Della went to the dining hall a little early to offer Holiday their help. Miranda had stayed behind to get all dolled up, in case Perry saw her.

Miranda and Della—the vamp in full moody mode, probably because she had to see her parents today—had bickered all morning. Kylie reminded them both to be on their best behavior around her mom and Sara. She honestly didn't care if they argued in front of her stepdad.

Well, maybe she cared a little, but Sara and her mom were more important.

They had just about gotten to the end of the path when someone called, "Wait up." Kylie turned, and Ellie, with a bright smile, came running up to join them.

Ellie grinned and reached over as if to hug Della. The fast embrace knocked Ellie's cap off.

Della backed up. "I'm not a hugger, Ellie. Nothing personal. But most vampires aren't huggers either."

"I'll work on that." Ellie grinned and snagged her hat from the ground. "Della voted me into her circle. I'm officially a member of the Shadow Falls vampire family."

"Cool." Kylie was happy for Ellie, but somewhere deep inside, this stood as another reminder that she didn't belong to any group.

Odd, how she'd helped Ellie do something that she couldn't seem to do for herself.

Della frowned. "It's nothing. Don't make a big deal of it."

"It is a big deal," Ellie said. "I was leaving today, but you guys changed my mind. Heck, you could have saved my life." She looked ahead and saw a couple of other vamps. "I need to run. But seriously, thank you!"

Della stared after her. "I still think she's way too touchy-feely."

Kylie watched Ellie run up and chat with the others. She wasn't sure why she believed Ellie was the vamp the death angels warned would die, but the tiniest bit of hope that she'd saved Ellie offered Kylie a shimmer of reprieve from her own troubles.

Or it did until about thirty minutes later, when Kylie saw the parents start to pour in. Everyone but her dad. Had he forgotten again?

Chapter Thirty

As the room filled with parents, Kylie really began to worry her dad was a no show. Her throat felt tight, her heart started breaking. Wanting to get away from the crowd, she escaped outside and went to sit on the office porch . . . to wait. If he didn't show, it wouldn't matter, she told herself. It wasn't as if he hadn't let her down before.

So why did it hurt so much?

It wasn't until she got settled in her chair that she remembered she was still being shadowed. She wasn't supposed to leave the dining hall without Holiday.

She started to get back up when she heard, "Hello, Miss Galen."

The female voice startled her and she yelped.

She turned in the chair and found herself staring at Lucas's grandmother Mrs. Parker. The fact that Lucas's grandmother knew who she was was a surprise.

"I'm sorry, I didn't see you. You startled me," Kylie said, still holding her hand over her heart. "It must run in the family." She smiled. "Lucas is always sneaking up on me."

"It's a werewolf thing." She motioned to the chair. "Do you mind?"

"Of course not." Kylie leaned back in her chair and tried to ap-

pear relaxed. But she got the feeling that this wasn't just an acciden-
tal encounter. What could Lucas's grandmother want with her?

The woman sauntered across the porch. For someone who moved
so slow, it surprised Kylie that she did it so silently and with an amazing amount of grace. She lowered herself into the chair, and even the
wood didn't creak. She folded her aged hands in her lap, looking the
epitome of propriety. She stared out for a few minutes, whether looking at the sky or the woods, Kylie didn't know.

The silence seemed awkward, but Kylie got the feeling it would
be rude to rush her. For a second, she stared at the woman's hands,
remembering the hands of the elderly woman who had come into
the camp pretending to be her grandmother.

Mrs. Parker glanced at Kylie. "My grandson is quite smitten with
you."

Smitten? Kylie didn't know people still used that word. But since
the woman was well over a hundred, Kylie supposed it fit her vo-
cabulary.

"Uh, I . . . like Lucas, too."

She nodded and leaned in a bit. "He mentioned that you knew
him when you two were young."

"Yes." The concerned look on the woman's face told Kylie what
this might be about. Most supernaturals believed that a supernatural raised by rogue parents was unsalvageable—once a rogue, always
a rogue. For that reason, Lucas had lied and stated he'd been raised
by his grandmother all his life. "But I would never tell anyone that
he lived with his parents."

"Good," she said. "He has high hopes of making something of
himself. He is being considered in line to be a grand leader of the
pack—to sit on the werewolf council—and this news could tarnish
his reputation." She tightened her brows and studied Kylie's pattern
and frowned.

"I'm sorry," Kylie said, assuming the woman's frown was about Kylie's unwillingness to let her see past her pattern. "I don't mean to be rude. I still don't know how to open up. I'm assuming Lucas explained my situation. That I'm not sure what I am."

"Yes. Lucas enlightened me on the matter." She continued to study Kylie. "Tell me, Miss Galen. Do you think you're werewolf?"

The question hung heavy in the air, reminding Kylie that Lucas had asked much the same question. Kylie's stomach knotted, and instantly she suspected what this conversation was really about. Obviously, his pack weren't the only ones wanting him to stay away from her. "I'm not sure."

Mrs. Parker smiled. "For your sake and my grandson's, I hope so."

"What do you mean?" Kylie asked, even though she suspected.

Leaning forward, she touched Kylie's shoulder. The touch was warm like Lucas's, and while Kylie wanted to pull back, she felt no animosity in the older woman's hand, nor did she see it in her eyes. There was only concern and love for her grandson. "The bloodline running in my grandson's veins is pure. His life mate will have to be one of his own kind."

"And if she's not?" Kylie asked.

"If she is part were, but shows loyalty to her heritage, they may overlook her lacking. But if she is not from our blood, then not only will he be forced to step down from his place, but the pack will no longer accept him as one of them. A were must never put another being who is not of our blood before he puts his own people."

"That sounds like racism," Kylie said.

The woman shrugged. "I cannot speak of what is right or wrong. I only speak of what is. Oddly enough, it is to correct a wrong that Lucas has fueled his long held desire to be a part of the council. Since Lucas was seven and came to live with me, he has been forced to lie to his own people and to the world about his upbringing. His goal has been to make it to that respected place and then change the views of our people about children born to rogues. He aches to show that the mistakes of the parents are not always passed down to the innocent child."

She rose from the chair as silently as she sat.

"Hey, pumpkin! There you are." Tom Galen's voice filled Kylie's ears, but she couldn't look away from Mrs. Parker's face to say hello to her stepdad. Was the woman really telling Kylie that if she wasn't werewolf, then she and Lucas couldn't get married?

Heck, she hadn't even officially agreed to go out with him. Marriage was a long, long way from here.

Footsteps sounded on the porch steps.

"I will go and let you visit with your company," Mrs. Parker said, and she nodded politely at Kylie's stepdad and walked off.

"You okay?" he asked, looking oddly at the elderly woman as he dropped into the chair she'd just vacated. "Is something wrong?"

"No," Kylie answered, and tried to push away her concern about Lucas's grandma so she could deal with her concern about seeing her stepdad again.

The visit with her stepdad wasn't as awkward as Kylie had thought. Then again, maybe it was just that after the extremely awkward visit with Lucas's grandmother, Kylie's awkward meter was malfunctioning.

Before Holiday missed her, Kylie moved her dad into the dining hall. Poor Holiday skirted from one group to another, trying to keep the peace.

As Kylie expected, her stepdad asked about her mom. Kylie didn't tell him about the business lunch/date her mom had gone on. He talked about some of the trips they'd taken on their father/daughter outings. Then he asked if she thought maybe they could go on another one soon.

Kylie hadn't said yes, but she hadn't said no. "I'll have to look at my schedule." For once, telling the truth—that some old vampire either wanted her to marry his grandson or planned to kill her—wasn't for the best.

When the time got close for him to leave, Kylie motioned to Holiday that she was going to walk her dad to his car, and Holiday's gaze shifted to Perry, who then followed them out.

When they reached the car, she hugged her dad. It didn't feel as awkward as the hug she'd given him the last time he'd come out for Parents Day, but there were still undercurrents of sadness to it.

"I love you," he whispered.

"Me too," Kylie said, and it was true. She loved him.

Before she released him, she realized he felt thinner. When she pulled away, she asked, "Are you eating okay?"

"Restaurant food isn't as good as your mom's cooking," he said.

"I miss her pancakes," Kylie said.

"I miss her." He gave her hand a tight squeeze. "If she asks about me, tell her I said that."

The loneliness she saw in his eyes gripped Kylie's chest. But he'd brought this pain on himself. None of this would have happened if he hadn't decided to bang his intern.

Mistakes. People make them. And most of the time, they had to pay for them. Was her stepdad destined to live alone the rest of his life because of his foolish decision to cheat on her mom?

"You okay?" Holiday asked as Kylie walked back inside, followed by Perry. "Did you survive the visit?"

"Yeah. It was sad, but seeing him is getting easier." Kylie looked around to check on Miranda and Della. Both looked miserable sitting like little soldiers with their respective parents.

Then she found Lucas. He sat attentively, hanging on every word his grandmother said. Evidently, the woman held a big influence over his life. But was it big enough that he wouldn't marry someone he loved because they weren't werewolf? Did Lucas even consider that a viable concern? Or was his grandmother just mentally stuck in the 1800s and thought it should be a consideration for Lucas?

Kylie looked at Holiday. It wasn't the place to ask, but the need to know was strong. "Do you think that supernaturals worry about who they'd marry because of bloodlines?"

Holiday's brows arched at Kylie's inquiry. "What brought on that question?"

"Curiosity," she lied.

Suspicion lurked in Holiday's eyes. She looked at Lucas and his grandma. The camp leader hesitated before looking back at Kylie. Kylie could tell Holiday searched for the right way to word her answer.

"I think that it might be more of a concern to some species than others," Holiday finally said.

"Like werewolves?"

She nodded. "They are the ones who have fewer mixed marriages than all the others. But it's changing. Today there are five times as many were mixed marriages than even ten years ago."

She tightened her mouth in a disapproving manner. "But those kinds of worries can wait for another ten years, young lady."

Holiday was right. It was a stupid thing to think about now. Stupid thing for Mrs. Parker to bring up, too. Kylie wasn't even seventeen. She didn't sit around and fantasize about getting married. Her dream with Lucas was a steamy make-out session, not going to a preacher to exchange vows. But stupid or not, Kylie knew she wasn't finished thinking about it.

"There she is!" a feminine voice called out, and without a doubt Kylie knew it was Sara.

Thirty minutes later, while her mom grabbed a soda, Kylie sat with Sara, feeling as if everyone in the dining hall watched and listened.

Because everyone had been talking about her latest superpower gift of healing her old best friend, Kylie knew all the campers were guessing this was Sara. It wasn't that she was ashamed of healing Sara; Kylie just didn't like being the center of attention.

Sara still looked thin, but everything from the shine of her brown hair to her complexion said she was okay. Sara kept glancing around at everyone and asking who was who.

"Is that your roommate?" She pointed to Miranda, sitting with her family.

"Yes," Kylie said. "I'll introduce you to her later."

"Where's the other one? The grumpy one?"

Della, across the room, shot Kylie a smirk. "She's over there," Kylie said, and pointed.

Because Della was still glancing at them, Sara waved. "She looks like a b with an itch."

Kylie's mouth dropped. "She's not. She's one of my . . ." Kylie almost said best friends, but she realized how awkward that might be. Sara used to be Kylie's best friend. "She's one of my good friends here."

"I remember you saying—"

"That was a long time ago," Kylie insisted, and hoped Sara shut up before Della got her feelings hurt.

"So, you're feeling better now?" Kylie tossed out the first thing she could think of to change the subject. But from the sparkle in Sara's eyes, Kylie realized it was the wrong question. Obviously, Sara was dying to bring up the whole "you healed me" topic.

"I think you know the answer to that better than I do," Sara said.

"Know the answer to what?" Her mom sat down next to Kylie.

"Nothing," Kylie said.

Sara let her gaze move around the room again. "Who's the hot black-haired guy who keeps staring at you?"

Kylie looked in the direction that Sara nodded. So did her mom. Lucas was staring at her, and he smiled. His grandmother must have left, because he sat alone. Then, as if he saw their gaze as an invitation to join them, he started over.

No. No. Panic stirred in Kylie's gut. At first, Kylie didn't understand why she didn't want Lucas to meet Sara. Then she remembered that Sara had always been the biggest flirt. Kylie didn't want Sara making a play for Lucas. Not so much because she worried Lucas would respond to it, but because Kylie didn't want Lucas thinking Sara was a party girl.

Old life meets new life, and Kylie didn't want either to look unappealing.

She picked up her glass of water and drank just to have something to do with her hands.

"You must be Sara." Lucas extended his hand.

Sara slipped her hand into Lucas's. "That's me. And you are?"

"Lucas Parker, Kylie's boyfriend."

Boyfriend? Kylie's breath caught. The water slipping down her throat went down the wrong pipe. She started coughing so hard, the sound bounced around the high beams of the dining hall. If that wasn't bad enough, her mom, who'd been sipping on a diet soda, did the same thing.

Crap! If there was one person in the dining hall who hadn't already stared at them, they did now.

Holiday walked over, studying Kylie and her mom as they both worked on getting air into their lungs. "Everything okay?"

"Yeah," Kylie managed to say, and felt some water drip from her nose. Oh, wasn't that just lovely. She wiped it away.

"How about we get some fresh air?" Holiday asked. "Why don't we take Sara and your mom to your cabin?"

"Yeah," Kylie said, and they all stood up.

Lucas seemed to sense he'd done something wrong, and he looked at her in confusion. "Well, I'll let you four go. I'll see you later."

Kylie nodded.

Lucas looked at her mom. "It was a pleasure to see you again, Mrs. Galen."

"You too," her mom said, and looked at Kylie with all kinds of parental concerns that involved boyfriends and the unspoken word . . . sex.

They hadn't gotten out of the dining hall before her mom leaned in. "Boyfriend? What have you not been telling me?"

Just great, Kylie thought. Now her mom would probably start mailing her the sex pamphlets.

Sara leaned in and whispered in her other ear, "He's hot."

"I know," Kylie whispered back.

"Not hot like good-looking. I mean hot like you were that day you touched me."

Kylie didn't know what to say to that. When they got to the door of the dining hall, Kylie reached for the knob, but the door swung open first and nearly knocked her down. She jumped back.

Derek and his mom came inside. Derek's gaze shot to Kylie and his eyes tightened as if her nearness hurt him. Then a look of concern filled his eyes when he noticed Sara.

"Look, Derek! It's Kylie!" Mrs. Lakes almost shouted, and again Kylie felt everyone in the room staring at her.

Without any advance warning, Kylie became locked in an embrace with Mrs. Lakes. Thankfully, she was a fast hugger.

Derek looked at Sara. "You must be Sara."

"That's me," Sara answered with her flirty smile. "Who are you?"

"This is Derek," Kylie said, and made quick introductions, which included her mom.

Mrs. Lakes waved her hand back and forth between Kylie and Derek. "I think they're sweet on each other. Isn't it cute?"

Several gasps came from the crowd behind them, probably the vampires listening in. Kylie felt her cheeks break out in embarrassment.

"Mom!" Derek rolled his eyes.

"I'm just saying the truth, honey. She's all you talk about."

Derek's face turned bright red.

Kylie's mom arched an eyebrow and eyed Kylie as if to say she would be certain to send those sex pamphlets now.

Sara chuckled.

And Kylie just wanted to die. Right there, right then. Especially when she looked back and saw Lucas taking it all in and frowning.

Chapter Thirty-one

"Why don't you girls walk ahead?" Kylie's mom said as soon as they got outside the dining hall. "I know Sara is dying to have some girl talk."

Kylie wasn't fooled. Her mom obviously was dying to discuss something privately with Holiday. Probably about Kylie having two boyfriends.

As Sara and Kylie started walking, Sara squeezed Kylie's arm. "Two guys? You've got two guys in love with you? Start talking, girl."

"Did Kylie's dad come this morning? I'm so worried about their relationship." Her mom's words seemed extra loud.

Kylie stopped and looked back. They were well over a hundred feet away and there was no way she should be hearing this. But she was. The sensitive hearing was back, and this time she was grateful.

"Yes," Holiday answered. *"He did come. They seemed to have a good visit."*

"Kylie?" Sara said. "Come on, tell me what's going on."

Kylie looked back at Sara and started walking again. "I . . . it's hard to explain."

"Good," her mom said. *"I'm a bit concerned about Kylie and, well, the boys. I've read when a girl has issues with her father, they find themselves having . . . acting out with boys."*

Well, at least Kylie now knew it wasn't just her. Her mom couldn't say the word *sex* to anyone.

"Do you supervise them and make sure there isn't anything happening that shouldn't be happening?"

"Well, try," Sara insisted. "Talk to me. I'm dying to know."

"Know what?" Kylie asked, failing miserably at keeping up with two conversations.

"Have you lost it yet?" Sara asked.

"Your daughter has a good head on her shoulders," Holiday answered. *"I don't think you need to worry about Kylie."*

"Lost what?" Kylie asked Sara, and then suddenly she knew what Sara was asking.

Apparently, the two conversations going on at once were about the same thing. Sex. "No. I haven't lost it." Annoyed at Sara's question, she remembered how close she and Sara had once been. They had told each other everything—no secrets. Sort of like she now did with Della and Miranda.

The awkwardness of having her old life cross paths with her new hit again. And in about fifteen minutes, Della and Miranda would meet them at the cabin. How awkward was that going to be?

Probably very.

"But they're so hot," Sara said.

"Yeah. They are."

"So which one do you really like?"

Both. The truth echoed in her head. Kylie inhaled. "Lucas," she said.

"Yum." Sara grinned, then shrugged. "Now, can you please tell me what you did to heal me?"

Kylie recalled the advice Holiday had given her. Just deny it. "I don't know what you're . . ." She started hearing the conversation between Holiday and her mom heat up again.

"Can I ask you a strange question?" Holiday asked her mom.

"I guess," her mom said.

"Do you have any American Indian blood in your family tree?"

"Why would Holiday ask that?" Kylie muttered.

"Why would who ask what?" Sara looked at her strangely.

Kylie shook her head. "Nothing."

"So start talking," Sara said. "And don't even try to deny it. I remember clearly how you rubbed my temples and how hot your hands got when you did it. And I felt it. I felt something happening inside me."

Sara came to a sudden stop and caught Kylie's hands in hers. "They're not hot now. So do you only get hot when you heal people? But why was . . . What's his name—Lucas—why were his hands hot?"

Kylie pulled her hands free, trying to remember what lie she'd given to Sara about her reasons for rubbing her temples.

"That is a strange question," her mom said. *"Why would you want to know that?"*

Sara let out a frustrated breath. "And don't tell me it's because your mom used to do it. Because I asked her about that on the ride up here, and she denied it. Said she couldn't remember rubbing your temples to help your headaches."

"Shh," Kylie said to Sara, not wanting to miss Holiday's answer.

But Sara didn't get quiet. Instead she let out a bloodcurdling scream that could have awakened the dead.

And she continued to scream. The sound pierced Kylie's eardrums. She went on instant alert, but she didn't know why. Her gaze started flipping from side to side, trying to find the source of danger.

Was it the eagle again? The evil-eyed deer? Was there another sinkhole, or had Perry gone unicorn again? Kylie was prepared for just about anything.

Tense to the max, she didn't know if she should prepare herself to fight or run. Then something butted up against her jeans-covered calf.

She glanced down.

Okay, she was prepared for about anything but Socks. Her skunk/cat was supposed to be locked up at Holiday's cabin. And just to make matters worse, her mom and Holiday came running to see what was wrong.

Within two seconds, her mom started screaming with Sara, while Kylie glanced back at Holiday.

"It's probably rabid," her mom screeched. "Get away from it, Kylie. Get away!"

"It's okay," Holiday spouted, but obviously she wasn't heard over her mom's wailing.

Kylie followed her mother's orders and stepped back. But Socks wasn't having it. He followed and pounced at Kylie's tennis shoe.

Sara squealed and darted across the path and hid behind Kylie's mom. Socks, suddenly frightened by the ruckus, shot back across the path and scampered up Kylie's leg. Unsure what to do, she held the scared pet with caution.

"Drop it! Kylie!" her mom screamed. "Drop that vermin this minute!" Then she bolted forward as if to knock the animal from Kylie's arms.

"Mom, it's okay," she said, though it was anything but.

Socks hissed, then swiveled in Kylie's hold and buried his pointed little nose in her armpit. Kylie didn't completely panic until Socks lifted his black-and-white fluffy tail straight up in the air and aimed it at her mom.

"No!" Kylie swung around and started talking sweetly to Socks. "Don't do it. Don't do it," she whispered.

"Everybody, step back," Holiday said, speaking more forcefully this time. "The skunk's not rabid. He's my pet."

Kylie looked back over her shoulder to see her mom gawk at Holiday in sheer horror. "You have a pet skunk?"

"Yes," Holiday lied, and almost sounded honest. "I know, it sounds kind of strange."

"Kind of?" her mom asked, eyes still wide with shock.

Kylie pulled Socks closer and continued to whisper what she hoped were calming words close to his ear. But who, she wondered, was going to whisper calming words to her? This, was exactly why merging her old life with her new was such a bad, bad idea.

"Well, that went well," Holiday said an hour later as they watched Kylie's mom and Sara drive out of the Shadow Falls parking lot.

Kylie, her chest so tight that she thought a few ribs had cracked, looked at Holiday in shock. "You're kidding me. I'm practically told I'm not good enough for Lucas by his grandma. My dad's miserable. My mom thinks I'm having sex with two boys. And she thinks you're an idiot who keeps a skunk as a pet."

"I had to come up with something," Holiday said. "He must have snuck out when I left and I didn't see him."

"Don't forget that it couldn't have gotten any more awkward between Sara and Miranda and Della. They barely spoke to each other. And . . ." Tears filled Kylie's eyes. "And if I ever wondered if you really kept things from me, I know the truth now. What's this crap about you wanting to know if I'm part American Indian?"

Holiday's face flashed with guilt. "I was going to tell you. Honest. There just hasn't been time."

"Yeah, you're always going to tell me something after the fact." Kylie batted at the tears rolling down her cheeks. "I'm sick and tired of all the secrets around here, Holiday. I'm tired of being kept in the dark. I'm tired of not knowing what I am. It's not fair, and I'm not going to tolerate it anymore."

It was Wednesday night. The last few days had passed by in a blur. Kylie had gone into a frenzy trying to dig up her family tree. Holiday had explained that there was an American Indian legend about certain descendants of an Indian tribe having been touched by the gods. And that these mere humans would carry the gift with them for generations.

If Kylie had that blood running in her veins, it would explain how she could be a protector and still be half human. Kylie didn't know why it was so important to her to find out her heritage. It wasn't as if it would get her any closer to discovering what she was. But it might explain why she seemed to have certain gifts. Then again, maybe it was because it was the only lead she could work on right now.

The ghost showed up three or four times a day but still wasn't talking. Lucas showed up two or three times a day, too. And they weren't doing much talking, either. But on the plus side, they were doing a lot more kissing.

She hadn't said anything about what his grandmother told her. Partly because he already seemed so tense—no doubt because of the approaching full moon. And the other part because she was afraid of his answer.

She was afraid he'd tell her his grandmother was right. That he could never consider marrying her if she wasn't a werewolf.

Yeah, it still seemed stupid that she'd worry about it at this point in their relationship. But then, Kylie kept coming back to the fact that being girlfriend and boyfriend was supposed to be all about finding that one person you'd spend your entire life with.

Should she live for the day or plan for the future? And should she start something when she knew it wouldn't and couldn't last? Could she risk giving her heart to someone who could never truly be hers?

Earlier that night, when Lucas came by, they'd sat on the porch, kissed, and stared up at the moon. "You don't feel anything when you look at it?" he'd asked her.

He no longer tried to hide the fact that he wanted her to be were. And it was getting harder for her to pretend that it didn't bother her. Not that it changed how she felt about him. Everything from his smile to his blue eyes to the way he kissed—it all captivated her. The time she was close to him was about the only time she really felt at peace.

Kylie remembered telling Holiday she needed a touchstone, something that felt completely right. Lucas had become her touchstone. In some ways, he was like the falls. When she was close to him, when she felt his warm touch on her, all her problems seemed so much smaller.

But when he wasn't close, those problems came back to sit on her shoulders and eat away at her sanity. Eventually, Kylie knew they needed to talk about the whole bloodline issue. And even his question about her going out. Although she got the feeling he assumed she'd said yes. Looking back, she realized that considering their conversation that day, he might even have reason to believe it. So she'd let that one slide, but the bloodline issue wasn't that easy to drop.

But for now, she decided to just let it be.

"Hey!" Della's voice snapped Kylie back to the present as she walked out of her room. "Is Miranda back yet from her make-out session with Perry?" She plopped down at the kitchen table behind where Kylie sat at the computer desk.

"Not yet." Kylie glanced back. Della looked bored or depressed. She'd been extra quiet lately. Ever since Parents Day.

"What are you doing?" Della asked.

Worrying. "My mom finally got me my great-grandmother's maiden name. I thought I'd put it in the database on that genealogy Web site and see if I get anything."

"Why don't you just put a feather in your hat and call yourself an Indian?"

Kylie frowned. "That's not nice."

"Sorry," she muttered. "I'm in a pissy mood."

"Why?" Kylie stood and grabbed two diet sodas from the fridge and then dropped back down in the kitchen chair.

Della took the drink Kylie slid over to her and popped the top. It fizzed and she pressed her lips to the rim of the can to catch the overspill. When she looked up, she had tears in her eyes.

"What's wrong?" Kylie asked.

Della made a little hiccup noise, and Kylie realized that the vamp was crying. She stopped herself from going over there and hugging Della, because she knew Della hated that.

"Della? Tell me what's wrong." And instantly, Kylie got tears in her eyes, too.

Della swiped at her cheeks. "I miss it. It's just like Ellie said. I miss being normal. I miss living with my family. I know I'm lucky to be here. Lucky to have you and Miranda as my best friends. And I'm happy that you've got Lucas and Miranda has Perry, but it just makes me miss Lee, and it hurts so bad sometimes. And I know I should try to go for Steve, but I'm not ready." She hiccuped again and more tears slipped from her dark lashes onto her cheeks. "I miss it. All of it. I miss being human."

Kylie started crying in earnest now. Not just for Della, but for herself. "I know," she said. "I miss it, too."

The next morning, Kylie woke up staring at the back of Della's head. Because Della was the only one with a full-size bed, they had ended up going to Della's bed and talking until they'd fallen asleep. Something moved at Kylie's back and she quickly rolled over and stared at a yawning Miranda.

"What are you doing here?" Kylie asked.

"I thought it was a spend-the-night party and I wanted to come," she said. Then she popped out her bottom lip. "You two didn't even wait up on me."

"You were late," Kylie said, and yawned.

"I know." Miranda grinned. "We had such a good time. We went swimming at the lake. Just the two of us. It's almost a full moon and it was so romantic."

"You went skinny-dipping?" Della asked, and rolled over, sounding half-asleep.

"No. But he did. Only because he thought I was going to." Miranda giggled. "I wore my bathing suit under my clothes, because he said we were going to the lake. And when I started pulling my jeans off, he thought I was taking it all off and he took his off and dove in really fast."

Kylie and Della started laughing.

"But I didn't see anything. Plus, he made me turn around when he got out and pulled his shorts back on."

The three of them stayed in bed, giggling, until they were almost late for breakfast.

It was a good morning. Not quite as mind-easing as being with Lucas, but Kylie had to admit that Della and Miranda were becoming her touchstones as well. Right now, she felt capable of facing another day of problem solving.

But the good mood took a nosedive when they walked into the dining hall and everyone turned and stared at them.

No, not at all of them. Just at Kylie. Or rather, they gaped at her forehead while tightening their brows. Obviously, her pattern was doing something weird again.

"Damn!" someone said. There were several gasps, a couple of whispers, and a few people even dropped their forks. Then came the dead silence—the kind of silence that screamed disbelief.

Della and Miranda both turned toward her and tightened their brows.

Miranda's eyes widened in shock. "Oh, my!"

"Shit," said Della.

"What is it?" Kylie asked.

Della swallowed and leaned in. "You finally opened up. Your . . . your pattern is readable."

Chapter Thirty-two

"What am I?" Kylie gripped Della's arm. "I need to know." Holy hell, she'd been waiting for the answer to this question for months. "Please, Della!"

"You . . ." Della shook her head. "You're human. One hundred percent human."

"Not funny." Kylie wanted to believe Della was teasing her, but the look on her roommate's face said otherwise. But how could she be human after everything that had happened to her? She remembered crying last night and telling Della she missed being human. Missed being normal. Had she willed it to happen?

Kylie darted out the door and ran as fast as she could to the office.

Not even Holiday's closed office door slowed her down. She barged in. Burnett and Holiday jumped apart as if . . . they'd been kissing. Oh, my God. The image of what she'd seen for a flicker of a second played in Kylie's head.

Burnett and Holiday were kissing. Any other time, Kylie might have yelped with joy.

Not now.

"We were . . . we were just . . . ," Holiday stuttered.

Kylie didn't care. Her heart pounded. Her mind tried to make sense of the fact that she was fully human. How was that even possible? What did it mean?

Even as she asked herself the questions, she knew the answer to the last one. Being human meant leaving Shadow Falls. Holiday. Burnett. Miranda. Della. Lucas. Perry. Derek. Jonathon and Helen. All of them. It meant walking away forever from her new life.

Tears filled her eyes.

"What's wrong?" Holiday asked.

It meant never helping another lost soul. It meant going back to her old life, where she never felt as if she belonged.

Okay, she had missed her old life. She had. But right now, she knew with twenty-twenty clarity that she would miss her new life more. These last few months, as hard as they had been, she'd come closer to knowing her true self than she ever had before. Maybe she still didn't know what she was, but in so many ways, she knew more about *who* she was.

"Kylie? What is it?" Holiday insisted.

"What the hell does this mean?" She pointed to her forehead.

Holiday and Burnett looked at her and their eyebrows twitched. The shock she saw in both their eyes didn't help Kylie's confusion. The knot in her throat grew to the size of a large frog.

Thirty minutes later, Kylie still sat on Holiday's sofa, with her legs pulled up to her chest, her forehead against her knees. She was dry—cried out.

The camp leader sat beside her. Holiday's hand rested on Kylie's back and sent waves of calm washing over her, but it didn't chase away the fear that swelled in her chest. She'd caused this herself. Brought this on herself. She'd somehow tapped into a power she didn't know she had and turned herself back into a human. Was it irreversible?

Kylie lifted her head. "I didn't mean to do it."

"Do what?" Holiday asked.

Kylie's throat felt raw. "Della and I were talking about how we wished . . . we wished we were human again. That we missed being normal, and—" Her breath caught. "And I do miss it, but right now it's so clear that I would miss this new life more. I don't want to be human, Holiday."

Empathy filled Holiday's eyes and she smiled. "I don't know what's happening. I don't understand it. But if there is one thing I'm certain about, it's that you are not human, Kylie. Well, not just human."

"But what if the death angels are trying to teach me a lesson? What if they got pissed at me for being ungrateful and this is my punishment?"

Holiday shook her head. "I've never heard of them turning someone into a human for punishment. And believe me, there isn't a supernatural alive who hasn't had moments of wishing they were human. That's perfectly normal."

"Really?"

"Of course. We live in the human world. The grass always looks greener on the other side. Truth is, sometimes it *is* greener. But we can't change what we are simply by wishing it was so."

Kylie nodded. "So you think this is just a fluke?"

"I don't know. But if I were guessing, I'd say it will change just like it's changed numerous other times."

"Will I not have any powers until it changes back?"

The question seemed to stump Holiday. "I . . . Wait. Can you still feel me attempting to alter your emotions?" Holiday rested her hand on Kylie's shoulder.

She felt the warmth leak from Holiday's touch through her shirt and flow into her skin. Then the soft heat seemed to form a bubble that flowed into her chest cavity, where it morphed into a soothing wash of emotion.

"Yes," Kylie said.

"Then I'd say nothing else has changed."

"So humans can't sense your touch?"

"No."

Kylie inhaled and found a little inner peace. Then she looked at Holiday. "Do you think I'll ever figure out what I am?"

"Of course you will." Holiday paused. "I didn't want to mention it because it's not a sure thing, but Burnett told me that the real Brightens, in Ireland, confirmed their plane reservations back to the States for the middle of September."

Kylie's heart skipped a beat. "Do they know about me?"

"Not that we know of. Burnett did some checking on the phone number for the caller the detective spoke to the day he'd thought he'd been talking to the Brightens. It wasn't their phone. The call was made from a cell phone, a throwaway, they call them. They can't trace it."

"But Burnett knows how to reach the Brightens now? I could call them, couldn't I?"

Holiday frowned. "I don't think this is something you want to talk about over the phone, Kylie."

Holiday was right, but Kylie was just so damn tired of waiting. She reached back and rubbed the tension in her shoulder and wished Burnett were still here. He'd cut out shortly after she'd started to cry. She wasn't sure if he'd been frightened by her tears or frightened by the thought of her asking him about what she'd seen when she'd walked in on them.

Kylie glanced at Holiday. "So . . . you and Burnett?"

Holiday rolled her eyes. "It was just a kiss, Kylie. Don't make it out to be something more."

Kylie let a slight smile work its way to her lips. Right now, she could use any good news at all. "Was it a good kiss?"

"Just a kiss and . . . a mistake. We were talking about Perry and

Miranda, about how sweet it was. The moment got away from us and . . . Definitely a mistake."

"Why, Holiday? Why can't you give the guy a chance?"

Holiday frowned. "The only reason I let this happen was . . . my guard was down because . . ." Kylie saw the shadows of pain in Holiday's eyes.

"You're afraid Burnett's the one in the casket?"

She nodded.

"Which means you care about him. Can't you see that?"

"I care, but caring for someone isn't enough. And we work together. Romance and work never go together."

"It could if you wanted it badly enough."

"Then I guess I don't want it that bad," Holiday said sternly. But Kylie knew that it was a lie.

And she suspected Holiday realized it, too.

They sat silently for a few minutes. "About the whole funeral vision thing . . . ," Kylie said.

"Yeah?"

"I think . . . I mean, there's a chance I fixed it."

Holiday studied her. "Fixed what?"

Kylie didn't feel right telling Holiday that Ellie had been going to run away. "I might have done something that took someone out of danger. So maybe a vampire won't die."

Holiday frowned. "I'd love to think that's true. But you can't change Fate."

Kylie recalled that those had been the words the ghost had whispered, but she refused to believe. "Then maybe it wasn't really Fate," she said.

"I wish I could believe that," Holiday said.

"I do believe it," Kylie said. But there was a part of her that doubted.

And when she let herself think about it, it tore her apart.

Holiday's phone rang. The camp leader picked it up, looked at the caller ID oddly, and then took the call.

"What's up?" Holiday asked, and then glanced over at Kylie. "She's fine." Holiday paused. "I'll tell her." She hung up and met Kylie's eyes. "That was Derek. He wanted to tell you that if you needed to talk, he's here for you. As a friend. He insisted I add that last part."

Kylie nodded and her chest swelled with emotion.

A knock came at the door. Holiday looked at Kylie. "Are you up to company? Derek's not the only one worried."

Kylie nodded.

"Come in," Holiday said. Della and Miranda popped into the office, their gazes filled with concern. Behind them came Lucas, Perry, Helen, and Jonathon.

"I'm fine," Kylie told them, but more tears filled her eyes. Tears because she knew that these people weren't just her friends. They were her family.

"We love you," Miranda said, her eyes tearing up. "And we want you to know that we don't care what you are."

Later that night, Kylie received another sign that her human brain pattern hadn't changed things. At first, she thought it was just a dream. She was watching Jane Doe resting in bed, running her hands over her pregnant belly, and staring at the sleeping man beside her. *"I love you,"* she whispered. *"But I have to do this."*

Then things changed and Kylie was Jane. She slipped quietly out of the bed. Her body felt cumbersome with the round, heavy weight around her middle. Her heart felt broken, heavy. Kylie couldn't ever remember feeling so much sadness, as if she were about to lose something more precious than life.

She moved out of the dark room, looked back one more time at the sleeping man. Whoever he was, Jane loved him.

"I'm sorry." The two little words tumbled out of her mouth. The man rolled over, and Kylie got a quick glimpse of his face. Pale complexion, thick, dark brown—no, not really brown, but auburn hair.

Something about his face made Kylie want to continue to stare at him, but she had no control over what happened in these visions. Reliving Jane Doe's past, she turned and walked out. She moved to a closet, grabbed a long black coat, and slipped it around her body. Then she pulled out a suitcase—an old-fashioned piece of luggage, no wheels. Carrying it made walking while pregnant feel even more awkward.

Why are you leaving if you love him? The question flowed through Kylie's mind, but the vision continued, leaving the question hanging in the air unanswered.

With tears now streaming down her face, she walked out of the small house. A car, with its headlights off, pulled up to the curb. She got inside. Kylie wanted to see who was driving, but Jane was too busy crying, too busy trying to deal with a broken heart, to care about the driver.

"You're doing the best thing," a woman's voice said as the car pulled away. *"He wouldn't understand."*

The vision went black. Kylie tried to wake up but got pulled back in.

And not to a good place, either.

There was light now, but she didn't care. She was in too much pain. Something was ripping her insides apart. It reminded Kylie of the worst menstrual cramp she'd ever had. Her body contorted with pain. Her back arched and she screamed.

"It's not coming," someone said. The pain in her abdomen eased and she became aware of the emotional pain in her chest again.

"Don't let my baby die." She raised up on her elbow.

The man standing between her opened knees met Jane Doe's eyes. *"I'd have to take it by C-section."*

"*Then do it!*" Jane screamed.

"*I'm not prepared for that. I don't have any anesthesia.*"

"I don't care," Jane said. "*Don't let my baby die. I can take it. It's not like I'm human.*"

The man looked at the woman sitting beside him. "*Get me a knife.*"

Chapter Thirty-three

No! Kylie screamed in her head, even as Jane Doe dropped back on the bed and resigned herself to being cut open with nothing to dull the pain.

"Kylie? Wake up!"

Kylie felt someone shake her. Still screaming, she opened her eyes and saw Della and Miranda standing over her. She managed to stop screaming but couldn't stop shaking.

"Should we get Holiday?" Miranda asked, looking worried.

Kylie shook her head no. "I'm okay." She rolled over and dried her tears on the blanket. "Go back to sleep," she muttered. Her heart still carried the panic from the vision, and she could feel the cold. Jane was here.

Della and Miranda looked at each other as if unsure what to do next.

"Go," she repeated.

As soon as they left, Kylie sat up. Jane sat on the edge of the bed. Her abdomen gaped open and blood spilled onto the tops of her bare thighs. *I didn't kill my baby. I loved him.*

"I know. I saw." Kylie hated to ask, but finding answers was why

Jane had come to her. "Did the baby die? Is that what happened? Did your baby die during childbirth?"

Jane looked at Kylie again. *"No."* She smiled, and instantly the blood on her hands disappeared and she was dressed in a pretty sundress with big yellow sunflowers. *"He lived. My baby lived. I made sure he was okay. And then I went back home."*

"Where was home?" Kylie asked. "Home to who?"

She blinked and then looked up. *"I don't know. I can't remember."*

"I'm a little confused," Kylie said. "Did you die during the birth?"

"No, I already showed you how I died. They killed me." And then she faded.

It took Kylie forever to fall back to sleep, and when she did, another dream had her in its trap. Immediately, she recognized what was going on. She hadn't moved into the dream, someone had come into hers.

She waited just a fraction of a second to make sure it wasn't Derek, then she saw him. Red. He stood by the lake.

"I'm not trying to fool you this time," he said.

"Leave me alone!" she snapped.

"I need to tell you . . ."

Kylie woke up in a panic in her bed. Red was gone. "Don't come back!" she said, and hugged herself, proud of how quickly she'd woken herself up.

The next four or five days at Shadow Falls were all about getting the camp ready to become a full-blown school, and that was fine with Kylie. Holiday was busy interviewing a few more potential teachers while a construction group—all paranormals—built a few large classroom cabins. Another all-paranormal crew put heating units into the cabins.

Kylie was still being shadowed. Because nothing else had happened, she'd started to feel guilty about piling on to everyone's busy schedules. On Friday morning, she took off to Burnett's office to suggest he call a halt to the shadowing. He disagreed.

"If anything, this is the time to be more careful," he insisted.

"Why?" Kylie asked.

He frowned. "For starters, how about because this place is a revolving door right now? I don't like strangers being here."

Kylie felt a shiver run down her spine. "You think someone working here could really be working with Mario?"

If so, that might explain Miranda's growing feeling that someone was lurking around their cabin. She'd started putting protective spells on their cabin every day now and had even gone to Holiday and Burnett with her concerns. Concerns they'd listened to but didn't feel held a huge threat. Or at least Kylie had assumed until now.

Burnett, all two-hundred-plus pounds of muscle, leaned back in his office chair. "I've checked everyone's credentials a dozen times." He reached for a heart-shaped stress ball with the words *Donate Blood* and squeezed it. "Maybe Holiday's right, and I'm being overly cautious, but I'm not taking chances."

Burnett turned his head to the side as if listening to something from outside the cabin. He frowned. "Another were is at it again. I'll be so friggin' glad when tomorrow's full moon is past. Excuse me." He shot out of the room.

Kylie ran out of the cabin after him, afraid Lucas was involved in whatever was happening. While normally she wouldn't consider Lucas getting into trouble, these last few days, he'd been extra tense. Last night when he'd come by her cabin to say good night, he'd barely kissed her.

When she'd asked if something was wrong, he'd reminded her that the closer he got to the full moon, the more he turned to his instinct instead of logic. Then he'd reached out and passed a single finger over her lips. "You are temptation in its purest form, Kylie Galen."

There was a part of Kylie that wanted to give in to that temptation, but another part of her still resisted. And as much as she wished it weren't true, she knew her reason for holding back had to do with Lucas's grandmother.

The moment Kylie hit the edge of the porch steps, Della showed up. "Ellie and Fredericka are going at it."

"Why?" Kylie asked.

"Supposedly, Ellie overheard the she-wolf talking bad about you and decided to teach Fredericka a lesson. You know, I hate to admit it, but Ellie's growing on me."

"Oh, crap. Where are they?"

"By Ellie's cabin."

Kylie took off. By the time they got there, Burnett had Fredericka, and Lucas was holding Ellie back. Ellie was bleeding, and from the glow in her eyes, she wasn't finished fighting.

"Let go of me!" she growled at Lucas. "I'll teach that dog—"

"Calm down," Lucas snapped. His own eyes were a bright orange. "She'll tear you apart. You can't win a fight with a were the day before a full moon."

"Watch me!" Ellie tried again to pull away, her fangs showing.

"Stop! Or I'll teach you a lesson myself," Lucas growled, his body growing tenser and his eyes brighter. Obviously, with his own body feeling the effects of the coming full moon, he shouldn't be the one trying to break up a fight.

"Why?" Ellie countered. "Why are you protecting that she-wolf? You should be helping me kick her ass. I thought Kylie was your girlfriend. Where does your loyalty lie? With that she-wolf, or with Kylie?"

Lucas paused; the question seemed to catch him off guard. "I'm trying to save your life, though I'm not sure it's worth much."

"Because I'm not were?" Ellie spit back.

"Enough!" Burnett roared.

Lucas let go of Ellie. The pissed-off vamp stepped back, but her eyes stayed bright. Then her angry gaze found Kylie. "You have definitely chosen the wrong guy. Derek would never defend someone who said those things about you. Never!"

Kylie's gaze locked with Lucas for a moment, and then she turned and walked away.

That night, Kylie awoke to the smell of roses. Before she opened her eyes, she checked the temperature to make sure it wasn't Jane. Or worse, another vision. But nope. No cold. Just the sweet floral scent.

"Hey, beautiful," said a familiar male voice. She opened her eyes.

Lucas knelt beside her bed, holding a bouquet of roses in his hands. She sat up and saw more roses all around the room. "What did you do, rob a florist?"

He gave her his bad-boy grin, and Kylie felt her heart melt just a little. "No, but let me just say that my grandmother is going to be really pissed when she sees her garden in the morning."

She grinned and then remembered she was mad at him. And yeah, it might not have been fair to be mad when all he'd done was do the right thing by breaking up the fight, but Ellie's words had stung and stung deep. And Kylie had been nursing a bit of a broken heart ever since.

It didn't help that Kylie knew, once he shifted into wolf form, he would run off into the woods with Fredericka fast behind him. So when he'd dropped by earlier that day to see her, she'd told him she'd had a headache and was going to bed.

But he was back now. And this time, he hadn't gotten her permission first to come into her room.

"Scoot over," he said.

Kylie arched a brow, remembering his caution about not getting too close to her before the change. "Is that a good idea?"

"I'll behave. I've made sure of it. I just want to hold you and apologize."

"For what?"

He took a rose and ran it down her nose and over her lips. It felt soft against her skin—a bit like velvet.

"I'm sorry that Fredericka is being such a bitch. Sorry for how things may have looked. I wasn't defending Fredericka. I was trying to keep Ellie from getting hurt."

There it was again. The fact that he'd been doing the right thing. And she knew it was true.

"But . . ." He set the rose beside her pillow. "I got to thinking about how I'd feel if it were you defending Derek. I really wouldn't like that." He scooped her up in his arms and moved her over and then crawled in beside her.

His warmth came against her side, and his lips brushed against her cheek. "You are the most important thing to me, Kylie. There isn't anything about you that doesn't fascinate me. The way your eyes light up when you smile. The sound of your laughter." He picked up the rose and ran it across her mouth again. "The shape of your lips. The way they feel against mine."

The rose moved up. "Your nose. The way it turns up on the end."

"It doesn't turn up that much." She'd always hated her nose.

"Maybe it does just a little." He grinned. "But it's so damn cute. And I love the way you sneeze."

"Now you're taking it too far." She giggled.

"Seriously, I love the sound you make when you sneeze. It sounds more like a puppy than human. A very cute and sexy puppy."

His smile faded and his blue eyes stared right at her. "For the first time in my entire life, I'm not looking forward to shifting. Because . . . then I won't be able to kiss you like this." His lips melted against hers, but he ended the kiss too quickly. "I'll be out there. And you'll be in here. And instead of enjoying the thrill of being free of this body, I'll be missing you."

He kissed her lightly on the lips again. "So, please. Please, don't be angry at me. I didn't mean to make you feel bad, or to make you feel as if anyone else is more important to me than you. Because they aren't. I'd kill for you, Kylie Galen. But more than that, I'd die for you."

She felt a tear roll down her cheek. "You'd better not die on me, Lucas Parker."

He caught the tear and wiped it away. "Am I forgiven?"

"Yes. You're forgiven." She reached up and wrapped her hand around his neck and pulled him in for a kiss. His mouth devoured hers, his tongue swept across her lips. After several long, delicious moments, he kissed his way down to her neck. It tickled, it tingled, and before long, she heard the soft humming sound emanating from him. She liked hearing it. Liked knowing she made it happen. Liked how her inhibitions faded while listening to it.

His hand slid up under her tank top, touching bare skin. Touching the edges of her breasts, and then his hands moved higher. His warm hands felt like sunshine against her skin. She closed her eyes, loving how it felt. She wanted this.

He broke the kiss and jerked his hand away. "Okay, it's time for me to go now."

He jumped out of the bed and frowned down at her. "I'm sorry."

She bit down on her lip to keep from telling him it was okay. To keep from asking him to get back in bed. Instead, she whispered, "I'm *not* sorry."

He gazed down at her. "You are so damn beautiful. And if I don't leave now . . ." He started out.

"Lucas?"

He turned around. "Yeah?"

"Thank you for the roses."

"You're welcome." He looked back at the door. "I should probably go before I run out of time."

"Out of time?" she asked.

He shrugged. "I told Della to kick my ass out if I stayed more than twenty minutes." He looked at his watch. "And knowing her—"

"Time's up!" Della pounded on the door with so much force, Kylie was amazed the door didn't break down.

Lucas grinned. "I knew I could count on her."

Kylie laughed.

Once he'd gone, she leaned back in bed, stared at the ceiling, and just breathed in the scent of roses, trying to remember every word he'd said. She wanted to remember this night forever.

Several days later, with her stomach gnawing on her backbone and Jonathon, her shadow of the day, in tow, Kylie set out to the dining room to get some breakfast.

Life had calmed down. A little, anyway. With the full moon behind them, Lucas was back to his normal, patient self. And he was being amazingly attentive, too. But if Kylie were honest, she sort of missed hearing his hum.

Not that she didn't enjoy his sweet side. He'd even brought her more roses last night. If Mrs. Parker didn't have reason enough to dislike her, Kylie figured the she-wolf's decimated rose garden would seal the deal.

Even Kylie's ghost was calmer. Jane Doe still made regular visits, but the ghost was back to giving Kylie the silent treatment. Which was fine for now.

Kylie ducked under a low-hanging branch on the trail and picked up speed.

"No! And I can't believe you'd even suggest it!"

Holiday's voice rang in Kylie's ear a good three hundred feet from the office. Kylie stopped and looked around to make sure the camp leader wasn't standing nearby.

She wasn't.

It must be the gifted hearing again. It had come and gone several times since her mom and Holiday's little discussion during Parents Day. Curious, Kylie looked at Jonathon to see if he'd heard it, too.

"What is it?" he asked.

"I thought I heard something. Did you hear it?"

"Hear what?" He started looking around. "That damn blue jay isn't back, is it? I'm telling you, it's a sick bird."

The bird had returned three more times. Jonathon had been present for two of them. "No. I thought I heard Holiday."

Jonathon tilted his head to the side as if putting his own sensitive hearing to the test. "I don't hear her."

So, was her hearing stronger than a vampire's? What did that mean? Especially when she still had the brain pattern of a human.

"It's not like I have a choice," Burnett said.

Great. They were fighting again. About what this time? Kylie wondered, and continued on to the dining hall. If she had to guess, Holiday was just finding another excuse to try to put some distance between her and Burnett. Since Kylie had walked in and found them kissing, she hadn't seen the two within fifty feet of each other.

"You have a choice," Holiday said. *"You go back and tell them that I said hell, no."*

"It's a couple of tests. They wouldn't take long and they could clear up everything."

"I said, no!"

"Now I'm hearing Holiday," Jonathon said. "She doesn't sound too happy."

"Don't you think this should be Kylie's decision?"

"What should be my decision?" Kylie muttered, and changed direction and started walking toward the office.

"No!" Holiday said.

"She wants answers. And this could give them to her."

Kylie moved faster. *What answers?* It didn't matter, she realized. She'd take any answers she could get.

"I won't allow it!"

"Won't allow what?" Kylie stormed into the office, leaving Jonathon behind.

Holiday and Burnett swung around. Holiday pointed to the door. "Get out!" she told Burnett.

"No!" Kylie stepped in front of him. "He stays. This is about me, and I need to know."

Holiday looked at Burnett with anger, then she looked at Kylie. "You wouldn't understand this."

"Why don't you try me?" She looked at Burnett. "Start talking."

He cut his gaze to Holiday.

"The FRU wants to run some tests on you," Holiday said. "To see if they can figure out what you are."

Hope rose in Kylie's chest. "I thought there weren't any tests that could tell me this?" She remembered asking Holiday that question before.

"There aren't!" Holiday said. "They just want to play around in your brain to—"

"I'll do it," Kylie said.

"No!" Holiday looked horrified. "I refuse to let them use you as some kind of lab rat. There are no guarantees that these tests are safe, and they may not even work."

Kylie looked at Burnett. "Are they safe?"

Burnett stared at Holiday, his eyes getting a pissed-off amber color. "I wouldn't let them do anything to her that's not safe," he growled. "Do you have that little faith in me?"

"I have that little faith in the FRU. History repeats itself."

"What kind of tests would they be?" Kylie asked.

"Just some CT scans," Burnett said.

"No!" Holiday turned back to Kylie. "They'll use you as a guinea pig."

"They're not going to hurt her," Burnett said.

"I know, because she's not agreeing to it."

The cold came into the room so fast that Kylie's breath sent tiny flakes of ice falling from her lips. Jane materialized, and at the same time, the three light bulbs in the fixture overhead burst. Shards of glass rained through the air.

"What the hell?" Burnett looked up and took a step closer to Kylie.

Holiday's crystals hanging throughout the room started swaying, sending rainbow colors spiraling around them.

The laptop computer on Holiday's desk started beeping, making serious malfunctioning noises.

"You stay away from her!" Jane shot across the room to stand between her and Burnett.

"Run, Kylie!" Jane yelled in the same tone she'd used to warn Kylie about the sinkhole.

"What's wrong?" Kylie demanded.

"He's wrong!" Jane yelled.

Holiday looked around the room. "What's happening, Kylie?"

"I think she thinks Burnett is trying to hurt me."

"Tell her to leave," Holiday insisted.

"Jane, you're going to have to go."

But Jane wasn't listening.

Burnett took another step closer to Kylie. Jane screamed and then jammed her hand inside his chest. Not only could Kylie see

Jane's hand, she saw the inside of Burnett's chest. And she watched in horror as Jane's hand closed around Burnett's heart.

"No!" Kylie screamed.

Burnett's gaze shot to Holiday. He reached for his chest.

"Stop it!" Kylie said.

Burnett dropped to the floor in a dead thud.

Chapter Thirty-four

Thirty minutes later, with Jonathon sitting under a tree a few feet away, Kylie sat on Holiday's porch, swatting away bugs and listening to Holiday, the doctor, and Burnett from inside the office.

"He asked you to take your shirt off," Holiday said.

"I don't need to take my shirt off," Burnett snapped. *"I'm fine."*

His voice was loud and clear, and he did indeed sound fine.

Not that it made Kylie feel any better.

"Maybe. Maybe not," Holiday said. *"We'll know as soon as you disrobe and let the doctor examine you."*

In a few minutes, Holiday came out and plopped on the porch beside Kylie. She had tears in her eyes. "I don't know why I'm worried about him. He's too pigheaded and stubborn to die."

Kylie laced her hands together. "I'm so sorry."

Holiday shook her head. "It wasn't your fault."

"You told me to get rid of her when I first told you about her. I refused, and she could have killed Burnett."

"She didn't want to kill him. She just wanted to get him away from you."

"Maybe I've been wrong all along. Maybe she is evil."

Holiday put her arm around Kylie's shoulder. "She wasn't evil. I felt her presence and her emotions. She was concerned about you. She did this to protect you, Kylie."

"Yeah, but, protect me from what? Did she really think Burnett was going hurt me?"

Holiday sighed. "She probably picked up on what I was feeling. I overreacted." She tightened her arm. "I mean, I refuse to let you be tested by the FRU. But I shouldn't have wigged out like that."

"You don't trust Burnett?" Kylie asked.

She shook her head. "I don't trust the FRU."

"Why? And if you don't trust them, then why are they involved with the camp? Besides, if they can really do some simple tests and tell me what I am, I want to do it."

Holiday closed her eyes for a second. "Don't take this wrong, Kylie. I'm not against the FRU. God knows we need them to keep things right. But they have no business testing people."

"But if they can really—"

"I can't let you do it. If they want to tell me the name of the test they want done, I'll ask our doctor if he can order it. But it will be under his care and his care only."

Kylie heard so much in the camp leader's voice. So much she wasn't saying. "Okay, what is it you're not telling me?"

It took a minute before Holiday finally sighed and started talking. "It was over forty years ago. It involved only one small branch of the FRU that has been shut down, and charges were brought against a lot of people. They were doing scientific tests on supernaturals. Something about figuring out genetics. The subjects were forced into doing it, and some people never completely recovered from the tests. It's not as if I think they're doing it again, but I refuse to have you go there so they can poke and prod you to find answers."

Kylie looked at Holiday. Bits and pieces of Jane's vision started replaying in her mind like an old movie. And everything suddenly made sense. "The FRU killed Jane Doe. They killed her and then they buried her with Berta Littlemon in the Fallen Cemetery."

Holiday's eyes widened. "You can't know this for sure."

"I do," Kylie said. "In the vision, Jane was called a subject. Her husband was one, too. And the doctor was a vampire. They mentioned her not having a pattern."

Kylie pulled her knees up and hugged them, trying to wrap her head around everything as it all came together. She didn't understand how Jane's baby fit in, but on some things she was clear.

"No wonder she went after Burnett," Kylie said. "She thought he was trying to do to me what the FRU had done to her."

Kylie was disappointed that Jane Doe was a no-show the next morning. Kylie had hoped now that she knew about the FRU, she could help Jane remember other things, like her name. That together they could figure out what it was Jane needed in order to cross over.

But dead people, just like the living, rarely did what Kylie wanted them to do.

A knock sounded at her door. "Come in."

The door opened and Miranda and Della both squeezed through the opening and shut the door extra quickly behind them.

"What is it?" Kylie asked.

"There's three guys here working on putting in the heating unit," Della said.

"And they're yummy," Miranda said. The contractors who worked around Shadow Falls had become a popular subject for all the female campers. Especially when they took their shirts off in the afternoons.

"As yummy as Perry?" Kylie teased. Lately, Miranda had been spending almost every free moment with the shape-shifter.

"Not quite as yummy," Miranda said, and then grinned. "But close."

"Well, thanks for the warning. I'll get ready to be awed."

"Just don't come out wearing nothing but a towel," Della said, also grinning. "Unless you're into that."

A few minutes later, Kylie walked out fully dressed, hair combed, and the only thing she'd added in honor of their company was a touch of lip gloss.

Miranda sat at the table, sipping a glass of orange juice, Della had a glass of blood, and two of the guys were down on the floor on their knees, saws at their sides and some kind of heating vent beside them.

As much as Kylie hated to admit it, Miranda was right. They were yummy. Both were in their early twenties, had dark hair, and wore tight T-shirts that showed off their dark tans and lots of muscles.

They looked up and met Kylie's eyes. Kylie tensed when they pinched their eyebrows at her, but she did the same thing. They were both werewolves. She saw the shocked look in their eyes when they saw her brain pattern.

"I'm the token human," she said.

Della and Miranda snickered. The two guys smiled and went back to work. No doubt they had orders from Burnett not to flirt with the female campers.

Kylie went to the fridge to get her own glass of juice. She heard Miranda's door open, and the third contractor joined them. Kylie turned around and peered at him under her lashes. This one was equally hot. Black hair. Wide shoulders. Thin waist.

His gaze met Kylie's and her juice slipped from her fingers and shattered at her feet.

His hair had changed. His name, Red, probably a nickname, no longer fit, but his eyes hadn't changed. The image of him appearing in her dreams, and of him staring at her in the mirror with blood dripping down his chin, filled her head. Then the image flashed, and she saw him plastered on her windshield and ramming his hand through her car window. As if that weren't enough, she saw the image of him staring at her while she was chained to the chair when he and his grandfather abducted her.

"Della?" Kylie said in an even voice, hoping she could warn her before the shit hit the fan.

But Della didn't answer. Kylie turned. The vamp still sat at the table, her glass at her lips. A few drops of blood hung in the air between her lips and the edge of the glass. Della didn't breathe. Didn't move. She looked frozen.

The shit had already hit the fan.

Kylie's gaze shot to Miranda, who was also frozen, a finger at her ear as if to brush back a strand of hair.

Ditto for the two guys on the floor.

"It's just you and me, Kylie," the rogue said.

She refocused on Miranda and Della. "Whatever you've done to my friends, you'd better undo it," she growled, and her blood fizzed with fury.

"Don't get worked up. They are fine. As soon as I release them, they will go back to normal and not remember a thing." He looked back to the table and then to her.

"So do it!" Kylie said.

He sighed. "I've never seen anyone who cared so much about others."

Though she wasn't sure why, Kylie checked his brain pattern. He was a werewolf. But how was that possible? He was a vampire. She tried not to show her surprise, but he saw it.

"What are you?" Kylie went ahead and asked.

"I'm the same thing you are. Just born a few minutes later than midnight." He took a step closer. "That's why we belong together. We're soul mates, Kylie. That's what we are."

She tightened her brows again, and this time he was human. Her heart thudded in her chest. "I'm not your soul mate. I'll die first."

"That's why I'm here." He took another step toward her.

She backed up. "You're here to kill me?"

"No." He stopped moving. Something about his answer and his tone rang true. "I'm here to protect you. Though you don't make it easy."

The sound of thunder rumbled from outside. He glanced out the window, and when his gaze came back to hers, Kylie knew something else.

"You were the eagle," she said. "And the deer. You're a shape-shifter?" And if they were the same, as he said, did that make her a shape-shifter, too?

"No. I mean, yes. I was the deer and the eagle, but I'm not a shape-shifter."

Then another thought hit. "You protected me, but you killed those innocent girls in Fallen. Why?"

He cut his eyes downward. "Would it upset you terribly if I said it was to impress you?"

"Impress me? You're sick."

"But they were mean to you and your friends."

"They didn't deserve to die."

"I know you feel that way now. I didn't really know you then. Now, I do. I wouldn't have done it if—"

"You don't know me now."

He shrugged. "I sometimes don't understand you. But I have watched you. You are an interesting study. I have always wondered what it would have been like . . . to have been born at midnight. Funny how just a few minutes on a clock can make a difference. I sometimes wonder if maybe—" The sound of thunder shook the cabin again.

Kylie could swear she saw regret in his eyes. But maybe not. The light in the cabin had been chased away by dark shadows. Kylie sensed the shadows were there for her.

Lightning flashed from the window. "I don't have a lot of time," he said, "but I wanted to tell you—"

"I will not go with you!" She might not win the battle, but she'd go down fighting.

"No, not this time. I'll come back for you later. Like I said, I'm here to protect you."

"From what?"

He glanced at the two contractors, frozen, not breathing, the same as Della and Miranda. "They want you dead."

Did he mean the two guys? "Who wants me dead?"

"The others. My grandfather and his friends. The others like us."

"Like us how? And why would they want me dead?"

"They are impatient and afraid of what you might be able to accomplish if you don't join us. But I will hold them off until you come around. But you must change your mind, soon."

He pointed to the taller of the guys on the floor, still frozen, as if they were working on the vents in the floor. "This guy, he was sent here to kill you. I had a wizard friend of mine peek into the future, and learned that your other friends would have gotten here in time to save you. But"—he pointed to the table—"the little witch wouldn't have made it. And for some crazy reason, I felt compelled to stop that from happening. I knew how much it would hurt you if she died." His brows creased as if he were confused. "It was an odd feeling, wanting to save her, caring if she died, because it's not like me to care. But . . . because of you, I did. I cared."

The words *Someone lives and someone dies* whispered in Kylie's head again.

"No!" This couldn't be happening. It just couldn't.

Then the sound of footsteps hitting the front porch vibrated the floor beneath her.

"Until later." He disappeared.

The door swung open and hit the back of the wall with a loud whack. Burnett, Lucas, Perry, and Derek rushed in.

"What the hell?" Della leapt out of her chair. Miranda dropped her juice and it splattered to the floor. Kylie's heart sighed when she saw they were okay. And yet . . . somewhere deep down, she'd believed him when he'd said they would be.

But did that mean she also believed him about everything else? Was she like him? She looked at Miranda and considered the possibility that she might have died had the rogue not intervened.

"You two!" Burnett said, pointing to the two men on the floor. "Come with me."

They stood up slowly. Then the taller one, the one the rogue had pointed to, leapt at the closed window. Glass shattered, wood splintered, and then he was outside. Burnett and Lucas went after him.

Chapter Thirty-five

"It doesn't make sense," Burnett growled an hour later as he paced back and forth in Holiday's office. Kylie agreed. Nothing made sense anymore.

They had caught the guy who'd been hired to kill her. But his information offered zero help in finding the person who'd hired him. They were no closer to finding the real culprit now than they'd been before.

Kylie, however, felt closer than ever to finding answers. No, she didn't know what she was, but at least she knew there were others like her. Question was, were they all evil? Was she the only one who'd been born at midnight?

"If he had wanted to take you, why didn't he?" Burnett stopped pacing in front of Holiday and Kylie on the sofa.

"He didn't say . . . exactly," Kylie said. "He said he would eventually convince them that I wasn't a danger to them. As if he thought he could change my mind about going with him."

"That's stupid," Burnett said.

Kylie decided to ask the question that had been bugging her for a while now. "How did he freeze Miranda and Della and the other two?"

Holiday answered, "There are some wizards and very strong witches and warlocks who can stop time."

"Do you think that's what he is? What I am?"

Holiday shrugged. "I've never heard of a witch or a wizard being able to change their brain patterns."

"Because it's impossible," Burnett snapped.

"Not really." Kylie pointed to herself.

Burnett closed his eyes and took a deep breath. "This whole thing is friggin' unbelievable."

Holiday stood up. "Which is why you can't report this to the FRU."

Burnett looked at her as if she'd lost her mind. "They have to be told."

"Why? They know someone is trying to kill her. We tell them about that, not about the changing brain patterns."

"Why would we keep it from them?"

Holiday crossed her arms. "Because it will give them more of a reason to take Kylie and use her as some kind of lab rat."

Kylie's gaze shot from Holiday to Burnett. "Did they ever say if they would allow Dr. Pearson to do the tests?"

Burnett's grimace deepened. "They said regular hospitals don't have the necessary equipment."

"Which is exactly what I thought," Holiday blasted. "We have no idea if those tests are safe."

"They said they were." But Burnett's tone had lost its force, and Kylie wondered if he believed it anymore.

"They killed the spirit I'm helping," Kylie said.

"You don't know that for sure."

"Yes, I do. And if you need proof, dig up the grave. Her body is in there."

Burnett swore. "The FRU is not the enemy, Kylie. I admit they've made mistakes in the past, but that was then."

"Right," Holiday said, her tone still sharp. "But they'll sacrifice one if they think it will benefit the whole." She pointed at Kylie. "One of my teens will not be that sacrifice. And if you can't accept that, then walk out of here right now. Because we can't work together."

His gaze shot to Kylie, then back to Holiday. "Do you realize what you're asking me to do? To betray my oath and keep information from the FRU?"

"It's your choice," Holiday said.

.Burnett closed his eyes, shook his head, and walked out of the office. Kylie didn't know if that was his answer, but from the sheer pain on Holiday's face, she certainly believed it.

When Kylie left Holiday's office after their meeting, Lucas was waiting. He'd gotten himself assigned shadow duty. He took her down to the stream and they stretched out on the warm grass and tried to find shapes in the clouds. Between finding everything from George Washington to dinosaurs in the sky, Kylie told him about Burnett and Holiday's argument.

"Burnett wants to tell the FRU, and Holiday thinks that will give them more reason to take me in for tests."

Propping up on his elbow, he stared down at her. "How do you feel about being tested?"

"I don't know. Part of me wants to do it if they really think it would give me answers, but Holiday's adamant that it could be dangerous. And I've always trusted her." And then there was what happened to the ghost.

"More than you trust Burnett?" Lucas asked.

"Maybe a little." Kylie looked into his blue eyes. "Do you think I'm wrong?"

"No. I probably trust Holiday more, too." He traced her lips with his finger.

"I just can't stand the thought of them fighting," she said, loving the feel of his touch, but her heart wouldn't let go of the problems at hand.

"That's between them," Lucas said.

"But it's about me. And I know they care about each other. I don't want to be the reason they gave up."

"You don't know they're giving up. I heard Burnett went back to the FRU offices to interrogate the captured were again. He'll be back."

"I hope so." But her heart wasn't so sure.

He leaned down and gently pressed his lips to hers. It was a soft, warm kiss. When he pulled back, his eyes held touches of amber color and she knew whatever thought had crossed his mind had stirred his anger.

"You know, I won't let that rogue have you. You're mine."

"I know," Kylie told him. What she didn't say was that she was worried no one might be able to prevent the rogue from carrying out his promise. So far, nothing had stopped him. Sure, if he was telling the truth about them being the same type of supernatural, and she believed him—she didn't understand it, but she believed him—then she was equally powerful. But if Holiday was right and she was a protector, then she would be able to use those powers only to protect others. That meant she was completely vulnerable to his whims.

It wasn't a good feeling. But she refused to cater to defeat. And she meant what she'd told the rogue. She would die before she became a part of some evil gang.

But she wasn't dead right now. And the proof was in how alive Lucas made her feel.

"Kiss me again," she said.

He grinned. "Is that a request or an order?"

"Both."

"Well, in that case . . ."

. . .

The next day, Burnett still hadn't returned. Holiday was moody, and Kylie had a raging headache. Lucas had found her earlier and told her his grandmother was ill and he was going to check on her. At around four, Kylie gave up and asked for permission to go lie down. Della, on shadowing duty, followed Kylie back to the cabin.

She didn't know how long she'd been asleep when the cold hit. She opened her eyes, feeling the icy mist on her breath. Jane was here.

"Thank God, you're awake," a feminine voice said. But it wasn't Jane's voice.

Kylie shot up. Through a curtain of hair, she saw Ellie standing at the foot of her bed.

"How did you get in here?" she asked.

Elle shrugged. Kylie glanced at the window she'd left open.

Kylie pulled the blanket up closer to her chest and looked around the room for Jane. She hadn't appeared yet, but she was here. Chill bumps climbed up and down her arms. Jane hadn't been here the last few days, and Kylie hoped she was finally ready to talk. "You know what, Ellie. This really isn't a good time. I have some business to take care of."

"But I need you to go to Derek," Ellie said. "He's upset. Not right."

Kylie studied her closer.

Ellie frowned. "You have to go to him." She shook her head. "I'm afraid he's hurt."

Kylie yanked her covers off. "Hurt? Where is he?"

"At the park about a half mile past the stream where the dinosaur tracks are."

"Why's he there?" Kylie asked.

"I don't know, but he needs you."

"Why does he need me?" Kylie slipped her tennis shoes on. "Has something happened?"

"I don't know," Ellie said. "I'm confused."

"Is he hurt?" Kylie's heart gripped in fear for Derek.

"No. I don't think so."

Ellie wasn't making sense. Kylie worried it might be a ploy to get her and Derek together. But something about the panic in Ellie's voice said differently.

"Let's go." Ellie moved toward the window.

"I have to get Della. She's my shadow, remember?"

"Hurry."

Kylie moved to the door and looked back again for Jane. She hadn't manifested, but her deathly cold still chilled the room. *I'll be back shortly,* she told the spirit in her head. *Please don't leave. We need to talk.*

Jane didn't answer. No surprise. Kylie walked out her bedroom door and Della looked up from the computer.

"You're slipping," Kylie said.

"How am I slipping?" Della asked.

"Ellie's here. "

"Shit! I am slipping." She stomped into Kylie's bedroom as if ready to give Ellie hell. Not that Kylie worried too much. Della and Ellie had bonded since Della invited her into her vampire circle.

Della came right back out. "Did she leave?"

"No way!"

Kylie stormed back into the bedroom. But Della was wrong. Ellie stood in the same place she'd been standing when she left. "You have to hurry."

"Maybe you dreamed it," Della said, stepping into the room.

The cold in the room pressed against Kylie's skin again. Kylie stared at Ellie. Her heart rolled over and tears crawled up her throat. No!

"What happened, Ellie?" Tears slipped onto Kylie's cheeks. "Is Derek okay?"

"I don't remember." Ellie sounded befuddled.

"Kylie? Is this a dream?" Della asked.

More than anything, Kylie wished it were. She looked at Ellie.

"What happened?" she asked again.

"You have to hurry. I'm worried about Derek."

Fear suddenly set in. Fear for Derek. Fear she might be too late to save Ellie and Derek. It didn't matter how much of her soul she'd have to give to save them. She'd give it.

"What's going on?" Miranda walked in.

"She's freaking again," Della snapped.

Kylie, with tears in her eyes, looked at Miranda. "I need you to call Holiday. Tell her Della and I are going up to the park past the dinosaur tracks. Derek's there and he might be hurt. Come on," Kylie said, and started to run.

Della caught Kylie by the arm. "What's going on?"

Kylie drew in a shaky breath. "Ellie's dead at some park close to here. And Derek was with her. We have to go before it's too late!"

Miranda let out a sob.

"How? What happened?" Della's eyes widened with emotion.

Kylie didn't have time to explain. Ellie bolted out the door, and Kylie went after her. Della's footsteps thudded against the earth as she came behind her.

Kylie never slowed down. Neither did Ellie or Della. When they got to the dinosaur tracks, they crossed the creek and jumped a fence into the park grounds. The path went uphill quickly, but Kylie kept up with no problem. Her blood fizzed with the strange kind of energy she got when she was protecting someone she loved. She just prayed it wasn't too late.

"It's just around the bend," Ellie said. She'd been quiet during the run. Then she suddenly stopped. Panic filled her gaze. *"Oh, my God. I remember."*

"What?" Kylie stopped beside Ellie.

"What? What?" When Della met Kylie's gaze, she must have realized she hadn't been talking to her, and she simply nodded.

"I followed someone here," Ellie said. *"I spotted him running from the camp. I was almost here when I heard someone behind me. It was Derek. That's when the person I'd followed attacked."*

"Who was it?" Kylie's mind went to Red. "Was it a young guy, red or brownish hair?"

"No, it was an old dude. Vampire."

Mario. They never had a chance!

Kylie's chest filled with pain. And guilt. This was all her fault. "Where's Derek? Where's your body?" She had to save them.

Ellie pointed to the side of the mountain. It looked as if it had recently been disturbed. Loose rock lay around the ledge. *"Derek came around the bend and a bolt of lightning struck. He was slammed against the rocks. His head was bleeding, but he was breathing. But then more lightning struck. I picked him up and put him in the small cave and moved the rocks in front of him. I was doing that when . . . everything went blank."*

Kylie ran to the edge of the cliff and started moving the loose boulders.

Della moved in. "What are we doing?" Worry filled her expression.

"He's behind here," Kylie said. They moved the rocks to the side. Rocks that weighted well over four and five hundred pounds. Her strength didn't even surprise her; she thought only of Derek and Ellie.

"Oh God!" Della took a step back.

Kylie saw Ellie's mangled body lying between the rocks. Kylie's breath caught, and her tears started falling faster. She picked up Ellie and moved her to the side and rested her body on the rocky path.

"She's dead," Della said.

"Keep moving the rocks," Kylie ordered Della, and with everything Kylie had she prayed Derek was still alive. Prayed she could bring Ellie back.

She laid her hands on Ellie's battered body and sent up prayers that this worked. She closed her eyes, concentrated, and moved her palms over the injuries, as she had with Lucas and with Sara. Blood, Ellie's blood, coated Kylie's hands. She cried harder and tried harder, but no matter how hard she concentrated, her hands didn't heat up.

Suddenly, Ellie was sitting beside her body. *"It's too late. Look."* Ellie pointed up at the sky. The sun was a big ball of orange. *"I see my mother up there. She's waiting for me."*

"No," Kylie said. "Don't go. I'm trying to bring you back."

"But I want to go with her. I've missed her."

"No!" Kylie screamed again.

Ellie's spirit stood. *"Derek's okay."* She pointed back to Della as she moved the rocks. *"But I have to go. Thank you, Kylie Galen. Thank you for being my friend. Thank you for teaching me to think beyond myself. Thank you for everything."*

"Please don't," Kylie begged. But it was too late. Ellie's spirit started floating up toward the setting sun and Kylie knew it was hopeless.

"I got him," Della yelled. "I got Derek."

Kylie bolted to him. He was unconscious but breathing. She found the wounds on his head and pressed her hand against them. More blood oozed between her fingers, but she didn't care. Her hands grew hot and she felt the heat of her palms sink into Derek's scalp.

"Did you save Ellie?" Della asked.

"No, I'm sorry," Kylie said, and stared at Derek.

"Holiday and the others are coming," Della said, and when Kylie looked up, Della had tears running down her face.

"I tried to save her," Kylie said. "I really tried."

Derek suddenly jolted up. "What happened?"

Kylie stood. Derek looked at her and then pain filled his eyes. "Ellie?"

Kylie put a hand over her mouth and more tears flowed.

Derek ran out and found Ellie's body. He knelt beside her and Kylie saw his eyes fill with tears of rage. "Who did this?"

Guilt swelled in Kylie. "It was the old vampire, the one after me."

Holiday and about a dozen of the others came moving around the bend of the ledge. Kylie looked for Lucas, wishing he were here to hold her, but then she remembered he'd gone to see his grandmother.

She turned and faced the cave, her emotions too raw. She heard several of the campers gasp and some cry. No doubt they were seeing Ellie's body.

Holiday moved in and placed a hand on Kylie's shoulder.

Tears streamed down her face; she held out her bloody hands and gazed at Holiday. "What good is this gift, if I can't save those I want to save?"

Holiday didn't try to answer; she just wrapped Kylie in her arms and held her close.

"We need to go before it gets dark," Holiday finally said.

Derek picked up Ellie's body as though she were a rag doll, then Kylie saw him reach back down for her LITTLE VAMP cap. He tucked the cap under his arm and carried Ellie down the steep path.

They walked for about five minutes; no one spoke. Derek dropped Ellie's cap, and the wind blew it past Kylie. Kylie heard him ask someone to pick it up. At the very back of the single-file line, and feeling numb, Kylie turned to go grab the cap. She saw it only about twenty feet away. She moved in, almost ready to reach for it, when a big gust of wind moved it closer to the edge.

Kylie moved another couple of feet. The wind took the cap to the very edge. It hovered there, half on and half off the ledge.

Only then did Kylie sense the unnaturalness of the breeze.

She wasn't alone.

The sound of a dry branch snapping had never sounded scarier. Someone stood behind her. And less than two feet in front stood . . .

death. She had no idea how deep the cavern went, but she suspected the fall would be fatal.

Breath held, thinking any second she would feel someone give her that fatal push, she turned. The old vampire Mario and two other elderly supernaturals stood there staring at her with cold, calculating gazes. All three were dressed like monks, their dark robes stirring in the wind.

"Kylie Galen," Mario said. His voice sounded as aged as he looked, but the sense of power could not be overlooked. Was this really what she was? She studied Mario; closer, his eyes were black, coal black. She saw only evil, and the idea that she shared anything in common with these people disgusted her. "So we meet again."

She took a small step back, closer to the ledge. "Much to my misfortune," Kylie said, and she felt the heel of her tennis shoe find the edge of the embankment.

" 'Tis true, my dear," he said. "Although, if you are so inclined as to save yourself, join us now. Pledge to us your allegiance and you will live. My grandson will make you a good husband."

"What are you?" She tightened her brows and saw into their patterns. Mario was vampire, the bearded one was warlock, and the other carried the pattern of a werewolf. But all three patterns were dark and ominous.

"Join us and you will have your answers."

Kylie swallowed and sent up a little prayer. She prayed for help. Then she prayed for forgiveness for anything and everything she'd ever done wrong. Then she prayed for courage. She took another step back until her feet hit nothing.

Chapter Thirty-six

Gravity grabbed Kylie from below. Her breath caught at the same time a hand caught her arm. Her heart throbbing in her chest, she looked up into the face of her rescuer. Red.

He jerked her back to safety.

She found her footing, beside him. But her mind raced as she realized he'd saved her. "Hello, Kylie," the rogue said.

She just stared at him, not sure what to say.

"She made her choice," said the bearded man standing beside Mario. His dark brown robe fluttered in the wind as he raised his hand and pointed those long, aged fingers at her. She stared in something akin to horror as flames came from the tips of his fingers.

Red jumped in front of her, and the old man's flames stopped. "I told you I would change her mind. Give her time. She's too good to kill."

"She has made her choice," Mario said. "Her time is up. Move out of the way. Let her plummet to her death."

"No," Red said.

Kylie stared at Red, confused by his willingness to protect her. And yet hadn't he been doing it all along?

"You dare to disobey me in front of my peers?" Mario growled.

"I dare," Red said. "I've spent my entire life living by your rules. You murdered my mother. You forced my father to run away. I've accepted that all my life, and I have asked nothing of you but this. Spare her. For me."

"She cannot be spared," said the other old man. "She will bring us down."

"She won't. I'll take care of her," Red said. "I'll change her mind, I'll convince her." There was pleading in his voice.

"The decision is made," the bearded man said.

The second old man raised his hand, and a surge of wind picked her up from the ground and knocked her back toward the edge.

She felt herself falling. Felt the air part as her body descended. Fear made her tense; grief for everyone she loved chased off the fear. She saw faces in her mind's eye that she would miss. Things she would never do. She saw Lucas's face and then Derek's. She saw her friends— new and old. Then she blinked, unable to breathe. She saw the sun setting and found an odd sort of calm settle within her. The colors in the dusk sky filled her mind with a surge of calm. She'd be able to be with Daniel and Nana.

Something or someone caught her again. Her memory shot back to being caught by Perry. The grips around her wrist were not human. The jolt brought air into her lungs. Had Perry come to save her?

"I have you. Hold on!"

But the voice didn't belong to Perry. It was Red.

A bolt of lightning shot past them, so close that Kylie felt the sting of it.

In seconds, the huge bird landed back on the ledge and set her gently on her feet. There were no sparkles as he changed back to human form. He was more than just a shape-shifter.

"You okay?" he asked.

Kylie looked at him through the tears in her eyes and nodded. She remembered him saving her from the snake. From the lightning strike in the woods and then trying to save her from the sinkhole. She'd never said thank you, never considered needing to, because all she saw in him was evil. But then he'd saved Miranda, too.

"I don't even know your real name," she managed to say.

"Roberto." He smiled. "I managed to snag this." He handed her Ellie's cap.

Right then Kylie knew. Red . . . Roberto wasn't all evil.

"Thank you," she said.

He stared at her as if he didn't know how to respond. Then he reached out and brushed a tear from her cheek. "You are even pretty when you cry."

"No, I'm not. I get all red and—" A bolt of lightning shot down from above. Roberto pushed her away. Her back hit the rock wall behind her. He looked prepared to run, but before he did, the lightning struck again. It hit him. The ground beneath her shook at the impact. The smell of burned flesh filled her nose.

Kylie dropped to her knees. Panic clawed at her throat. She didn't want to see it, but she couldn't look away. Roberto's eyes turned blood red, and his body contorted backward; something that looked like smoke billowed out of his mouth, and Kylie knew it was his soul. And then he fell. The sound of his soulless body hitting the hard earth was pure sadness.

She moved to try to save him.

"Don't." The sound of his voice startled her. She looked at him. His spirit stood several feet from his body, gazing toward the dusk-filled sky. *"I don't want to stay."* Purples, shades of bright pinks, golds, and shades of gray now laced the sky.

"Do you see them?" he asked.

For a second, she thought he meant his grandfather and the two other men, but then she did see, and she understood. Angels were dancing in the painted sky; like birds, they moved gracefully in the wind.

Kylie nodded. "I do." But she still had to try. She laid her hands on his body. And concentrated. Nothing happened. Her hands would not heat up. Giving up, she finally gazed up at his spirit.

"Why would you want to save me?" his spirit asked.

"Because you saved me," she said, and looked up.

He gazed back at her, and all hints of evil were gone from his eyes. What she saw was a person who never had a chance. A boy raised into evil, taught evil, and never loved. *"I understand now,"* he said. *"I was wrong, Kylie Galen. You are not my soul mate. But because of you, I have saved my soul."* Then slowly his spirit was taken, pulled up by the sky. He became part of the colors in the dusky sky. Part of the beauty, part of something that was eternal. The death angels took him at the last second of dusk.

Kylie wasn't sure how much time passed, but the colors of the sky had turned black when another *whoosh* of wind hit. What was a flash in the night suddenly became a body, crouched down only a few feet from her. Kylie scooted back and then recognized Burnett.

"Are you okay?" he asked.

Kylie nodded.

"I need to get you out of here, now." He pulled her up.

She looked down at the body near her feet. And realized his eyes, empty, dead, were open. She lowered herself and closed his lids.

When she stood up, she told Burnett, "He died saving me."

"Then maybe hell will be easy on him." Burnett picked her up.

"He didn't go to hell," Kylie said.

She didn't know if he heard her. It didn't matter. She knew.

Burnett carried Kylie back to the main office, where Holiday paced across the front porch. He set Kylie down.

"Thank God!" Holiday ran to Kylie and hugged her.

"Thank you," Holiday said to Burnett, but when she released Kylie, he was already gone.

Her frown deepened, but her expression changed and she met Kylie's eyes. "Are you okay?"

Kylie nodded and tried not to cry. "Is Derek okay?"

"He's resting."

Kylie nodded.

"What happened, Kylie? You were there one minute and then gone the next."

Kylie pulled out Ellie's hat from her jeans pocket. "I went back for this, and . . ." The tears she didn't want to cry came anyway, and she told Holiday the whole story.

Kylie wasn't asleep when she heard the knock on her door several hours later. She heard Della answer it. Then she heard Lucas's voice. He came into her bedroom and pulled her against him, and Kylie held on to him like a life preserver. She needed his strength. Needed to feel his arms around her. They stayed like that for hours, not kissing, not making out, just holding on to each other.

The next morning, the mood at the camp was somber at best. Everyone missed Ellie. They missed Burnett. They missed Derek. He'd left for the weekend to stay with his mom. Kylie was almost afraid to see him. Ellie's funeral was set for next week because the FRU wanted to do an autopsy. Kylie knew that no one at the camp blamed her, but she couldn't quite keep from blaming herself.

Holiday, sensing Kylie's emotion, had taken her to the falls. It was there, behind the wall of water, that Kylie felt most of the ugliness of guilt lift. She asked the question why, why it had to happen. The answer came in a feeling. Fate had called Ellie home. Fate was still pissing Kylie off. But some of the guilt did fade.

Holiday worked like crazy to keep the camp running and do interviews for teachers. It was too much for one person, though. So Kylie got together with a couple of the other campers and assigned jobs. One person oversaw the contractors, while another answered calls at the office.

Holiday almost protested but then threw in the towel and accepted their help.

On Thursday afternoon, when Lucas had her for shadow duty, Kylie asked if he'd seen Burnett.

"No, but he's around," Lucas said. "He's set guards around the camp in case anything else happens."

Kylie hoped nothing else would happen. According to Miranda, whoever had been hanging around was now gone.

Apparently, so was Kylie's ghost, because she hadn't appeared in days.

The next afternoon, Kylie was sitting on the front porch when Derek walked up. He must have returned early.

The lingering guilt she felt at Ellie's death bubbled to the surface. And when she saw that he still had shadows of grief in his eyes, she felt her guilt swell to the point of pain.

He lowered himself beside her. "That's what I came to see you about."

She looked at him, unsure what he meant. "I knew you would feel responsible for this. And I just wanted you to know that Ellie made that choice when she took off after the intruder. I made the choice to follow her. It's not your fault. You would have done the same for anyone in this camp."

Kylie felt a knot form in her throat. "But he was here because of me."

"I know. I'm sure Ellie knew it when she went after him. But it didn't stop her. And she would be so unhappy if she knew you blamed yourself for her death. It would be a dishonor to her memory if I let you keep blaming yourself. She liked you. She liked you a lot."

Kylie felt a few tears roll past her lashes, and Derek put his arm around her. It wasn't a boyfriend kind of hug, just a hug from a friend who was offering a warm touch of comfort. And it felt really good.

When the next day came and Jane was still a no-show, Kylie went to Holiday with a request.

"No." Holiday shoved herself back in her desk chair.

"But I need to see her, and I know she's there."

"Don't you remember what happened the last time you went?"

"I remember I survived," Kylie said. "I also remember I ended up helping another lost soul, and I learned something when I was there. I need to go, Holiday."

Holiday slapped her pen onto the desk. "Someone is trying to kill you."

"*Was* trying," Kylie said. "I think Miranda is right. They're gone right now."

"Why would they leave?"

"I don't know. But I refuse to live my life in a prison."

"This isn't a prison," Holiday said.

"It is if I can't ever leave."

Holiday scowled. "If I say no, you're still going to go, aren't you?"

Kylie gave the question some thought and answered honestly. "Probably."

"Fine. I'll clear an hour after lunch and we'll—"

"I don't think you should go," Kylie said.

"Why?"

"I've been there. They know me, and if you show up, it might confuse things. I think you scared Jane Doe. She might not show herself if you're there."

Holiday's frown deepened. "There is no way in hell that I'm letting you go by yourself."

"Not by myself," Kylie insisted. "You could call Burnett."

Holiday frowned, but Kylie knew she wouldn't say no. Not when it involved someone's safety. And yes, this might have been a bit of a ploy to get them back together again, but it was killing Kylie to see Holiday so miserable.

Besides, Kylie did want to help Jane Doe.

Burnett agreed to the plan. But after Ellie's death, he said he wasn't going in with just the two of them. Lucas wasn't there. He'd driven into Houston to get the contractors their supplies. He wouldn't be back until three. So Burnett recommended Derek and Della.

Derek looked thrilled when she asked if he would go with her. He'd agreed before she told him where they were going.

"It's the cemetery," she said. "And there will be ghosts there."

"No problem."

Della hadn't been so thrilled. But of course, after grumbling, she agreed to go.

When they arrived at the Fallen Cemetery gates, Della grumbled some more. Derek put his warm hand against Kylie's back and whispered, "It's okay. I'm here."

Obviously, he'd read her misgivings about making the trip. Sure, she'd put up a good front with Holiday, but it didn't mean she wasn't scared. She could still remember how terrified she'd felt when the ghosts had charged her all at once.

"Thanks." Then she mentally pulled up her big-girl panties and walked through the gates, with Della on one side of her and Derek and Burnett on the other.

Sun and shadows danced across the graves at the same time the unnatural cold fell upon them like an invisible cloud of fog.

Derek leaned in again. "I need to talk to you . . . when we can steal a minute. It's important. Please."

She nodded.

"*It's her. She's back . . .*" Kylie heard one voice and then a merge of voices, male and female, young and old.

"*She said she'd come back.*"

"*And I thought she was just bullshitting us.*"

"*I told you she wasn't lying.*"

Tension pulled at her skull, forecasting a headache. But the spirit of the old man's wife manifested and the voices retreated.

"*My husband got his medicines right, thanks to you.*"

"That's good," Kylie said out loud.

"What's good?" Derek asked.

"She not talking to you," Della said. "Freaky, isn't it?"

"It's not that bad," Derek said, but Kylie saw him cutting his green eyes from side to side, as though he wondered where the spirits were. Burnett remained silent, standing stoic. He'd hardly spoken since he'd met them at the front of the camp.

Why haven't you passed over? Kylie asked this question in her head as she ambled down the path between the tombstones.

"*I decided to just wait on him,*" Ima said. "*But Catherine passed on. That was the woman you helped. Her kids came here. I heard them say they're planning on changing her tombstone to show her real name. That was nice of you to do that.*"

Kylie nodded. *Have you seen the other one? The one you call Berta Littlemon?*

"*She was just here. She's been a basket case since they took her away.*"

"Took her away?" Kylie asked aloud again.

The spirit just shrugged and said, "*There she is. Sitting by the grave.*"

"I'm going to be right over there." Kylie pointed to the grave where Jane sat on the ground.

"As long as we can see you," Burnett said.

Kylie moved over to Jane. The ghost looked up and the sun hit her face. She had tears webbing her dark lashes. She didn't have on any makeup. She looked young. And pregnant.

"Are you okay?" Kylie sat down next to Jane.

The spirit looked back at the grave. *"I want to remember so badly. But my brain doesn't work. Sometimes I feel as if the answers are right there, but I can't reach them. Then I remember something and it disappears. Why doesn't my brain work right?"*

Kylie hesitated. But Jane deserved to know. Just like Kylie deserved to get her own answers. "I don't know everything, but I know some."

"What?" she asked.

"There's an organization called the FRU. They're like the government for supernaturals. According to the leader of our camp, several years ago, the FRU were doing tests, something about genetics. I don't know what kind of tests they ran, but from the vision I had, I think you were one of the ones they tested, and they operated on you. You had your head shaved and had stitches. In the vision, you looked paralyzed. I think something went wrong with the test they did, so . . . they killed you."

Jane put her hand over her trembling lips. *"I remember I showed you that. They put a pillow over my face."*

"Yes," Kylie said.

"I didn't want to do the tests, but . . . my husband. What was his name?" she asked Kylie.

"I don't know."

Jane shook her head. *"He insisted that we do it, so they would leave us alone."*

"Who would leave you alone?" Kylie asked, wanting to make sure they were still talking about the FRU.

"The organization that you said. If we didn't agree to be tested, they'd imprison us."

"Why?"

Jane paused again. *"I can't remember. But I think it was because we were different."* She looked at the grave. The dirt around the tombstone had been disturbed. *"He took me away. He dug me out of the ground."*

"Who did?" Kylie leaned closer.

"That bad man."

"What bad man?"

"The one who wanted you to be tested."

"Burnett?" Kylie asked. "He took you away?"

She nodded. *"I don't like him."*

Kylie stared at the grave, trying to figure out what that meant. "He's not bad," she said. But why would he dig up Jane's body? Was it to prove what the FRU had done? Or was it to protect the FRU from her accusations?

"He looks bad." Jane pointed toward the path.

Kylie looked up. Burnett stopped in front of her. "I can explain it."

Kylie stood. "I hope so."

He frowned but didn't explain, so she decided to start asking questions.

"Why did you take Jane Doe's body?"

He hesitated. "I thought you wanted to know who she was."

Kylie sensed he was speaking only half the truth. "Do you know who she is?"

He nodded. "I was going to tell you, as soon as I had a little more information." He paused again. "But I guess now is fine. Her name is Heidi Summers."

Kylie looked around for the spirit. She didn't see her, but she could still feel the cold. Whether it was from Jane or someone else, Kylie didn't know.

"I have an address, too. She lived a couple of miles from here. I thought you'd want to go there."

"Yes," Kylie said. "Is her family still there?"

Burnett started walking, and Kylie followed him. She saw Derek and Della waiting for them by the gate.

"The house is listed to Malcolm Summers," Burnett said. "So I'm assuming it's her family."

Kylie caught her breath when a hundred or more souls lined up on each side of the path. They all reached out for her and started talking at once. Her head started to pound. The icy feel of their touches stung like thousands of needles.

She felt herself being pulled in a thousand different directions.

"Help me."

"No, help me."

"Stop it!" the spirit of the old man's wife screamed. *"If you're not nice, she won't come back."*

The jabbering stopped. They brought their hands to their sides, but they didn't leave. They stood completely still and watched her with soulless eyes—all wanting, needing her to do something for them so they could cross over.

But there were too many to help. Guilt filled her chest. She breathed in the frigid air and forced herself to concentrate on the one she could help. Jane Doe.

"The Summers family. They're supernaturals, right?" Kylie asked, unsure what she would say to them. But if they were supernaturals, perhaps it wouldn't be so hard.

Burnett frowned. "They aren't registered supernaturals."

"You think they're rogue?"

"Not everyone unregistered is rogue. But they could be."

Derek moved in beside Kylie, appearing concerned. He brushed the top of his hand against hers. She felt the calm he offered and appreciated the assistance.

Burnett turned to Derek and Della as soon as they walked out of the gate. "I called Holiday and asked her to pick you two up. I'll bring Kylie by later."

Kylie and Burnett got into his Mustang. As she watched Della and Derek get smaller in the rearview mirror, the craziest thought struck. What if Burnett took her to the FRU to get tested? What if Jane was right? What if he wasn't a good guy?

Chapter Thirty-seven

Neither of them spoke during the ride. The silence seemed heavy, but not that unusual, or so Kylie reminded herself. Burnett had never been Mr. Chatty.

But with every roll of the tires, Kylie's uncertainty rose. She glanced at Burnett, again sitting silent in the driver's seat.

"You seem nervous," he said.

"Should I be?"

He appeared confused. "I thought you wanted to see them."

She nodded, but the memory of Jane and her surgery hit harder. Oh sure, Kylie's heart told her Burnett was a good guy, but she could also remember Holiday saying that the FRU weren't above sacrificing one person if they thought it was for a good cause.

When Burnett parked his Mustang in front of a small white-framed house, the same house Kylie had seen in her visions, a wave of shame hit for ever doubting Burnett.

"I tried to call them, but no one answered," Burnett said. "Of course, I'm going to go in with you, but I'll let you explain things however you see fit."

Two minutes later, after receiving no answer to their knock, a woman, looking all of ninety years old, stepped out of the house next door.

"Can I help ya?" She came toward them, moving amazingly fast for someone her age.

Kylie, thinking she felt a whisper of cold, immediately checked the woman's pattern. Burnett did the same. The woman was human.

"We're looking for Mr. Summers," Burnett said.

"Well, you're too late. He and his sister-in-law flew out this morning. Went to Ireland."

Ireland? Was it a coincidence that the Brightens were there now? Kylie looked at Burnett and saw the same question in his eyes.

"Why did they go there?" Burnett asked.

The neighbor grinned. "Said he was looking for something he lost a long time ago. Said it was more valuable than gold and he figured it might be there."

"Do you know when he plans to return?" Kylie asked.

"I'm supposed to water the plants and feed the cat for a week."

Burnett started moving back to the car. "Thank you, ma'am."

"Did you want to leave a message?" the neighbor asked.

"We'll come back." Burnett smiled and waved.

Kylie got into the car, sank into the seat, and wanted to kick and scream with frustration. More questions and zero answers. She was friggin' tired of this.

Burnett started the car. "Let's drive over to the next block and come back on foot."

"Come back for what?" Kylie asked.

"I figured you'd like to go inside," he said. "See if we can learn anything."

"Isn't that against the law?" Kylie asked.

His eyes widened. "Only if we get caught."

She bit down on her lip so hard, she tasted blood. "Do you, like, have any 'get out of jail free' cards if we do get caught? I wouldn't look good in prison garb."

He patted his pocket. "I think I brought two with me."

The house smelled like herbs. Rosemary. Maybe a little thyme. The furnishings were old. Lots of antiques, expensive-looking things, but nothing too showy. When Kylie stepped into the hall, she spotted the closet Jane had pulled her suitcase from. Right then, she felt the cold come down on her.

She stopped abruptly. Burnett bumped into her from behind.

"Something wrong?" he asked.

"You mean other than the fact that we just broke into someone's house?" She knew he didn't want to know they had company.

"It's fine," he said.

"Right." She moved into the bedroom. Jane Doe, aka Heidi Summers, sat on the bed, staring at the photos on the bedside table.

Kylie studied the woman's face behind the frame. "It's you."

"What's . . . Never mind, I'll wait out here." Burnett must have realized she wasn't talking to him and wanted nothing to do with the ghost.

Considering what had happened to him the last time, Kylie didn't blame him.

"Me and Malcolm." Heidi said the name with so much love. *"I remember."*

Kylie picked up the picture. She recalled feeling something odd when she'd seen the man's face in the vision. The same thing hit her again. Then chills shot down her spine. Not from the cold this time, but from the realization.

"Burnett?"

"What?" He barged into the bedroom as if ready to fight.

She held out the picture. "That's him."

He took the picture. "Who?"

"That's the same man who came to the camp. The one who claimed to be my grandfather."

Burnett scanned the photo. "Are you sure?"

"Completely."

Heidi stood up. *"It was him, wasn't it? I remember. And that was my sister, too."*

Her sister? Kylie remembered the woman, remembered feeling a connection. "Why would they come to the camp and pretend to be my adoptive grandparents?" Kylie asked, and she meant the question for both Burnett and Heidi.

"I don't know," Burnett answered.

Heidi stood there as if trying to think. *"Wait. They were from Ireland. And the neighbor said—"*

"Who was from Ireland?" Kylie asked, and saw Burnett leave again.

"The people who adopted my boy. I gave him up for adoption. I went to a doctor who placed children with good parents. The doctor was human, but he knew about supernaturals. I remember there were complications, I had to have a C-section, and the doctor didn't want to do it because he didn't have the supplies to put me under; I made him do it anyway. I couldn't let my baby die. I knew whatever pain I experienced would be better than knowing I'd robbed my son of his chance at life. Then I made sure he would go to a good family." She sat up straighter. *"Malcolm's looking for our son."*

Tears filled Kylie's eyes as the truth swirled around her heart, making her dizzy. Heidi Summers was Daniel's birth mother. She was Kylie's grandmother. And Malcolm Summers, her real grandfather, and her grandmother's sister had posed as Daniel's adoptive parents. Why? Why not just tell her? More questions.

"He's going to find our boy. And they'll be a family, the way we should have been."

The pain of everything her grandmother had endured suddenly swamped her. Knowing she would have to tell Heidi that Daniel was dead cut like a knife.

But she had to tell her, didn't she?

"He won't find him," Kylie said.

"How do you know?"

Kylie wiped the tears from her eyes. "He's not in Ireland."

"Why else would Malcolm have gone to Ireland?"

"He went to find the Brightens."

Heidi sank back on the bed, as if trying to absorb what Kylie said. *"Yes, that was their name. They adopted my boy."*

Kylie nodded. "But your son isn't with them."

"Where is he?" She jumped off the bed. *"Take me to him. I want to see him."*

Kylie's breath caught. "He died a long time ago."

"No!" she yelled. *"He lived. I went to see him right before they forced Malcolm and me to go to that place for tests. It was a few months after I had given birth. My son was fine. So healthy."*

"He didn't die when he was a baby," Kylie said. "He grew up, met a woman whom he fell in love with, and then he joined the army. He died when he was twenty-one while on a mission, trying to save a woman. He was a hero. You should be proud."

Heidi dropped back on the bed. *"Are you sure?"*

"Yes." Another wave of tears filled Kylie's eyes. "I'll bet he's waiting to meet you on the other side, too."

She looked up as if she could see heaven. *"Did you know him?"*

Kylie nodded. "Only his spirit." She felt tears begin to roll down her cheeks. "He's my father."

Heidi's eyes rounded. *"That would mean that you . . ."* She reached out and touched Kylie's cheek. *"I should have known. You look like Malcolm. Blond hair instead of red, but those eyes . . ."* A tear slipped from her cheek. *"I think . . . a part of me did know."*

Kylie blinked. "I have so many questions to ask you, so many things I want to know. First, what are we?"

"What do you mean?"

"We're supernatural, right?"

She hesitated, as if she had to think. *"Yes. That was why they took us in to do those terrible tests."*

"So, what are we?" Kylie held her breath, waiting, hoping for her answer.

Heidi frowned as if trying to think again. *"I . . . can't remember. I'm sorry. But . . ."* She pointed to the picture. *"Malcolm will remember. The man never forgets anything."*

Heidi stood up. *"I have to go to my son now. I need to tell him that I love him. That's why I stayed here. To tell him how sorry I am that I gave him away."*

"Why did you do it?" Kylie asked, hoping something would jog her memory. "Why did you give him away?"

She tilted her head as if to think again. *"Because they wanted the little ones more than they wanted us."*

"Who?" Kylie asked. "The FRU?"

"Yes," she said. *"It was the only way to keep him safe. If I'd run with him, they'd have found me. So I gave him away. I told Malcolm I lost the baby. I had to do it. He trusted them. He said they wouldn't hurt our baby and they would just study him for a little while. But I didn't believe them. So I gave the baby away, I lied to Malcolm, and then I came back because I loved him so much."*

"Why did they want to study the baby?" Kylie asked.

"I don't remember . . . Wait, it was because we were different and they didn't like it."

"How were we different?"

She shook her head. Her brow wrinkled. *"Everything is still so messed up. I remember some things and not others. Malcolm will know."*

She leaned down and pressed a hand to Kylie's cheek. *"I'm going to see my boy. But you, Kylie Galen, are everything I would have wanted in a granddaughter. I must go now."*

Kylie wanted to scream no and beg Heidi to stay, that she had more questions. But it was too late. Heidi had already disappeared.

Fifteen minutes later, Kylie sat silently in the Mustang as Burnett pulled up to the camp. She'd told Burnett everything. About how Jane Doe was really her grandmother, and she'd given Kylie's father away for adoption because the FRU were taking children like them to study. He put the car in park and looked at her. "So you think he went to find the Brightens?"

Kylie nodded.

"I'll see if I can find Malcolm Summers in Ireland. But there's a good chance you might have to wait until he gets back."

Kylie nodded, not liking being this close and still so far away. She reached for the door handle and then looked back at Burnett. "You're not coming in?"

He frowned. "No."

She hesitated to ask but then went for it. "Are you ever coming back?"

He gripped the wheel. "I don't know."

"Why?"

He stared straight ahead. "It's what she wants. She doesn't trust me anymore."

Kylie swallowed. "Neither did I."

He arched a brow at her.

"When you were driving me to the house, I was afraid that you were taking me to be tested."

He frowned. Hurt lingered in his eyes.

"But that's because I saw what the FRU did to my grandmother. I lived bits and pieces of it through her, and when someone lives through something bad, it's hard to trust. I don't know exactly what happened to Holiday with that other vampire, she won't even talk to me about it, but it must have been bad. It scared her and now she's scared to love again. But if you just hang in there . . ."

"I have hung in there. I'm done."

They sat there staring at each other for several long seconds. "I should go," he said finally.

Kylie got out. As she watched Burnett pull away, the emotions playing in her heart were the same as the ones she'd felt the day she watched Tom Galen drive away with his suitcases.

Shadow Falls was her family. They'd already lost Ellie. They didn't need to lose Burnett, too. But for the life of her, she didn't know how she could change this.

Lucas met Kylie at the gate. More than anything, she needed a hug. She wanted to tell him what she'd learned, but what she got was his anger.

"Why didn't you wait on me?" he demanded.

Maybe it was because her emotions were already on the edge, but she just started walking away.

"Damn it!" Lucas said, and moved in step with her. "Why in the hell would you go back to the cemetery, anyway? And why would they allow Derek to go with you?"

"Because I needed answers. And because Derek is my friend. Just like Fredericka is yours!"

He caught her by the arm. "Do you know how worried I've been?"

"Yes," Kylie snapped. "You were as worried about me as I am about you when you run off and play wolf for a night."

He looked stunned. "I can't help what I am, Kylie."

"Neither can I, Lucas." Tears sprang to her eyes. "I don't know what I am, but I know that what I do is deal with ghosts. And if you can't accept that, then maybe you can't accept me."

"I didn't say that," he insisted. "I just want—"

"You want me to be werewolf," she said. "You want me to be were-wolf so your family and your pack will accept me. But right now, it's not looking good that you'll get what you want. So maybe you need to think about that, too."

She took off.

He caught up with her. "I'm sorry," he said. "It's just I can't stand the thought of something happening to you. And . . . nothing is going to change between us, no matter what you are." He lifted her chin and met her eyes. "Don't you know how I feel?"

He pulled her against his chest, and Kylie let him. She buried herself in his warmth and tried to believe that he spoke the truth, but she couldn't lie to herself. She knew Lucas wanted to believe it, but she wasn't completely convinced that it would be the case if his grandmother really got involved. Kylie wasn't even sure it was fair of her to ask him to make that choice.

Kylie awoke very early Tuesday morning. Her first thought was that today was Ellie's funeral. She recalled the vision she'd had about it and wondered if it was fair that she had to live through it twice.

She ran a hand over her face. Her alarm hadn't gone off. So why was she awake?

The cold suddenly fell on her like a blanket of ice. "Heidi?" She sat up so fast, her head spun. "Is that you? I have more questions to ask."

No answer came. Kylie sat there, waiting. Through the haze of darkness, she saw a figure appear at the end of her bed. "Heidi?" she asked again.

Kylie turned on the lamp. The light filled the bedroom and illuminated the spirit, who stood with her back to the bed. It wasn't Heidi. Kylie couldn't even tell if this ghost was male or female. Somehow he/she looked . . . deader than the others. Sure, they were all dead, but for some reason even the matted hair looked deader than the hair of other spirits.

"Hello," Kylie whispered.

The spirit turned around, and Kylie stopped breathing. Worms, maggots, and creepy insects crawled in and out of the eye sockets, eating away at what little flesh still clung to the face.

Screaming, Kylie slammed back against the headboard.

"Can you help me?" A stream of worms cascaded from the spirit's lips as she spoke, and they landed on Kylie's blanket.

"I . . ." Kylie kicked the covers to stop the gooey-looking creatures from crawling toward her. "I might, but can you do something about your face? Now!"

Della bolted into the room. "You okay?"

Kylie glanced back at the foot of her bed. The ghost was gone. Relief washed over her. "I'm fine," her voice squeaked out. Remembering the maggots—and not one hundred percent sure the ghost had taken them with her—Kylie leapt up, yanked the covers off the bed, and tossed them on the floor. She backed away from the pile of bedding.

"Yeah. You look just fine," Della said sarcastically.

Kylie jumped from foot to foot and brushed off imaginary maggots that she felt crawling on her skin.

Della stood there in Mickey Mouse pajamas, staring at her as if she didn't know whether to laugh or run.

Kylie stopped dancing and tried to breathe normally. "If I die, promise me I'll be cremated."

Della frowned. "Die?"

"Not that I'm planning to die anytime soon." She gave her arm one more swipe. "But still."

Della shook her head. "I don't know why you pretend you're okay."

Kylie wrapped her arms around herself. "Me either."

Kylie didn't go back to sleep. She wasn't sure if she'd ever sleep in that bed again. Instead, she dressed and waited for Della and Miranda to go to the sunrise service.

The service happened just as it had in the vision. Only the grief felt deeper, especially when Kylie saw Derek, tears in his eyes, holding Ellie's hat.

Holiday kept looking over her shoulder. Kylie knew she was looking for Burnett. It wasn't until Chris started talking that Burnett slid into the chair next to Holiday.

She saw the two of them look at each other. Kylie wasn't sure what kind of look it was—other than sad. Sad seemed to be the mood of the day. Well, for everyone except the blue jay who kept flittering by, spouting out song as if wanting to impress her.

Only she wasn't impressed.

When the ceremony ended, Lucas took her hand to walk her to the dining hall, where they planned to have a celebration of Ellie's life. Everyone was going to tell Ellie stories.

But Burnett stopped her. "I need to talk to you and Holiday a minute."

Lucas said he'd meet her in the dining hall. Then Holiday and Burnett and Kylie walked into the office.

"Is something wrong?" Kylie asked once Burnett closed the door.

He pulled an envelope from his suit jacket and handed it to Kylie.

"What is that?" Holiday asked. From her tone, she seemed to think it had to do with Kylie having tests.

"It's the location of her grandmother's body."

"You had her buried in her own grave?" Kylie asked.

"Not exactly." He paused. "Let's just say that if the FRU try to force you to undergo any tests that you aren't comfortable with, you can use this to . . . insist that you prefer not to participate."

"So you think they'll push for Kylie to be tested?" Holiday asked.

He frowned. "I'm under the impression they will, yes."

"You told them about what happened?"

"I haven't told them anything since you asked me not to."

"So the FRU doesn't know you removed the body?" Holiday asked.

"No." His gaze met Kylie's. "What they did to your grandmother was wrong. And while the agency has admitted to some wrongdoings with some of the testing that went down in the sixties, this is one skeleton they wouldn't want brought forward."

"Why did they do it?" Kylie asked.

He shrugged. "The information I could find was very vague. Supposedly, there were a small number of supernaturals who were genetically different from the rest."

"So we still don't know what I am?"

Burnett's expression tightened. "I'm afraid not."

"Except a genetic freak," she muttered.

Holiday sat beside Kylie on the sofa and reached for her hand. "Don't say—"

"I'm assuming it's just the opposite," Burnett broke in. "They wouldn't be interested in something that wasn't working correctly. Just the fact that you can appear human would be considered an advantage. That could be all there is to it, or it could be more."

"What advantage is there to appearing human?" Kylie asked.

"A lot. Right now, supernaturals aren't allowed to run for any political office."

"That doesn't seem fair," Kylie said.

"It probably isn't. But what they did to your grandmother wasn't fair either. However, I do have some news." His expression seemed to change, but to what Kylie wasn't sure.

"I actually spoke with Malcolm Summers. Your real grandfather," Burnett said. "And before you ask, we didn't discuss any details. I was afraid if I started asking too many questions, I'd scare him off. I told him you wanted to meet him."

"And?" Kylie gripped Holiday's hand. *What if he said he didn't want to meet me?*

Chapter Thirty-eight

Burnett continued, "He said he was getting on the next flight available back to Texas. It may be Thursday before he arrives."

Kylie got tears in her eyes. "It's really going to happen, isn't it? I'm finally going to get my answers." She still felt fear, but less than before. She needed her answers. Deserved them.

"It looks like it," Burnett said.

Kylie jumped up, stopping herself just before she wrapped her arms around him. "May I hug you?"

He grinned and grimaced at the same time. "Make it quick."

She did. When she backed up, Holiday watched with tears in her eyes.

Burnett nodded at Holiday. "And this is for you." He pulled out another envelope and handed it to her.

"What is it?" Holiday asked, sounding unsure.

"It's a donation to help cover future costs for Shadow Falls . . . and my resignation."

Holiday stiffened. "That's what you want?" She sounded so hurt that Kylie's heart gripped.

"It's what you want," he said.

"I didn't ask you to resign."

"The hell you didn't!"

"Should I leave?" Kylie asked.

But no one was listening to her, and Burnett was blocking the door.

"Hello?" Kylie said, but they were too busy staring daggers at each other to pay attention to her.

"I said, if you couldn't understand my not letting Kylie go in for tests by the FRU, then you'd best leave."

"Because you don't need me anymore now that you have other investors lined up, right?" Burnett sounded hurt.

"What investors?" Holiday asked.

"Don't lie to me, Holiday! I saw the file. You have four possible investors waiting in the wings."

"You went through my desk?"

"I wasn't snooping! I had to pay the bills while you were away, remember?"

"Well, next time you go rummaging in my desk, you should read the dates on the paperwork!" She went to her desk, opened her drawer, and tossed the file at him.

"What's that supposed to mean?"

"I didn't find these people just now. I found them before you signed on."

He stared at her in growing confusion. "You said the only reason you chose me was because you didn't have anyone else."

"I didn't say that. You assumed it."

Burnett stared at Holiday. "Are you saying you chose me over these other people?" He moved closer, leaving a slight opening to the office door.

"I'm gonna just slip out now." Kylie took a step forward.

They ignored her. And Kylie hesitated for just a second.

"So you care about me," Burnett grumbled. "Why the hell can't you admit it, Holiday?"

"Hiring you was a business decision, Burnett."

"Bullshit!" Burnett said. "Each one of them has more money than I do."

"A business decision, not a financial one."

"Is that why you kissed me?" he demanded.

"I did no such thing. *You* kissed me."

"And you enjoyed it!"

"I'm out of here." Kylie eased around Burnett and walked out, but she carried with her a smile and a lot of hope. She was pretty sure Burnett wasn't quitting now. And in two days, she would have answers from her grandfather Malcolm. God, she hoped it was true.

"Hey." Derek met her on the porch.

"Hey," she said, still smiling.

He stopped, obviously hearing Burnett and Holiday bickering in the office. "Is everything okay?"

Kylie chuckled. "They're arguing. So it's pretty much back to normal now."

"Better than when they weren't talking to each other."

"My thoughts exactly," Kylie said.

Derek studied her. "Can *we* talk?" He motioned to the two rocking chairs.

"Sure."

She sat in the first chair. He took the other. For a second, she got the image of them here before. Of him moving in and kissing her while she reclined in the chair.

She pushed that image away. They weren't kissing now. They were just talking. Two friends, talking.

He started to speak, but then his eyes widened. "You got good news?"

She grinned, knowing he'd read her mood. "My real grandfather is coming to see me in a few days."

"Damn!" His eyes filled with contentment for her. "You'll finally get your answers. Kylie Galen will know what she is. No more mystery."

"I hope so." An odd thought hit: What would her life be like when her quest changed? A wash of cold moved in behind her. She glanced back and just as quickly turned back around.

"I heard about your grandmother," Derek said. "And the rogue vampire. He really sacrificed himself for you?"

"Yeah." Her emotions took a nosedive. "All I saw in him was evil, Derek. But it wasn't true."

"It wasn't just you," he said. "That's what I saw, too. So I get how that makes you feel."

She sighed. That was the thing about Derek. He always understood her feelings.

"Thanks." Someone walked past, and for a crazy second she thought it was Ellie. But of course, it wasn't.

"I miss her, too," Derek said, reading her again.

Kylie looked up toward the sky. "Sometimes, I just wish heaven wasn't so far away."

Things grew quiet. When she looked back, Derek was staring at her. Staring at her the way the old Derek used to stare. The gold flecks in his eyes brightened against his green irises. She felt the world go fairy tale around her, and she noticed things. Things like how his shoulders looked like a soft place to rest her head.

"You were right, you know."

"Right about what?" she asked.

"Me pushing you away. It was the stupidest thing I've ever done. Then the mistake with Ellie, I . . . messed up, Kylie, and it hurt you. I'm sorry. So damn sorry."

"That's history," she said, and another silence fell upon them.

"I talked to Holiday," he whispered.

His soft-spoken words had Kylie realizing that Holiday and Burnett weren't arguing anymore. Were they busy doing something else?

"Talked to Holiday about what?" she asked.

"About why I was feeling supercharged emotions around you."

Kylie bit down on her lip. She didn't need to know this now, did she?

Derek sensed her feelings. "I'm not expecting you to do anything. I just want you to know."

"Know what?"

He hesitated. "Holiday said that sometimes, when a fae really cares about someone, their emotions can become blown out of proportion. Most times, the problem goes away after they accept their feelings. So that's what I'm doing. Accepting it."

She opened her mouth to speak but didn't have a clue what to say.

He cupped his jeans-covered knees in his hands. They were jeans that fit him really well, too.

"I'm in love with you, Kylie." He looked almost embarrassed by the admission. He jumped up, took one step away, then swung around and faced her again. "I don't expect you to say it back, and I don't think this will change your mind about anything. But you deserved to know. And I needed to tell you because . . . I've never felt this way before—for anyone."

Kylie sat there, his words running around her head, feeling . . . Okay, what did she feel, exactly? First was confusion. Then came fear. Derek loved her. Her heart tightened.

She glanced up into his eyes and saw he was reading her emotions. Every one of them.

"I should leave now," he said, but he leaned down and pressed the quickest of kisses on her cheek. It reminded her of how Perry had kissed Miranda that night in the parking lot. Romantic. Sweet.

She just watched him leave. Then she fell back in the rocker and tried to decipher the emotions swelling in her chest.

"How can everything feel so right and yet wrong at the same time?" she muttered.

"Life's weird like that." The rocker beside her, the one Derek had just left, creaked slightly.

Kylie glanced over at the reclined spirit and frowned. "Things aren't going to get any easier, are they."

The spirit chose not to answer.

"Look," Kylie said, and pulled her knees up in the chair. "I don't have a lot of rules. But I told you, you're gonna have to do something about that face."

The ghost's face magically started healing, becoming normal. Kylie gasped. It wasn't seeing it happen that shocked her; it was the face. She recognized it.

"God, no."

The ghost disappeared. Kylie shot up to go find Holiday when another voice spoke behind her.

"Kylie?"

Recognizing Daniel's voice, she swung around. "Daddy," she said, and hugged him.

His cold arms came around her. When she pulled back, she saw he had tears in his eyes.

"That's the first time you called me that."

"I guess it just took me a while," she said.

He smiled and touched her face. *"I met my real mother for the first time. She sure was proud of her granddaughter."*

"She seemed sweet. She loved you so much."

"I know," he said. Suddenly he faded a bit. *"I don't have much time, Kylie. But I found the answer you wanted."*

"What answer?" she asked, scared to believe.

"What we are. My mother finally remembered."

"And?" Kylie held her breath.

"We're chameleons."

Kylie shook her head as she tried to grasp what he meant. "We're lizards? What does that mean?"

He faded a bit more. *"I don't know."*

"We can change our patterns. Is that what it means?" she asked.

"I have no more answers," he said. *"But soon. Soon we will discover this together."*

"Together?" she asked.

He nodded, and the cold and what vapor was left of his visual spirit faded even more.

"I'm going to die?" she asked as the icy tremors prickled her skin.

He didn't have the chance to answer, but she could swear she saw him shake his head. Or maybe it was just wishful thinking.

She stood there on the porch, trying to breathe, trying to come to terms with what she had learned. She was a chameleon. She might be about to die. And . . . she remembered the face of the ghost—the one who showed up before her father. She might not be the only one who was going to die.

"Holiday?" Kylie called out as she stormed back into the office.

Life really wasn't going to get any easier.

Whispers at Moonrise

To my editor, Rose Hilliard, and my agent, Kim Lionetti, for helping me reach my writing goals. To my husband for cooking the dinners, for doing the dishes and the laundry, so I could put in the hours to make deadlines and work toward making those dreams come true.

Acknowledgments

So often in this life, we spend so much time telling people when they do something wrong, from the waitress at the restaurant to the bagger at the grocery store. We forget to tell those people who just get it right. So I'd like to tip my hat to one organization and a bunch of individuals who have gotten it right.

To Romance Writers of America for creating an organization that provided me with the knowledge to move up the ladder in this career. To Rosa Brand for her awesome videos and friendship. To Faye Hughes and Kathleen Adey for assisting me in getting it all done. Thanks for all you two do. To all my writing peeps whose support is essential to making this mostly solitary career into one with a group of peers who are there to laugh and cry with, and keep each other inspired. A special thank you to another writing peep, Susan Muller, for the hour of walking, talking, and laughing we do most every day. To my parents, Pete Hunt and Ginger Curtis. You must have done something right because I didn't turn out too bad. Well, I'm not perfect, but for the most part, you must have raised me right. To my kids, who haven't turned out too bad, either. I'm proud of you both. And because as I write this, it's almost Father's Day, thank you to Jason, my son-in-law, for being a champion daddy to my precious granddaughter. A big thank you to the fans who have recommended my series to others. And my gratitude goes to those fans who have taken the time to e-mail me and tell me that my books have touched them in some way. Those e-mails help keep my joy of writing alive and kicking even when deadlines are kicking me in the butt. Thank you to each and every one of you for getting it right.

Chapter One

Kylie Galen stood on the porch outside the Shadow Falls office, panic stabbing at her sanity. A gust of late August wind, still chilled by her father's departing spirit, picked up her long strands of blond hair and scattered them across her face. She didn't brush them away. She didn't breathe. She just stood there, air trapped in her lungs, while she stared through the wisps of hair at the trees swaying in the breeze.

Why does my life have to be so damn hard? The question rolled around her head like a Ping-Pong ball gone wild. The answer spun back just as quick.

Because you're not all human. For the last few months, she'd struggled to identify the type of non-human blood that rushed through her veins. Now she knew.

According to her dear ol' dad, she was . . . a chameleon. As in a lizard, just like the ones she'd seen sunning themselves in her backyard. Okay, so maybe not just like those, but close enough. And here she'd been worried about being a vampire or a werewolf because it would be a little hard to adjust to drinking blood or shape-shifting on full moons. But this . . . this was . . . unfathomable. Her father had to be wrong.

Her heart pounded against her chest as if seeking escape. She finally breathed. In, and then out. Her thoughts shot away from the lizard issue to the other bad stuff.

Yup. In the last five minutes she'd been slapped with not one, not two, not even three, but with four oh-crap eye-opening revelations.

Well, one thing—Derek's confession that he loved her—couldn't completely be called bad. But it sure as hell couldn't be called good. Not now. Not when she considered them history. Not when she'd spent the last few weeks trying to convince herself that they were just friends.

Her mind juggled all four disclosures. She didn't know which to focus on first. Or maybe her mind did know. *I'm a freaking lizard!*

"For real?" she spoke aloud. The Texas wind snatched away her words. She hoped it would take them all the way to her father—wherever the dead who hadn't completely passed over went to wait. "Seriously, Dad?"

Of course, Dad didn't answer. After two months of dealing with one spirit or another, the whole ghost-whispering gift and its limitations still managed to piss her off. "Damn!"

She took another step toward the main office's door to unload on Holiday Brandon, the camp leader, then stopped. Burnett James, the other camp leader and a cold to the touch but hot to look at vampire, was with Holiday. Since Kylie couldn't hear them arguing anymore, she figured that meant they might be doing something else—like sucking face, swapping spit, doing the tongue tango. All phrases her bad-attitude vampire roommate Della would use. Which probably meant Kylie was in a bad mood. But didn't she deserve a little attitude after everything that had happened?

Clenching her fists, she stared at the office's front door. She'd inadvertently interrupted their first kiss and she didn't want to do the same with their second. Especially when Burnett had threatened to resign from Shadow Falls. Surely Holiday could change his mind. Couldn't she?

Besides, maybe Kylie needed to calm down. To think things through before she ran to Holiday in bad-attitude hysterics. Her thoughts shifted to her latest ghost issue. How could a ghost of someone who was alive appear to Kylie? A trick, right? Had to be a trick.

She glanced around to make sure the ghost had really gone. The cold had vanished.

Turning, she shot down the porch steps and headed around to the back of the office. She started running, wanting to experience the sense of freedom she got when she ran, when she ran fast, ran non-human fast.

The wind picked up the black dress she'd worn to Ellie's funeral and sent the hem dancing against her thighs. Her feet moved in rhythm, barely missing the Reeboks she usually wore, but when she arrived at the edge of the woods, she came to an abrupt halt—so abrupt that the heels on her black dress shoes cut deep ruts into the earth.

She couldn't go into the woods. She didn't have a shadow—the mandatory person with her to help ward off the evil Mario and his rogue buddies if they decided to attack.

Attack again.

So far the old man's attempts at ending her life had proved futile, but two of those times had resulted in the death of someone else.

Guilt fluttered through her already tight chest. Fear followed it. Mario had proven how far he'd go to get to her, how evil he was when he'd taken his own grandson's life right in front of her. How could anyone be that wicked?

She stared at the trees and watched as their leaves danced in the breeze. It was a completely normal slice of scenery that should have put her at peace.

But she felt no peace. The woods, or rather something that hid within, dared her to enter. Taunted her to move into the thick line of trees. Confused by the strange feeling, she tried to push it away, but the feeling intensified.

She inhaled the green scent of the forest, and she knew.

Knew with clarity.

Knew with certainty.

Mario wouldn't give up. Sooner or later she would face him again. And it wouldn't be serene, tranquil, or peaceful. Only one of them would walk away.

You will not be alone. The words echoed deep within her as if to offer her peace. No peace came. The shadows between the trees danced on the ground. Calling her, beckoning her. To do what, she didn't know.

Trepidation took another lap around her chest. She dug the heels of her shoes deeper into the hard dirt. The heel of her right shoe cracked—an ominous little sound that seemed to punctuate the silence.

"Crap!" She stared down at her feet. The one word seemed yanked from the air, leaving nothing but a hum of eeriness.

And that's when she heard it.

Someone drew in a raspy breath. While the sound came only at a whisper, she knew that the owner of this breath stood behind her. Stood close. And since no chill of death surrounded her, she knew it wasn't from the spirit world.

The sound came again. Someone fed life-giving air into their lungs. Odd how she now feared the living more than she feared the dead.

Her heart thudded to a stop. Much like the grooves left in the earth by her three-inch heels, her growing dread left ruts in her courage.

She wasn't ready. If it was Mario, she wasn't ready. Whatever it was she needed to do, whatever plan or fate she was destined to follow, she needed more time.

Chapter Two

"Are you . . . okay?"

The voice. Not Mario. Derek's voice.

His familiar tone had her initial panic fading, but only for a second. *I'm in love with you, Kylie.* The words he'd spoken less than fifteen minutes ago flowed through her head, bringing with them another emotional storm that made her mind and heart spin. Derek loved her. But what did she feel?

She shifted slightly, and the heel from her right shoe fell off, making her off balance. That's how her life felt—as if it had lost a heel, and her only choice was to limp along.

"What's wrong?" His voice rang with concern.

I'm fine. The words perched on the tip of her tongue, but she swallowed them. Derek, half-fae, could read her. To lie to him about her emotional state was futile. So she turned around and faced him.

"What are you doing here without a shadow?" Derek asked. "You know you're not supposed to be without a shadow in case that freakish rogue returns."

Meeting Derek's gaze, she spotted the panic brightening his eyes. She knew the panic she saw was her own as well. When she hurt emotionally, he hurt. When she experienced joy, he lived it, too. When she feared something, he feared it for her. Considering her emotional state these last few minutes, he must be in hell.

His chest expanded behind the fitted dusty green t-shirt. He held a hand over his hard stomach as he sucked air into his lungs. His dark brown hair appeared windblown, and his bangs clung to his forehead. A drip of sweat rolled down his brow. For a second, all she could think about was falling into him, letting his calming touch chase away the apprehension inside her.

"Is it . . . what I said?" he asked. "If it is, I'll . . . take it back. I didn't tell you that to tear you apart inside."

One couldn't take back an admission of love, she thought. Not if he really meant it. But she didn't say that. "It's not what you said." Then she realized that, too, was a lie. His confession played havoc with her emotions. "Well, it's other stuff, too."

"What stuff?" His words came out breathlessly. His eyes searched hers and she saw the gold flecks in his irises brighten. "I sense you're terrified and confused, and—"

"But I'm okay." She noticed again his winded state, as if he'd just run a mile to get to her. *Had he?* "Where were you?"

He took in another deep gulp of oxygen. "My cabin."

Over a mile. "You felt my emotions that far away?"

"Yeah." He frowned as if he hoped she didn't blame him. She didn't like that her emotions were an open book for him to read, but she didn't blame him. He'd told her once that if he could stop reading her, he would. She believed him.

"I thought you said it was lessening," she said. "Does it still make you crazy?"

His left shoulder shifted upward a couple of inches. "It's still strong, but it's not overwhelming like before. I can handle it, now that I . . ."

Now that he'd accepted he loved her. That's what he'd told her.

That's why their link had grown so strong. Her chest grew heavy with indecision again. It was a good thing that one of them could handle it. Because she wasn't sure she could deal with this. Not with him loving her. Not with any of the revelations she'd been given. At least right now.

"What's wrong?" He stepped closer. So close she could smell his skin—earthy, honest, real.

The temptation to walk into his arms washed over her. She longed to feel the up and down motion of his chest as he breathed, to let what was in the past be what was in the future. Closing her hands into tight fists, she limped past him with her one broken heel, went to a tree, and lowered herself down to the ground. The earth felt cooler than the heat in the air. The blades of grass tickled the back of her legs, but she ignored it.

He didn't wait for an invitation; he lowered himself beside her. Not close enough that they touched, but close enough that she thought about touching.

"So it's more than one thing?" he asked.

She nodded and the decision to confide in him seemed already made. "My dad appeared to me." She bit down on her lip. "He told me what I am."

Derek looked puzzled. "I thought you wanted to know."

"Yeah, but . . . He said I'm a chameleon. As in, a lizard."

His brows pinched and then he chuckled.

She didn't appreciate his candor. Her panic came back three-fold. She'd wanted to know what she was so the others would accept her, so she would fit in, but what if she ended up being something that honestly made her a freak?

"I hate lizards," she blurted out. "They're right up there with snakes—evil little bug-eyed creatures scurrying around in the dirt and eating creepy-crawly things." She stared out at the woods again, imagining a brigade of lizards staring back at her. "I saw a program once that showed a long-tongued lizard eating a spider in slow motion. It was gross!"

Derek shook his head, all shades of humor fading from his eyes. "I've never heard of supernatural lizards. Are you sure?"

"I'm not sure of anything. That's what's so scary. Not knowing." She shivered. "Seriously, devouring blood is preferable to having one of those long tongues and dining on insects."

"Maybe he got it wrong. You said ghosts have a hard time communicating."

"At first, yes, but now my dad makes perfect sense."

Derek didn't look convinced. "But what do you think a chameleon supernatural is, or does? All I think they could do is change colors."

Kylie let his words run around her brain for a second. "Maybe that's it?"

"You can change colors?" Doubt showed on his face.

"No. But maybe I can change my pattern. Like how my grandfather and aunt appeared human. And like how I appear human now."

"Or . . . maybe your father's having a relapse and he's just confused. Because I've never heard of any supernaturals who could change their brain patterns."

"What about me?" she asked. "What about my grandfather and aunt?"

He shrugged. "Holiday said it was probably a wizard who cast a spell for your grandfather and aunt."

"Did he cast it on me, too?" Kylie asked.

"No, but . . . Okay, I don't have the answer." He frowned. "And I know that frustrates you. But didn't you tell me that your real grandfather was coming to visit? I'm sure he'll clear it up."

"Yeah." She bit down on her lower lip.

Derek studied her. "There's something else wrong, too?"

She sighed. "When I asked my dad what it meant about being a chameleon, he said we'd figure it out together."

"And that's bad because . . . ?"

Kylie stated the obvious. "He's dead, and he's limited to earthly visits, so does that mean that I'm going to die soon?"

"No, he didn't mean that." Derek's tone deepened with conviction.

She started to argue that he couldn't say that with certainty, but because she wanted to believe him, she bit back the words. Taking a breath, she stared down at the grass and tried to find peace in knowing that her grandfather was going to come in a couple of days. Tried to find peace in having spilled her troubles. And she did feel slightly better.

"Have you asked Holiday?" He leaned in and his shoulder bumped into hers, his warmth, his soothing touch chasing away some of her angst.

She shook her head. "Not yet. She's still in the office with Burnett." And Kylie still hadn't mulled over the whole ghost issue. If someone's ghost appeared to you when they weren't dead, what did it mean? The possible answers started her heart shaking.

"I think this is kind of important," he said.

"I know, but . . ."

"There's something else, isn't there?"

She glanced up. Was he reading her emotions or her mind? "Ghost problems," she said.

"What kind of problems?"

Of all the campers, Derek was the only one who didn't run away at the mention of ghosts. "This person isn't dead."

"So it's not a ghost." Derek looked confused.

Kylie bit down on her lip. "Yes . . . I mean, at first the spirit had the whole zombie thing going on—hanging flesh, and worms—but then it changed. And when it did, the face turned into someone I know."

"How could that be?" he asked.

She paused. "I don't know. Maybe it's a trick."

"Or not," Derek said. "You don't think someone's going to die?"

Not anyone else, she wanted to scream. "I don't know." She yanked a few blades of grass from the ground.

"Who is it?" he asked. "Not someone here, is it?"

Kylie's chest tightened. She didn't want to say it—afraid that if she said it aloud, it would make it so. "I just need to think it through."

Derek paled. "Oh, crap! Is it me?"

"No." She tossed the blades of grass and watched them whirl in the wind on their descent.

When she looked back at him, she could feel him reading her emotions, deciphering their meaning. "You care a lot about this person." His brows pinched. "Lucas?" She heard the pain in his voice from just saying the name.

"No," she said. "Can we drop it? I don't want to talk about it. Please."

"So it is Lucas?" Derek asked.

"What's Lucas?" A deep, irate voice suddenly spoke up.

Kylie looked up and saw Lucas step out of the trees. His eyes were an angry orange color. She flinched with guilt for a just a second, then fought it back. She hadn't been doing anything wrong.

"Nothing," Derek bit out when Kylie didn't speak. He stood up and took one step toward the office. Pausing, he looked back at her, and then glanced at Lucas. "We were just talking. Don't go all were on her."

Lucas growled. Derek walked away, appearing unaffected by Lucas's anger. Kylie grabbed another handful of grass and yanked it from the ground.

"I don't like this." Lucas stared down at her.

"We were just talking," she said.

"About me."

"I was telling him about a spirit and that . . . it looked like someone I care about, and he asked if it was you. You should feel good that he knows I care about you."

Lucas's scowl deepened. Was it because of Derek or because she'd mentioned ghosts? Lucas's inability to accept her working with the spirits hurt.

"He has feelings for you," Lucas countered.

I know. "We were just talking."

"It makes me crazy." His eyes glowed a deep, burnt orange color.

"What makes you crazy? Me talking to Derek, or me talking about ghosts?"

"Both." His voice rang with such honesty that she found it hard to condemn him for it. "But mostly it's the thought of you spending time with that fairy."

She flinched at his insult toward Derek. Then, unsure what to say, she stood up. Forgetting about her missing heel, she almost tripped. He caught her by the elbow.

She met his gaze, still marked by his were anger. But his touch was tender and caring, with no hint of the fury she saw in his eyes. She remembered that some of his reactions were instinctual, which meant he shouldn't be held accountable. Another part of her knew that instinctual or not, it didn't make it right.

She sighed. "We've already talked about this."

"Talked about what?" he asked.

"Both things. I help spirits, Lucas. That's probably never going to change."

"Yeah, but they scare the shit out of you. They scare the shit out of me."

Kylie tensed. "You think your shifting into a wolf doesn't scare me?"

"That's not the same. They are ghosts, Kylie. That's not . . . not natural."

"But turning into a wolf is completely natural," she said with sarcasm.

He exhaled. "Okay, coming from someone who's lived their life as a human, I can see your point. And while I'm sure I'm never going to love the ghost whispering part of you, I'm working on accepting it." His tone told her how hard that was for him. "But accepting that you're spending time with Derek isn't easy when I know if he were given the chance, he'd steal you away in a snap."

She swallowed raw emotion and touched his chest. His warmth soaked through his shirt and into her hand. "I know how it feels. Because I feel the same way when I see you with Fredericka. And that's the reason I know I can't tell you to push Fredericka away."

He placed his palm over her hand and a soft pleading filled his gaze. "That's different. Fredericka is part of my pack."

She shook her head. "And Derek's a friend."

"Exactly. That's what makes it different. A friend isn't the same as a pack member."

"It is for me." She shook her head. "Think about it. You're loyal to pack members. You would defend them. You care about them. That's the same way I feel about my friends."

"That's because you're not a were. Or at least not yet." He snaked his free hand around her waist and tugged her a little closer. "Hopefully, soon, it will all make sense to you."

I'll never be a were. She stared up at him. The evidence of his anger had faded from his eyes and she saw affection in their deep blue depths. He cared about her. She knew that with certainty. And maybe for that reason, she wavered about telling what she knew. Instantly, it hit her that she hadn't hesitated to tell Derek. Why could she confide in Derek and not Lucas? Bothered by the thought, she forced herself to say, "I'm not a were."

"You don't know that," he said. "The fact that you developed more before a full moon and had mood swings has to mean something."

She shook her head. "I'm not. I know what I am."

His eyes tightened in confusion. "You . . . How do you know?"

"My father appeared to me again. He said I was a chameleon."

Puzzlement filled his gaze.

She frowned. "I don't know exactly what it means."

"That doesn't make sense." He released her. "There's no such thing. Just because some ghost said—"

"It wasn't just 'some ghost.' It was my father."

"And your father is a ghost." Whether he meant it to or not, it sounded like an insult.

His words and his attitude stung. She pulled her hand from his warm chest. All the emotional havoc from earlier whirled inside her.

"I know he's a ghost," Kylie said. "And I wish he wasn't dead. I wish I knew what he meant. I wish that you could accept me for what I am. But I can't change the fact that my dad died before I was born. I can't help that I don't understand what he meant. For that matter, I don't understand a tenth of what's happening in my life right now. And I have a feeling you will never be able to accept me for what I am."

"That's not true." His expression hardened with denial.

"Yes, it is." She turned and limped away.

She heard him ask her not to go. She ignored his plea. Then, stopping, she reached down to remove her shoes. As she straightened, her gaze caught on the row of trees—on how their leaves stirred even when no wind blew. She felt again the unexplainable sense that she was being lured to enter. As tempting as it was, she walked away. Walked away from the forest. Walked away from Lucas.

And both somehow felt wrong.

Chapter Three

Kylie's bare feet moved quickly against the earth as she ran. She heard the blend of voices coming from the dining hall where everyone had congregated after Ellie's funeral. Ellie, who'd died at the hands of Mario.

Another wave of guilt washed over Kylie. She ran faster. She didn't want to join the crowd. She wanted . . . *needed* . . . to be alone.

She'd almost made it to her cabin when she felt a whoosh of air fly past her. A vampire whoosh. Maybe a vampire on the hunt.

Kylie pushed herself to run faster and mentally prepared herself to fight. Not that she stood a chance of winning a battle with a vampire. Whatever super strength she had only served her when she was helping others.

A *protector*, the other supernaturals called her. But how could they call her that when she hadn't protected Ellie? Even Kylie's healing abilities had failed. How unjust was it that she could save a bird, pull it back from death, and yet couldn't save a friend? She would have paid the price. It wouldn't have mattered how much of her soul she'd had to give to save Ellie.

She felt it again—that flash of air as something swooped past.

This time she saw a curtain of straight black hair billow in the wind. Definitely a vampire.

But not one on the hunt.

Della appeared beside her, running at the same breakneck pace. But being vampire, she moved with ease, as if she were taking a leisurely jog.

"What's wrong?" Della's dark hair, hinting at her Asian bloodline, flew behind her like a flag.

"*You* are what's wrong." Kylie came to a jerky stop. "I hate it when you fly by me like that and I can't tell it's you. I feel threatened. I feel like . . . prey."

"Well, damn," Della said in her everyday bad-attitude voice. "Excuse me for being concerned. I heard you running like hell and thought someone was chasing you."

"Sorry. No one is chasing me." Kylie's gaze shot back to the woods. *They're just taunting me to step into the woods and face them.* But who was it, and for what reason? Earlier she'd assumed it was Mario, but could she have been wrong about that?

"What happened?" Della asked.

Kylie pulled her eyes away from the woods. "Nothing."

Della tilted her head to the side, as if listening to Kylie's heart, listening for signs of deception. Della rolled her eyes. "Liar. Liar. Pants on fire."

Kylie groaned. "Fine. I'm lying. And if I were wearing pants, they'd combust and burn my ass."

"Wow. You are in such a lovely mood. What took a bite out of your attitude?"

"You did." Kylie flinched at the sound of her sharp tone.

Della grinned as if enjoying Kylie's anger. Kylie started walking.

"Who's supposed to be shadowing you?" Della asked.

"I don't know." Kylie's gaze shot to the woods and the sensation hit stronger than ever. She took off running down the path, push-ing herself harder. She didn't stop until she got to her cabin. Her stomach cramped from running. She dropped down on the edge of their porch.

"So what happened?" Della, not even breathing hard, plopped down beside Kylie.

Something in the woods is calling my name. That sounded crazy. Kylie couldn't say it. She looked at Della. Her roommate's slightly slanted black eyes appeared genuinely concerned, and that made Kylie feel like a bitch.

"Sorry. I'm in a bad mood."

"Which is so rare," Della said. "I kind of like it."

Kylie rolled her eyes and pushed back her reservations. "Have you ever heard of chameleons?"

"Yeah," Della said.

"You have? What do you know about them?"

"They're lizards that change colors. According to Chan, they don't taste too bad. In Hawaii, the local vampires sell their blood. It's supposed to be as good as O negative."

"No." Kylie pulled her knees up and hugged them.

"No, what?"

"I mean . . . chameleons as a type of supernatural?"

"A lizard supernatural?" Della laughed.

Kylie jumped up.

"Hey." Della popped up beside her. "What's wrong with you?"

Kylie yanked open the cabin door and looked back at Della. "Everything is wrong."

"Is this about Ellie?" Della's voice hinted at an emotion that the vamp kept hidden.

Kylie's heart gripped tighter. "Yes, it's about Ellie. It's about me being a lizard. It's everything."

"You're a lizard?" The seriousness faded from Della's eyes, and she grinned.

Kylie stormed through the door, then swung around. "Yeah, you're a vampire, and I'm a lizard, so just friggin' get used to it."

Della's smirk faded. "Have you been smoking something? Seriously, I think you're a werewolf. This new snarky attitude is a dead giveaway."

"And vampires aren't snarky?" Kylie rolled her eyes.

"No, we're pissy. Snarky and pissy are two totally different things." Della moved inside. The vamp's attempt at humor was to help, not hurt.

But Kylie wasn't in the mood. "I'm not a werewolf." Tears stung her eyes. "If I were, then Lucas would be happy and all would be right in the world."

Della's mouth dropped open. "You're serious. Who told you that you were a lizard?"

"My dad."

Della's eyes widened. "You're shitting me."

"No shitting."

Della fell into the sofa and her gaze darted around the room. "Is he here now?"

"No."

"Good." She slapped her hands on her thighs. "Maybe he was smoking something."

Kylie rolled her wet eyes. "Would you please stop making wisecracks?"

Della snatched up a sofa pillow and tossed it at Kylie. "See, there's the werewolf attitude coming out again."

Kylie swung around to go into her room, but before she got to the door, Della shot in front of it. It was freaky how fast a vampire could move.

"Fine," Della said. "I'll try to be serious, but . . . it's crazy. I know you don't want to believe this, but someone's pulling a practical joke on you. There's no such thing as a lizard supernatural. Just ask her."

"Ask who?" The cabin's main door slammed as Miranda stepped inside. Her blond hair hung loose, streaked with pink, green, and black. Kylie didn't know if Miranda used her Wiccan powers to color her hair or Nice 'n Easy.

Miranda frowned. "Why did you leave me?" she asked Della.

Della made a face. "Sorry. Kylie's having a crisis. I can only be Superfriend to one of you at a time."

Miranda looked at Kylie. "What kind of a crisis?"

Ordinarily, Kylie shared everything with Miranda and Della, but at this moment she wished she'd kept her mouth shut. All this time she'd longed to know what she was, thinking it would solve everything, and yet here she was, supposedly knowing, and feeling more confused than ever.

"A tasty reptile crisis." Della giggled, put her hand over her mouth, and then looked apologetically at Kylie. "Oops."

"What?" Miranda asked.

Della propped one hand on her hip. "Tell Kylie there's no such thing as lizard supernaturals."

"Perry can change into a lizard." Miranda's eyes brightened with pride. "Yesterday he shifted—"

"Please, not another Perry story." Della pressed both her palms against her stomach. "I swear, I'll hurl."

"You are such a bitch," Miranda snapped.

"I'm not a bitch. I'm just sick of hearing Perry stories. 'Perry's pinky toes are so cute. Perry's got the most charming freckle behind his right ear.'"

"You're just jealous! Because you don't have a boyfriend and Kylie and I do!"

Did. Kylie *had* a boyfriend. She wasn't sure what was going to happen with her and Lucas now. His pleas for her not to run off echoed in her heart.

"Jealous?" Della roared back at Miranda. "Please, I'll chew out my own heart before I become lovesick like you."

Miranda held up her hand and wiggled her pinky—a sure sign a spell was about to spill from her lips. Della's eyes brightened and her canines came out to play.

"Stop!" Kylie looked from one to the other. She couldn't take it anymore. "Oh, hell, don't stop. You two have been threatening to kill each other since I got here, and it's driving me mad. So just kill each other and put me out of my misery." Inside, Kylie flinched again. She didn't mean it. Not even now, when furious, but maybe a little reverse psychology would fix these two.

Miranda and Della stared at Kylie as if she'd lost her mind, and they could be right, but it was partially their fault. Their arguing had caused her to go nuts.

"Come on. What are you waiting for? Kill each other. And make it entertaining." She crossed her arms over her chest and stared daggers at the two of them. Her right foot started tapping, just like her mom's tapped when she was about to blow a gasket.

Della's eyes returned to their black color and her canines disappeared under her top lip. Miranda dropped her threatening pinky. So reverse psychology did work. Ha. Who knew?

"What's wrong with her?" Miranda asked Della as if Kylie were too mentally unstable to ask.

"Nothing's wrong with me," Kylie answered, frustrated beyond her limits. "It's what's wrong with you two."

Della glanced at Miranda and shrugged. "She thinks she's a lizard."

"A chameleon," Kylie corrected.

Miranda rolled her eyes. "Poor thing. She's acting like a werewolf."

Della shot Kylie a smirk. "I told her that. But did she listen to me? Hell, no."

"I'm not a werewolf." It didn't matter what Kylie now wished she was.

"If you are, it's okay," Miranda said. "We've vowed to love you anyway."

Kylie dropped down onto a living room chair while her two best friends stared at her with a mix of pity and leeriness. They thought she was crazy. Heck, maybe she *was* crazy. She thought the woods were calling her name and she believed she was a reptile. She leaned back and stared at the ceiling.

"I'm a chameleon," she said, hoping that saying it would bring some kind of instinctual understanding. She held her breath, waiting for an epiphany—an internal knowledge that would make her right with the world.

Nothing came. And nothing felt right. Not her being a lizard, not seeing a ghost with the face of someone who was alive, not with her dad suggesting she would soon be making a trip into the afterworld, and especially not Derek's confession of love.

Nope. Nothing felt right. She moaned.

"Get her a Diet Coke, Della," Miranda said. "Maybe the sugar will give her some brainpower."

"It's fake sugar," Della answered.

"I know. But haven't you ever heard the saying fake it until you make it?"

"Ugh, forget the soda. I'm going to bed." Kylie popped up from the chair and went into her room, slamming the door so hard it rattled on its hinges.

From behind the door she heard them say in unison, "Definitely werewolf."

• • •

She hadn't gotten to her bed when she heard a loud commotion from the living room. Had Miranda and Della finally decided to really duke it out? Feeling guilty for encouraging them, she went to stop them but stilled when she heard voices.

"Where's Kylie?" Burnett's deep tenor spilled through the walls at the same time that her phone started ringing.

She pulled her phone from her pocket and jerked open the door. Burnett stood there with his hand raised to knock. Both anger and a thread of guilt filled his expression.

"Something wrong?" Kylie's ringing phone hummed in her hand.

"Are you okay?"

"Why wouldn't I be?" Had something else happened? At this point, nothing could surprise her.

Chapter Four

"You left without telling me." Burnett's mouth thinned with his reprimand.

"I did not." Kylie saw Della and Miranda behind Burnett, wearing concerned expressions. No doubt, it wasn't wise to disagree with Burnett.

"You were in the office and then you were gone," Burnett barked. "I was supposed to be shadowing you."

"That was almost an hour ago," she said. Had he just now realized she was gone?

The ringing of her phone drew her attention and she pulled it up to see who was calling. Holiday's name appeared on the tiny screen. Then the camp leader, phone pressed to her ear, stormed into the cabin.

"You found her." Relief filled Holiday's eyes and she folded her arms over her stomach and breathed as if she'd run all the way here.

"You shouldn't have left without telling me," Burnett said to Kylie.

Holiday shut her phone off and silenced Kylie's cell. Kylie stared at the camp leader, recalling the ghost issues that she needed to talk to her about. *How could someone alive appear as a ghost?*

"I was in charge of you." Burnett continued his tirade.

Kylie glanced at Burnett as she set her phone down on the end table. She should probably keep her mouth shut, but her bad mood prevailed. "You can't blame me. I told you I was leaving. Not once, but twice. You two were too busy being pissy with each other to hear me." When her own hostile words rang in her ears, she worried maybe Della and Miranda were on to something about her being werewolf.

Holiday stepped closer. "We weren't arguing."

Really, Kylie thought, noticing that Holiday's shirt was on inside out. Not arguing, huh? So what had they been doing that led to Holiday wearing her shirt inside out? All Kylie's frustration lessened and she almost smiled. Almost.

"Yes, we were arguing," Burnett confessed, as if suddenly remembering.

"We were just discussing things." Holiday sent Burnett a look that said, *Don't disagree with me on this.*

"We were discussing it heatedly." Burnett received another hard stare from the redheaded camp leader.

"I'll say," Della mouthed off. "I heard you all the way in the dining room. And I'm not so sure it was my vampire hearing that caught it."

"Yes, it was," Miranda piped up. "Because I didn't get to hear a thing. Then again, I was probably talking with Perry." She got a faraway look in her eyes. "I love talking with Perry."

Della moaned.

"That said," Miranda continued, "nothing is as fun as a good argument. So if someone would like to fill me in, I'd appreciate it." She rubbed her hands together. "Just the good parts."

Burnett exhaled in frustration. "We were just—"

"What we were doing isn't important," Holiday blurted out, blushing.

"So you weren't arguing?" Miranda looked intrigued.

Kylie almost smiled again. Holiday was right. What they were doing wasn't important. The thing that mattered was that they'd made up. The thing that really mattered was if Holiday had managed to talk Burnett out of resigning his position. Shadow Falls needed him.

Holiday needed him.

Everything inside Kylie told her that the two of them were meant to be together. Unfortunately, Holiday resisted the idea of her and Burnett becoming an item. And while she hadn't completely admitted it, Kylie suspected it had everything to do with Holiday's vampire fiancé who'd broken her heart when he left her at the altar. Kylie also sensed there was more to that story than Holiday let on. Not that being left at the altar wasn't bad, but something told Kylie it had been something even more emotionally damaging. Why else would Holiday reject Burnett's love?

God knew it wasn't easy for a vampire to take rejection. Kylie had told him he needed to be patient. Holiday couldn't continue to hold out. Not when Burnett was practically perfect. Tall, dark, moody enough to be fascinating, and with a good heart. Sure, being vampire, he didn't go around passing out good cheer like Holiday did. But he cared.

Did Holiday finally come to her senses?

"Are you staying on at Shadow Falls?" Kylie asked Burnett, breath held in hope.

Burnett glanced at Holiday and damn if he didn't almost smile. "I'm staying."

"Yes!" Miranda and Della high-fived each other and did a little victory dance.

A sense of rightness filled Kylie's chest. Maybe today wouldn't go down in history as the worst day in her life, after all.

Burnett, being his slightly brooding self, didn't seem to share her roommates' joy, but Kylie spotted relief in his eyes. "Next time you are under my charge, don't walk away without my permission."

Kylie nodded, too happy to care if she wasn't at fault.

"Even if you have to knock me over my head twice to get my attention," he continued, taking most of the blame on himself. Kylie's smile widened. As stern as Burnett could be, he wasn't unfair.

She watched Burnett start for the door, and Holiday turned to go with him. Again, Kylie couldn't help but wonder how far things had gone in their time together. Had their clothes been half off when they suddenly realized she was gone?

Holiday looked back at Kylie. Their gazes met and held.

Just from the quick glance, Kylie knew that Holiday, an empath like Derek, had read the swarm of emotions playing hide and seek in her mind. And not the happy ones.

Kylie seldom got anything past the fae. Not that Kylie attempted to hide a whole heck of a lot from Holiday. The bond they shared had moved past friendship. Holiday was family—not the kind you were born with, but the kind you were lucky enough to choose.

"I need to speak to Kylie." The warmth in Holiday's tone had Kylie's chest tightening and she wondered what she'd ever do without the woman in her life. She hoped she never had to find out. The thought sent a shiver down Kylie's spine.

Burnett acknowledged all of them with a farewell glance, and then left.

As soon as he walked out, Della turned to Holiday. "Maybe *you* can talk some sense into Kylie. She thinks she's a lizard."

Five minutes later, Holiday and Kylie sat on the edge of the porch, their bare legs dangling over the edge. The camp leader had changed from the dark dress she'd worn at Ellie's funeral to a pair of cutoff jeans and the yellow shirt that she wore inside out.

Kylie's black dress flared across her thighs, landing right above her knees. If she stretched out her feet, her toes would brush against the grass. She usually liked how the light tickle felt, but for some reason it now reminded her of sitting with Derek earlier out beside the tree.

Pushing that thought aside, Kylie stared down at their feet. Holiday had on a pair of sandals, and her toenails were painted a soft pink.

"What happened?" Holiday asked, concern deepening her tone.

"I don't know where to start," Kylie said.

"How about with the whole lizard thing? What's Della talking about?"

Kylie bit down on her lip. "Before I get into all that, what happened between you and Burnett?"

Holiday glanced away. "He's staying on."

"I know that." Smiling, Kylie bumped her shoulder with Holiday's. "Did anything good happen?"

Color brightened Holiday's cheeks. "I don't feel comfortable talking about this."

"Wow. It must have been good, then," Kylie teased.

Holiday frowned, which meant whatever happened hadn't changed much. Some clothes might have come off, but Holiday's reservations hadn't.

"We didn't . . ." Holiday dropped her face into her hands. "I'm confused, okay? I need Burnett at Shadow Falls. He's strong in all the areas that I'm lacking. And where he's lacking, I'm strong. But . . ."

"But you're scared to admit you care about him," Kylie said, even when her gut told her she needed to back off.

"You don't understand," Holiday said.

"That's because you haven't told me everything," Kylie accused, and she got that sensation again that there were things, emotional things, Holiday kept bottled up inside her.

Holiday sighed. "This is something I need to work out myself. I know we're close and I love that you care." She put her hand on top of Kylie's. "I feel that you're only trying to help, but I need to go solo on this one. And I'm asking you to accept that."

Kylie nodded, knowing she had to respect Holiday's wishes, but not liking it.

"Now, let's get back to you." She bumped Kylie's shoulder with hers. "Talk to me."

Taking a deep breath, she told Holiday about her dad's visit—both the chameleon stuff and the part about them figuring it out together . . . *soon.*

Concern and confusion filled the camp leader's eyes. "Okay, about your dad saying you will work it out together—I don't think it means what you think. Time doesn't mean the same thing in the spirit world."

Kylie considered what Holiday said. "It's not that I don't believe you, it's just . . . there was something about the way he kept saying 'soon.' And he was happy about it."

Holiday shook her head. "Your dad loves you. And I think if he knew you were going to die too soon, he'd be panicking. And the last thing he would do is share that news with you."

It hurt to say it aloud, but she did it anyway. "If I'm going to die, I should know."

"It doesn't work like that. I mean, there are a few people who are able to know of their death and use the time wisely. But when you start planning for the end, most people instinctually stop living for tomorrow. Living for the day is beautiful—too many of us don't do it enough—but to live fully, we must live for today and tomorrow. Think about it, if you knew you were going to die in six months, would you start a project that you knew you couldn't finish? Would you go to school to learn to be a doctor? Would you have a child, knowing you would leave it alone too soon? People miss out on so much if they stop living for tomorrow."

Holiday's little speech sent Kylie right into the lap of another problem. Her ghost problem. She tried to think about the best way to approach it.

"Now, about the whole lizard thing," Holiday said, taking Kylie's thoughts in another direction. "I've never heard of a chameleon supernatural. And while I'm inclined to tell you that he got it wrong, I wonder . . ."

"Wonder what?" Kylie asked.

"I don't know for sure, I'm just—"

"I know," Kylie said. "You're just speculating, guessing, but since I'm feeling pretty clueless, I'd like to hear it."

"I was going to tell you." Holiday's expression told Kylie she needed to be patient.

She'd grown tired of being patient. And yes, she knew that on Thursday, her grandfather Malcolm Summers was coming, and hopefully he'd make sense of all this for her. But that meant a couple more days of not knowing.

"So just tell me. Please." Kylie softened her tone because being impatient might be understandable, but blaming others for it wasn't.

Holiday inhaled. "Maybe he referred to you as a chameleon because your pattern hasn't matured to what it really should be. It's still changing, like a chameleon changes colors."

"But he said I was a chameleon like he was telling me that I was a vampire or witch. Is it possible that there's another type of supernatural race that no one knows about?"

Holiday paused. "My gut says no. The history of supernaturals is documented in books as old as the Bible. But . . . I admit I'm baffled. It seems that whatever is causing this is probably hereditary because of your real grandfather and great-aunt's ability to change their patterns to human. But even that is completely off the chart weird. I'm still thinking it was Wiccan related but . . ."

"Or . . ." Kylie considered Holiday's words. "Maybe that's what it means, the whole chameleon thing. I was talking about this with Derek earlier. Maybe chameleons can change our species. Like a chameleon can change its colors."

Holiday paused as if thinking. "But DNA doesn't work that way. You can't have more than one string of DNA. It isn't possible, because supernaturals only have the DNA of the dominant parent."

Kylie bit down on her lip. "Then maybe it's not the species that really changes, but just the pattern. And in a way it makes sense because a chameleon doesn't turn into a rock, it just changes its colors so it looks like a rock."

Holiday's brow wrinkled. "But . . ." She shook her head.

"But what?" Kylie wanted to know everything Holiday considered.

"It just doesn't feel right. If this ability to hide your pattern actually exists, why haven't other supernaturals heard about it?"

"Maybe we have heard about it," Kylie said. "Maybe this is exactly why they tested my grandmother. You mentioned once that you'd heard about those tests. Did anyone say what the tests were for?"

"Not specifically," Holiday said. "Something about understanding genetics in some supernaturals. But that they went wrong."

"That's an understatement," Kylie muttered. "They killed people." *Killed my grandmother.* Kylie couldn't understand how someone could do that—take a life. For that matter, how could Mario kill his own grandson? Or kill Ellie, who never did a thing to harm him? Or anyone else for that matter?

"I know." Holiday sighed as if sensing Kylie's grief. "Which is why I refuse to let them test you. I don't think the FRU is evil, Kylie. I just don't trust them to not take too many risks with you to find answers. Whatever is going on, we'll figure it out sooner or later."

Kylie sure as hell hoped so. Because right now, it didn't make a lick of sense to her. She gazed back at Holiday. "Is that why you can't trust Burnett? Because he's part of the FRU?"

Holiday looked perplexed. "I trust Burnett."

Kylie arched a brow in disbelief.

"I trust him with Shadow Falls," Holiday confessed.

Just not with your heart. And how sad was that? Kylie thought.

"I wouldn't have him working here if I thought there was a chance he would betray you or any of my students."

"I know," Kylie said. "And I trust him, too. I mean, the whole FRU thing with my grandmother scares me, but I trust Burnett."

Holiday met Kylie's eyes again. "I know that waiting for answers is hard on you. But hold on to the hope that your grandfather will come on Thursday and—"

"What do you mean 'hold on to the hope'? He told Burnett he was coming, right?" Seeing disappointment flash in Holiday's eyes, Kylie's heart sank. "What happened?"

"Burnett tried to contact him again and . . . your grandfather's phone has been disconnected. But it could mean nothing."

"Or it could mean that he's decided not to communicate with me." A knot rose in Kylie's throat.

"Don't get worked up over it until we know."

Kylie pulled her knees up and dropped her head on them, trying not to cry. Was her hope of discovering the truth now slipping away?

Holiday rested her hand on Kylie's shoulder. A sweet calm came with the touch, and while it soothed Kylie's panic, it didn't change anything. They sat there for several minutes, not talking, Kylie trying not to cry and Holiday doing what she did best—offering emotional comfort.

The soft breeze whispered past and somehow Kylie's mind shifted from one problem to another. "Derek told me he talked to you about . . . things."

Holiday brushed a strand of hair off Kylie's cheek. "I'm sorry. I imagine that came completely out of left field."

Kylie nodded. "What am I supposed to do with that information?"

"I don't think you have to do anything."

Kylie exhaled. "It makes me feel crazy and sad, and I start questioning things. And Lucas is jealous of him and I don't blame him for being jealous because I feel the same way about Fredericka. But . . ."

"But you care about Derek," Holiday finished for her.

"I do. I'm just not sure if what I feel for him is what I feel for Lucas. Does that make sense?"

"Perfect sense," Holiday assured her. "You'll figure it out."

"Will I?" Angst rose inside Kylie again. "Everything in my life is a huge effing question mark. I'm tired of not being sure of *anything*. And then the ghost . . ." Kylie let the words fade.

"You have a problem with a ghost?" Holiday asked. "Is it your grandmother? Have you asked her about what your dad said?"

"No, it's not her." How much should Kylie tell Holiday? "At first, the spirit showed up looking like a zombie, hardly even had a face. I insisted she fix that. But . . . then the face she got was . . . someone who wasn't dead."

Holiday bit down on her lip. "Are you sure she isn't dead?"

"I'm sure." *Extra sure.*

"Well," Holiday continued, "it could be one of two things. The most likely answer is that you have a ghost with an identity crisis."

"Seriously? Ghosts can have an identity crisis?" Kylie asked.

"Afraid so. They may not even know what they looked like. Or they may not have liked how they looked, so they plaster the face of someone else on their ghost bodies. Most of the time, they use the face of the ghost whisperer. And seeing your face on a ghost . . ." Holiday shivered. "Not good."

"I can imagine," Kylie said, but she didn't want to imagine it. She already had too much on her plate. "What's the other thing it could be?"

"It's rare," Holiday said. "But did you see *A Christmas Carol*?"

"Yes." Kylie recalled the plot. "The Scrooge thing, right?"

"And the ghost from the future," Holiday said.

Kylie's breath hitched. "This person could be about to die?" Sure, the thought had crossed her mind, as it had Derek's, but not until Holiday said it did it feel real. No, Kylie refused to accept it. She'd seen too much death already.

"Is this one of the things I can change?" Kylie asked, panic building in her chest.

"Probably not." Holiday frowned. "Is it someone you know well?"

Kylie didn't answer. She couldn't. She just kept reminding herself that Holiday had said it was rare.

"Is it someone from Shadow Falls?" Miranda's voice piped up from behind them.

Kylie turned to see Miranda standing in the doorway behind them.

"Sorry," Miranda said. "I didn't mean to eavesdrop . . . but is it someone from here?"

"No," Kylie lied.

"Oh, good." Miranda did a dramatic swipe of her brow. "Your phone's chirping." She held out the phone. "It's your mom. This is like the third time she's called in the last five minutes."

"You should call her," Holiday said. Then the camp leader's phone rang. She glanced down at the number. "It's Burnett."

Holiday and Kylie stood at the same time. Kylie reached for her phone from Miranda as Holiday answered hers.

"Hello." Holiday paused. The worry wrinkle between her eyes appeared. "About what?" Her tone had Kylie hesitating to make her own call. "Let's talk before you go. I'm on my way." Holiday hung up.

"What's wrong?" Kylie asked.

"I—I'll talk with you when I know something." Holiday took off, but her answer had Kylie suspicious that the call had something to do with her.

"That didn't sound good," Miranda said.

Just great, Kylie thought. How much more could she take?

Chapter Five

"Are you okay?" Holiday's voice stirred Kylie awake about an hour later. After trying to call her mom numerous times and leaving several messages, her mind and heart gave up and she went to bed and took a nap.

She looked at Holiday perched on the end of her bed. Sitting up, Kylie yawned and brushed her hair from her eyes. "I've been better."

"Life can be so hard sometimes."

"Tell me about it." Kylie remembered the call from Burnett. "Is everything okay? What happened?"

Holiday stared at her with a vacant expression. "Who's Burnett?"

The cold in the room sent chills spidering across Kylie's back. She blinked and focused again on the woman's features. There was no doubt about it. She was Holiday.

Anger, fear, and frustration swarmed through Kylie's chest. "Okay, let me make something clear. When I told you to fix your face, I meant for you to get your own face, not borrow one from someone else."

The spirit pressed her palms against her cheeks, and her eyes widened. *"Is this not my face?"*

"No, it's not! It's the face of someone I care a lot about, and, nothing personal, but I don't like seeing you wearing it."

"I'm so confused."

"You have an identity crisis," Kylie offered, wanting more than anything to believe it.

"An identity crisis," the spirit repeated.

"Yeah, and you need to figure out who you are and what it is you need from me, because I can't help you if you don't."

"It's mostly a blur." She pursed her lips in the same manner Holiday did when she was thinking really hard, and damn if the resemblance wasn't uncanny. Even the green color of her eyes matched perfectly.

"Maybe you're right," the spirit said. *"I remember always feeling as if I lived in someone else's shadow."*

"That's good," Kylie said, relief allowing her to breathe deeper.

"Good that I lived in someone else's shadow?" The ghost frowned. *"I don't see it as a good thing."*

"No, I . . . I mean it's good you can remember stuff." And right then, Kylie remembered something, too. One quick and easy way to assure herself that this spirit wasn't Holiday Brandon. Kylie tightened her eyes and focused on the ghost's forehead.

The whimsical pattern, like the face, matched Holiday's to a T. Kylie's chest swelled with concern. "You're a fae?"

The spirit propped one bent knee up across her leg, put her elbow on her knee, and then dropped her chin in the palm of her hand. The gesture was so Holiday that Kylie's heart skipped a beat.

"Yup, that's what I am." She tightened her brows and gazed at Kylie. *"Oh, my, what are you?"*

Kylie hesitated. "I'm a . . . chameleon."

The spirit made a face. *"You're a lizard?"*

Kylie frowned, but her concern wasn't about herself. "Do you remember your name?" Kylie held her breath.

The spirit met Kylie's eyes and her brow tightened in puzzlement. Then she stood up and walked to Kylie's window. Staring out in silence, she finally turned around. *"Someone is looking for you."*

"Do you remember your name?" Kylie repeated her question.

Pulling her red hair over her shoulder, the spirit twirled it into a rope. The exact same way Kylie had watched Holiday do just a little bit ago. The ghost looked back. *"They want you to come to them."*

Kylie's chest tightened a bit. "Let's talk about you right now," Kylie said, making a mental decision to focus on one problem at a time.

"But you are so much more interesting. There's all this mystery around you. A lot of questions to be answered. I can feel your emotions, you know. That's what faes do. We feel what other people feel."

"I know," Kylie said, frustrated and scared about the spirit's real identity, but she fought the angst back so she could learn more. Because if she was Holiday, then maybe Kylie could do something, change something to prevent . . .

"I used to be able to touch people and make them feel better, but that went away."

"Why did it go away?" Kylie asked.

She frowned. *"I'm not completely sure. I think I did something bad."* The ghost's bright green eyes filled with tears. *"I hurt people."*

Kylie sensed the spirit's pain, her remorse, but she couldn't deny feeling a bit of reprieve from the confession. Holiday wouldn't do anything wrong. She was too good-hearted. Cared too much.

"Maybe you didn't mean to hurt them," Kylie said, wanting to help. She wrapped her arms around herself as protection against the chill that accompanied a spiritual being.

"I don't know. I think I was angry." The spirit stared at the wall as if lost in thought and then she reached up and touched her throat.

Kylie noticed the painful-looking bruises around the ghost's neck.

"What happened to you?" Kylie asked, a knot forming in her throat at the thought of being choked to death.

The woman looked back at Kylie, her eyes still wet with emotion. *"I'm dead."*

Kylie nodded. "I know." She waited a second. "What happened?"

The spirit shook her head. *"It's like bits and pieces of a bad nightmare. But I think it has something to do with why I'm here. I mean, I should have left by now . . . We . . . supernaturals don't hang around."* She looked down and her image started to fade. *"I need to go figure this out. I think it's important."*

"I'll help you any way I can," Kylie said, remembering Holiday saying the same thing about very few non-humans hanging around after they died. "If you can tell me your name, I might be able to find something on the computer that will help us."

The spirit moved to the window and touched the pane of glass. A layer of ice appeared on the window, the frost blurring the view outside. *"You'd better start figuring out your own problems, too."*

"I'm trying," Kylie said, again seeing Holiday's personality in the spirit and not liking it. "What's your name?" Kylie insisted.

The spirit's figure faded at the same rate as the ice on the window. Then she spoke. *"I think it's Hannah or Holly. Something like that."*

"No," Kylie said, her own voice little more than a whisper.

She then grabbed a clip and put her hair up, determined to go see Holiday, not even sure what she would or wouldn't tell the camp leader. Kylie just needed to see Holiday alive.

Kylie moved out of her room and found the main room in the cabin empty. She started for the door and stopped. Who was supposed to be shadowing her? Not that Kylie really cared. She was just going to the office, but she'd already gotten in trouble once with Burnett about the shadowing business, and she didn't want to go for two.

"Della?" she called out.

No answer came back. Was something wrong?

"Hey." Miranda popped out of her bedroom a second later. "Della had a meeting with Burnett. I'm on shadowing duty." She said it with pride.

Kylie nodded. "Good. Let's go to the office."

"Why?"

"Because I want to talk to Holiday."

"About what?"

"About something."

"Got a 'tude, do ya?" Miranda made a face as if she'd just had to swallow something really disgusting.

Kylie started to smart back, but caught herself. It was understandable that she was in a bad mood, but it didn't give her the right to take it out on her friends. "I'm sorry. I know I've been cranky today. But I've just got a lot of crap on my plate."

"I know," Miranda said in an apologetic tone. "The funeral put us all in a bad mood. But then with your whole lizard crisis, I mean, I'd be in an extra-bad mood if somebody told me that I was a reptile. Which is why I haven't raised my pinky at you one time."

"And I appreciate it," Kylie said, and then realized what Miranda had said. "What did Burnett want to talk to Della about?"

"Beats me."

"Was she upset?" Kylie couldn't help but worry that it had something to do with whatever Holiday was so upset about when she spoke to Burnett earlier. And Kylie hadn't forgotten that at the time she'd gotten the impression it was about her.

"Not really. Between you and me, I think Della's got a crush on Burnett. She just glows when Burnett asks her to do something."

"No, she doesn't. She knows he's totally into Holiday."

"Then why doesn't she go for Steve? She's jealous of us having boyfriends but won't go after Steve. And lately I noticed the same thing you did. That shape-shifter stares at her all the time. He's hot for her."

Kylie motioned to the door. "She doesn't go for Steve because she's still in love with Lee."

"Yeah, I guess that could be it, too." They walked out and started down the path toward the office. "You know, I could put a hex on him."

"On Steve?" Kylie asked.

"No, on Lee. I could easily give him warts. And I could put them some place it would really scare the piss out of him. If you know what I mean."

Kylie shook her head. "I don't think Della would want you to do that."

"She might if we caught her in the right mood."

"I wouldn't even chance asking, because if she's not in the right mood, it might really tick her off."

"Yeah, I guess." They continued down the trail. "Do I really talk about Perry all the time?"

Kylie looked at Miranda. "Yeah, but it's not as bad as Della makes it sound. I'll bet I talk about Lucas all the time." She remembered she'd walked away from him today. Was he going to be angry at her? Did he have a right to be?

"Actually, you don't. But you used to talk about Derek all the time."

Kylie frowned, not liking how that sounded.

"Oh, that reminds me, he came by to see you when you were sleeping."

"Derek came to see me?"

"No, Lucas."

Embarrassed that she'd misunderstood, Kylie bit down on her lip. "Why didn't he wake me up? Why didn't you guys wake me up?"

"He told us not to. He peeked in on you and said to just tell you he came by. Actually, it was kind of sweet. He stood in the doorway watching you for several minutes. He kind of looked sad. Or sappy. Like he was totally in love with you. Della was waving her hand under her nose as if to say he was emitting all kinds of pheromones." Miranda grinned.

Kylie's heart hurt so much she couldn't grin back. Guilt spiraled through her, both for not talking about him as much as she had talked about Derek and for walking away from him earlier when he tried to talk to her. At the time, she'd felt justified, but hindsight always gave her another viewpoint. Was she being too hard on Lucas?

Probably, she admitted. She'd been crabby lately. Hence why Miranda and Della were accusing her of being were. Something she needed to remedy.

She made up her mind. After she spoke with Holiday, she was going to find Lucas and apologize for leaving him like that. She quickened her pace down the trail. The trees on both sides seemed to grow closer together. And Kylie felt it again—the feeling of someone calling her. Luring her to step out into the woods. She stopped and looked out at the line of trees.

They want you to come to them. She heard the spirit's words whisper in her head.

Who was out there? Was it Mario?

Suddenly, she wasn't so sure. It didn't feel evil. It felt . . . She didn't know how it felt, honestly, only that it wasn't completely evil. However, it still scared her to the point that her breath came short, and a chill ran up her spine and tingled at the base of her neck.

"What?" Miranda asked, a note of fear in her tone. "Your aura is going all sorts of strange colors on me."

"Nothing," Kylie lied. She turned and started jogging to the office. As her feet pounded the path, little clouds of dirt floated up. She blinked the dusty air away and that's when she saw the moon—

half full, but bright. And it looked as if it just suddenly appeared in the sky.

Moonrise, she thought. She felt again the whispers echoing in her mind. Whispers she couldn't understand, whispers that both lured her and frightened her.

"Is it a ghost?" Miranda asked, her feet pounding the path as her multicolored hair danced in the wind. "Is it?"

"No," Kylie said, able to speak without huffing.

"Then can you slow down? Because I'm not like you and Della. I mean, I could cast a spell and maybe I could run faster, but that would take some time. And the last time I tried it, I turned myself into an antelope."

"We're just about there," Kylie said, but, remembering how she hated having to work so hard to keep up with Della, she did slow her pace. Suddenly, a whoosh of air blew past them. Kylie's first thought was vampire, but then Perry, in his huge prehistoric bird form, landed in front of them.

Miranda, even huffing and puffing, squealed with pleasure. Perry took his right wing and wrapped it around the little witch, pulling her into his chest and giving her a warm bird hug. Then he cooed, sounding like a dove. As sappy as it was, and even in her bad mood, Kylie's chest tightened. And the tender smile she spotted in Miranda's expression sealed the deal. Love was a wonderful thing. Kylie wanted it. All of it. Complete devotion. All the sappy, crazy feelings.

Images of both Derek and Lucas filled her head. Oh, hell, could she be in love with both of them? Was that even possible?

Perry released Miranda and stepped back. Sparkles started falling around him like iridescent snow. In seconds, human Perry appeared. His sandy blond hair clung to his forehead as if he'd worked up a sweat. His eyes were blue. Bright blue. He wore a pair of black jeans and a T-shirt that read, WHAT DO YOU WANT ME TO BE?

"I was just coming to get you," Perry said, shifting his gaze from Miranda to Kylie.

"Me?" Kylie asked. "Why?"

He shrugged. "They told me to. Ordered me to."

"Who?" Kylie asked. "Who told you to get me?"

"Duh. Burnett and Holiday. I don't take orders from anyone else. Except maybe Miranda." He grinned at Miranda.

"Is something wrong?" Kylie asked.

He looked back at Kylie. "I don't know. But I know your mom showed up and she's fit to be tied. Giving Holiday hell."

"My mom's here?" Kylie asked, feeling confused.

Perry nodded. "Sorry."

Kylie took off at a heated pace. Worry had her feet hitting the dirt and leaving a cloud of dust in her wake.

Chapter Six

Kylie ran directly into Holiday's office. Her mom stood in front of Holiday's desk, making some declaration. Holiday sat behind the desk, listening to the declaration. Burnett stood stoic, taking it all in. Kylie barely gave him a glance. She focused on her mom, who swung around and . . .

Kylie was engulfed in a quick but desperate hug. Over her mom's shoulder, Kylie's questioning gaze shot to Holiday, who stood up. Her mom backed up.

Kylie continued to stare at Holiday. The briefest of memories of the spirit pulled at Kylie's heart. How could they be so identical and not be the same person? Kylie told herself to deal with one thing at a time. So she refocused on her mom. The look on her face scared the crap out of Kylie. It was the same look her mom had when her grandmother had died.

"What's wrong?" Kylie's mind searched for possibilities and her breath caught as one hit. "Is Dad okay?"

She might still be angry at her stepfather, might not have forgiven him for his infidelity with his young intern, but Kylie loved him. She'd never been surer of that fact than right now. Now, when she imagined the worst—imagined her mother telling her that there had been an accident. That Kylie would never get another long hug from the man or go with him on a father/daughter trip.

"Your dad is fine. It's you that isn't." Her mom's gaze shot over Kylie's shoulder and then back at Kylie. "Why didn't you tell me you were sick?"

"I'm not sick."

"You had some headaches. And those nightmares, remember?" Holiday spoke in a certain tone that Kylie didn't quite understand.

Her mom's gaze flipped from Kylie's face over her shoulder again and for some reason it made Kylie turn around. Sitting on the sofa was a man she didn't know.

"I . . . don't understand," Kylie said, and looked back at her mom.

"It was in my records," Holiday said, again in a tone that seemed to mean something. "I put it in the files and the administrators thought maybe your mom should be contacted. To see if perhaps you needed testing."

Kylie continued to stare at Holiday.

"They called me and asked if they had my permission to test you. Baby, are you okay?"

Test me? Administrators?

Oh, hell, the dots started going together. It wasn't any administrators. It was the FRU. They were trying to get her mom's permission to test her.

"I'm fine," Kylie said. "I don't need to be tested." Fear shot through Kylie. Her gaze shot to Burnett. He looked at her, straight on. No guilt. And she sensed he didn't have any part in this. She remembered the phone call and suspected that this was what it had been all about. Her gaze shot to the man on the sofa. Was he from the FRU? Was this the bastard who wanted to use her as a lab rat like they'd used her grandmother?

"Who are you?" she asked before she could stop herself. Then she tightened her eyes and checked out his pattern. She blinked and did it again when he came up human.

"This is John," her mom said. "We were out having dinner when I got the message from Mr. Edwards that you've been blacking out."

"John?" Who the hell was John? Kylie looked at her mom. And damn if her mom didn't look guilty.

"He's the client that I had lunch with the other day, remember? I told you about him."

Kylie did remember. He was the guy who was going to ruin all the chances of her mother and stepfather getting back together.

"As I've explained," Holiday continued, "Kylie hasn't actually been blacking out. I think I might have just made it sound a bit worse than I intended in my reports. And when someone read them, they interpreted things wrong."

Emotion fluttered around like trapped birds in Kylie's chest. Holiday glanced at her and Kylie got the feeling the camp leader was trying to communicate something to her. But damn, Kylie couldn't read minds. She couldn't even read emotions.

"Didn't Kylie have night terrors at home?" Holiday asked.

Kylie suddenly thought she understood what Holiday wanted. "Yes. They were just night terrors, Mom. I didn't pass out. You remember how out of it I get when I have one of those. I'm not sick. I don't need testing. Besides, you already had me tested, remember?"

"But I didn't think you were having them anymore."

"I've only had a couple. And I'm fine. Look at me, I'm fine." She held her arms out, mentally searching for a way to prove it. "I can touch my toes; I can touch my tongue to my nose." It was a little rhyme she and her mom said when someone asked if they were okay.

"But why would Mr. Edwards want to run tests on you?"

Holiday leaned forward in her chair. "Oh, don't listen to him.

He's just overcautious." She smiled, doing her best to sound convincing. "But if you would like to schedule Kylie for some tests with your own doctor for your peace of mind, I'd completely understand. I mean, nothing against the doctors here, but I would hope you have a good relationship with your own physician."

"Do you think I should?" her mom asked Holiday with her worried maternal look.

"Actually, no, I don't. I think Kylie's fine. With only two occurrences of the night terrors, I think she's doing great."

"I *am* doing great," Kylie persisted. "I'm fine. I promise. Please, Mom. I don't want to go through those tests again."

Her mom ran her palm over Kylie's cheek. "Do you know how scared I was? Oh, Lordie." Her mom looked back at Holiday. "You should consider having a serious talk with Mr. Edwards. I swear, the way his message sounded, you would think Kylie was in serious trouble."

"I'm sorry that scared you." Kylie looked at John over her mom's shoulder.

The man stood up, moved forward, and rested his hand on her mom's shoulder. Kylie had the oddest desire to slap his hand away and tell him he didn't have the right to touch her mom.

"Hello, Kylie," John said.

Kylie took in his suave smile, brown eyes, and matching chocolate-colored hair that was styled to perfection. She so wished she could find something ugly about him, but nope. He wasn't ugly. He wasn't completely older-guy hot like Burnett, maybe because he was a tad older, but he had the whole distinguished-looking thing down pat.

"I wish our first meeting could have been under different circumstances," he continued, "but I've been hoping to meet you. Your mom has told me so much about you."

Funny, Kylie thought, her mom hadn't told her so much about him. Well, she'd told her about having lunch and that he'd said he might call her again, but she'd neglected to say he had called. Probably because she knew Kylie had mixed feelings about her dating. Ahh, but right now, they weren't so mixed.

Kylie didn't like him. However, because she didn't have a reason—except her gut feeling and maybe her wanting her mom and stepdad back together—she was going to have to suck it up. Be nice. What was it Miranda had said? "Fake it until you make it." Could she learn to like this guy?

"It's nice to meet you." Kylie plastered a warm expression on her face. But she worried he could tell it was a sham.

"The pleasure is all mine," he said.

Kylie just smiled. He was completely right about that.

For the next half hour, Kylie sat in the meeting room in the office and visited with her mom and smarmy John and pretended like everything in her life was just peachy. Peachy and Smarmy. Phrases that Nana, who'd passed away about three months ago, would have used.

Weird how Kylie seemed to be channeling her right now. She'd love it if Nana would pop in for a visit. *You there, Nana?* Kylie asked in her head while John rattled on about the years he'd lived in England.

Nana didn't answer. But Kylie got the oddest sensation she was close.

"I've always wanted to see England," her mom said, holding on to every word the man said.

"We can fix that," John added with enthusiasm. "I have a trip scheduled next month. Why don't you take some time off and come with me?"

"Really?" her mom said. And damn if Kylie wasn't thinking the same thing. *Really?* The man wanted her mom to go to England with him. She didn't even know him. And would he expect her mom to share a hotel room with him, too? No way!

"Mom's work schedule is pretty demanding. She won't be able to make it," Kylie declined for her mom, before she realized she shouldn't have a say in the matter.

Her mom's mouth dropped open at Kylie's declaration and she shot Kylie a that-was-rude scowl. "Well, my work is demanding, but I might be able to get a few days off." She cut her eyes back to Kylie, warning her not to speak up.

"Great," John said, as if he missed the silent tension.

"Great," Kylie repeated, her smile so stiff she didn't think her lips moved.

"Speaking of schedules." Her mom looked at her watch. "We should be heading home. It's almost a two-hour drive. And I do have to work tomorrow."

Her mom gave her a quick hug. And for her hug-impaired mom, it was pretty good. When Kylie pulled back, she mouthed the word *sorry*. And she was sorry. She didn't want to hurt her mom's feelings, even if she didn't like this guy.

The look her mother sent her was one of pure understanding. Which only made Kylie feel a little worse.

Leaning in again, her mom whispered, "Love you."

"Love you, too." Kylie went back in for another hug, and this time she held on a little tighter and for a second longer.

When she walked them out and passed by Burnett's office, she saw his six-foot-plus frame seated at his desk. He pretended to do paperwork but no doubt his super-hearing ears had been tuned in the entire time. And that was fine, she didn't have anything to hide, but as soon as Mom and the creepy guy left, Burnett had better be up for more than listening. He had a lot of explaining to do.

She had known the FRU wanted her tested, but she hadn't believed they'd go so far as to contact her mom. And if they would go that far, what was next? Would her mom's refusal to have Kylie tested be the end of it? For some reason, Kylie didn't believe so.

When Kylie returned a few minutes later, Holiday and Burnett were waiting on the cabin porch.

"What's going to happen now?" Kylie asked.

Burnett frowned and led them into Holiday's study. "I don't know. I'm stunned that they did this. They called me to come in and talk about changing your mind. I told them that you'd already declined. Someone said you weren't of legal age and suggested they go through your mom. I pointed out that your mom wasn't supernatural and how that could lead to too many questions. I thought I'd convinced them it wasn't the route to take. But when I got back here, Holiday was on the phone with your mom. They must have called your mom the minute I left the office."

Holiday sat down on the sofa. Kylie joined her. When Holiday reached for her hair and twisted it into a rope, Kylie remembered the reason she'd come to the office in the first place. Her gaze went to Holiday's neck and she remembered the spirit's angry bruises. Fear for her friend took a lap around her heart.

"Lucky for us, your mom bypassed calling the FRU back and came straight to us," Holiday said. She met Kylie's eyes. "It's going to be okay," she said, obviously reading Kylie's concern.

"I hope so." Kylie slumped back against the sofa.

"You're still upset about what happened earlier," Holiday said.

"What happened earlier?" Burnett took a step closer.

"I didn't get a chance to tell you . . ." Holiday explained about Kylie's father telling her she was a chameleon.

Kylie waited for disbelief to appear on the vampire's face, or the *you're a lizard* response everyone else had given her. When Burnett didn't offer up either, suspicion settled in.

"What do you know?" she demanded.

His eyebrows pinched. "The word *chameleon* was mentioned in the documents I found about the test responsible for your grandmother's death."

"What did it say? Did it explain how I can have a human pattern and still be supernatural?" Kylie asked, annoyed he'd kept anything from her. Kylie saw Holiday frown as well.

Burnett's gaze went from Kylie to Holiday and concern pulled at his frown. "They didn't explain anything. One of the doctors used the word *chameleon* in his notes. It didn't make sense; as a matter of fact, I wondered if it was a typo. I didn't have the original documents. Just one doctor's notes made while referring to the other documents."

"But at least this proves it," Kylie said.

"Proves what?" Burnett asked.

Kylie gazed from Burnett to Holiday. "That this is what being a chameleon is. Having a pattern that says you're one thing when you're not. I mean, we know I'm not all human." She pointed to her forehead. "And yet my pattern says I am. Of course, it doesn't tell me squat about what I really am."

"I don't think we've proved anything yet," Burnett said. "Yes, I think somehow these two things mean the same thing. I just don't think we've proven what they mean, yet."

Holiday's expression said she agreed with him. "I've been thinking," Holiday said. "Maybe your . . . pattern issues are somehow linked to you being a protector. I don't think there's ever been a part-human protector that we can compare you to."

"I hadn't thought about that," Burnett said. "That could be it."

"But what about the whole chameleon thing?" Kylie asked.

"I don't know," Holiday said. "I'm just saying it could explain your pattern issues."

Kylie's mind ran around everything that was said. The more she thought about it, the less sense any of it made. "I want to read those files."

"I'm sure by now the few files I was able to pull up have already been hidden."

"They killed my grandmother and got away with it, and now they're trying to do the same to me."

"The people who did that were either let go or have retired." His frown deepened. "I know that's how it looks and I agree you should decline testing, but I don't believe they would intentionally jeopardize your life."

"We don't know that." The firmness in Holiday's tone reminded Kylie of her mom's voice in maternal mode.

"Which is exactly why I've done what I have," he said. "Why I'm basically going against my oath to the FRU. I'm on your side. What else can I do to prove that?"

"Please," Kylie said. "I don't want you two arguing because of me."

"You don't have to prove anything." Holiday blushed with guilt. "I'm sorry. I just get so furious on Kylie's behalf."

"I know. I feel it, too." Burnett glanced at Kylie. "And we weren't arguing." He turned and focused on Holiday for a second. "This time we really were just discussing. Right?"

"Right." The slightest of grins appeared on Holiday's lips when she met his gaze.

Kylie grinned, too, even as emotion filled her chest. She was so lucky to have these people on her side. But her smile only lingered a second. "What will their next move be?"

Burnett exhaled. "Chances are they still may attempt to change your mind. Convince you that it's for a greater good. That's what I thought the plan was when I left."

"And is that when I tell them I know about my grandmother? Threaten to expose them if they don't back off?" Kylie asked.

Burnett had taken it upon himself to move Kylie's grandmother's body just in case someone in the FRU decided to hide the evidence of what had happened. In his own words, this would give Kylie some leverage to use against the FRU if they tried to force her to do something she didn't want to do.

"I would just say no, and then if they push, bring up your grandmother's remains." His expression tightened and concern flickered in his eyes. The same emotion reflected in Holiday's gaze.

"What will happen if they find out you were behind the moving of her body?" Kylie asked.

"They won't find out. I covered my tracks," he said adamantly. Maybe too adamantly, as if saying it with conviction would make it so.

"They'll suspect you because you work here. Because you're close to me," Kylie said.

"They might, but they'll have to prove it. And I haven't left any proof for them to uncover."

Kylie hoped that was the case. She glanced at Holiday again and remembered the ghost.

Holiday reached over and put her hand on Kylie's. "Is something else wrong?"

"No. Just this."

"You sure?"

"Do I need more?" Kylie's gaze shifted to the window. She could see the dusk sky going black, but she could still make out the tops of trees swaying ever so slowly.

Her gaze shot back to Holiday and she suddenly felt the need to come clean. "I feel as if I'm being called to something." She motioned to the window. "Something's out there calling me. But I'm not sure what."

Holiday looked confused. "Like being called to the falls?"

"Yeah," Kylie said. Only it felt a lot bigger than that.

"Then let's make a plan to go." Holiday leaned forward. "Do you think tomorrow's soon enough?"

Kylie started to clarify that she wasn't sure it was the falls calling her, but she didn't know how to explain it. So she just nodded.

"I'll go with you," Burnett said.

"Inside the falls?" Holiday looked back at Burnett.

"If you think I should, I will."

"The thought of going to the falls doesn't bother you?"

He shrugged. "I've been there before."

Holiday looked at Kylie and then back at him. "I know. And I find that baffling. Most supernaturals can't seem to force themselves to enter."

A small grin tightened the corners of his eyes. "Like I've been telling you, I'm special."

Holiday sighed. "But the falls—"

"Are not a problem." He cut her off and focused on Kylie. "Why don't I walk you back to your cabin? Della's on shadow duty. I told her I'd see you back." Burnett's diversion of subject appeared to be a deliberate ploy to avoid talking about the falls. What was Burnett hiding? The same question seemed to brighten Holiday's eyes as well.

"She missed dinner," Holiday said.

"All I want is a sandwich and we've got that at the cabin."

Holiday gave Kylie a long hug with warm calming emotion.

The effects from the hug lingered until she and Burnett started down the dark trail and he asked, "Would you like to explain why you lied to Holiday?"

Chapter Seven

"I didn't lie." As soon as those words were out Kylie recalled she'd indeed lied when Holiday asked if there was something else wrong. Damn, she should have remembered that Burnett could hear her heart racing if she lied.

She continued walking. He glanced down with one brow arched in disbelief. "Try again."

Kylie frowned. "It's a ghost issue. I'm just trying to figure it out myself." No way in hell could she tell Burnett about the ghost looking like Holiday. Burnett would freak. Then again, maybe he wouldn't. Maybe he wasn't so afraid of ghosts as he pretended to be.

"What is it that you're hiding from her about the falls?" she asked.

His arched brow lowered. "I'm not hiding anything."

"You can go into the falls when the others can't."

"It baffles me as well," he said. "Though I don't exactly feel comfortable there."

"You didn't feel called to go there?"

He hesitated. "Maybe a little." They walked in silence for the next four or five steps.

"Why didn't you tell Holiday?" Kylie asked.

He cut her a sly look. "Maybe I'm trying to figure it out for my-self." He used the same words she'd used on him.

"Okay." She rolled her eyes.

In a few minutes, he spoke again. "I thought you could talk to Holiday about the ghost issues."

"I can. But I'd like to handle it on my own if I can." It was the truth, so she didn't worry about what he'd hear beneath her words.

He nodded. As they neared the cabin, Kylie remembered she'd wanted to visit with Lucas. "Can Lucas take over shadowing me for a while this evening? I need to speak to him about something."

Burnett seemed to consider it. For a second, it appeared as if he might refuse. "Okay, but don't go into the woods."

His answer had her wondering. "Is the alarm working?"

"Yes, but in certain weather conditions, someone might be able to get into the forest without being picked up."

She nodded.

"Have you seen anyone?" he asked.

"No."

He stopped. "Are you sure?"

"I'm sure," she said. "Sometimes I just . . . the woods scare me a little."

"Then listen to your fears and avoid them."

"That's my plan." Kylie looked at the line of trees and the dark shadows beyond them. She didn't feel anything. Maybe what she'd felt earlier was just her overactive imagination.

Kylie spotted her cabin nestled in the trees. The lights were on and a golden hue spilled out the windows. She saw Della's shadow pass in front of the window and remembered . . .

"What did you have a meeting about with Della earlier?"

"Just FRU business." He sounded purposely vague.

"Is something wrong?" she asked.

He shook his head. "No."

"Are you having her do something for the FRU?"

"It's possible. Why?"

Kylie frowned. "Considering the FRU is causing me such a head-ache, I'm not thrilled about you getting my friends involved with them."

He stopped, dropped his hand into his jeans pockets, and shook his head as if in frustration. "The FRU is an organization meant to help the supernatural people, just like the police help humans. There have been dirty cops and even groups of cops that have done bad things, but we don't stop trusting the force as a whole."

"I might if they killed my grandmother," she said honestly.

His expression tightened. "I don't agree with everything the FRU does, but without the FRU, the world would be in chaos. The races would all be against each other, killing and maiming each other. The human race would be viewed as a food source."

Kylie shivered at his description.

"If you can't trust the FRU, at least trust me on this," he said. "The good the FRU does far outweighs the bad."

"I'll try to see it like that." But she didn't promise anything. She couldn't.

"You could have just called him," Della said, moving down the dark path toward Lucas's cabin about an hour after Kylie had returned. Kylie got the feeling that Della was a little annoyed that Kylie wanted to spend the evening with Lucas instead of hanging out with her. Especially when Miranda had run off with Perry. But Kylie's guilt over walking away from Lucas earlier made seeing him feel imperative.

"I kind of wanted to be the one to take the initiative." Kylie noticed the moon, a bright silvery white, a little over half full, hanging overhead. It was a pretty night. The temperature had dropped to the low eighties, making it almost comfortable.

"Why? What did you do wrong?"

"I got mad and walked off earlier."

"Was that why he was so sappy-eyed when he came by while you were asleep?" she asked.

"I guess." Kylie gave the line of trees a good long stare and felt nothing, which felt really good. Then she looked back at Della. "What did Burnett want to talk to you about today?"

"Nothing really."

Kylie looked at her. "You know, when you're friends with someone for a while, you don't have to hear their heartbeat to know they're lying."

Della made a face. "Yeah, but I thought that would be more polite than telling you to bug off."

Kylie frowned. "Are you going to do something for the FRU?"

"How did you know?"

"They already had Lucas and Derek do stuff. It just seemed logical. Not that I like it." She remembered Burnett saying the FRU wasn't all bad, and tried to give herself an attitude adjustment, but she couldn't completely let herself trust them.

"I think it would be kind of cool to work for them," Della said. "It would give me a reason to kick some asses every now and then."

"Do you trust them?" Kylie asked.

"I trust Burnett," Della said, and studied Kylie. "Don't you?"

"Of course I do." She hadn't told Miranda or Della about Burnett moving her grandmother's body. It just seemed like something that she shouldn't tell anyone. "They went to my mom to see about testing me."

"Oh, shit, I remember Miranda saying that your mom was here, but I forgot about it. What did your mom say? God, did they tell her you were supernatural? I'll bet it totally freaked her out."

"No, they told her they were worried because I had headaches and passed out and they advised her to have me tested. Holiday explained it was just the night terrors and advised against it."

"Oh, hell. What did Burnett say?"

"He's not for me getting tested either."

"Good," Della said. "I mean, I wouldn't want anyone probing around my head. Not after hearing what happened to your grandma." Della stopped and looked at Kylie. "Do you not want me to work for them because of this?"

Kylie got the feeling that Della would really give up her chance to work for the FRU because of Kylie's opinion—even when it was clear that Della was excited about the possibility. Her appreciation for Della's devotion swelled in her chest.

"No," Kylie said. "But . . . I do want you to be careful."

"I'll be careful." Della rubbed her hands together. "I'm glad you figured it out. I've been dying to tell someone. It'll be so cool."

They got to Lucas's cabin. The lights were on. Kylie knocked on the door while Della hung back by the porch steps. Steve, the shapeshifter who had a crush on Della, came to the door. With everything happening, Kylie had forgotten he roomed with Lucas. And so had Della, Kylie realized, when she heard the vamp draw in a quick breath.

"Hey," Steve said.

"Is Lucas here?" Kylie asked.

His gaze shifted behind Kylie and his expression changed. Kylie knew he'd spotted Della. "Uh . . . yeah. I mean, no. He left a few minutes ago with Fredericka."

"Oh." Kylie tried not to let it show that the news bothered her as she turned to leave.

Steve called after her, "He'll probably be back shortly."

She turned back. "Do you mind if we wait for a while?"

"No." His eyes lit up as he looked at Della. "Come in if you want."

Della cleared her throat in a sound that said hell no.

"Can we just sit out on the porch?" Kylie asked. "It's a nice night."

"Yeah." He stepped out. His brown hair hung across his brow. Even in the dark, Kylie could make out that his eyes were dark brown, and they were filled with interest as they cut toward Della.

When Kylie turned around, Della didn't look too happy, but she sauntered forward. "We shouldn't wait long." She plopped down on the steps.

"Just a bit." Kylie lowered herself beside the unhappy Della. Steve sat down on the side of the porch. No one said a word.

"I heard some of the new teachers were at dinner tonight." Kylie tossed out the conversation starter, hoping not to slip into angst over Lucas traipsing through the woods with Fredericka.

"Yeah," Steve said. "The English teacher, Ava Kane, seems nice. She's half-witch and half-shape-shifter."

"Why don't you just admit that you like her because she has big tits?" Della said.

Even in the dark, Kylie could see Steve's face redden. "I . . . won't deny she's pretty, but that's not what I meant."

Kylie shifted her foot and kicked Della.

"Ouch!" Della glared at Kylie. "Why did you do that?"

"When are classes supposed to start?" Kylie asked, and no one answered—Steve probably because he was afraid to get in trouble again and Della because she was too busy rubbing her kicked ankle.

Steve finally cratered. "I think next Monday."

"Were there any other teachers there?" Kylie looked at Della to answer.

"Yeah," Della added. "A Hayden Yates. He's half vampire, half fae. I think he's going to teach science. He seems okay."

"And?" Steve asked, his tone deeper, even if it was just above a whisper.

"And what?" Della asked.

He stiffened his shoulders. Which Kylie had to admit were pretty broad. The guy was cute. Why wasn't Della at least being nice?

"Why do you like Mr. Yates?" Steve asked. "His sexy body, or do you pretend it's his mind?"

Damn, Kylie thought. These two were as bad as Della and Miranda. Or Burnett and Holiday.

Della scowled at Steve and then looked at Kylie. "I'm out of here."

Embarrassed, Kylie looked at Steve. "Thanks. Can you tell Lucas that I came by?"

"You could probably find him." Steve stood up. "I think they were going down to the clearing by the stream."

"Oh," Kylie said, and took off after Della. Kylie's chest pinched with jealousy as she remembered her and Lucas going to the stream. She was so fixated on trying not to feel the green emotion ping-ponging in her heart, she hadn't realized they were heading the wrong way.

"Where are we going?" Kylie asked.

Della glared at her. "To the stream, idiot. And don't for one minute pretend that you don't want to know what he's doing down there with that she-wolf. If he was my boyfriend, I'd go grab him by the scruff of his neck and teach that wolf a lesson he wouldn't forget. He'd be whimpering like a pup before I let him go."

Kylie continued to follow Della while holding an out-and-out debate in her head over the wisdom of continuing or turning around. If she went to the stream, would Lucas think she'd come because she was jealous? But if she didn't go and Steve told him she'd dropped by and hadn't come, would he think she'd gone home because she was jealous?

Okay, the only thing that came out of that mental debate was knowing that she didn't want Lucas to think she was jealous.

Even though she was.

But did that mean she was wrong?

Or was Lucas wrong? Wrong for taking off in the dark to spend some time with Fredericka by the creek? Was he right now rolling on the grass with Fredericka, kissing her the way he'd kissed Kylie when he'd taken her to the creek?

Or was it as innocent as her getting caught behind the office with Derek?

Kylie looked up at the moon. The glow seemed extra bright and she felt that odd sting on her skin. Just like she felt on the full moon.

She inhaled deeply and told herself she was imagining things.

"Quit trying to talk yourself out of going," Della said.

"How do you know that's what I'm doing?"

"Because I can see it on your face. And because you couldn't walk any slower if you were a turtle on crutches."

"I just don't want to come off like a psycho girlfriend."

"If he's making out with her—or worse, playing hide the salami—then he deserves you coming off like a psycho. Hell, I'll join you and we'll both go psycho on his ass."

"I don't think he's doing that." As if saying it helped her believe it.

"You didn't want to think Derek did it, either." Della sighed as if she regretted saying the words. "No disrespect to Ellie and all, but it was still wrong."

Kylie's chest tightened at the mention of Ellie's name. "That was different."

"How is it different?" Della asked. A low-hanging limb swung back and Kylie caught it with her arm with complete ease. "I think it adds up to the fact that all guys are scum. Maybe we weren't even supposed to mate with them."

"Derek and I weren't together."

"Maybe you hadn't said you were together. But in your heart, you were together."

Kylie remembered what Miranda had said about her talking about Derek more than she did Lucas. Suddenly she didn't want to talk about her screwed-up love life. So why not talk about Della's screwed-up love life? It seemed like the perfect diversion.

"You could have been nicer to Steve."

Della swung around, attitude in her body posture. "I was nice."

"No, you weren't. You accused him of liking the new teacher's tits."

Della resumed walking. "You should have seen him ogling her, it was embarrassing."

"It kind of sounds like you're jealous, which says you like the guy," Kylie pointed out.

Della started walking faster, her pace matching her mood. "I don't like him. But I'll admit he has a nice butt."

"And you said you were going to try to be more approachable to his nice butt," Kylie reminded her.

"I tried. It didn't work out. I guess his butt isn't that nice."

Another branch came back, and the instant Kylie caught it in her palm, she remembered. She stopped and looked up through the trees at the sky. A few stars twinkled back as if laughing at her.

"Crap," she muttered.

"What?" Della looked back over her shoulder.

Kylie glanced around. The moon's glow cast a silver shine through the trees and shadows danced on ground.

"I just remembered."

"Remembered what?"

"I'm not supposed to go into the woods." Kylie inhaled the verdant scent of the trees and the moist earth. Then she internally searched for that feeling of being lured, beckoned as she had been earlier. It wasn't there. So maybe all those feelings were just her over-active imagination. Oh, yeah, she wanted to believe that.

Nevertheless, she'd disobeyed Burnett's orders. Maybe not on purpose, but she didn't think he'd find that excuse acceptable. "We should go back."

"But we're almost there. And you've got me—a badass vampire—with you. Nothing's going to happen. And don't you want to know if Lucas and Fredericka are doing the hokey pokey?"

Kylie caught another branch coming back at her. "If Burnett finds out, he's going to be pissed."

"Then we won't tell him. Trust me. It's gonna be fine."

Against her better judgment, Kylie continued taking steps with Della. The crickets did their thing and an occasional bird called out. In the background, Kylie could even hear the sounds of the wild animals in the park. Normally when the night sang, it meant all was well. It was in the quiet that things jumped out of the shadows. When evil seemed to appear.

Inhaling the night air, she continued moving, jumping over a few patches of thorny bushes and ducking under low branches.

"Crap," Della hissed, and came to an abrupt stop.

"What is it?" Kylie asked, and that was when the forest went silent. Not dead like in ghost silent, but dead like in threatening.

"The next time I tell you to trust me, don't." Della looked back over her shoulder. Her eyes were bright green and her canines extended. "We've got company."

Chapter Eight

"We should run." Kylie's voice was nothing more than a whisper. Her heart throbbing in her chest sounded louder.

"When things run, they get chased," Della answered. "I'd rather do the chasing."

"Smart girl," a deep voice answered back. And just the sound of it sent chills down Kylie's spine.

Three silent figures stepped out from the shadows. The only noise filtering through the thicket of trees was Della's hiss. Kylie moved to stand next to Della in case they attacked. Her mind still played with the option of running. A good option. But first she had to convince Della.

The slight sound of twigs being snapped under footsteps sounded at their backs. They were surrounded.

Time to find a new option.

Even with only the half moon lighting the path, Kylie was able to check the patterns of the three men fronting them: werewolves. The edges of the patterns were dark, as if their intentions were not good natured. That could only mean one thing: rogues.

The bigger man in the middle stepped closer. Della hissed harder. Kylie felt her blood fizz with the need to protect the little vamp. As badass as Della considered herself, this was no fair match. Not that the rogues would care.

"I will kindly ask you to leave," Kylie said, not sure where her bravado came from, but it was there, and she'd be damned if she wouldn't use it. "You're trespassing. This is Shadow Falls property." She stood with her shoulders back, her chin up. Knowing they could smell fear, she tried not to let the seed of that emotion grow any bigger.

Kylie saw Della, poised to attack, and Kylie touched her elbow, hoping to convince the vamp to wait. Maybe they could talk their way out of this.

"Leave now, or I'll rip your throat out first," Della said to the man facing her.

That wasn't the kind of talk Kylie had in mind.

"We did not come here to do harm," the guy in the middle said to Kylie, and then he cut Della a smirk as if mocking her threat. "But if provoked, that could change."

Della hissed louder.

"Then leave." Kylie's gaze moved over him. She got the feeling the one who spoke was the leader. He didn't look old, but things like the gray at his temple and the fine lines around his dark blue eyes told her he was older than she'd first assumed. Caught by his eyes, her mind tried to place him. She felt him staring, doing the same with her, and then his eyes pinched as he read her pattern.

As sudden as a flicker of light, she knew who he was. She sensed he recognized her as well. That kernel of fear lingering in her gut grew. This man didn't value life. He'd already proven that to Kylie once.

He took another step forward. Della tried to jump in front of him, but Kylie grabbed her.

"Let me handle this." The sizzle in Kylie's blood—the sizzle that came when her need to protect arose—grew stronger.

"I'm not here to spill blood," he insisted.

"Then leave," Kylie demanded.

"Yeah, tuck your tail between your legs and run," Della bit out.

A threatening growl came from behind them. Della swung around, yanking away from Kylie's hold, her eyes glowing brighter. Fear took another lap around Kylie's heart. Not fear for herself, but for what was about to happen. Her blood now buzzed as it moved into her veins. She kept her focus on Della. If anyone put a hand on her, this would not end well.

"Calm down," the leader spoke, and Kylie sensed he spoke to her as well as to his own men. "I just came to speak to my son."

"Then speak to him." A new voice rang out from the trees. "But you and your guards back away right this minute." Lucas's voice, deep and menacing, came from Kylie's right. When she turned, she saw that his eyes glowed burnt orange. She watched him lift his head ever so slightly to pull air in through his nose.

She knew then she'd lost her battle trying to hide her fear. Lucas had smelled it as the others probably had. But she wondered if they picked up on the fact that she hadn't feared the fight. She'd feared the emotional havoc it would've caused. Killing your boyfriend's father couldn't be good for a relationship.

"I said, back off," Lucas ordered.

When the three men didn't back up, Della spoke up again. "You heard him, you jackasses. Back off."

Lucas suddenly stood on the other side of Kylie. His warm forearm brushed against her shoulder, leaving no doubt of his loyalty to her, even over his own father. The thought warmed her heart, even as it thudded with panic.

More werewolf campers stepped out from behind the trees. They didn't appear aggressive, but just their presence spoke of their loyalty to Lucas.

"It appears I'm not the only one who brought his guards," Mr. Parker said.

"If I need them, they'll back me," Lucas said.

A low growl came from one of the weres bracketing Lucas's dad. Mr. Parker glanced over at him. "There will be no trouble tonight."

While still leery, and with the tension so thick it made breathing difficult, Kylie heard the command in the man's voice and sensed his men would not defy him. The surge of adrenaline storming in her veins lessened.

Will, another camper and one of Lucas's friends, moved in closer. Somewhere in the back of Kylie's brain, the realization hit. Lucas hadn't been alone with Fredericka. A thread of guilt over doubting him rose in her chest.

As if thinking of the girl brought her here, Fredericka walked out of the line of trees and into the small clearing.

"Mr. Parker," Fredericka said in a light tone, breaking the tight tension. "What a pleasure to see you again." The she-wolf shot Kylie a slight smirk, as if wanting Kylie to know she was friends with Lucas's dad.

"The same here," the man replied with disinterest. He paid Fredericka no heed. He hadn't stopped studying Kylie's pattern. She felt the slightest bit worried that it was doing something strange.

"So the rumors don't lie," Mr. Parker said, sounding perplexed.

"What rumors?" Kylie asked.

"I can see why my son is intrigued by you. A shame that you are not one of us."

Kylie's chest tightened at the implication. As if her relationship with Lucas was doomed.

"Enough," Lucas said. "I think—"

"You are one strange bird, Kylie Galen." Mr. Parker tightened his brows as if to get a closer look at her pattern.

Kylie tilted her chin up a notch. Not a bird, Kylie thought. A chameleon. And an inexplicable sense of pride filled her chest. For the first time, Kylie accepted that while she knew nothing of what being a chameleon meant, there was value in the little knowledge she had.

Lucas turned to face Della. "Both of you go back to your cabin." His gaze settled on Kylie. "I'll see you later."

Resentment at being told to leave stirred in Kylie's gut, but logic intervened and she sensed his intention came from his need to protect her and not to control her. Then she realized that if she resented his authoritative tone . . . She glanced at Della.

"I'd rather help you send these guys off," Della growled.

Kylie spoke up. "We should go."

Della frowned, but her expression said she'd concede. "Fine. I didn't want to hang out with these dogs anyway." She snarled at the intruders.

One of Mr. Parker's guards took a defensive step forward, and both Kylie and Lucas moved in a step. That one step left little doubt that neither of them would allow the guard to touch Della. Kylie didn't miss the frown that Lucas sent Kylie, as if to say he didn't want her taking the protective role. But that was what she was. A protector. A chameleon protector.

Della scowled at both of them, as if to say she didn't need their protection.

"Go. Please," Lucas said.

Kylie motioned for Della to follow her.

As they walked away, Kylie couldn't resist looking back. She saw Lucas, his posture defensive as if his father brought out the worst in him. Her thoughts went to both her own father and her stepfather. Neither of them put her on the defensive. Yeah, her stepfather had made some bad mistakes, and Kylie might still be working on forgiving him, but deep down she knew he loved her. And with her real father, Daniel, well, he cared so deeply he hadn't even let his death separate them.

Kylie sensed Lucas had never felt any affection from his father. Her heart hurt for him, and her blood heated with the need to defend him.

But defend him against what? What was it that had brought Mr. Parker to camp? Something told her it wasn't just to give Lucas a hug. Was something wrong with Lucas's grandmother? His half sister?

A shame that you are not one of us. His words echoed in her head and heart. Could he be here about her? Protesting the fact that Lucas was . . . intrigued with her?

"Burnett's going to be so pissed about this," Della huffed, her hurried pace matching her angry tone.

Kylie nipped at her lip with worry, before expressing her thoughts. "Which is why you aren't going to tell him."

Della looked at Kylie. The vamp's eyes were still bright with fury. "They are rogues."

"But he's Lucas's father." And the thought of Lucas having to deal with Burnett after already having to deal with his father seemed unfair.

"It's against regulations."

"Just like it was for Chan to show up," Kylie reminded her. "And like Chan, Mr. Parker didn't hurt anyone. He just wanted to talk to his son."

Della let out a breath of frustration. "You know, I really hate it when you do that."

"Do what?" Kylie dodged a vine swinging back.

"Use logic and rub my nose in the fact that you're right."

"I didn't rub your nose in it."

"Maybe not. But I still don't like it."

They walked a few minutes without speaking. "Thanks for not telling," Kylie said, knowing that was what Della meant.

They moved through the dense vegetation with only the night's song whispering through the trees. Finally, Kylie spoke up. "Lucas wasn't alone with Fredericka."

"Yeah, I figured that one out, too," Della said. "But . . ."

"But what?"

"I don't know. I mean, I kind of feel as if I sort of encouraged you to go with Lucas and maybe I was wrong."

"Wrong?" Kylie grabbed Della by the arm. "Do you mean wrong to push me, or wrong for me to go after Lucas?"

Della frowned. "Both."

"Why would you say that?" Kylie asked, hurt that Della would make such a statement—especially when her heart was already so confused.

"It's not that I don't like Lucas, I do. But he's werewolf and you're obviously not. I admit I thought you were before. But tonight when we were surrounded by weres, I could just tell that you weren't like them. And after what his grandmother said and now after what his dad said, I think his family and his pack are going to stand in your way."

"He told me he doesn't care what they say." And she believed it. She did.

Sadness filled Della's eyes and Kylie felt the emotion resonate within herself.

Della exhaled. "That's what Lee said, too. And look what happened with us."

It's not the same thing.

While Kylie waited on her porch for Lucas to show up, she contemplated what Della had said and thought about her day from hell.

She'd spoken to her mom, who needed reassurance that Kylie was okay. She'd spoken to Holiday, who needed the same thing. Then her phone chirped again. Derek, this time, wanting the same thing.

"Hey, I just wanted to check in," he said.

It was funny, really, how well she knew him. She knew what he felt without his ever having to say it and so she knew why he'd called. He'd obviously sensed some of her earlier emotions. "I'm fine."

"If you need to talk or anything, I'm here." He sounded so wistful, she felt her heart grow tighter.

"I know," she answered. "And I appreciate it."

"Did you ever figure out the whole ghost issue?"

"Not yet," Kylie admitted, her tone echoing some of the frustration she felt.

"Did you talk to Holiday about it?" he asked, sounding genuinely concerned.

"A little," she said. "But I wasn't . . . I only skimmed the surface."

"Oh, shit!"

"What?"

"That's who it is, isn't it? That's whose face the ghost has stolen. It's Holiday."

Kylie closed her eyes. "Yes, but please don't say anything. I'm trying to figure it out before I take it to Holiday."

"Is she in danger? Does this mean . . . anything?"

"In a roundabout way, I asked Holiday, and she said it was unlikely. But . . ."

"But what?"

"It's just scary," Kylie admitted. "Seeing her as a ghost when she's not dead."

"Hell yeah, it's scary. And you shouldn't have to figure it out all by yourself. I'm here for you. I don't know how to help solve this, but whatever it takes, I'll do it."

"Thanks." She leaned back against the cabin wall, and right then she was hit by a wash of cold. Dead cold.

"And I don't expect anything in return," he said. "I accept we're just friends."

"Thank you." The spirit, identical to Holiday, stood over her, looking down with a frown on her face. "I should go."

"Something wrong?" he asked, and she couldn't help but wonder if he could feel her now.

"Just . . . got company."

"Lucas?" His tone expressed exactly how he felt about the werewolf.

"No. The ghost."

"Oh. So, I'll let you go. But Kylie . . ."

"Yeah?" She stood because she didn't like having the spirit staring down at her.

"I'm here if you need me." He sounded so genuine.

"I know," she said, feeling the words vibrate in her chest. She hung up and met the woman's green gaze.

"I think you should pick him," the spirit said.

"Say what?"

"Between him and the werewolf. I like him. He's fae."

Kylie bit back the frustration. "I think I'd better decide that."

"Just a little advice," the spirit said.

Kylie studied her. "Did you discover anything?"

"Not really, but I remember some stuff."

"What kind of stuff?"

"Scary stuff."

"Can you tell me about it?"

The spirit studied Kylie with the same kind of concerned look Holiday always did.

"I don't think you need to hear it. You're . . . young."

Kylie rolled her eyes. "You came here for me to help you. I can't help if you don't tell me things."

She blinked. *"I don't know if that's true."*

"What's not true?"

"That I came to you to help me." She stood silent for a long moment. *"I think I came to you to help someone else."*

"Who?"

"I don't know exactly. But I sense it."

"What do you sense?"

"That danger is right around the corner." Her eyes filled with worry.

"Can I stop it from happening?"

She tilted her head to one side and considered the question. *"I think so. I think that's why I came. So you could stop it."*

Kylie's heart filled with hope. Surely, if it wasn't possible to help, the spirit would have known. So even if this was Holiday, maybe Kylie could save her. Maybe the person the spirit was supposed to save was herself and she just didn't realize it. "Have you figured out your name yet?"

She shook her head. *"I just keep getting the same thing. I think it's Hannah."*

"Please tell me what you know. It might be important."

She shook her head. *"I'm not ready to talk about it. And it's not a whole lot. Just . . . flashes of stuff."*

"Why aren't you ready to talk about it?"

The spirit turned and stared at the woods as if she'd heard something.

Kylie followed her gaze. She didn't see anyone, but oddly, the feeling she'd felt earlier had returned. Someone was out there. Calling for her.

Who are you? What do you want? She asked the question in her mind.

"They want to talk to you," the ghost said.

"Who?" Kylie asked. "And you said 'they,' so how do you know there's more than one?"

"I just somehow know there's more than one. But if I don't know my own name, how could I know theirs?"

"Have you seen them? Do you know what they want with me?" She shook her head. *"I just sense them. Calling you."*

"Do they mean to harm me?" she asked.

"I . . . can't say for sure. But they don't feel evil."

"They don't really feel evil to me, either." Or maybe she just wanted to believe it. She moved down the steps. She'd almost reached the woods when someone caught her arm—someone warm, someone alive.

Chapter Nine

Kylie swung around, her heart bouncing off her stomach all the way up to her throat.

"Where are you going?" Lucas asked.

"Nowhere." She swallowed the panic. "I was waiting on you and thought I heard something." It wasn't completely a lie; she'd heard it with her heart.

He pulled her against him. "That's when you go inside the cabin, not into the woods. Even normals know that from watching those phony horror shows."

She rolled her eyes. "I would've gone inside if I thought it was evil."

"But sometimes you don't know." He slid his hand down to her waist.

She agreed with him on that point and probably needed to remember it, too.

Yet remembering anything became harder with him this close. So close she felt him breathe. The soft touch of his palm warmed her skin beneath her clothes. The tenderness and heat created a trail of tingling sensation.

He dipped his head down and gazed into her eyes. "Do you have any idea how I would feel if something happened to you?"

"Probably the same as I'd feel if something happened to you," she said. "What did your father want?"

He frowned. "It's Clara, my half sister. She ran off again. She told him she was coming here, but he suspected she went back to her boyfriend."

"I'm sorry. What are you going to do?"

"I don't know." He sighed. "I've already gone after her twice. She said she wanted to come here. But maybe she lied. If I bring her here against her will, what's going to stop her from running off?"

"Is the boyfriend that bad?"

He grimaced. "He's rogue and heavily into a gang."

"And that automatically makes him bad?" She'd learned that not all supernaturals were registered, and to some people that alone made them rogue, but not all unregistered supernaturals were bad, either. Della didn't consider Chan evil. And Kylie chose to believe her grandfather and great-aunt weren't bad. "Are all gangs bad?"

Her question seemed to give him pause. "Not necessarily, but even the gangs that aren't completely unethical are generally into something illegal."

"Drugs?" Kylie asked.

"And other stuff."

Kylie remembered how badly she'd felt for Lucas when she'd seen him looking so defensive facing his own father. She remembered he'd stood up for her against his own family. Her heart hurt for Lucas. "If your half sister is anything like her half brother, she'll do the right thing." She stepped up on her tiptoes and pressed her lips to his.

It was late. It was dark. But the moment seemed so right. What was meant as a quick kiss lingered and became more. Much more. He deepened the kiss and she leaned into him. She felt his body come closer to hers, hard in all the places she was soft.

She heard the purring sound that a were made when he was close to a potential mate. She became almost hypnotized—lured by the sound, tempted and enticed by all that could follow.

He tasted so good, felt so good. She wanted more. She wanted to feel more. To taste more. To experience more.

Then the magic ended when he pulled away. He brushed his hand over her cheek and while his blue eyes held the heat of passion, she could tell his mind was chewing on something else. "I'm sorry that my dad scared you."

She fought the desire to tell him to just start kissing her again. "It's okay," she said, and tried not to sound disappointed.

"No, it's not." He caught her hand and moved to the porch.

"He stated right away that he wasn't there to cause harm," she said, wanting to soothe Lucas. Wanting to make this easier.

"And you should never believe him," he said.

A whisper of fear settled in her chest. They lowered themselves down on the porch so they could lean against the cabin.

He brushed his thumb over her lips. "I don't want my father anywhere around you."

She looked into Lucas's serious gaze. "He hurt you?" The need to protect him made her blood run faster.

"Not me. I'm his son. But he considers anyone else fair game."

"If he's that bad, why do you go there? Why have anything to do with him?"

"For Clara, mostly. But then . . . I need him right now."

"Why?"

"His approval will go a long way to help me get into the were council."

The council he couldn't get on if he married her. The thought shot a wave of apprehension through her and she remembered what Della had said about things not working out between them because of his family and his pack. She pushed that thought out of the way and tried to understand. "But if that's who they look to for approval, then why would you want to be on that council?"

He closed his eyes for a second as if explaining was difficult. "If I make it on the council, then I can change things."

Kylie recalled his grandmother telling her that he wanted to change how the world viewed children raised by rogues.

"But until then, I have to convince him that I see things his way."

"What things?"

He shook his head slowly. "Things I don't think you even need to know."

Kylie frowned, not liking being shut out of his world, even if she wasn't sure she wanted to belong to it. She'd bet that Fredericka knew everything. "But I do need to know. I want to be a part of your life. I don't want to be shut out." *I don't want your pack or your family keeping us apart.*

His eyes tightened. "I'm not shutting you out. I just prefer that you know this Lucas."

She digested his words. "There can only be one Lucas."

"There is only one. One real one. But I have to play games with my father and the council. I have to convince him that I'm on his side."

She shook her head. "I don't understand."

"And I don't expect you to."

She dropped her hand from his arm. "That's not right. How would you like it if you thought I kept things from you?"

A frown pulled at his lips. "You do keep things from me. Things about your ghosts." His eyes brightened with frustration. "Things you talk to Derek about and not me. And you're right, I don't like it."

She considered his words and knew they were true. "I only keep things from you because you don't want to know about them. They make you crazy."

He nodded, and acceptance filled his eyes, but she could tell it cost him emotionally. "And believe me when I tell you that the things I keep to myself are things you wouldn't want to know either."

She looked deep into his eyes, hating this conversation, but only because she cared so much about him. "Secrets between people can't be good. It can keep them apart. Why don't we just tell each other everything?"

"Sometimes what we don't know protects us. It can't hurt us if we don't know it." He leaned his forehead against hers. "I can promise you this, Kylie Galen. I'll do whatever I have to do, but I won't let this hurt you."

She frowned. "What do you mean by whatever you have to do?"

"Just that. I won't let what's happening in my messed-up life hurt you."

His words scared her. But the fear was more for him than for herself. "I'm not some fragile little girl. I'm not the same girl whose window you peeked into."

The playfulness in his eyes was both sexy and warm. "Oh, I've noticed."

"I'm serious."

"I know. But you're still my girl, and I want to protect you."

She rolled her eyes in frustration. "I'm the protector. That's what I do," Kylie insisted.

"I know. You're amazing and can do amazing things. And you've already saved my life. But as a protector, the one thing you can't do is protect yourself. So please don't try to stop me from doing it."

Kylie woke up before the sun the next morning. The only thing she was aware of was Socks sleeping on her stomach, his pointed skunk nose resting between her breasts. She lifted her head and stared at the little guy. He opened one of his beady eyes and then the other, and stared up at her with adoration. The kind of look one got only from a pet.

The kind that said pure love and acceptance.

The silence in the room was loud. Unsure about what had awakened her, she pulled her arm out from under the thin cover to measure the temperature. No cold. No ghosts.

And then she heard it. Or heard her.

"Kitty, kitty," Miranda called from the slightly opened bedroom door. "Come on, Socks. Don't you want to be turned back into a kitten?"

Socks sprang to his feet, leapt to the floor, and scurried under the bed. Kylie wasn't sure if his annoyance was at Miranda for constantly trying to change him back or if he perhaps didn't want to change. Considering Kylie had changed a whole hell of a lot these past few months, she couldn't blame Socks. Change was scary.

Miranda pushed open the door a bit more. "Come on, don't make it hard on me."

Kylie leaned up on her elbow and yawned. "I think he's scared."

Miranda moved in a little more. "I think I got it figured out. I just need to take him outside and into the first morning light."

"Hmm." Kylie rose up, putting her bare feet on the cold wood floor. Too cold? She did another visual sweep to check for ghosts. Nope. She had a ghost-free zone happening.

"Sorry I woke you up. I thought I could just sneak in and grab him." Miranda seemed wide awake and in a good mood as she plopped down and gave the mattress a little bounce.

"No big deal. I was practically awake anyway," Kylie lied. In truth, it had been a pretty sleepless night. After Lucas had left, Della had retired to her room and Miranda hadn't come home, so Kylie had grabbed Socks and gone to bed. Not to sleep. That would have been too easy. She'd tossed and turned for hours, juggling her problems like balls, and not really solving a single one of them.

However, she had to admit, she'd gotten used to thinking of herself as a chameleon. And was thrilled it was one day closer to Thursday, when her real grandfather would visit.

Or at least she prayed he'd visit her.

Remembering her difficulty falling sleep reminded her that the last time she checked the clock, at around three AM, Miranda still hadn't come back.

"So, are you going to fill me in?" Kylie asked.

"Fill you in on what?" Miranda's smile tightened with mischievousness. Kylie studied her friend closer. She wore the same clothes she'd worn to her date last night. Had Miranda woken her to try to transform Socks back into a kitty, or did she need someone to talk with? Not that Kylie minded. She'd woken Della and Miranda up many nights, mostly with dreams or those scary visions—but if she had just needed to talk, she knew they'd be there for her.

"Just what time did you get home, young lady?" Kylie asked in a teasing voice.

"Early. I swear." Miranda giggled. "Early this morning."

"Details. I want details." Kylie rubbed her hands together, mimicking Miranda.

"Don't get too excited," Miranda said. Then she sighed. "We didn't . . . you know. But we did . . . well, you know."

Kylie let the riddle roll around her sleep-dazed mind and shook her head. "I think I get the first 'you know,' but I'm lost on the second 'you know.'" Still feeling the cold on the bottom of her feet, she pulled her legs up on the mattress. The darkness in the room felt lightened just by Miranda's presence.

"We kissed, we made out." Miranda's grin widened, and then she got that sappy lovestruck look on her face. "We fell asleep in each other's arms down by the swimming hole. He held me all night long, and I think I'm in love for real. It's like I know I belong there. In his arms."

Kylie remembered the times she'd fallen asleep in Lucas's arms. Awesome didn't begin to describe it. But had she woken up knowing for sure that he was the one? She couldn't remember ever feeling that way.

Then, realizing this was Miranda's moment, she pushed her self-indulgence away. "Well, I'm thrilled for you." And Kylie was. Even if she was just a tad envious, too.

"I know *you* are." Miranda's smile faded. "I don't think Della will feel the same way."

"Of course she will," Kylie said. "She just has a hard time showing it. Remember how she kept encouraging you to make up with Perry when you were mad at him?"

"I guess," Miranda said, not sounding convinced. "I mean, I feel as if I can't say anything about Perry around her now. I get that she's hurt about Lee and I don't want to make her feel bad, but I also want to be able to talk to her about what's going on in my life. And right now what's going on in my life is all about Perry. Seriously, I don't want to have to walk on eggshells around her."

"And I think you're just worrying too much. Believe me, in a day or two things will be back to normal and you guys will be threatening to rip each other's limbs off for a reason that has nothing to do with Perry."

Miranda exhaled. "You make it sound like we argue all the time."

"Not all the time," Kylie said. "Just most of the time."

Miranda shrugged. "Anyway, do you think you can help me snag Socks so I can see if I got the spell right? Perry listened to me practice for an hour. I want to fix this." Miranda frowned. "I feel like a screw-up."

"You're not a screw-up." Kylie looked down at the floor. "Come here, Socks. Come here, baby."

Miranda fell back on the mattress. "I feel like one, especially when my Wiccan sisters tease me about it. I suck at being a witch."

"They tease you about Socks?" Kylie asked.

"Yeah, not that I blame them. I messed up."

"Screw them," Kylie said. "You should figure out how to curse them with a dose of dyslexia and see how they deal with it."

"They're really not being mean," Miranda said.

"But it hurts you." Anger for Miranda burned Kylie's chest. She hated bullies. Hated people who put other people down so they could feel better about themselves.

Miranda popped back up. "But they're just teasing." She knelt and tapped her fingers on the floor. "Here, kitty, kitty."

Miranda's words seemed to be sucked up by the shadows in the corners of the room. Kylie lowered her foot from the bed and swiped her heel against the bed ruffle.

She waited to feel Socks attack her ankle. The only thing she felt was an icy cold leaking from beneath the bed skirt. An icy cold that gave Kylie a bad feeling.

She looked at Miranda. "Why don't you go outside and I'll . . . I'll bring him to you. He'll probably come out when you leave." For some reason the room seemed to grow darker. Kylie hoped Socks was all that would come out.

Miranda stood. "I don't know why he doesn't like me," she muttered, and walked out.

Kylie cautiously stood and stared down at the bed ruffle. "Socks? Kitty?"

No little skunk came scampering from beneath the bed. No soft meow whispered from beneath to let her know he was okay.

Taking a deep breath, she got on her hands and knees and stared at the unmoving ruffle. She fought the temptation to breathe on it. For some odd reason, she wanted to see something move; the odd stillness of the material didn't feel right. Nothing felt right.

She reached for the cotton material to peer beneath it, praying all she'd find was one scared skunk. Kylie's fingers almost touched the ruffle when a sound—a moan or a strangled cry—whispered from beneath the bed. She jerked her hand back. Her breath caught. That didn't sound like Socks at all.

An icy and unnatural cold snaked from under the bed. Steam billowed out from the bed skirt. Fear, ugly, raw fear filled her chest. She glanced back at the door. Wished she could leave. Knew she couldn't. Instinct told her Socks wasn't alone under that bed.

Still on her hands and knees, she took one tiny knee shift backward. How many times as a child had she feared a monster under the bed? How many times had her mom promised that monsters didn't exist? That moan sounded again.

Her mom was wrong. A monster, or something equally scary, lurked right under Kylie's bed.

She couldn't blame her mom for the lie. Mom didn't know.

But Kylie did.

Not that it mattered. Unwilling to abandon her pet, trying to settle her pounding heart, she reached again for the bed skirt. Right before her two fingers caught the cotton fabric, a hand shot out.

Her own scream faded into the shadows as the cold, dead hand grasped Kylie's arm and yanked her forward.

She fought for freedom, clawed at the fingers, twisted her arm, anything to pry it loose. Nothing worked.

"Help!" she screamed, but no one answered. The clasp around her wrist tightened, dragging her closer. The last thing she saw was the bed ruffle sliding over her face as she slipped into dark oblivion. Her last thought before her mind went numb was that she was finally going to meet the monster living under her bed.

Chapter Ten

Kylie lay flat on her back, cloaked in darkness. Deep, black darkness. *Just a vision. It's not real. Not real.*

Something on each side of her pressed tight against her forearms. It felt real. She tried to move, but couldn't. Fear swelled inside her. She tasted the bitterness of it on her tongue.

Disoriented, she tried to make sense of it. Inhaling, she smelled the earth. Wet, moist dirt. She wasn't under the bed. Where was she? An answer came and she wished it hadn't. She was buried. Another scream filled her throat, but logic told her this wasn't real. *Just a vision.*

But from who? And what? Holiday?

The sound of Kylie's own breath leaving her lips sounded too loud. Instantly, she realized she wasn't alone. It wasn't the sound of someone else breathing. No one breathed but her. Yet the grip on her wrist hadn't loosened. Whoever had dragged her under here hadn't left—someone still clung to her wrist as if that person's very life depended on it. Unfortunately, Kylie knew it was too late. Only she was alive.

"Why am I here?" She tried to move again but felt somehow constricted.

No answer came.

Blinking, her vision slowly adjusted to the darkness. She saw the pattern of old wood a few inches from her face.

She tried to pull her wrist away from the tight grip, but the hold only tightened.

"Oh, shit. What have you guys done?" A familiar voice echoed in the darkness.

Holiday.

"I'm in here," Kylie called out. Only this time no words left her mouth. She couldn't speak.

"Cara M. said she could help us get out of here," another female voice answered.

Footsteps sounded above. The wood panel creaked. Dust and dirt sifted down on Kylie's face. She blinked the grit from her eyes and tried to hold her breath so she didn't choke.

"He's leaving," someone whispered.

Kylie blinked, and when she opened her eyes, everything had changed. She stood in an old dilapidated cabin, staring down at the creaky wooden boards beneath her feet. Then, as if the floor faded, Kylie saw what lay hidden below.

Three decaying bodies lay positioned shoulder to shoulder. A scream spilled from Kylie's lips. She tried to run, but her feet felt frozen. She tried to look away, but couldn't.

One corpse was a woman with dark hair, probably in her early twenties, wearing a nightgown. The second was a blond around the same age wearing a familiar waitress outfit with a nametag on it that read CARA M. And the third . . . Oh God! Holiday.

Tears filled her eyes. Kylie screamed louder when she realized she once again lay flat on her back. Darkness swallowed her up. Panic tightened when she felt something moving at her side. Adrenaline surged through her veins. She leapt up and banged her head so hard, it rattled her brain. She collapsed on her back again.

"Where the hell are you?" A voice echoed around her. A familiar voice. Della's voice. "Mofo!" Light suddenly filled Kylie's vision. "What are you doing under there?"

Kylie gasped, swallowed her scream, and realized she lay on her bedroom floor with a shivering Socks plastered to her side.

"You are just too friggin' weird." Della, looking half-pissed and half-asleep, stood over Kylie holding the bed up above her head. Yes, the whole twin bed—frame and mattress. Holding it up as if it were nothing more than a lightweight piece of foam.

Socks let out a pathetic meow.

Afraid Della might drop the bed, Kylie snatched up the little skunk and lunged to her feet. Her knees wobbled; the skunk trembled in her arms. She glanced down, praying it would be her bedroom floor and not a grave.

No grave. No dead girls. No dead Holiday.

Kylie inhaled. As much as she wanted to push the gruesome memory from her brain, she couldn't. Something in the vision might help her. Help her figure it out so she could prevent it from happening. Help her save Holiday's life.

"What the hell is going on?" Della asked again. "Or do I not want to know?"

"Sorry. Bad dream." Kylie's voice shook.

Della dropped the bed. It banged and clattered on the floor.

"Is there a ghost here?" Della glanced around, obviously not believing Kylie's bad dream excuse.

Kylie took a second to feel the temperature. "No," she said honestly.

Della studied her, her expression softening. "Are you okay?"

Kylie nodded and watched Della's frown return.

"And you aren't going to explain this?" Della asked.

Kylie shook her head. Della really didn't want to know.

"Then good night!" The little vamp shot out of the room, leaving as quickly as she'd come.

Kylie breathed in. Breathed out. Tried to calm her racing heart.

She tried to see the bright side—the bright side of being in a grave with three decaying bodies.

Not an easy task.

However, at least she had something to go on. But would it help her? Oh, God, it had to, didn't it?

She pulled Socks closer, offering comfort and trying to take comfort in holding something as scared as she was. It might have worked if the loud knock on her window didn't have her heart slamming against her rib cage. Kylie jumped clear across the room.

Another scream rose in her chest, but before she released it, she spotted Miranda peering through, her palm pressed against the glass.

"You coming?" she yelled. "We're going to lose the first light."

The cold filled the room. And so did the spirit. Kylie looked over at the ghost who looked just like Holiday. *"I'm so sorry. She shouldn't have done that."*

Kylie tried not to envision Holiday, or God help her, the Holiday lookalike, as she had appeared in the grave. "It's okay," Kylie said, and she meant it. She could do this. If hanging out with dead people would save Holiday, she'd do it. Heck, she'd dance with the dead if it meant saving Holiday.

"I need to know things," Kylie said. "You need to show me things so I can figure out how to help you."

"Show you what?" Miranda asked.

Kylie ignored Miranda.

The spirit shook her head. *"I told you, I don't think I'm the one you have to help."*

And wasn't that just like Holiday, Kylie thought, too damn stubborn to accept help. Even in ghost form.

"The only help I need is you to bring out Socks," Miranda called from the window again.

"You should go," Holiday said. *"That little fellow would like to be a cat again."*

Kylie looked at Miranda and then back to the spirit. "How do you know what he wants?"

"It's one of my gifts; I can communicate with animals."

"No, you can't," Kylie said. Or Holiday couldn't communicate with animals. Did supernaturals who passed over change their gifts? Kylie didn't think so. Did that mean this wasn't Holiday? And if so, who was she?

"Fine, you want him to stay a skunk," Miranda said in her irate voice.

Socks chose that moment to put his paw over his eyes and Kylie moaned.

A few minutes later, Kylie walked out behind the cabin with Socks held close to her chest. It was still dark and quiet, as if the world hadn't woken up yet. Unlike her, the world didn't get woken up by witches or visions of dead people.

The air held an early morning chill, one of the first signs that summer had outworn its welcome and fall waited nearby to fill its shoes.

When she took another step, she felt it. The calling. Her gaze shot to the edge of woods. Her heart raced and the temptation to move closer whispered her name like an old friend.

Kylie took one step, almost answering the unexplainable yearning, but Miranda's voice pulled her back. "What took you so long?"

"I had to get him out from under the bed," Kylie said, not in the mood to do this, but she remembered the insecurity in Miranda's voice when they'd talked earlier about the other witches giving her a hard time about the goof. Since the first morning light lasted only a few minutes, it was a small price to pay for Miranda's happiness. Then Kylie would sit down and rehash what she'd gotten from the dream. Something in there had to help her make sense of the visions.

Miranda, holding her little black pouch of magic herbs, led Kylie around to the back. "I haven't mistreated him. I have no idea why he doesn't like me."

"I know." But after a month of Miranda following the skunk around trying different spells, Socks had grown leery of her. Kylie would have grown leery of her, too.

Miranda looked up at the eastern sky and saw the light. "It's time." She did a little happy dance. "Put him down."

Kylie gave Socks's black-and-white fur a soft stroke. As crazy as it sounded, she would miss his skunk side. Savoring the sight of him in skunk form one last time, she set him down and backed up, giving Miranda space to work her magic. Of course, Socks started following her, not wanting to be left behind.

"Stay," Kylie said, and motioned for Miranda to start.

Miranda began chanting. Something about light and your true self. Socks started forward again. Miranda waved at Kylie to catch him. Kylie spoke gently to the skunk and he stopped moving. Then, reaching into her bag, Miranda pulled out a pinch of a strange herb-like substance. She tossed it in the air over Socks; a few pieces popped and sizzled as they rained down around him.

Kylie held her breath, waiting to see her beloved pet transform into a feline. But nope. The little animal with a white stripe down his back remained in his skunk form.

Miranda frowned up at the sky and commenced chanting again. She tossed more herbs in the air. This time, Socks rose up on his short skunk legs and swatted his tiny paws at the sparkles.

Yet even after all the sizzle of crackling herbs, he remained the same black-and-white skunk. Miranda looked back at the sky as if desperate and commenced another chant.

She held up her little black bag over his head and just shook it down on the animal.

Socks spotted the string hanging from the pouch and leapt up in the air to catch it. When Miranda pulled it back, Socks started to leave.

"Stop him!" Miranda's frustration rang loud and extra clear.

Kylie knelt and waved the little guy back. His beady black eyes looked at Kylie with confusion. Empathy for her pet filled her chest.

Miranda started to chant again.

Socks tried to escape again.

Miranda insisted Kylie stop him again.

It continued for several more minutes until Kylie held up her hand. "This isn't going to work."

"It has to," Miranda said. "I only have another few minutes of first sun. Just keep him there."

As if Socks understood, he darted between Miranda's legs.

"No," Miranda said.

Kylie caught the confused animal. "I think he's had enough," she offered in her most sympathetic voice.

"But he's still a skunk. Put him down. I can do this. I *have* to."

Kylie understood Miranda's need to prove herself, but . . . "Can't you try again tomorrow?"

"One more chant. Really quick, please? All he has to do is stand there."

Relenting, Kylie set Socks down and Miranda went back to reciting some fancy spell.

When Miranda stopped and Socks was still a skunk, Kylie gave Miranda a look of condolence. "It's okay. We'll try another time," Kylie said, beginning to lose her patience.

"Wait. I forgot to bless the light and wind." Miranda paused as if recalling the words.

Kylie held her hand out, pinky first, and muttered, "Why can't you just wave your pinky at him and say, 'Change back into a cat'?"

The pieces of herbs left on the ground shot up in the air. They crackled and popped around the little skunk and then started swirling around him like a tiny tornado. Socks, raised up on his hind legs, swatted at the bits of herb.

And then, just like magic—well, it *was* magic—Socks the skunk disappeared and Socks the feline appeared.

Miranda gaped at Kylie. "How did you do that?"

Kylie's gaze shot back to her kitten, still batting at the sparkling herbs floating around him. "I didn't do that!" She stared at Miranda.

"Oh, my gawd!" Miranda squealed.

Someone whisked past them in a blur.

"What the hell is it now?" Della came to a jolting stop by Miranda.

"She's a witch." Miranda pointed at Kylie. "You're a witch."

Kylie shook her head. She was a chameleon. "I didn't do that. It was you. Just . . . a delayed reaction."

"No. You're a witch. Right now, you're a witch."

Della rolled her eyes. "What the hell?"

"I'm telling you, I didn't do that," Kylie insisted.

And she hadn't. Had she?

Della squinted at Kylie.

"Mofo!" Della said.

Miranda slapped her forehead a couple of times. "Your pattern says you are a witch."

"What's wrong?" A deep voice came from behind Kylie.

Kylie turned around. Derek, looking disheveled as if he'd climbed out of bed in a hurry, came running up.

"She's a witch," Miranda screeched.

"No," Kylie said. Swinging around, she stared at Socks, still in feline form. Her father had told her she was a chameleon. Her father would know, right? Sure, she hadn't wanted to be a lizard at first, but she'd accepted it. Besides, why would her father lie?

From the corner of her vision, she saw Derek move in front of her. His brow pinched.

"It's not true, is it?" Kylie waited for Derek to deny it.

Doubt filled her. Had Daniel lied? Had her grandmother just been confused when she told Kylie's father they were chameleons? But why would Burnett have heard of chameleons if they didn't exist? Why did her life have to be so damn difficult?

"Tell me already!" Kylie insisted. "Am I a witch?"

Chapter Eleven

Derek nodded. "It's true. Your pattern says you're a witch."

Miranda folded her arms against her chest. "Don't you want to be a witch?" She sounded offended.

"Of course she doesn't want to be witch," Della mouthed off, still looking pissed at being woken up. "It's boring as hell. You don't do anything but throw herbs around and the only way you can fly is on a broom."

"It's not boring! And I do not fly on a broom! I swear, one witch did that and now we all get stereotyped." Miranda's eyes tightened with anger.

"Admit it," Della said. "If you had the power to change yourself, you'd be a vampire."

Miranda vehemently shook her head. "Who would want to be a bloodsucking, cold bitch with fangs!"

Kylie stared at the two of them verbally sparring, tossing insults so fast she couldn't even keep up. Then, too befuddled to intervene, she grabbed Socks before he wandered off in the woods.

Her gaze shifted back to the trees. The woods still called to her. What the hell was going on?

Her mind whirled as she headed to the cabin. Derek fell in step beside her. His shirt, left unbuttoned, fluttered open, exposing his hard abs. Not that she really noticed. Okay, so she noticed, but it didn't mean anything. Except that she was female and females found shirtless guys appealing.

"You're feeling confused," Derek stated.

"Yup." She didn't slow down. She couldn't. She was too annoyed that she found him so appealing. Too annoyed at the damn woods calling her like an old friend to come out and play. She didn't have any old friends. Not anyone looming in the woods.

"You're feeling betrayed," he said.

"Yup. Well, sort of." She continued to the cabin and snuggled her kitten to her chest. Her heart ached and the beginning of tears stung her eyes.

"And you're scared."

"Three out of three," she said. Yet all she felt now was . . .

"Frustrated." Derek finished her thought for her.

She stopped and looked him dead in the eyes. "You don't have to tell me what I feel. I know what I'm feeling."

"And you're in a pissy mood," he added with a smile. When she didn't respond in kind, his humor faded. "Sorry. I'm just . . . I want to understand."

"You know what I'm feeling; what more do you need to understand?" She stormed up the porch steps with Socks tucked under one arm, and yanked the door open so hard it made a loud banging sound when it hit the wall. Socks flinched. Derek followed her inside.

"I know your emotions, but I can only guess the reasons for them."

She dropped down on the sofa and held Socks in her lap. "Look, I'm in a really bad mood right now, and I suggest you might want to leave."

Derek dropped down beside her. He ignored what she said and continued, "For example, I know you're afraid, but what are you afraid of? Are you frustrated because you're a witch, or because your two best friends can't stop biting each other's heads off? And who are you feeling betrayed by right now? Is it me? Is it about . . ."

"No," she said before he mentioned Ellie and Kylie had to deal with those emotions as well. "It isn't you." Or maybe it was a little, she thought, remembering Miranda's comment about how she'd talked about Derek all the time.

"Is it about Lucas?" he asked. "You can tell me if it is. I want to help you and if it means listening to your issues with him, I'll do it."

She pulled Socks closer. "It isn't Lucas." But then she remembered their meeting last night, when Lucas had admitted to keeping secrets from her.

A long pause filled the room. Derek leaned in, his shoulder touched hers, and his emotional healing abilities flowed over her like a welcome breath of fresh air. Kylie had no doubt that the touch was on purpose, that he'd meant to help her.

She stared at Socks, then at Derek, trying to slow down her emotional overload. Trying not to be a bitch.

"Tell me what you're afraid of. I want to help." He stared at her forehead. "Does being a witch scare you?"

"I'm not a witch," she said before she could stop herself. Even with his warm calm flowing though her, she felt her frustrations build. Then she recalled Socks's magical transformation. Had she done that?

"At least, I don't think I am. It's not that I don't want to be a witch, it's . . . Why would my father tell me I was a chameleon if it wasn't true? I don't think my grandmother would make that up. And why would Burnett have heard about the species, if they didn't exist?"

"Burnett heard about it?" Derek asked.

She nodded. "Nothing concrete, just read it in some of the reports." She touched her forehead. What did all this mean? "Is my pattern really showing that I'm a witch?"

He nodded, as if afraid to disappoint her, then asked, "What's going on? I woke up this morning after a terrible nightmare. I couldn't remember it, but the point of it was that you were in trouble. When I was alert enough, I realized that maybe you really were in trouble and I'd just dreamed what I was reading from you. Then I felt all these other emotions from you. Is this about the ghost? Holiday's ghost?"

The vision she'd had flashed in her head like a bad movie clip. She closed her eyes, trying to shut it off, and searching for what to say to Derek. Tell him, or not tell him?

"I had a vision," she finally said, needing to confide in someone—needing to filter though everything she'd learned from the vision. "There were three bodies in a grave."

"Three? So it's like a serial killer?"

Socks moved from her lap and tucked his face into the curve of her arm, almost as if he understood what Derek had said. Kylie brushed her hand down his soft black feline fur. Feline. Had she done this? Had she changed him back?

"I think so." Kylie bit down on her lip and pushed those questions away to concentrate on something more important. "Holiday, or the one who looks like Holiday, was one of them." She recalled all the things her gut insisted might be important. "They were buried below some kind of an old cabin." Her chest tightened. "Seeing Holiday like that was . . . hard."

"I can imagine," Derek said. "Didn't you tell me that the visions were like puzzles to help you figure things out?"

She nodded. "But it wasn't the one who looked like Holiday that brought me into the vision. It was one of the other girls. I think she wants to be found, so they can leave the makeshift grave. So I'm still not sure if the vision is going to help me. Or maybe it can. I don't know." Her chest clutched. "Why can't they just tell me what they need?"

"Maybe if you tell me about it, I can help figure it out."

She looked at Derek. "How?"

"I worked for a PI. I sort of know how to dig things up. I'm good at it."

Kylie scratched Socks under his kitty chin as she tried to think of anything that might help them understand the vision. "One of the girls had on a waitress uniform. Like from a diner or something. For some reason, the uniform looked familiar. And she had a name tag on that said 'Cara M.' The others even called her Cara M., not just Cara, as if they didn't really know her but were calling her that because of her name tag."

"That's good," Derek said. "Maybe you should make a list of all the dinerlike restaurants you've been to lately. I'll go online and see if I can find what their uniforms look like."

As Kylie's mind tried to latch on to any other details that might help, she recalled the spirit's visit right before she'd gone outside to bring Socks to Miranda.

"What's puzzling you?" he asked, sensing her emotions.

Kylie watched her kitten—still finding it hard to believe that he wasn't a skunk anymore—leap down from the sofa. "The spirit told me that Socks wanted to be changed back into a cat. When I asked how she knew that, she said that she could communicate with animals."

"Holiday can't read animals." Derek's eyes widened. "Wait. She can't, but she knows someone . . . someone close to her that is full fairy and actually had a little of the ability to do so."

"Are you sure?" Kylie asked.

"She told me during one of our counseling sessions."

"Did she say who it was?"

"No, but . . . I got the feeling it was someone close. I also got the feeling that it was someone who'd hurt her, because I felt her emotions when she talked about her. And then she changed the subject."

Kylie nodded. Holiday was good at changing the subject when it came to something personal. "So, if this person was close to Holiday, then it would be understandable why she would take on Holiday's appearance as a ghost." Kylie chewed on that thought for a moment, feeling some relief. And it gave her the first real hope that Holiday wasn't in danger.

Kylie sighed. The early morning sun must have risen higher, because she watched as the first gold rays spilled through the window and cast shadows on the wood floor. "So how do we find out who this person is?"

"I can bring it up again in our next counseling session with Holiday. It's this afternoon. Like I said, she didn't want to talk about it, but maybe I can sneak it into the conversation."

Derek's words pulled Kylie away from the problem at hand. "You get counseling sessions from Holiday?"

He frowned. "Not counseling like my-head's-messed-up counseling. We just chat . . . like you two do."

"I didn't mean it was a bad thing. I just didn't know you met with her regularly."

"I have since I came here."

"I knew you were in the beginning, but I didn't think you still did."

"I didn't for a while. But since I've been back . . . I see her now."

Before Kylie could stop herself, the question slipped out. "Do you talk about me?"

"Some," he admitted, looking guilty.

She almost asked for details, but wisdom slipped in. She didn't need to know. Especially if it was about his feelings for her. The less she heard, or even thought, about his confession of love, the better off she'd be.

Her gaze, as if it had a mind of its own, lowered again to his bare chest. Reprimanding herself, she popped off the sofa. "I think I'll go talk to Holiday now about this whole witch issue."

"Are you going to mention the vision?"

She considered the question, but her heart said no. The message came with such certainty that she wondered if she wasn't getting some divine advice. "Not yet. If I don't get anything in a day or so, I think I should."

He nodded. "I'll get busy later trying to figure out what I can." He stood up. "Let's go." The sun spilling though the window hit his chest, making his bare skin look even more golden.

"That's okay," she sputtered. "You don't have to . . . tag along."

Disappointment flashed in his green eyes. "Yes, I do. I'm your shadow until after breakfast."

Oh, great. Her gaze slipped down to his open shirt again. Was she going to have to look, or try not to look, at his chest all morning? "Then at least button your shirt." The words were out before she realized how that sounded.

The disappointment in his eyes vanished and a sexy twinkle took its place. The twinkle brought out the gold flecks in his irises, which she used to admire so much.

"Why?" he asked. "Does it bother you?"

She glared at him. "Don't go there." Then to make her point even clearer, she held up her pinky at him. "I might have powers you don't want to mess with. And since I don't know how to use them, I could really mess a person up. By accident, of course."

He held up his hands in complete submission. "I won't go there. I swear." But the sexy grin on his lips remained as he started buttoning his shirt.

Freaking great, Kylie thought. He'd probably read her emotions and assumed she still found him attractive. Which she did, but not in the way he thought. Okay, so it was in the way he thought but it didn't mean anything. Or so she tried to tell herself as she took off for the front door.

Derek followed right behind her.

When they walked past her two roommates still tossing threats at each other, Kylie didn't even look back. If they were really going to tear each other's body parts off, they would have done it by now. Right?

"Don't panic," Holiday said after Kylie walked in, pointed to her forehead, and explained she might have pulled off a bit of abracadabra and changed Socks back into a kitten.

"Panicking is never good." But she couldn't stop staring at Kylie's pattern.

It might not be good, but Kylie could see panic in Holiday's eyes. Well, maybe it wasn't so much panic as it was sheer befuddlement. No doubt Kylie shared the same expression. Though hers probably *was* panic. And not all because she'd turned into a witch. It was more about seeing Holiday, and the images of the vision that were now popping up like flash cards in her mind. The vision Kylie still sensed she didn't need to share with the camp leader.

"Okay, exactly what happened?" Holiday asked.

"Just what I said." Kylie plopped down in the chair across her desk. "Miranda was trying to change him back with all these fancy spells, but not having any luck. I was concerned about Socks; he didn't want to be there. So I pointed my pinky at him and blurted out something like, 'Why can't you just say, change back into a kitten.' And it happened."

Holiday nodded and continued to stare at Kylie's pattern as if she expected it to change.

"Am I really a witch?"

The fae's brow puckered. "Yes. But . . . yesterday you were a human and before that you were . . . a pattern no one could recognize."

"So you think it'll go away?"

Holiday looked apologetic before she even spoke. "I don't know for sure but . . . more than likely, you're a witch. I mean, if you really have powers."

"But the powers could go away, too." Kylie sighed.

"But . . . if you have powers then you obviously have the witch DNA. Unlike a pattern, DNA is pretty permanent," Holiday said, but she didn't sound sure of anything. "Then again, witches don't have speed the way you have when you run, or sensitive hearing. Most wouldn't have the type of healing gifts you have, either. And very few of them dreamscape." Now Holiday was thinking out loud more than talking to Kylie. "Of course, it could all be related to you being a protector. Or it might be because of the hybrid mix. Some hybrid mixes have—"

"How about ghost whispering? Do witches have that?" Kylie asked.

"A few have it, but not all." Holiday touched her chin, as though completely puzzled. "But what's really odd is that you're appearing to be a hundred percent witch now. But I guess your being a protector could maybe . . . affect that."

She slumped back in her chair as if stumped. "Have you tried to see if you could do anything else?"

"Do what?" Kylie asked.

"Magic?"

"No," Kylie said. "What if I screw something up? Like Miranda does. I could turn someone into a kangaroo or even something worse."

"I doubt you would do that. Why don't you just try to move something?" Holiday pushed a leather, heart-shaped, sand-filled paperweight to the edge of her desk.

"I don't know." Kylie bit down on her lip. "It's totally freaky."

"Not really. Just try." She made a funny face. "And be prepared to duck if we have to."

"Oh, that makes me feel so much better," Kylie said.

Holiday grinned. "Try it."

Kylie took in a deep breath. Then, pointing her pinky at the red heart, she said, "Move."

Nothing happened. Kylie exhaled and grinned. "See, I'm not a witch."

Then the paperweight started to jiggle . . . or beat. At least that's what it looked like it was doing. Beating, pumping, as if it were a real heart.

"Shit!" Kylie said, and either there was an echo in the room or Holiday spurted out the same word. "Did I make it come alive?"

Holiday didn't answer; she was too busy watching the throbbing heart. Then the thing floated up and shot across the room. "Duck!" Holiday screamed.

Kylie dropped to the floor just as the paperweight whizzed past. Unfortunately, Burnett walked into the room.

The heart went right for him.

Chapter Twelve

The heart paperweight hit him in the chest. Shocked, he tried to catch it, but missed. It bounced off his wide, masculine upper body and whizzed off. It stopped in the middle of the room, hung in the air like something filled with helium, and then it rocketed forward, aiming again for Burnett. And like the first time, it didn't miss.

But this blow was much . . . much worse.

Right in the crotch. Or as Della would say, his "boys" took a direct hit.

"What the hell!" he growled. He doubled over in pain. The heart moved back, and he snatched the leather-covered, sand-filled paperweight from the air, and squeezed it until it burst. Unfortunately, when the sand exploded from his tight fist, it regrouped in the shape of a heart and managed to hover in the air.

"Is Miranda in here?" Burnett growled, still doubled over.

Kylie, realizing the screwed-up witch he sought was her, raised her hand and said, "Stop." When nothing happened, she remembered to extend her pinky. "Stop!"

The sand fell to the floor and scattered like . . . well, like sand.

Holiday sat back up in her chair, looking too stunned to speak.

Burnett, fist still pressed into his thigh, rose up to his full height.

"Damn!" Holiday muttered finally.

"Damn!" Burnett echoed.

Kylie looked from the shocked Holiday to the hurting vampire. Kylie thought his outburst was due to the pain, but nope. He stared at her forehead.

"Interesting," said Holiday.

"Strange," Burnett followed, never taking his eyes off Kylie's forehead.

"Just lovely!" muttered Kylie. Their dumbfounded expressions were a foreshadowing of what was to come at breakfast. Leave it to Kylie to be the mealtime freak-show entertainment.

"You're a witch," Burnett said in disbelief.

"Appears that way," Holiday agreed.

"No. I'm a chameleon." And each time Kylie said it, she believed it a little more. It didn't matter that she could reverse spells and turn animals back into their normal form, or that she'd sent a heart flying around the room and ball-busted a vampire. Her father told her she was a chameleon and she believed him.

"Maybe chameleon means something else," Holiday said. "Maybe it has something to do with you being a protector. For that matter, all the other gifts could be due to that as well." The camp leader's phone rang. As if needing a distraction, she eyed the caller ID. Raising her gaze, she met Kylie's gaze with empathy.

"What now?" Kylie bellowed.

"It's . . . Tom Galen, your stepfather."

Just lovely, Kylie thought. A call this early couldn't be about anything good. So, what new disaster did he want to add to the mix?

"Is everything okay?" Derek shot inside the office door. "I heard a commotion," he muttered.

"No," Kylie said just before Holiday answered the call. "At this particular moment, I can't think of one single thing that's okay."

After breakfast, Kylie and Miranda walked out of the dining hall to head back to the cabin. Della had some kind of meeting with Burnett. Kylie had begged out of Meet Your Campmate hour due to her sucky start of the day. Plus she was supposed to go to the falls with Holiday and Burnett as soon as Burnett talked with Della.

"They like you. They're just surprised," Miranda said, apologizing for the entire witch group, who'd done nothing but gape at Kylie's forehead during breakfast. "I mean, we all thought you were vampire or werewolf. Some people had bets on you being a shapeshifter, but none of us ever thought you'd turn out to be one of us."

"You seriously took bets on what I was?" Kylie asked.

"A couple of warlocks started it." She frowned. "Sorry. If it makes you feel better, I lost five bucks."

Kylie shook her head in disbelief. Not that it was just the Wiccan gals or guys reacting. The entire Shadow Falls breakfast crowd had ignored their runny eggs and raw bacon and had eyes only for Kylie's newly emerged witch brain pattern. Or they had until Della, bless her cold heart, tried to help.

The vampire had vaulted up in the air a good five feet, landing with big thump on top of the table—her black tennis shoes landing half on and half off several campers' trays of food. Then with concern for Kylie, Della announced that Kylie had just whispered a curse and anyone gawking at her forehead would be turned into a flatulent goose.

It was, of course, a bald-faced lie. Since Kylie had sent the heart paperweight zipping around the room, she'd been superconscientious about not moving her pinky. Not an easy feat either when trying to fork up runny eggs. Nevertheless, her two pinky fingers were on time-out until Kylie figured out the witch thing.

Kylie stopped out front of the office and debated popping in and asking Holiday if she'd ever gotten in touch with her stepfather. The two were playing phone tag. Kylie also wanted to check and see if Burnett had heard from Malcolm Summers, her real grandfather.

He'd told Burnett he would be here tomorrow, but what were the chances of that happening now when he'd had his phone disconnected and dropped off the face of the earth? Kylie suspected it was because of Burnett's tie with the FRU. Then again, maybe he just didn't care about her. It wasn't as if he'd even known his own son, her father.

That thought stung until she realized it didn't make sense. If it were true, why would he and her aunt have come to the camp pretending to be her father's adoptive parents? The fact that they'd come disguised as humans reinforced that he didn't trust someone at Shadow Falls. And that someone had to be Burnett because of his connections to the FRU.

"Don't you just love Della?" Miranda asked. "She's a pain in the ass, but when it's about protecting us, she steps up to the plate, or on the plates." She giggled. "I'll bet she stomped on about six breakfast platters this morning."

"I know. She's great." Even if the plan backfired.

"I mean, really? A flatulent goose? Where does she get these ideas?"

"I wouldn't know," Kylie muttered. Frankly, she wasn't even completely sure what flatulent meant. Nevertheless, feeling overwhelmed, she decided to chalk it up to a learning experience. Not only did she have a word definition to look up, but she'd learned another important lesson—that being stared at wasn't any worse than when people refused to look at you. Nope, not one person chanced even giving her a quick peek after Della's warning. Flatulent must be really bad.

"This is still so cool. You are a witch like me!" Miranda rubbed her hands together with complete glee.

Kylie wished she shared Miranda's optimism. "I still don't believe it. I don't care that even Holiday half believes it," Kylie said, and then added, "You do know it could change, right? I was all human and now I'm not." And her dad told her she was a chameleon. She believed him.

"But this is the first time you've shown a real supernatural pattern, so it's probably real." The little witch did a butt-wiggling victory dance. "Aren't you over-the-moon excited?"

For Miranda's sake, Kylie plastered a smile on her face, but the over-the-moon comment repeated in her head, reminding her of a certain werewolf.

"I wonder why Lucas wasn't at breakfast," she said aloud. Not that she was all that eager to tell him the news.

"I don't know," Miranda said, still wearing her toothpaste ad smile. Then her smile faded. "Are you worried he'll be disappointed that you aren't were?"

"No," Kylie said, not sure if it was an out-and-out lie. She wasn't worried he'd be disappointed; she was worried he would be devastated. Her heartstrings gave her a few emotional pulls and a knot tightened in her throat.

"Is there any legendary bad blood between weres and witches?" Kylie asked.

"Nothing that I know of," Miranda said. "I mean, weres don't typically like any race but their own. But they don't dislike witches as badly as they do vampires."

Kylie supposed she should be grateful she hadn't morphed into a vamp.

Then again, she had a feeling nothing other than her turning into a were would make her acceptable to Lucas's family and pack. Could their relationship survive the prejudices?

"Do you want to go to the cabin and try out a few spells?"

"Oh, hell no! I don't want to goof anything up."

"You won't," Miranda said. "I'll be with you. I won't let you mess up."

Right, like you've never messed up. The words shot from Kylie's brain and landed on the tip of her tongue, but she managed to swallow them. Just because she was hurting didn't give her the right to hurt others.

"You're just nervous. You gotta trust me." Miranda's bright smile widened even more. "We witches have to stick together."

"Sorry," Kylie said. "I've already managed to zap Burnett in the balls with a paperweight. I'm taking the day off."

"Seriously? You did that?" Miranda snorted with laughter, causing frowns from the group of weres walking past.

Kylie spotted Will and called out. "Will?"

The dark-haired, brown-eyed teen turned around and appeared annoyed. Was it rude to call a were's name? Or was his expression due to more personal reasons? Were all of Lucas's pack members going to start giving her the cold shoulder?

"Yes?" His tone matched his expression.

Kylie moved a few feet away from Miranda. Standing in front of Will, she tried not to let his discontent intimidate her. "Lucas wasn't at breakfast. I was wondering if you know where he is."

Will glanced at the woods, as if stalling. While Kylie couldn't read minds, it was almost as if he were trying to come up with a lie. Why?

"Is something wrong?" she asked.

He motioned the other weres to go ahead. Then he waited for them to get out of hearing range before he spoke.

That had to mean something was wrong, didn't it?

"Lucas was summoned by the Council," Will finally said.

"Is that a bad thing? Is he in trouble?"

"I . . . don't know. That's between him and the Council."

Concern pricked at Kylie's mind. "Do you know when he'll be back?"

"No." He shuffled his feet against the rocky path, then glanced off at the woods again before facing her. "I'm sorry," he added, and something about the tone in which he offered the apology, even the sincerity in his eyes, told Kylie he meant it—but why? For what was he apologizing?

"What are you not telling me?" she asked. "Please just tell me."

"If you have questions, you should ask Lucas, not me."

"So something is going on?" She stepped closer, feeling her heart beating against her ribs. Without warning, her gaze shifted to the woods, and she felt it again. As if the trees were calling her name. But with her heart stuck on her concern for Lucas, she focused on the problem at hand, and on Will. "Is it about me?"

Will's discontent grew more noticeable in his frowning expression. "I don't know. I have to go." He walked away. She watched him leave, silently, and got a nagging feeling that something was brewing.

Will disappeared down the path. Kylie's heart remained on Lucas, but her gaze shifted back to the woods where the trees slowly stirred in the gentle breeze. It was the oddest feeling, like being really thirsty and seeing a glass of water. This feeling, the calling, was even stronger than the call to the falls.

What the hell was going on?

Miranda cleared her throat, and Kylie glanced back at her roommate. "Are you okay?" Miranda asked, and moved closer.

Kylie rolled her eyes. "Why does everyone ask that question when it's obvious that I'm not?"

"Probably wishful thinking," Miranda answered, bumping Kylie with her shoulder, and smiling in sympathy. "Don't worry. If Lucas likes you enough, things will work out. It did for Perry and me."

Kylie breathed in. Then she breathed out. She started walking again, consciously fighting the temptation to take a flying leap into the woods—to figure out who it was and why they wanted her attention so desperately.

They walked another five minutes without talking. Kylie concentrated on the rhythmic sound of her own footsteps, which created a sense of calm. But the scream, a cry of sheer panic, pretty much shot that calm all to hell.

Kylie stopped so fast she nearly tripped and grabbed Miranda's elbow to steady herself. The sound came from the very place she felt lured—the woods. Deep in the woods.

"What is it?" Miranda asked.

Kylie looked at her. "You don't hear that?"

Miranda tilted her head. "Hear what?"

Kylie stepped a foot or two closer to the woods and tried to identify the voice of the screamer. The high-pitched sound told Kylie it was female, but there were no notes of familiarity to it. None.

It didn't matter. She felt it—the familiar fizz, the telltale buzz in her blood that happened when she moved into protective mode.

Her breath caught in her throat; everything inside her said someone needed her. She had no choice but to answer the cry for help. She bolted toward the woods.

"Kylie!" Miranda screamed out. "Don't run!"

Right before Kylie entered the thicket of trees, she called back for Miranda to go get help.

And fast.

Chapter Thirteen

Kylie ran like the wind.

Nothing slowed her down. Nothing could.

Not the thick underbrush.

Not the overhanging limbs.

Not even the seven-foot barbed-wire fence telling her she was leaving Shadow Falls property. *Don't you dare leave Shadow Falls property.* She heard Burnett's warning ring in her head, but she ignored it. She followed the screams.

She even ignored her fear that she was running full-speed ahead into a trap set by Mario and his friends. It didn't matter. She was a protector. She had to protect.

After several minutes of running on pure adrenaline, her breath heavy, she sensed the scream and the screamer getting closer. Then she saw it.

Not the screamer.

She saw the fog—the thick, low-hanging cloud that moved over the underbrush, as if swallowing the ground up. It moved in a way that said the force behind it was more than Mother Nature. This was some unnatural power.

A power that traveled at breakneck speeds.

Logic told her to run, but the screams grew louder, and instinct kept her feet moving right into the mouth of the fog. Movement to the left caught her eyes. A girl raced to escape the thick mist. Her long black hair stirred around her head, reminding Kylie of the picture of Medusa she'd seen in a Greek mythology book.

Still a distance away, the girl's gaze met Kylie's. Relief sparked in the runner's eyes. Doubt sparked in Kylie.

Was this real, was the girl real, or was this another vision? Was the girl truly running for her life, or was she running from a death that had already claimed her?

Questions bounced around Kylie's mind as her feet hit the earth. Faster, she told herself when she saw the fog almost at the girl's heels. "Run faster," Kylie screamed.

Dead or alive, helping the stranger felt essential. The sound of the girl's rapid footfalls echoed through the trees, until her speed helped her escape the mouth of the fog.

Then, as if in slow motion, the girl tripped, lost her footing, and hit the ground. Hard.

The thud of her fall bounced off the trees.

Kylie watched in horror as the fog moved in. She pushed herself, sensing the need to reach the girl before the strange fog. The fizz in her blood gave her strength.

Coming to a sudden stop beside the lifeless body, Kylie snatched the unconscious girl into her arms. She weighed next to nothing. When Kylie looked up the fog was almost upon her. Running on instinct and perhaps panic, Kylie shot off.

Her feet pounded the underbrush into the ground. She hadn't gotten ten feet when the feeling of being lured hit her again. *Come to us. Come to us.* The wind, the trees, everything whispered the same message.

She stopped running. Her breaths came short, in and out. She swung around. "What do you want? Who are you?"

Her heart slammed against her rib cage. Cradling the girl closer, Kylie stared at the fog.

The thick gray cloud hovered twenty feet back, pulsating as if a heart beat within. The air around it stirred as if it breathed.

That's when she stopped being able to breathe, because . . . because freaking hell, fog wasn't supposed to breathe. Fog wasn't supposed to be alive.

Before Kylie could react, the cloudlike air shifted and separated into two different masses. While she didn't sense an evil presence, she could no more deny the fear biting at her backbone than she could deny her own need for oxygen. Part of her instinct screamed to run, another part screamed to stay.

The fog inched back a few more feet as if it sensed Kylie's dread.

So she waited.

She watched.

She listened.

Listened to her name being called.

Kylie. Kylie.

Listened to the words spoken that came with the wind—whispered softly like a breeze stirring in the leaves. *We mean you no harm.*

"Who are you?" Kylie called out.

The girl in Kylie's arms shifted. The weight that had felt lifeless now stirred with life. Glancing down, she saw that blood oozed from the girl's brow. The need to get her help pulsed through Kylie's veins. She looked up again at the fog. The two different masses had taken shapes. Humanlike shapes.

Don't go.

Kylie's instinct to move the girl to safety swelled in her chest. To face the unknown alone was one thing. To do it with a bleeding girl in her care was another.

"I have to," Kylie answered, and turned to leave. She got only a few feet.

Stay.

There was something about the voice, a male voice. She glanced back over her shoulder; air caught in her chest.

Her grandfather? Was that not him? Then Kylie saw the woman and recognized her as her grandmother's sister. Tears filled Kylie's eyes.

She started to turn back but the girl in Kylie's arms screamed. She looked down. The girl's eyes shot open. Her dark blue irises stared up in bafflement and sent a bolt of familiarity rocketing through Kylie.

But she had no time to ponder. The blood oozing down the face of the girl came down faster. Kylie's instinct to get the girl to safety made her own blood sizzle. How badly was this stranger hurt?

"Release me!" the girl ordered in a low growl, and tried to squirm free. "Release me!" she screamed again, and started to fight this time. Her strength told Kylie this was no human. Without Kylie's protective powers, the girl would have easily won her freedom, but not now.

"In a minute."

Kylie took flight—holding the squirming blue-eyed stranger close. *I'm sorry.* Kylie spoke the words in her head and prayed they would be heard by those she'd just left. She'd had no choice but to leave. Her need to protect bit down stronger than her own quest.

Clutching the screaming stranger in her arms, Kylie jumped over the barbed-wire fence. Once on Shadow Falls property, the silence in the woods seemed louder than the girl's protests. Without warning, Kylie felt one, two, and then three whisks of air fly past her.

Then Burnett, Della, and a large bird—Perry—appeared beside her, all three moving at Kylie's pace.

Kylie stopped running. So did the others. Tiny sparkling bubbles appeared beside Perry as he morphed back into human form.

The three of them stared at Kylie, or rather, they stared at the screaming girl in Kylie's arms.

"Who is she?" Burnett asked.

"Don't know." Kylie's breaths came short, her mind on her grandfather and great-aunt. "She was running from—"

"She's a were," Della interrupted. "I could smell her as soon as we passed."

The girl stopped struggling against Kylie's hold. Her voice deepened as she met Kylie's eyes. "Release me now! Or you will regret this with your dying breath." She raised her head and glared at Della and then Burnett. "All of you will regret it!"

Burnett spoke directly to Kylie's package. "Give me your word that you will not run."

She glared at him.

"If you do, I'll catch you and I'll be really pissed off."

"If you're fast enough," the girl quipped.

"Oh, he's fast enough." Perry tossed in his two cents. "When he was fifteen, he chased down a shape-shifter in antelope form and kicked his antelope ass. There wasn't enough of that animal left to make a rug."

"Fine," the stranger bit out. "I won't run."

Della moved in and stared at Perry. "You knew Burnett when he was fifteen and chasing antelopes?"

Releasing the girl, Kylie's gaze collided with the antelope ass kicker himself. His expression prepared her for what came next. "I thought I made it clear you were not to go into the woods."

Kylie nodded, but she refused to be reprimanded for doing what, for her, was as natural as breathing. "Someone was in danger."

"*You* put yourself in danger." His gaze shot back to the girl. "What were you running from?"

"Fog." The girl wiped away the blood that oozed from her forehead. "It chased me."

"Fog chased you?" Della snickered. "You smoking something?"

"She's telling the truth." Kylie almost told them about her grandfather, but something compelled her to think first . . . speak later.

"Who are you?" Burnett asked the girl.

"Who are *you*?" the girl countered.

"Definitely were with that attitude," Della muttered.

Perry laughed, then waved at the girl. "You're bleeding. It's dangerous to bleed in front of vampires."

"Don't worry," Della said. "Were blood is nasty."

The girl shot Della a cold look. Kylie got the feeling again, that something about this stranger was familiar.

Burnett spoke next. "I'm Burnett James, the camp leader of Shadow Falls, and you are trespassing."

"You're . . . Burnett?" The girl showed the first bit of insecurity.

"She wasn't trespassing," Kylie spoke up. "I brought her across the property lines."

The female shot Kylie a look of surprise. "I don't need you to defend me."

"I wasn't. Not really."

Burnett's body posture hardened, but his scowl targeted Kylie. "You left Shadow Falls property?"

"I heard her screaming." The bleeding stranger pinched her brows, trying to read Kylie's pattern. Was she still a witch? Or was her pattern doing something else weird?

"You . . ." The girl shook her head. "You're a witch. How could you . . ."

Well, that answered that question, Kylie thought.

The girl turned her blue eyes back on Burnett. And just like that, Kylie knew who she was. The color of the eyes, the way she tilted her head, even her body language hit the mark.

"I'm—"

"Lucas's sister," Kylie said.

"Yes." She focused on Kylie again. "I'm Clara Parker. Who are you?"

"Kylie Galen," Kylie said.

Surprise widened the girl's eyes. "But you're a witch? I thought . . ." She paused. "And you ran and have strength like you're either a were or . . . a vamp." The last word came out sounding like an insult.

Della growled. Burnett's frown tightened.

The frustration of the whole witch issue came rushing back. "I'm just an evolving piece of art. Just call me the mealtime freak show here at Shadow Falls."

"You're not a freak," mumbled Perry. "I'm the resident freak," he said with pride.

Clara continued to stare at Kylie, and then she said, "Why was that fog chasing me? Did you do that with magic?"

"No, I didn't do it."

Burnett focused on Clara. "Your family is worried about you."

Clara rolled her eyes. "They worry too much. I told them I was coming here."

"You were expected two days ago," Burnett reprimanded. "And just so you know, if you plan on staying on at Shadow Falls, we don't like changes in plans without going through the proper channels."

Clara arched her chin up as if to offer Burnett some lip. Remembering it was Lucas's sister, Kylie intervened. "I'm sure she'll adjust. Lucas will fill her in."

"Where is my brother?" Clara insisted.

"He was called to visit the Council," Burnett answered.

Kylie looked at Burnett and wondered if Lucas had told Burnett. If so, why hadn't Lucas told her?

"Is something wrong between him and the Council?" Clara asked Burnett.

Kylie recalled Will's odd behavior earlier when Kylie asked the same question.

"Not that I know." Burnett stood stoically for a few seconds, and then asked Clara, "How badly are you hurt?"

"Just a scratch," Clara answered.

"She passed out," Kylie said.

"Did not," insisted Clara, as if it would make her look weak.

Kylie started walking back to the clearing. Everyone fell in step with her. The sounds of the woods returned to normal, but Kylie barely noticed. Her mind chewed on what she'd seen when she'd looked back the last time, and tried to decide what if anything to share with Burnett. Glancing briefly over her shoulder, she tried to listen with her heart to see if she still felt her grandfather and aunt calling. Were they still there? Or had they left?

The sensation lacked the earlier power, but she still felt it.

"Perry," Burnett spoke up, "you and Della go ahead and make sure Clara gets to the office to be seen by Holiday." Burnett's demanding voice bounced off the trees and caused another wave of silence. "Kylie, I want a minute with you." His tone left little doubt that the minute wouldn't be pleasant.

Kylie stopped walking. Perry shot Kylie a look of pure sympathy. "She was just trying to help," the shape-shifter offered.

Della spoke up. "And nothing happened. All's well that ends well, right? You can't get mad when—"

"Go," Burnett ordered.

Della grunted, and Perry sent Kylie another look of empathy. She loved both of them for feeling the need to intervene, but she could handle this. She hoped.

"I'll see you," Kylie said when Perry appeared poised to argue.

As they walked away, Kylie inhaled a deep breath of wood-scented air. Burnett stepped beside her. They watched the three others move ahead. Clara glanced back. Her gaze expressed more curiosity than concern.

"Is she in trouble?" Clara asked, her voice getting softer as the distance between them increased.

"Let's just say, I wouldn't want to be her right now," Perry answered.

"And your wolf ass is the reason she's in trouble," Della smarted back.

"I didn't ask her to help me," Clara countered.

Kylie waited before she spoke to Burnett. "I shouldn't be reprimanded for doing what I was supposed to do."

"You could have been killed. It could have been a trick to lure you away from Shadow Falls."

"It wasn't. Clara thought she was in danger. I felt her fear and reacted."

"She thought she was in danger?" he asked, picking up on Kylie's slip of the tongue. "Are you saying she wasn't?"

When Kylie paused, Burnett continued. "Exactly what was it you two were running from?"

A need to tell the truth filled her chest, but another need—the need for answers—kept her quiet. "Like I said before. It was fog," Kylie answered, confident that her response wouldn't read as a lie. Her words were true.

Just not the whole truth.

"Did you sense it was evil?"

"I was scared," she admitted again. A shiver rushed down her spine. Not from fear, but from the cold that came when the dead neared. She glanced around, trying not to let on that they had company. The ghost, Holiday's look-alike, peered at them from behind a tree.

"But . . . ?" Burnett asked, sensing she wasn't finished.

"But I didn't sense it was evil." A whisper of guilt came, but if she told Burnett her grandfather and aunt had attempted to see her without permission, what would Burnett say?

"I'm trying to protect you. I can't do that if you don't follow my rules."

"I don't normally break your rules." The cold grew colder and she cut her eyes to where the ghost had been. She'd disappeared. In a flash, the Holiday look-alike stood beside Burnett, looking at him as if she recognized him. The thought sent a tremor of fear through Kylie's heart.

"It could only take one broken rule and it would be too late."

Kylie bit down on her lips, fighting the cold. "I'm sorry." *For upsetting you, not for going.* "I heard the scream and I felt called to help."

"Next time, before answering that call, get me."

"I'll try." She shivered in spite of her attempt not to.

"I think you could do better than try," he countered, then he looked up as if questioning some higher power. "Explain to me why I wanted to be a part of Shadow Falls."

"I can answer that," Kylie said, feeling bad for making him angry. "Because beneath that crusty exterior of yours, you care about us. And you love the other person who runs this place." Kylie glanced at the ghost, wondering if she would react to the words.

The spirit's gaze widened. *"Do you mean . . . ?"*

Burnett frowned, but he didn't try to deny it.

Kylie would've been happy that he'd come to terms with his feelings for Holiday if she didn't have the ghost staring as if . . . as if the confession of love had affected her.

The spirit looked at Kylie. *"He's in love with the camp leader?"* Panic laced her tone. Did the spirit now know she was Holiday?

What's your name? Kylie asked in her head.

"I told you," the ghost answered.

"I'll never get used to this." Burnett started walking.

"Get used to what?" Kylie caught up with him, her attention

more on the spirit who walked beside the vampire, staring at him with surprise.

"The ghosts," Burnett blurted out as if the words cost him.

Kylie stopped and grabbed him by the elbow. "You can feel them?" she asked. Generally, only when a spirit was trapped in a small room could a non–ghost whisperer feel them.

"No," he said.

Kylie stared at him.

"Fine. Maybe I feel them a little. It's probably more about the look you and Holiday get in your eyes when they're around," he confessed. He looked around. "Is she gone?"

"How did you know she was a female?" Kylie asked, realizing the spirit was gone.

His jaw clenched. "I could smell her," he said, as if it were some kind of a sin.

"You can? I didn't think . . . I mean, I didn't think vampires had ghost-whispering gifts."

"I didn't think so either." And he didn't sound happy about it. He shot off walking again, only faster—his pace reflective of his mood.

Kylie kept up, but barely. "Does Holiday know?"

"Know what?" He didn't even look at Kylie.

"About you detecting ghosts? She was curious as to why you could go into the falls and—"

"No, she doesn't know," he said. "And don't mention it. I'll tell her later." Worry tightened his jaw.

They walked in silence for a second. "I didn't mean to cause trouble by going after Clara. I just reacted to my internal instinct."

"Sometimes our internal instincts can be skewed," he added.

She wondered if he was talking about his ability to smell and sense ghosts as well as her protective instincts. "I'll try to do better next time."

"Thank you," he said, as if conceding to what she offered.

They continued forward. The wind stirred the trees.

"Can you tell me more?" he asked.

"About ghosts?"

"No. About the fog. I'd like to forget about the ghosts."

Kylie remembered how she'd felt when she first learned she could detect the dead. She could relate to his feelings. Sometimes she'd still like to forget about her ability.

"Did you sense it was Mario?"

"No." Kylie went over the details, careful not to leave anything out except the ending. No doubt he would question Clara later. But Kylie was almost certain Clara hadn't seen anything that would give the secret away.

"It has to be Mario and his buddies again." Burnett's fist clenched as he walked.

Kylie hesitated to say anything, knowing if she slipped up and lied, he would know. But neither did she want Burnett to worry too much. "Remember I said it didn't feel evil."

"It has to be them." He looked at her directly, a stern, fixed stare. "You do not go into the woods, with or without a shadow. You understand?"

She nodded. She understood, but she didn't say she would comply.

"It has to be some witch or wizard behind this." His brows pinched. "You don't think that you accidentally caused the fog, do you?"

"No," Kylie insisted.

"You sure? With the other incident—"

"It was different." Her cheeks warmed, remembering the incident.

Their pace slowed. The trees and underbrush seemed to soak up the sound of their footsteps. Kylie's mind returned to Clara, and from Clara, it moved to the girl's brother.

"Can I ask you something?" Kylie asked.

"If I said no, would it stop you?"

"Probably not." She debated on how to word her question.

"If it's about anything concerning Holiday and me, I've been ordered to plead the fifth."

She grinned. "Don't worry, the inside-out shirt the other day pretty much told me what I wanted to know about you and her."

The stern-looking vamp half smiled again. His smile faded. "It's not about ghosts, either, is it?"

"No. It's . . . When a Council calls someone in for a meeting, is it bad news?"

"You're talking about Lucas?" he asked.

She nodded.

He moved a limb out of his way, holding it back so it wouldn't hit Kylie. "It can be, but not always."

"Do you know what it is they want with Lucas?" She pushed another limb away.

"No, I don't." His words rang completely honest.

"Are you concerned?" Kylie asked.

He hesitated. "Yes."

"Why?"

"I respect Lucas's need to become a part of the Council so he can help bridge the problems between the weres and the FRU, but I don't want the Council to have too big of an influence over him."

"You don't trust Lucas?" Kylie asked.

"If I didn't trust him, he wouldn't be here. My problems stem from the fact that the were council and the FRU have issues. In general, the were community is less compliant to work within the FRU's rules. It goes back to the pack mentality."

"But couldn't that be because the FRU considered werewolves lower-class citizens?"

"That has changed," he said. "But I'm sure that plays a big part in their behavior, and I can assure you that the FRU treats all were situations with that in mind. However, prejudices stem from both sides.

One of the reasons they were viewed as outcast was because they viewed others as the same."

"So it's a 'which came first, the chicken or the egg' kind of thing," Kylie said.

"I guess it doesn't matter," he said.

When they arrived at the clearing, Burnett looked at her. "I'll walk you back to your cabin. If Della or Miranda isn't there, I'll get someone else to shadow you for the time being. Holiday and I will be there shortly to go to the falls. But until I investigate this whole fog thing, you're not to leave that cabin without me knowing where you are and who you are with."

She flinched slightly at his tone and new demands. Surely he was exaggerating. "Do you mind if I go back to the office with you?" Kylie asked. "I'd sort of like to check on Clara."

He hesitated, but nodded, and they started down the path to the office. Kylie gave the woods one last glance and felt nothing. Had they already left?

Her gut instinct said they had. Question was, would they come back? And if so, could she find a way to go to them?

Before Kylie stepped up on the porch, she heard Lucas talking. "You can't keep doing this!" His voice carried.

Kylie wasn't sure if it was her sensitive hearing or if he was talking that loudly. Considering how private werewolves were, she suspected the former.

"What did I do?" Clara asked. "I told them I was coming here and I did."

"Where else did you go? Did you go see Jacob?" Lucas's tone came out tight.

"Of all people, I would assume you could understand my need to see who I wanted to see."

"As strange as it is, I think Dad's right about him."

"Really, are you going to let him choose your lifemate? Wasn't that what you two were arguing about when you were back there? Your affection for Kylie?"

Kylie's breath caught. Lucas had argued with his dad about her?

"We're talking about you," Lucas snapped.

"I'm here, isn't that what matters?" Clara asked. "Isn't that what you want?"

"What I want is for you to quit playing games, Clara. I'm trying to help you."

"Games? Please, you are the biggest game player of them all. You play games with the Council, with Dad, with your mom, and with Grandma. You even play them with Fredericka. I'll bet you're even playing games with that witch of yours."

"I'm not playing games, and I don't have a witch."

Kylie hesitated as they moved closer to the cabin's steps, and from the look Burnett sent her, she supposed that he, too, was hearing the conversation.

"I could still walk you to the cabin," Burnett offered, and from his tone, Kylie sensed he understood how this might be hard for her. His concern should've been touching; instead she didn't like knowing everyone knew her business. She preferred her private life to stay private.

"I'll have to face him sooner or later," Kylie said, glancing away.

But even Kylie had to admit, later sounded really tempting. Yet she squared her shoulders and continued walking, her gut tight at the thought of Lucas's response to her being a witch.

Chapter Fourteen

As Kylie and Burnett took the steps up to the office, Kylie suddenly wished she hadn't come.

Behind the door, Clara continued arguing with her brother. "I think she might have been the one who sent the fog after me. She pretended like she rescued me, but maybe the witch was just—"

"You think who sent the fog after you?" Lucas demanded.

"Kylie!" Clara fumed.

Kylie's breath hitched.

"Kylie isn't a witch," Lucas said.

Burnett pushed open the office door; Clara and Lucas, positioned in the entryway, turned around. Kylie prepared herself for his reaction.

"I am for the time being." Kylie decided to expose her cards and worry how the game would be played later.

"You're what for the time being?" Lucas asked, unaware that Kylie had been privy to their conversation.

"A witch," she said.

Lucas stared at her forehead. Shock, confusion, and disappointment flickered in his eyes. "What . . . Witches don't have speed. They can't run . . . like you run."

"Confused the hell out of me, too," Clara said. "That's when I realized she probably cast a spell, and if she cast that spell, maybe she did it all."

"I didn't create the fog," Kylie said. Was Clara really already turning on her?

"So how did you know where to find me? And don't lie again and say you heard me. I wasn't close enough for you to hear my screams."

The accusation stung, but Kylie tried not to take it to heart. Clara had reasons for being suspicious. Witches weren't supposed to be able to run like lightning or have super hearing. Which validated Kylie's belief that she wasn't a witch.

But if her grandfather and aunt could turn themselves into fog, did that mean they belonged to the Wiccan species? She didn't think shape-shifters could change into fog, could they? Doubt pulled at her mind.

"Kylie isn't your normal witch." Burnett came to her defense.

Lucas glanced at Clara, to Burnett, then back at Kylie. An apology replaced the stunned disbelief in his eyes.

He continued to gaze at her, but spoke to his half sister. "If Kylie says she didn't do it, she didn't do it."

"You take her word over mine? Now I see our father's concern." Clara's tone rang heavy with accusation. "How can you call yourself a leader of our people when you stand up for a witch over your own kind, own blood?"

Lucas's jaw tightened. "My belief does not come from her words. I know the facts. Kylie has sensitive hearing. She could hear your screams from miles away."

"Witches don't have—"

"As Burnett pointed out, I'm not a normal witch." Kylie gazed at Lucas. Why couldn't he have simply declared he believed her? Was a were's loyalty to his pack so restrictive that his faith in her held no credibility?

Feeling Clara's stare, Kylie continued. "Apparently, my brain has a bad habit of showing different patterns."

"Then there's something seriously wrong with your brain." Clara's tone made her words even more of an insult.

Kylie waited for Lucas to correct Clara. When his gaze found hers, she could swear she saw an apology flash in his eyes, but he remained silent.

And just like that, she knew why. Because to do so would be putting her before Clara. Because Kylie wasn't a werewolf, she wasn't supposed to matter to Lucas. Or at least not matter as much as one of his own. The realization brought with it a wave of pain that caused her chest to clutch. She told herself she didn't need him to defend her, that she knew he cared, so what did it matter that he remained silent?

"My mind is fine." Kylie met Clara's eyes and then briefly glanced at Lucas. Yup. Kylie's mind would be okay; it was her heart she worried about right now. Because while it shouldn't have mattered, it did.

A lot.

"Why weren't you scared of what you saw?" Clara asked.

Unsure what Clara meant, Kylie paused. Had the girl seen more than Kylie knew? "Who says I wasn't scared?"

"Kylie's a protector," Burnett intervened.

Clara's eyes widened. "No shit?"

Uncomfortable at the girl's stare, Kylie suddenly wanted to escape. "I should go." She turned to leave.

Burnett gently caught her by the arm and, as crazy as it seemed, she felt empathy in his cold touch. He leaned in and whispered, "Not until you have a shadow."

"I'm here." Holiday stepped through the door. "I took a short walk to give Lucas and his sister a few minutes to talk." Her green eyes went to Kylie as if she sensed the emotional storm brewing inside her. Holiday motioned for Kylie to follow her out.

Burnett looked at Holiday. "Stay close. There could still be danger around."

"Exactly what happened?" Worry filled Holiday's green eyes.

"We'll talk later," he said. "I need to chat with Clara while everything is fresh in her mind."

Kylie walked out, her heart breaking at Lucas's behavior and her gut worrying about what Clara remembered. Yet one glance at Holiday and Kylie remembered her vision and Holiday's possible demise. Heck, maybe Clara was right. Maybe something was wrong with her mind. Perhaps the stress of everything had finally driven her loony.

Was becoming a witch the first sign of insanity? Or was it just part of being a chameleon?

Kylie followed Holiday to the dining hall to grab a sandwich. Lunch had come and gone and so they had the place to themselves. They barely talked and the awkwardness didn't feel right. When they walked out of the dining hall, Kylie's gaze went to the woods to see if the feeling had left, or if she sensed her grandfather and great-aunt calling her. But she felt nothing.

Holiday reached over and touched Kylie's shoulders. "Talk to me."

Kylie absorbed the calm that Holiday offered and faced her. "I hate prejudices," Kylie said, knowing that only one of the problems at hand, Lucas, could be discussed with the camp leader. If she told Holiday who was in the woods earlier, she'd tell Burnett. And both of them would refuse to let Kylie go to them if they returned. But she had to, didn't she?

"I hate them, too," Holiday said, as if she knew exactly what prejudices Kylie referred to. "If there was one thing I could change in the world, that would be it."

Closing her palm, Kylie fought the feeling of disappointment Lucas's stance with Clara had given her. "You would think after being the target of prejudice, the were society would know how unjust it is."

"I think—"

"Can I please have a moment with Kylie?" Lucas's voice came from behind them. Just hearing his deep tenor caused another wave of pain to wash over her chest. She couldn't think of anything, or anyone who would have stopped her from standing up for him if the shoe had been on the other foot. And yet . . .

Kylie and Holiday turned around. The camp leader met Kylie's gaze, almost asking if this was what she wanted. She nodded.

"Fine, but don't go far." Holiday walked back to the porch and sat down on one of the rocking chairs.

Lucas took Kylie's hand and led her around to the back of the office. He didn't speak, and neither did she. He stopped by the tree, where they'd been earlier, and turned to face her. Not a word left his lips; he just stared.

What she wouldn't give to be able to read his mind. What was he thinking? Was he upset because she was a witch, was he sorry that he hadn't come to her defense? Was he realizing how hopeless this relationship was?

"Thank you for rescuing my sister," he said. "I'm sorry she's so ungrateful."

Kylie nodded.

He leaned down and pressed his forehead against hers. All she could see was his eyes, the blueness of them, the long dark fringe of lashes surrounding them.

"I hurt you." His voice came out even deeper than before.

She didn't deny it.

She continued to stare into his eyes and he didn't blink. The pain reflecting in his deep blue irises made her breath catch.

He closed his eyes and inhaled before speaking. "Have you ever known the right thing to do, but couldn't do it?"

She pulled back just a few inches. "Depends. What's the right thing to do?"

She posed the question even though she was afraid to ask. It wasn't the question that scared her, though. It was the answer. Because deep down, she sensed it. She had sensed it since his grandmother talked to her. She and Lucas had too many things standing in their way for them to make this work.

"I should let you go," he said. "I should put a stop to this . . . to us. Because until things change, everyone will be against us. And yet . . ." His head dipped down ever so slightly and his lips met hers.

So much emotion came with that brief kiss. And while she didn't think she had any room in her heart for more emotion, she felt it move inside her. His pain was her own. His fear was hers. She closed her eyes, fought the ache radiating in her heart, and just savored his touch.

He pulled back and ran his thumb over her lips. "And yet, how can I let you go when you're the thing that keeps me going? When the main part of the reason I want change is you?"

His finger swept over her chin, a sweet touch that nearly brought tears to her eyes. "I'm begging you. Please be patient with me. Trust me when I say that you have a place here." He took her hand and rested it on his chest. "I have to behave a certain way or it will get back to my father and the Council, but it's not how I feel." He paused a moment. "Please don't give up on me, Kylie Galen."

She could feel his heart beating. She could feel it breaking, too, right alongside her own. "I don't give up easily." It was the truth. If she was a quitter, she wouldn't still be at Shadow Falls.

He wrapped his arms around her, leaned against the tree, and pulled her flush against him. They stood like that for the longest time. Not talking. Not making promises. And Kylie couldn't help but wonder if it was because they both instinctively knew those promises wouldn't hold.

He finally pulled away. "I should go help Clara get situated."

Kylie loosened her hold around his waist. But she didn't want to. She didn't want to give him back to Clara or to Fredericka or to his father. As selfish as it was, she wanted him all to herself. Or maybe it wasn't that she didn't want to share him. Maybe she just didn't want to share him with people who were trying to keep them apart.

"Do you want to come with me?" he asked.

Clara would love that, Kylie thought. Not. "I'll let you two have some time alone."

"Thanks," he said as if he'd hoped she'd refuse. He smiled, but beneath the smile was a touch of disappointment. "So you're a witch. I never would have guessed."

"I'm a witch right now," she said.

He looked confused. "You think it will change?"

"Yes. Maybe." What did she believe? "I changed from that strange pattern to human."

"Yes." He stared at her pattern. "But this is a true supernatural pattern." Lucas's attention shot over his shoulder and he growled. Derek came around the office.

Derek's green gaze met hers. There was no apology in his eyes for interrupting them. Even his posture seemed to say he had a right to be here. "I need to see you, Kylie. It's important."

"About what?" Lucas asked.

Derek didn't look at Lucas. The fae's gaze never left Kylie, and while he answered the question, he spoke to Kylie. "It's about your ghost."

"Since when did you become a ghost expert?" Lucas asked.

Derek looked at the were for the first time. "Since I found out

Kylie needed help with them." His implication hung in the air. He supported her when Lucas didn't.

Lucas heard it as well. His eyes tightened and turned a light orange.

Before trouble started, she placed a hand on his back. "Go help Clara."

He didn't look happy, but his expression told her he wasn't planning on arguing.

Yet his next move surprised her. He leaned down and placed an affectionate kiss on her lips. The kiss seemed more about letting Derek know she was his girl than for her pleasure, but she didn't completely blame him.

There had been a time or two she would have loved to kiss him like that in front of Fredericka.

"What is it?" Kylie asked Derek as soon as Lucas moved around the office and was out of earshot.

Derek stared after Lucas and then back at her. "You're disappointed. What's disappointing you?" he asked, reading her emotions right on the mark.

"Nothing." She refused to talk about this with Derek.

"Is it Lucas?" he asked.

"Let it go," she insisted. "I'm with Lucas now."

Though for how long? The question whispered through her head.

A frown pulled at his lips. "I know. I screwed up and didn't realize that I loved you until it was too late."

She held up her hand. "Don't say—"

He reached out and laced his fingers with hers. The press of his palm against hers came with a soft warmth, a sense of calm, and endearment. She frowned at how tempted she was to just hold on, but knowing her emotions were completely out of whack right now, she pulled her hand from his. He was her friend. Just a friend.

"It's okay." He dropped his hand into his pocket. "I accept that it's my fault. And you don't have to tell me you love me." His gaze met hers. "But I can read you, Kylie, and I know you don't want to admit it, but you care about me, too."

"Stop it," she said. "I care about you like a friend."

"No." He continued to stare. "It's more. But don't worry. I know you care about Lucas, too. And that's my cross to bear because I pushed you right into his arms. And as long as you're happy, I can accept that. But if you're not—"

"Please stop." Kylie wanted to start singing "la la la" and cover her ears. And if it wouldn't have been so childish, she would have done it. Instead, she reminded him of the real matter at hand. "Didn't you say you had information about my ghost issue?"

He stuffed both his hands in his pockets. "Yeah. Good news, at least I think it is. But I guess some of it could be bad news, too."

"What?" She hoped it was more good than bad. She could really use some good news.

"I don't think your ghost is Holiday."

"But . . . how . . . what makes you think that?"

"I did some research on the Internet. Simple stuff." He hesitated. "I found out that Holiday has an identical twin. Her name is Hannah."

I think my name is Hannah or Holly, or something like that. The spirit's words echoed inside Kylie's head. "A twin? Why hasn't she ever mentioned her?"

Derek shrugged. "It seems a little odd, doesn't it? I mean, you would think she'd have said something about having an identical sister."

"Yeah." Kylie couldn't deny it hurt that Holiday didn't feel she could tell Kylie things, when she shared everything with Holiday.

"Do you still think this ghost is from the future?" Derek asked.

Kylie considered it. "No. She's dead." Just as the other girls were in the grave she'd seen in her vision. And just like that, Kylie's angst about Holiday not trusting her faded and Kylie's heart filled with sympathy. Kylie couldn't imagine losing a sister, let alone a twin. Was this why Holiday hadn't ever mentioned her? Did grief over her twin's death keep Holiday from ever talking about her sister?

Derek let out a deep breath. "Okay, here's something else that's weird. I couldn't find any death records on her. None. That's why I said this might be bad news."

"What are you saying?" Kylie asked.

Derek frowned. "Holiday might not know her sister is dead."

A knot of grief formed in Kylie's throat. "So I have to tell her."

"If you want, I could do it," Derek offered. "Or we could do it together."

Genuine concern filled his expression. She appreciated his offer, more than he would ever know, but she couldn't let him do it. As much as she dreaded being the bearer of bad news, Hannah had come to Kylie, and she should be the one to tell Holiday.

Then Kylie remembered something else Hannah had said. *I think I came to you to help someone.*

What exactly did Hannah need Kylie to do? Was telling Holiday about her death enough or did she need more?

Derek ran his hand down her arm. "Have you made a list of all the diners you've gone to recently?"

"Diners?" Kylie asked, unsure of what he was talking about. Unsure of why a simple touch could seem so wrong.

"You said one of the girls in the vision was wearing a diner uniform that looked familiar to you."

"Yes, I mean I remember, but no, I haven't had time to do it."

She took in a deep breath. "I'll get to it as soon as I get back to my cabin. I'll e-mail it to you."

"E-mail me the description of the uniform and the girls, too," he said.

"Hey." The sound of Holiday's voice had the knot in Kylie's throat doubling. She turned to face the camp leader and a chasm of empathy and hurt opened in her heart. And yet Kylie couldn't help but admit the relief of knowing that the dead girl wasn't Holiday.

Holiday's green eyes softened. "Something happen?"

For the life of her, Kylie didn't know how to tell her. "No," she lied, but for a good reason. The last thing Kylie wanted to do was just blurt out the news. Then it hit her, maybe she should talk to Hannah first. Perhaps she needed to know exactly what it was Hannah needed before she moved forward.

Holiday nodded, but disbelief flashed in her eyes. "Burnett got called to the FRU office and he insisted we hold off going to the falls until he comes back. I was hoping you could help me set up a few things in the dining hall. We're having a welcoming reception for the new teachers later this afternoon."

"Sure," Kylie said, and she met Derek's eyes briefly.

"Good luck." He mouthed the words and then he reached out and touched her, sending a much-needed current of calmness through her.

"Thanks," she whispered to Derek before she turned to join Holiday. They took a few steps and Holiday glanced over at Kylie with suspicion.

"Boy trouble?" Holiday asked in a low voice.

"Yeah," Kylie said, and it wasn't even a lie. While her heart was aching for Holiday, Derek's earlier words echoed in her mind and left a trail of uncertainty. *I can read you, Kylie, and I know you don't want to admit it, but you care about me, too.*

And the worst part was, he was right.

Chapter Fifteen

"If you want to talk about it, I'm here," Holiday said as they moved around to the front of the office.

"I know." Kylie gazed briefly at the woods, but the feeling from earlier, the feeling of being called, hadn't returned.

Holiday looked over at her and frowned. "Are you really okay? I mean, I respect your privacy. But lately you've been . . . closed off a bit. And I worry. Because . . . well, you usually trust me." Holiday rested her hand on Kylie's arm. Warmth and concern flowed from the touch.

Usually, I'm not dealing with a ghost who looks just like you, who I just found out is your sister, and I don't know if you even know she's dead.

"I don't mean to be closed off," Kylie said. "I'm just . . . between Lucas and Derek, and my grandfather changing his number, and the FRU trying to do experimental tests on me, and my mom dating, I'm a tad overwhelmed."

"And rightfully so," Holiday said.

Thinking about her mom dating led Kylie to think about her stepdad. "Oh, I almost forgot. Did you ever get in touch with my stepdad and see what he wanted?"

"Yeah, he called a while ago. He found out about the FRU saying you needed some medical tests and was concerned."

"Did the FRU call him, too?" Kylie asked, ready to panic that they hadn't given up their mission to treat her like their very own lab rat. Maybe even give her the same test that had killed her grandmother.

"No, and I asked because it scared me, too," Holiday answered, telling Kylie how accurate the camp leader was at reading her emotions. "He said he'd spoken with your mom."

"My mom? Really?" An unexpected smile spread across her lips. "So they're talking again? That's the best news I've heard all day. Maybe she'll dump the creep who wants to take her to England and give my stepdad another chance."

"Perhaps," Holiday said, as if wary of giving Kylie too much hope.

Kylie remembered that Holiday had dealt with the whole parental divorce thing, too. "How long does it take?"

"How long does what take?" Holiday asked.

"How long before you stop wishing they hadn't split? How long before you stop wanting to tell them to cut out the fighting and go back to the way things used to be?"

"I wouldn't know." Holiday sighed and offered a sympathetic smile. "I'm still waiting. I think when you grow up with them together, you just always assume they will stay together. But I do know I've reached a place where I know my parents are probably better off not being together. Nevertheless, I still have times that I remember how it used to be when we were a family, and . . . I wish things were different now. The sad truth is that we change. Parents. Siblings. And when that happens, people grow apart and—"

"But who we love shouldn't change." Or could it? Kylie's mind went from her parents' divorce to Derek, and then to the ghost issue. Then, suddenly, Kylie realized that this line of conversation might be the opening she needed to ask about Holiday's sister. "Did you go through it alone?"

"Alone?" Holiday looked confused.

"What I mean is, do you have any brothers or sisters?" Kylie asked.

Holiday was looking away so Kylie couldn't see her expression, but if the sudden flinch in the woman's shoulders was any indication, Kylie had hit a nerve. Why? What was Holiday not willing to talk about? Had Hannah and Holiday grown apart?

As another second ticked by, Kylie hesitated, not knowing what to do. Should she push for an answer, or just let the moment pass? After all, this wasn't just about her wanting Holiday to trust her, this was about helping Hannah cross over. Once she solved the whole ghost issue, maybe then she could focus more on solving her other issues.

"Unfortunately," Holiday said, ending the uncomfortable silence, "siblings are not always a help in this matter." She reached for her phone. "I just remembered I need to make another call. Can you head over to the dining hall? I asked Miranda and Della to help me, too. Della's taking over shadowing duty. I have a couple of banners to put up and there's some balloons to blow up. They're in the back of the dining hall, and I just wanted to get some tables set up to hold the appetizers. I should be over there in a few minutes. And hopefully Burnett will be back and we can take a quick run to the falls before the ceremony."

"Sure," Kylie said, disappointed. She sensed Holiday was running away so she could avoid answering any more of Kylie's questions.

Holiday arched another brow, obviously picking up on Kylie's discontent, and shook her head. "I still wish you'd talk to me."

And I wish you'd talk to me. "I'm fine." Kylie watched Holiday head to the office and when she turned around, Della was standing there.

"At your service, Miss Witch." Della grinned and stared at Kylie's forehead. "However, I won't deny that I'm disappointed. I mean . . . you liked the taste of blood, so I figured you'd at least be half-vampire."

Kylie rolled her eyes and pointed to her forehead. "I keep telling you guys, I don't think this is final."

"It looks final to me."

Kylie looked back at the woods and wished she felt that her grandfather was still there. Wished she could meet him face-to-face and finally get the answers she needed. But she didn't feel it. Didn't sense that something out there called to her to join it.

She looked back at Della. "And what was I last week? A human, right? And for how long? A few weeks?"

Della made a face. "Okay, I see your point. But this is the first real supernatural pattern you've shown."

"Yeah, and I'm betting it won't be my last. Let's just say, I think I've got ADD brain patterns. They never sit still. One comes, one goes."

"Damn," Della said. "Miranda's right. You really don't want to be a witch, do you?"

Kylie let out a gulp of frustrated air. "That's not it at all. It's just I was told—"

"That you're a lizard." Della made her sympathy face. Not one she used a whole lot, either. "Look, no hard feelings, but I think I'd believe you're a witch before I'd believe that you're a lizard. And if I may add one little thing, if you keep this not-a-witch front up, you're really going to hurt Miranda's feelings. She's already upset. And you know what she's like when she gets upset."

Kylie closed her eyes and inhaled. "I didn't mean to hurt her feelings. If I hadn't gotten the message from Dad saying I was a chameleon, I'd be ecstatic at the idea of being a witch." If frustration wasn't in the driver's seat of Kylie's emotions, surprise would have been behind the wheel. When had Kylie and Della traded places? Normally, it was Kylie calling Della on this offense. "Look," Kylie said, trying to explain herself. "Witch and fae were my top choices of species, but—"

"You didn't want to be a vampire?" Della sounded insulted.

Oh, crap, now Kylie had offended Della. Nothing was going right today. "Please," Kylie said, her frustration not just sitting in the driver's seat anymore, but revving up the engine. "I didn't say that, I just—"

"It's being cold that bothers you, isn't it?" Della asked, looking more hurt, but not mad. And Kylie guessed she should be thankful about that. A hurt Della was hard to deal with, but dealing with an angry and hurt Della was impossible.

"No, it's not being cold, it's . . ."

"It can't be the blood because you liked the taste of blood."

"I like the taste of it, but I don't necessarily like the idea of having to drink it, or the idea of having French fries taste like toad's butt, because that's exactly how you described it. But if I'm vampire, then I'll be happy." When Della's expression didn't change, Kylie added, "Truthfully, it would be cool to be able to fly like you guys do."

"It's very cool," Della said, her expression softening.

"Anyway," Kylie continued, "I'll be happy with whatever I am. I don't even care anymore. But right now, I trust what my dad said, and he said I'm a chameleon. Doesn't that make sense to anyone?"

"No," Della said matter-of-factly. "Sorry, but the whole 'I'm a lizard' thing sounds crazy. Maybe you should come to grips with the fact that you're going to end up just being like one of us. A normal supernatural."

Kylie's head was spinning. First, *normal* and *supernatural* didn't fit in the same sentence, but . . .

"When have I ever been normal?" she asked. "When has anything connected to me, to my powers and gifts and my forever-changing brain patterns, appeared to be normal?"

Della opened her mouth, to argue no doubt, and then shut it. The pause lasted a whole second. Which for Della was a long time. "Okay, you've made another good point, but . . ."

"No buts," Kylie said. "I'm either a freak, or maybe, just maybe, I'm some other type of supernatural. Something not very many people have heard of."

Della pursed her lips as if in thought. "And that would be totally cool, wouldn't it? To be something very rare. Of course, you're already super rare because you're a protector. Hey . . . maybe that's why your pattern went crazy in the beginning, because you're a protector. And you're the first part-human protector to ever exist. Which, like I said, is cool."

"No, I'm not the first. My dad was a protector." Kylie paused. "And it's not as cool as you think." After a second, Kylie added, "Holiday suggested being a protector could have made my pattern do stupid stuff, but . . ."

"But you want to be a lizard," Della said.

Kylie just rolled her eyes and gave the woods another glance. She didn't feel anything, but maybe if she stood among the trees and surrounded herself with the foliage, she would feel it. Her grandfather and aunt could be waiting for her. Her answers could be out there waiting for her. "Can we take a short walk?"

"I thought we were supposed to be helping Miranda and Holiday set up the dining room."

"Just a short one."

"Where to?" Della asked.

Kylie motioned to the woods.

"Oh, hell no! Burnett was very, very, *very* clear on that. You aren't supposed to go in the woods. He'd have my head on a platter. After he chewed my ass out."

Kylie looked around to see if anyone was within hearing distance. Super hearing distance. She didn't see a soul.

She still dipped her head down and spoke in a whisper. "I know who's out there and I need to talk to them."

"What . . . ? Who's out there?"

The sound of a door shutting filled the warm air. "You guys letting Miranda do all the work?" Holiday's voice came behind them.

Kylie turned around and saw her stepping off the office steps. "Just going in."

Della leaned in. "Don't leave me hanging like this."

"Later," Kylie said when she saw Holiday walking up.

"Later what?" Holiday asked.

Guilt stirred in Kylie's chest, but she forced herself to lie. "Later, I'll tell her my bucket of boyfriend woes." She forced a smile.

"Yeah, boyfriend woes," Della said, as if to add validity to Kylie's lie. "Two guys fighting for her heart." Della cut her eyes to Kylie, and the message in her friend's eyes said she'd be pressing Kylie to finish their conversation about the woods ASAP.

"What a bucket of . . . woe that is!" Della said with drama. But somewhere in Della's voice, Kylie heard something else. A bit of envy.

Holiday chuckled. From the camp leader's expression, Kylie sensed she'd picked up on Della's emotions as well. And that caused Kylie to worry. How much of Kylie's woes did Holiday sense? And how long could Kylie keep things from her? Just long enough, Kylie prayed, to know the right way to approach everything.

Holiday shrugged. "From what I hear, she's not the only one with boy troubles."

"Yeah," Della said with sass. "You and Burnett are filling the air with pheromones." The vamp waved a hand in front of her nose.

Holiday frowned. "I wasn't talking about me." She gave Della a pointed look.

"Me?" Della asked, in total bafflement. "I don't have a boyfriend, so how could I have boyfriend troubles?"

"You could have a boyfriend if you wanted one," Kylie muttered, and that remark got her a sharp jab of Della's elbow in the ribs.

Holiday grinned. "Rumor has it you were the cause of some friction down by the lake."

"What friction?" Della asked.

"Between Steve and Chris," Holiday said, and wiggled her brows. Leave it to Holiday to know what someone needed to hear.

Except in Kylie's case. Kylie needed to know about Holiday's sister, but getting Holiday to talk about it, without just blurting out that her sister was dead, seemed impossible. But if Kylie didn't hear from Hannah soon, or Holiday didn't start talking, then blurting it out might be her only option.

"No." Della shook her head, sending her shoulder-length black hair swinging. "It wasn't over me. You just heard it wrong."

Holiday half grinned and shrugged. "If you say so." She paused and grinned like she knew something no one else did. "Come on. Let's get the dining room whipped into shape for the reception." She draped an arm around each of their shoulders and started walking toward the dining hall.

They took about three steps when Della came to a sudden stop. "Really?" she asked Holiday. "It was over me? Chris and Steve were upset with each other over me?"

"I told you Steve liked you." Kylie almost chuckled at Della's shock.

But Della wasn't listening to Kylie. "You're not shitting me?" Della continued, focusing on Holiday, her head tilted slightly as if listening to see if she was lying.

"I swear." Holiday grinned. "My heart won't lie."

"They were fighting—?"

"I said friction," Holiday corrected.

"They're frictioning over me?" She chuckled and then stopped as if to let that piece of info sink in. "No. Not me. It has to be a mistake." But Della's eyes lit up with a spark of self-confidence.

Kylie grinned—even feeling the weight of all her problems pressing down on her, seeing Della beaming with "boy" pride felt good . . . and right. It hadn't escaped Kylie that Della felt left out with both Miranda and Kylie having boyfriends, but she hadn't sensed how big of a chunk that took out of Della's confidence until now. And after the vampire's heartbreak with Lee, Della deserved to feel "friction worthy."

Not that all friction was a good thing. The friction between Lucas and Derek sure as hell couldn't be chalked up as a positive. But for right now, Kylie just wanted to think about Della.

Five minutes later, Kylie realized Della was right. Miranda was upset. The little witch hardly spoke to her as they whipped the dining hall into shape. Of course, Miranda squealed with glee when Della told her about Chris and Steve having "tension." Feeling like a third wheel, Kylie finally walked up to Miranda and apologized for . . . Well, she wasn't sure what she was apologizing for, but she said the magic words, "I'm sorry," and asked Miranda if she'd go over a few spells with her later.

Miranda's eyes lit up. "I would be delighted. Just decide what spell you want to try. And you can trust me, I can do this."

The look of sheer contentment on the little witch's face told Kylie that Miranda's problem was more about Kylie's initial refusal of her help and the ding against her ego than believing Kylie didn't want to be a witch.

While rearranging the tables in the front, Kylie's phone chimed with an incoming text. It was from Lucas.

Still with Clara. Miss you. I'll probably be busy introducing Clara to the pack until later. I'm not going to be at the reception. I'll stop by and see you tonight before you go to bed. Thanks for understanding.

Kylie stared at the phone and sensed she would be seeing a lot less of Lucas now that Clara was here. Kylie inhaled and tried to tell herself that she did understand. That of course he would have to take time with his sister. But between his pack and now Clara, Kylie wasn't sure where she fit in.

Or *if* she fit in.

Fifteen minutes later, Kylie noticed that Della kept glancing at her. Kylie knew the vamp was chomping at the bit to get Kylie alone so she could finish their conversation about who was in the woods. But frankly, Kylie was having second thoughts about coming clean. Telling Della meant she'd have to tell Miranda. Not that Kylie didn't trust them to keep it a secret, but . . . she just didn't want to get anyone in trouble. Then again, considering that she never went anywhere without a shadow these days, she was going to have to trust someone. And she trusted her two roommates more than she trusted anyone else at Shadow Falls.

They were almost finished setting up for the event when Holiday's phone rang. Holiday stepped away to take the call.

Della came moving over so fast that she bumped into Miranda and nearly knocked her down. "Talk and talk fast," Della sputtered at Kylie.

"Talk about what?" Miranda rubbed her shoulder and frowned at Della.

"Shh!" Della held up a finger to silence Miranda and eyed Kylie with persistence. "Talk."

"Don't you shush me!" Miranda bit out.

Kylie exhaled and reached over and touched Miranda's arm, hoping to calm her, then she answered Della's question. "It's my grandfather and aunt. They were the fog."

"They were . . . the fog?" Miranda asked, her bad attitude with Della dropping along with her mouth.

When Kylie nodded, Miranda continued. "Then that proves it, you are a witch, because they have to be some dang powerful witches to pull that off."

"Wait. Why would they do that?" Della asked.

Kylie frowned, and looked again at Holiday standing across the dining hall. Kylie noted how the camp leader's gaze kept moving to Kylie and she suspected the phone call had to be about her.

Again.

Great. What was it this time?

"Earth to Kylie," Miranda snapped.

Kylie glanced back at her two roommates. "I'm not sure it proves anything at this point."

"But why would they chase Lucas's sister?" Della asked.

"I don't know." Then suddenly Kylie did know. "To get me to enter the woods. They've been calling me for a few days now but I thought . . . I thought it might be Mario and his friends and I didn't go. But I'll bet my grandfather knew if I thought someone was in danger, I'd—"

"Do they even know you're a protector?" Miranda asked.

"I don't know." Kylie's mind raced. "I know that Burnett talked with him, but I don't know what all he told them."

"I'm not buying all that," Della said. "Maybe it is Mario pretending to be your grandfather and aunt. Maybe this is just a trick to get his hands on you."

"I don't think so," Kylie said. "And right now I have to follow my gut. I've got too much going on, and it would be nice to get some answers about something."

"What else is going on?" Concern made Della's brows tighten.

Kylie hesitated. "Ghost issues."

"Which means we're not gonna be any help there," Della countered.

Exactly what Kylie thought, too. When it came to ghost issues, it was either Holiday or she was on her own. She recalled Derek, who'd told her he was willing to help her even though chances were he felt the same way about the spirits as the other supernaturals did.

Della piped up again. "But I thought your grandfather was supposed to come see you tomorrow. Why are they turning themselves into fog and sneaking in to see you if they could just show up tomorrow? And how did you know the fog was them?"

"He was supposed to come," Kylie answered. "But since then he's shut off his phone and hasn't contacted Burnett at all. And right when I left the fog took on human form and . . ." Kylie wasn't sure how to put it. "I recognized my grandfather and my aunt. I'm sure of it."

Della's expression hardened. "But if you're wrong, and if we go out into the woods and shit happens—"

"Go into the woods?" Miranda blurted out. "Oh, crap, no! Burnett said she wasn't to go into the woods. To not let her get close to the woods."

"I know," Kylie said. "But if I want answers to what I am, I'm going to have to go to my grandfather, and I don't think he's going to just walk into the camp, not when the FRU is crawling all over Shadow Falls. And after what the FRU did to my grandmother, I can't say I blame him for not trusting them. Heck, even Holiday doesn't trust them."

Miranda bit into her bottom lip. "But if you're wrong . . ."

"I'm not." And just like that, Kylie realized she couldn't put her two best friends in danger. The guilt she still harbored over Ellie swelled in her chest. "But just in case, I'm going in alone."

"No way!" Della said.

"All I want to do is walk a little ways into the woods. You guys can just stand at the edge. If I don't feel anything, I'll come right back out."

"And if you do feel something?" Miranda asked.

"Then I'll know it's them and I'll meet them."

"Oh, hell no! You are not going in alone," Della declared. "You're a protector. In case you've forgotten, that means you can't protect yourself."

"Della's right," Miranda said. "If you go, we all go."

"I don't think any of us should go!" Della said.

Holiday started walking over and, knowing the fae would be able to read the mood, Kylie looked at her two best friends. "Think happy thoughts. Quick. Before Holiday reads . . ." She let her words fade as Holiday drew near.

"What's up?" Holiday asked.

"Nothing," the three of them answered at the same time.

Kylie smiled and tried envisioning Lucas to instill a happy emotion, but Derek's image and his loyalty to her ghost issues popped into her mind. And instead of being happy, more angst filled her head.

Holiday quirked an eyebrow that read as disbelief, but she appeared to move past it and said, "That was Burnett. He's not going to make it back until right before the event and has insisted we postpone the trip to the falls until tomorrow. Is that okay with you?"

"That's okay," Kylie said.

And it was okay. Maybe now she could take that walk into the woods and get some answers—if they were still there. She just needed to figure out how to do it without Della and Miranda freaking out.

Chapter Sixteen

Kylie stood on the edge of the path, ignoring Della and Miranda as they argued over who was going into the woods with her and who was staying at the path. Little did they know, neither of them were going.

She couldn't put them in danger. Even if there weren't any danger, if Burnett found out, he'd give them hell. And hell from Burnett felt pretty dangerous. Somehow Kylie was going to have to figure out how to sneak away and do this on her own.

Besides, she wasn't even sure her grandfather and aunt were still there. Maybe moving into the woods would tell her, but not now. Still, she closed her eyes and listened with her heart. When she didn't feel even the slightest yearning to enter, she spoke in her mind.

Are you still out there?

"I'm here."

The words sounded at the same time as Kylie felt the cold. Not recognizing the voice, she snapped her eyes open. Standing in front of her was a blond woman, early twenties, wearing a diner uniform with a tag on it that read CARA M. Kylie's heart thudded faster when she realized this was one of the girls from the vision, the vision of being buried with Holiday's sister.

Letting go of a sigh, Kylie's breath turned to cold vapor.

"Damn!" said Della.

"Damn what?" asked Miranda.

"Kylie's got company," Della said. "White misty shit always snakes up from her lips when she's chatting with the dead."

"Oh!" Miranda took a step back and stared at Kylie. "Man, her aura is doing some crazy stuff again. This is so damn freaky. I'm so glad I'm not her."

Trying to shut out Della and Miranda, Kylie focused on Cara M. Kylie recalled Derek asking her to describe the uniform so she studied it for details. She snapped a picture of it in her mind—the V neckline, the checkered pattern around the bottom of the skirt—so she could describe it to him later. But why not just ask?

"Where did you work?" Kylie asked.

"I worked at my aunt's voodoo shop," Miranda answered. "Crazy crap happened there."

"She's not talking to you," Della snapped.

"Sorry." Miranda shrugged. "This is so freaky."

"Do you know the name of the diner?" Kylie continued to stare at the spirit.

"I . . . don't know," Cara M. answered. *"But can you please get us out of there?"*

Kylie frowned. "I want to, but I need to know where you are."

"But you do know. The other girl took you there. Don't you remember?"

How could she forget? "I saw you guys and you were under a building of some sort, like a wood floor, but I don't know where that is. What town are you in? Is there an address? Is it close to here?"

"Yes, it's close. It didn't take much time at all to get here."

Kylie considered what she said and asked, "But how did you get here? I mean . . . did you walk or . . . come spiritually?" Kylie hadn't considered how spirits traveled and she realized how little she knew about the whole ghost-whispering thing.

"I don't know," the spirit answered. *"But I can take you back there if you'd like."*

"No," Kylie blurted out. The thought of being trapped in the grave again was too much. She took a deep breath and remembered to talk mentally. *Can you tell Hannah I need to see her?*

"Who's Hannah?"

One of the girls with you. The one with red hair. Kylie could feel Miranda and Della staring and she purposefully turned her back so she wouldn't be disturbed.

"So her name is Hannah? How do you know her name? She's not wearing a name tag." The spirit glanced down at the name tag attached to her uniform. *"Do you know my name? They call me Cara M., but I don't remember being her. My life is like a vague picture book I once looked at and I can recall flashes of the images on the pages, but they never turn slow enough for me to recognize anything."*

That's not uncommon after death, Kylie assured her, remembering Holiday saying that the more dramatic the death, the less the spirit remembered. The thought of what these girls possibly went through sent real pain skipping through Kylie's limbs. Her heart clutched with the need to help them. To do whatever they needed to help them move on.

"Will I ever remember?" Cara M asked.

The spirit's question came with such sadness that the emotion swelled in Kylie's heart. *I'm not an expert, but from what I've seen, things usually come to you. Spirits generally hang around for a reason and once that's taken care of, they remember things, and then pass over.*

Cara appeared to consider Kylie's words and nodded. *"I think the reason is so we can get our own graves. I've never liked roommates. And it's really cramped in that grave."*

Unfortunately, Kylie could remember just how cramped it was. She shivered, feeling her shoulders pressing against the dead girls' bodies on each side. Pushing the thought aside, Kylie concentrated on the conversation and not the horror of what had happened.

I'm trying to get you guys out. But something told Kylie that while Cara M.'s only need might be to escape the makeshift grave, Hannah wanted something much more. But hopefully while solving Hannah's problem Kylie would help out all three of them.

Cara M. stood there as if deep in thought. *"Is it nice where I'll cross over to?"*

Kylie debated what to say, then went with the truth. *I've never seen it, but I think so.*

The spirit looked around, then slowly floated up a good six or seven feet. She hung in the air, causing a big swirl of fog to appear around her, reminding Kylie of a scary movie. After a few seconds, she glanced down at Kylie with eyes that seemed lost, hurt. *"It's nice here, too."* She floated back down to the ground.

"I think I recognize this place. Are we close to that place with the dinosaur bones?"

Hope stirred in Kylie's tight chest. *So you know about this place? Did you live near here?*

"I . . . think so. I see an image of swimming in a lake. There was a lot of laughter there. It must have been fun."

Yes, there's a lake. Can you see anything more? Where you worked? What town?

The spirit frowned. *"I can't."* Darker shadows started appearing beneath her eyes. Shadows that made her look sadder and somehow deader. *"Please get us out of there."* She started to fade.

Wait. Can you tell Hannah I need to see her?

"I can, but I don't know if she'll come. She's upset."

At what? Was Hannah's memory returning, too? The cold began to ebb away.

The ghost completely vanished and the Texas heat replaced the chill, leaving Kylie with even more questions than before.

"Is the ghost gone?" Miranda asked.

"Yes," Kylie sighed.

"Are we going in?" Miranda asked.

"Where?" Kylie asked, confused.

"The woods. Duh."

"Oh, no," Kylie said.

"Thank Gawd!" Della muttered, and all three of them started walking to the cabin. Kylie looked back one more time and wondered if she'd ever find all the answers she needed. In a way, her life was as much of a mystery as a ghost.

They had one hour before they had to be back at the dining hall for the welcoming reception. While still walking, Della and Miranda jabbered about getting ready for the reception. No doubt Della wanted to spruce up to impress both Chris and Steve. Miranda wanted to wow Perry.

Kylie tried to get into the spruce-up mood with them, but her enthusiasm came up short. Lucas wouldn't even be there, so who would she be trying to impress? A vision of Derek popped into her head and she pushed it back and felt guilty for even thinking it.

Trying not to think about Derek reminded Kylie that she'd told him she'd e-mail him the description of the diner uniform. As Kylie moved to the computer, her mind raced with the details she'd collected about what Cara M. had been wearing.

Kylie opened her web account and saw a whole buttload of e-mails: a few from her mom, a couple from her dad, one from Sara, and some spam, and then a few from accounts she didn't recognize.

Ignoring her incoming mail, she clicked on the button to send a new e-mail, typed in Derek's name, and then started typing the description of the waitress uniform. She recalled all the things she'd learned about Cara M. and found herself wishing she had someone to talk to about them. Then again, she did have someone—the person she was e-mailing. Derek.

Miranda and Della's laughter spilled out of Della's bedroom. Why did hearing them laugh make her feel lonely?

The answer bubbled to the top of her mind. Because they were giddy with the idea of romance, of getting all dolled up to impress guys. Right now, the idea of romance left Kylie feeling befuddled. It felt like Lucas was pulling away and somehow Derek was sneaking closer. And nothing felt right.

But she still felt lonely.

Remembering the e-mail from her mom, Kylie picked up the phone and dialed her number. The phone rang four times before her mom answered.

"Hi, Mom," Kylie said.

"Hey, sweetie," her mom answered, and the sound of her voice had Kylie feeling homesick. "Is everything okay?" her mom asked.

"It's fine. Why do you always assume when I call you that something is wrong?"

"I don't always assume that. Only sometimes. And this is one of those times. I must be psychic. So stop pretending and tell me what's up."

Heck. Maybe her mom was a supernatural.

"Nothing," Kylie said. "I just got an e-mail from you and thought I'd call you. You are always saying I don't call enough."

"True." Her mom paused. "What's the matter, sweetie?"

Giving in because lying sure as hell didn't seem to work, Kylie answered, "Just a bad day."

"You know if you change your mind about staying there for the school year, and want to come home, I could get you enrolled back in school here and—"

"I'm not going to change my mind, Mom. I love it here." *I belong here.* "I'm allowed to have a bad day, right?"

"Yes, just like I'm allowed to worry about you when you have a bad day."

"Well, don't worry too much." There was a sudden background noise on the line.

"Where are you?" Kylie asked.

"Out to an early dinner."

"Alone?" Kylie asked, hoping her mom wasn't out with Smarmy John, who wanted to drag her mom off to England and get her naked and between the sheets.

As soon as the thought came, Kylie tried to push it away.

"Uh, no." Her mom's answer came out sounding guilty. "Not alone."

"With John?" Kylie attempted to keep her disappointment from her voice, but didn't think she was successful.

The silence lingered a few seconds on the line.

"It's a yes or no answer, Mom. It shouldn't take you that long to reply." Kylie realized she sounded just like her mom, too. But damn, she was certain her mom had used the exact line on her at one time or another.

"Uh . . . yes," her mom's reply came out.

Kylie closed her eyes. As if her brain were on automatic pilot, the question slipped out. "You're not having sex with him, are you?" And even before the last word of the inquiry left her lips, she knew she was going to regret it.

Oh, yeah, regret times ten. Kylie felt her face turn red.

Her mom's breath caught and she started coughing. "Uh . . ." More hacking.

"Hello, Kylie." A male voice came on the line. "I think your mom choked on her wine."

Wine? Her mom was drinking wine at three in the afternoon?

Was he planning on getting her drunk and having his way with her?

"Kylie? You there?"

"Yeah." Kylie heard her mom telling John to give her the phone back. Kylie imagined her mom panicking thinking Kylie might ask John if they were having sex. Not that she would. The fact that she asked her mom was probably going on her most embarrassing moments list.

"Kylie?" Her mom must have snagged the phone back. "We . . . should talk later." Her voice came out squeaky, like a cartoon.

"Yeah. Later." Kylie disconnected and stared at the phone.

Okay, lesson learned. Her mom not only couldn't say the word *sex,* she obviously couldn't hear it, either. Did that mean her mom couldn't have sex? Gawd, Kylie hoped so. Lesson number two. Talking about sex with her mom made her queasy. Could she possibly suffer from the same affliction as her mom?

Resting her phone by the computer, pushing thoughts of her mom having sex from her mind, Kylie refocused on the computer and tried not to listen to her roommates giggling about something— probably something to do with sex, too. Moaning, she dropped her head down on the table, feeling the blood rushing to her cheeks, hoping the coolness of the wood would chase away the heat.

Her phone, placed beside the computer, chimed with an incoming text. Sitting up, she picked it up to get the message. Her heart did a little jolt when she saw it was from Derek.

His message read: *You ok? What's happening?*

Kylie closed her eyes. Could he sense everything she was feeling now? She dropped her head back on the table again, so hard she probably bruised her forehead. She took a few deep breaths and then sat up and started texting him back.

Fine. E-mailing you the description of the diner uniform now. U going to the reception?

She held her breath and waited to see if he'd answer.

I'll be there. U?

Oh goodness, did he think the question was like an invitation to hang out?

Was it an invitation to hang out?

Yes. Bye. Guilt set in. But at least the guilt replaced the embarrassment of asking her mom if she was having sex.

Kylie stared down at her phone. Why did texting Derek feel wrong? She shouldn't feel that way. They were just . . . friends. Heck, Fredericka was with Lucas five times more than Kylie was with Lucas. Ten times more than Kylie was with Derek. And Fredericka and Lucas had been lovers.

Trying to shake off the feeling, she finished the e-mail and hit send.

"Kylie?" Miranda called from the doorway of Della's bedroom. "Did you do it?"

Kylie looked over her shoulder and attempted to focus on Miranda's cheery voice. Frankly, she could use some cheer. Lately, it seemed she'd done nothing but chew on her problems. "Do what?" she asked a smiling Miranda.

"Stuff your bra. Did you do it?" the witch asked.

Kylie bit down on her lip and grinned as the memory filled her head. "Sara talked me into doing it in sixth grade, but I chickened out and hid behind a dumpster and got rid of the tissue before we got to school. She was livid when she saw me and she had super boobs and I didn't."

Miranda chuckled and Kylie could hear Della inside the room laughing as well.

Miranda gazed down at her chest. "I admitted that I did it for a while before I got them for real. But Della swears she never did it, but I can tell she's lying."

"I'm not lying," Della countered, popping out of her room. "Truth is, I might have done it if I hadn't seen Tillie McCoy bump into the locker with her size Cs and then walk down the hall with a square boob without realizing she'd smashed her boob stuffing." Della held her hand out in front of her chest. "Seriously, she had one boob out to here and one squared off to here. Crazy thing was, the guys still couldn't take their eyes off them. I don't think they cared one was square."

Kylie chuckled but what she really felt was embarrassment for a girl named Tillie whom she'd never met. "That would be awful."

"It was," Della said. "I think tissue sales dropped in town due to it, too. Seriously, the next day, all the girls in seventh grade had lost a couple of cup sizes and the boys were depressed for a month. That day I decided that being a member of the itty bitty titty committee wasn't the worst thing."

They all laughed again.

"You know boys stuff, too," Miranda said.

"Stuff what?" Kylie asked.

Della pointed to her pelvic area.

"Seriously?" Kylie asked.

"Seriously," Della and Miranda said in unison.

"They use socks," Della added.

"Socks? Why?" Kylie asked. "It's not as if we . . . check down there."

"They think we do," Della said. "Face it, guys have sex on the brain. Girls have romance on the brain."

"Sometimes I have sex on the brain," Miranda admitted. "Well, I mean, I think about it. Does that make me a slut?"

They laughed harder, Miranda included. Then Kylie shook her head, still trying not to imagine a guy with a sock in his pants. "We all think about it, but . . . that is just so . . . crazy!"

Della frowned at Miranda and pressed her hands on her temples as if she'd suddenly gotten a migraine. "Damn! Why did you have to bring up the sock thing? Now I'm going to be tempted to look at all the guys' zippers tonight to check for sock bulges."

"You're right." Miranda giggled. "It's like an accident on the side of the road. You don't want to look, but your eyes go there anyway." She hit the bottom of her chin with the back of her hand and tilted her head back. "We'll just have to keep our chins and eyes above the waist the whole time. Whatever we do, no bulge checks."

They all laughed even harder.

Best of all, the laughter reached down into Kylie's heart and eased her feeling of impending doom. And for that, she was grateful.

The dining hall smelled like cupcakes, which Holiday had the kitchen staff fix for the event. A group of campers hung out over by the appetizers, probably saying hello to the new teachers and a few of the new campers who'd come on board at Shadow Falls. Kylie had spotted one or two new faces the last few days, but hadn't actually met any of them yet. She had to face it; she didn't excel at meeting new people. But considering the first school year at Shadow Falls started next week, she'd have to meet them soon enough.

Standing beside Miranda, Kylie realized the place wasn't as crowded as she'd expected it to be. Probably because the reception wasn't mandatory. Nevertheless, over half the campers were present. Then Kylie noted that none of the weres were here. They'd obviously gone off to do their own thing. Again.

Another sweep of the room told Kylie that Derek hadn't arrived yet, either. She wondered if he was still doing Internet searches to see if he could find a diner in the area that Cara M. might have worked at before she'd been killed. The fact that he was helping her with a ghost issue filled her chest with something warm and scary.

Scary because she couldn't exactly define the warmth. They were just friends, she told herself again. And she found it harder to believe each time she said it, too.

Helen waved at Kylie from across the room. She had her arm around Jonathon. Kylie admired the relationship the two of them had found with each other. It was sweet and romantic. Kylie grinned and waved back. In spite of knowing her problems were still here, she felt . . . lighter, and the grin felt real, too.

Amazing how a little girlfriend-laughing time could raise your spirits. Though she did have to struggle not to look at guys below the belt to see if she detected any sock wearers. And just thinking about it made Kylie want to giggle. Unfortunately, Miranda spotted Kylie's stifled smile and, as if guessing what had caused it, the witch snorted with laughter. Then meeting Kylie's gaze, she pressed her hand under her chin and mouthed the words *chin up.*

Della, across the room, let out another laugh.

"What's so funny?" Burnett walked up beside Miranda.

"Nothing," Kylie said, then feared Miranda would tell him the truth. Miranda was good at blurting out the wrong thing at the wrong times.

Meeting Burnett's gaze, Kylie recalled he could detect a lie, so she quickly added, "Nothing I can share without . . ."

"Blushing?" he asked, looking from her face to Miranda, who glowed an embarrassed pink. The color almost matched her hair.

Afraid Burnett would want more of an explanation, Kylie added, "It's girl talk."

He held up a hand. "You don't have to explain. I really don't speak girl talk and every time I tried to learn it, I regretted it." He almost smiled and his expression softened with what looked like concern when he met Kylie's eyes. "Sorry I didn't make it back in time to go to the falls."

"It's okay," Kylie answered, and then, call her paranoid, but she asked, "The thing you had to do at the FRU, it didn't have anything to do with me, did it?"

"No," he assured her, sounding honest.

She nodded and then she went for a second question, although she was pretty certain she knew the answer. "No word from my grandfather?"

He shook his head. "I'm sorry." He sighed. "With all the things that have happened lately, I'm glad you're keeping your chin up."

Chin up. The words ran around Kylie's head. Miranda snorted another bit of laughter and faced the opposite direction. Kylie had to bite the inside of her cheek to keep from laughing. Then Della's chuckle sounded from across the room.

Wrinkling his brow, Burnett looked over at Della, who fell quickly back into vampire mode and wiped all signs of humor from her face. Burnett shook his head and focused on Kylie again. "If you can stop giggling, the new teachers are all eager to meet you."

"Me?" Kylie asked, his comment chasing the grin off her face. She shifted her gaze to the side of the room where the teachers congregated. They were indeed staring at her.

"Why would they want to meet me?" Kylie's I-don't-like-to-be-singled-out phobia reared its ugly head.

"They've heard about you," Burnett said as if it was obvious.

Kylie could only imagine what some of the campers had told them. Then an even worse thought hit. "Heard about me from whom? You mean, since they've been here, right? *Right?*"

Burnett looked uncomfortable with the questions. He glanced around, almost as if searching for an out, or perhaps searching for Holiday to answer the questions for him. When he didn't spot her, he looked back at Kylie. "I . . . Well . . . news spreads. People talk."

"People? You mean people outside of the camp? People outside of Shadow Falls are talking about me?"

He looked put on the spot, but he nodded. "Just the super-naturals."

Just the supernaturals? "So, the whole supernatural world knows about me?" The thought made Kylie want to find a hole to climb into. It was bad enough knowing the campers were always on "Kylie alert," waiting to see what her wacky brain pattern was going to do next, but to think she was the subject being discussed everywhere made her supernatural butt extremely uncomfortable.

"Perhaps not the whole supernatural world," he said as if trying to console her, and then hesitated as if reconsidering the wisdom of his answer. "I mean, I couldn't say if everyone—"

"Oh, it probably is everyone," Miranda said. "My mom said they were talking about you at Witch Council last week in Italy. And they didn't even know you were a witch then. You can imagine how they are talking now."

Kylie didn't want to imagine. Her chest suddenly felt hollow. "They were talking about me in Italy? You didn't tell me that." She bit down on her lip. "I'm such a freak that—"

"That's why I didn't tell you," Miranda said. "I knew you'd get all weird about it. And you're not a freak," she added. "You're a pro-tector. And being a protector is huge. Very newsworthy like a natu-ral disaster. Not that you're a disaster. I mean, like good news."

Nothing about this felt good. It felt more like a disaster. Not even a natural one.

"Word of a protector would be something people would talk about. But Miranda's right, it's not a bad thing." Burnett looked at Kylie and obviously read her erratic heartbeat and motioned to the crowd of teachers. "They just want to say hello. Not interrogate you."

Say hello to the camp's natural disaster, aka the freak. Kylie's heart raced.

"It's not a big deal," Burnett said.

Right. Only it felt like a big deal to her. Especially when she looked up and noted all three of the teachers gawking at her. Two were even twitching their brows, checking out her pattern—and their actions had encouraged several of the campers to do the same. She could almost hear the roar of thoughts. *Hey, anyone want a good laugh? Check out Kylie's brain pattern again.*

She heard someone say something about her still being a witch. Kylie supposed she should feel happy she had a pattern to check out—instead of one of those screwball shifting patterns that really freaked people out. But even knowing that didn't make her anxiety subside. She hated being in the spotlight.

Burnett, looking baffled at Kylie's emotional dilemma, leaned closer and whispered, "If you really don't want to meet them—"

"No, I . . . I'll do it." It was crazy not to. And she felt like an idiot for letting her insecurities be known. It wasn't that she completely hated meeting people, she just hated meeting people who already had a preconceived notion about her. And she sure as hell didn't like knowing that people in Italy were talking about her. Probably in Italian, and she couldn't even understand it.

Stiffening her backbone, she plastered a smile on her face, hoping to appear less like a freak than they considered her to be. It was, however, the same fake smile she wore when her mom took her someplace she didn't want to go—like to one of those mother/daughter days at work, or to one of those stuffy volunteer luncheons. What was it that her mom had said about that smile? Oh yeah: *You look like you just swallowed a mosquito.*

Yup, she was going to look like a freak, all right.

Chapter Seventeen

Kylie, practically holding her breath, suffered through Burnett's introduction of all three teachers. First was Hayden Yates, aka Mr. Yates to the students, who gave her a nod and a more than uncomfortable stare. The new half vampire, half fae science teacher shook her hand and held on for a second longer than she'd liked.

Considering his fae half was dominant, she was surprised she didn't feel any emotion-altering warmth from him. And although he didn't strike her as a pervert, something about him gave her just a bit of the creeps. She wasn't sure what it was, but she didn't like it, or him. Odd, because Kylie normally didn't make rash assumptions about people—with the exception of her mom's new boyfriend, of course. But that was a special case. That guy wanted to dirty up the sheets with her mom and that just wasn't okay.

Ava Kane, aka Ms. Kane, wore the title of English teacher. She was half-witch and half-shape-shifter, with shape-shifter being her dominant species. She seemed nice enough, but the way she kept twitching her brows, trying to see something different in Kylie's brain pattern, made Kylie uncomfortable. Exactly what did she think she'd find?

Collin Warren, a half-fae, half-human, was the history teacher and a geologist who came off as the quiet type. Odd, for someone with fae blood, because they usually seemed to have a certain amount of natural charm, but then again, perhaps not all half-fae inherited that talent. Kylie had heard that, on rare occasions, some human supernatural blends tended to be more human than supernatural, so perhaps that was the case with Mr. Warren.

Nevertheless, he smiled, said the proper things—"Nice to meet you"—but Kylie got the feeling he was as uncomfortable being put on the spot as she was. Which made her wonder why he'd want to be a teacher.

After everyone knew everyone's name, Kylie stood there, her smile still spreading her lips tight, and waited for something to end the awkward moment. Burnett finally intervened. "Well, I'm glad you all met."

Kylie spun around, thinking only of escaping. But one step forward, and she found herself surrounded by six or seven teens she'd never met. Obviously the new students. The blunt stares and open curiosity in their expressions made her catch her breath again. It was one thing to be gawked at by the regular campers, but newbies . . . Her heart raced and her palms began to itch. Hives were only a few minutes away.

Her swallowed-a-mosquito smile fell flat. And that mosquito she'd supposedly inhaled buzzed in her stomach. She didn't know if she could handle more brain gaping and uncomfortable introductions.

"Is it true that you didn't even have a pattern at first?" one of the girls, a witch, asked.

Suddenly, an arm fell across her shoulders. Before she looked at the owner of that appendage, she recognized Derek's warm touch. "I'm sorry, but you guys are going to have to meet Kylie later. I need to steal her away."

"Lucky guy," one of the new vampires said.

"Yeah, I am," Derek said, sounding possessive.

He guided her through the circle of new students. Moved her with confidence and with purpose—the purpose being to get her the hell away from the gawkers. But damn, she appreciated Derek being there so much. She leaned against his shoulder and heard him sigh.

"Hang in there," he whispered. "I'll get you out of here."

He glanced over his shoulder and she followed his gaze to see him looking toward Burnett. The vampire nodded as if giving permission for him to take her out.

She didn't breathe again until they walked out the dining hall door.

Derek's arm tightened as they left the building, as if telling her he didn't want to let her go. While she hated admitting it, there was a small part of her that didn't want him to let go either. But knowing what was right, she stepped away from his side. And then she met his soft green eyes.

"I'm sorry," she said.

"For what?" he asked.

For everything. For feeling things I shouldn't. "For needing to be rescued. It's crazy. I should be able to handle it. It's just that people stare at me like I'm . . ."

"Special?" He grinned.

"No, like I'm a freak."

He shook his head. "They don't think you're a freak. They're curious. And that one vamp was totally into you, but I'm sure it's still hard."

"Maybe when I know for sure what I am, then it won't be so hard." But she did know, didn't she? She was a chameleon. Was she starting to doubt her heritage like everyone else?

Derek's eyebrow rose. "You still don't believe you're a witch?"

"Not completely," Kylie said.

He nodded. "Well, that should all be cleared up tomorrow, right? When your grandfather comes."

That's when she remembered she hadn't told Derek about her grandfather cutting off his phone or about him and her great-aunt turning into fog. She started to spill her guts to him when she felt the sudden splash of cold.

The smear of condensation started to materialize next to Derek. The familiar feminine form taking shape told Kylie it was Hannah. But Kylie's breath caught when she saw the spirit had gone back to her zombie look. The beige dress she wore was in shreds and stained with mud. Her hair hung lifelessly around her shoulders. Part of her cheekbone was exposed where the skin had decayed and hung loose. And worms moved in and out of her ears.

Gross. Instinctually, Kylie took a step back.

"Not again." Panic filled Hannah's dead-looking eyes.

"What?" Kylie forced herself not to keep backing up. But the worms were falling off her at a rapid rate.

"Huh?" Derek took a step closer and one of the worms fell onto his chest.

Kylie brushed it off and then shook her head.

"Oh." His eyes widened with understanding. He took a small step back, not so much out of fear, but as if giving her space.

Kylie refocused on Hannah. But the spirit's gaze stay glued over Kylie's shoulder. She heard the dining hall door open behind them, and the sound of the crowd followed the door. Hannah continued to stare over Kylie's shoulder. Then, suddenly, her expression grew more panicked.

"No," Hannah muttered and her hands, more bone than flesh, grabbed Kylie by the shoulders. Worms went everywhere.

"Not again! Not again!" The spirit's touch sent wave after wave of icy tremors coursing through Kylie, who forgot about the worms. Pain shot from every nerve ending and her body stiffened from what felt like a brain freeze to her entire body.

"Is everything okay?" Derek moved in.

The throbbing through Kylie's body locked the air in her lungs. She wanted to scream. But she felt as if someone had her by the throat. Black spots started forming in her vision. She felt her knees start to fold. Derek touched her and just like that, the pain and the dizziness vanished. Blinking, she saw Hannah was still there, standing beside Derek.

Kylie breathed, then forced the words out. "Not again, what?"

Hannah didn't answer, didn't even look at her. Derek did, and he appeared concerned.

"Look, I need to know what it is you need me to do. Please, answer me." But the spirit, her frightened dead gaze locked over Kylie's shoulder, faded into thin air.

Derek brushed his hand down Kylie's arm. "You okay?"

Kylie nodded, savoring the warmth of his touch, and then she turned around to see who'd walked out of the dining hall, wondering if that was what had sent Hannah running. Burnett, the new teachers, and a couple of the new students stood by the door.

"Was that Hannah?" Derek whispered.

"Yeah," Kylie said, still trying to wrap her head around what Holiday's sister had meant by *not again*.

"You really okay?" he asked.

She touched her throat. "Yeah. I just don't know what it is that she needs me to do."

"I don't know if this helps, but I think I know where Cara M. worked."

"Where?" Kylie asked.

"When you told me that she could possibly be from around here, I Googled all the diners and cafés in the area. I found some photos and this old newspaper article about some place called Cookie's Café, right outside of Fallen. Have you ever been there?"

"No, I don't . . . Wait. Yes, my mom took me to this restaurant that was really just an old house. That must have been how I recognized the uniform."

"That's it. The house was built in the eighteen hundreds." He smiled as if proud he'd found the answer to at least part of the puzzle.

Kylie almost smiled herself, but then it hit her. What now? Even if all Kylie needed to do was find the bodies, how was knowing where one of the dead girls worked going to help her? Ordinarily, she could talk to Holiday about this but . . . she couldn't do that until she knew exactly what was going on. It would be unbearably cruel to tell Holiday her sister was dead when there was a chance Kylie was misinterpreting the visions.

Then another realization washed over her. She should probably go to the police. But she didn't have a freaking clue how to explain any of this. Which meant it might be up to her to try to solve the murders.

Not again. Not again. Hannah's words rang in her head. What was Hannah trying to say?

Oh, holy hell, Kylie didn't have a clue how to move forward. She wasn't an investigator. She didn't even enjoy watching TV shows about detectives. She glanced back up at Derek. "What should I do now?"

"I called the diner, just to ask if there had been a Cara M. working there, but it's a tourist place and they're only open on the weekends."

Kylie's mind continued to whirl with what she needed to do: "Oh, hell, I'm so out of my league on this."

"Don't worry," Derek said. "I'll help you. And besides, we have until Saturday to decide what to do next."

She looked up at him with complete appreciation. "How can I thank you?"

He grinned with pure sex appeal, the gold flecks in his eyes brightening. "I could think of a few ways."

She frowned.

He held up a hand. "Fine. Just smile a little more. That'll be payment enough."

Thursday morning, Kylie woke up when Socks bumped her chin with his nose. As she blinked away the fogginess of sleep, she stroked Socks's soft feline fur. The sun spilled through the window and she watched as the day's brightness and shadows flickered on the ceiling, fighting for space—a war of sorts between light and darkness.

As the battle took place, she felt her mood host a similar conflict. Her life seemed to be a mêlée of so many problems and yet so many possibilities. She'd lost Derek, but gained Lucas. She'd lost the bond with her stepdad but found Daniel. She'd lost being human, but was now supernatural.

And today was the day she was supposed to meet her grandfather and discover just what it all meant, but she doubted that would happen. A frown pulled at her lips and the darker side of her mood tried to take over.

Not that she'd let it win. She closed her eyes and tried to think positive thoughts. But her mind went to Hannah and the fact that Kylie shouldn't postpone telling Holiday any longer that her sister was dead. Just thinking about how that conversation would go took another bite out of Kylie's disposition.

Then her heart reminded her that Lucas hadn't shown up last night, despite the fact he'd told her he would. That pretty much made it official. The dark side, the bad mood, had won. Glancing back up at the ceiling, she couldn't help but notice there were indeed more shadows than sunlight.

For some crazy reason, she remembered Nana telling her to enjoy her childhood because soon enough she'd be an adult. Was this adulthood? To wake up every day and know it would bring both good and bad? To do things you had to do, even if you wished you didn't have to do them?

Then she recalled another piece of Nana's advice. *Just remember, sweetie, sometimes we can't change what happens, but we can change how we let those things affect us.*

"Easier said than done, Nana." Kylie inhaled a big gulp of frustration and the sweet smell of roses tickled her senses. Turning her head, she saw the single pink rose on her nightstand. The memory of Lucas having robbed his grandmother's rose garden and filling Kylie's room with roses sent her bad mood on time-out. Then, seeing the note beside the rose, she sat up and reached for the slip of paper.

Kylie,

Sorry I was late. Something came up and I had to go visit my dad. You were out like a light when I got here. But damn, you are so beautiful when you sleep. If Della hadn't heard me opening your window and poked her head in and shot me the bird for waking her up—she's impossible—I would have climbed in bed with you just to feel you next to me.

You have no idea how much I'd like that. To feel you against me. All of you.

Sweet dreams,
Lucas

Kylie reached for the rose and placed it to her nose. The sweet scent made her smile. Maybe the bad mood wasn't going to win after all.

. . .

Kylie reconsidered her positive attitude when a couple of hours later, she batted at the bugs swarming around her as she moved into the woods with Holiday and Burnett. But it wasn't the bugs causing the deterioration of her good mood. It was one certain dark-haired, blue-eyed werewolf.

Kylie should have been excited about going to the falls. She always felt better after a visit. But right now, she didn't want to feel better. She wanted to feel . . . mad.

Wait. She didn't *want* to feel it, she did feel mad.

Mad at the rose-leaving, note-writing were.

She'd completely let go of her aggravation about Lucas not showing up last night. She'd tried to set aside the fact that he'd practically told her he had to keep secrets from her. While she didn't like it, she'd even accepted that Fredericka, his one-time sex buddy, would always be within touching distance of him, when Kylie wasn't anywhere close enough to touch him herself. She had worked at overcoming the fact that his grandmother, his father, and even his entire pack, were against their being together.

She'd done a lot of setting aside, overcoming, and accepting. And after this morning, she realized that it might have been too much—because after not showing up last night, after hardly seeing her yesterday, he'd barely acknowledged her this morning in the cafeteria.

Another mosquito buzzed past and she swiped at the air, sending the pest headfirst into a tree. *Bzzz . . . splat!*

Couldn't Lucas have come over and had breakfast with her? She wouldn't have even blamed him if he'd brought Clara with him. But no, all she'd gotten was a smile, and even that smile had seemed somehow purposefully short. Then he'd joined the were table with all his other friends, his pack—people who clearly came before her now and probably always would.

Last night, he'd climbed into her bedroom way after midnight while she'd been asleep. He'd left her a rose and a sweet note, and this morning all she'd gotten from him was a half-assed smile. What was up with that?

She sure as hell didn't know. Who was she kidding? She knew exactly what was up. She wasn't good enough for him, because she wasn't a were.

That stung. Really stung. Then, to make matters worse, when Derek sat beside her, Lucas had the audacity to text her and say he didn't like it.

Right. He didn't like the fact that Derek had sat beside her, but he'd chosen not to sit with her. Instead, his sexy little butt was sandwiched between Fredericka and one of the new female weres, who was all over Lucas to the point that even Fredericka was unhappy about it.

Yeah, Kylie could hear Lucas telling her that he no longer cared about Fredericka. She could hear him saying that he hadn't asked the new girl to sit beside him, and she could hear him saying he had to be loyal to his pack. And maybe Kylie was wrong to feel angry, or maybe she wasn't so much angry as she was just tired of playing second fiddle.

Second fiddle sucked.

Another mosquito bit the dust when she swiped it off her cheek.

"You might want to slow down," Burnett said, moving up beside her with his long-legged strides.

Kylie glanced at him. He studied her briefly, then shifted his gaze back to the terrain as if expecting something to jump out at them. He'd been acting antsy since they walked into the woods, not that Kylie paid too much attention; her heart had been too busy fiddling with her second fiddle matters to care if Burnett had drunk too much caffeine.

"Seriously, slow down," Burnett said.

"Why?" Kylie asked.

He briefly glanced over his shoulder again. "As wonderful as faes are, they're slow."

Kylie sighed. She hadn't realized that she was moving at a fast sprint. A non-human sprint. A non-witch sprint, too. Which meant she wasn't really a witch, right? Glancing back, she saw Holiday power walking to keep up.

"Sorry." Kylie slowed down and noticed how Burnett kept looking around as if he expected something to jump out at them. Had something happened? And if so, did it have anything to do with her?

Holiday's footfalls sounded beside Kylie. She glanced from the nervous vampire to Holiday.

"Thanks for slowing down," Holiday said, sounding a bit breathless. In less than a minute, Burnett lagged behind them, just out of vampire hearing range. Probably at Holiday's insistence. No doubt she wanted to talk with Kylie, and Holiday didn't like knowing he'd listen in.

The verdant smells of the forest filled Kylie's senses. For the first time since she entered the woods she recalled her grandfather and the fog. She immediately tried to listen with her heart to see if she felt the calling sensation from before; it wasn't there. Then she wondered if somehow the whole fog episode was behind Burnett's edginess. Or even worse, had they tried to return and set off the alarms? Would Burnett even tell her about it if they had?

Probably not.

She looked back at Burnett. What did the vamp know?

Moving closer to Holiday, Kylie asked, "Can you tell me something and be honest about it?"

Holiday's footsteps on moist earth made squishy sounds, as if Kylie's question had added a weight to her step. "I don't lie to you."

"By omission you do. Not being up-front about something is as bad as lying." And then there was the issue of how little Holiday shared about herself. As much as Kylie confided in Holiday, it hurt to realize it wasn't a two-way street.

"I don't purposefully keep things from you." The truth in her tone hung in the damp air. They walked without talking for a few moments.

"What is it you want to know?" Holiday asked.

Kylie fought back her frustration with Holiday, knowing her anger with Lucas was affecting her attitude. "What's with Burnett? He seems extra alert. Has he . . . learned something that concerns me? Does he have news about my grandfather? Today was supposed to be the day he showed and yet . . . I don't think there's a chance in hell that he's coming. And no one is even saying anything about it, as if it never happened."

Holiday frowned. "Because we didn't think it would happen, we decided to downplay it. But Burnett and I talked earlier about it and he hasn't heard anything about your grandfather. But . . . I agree about him being . . . let's call it on the defensive. I asked about it. He says he's feeling jittery." Her tone seemed to say that Holiday didn't buy it.

And neither did Kylie. Something was up. But what?

As they continued over the rocky path, an unnatural cold seemed to sweep in with every other breeze. Someone, someone dead, was close by. She gave Burnett another glance over her shoulder and remembered their talk about ghosts.

Was that the issue bothering him?

Holiday slowed down and peered back with concern. A slight huff of air leaked from her lips and her expression shifted from concern to annoyance. Not just any kind of annoyance, but the kind that stemmed from the opposite sex.

The mood must have been contagious because Kylie's own thoughts ventured to her opposite-sex issues and she wondered if men weren't just created to drive women crazy.

A few more minutes down the path, Holiday spoke up. "Now it's your turn. What's up with you? And don't tell me nothing, because you have anger dripping from you like a leaky faucet."

Kylie frowned, too angry to deny her feelings. "Lucas is what's up."

"Boy trouble, huh?"

"Boy catastrophe is more like it. I'm not sure I can do this."

"Do what?" Concern sounded in Holiday's voice.

"Do Lucas," Kylie said.

Holiday made a funny face and raised one eyebrow.

"Not do him as in . . . get naked," Kylie blurted out, realizing what she'd said and thinking this was the cause of Holiday's odd expression.

"I mean, dealing with being the last thing on his to-do list. I mean him treating me as if I'm an afterthought in his life. I mean me feeling as if everyone he knows and cares about thinks I'm not good enough for him because I'm not a were."

Sympathy filled Holiday's eyes. "If it helps, I don't think Lucas shares the old beliefs of the weres. Most of the young weres don't agree with them, but there's pressure from the elders in their society to follow them anyway."

"I know," Kylie said. "And I also know that the only reason he's abiding by the stupid rules is because he needs his father's approval to make the Council so he can change things. But when he won't even smile at me for longer than a second, it hurts!" she seethed. "I guess that makes me a selfish twit for feeling this way." Her words resonated deep inside her and the guilt, like flies on a bad banana, started buzzing around her chest.

"No." Holiday cut her green eyes toward Kylie as they took the bend in the trail. "It doesn't make you selfish. It makes you normal. No one wants to be made to feel as if they aren't good enough."

"But I still feel like a selfish twit," Kylie said. The sound of the falls started playing in her ears, and even from this distance she felt the calming in her mood. "Or I feel selfish when I'm not feeling furious."

Holiday leaned in and brushed shoulders with her. "Your feelings are valid. Don't feel guilty. Sure, Lucas is making these choices for a reason. It's part of his quest, and we all must pay a price for following our own paths. But . . ." She paused in thought. "It's not always fair to ask others to pay that price." She glanced back at Burnett again.

Kylie sensed Holiday's words held a personal significance. In the last few days, Kylie suspected the relationship between Burnett and Holiday had gone backward. And she didn't think it was Burnett doing the backtracking.

"I think he'd be willing to pay it," Kylie said.

Holiday frowned. "I was talking about you and Lucas."

"Right," Kylie said. *But you were thinking about you and Burnett.*

They moved off the path and into the alcove of thick trees as they completed the journey to the falls. The moist smell of wet earth perfumed the air, the sound of rushing water played in the symphony of the woodsy sounds, and the serene ambience grew stronger.

Kylie's anger, her frustrations, all seemed lighter with each step. And when they arrived, it was . . . surreal. Each time, she seemed to forget how good it felt. They stood on the bank of the creek and stared through the misty air at the spray of water cascading downward.

Kylie heard Holiday draw in a deep, calm breath that matched her own.

"What is it about this place?" Kylie asked.

"Magic. Power." Holiday reached down to remove her shoes and Kylie did the same. "Back in the 1960s, there was actually a supernatural doctor in botany science who came here to prove that all this could be explained by some chemical compounds in some plant life. A natural drug of sorts."

"But how could that be when not everyone experiences it?" Kylie unlaced her shoes.

"Ahh, but those not welcome here generally feel the opposite, an uncomfortable sensation that urges them to flee. Which is why this scientist believed it was a chemical reaction. Meaning, the few supernaturals who experience positive emotions were just genetically inclined to react differently to the plant's compounds. Like how some groups of people react differently to drugs."

"And what did he find?" Kylie asked, intrigued by the subject, but no more believing it was a drug than she believed in Santa Claus.

Holiday pulled off her shoes and set them beside a rock and stood up, glancing down at Kylie with a slight smile on her lips. "Not a damn thing. After only a few weeks of working in the area, he and his teams suddenly gave up the grant that was going to pay for the project. Rumor was the Death Angels scared them away."

Kylie moved her gaze around the verdant and beautiful landscape. The mingling of mist and sprays of sunshine beaming down from above the trees spoke of the power and magic that Holiday had mentioned. The ambience that existed here was too reverent to be considered a drug, and the natural splendor too spiritual to be dissected and studied under the microscope.

"I can see how the Death Angels wouldn't like unbelievers digging around. I'm glad they chased them away."

"Ditto," Holiday said.

Standing up, Kylie's bare feet sank into the moss-covered bank. Wiggling her toes, she bent down and rolled up her jeans.

Right then something swooped down in front of her. She swallowed her scream when she saw it was the blue jay. The bird she'd brought back to life that had somehow imprinted on Kylie and kept stopping in for visits. Hovering right in front of her, it sang as if personally performing a ballad just for her.

"I'm not your mama," Kylie said. "Go, find your own way. Do what all birds do. Leave the nest, so to speak. Find a hunky blue jay to flutter after."

"That's sweet." Holiday chuckled.

"Maybe, but it's also weird," Kylie muttered.

With her jeans rolled up, she took a step into the creek. The cool water lapping around her ankles felt heavenly. Her heart that had moments earlier ached with raw emotion now felt lighter. Things, at least for right now, felt right. Her world felt manageable; her problems solvable. She eagerly embraced the feeling.

Yet if she'd learned anything from her visits to this special place, it was that even a manageable life didn't mean things would be perfect. A trip to the falls didn't fix anything. It simply offered one the strength to face the hurdles.

Life could still hurt like a paper cut right across the heart.

And she had a few paper-cut scars to prove it. A vision of Ellie filled her heart. Yet as a breeze carrying the misty coolness brushed Kylie's face, the ache faded into acceptance. Every new day was about opportunities. You couldn't always control life, just your response to it.

Stopping halfway across the creek, she turned to look at Holiday. The camp leader stood gazing back at Burnett, who stood in the trees. The expression on her face held concern, fascination, and something else.

Love. Burnett and Holiday were meant to be together. The feeling came on so strong and with such certainty that there seemed to be a message with it—a message Kylie couldn't quite read. Did it mean she was supposed to help make that happen? Or could she trust that if left alone, love would find a way?

And could she feel the same about her and Lucas?

Not that she was prepared to call it love. Nor had he called it that.

But Derek had. *I'm in love with you, Kylie.*

Kylie closed her eyes and tried not to think about anything other than the calm feeling that the falls provided.

Chapter Eighteen

Time seemed to stop as Kylie and Holiday sat side by side in the alcove of the falls. The wall of water diffused the incoming light; only the briefest rays of yellow sun passed through. And when they did, the light caught in the mist droplets and danced in the air. The water rushed down with a low roar, and tiny molecules of moisture brushed against their faces.

The thought occurred to Kylie that maybe now would be a good time to tell Holiday about her sister. If anything could help curb the sting of the news, it would be the magic of this place. Yet even with the peacefulness embracing her, the idea of telling Holiday about the death of her sister had Kylie's heart hurting.

Then a familiar chill filled the damp air. Hannah materialized, standing in the pool of water. Her green eyes, bright with tears and filled with sadness, focused on Holiday.

Oblivious to her sister's presence, Holiday stared at the wall of water rushing down. She rubbed her arms as though she were chilled, and then turned her head and met Kylie's eyes. "A visitor?"

Kylie nodded, her throat getting tighter with emotion when she glanced again at Hannah's tears.

Holiday shrugged. "That's odd. They normally don't come back here." She leaned back on the rocks and stared up at the cave ceiling, as if giving Kylie space to deal with the spirit.

"She hates me," Hannah said. *"And I don't blame her. What I did was unforgivable."* Shame now entered Hannah's wet eyes.

Kylie almost asked Hannah what she'd done, but decided to let her be the one to initiate the conversation. Kylie sat there in silence, feeling the cold of death that somehow seemed to blend with the calm of the falls.

She studied Hannah's emotion-filled expression and she knew the spirit had found her way through the confusion of death enough to communicate.

Enough to remember. Did she recall the moments before her death? The name of her killer perhaps? But all Kylie saw in Hannah's expression was regret.

Watching Hannah took Kylie back to her own near-death experience, to when Mario and his friends had knocked her off the ledge. She'd thought she was about to die. And she would have if Red, Mario's grandson, hadn't saved her and sacrificed himself in the process.

She remembered the regret that consumed her when she thought it was the end. Probably the same emotions Hannah felt now. Wouldn't everyone feel that way? Living, Kylie supposed, meant making mistakes, as well as garnering karma points.

While Kylie had never really defined her job/gift as a ghost whisperer, she supposed it entailed helping the spirits recall the good they'd done as much as helping them absolve any outstanding mistakes. It seemed that when you were alive, you spent most of your time trying to forgive others; upon death, it was yourself you mostly needed to forgive.

I'll bet you two were close, Kylie said. *I imagine you had a lot of fun as sisters.*

Hannah looked up at Kylie. *"We did. I just wish . . ."*

When Hannah didn't continue, Kylie asked, *What is it that I need to do for you? Is it just telling her about you? Is it getting you and the others out of the mass grave?*

"No, it's more." She paused as if still trying to remember. "*It can't happen again.*" Hannah's whisper echoed against the cave's rock walls and the cold of her presence built.

Kylie pulled one knee closer to her chest. *What can't happen again?*

Hannah stepped closer, looking lost in thought. "*I can't look at her without feeling . . . I was so wrong. So jealous. I got what I deserved. I deserved to die, but the others didn't. It has to stop.*" Even more tears filled her eyes. The sound of rushing water punctuated by the quietness of the mist-filled air added a strange kind of eeriness to the moment.

"*He wants her.*" Hannah took another step forward. Desperation filled her eyes. "*And you have to stop him.*"

Kylie's gaze shifted from the spirit's face and became captured by the still water that didn't even stir as Hannah inched forward. Her sad spirit stopped when she stood directly over Holiday, staring down at her with a mixture of love and regret.

Realizing what Hannah had said, Kylie asked, *Who? Stop who from doing what?*

Holiday's phone rang and Kylie looked over at her. The camp leader sat up, her brows pinched. "Okay, that's odd, too. Phones don't usually work in here." Pulling her phone from her pocket, she eyed the number on the screen.

Kylie heard Holiday's breath catch at the same time as Hannah's. The spirit let out a sound of despair and took off running through the falls. Her footfalls, though quick, fell silent on the rock floor.

Right before Hannah's spirit darted through the wall of water, she glanced back at Holiday, who stared transfixed at the number on the phone. Then she disappeared, taking with her the cold that she'd brought.

"Who is it?" Kylie asked Holiday.

Holiday shook her head. "It's . . . Blake."

"Who's Blake?" Kylie asked, somehow certain he was a clue to all this. Was he the one Kylie had to stop from doing something bad to Holiday?

Was Holiday's life in danger?

The hum of the rushing water was interrupted by the sound of someone running, splashing through the falls. Kylie and Holiday looked up.

Burnett, standing guard outside the falls, shot through the rush of water, his face etched with panic. His clothes were wet, and his dark black hair was scattered across his brow and dripping water down his face. "Where did she go?" He blinked, and then his gaze landed on Holiday. His eyes widened. He shook his head in pure confusion. "You just . . . ran out of here. How could you . . . ?"

"What?" Holiday asked.

Burnett just stood there, his complexion paler than its normal olive color, staring as if he'd seen a ghost.

Kylie suddenly realized that was exactly what had just happened. Burnett had seen Hannah.

Oh, shit, Kylie thought. Burnett not only could smell ghosts, he could see them, too.

"How could I run where?" Holiday asked again, tucking her cell phone back in her pocket. "You're not making any sense."

Kylie didn't know what compelled her to do it, but she glanced at Burnett and shook her head, indicating that he shouldn't tell Holiday about what he'd seen.

He opened his mouth and then closed it and studied Kylie. She shook her head slightly again and she knew he'd understood.

He focused on Holiday again. Then, still looking perplexed, he answered, "I misspoke. I thought I heard you call me."

"No," Holiday said. "I didn't."

"Fine," he blurted out, and in a blink of an eye he shot back through the wall of water.

Holiday stared wide-eyed at the spot where he'd stood a flicker of a second earlier. "I know you told me he'd come back here and it's not as if I didn't believe you, but I guess I had to see it to wrap my head around it. I don't . . . I've never seen anyone be able to come back here who wasn't blessed."

Kylie's mind raced with what to say, but then she remembered Holiday's phone call and the anguish in Hannah's expression when she'd rushed out. Then Kylie recalled the distinct feeling that whoever that caller was had something to do with Hannah and could be the person the spirit seemed to be so worried about.

"Who's Blake?" Kylie asked again.

"Don't you have an appointment with one of the new teachers?" Burnett asked Holiday fifteen minutes later as they came to the clearing of the woods after they walked back from the falls. "Why don't you head back to the office and I'll see Kylie to her cabin?"

Kylie cut her eyes up at Burnett and she knew his game plan. He wanted her alone so he could interrogate her about what had happened at the falls. She could tell by his silence and the color of his eyes that the interrogation wasn't going to go easy.

"I still have half an hour if you have something else to do." Holiday studied Burnett with open curiosity, probably confused about his change in eye color. On the walk back, she'd come out and asked him about his ability to walk into the falls. He'd shrugged and said he hadn't given it much thought.

Which was a huge, honking lie. He'd obviously thought about it a lot. And he'd gone back to thinking about it because he didn't speak again for a while. With silence following them as they made their way through the woods, Kylie had done her own thinking, or worrying. Trying to figure out the mystery of Blake with each step, she'd fretted until she'd chewed her bottom lip sore.

When asked about the caller earlier, Holiday had danced around the truth with her answer: "Someone I used to know."

That hadn't told Kylie squat. She'd been tempted to blurt out a list of questions.

Did Blake also know your twin sister that I'm not supposed to know about?

Do you think this Blake character could have done something to your sister, like kill her?

Do I need to tell Burnett about Blake just in case he is the person that I'm supposed to not let hurt you?

Oh yeah, Kylie had a lot to fret over, including the upcoming interrogation from Burnett.

"Nah," Burnett said. "I'll see Kylie to her cabin. You go relax."

Holiday's brow tightened in a total non-relaxing way and she looked at Kylie as if she might know why the vamp was acting so weird. Kylie shrugged.

"Okay." Holiday walked toward the office.

Kylie started the trek to her cabin and made a bet with herself on how long it would take Burnett to start hitting her with questions. One minute? Two?

"Start talking!" Burnett ground out less than twenty seconds later.

Okay, so maybe she overestimated his patience.

He stopped walking and looked at her, his expression one big scowl. "Who was that at the falls who looked like Holiday? Did you use your witch powers to do that?"

Kylie hesitated, unsure how to answer him. She remembered how she'd felt learning she'd be spending the rest of her life hanging out with dead people.

"I didn't do anything."

"Then who was it?" he demanded. "And why did you feel the need to keep this from Holiday?" When she paused, he added, "Now, Kylie! I want answers. And don't forget that I can tell when you're lying."

She exhaled. Understanding his frustration, but . . . "It's Holiday's twin sister."

His brows pinched in confusion. "Holiday has a twin?"

Kylie nodded.

Burnett looked off for a second, then back at her. "Why wouldn't she have ever mentioned this?" He ran a palm over his face, frustration and disappointment filling his eyes. He blurted out his own answer. "Because she doesn't confide in me about anything."

His gaze shot back to Kylie. "But wait. How could this twin be in the camp without setting off the alarms? I checked my phone when I went back outside the falls. The alarms hadn't been triggered and there was no bad weather to make me believe someone could have fooled the system."

"She didn't fool the system. She . . ." There wasn't an easy way to say this, but she still paused to try and find the right words.

"She must have," Burnett continued. "How else would—?"

"She's dead," Kylie said, feeling the pressure to answer under his intense scowl. "Holiday's sister is a ghost."

Chapter Nineteen

"Her twin is dead?" Burnett's tone rang with empathy. "How? What happened?"

Kylie felt a warmth in knowing that he thought of Holiday first before realizing exactly what this meant—not that she didn't expect him to see the obvious any minute now.

Or maybe less than a minute. His eyes widened with hints of panic and his mouth became slack.

"No! She can't be . . . because I can't . . ." He shook his head. "No."

"It's not much different than smelling them. And you already knew that you could do that," Kylie said, hoping to ease the shock.

"It's a hell of a lot different." He raked a hand through his hair. "How could . . . I'm vampire and we don't . . . We don't see spirits."

"I know. I remember Holiday saying that." Kylie paused. "What's even stranger is that you saw her, and normally only the person connected to the spirit sees them. I don't see Holiday's ghosts and she doesn't see mine. So why would you see Hannah?"

"I'm not supposed to see any of them!" he bellowed. "I'm vampire. Very, very few vampires are given this secondary power."

Kylie twitched her brows at Burnett's pattern. "Maybe you're not a hundred percent vampire. Your great-great-grandma could have been a hybrid, and it just kind of popped up now."

He slapped his forehead. "Does my pattern not look all vampire?"

Kylie shrugged. "Yes." She looked at him with empathy. "But considering what I've been through, I've kind of learned not to put a lot of stock in what someone's pattern shows."

He stared at Kylie as if she'd morphed into something evil. "That only happens to you."

"Yeah. Sometimes it feels that way." She found his comment somewhat humorous. She did another shrug, biting back her smile because she didn't think what little sense of humor Burnett had was functioning right now.

"However," Kylie continued, "we can't deny that something's going on. Your pattern says all vampire, and full-blooded vampires aren't usually ghost whisperers."

"Maybe it's punishment because I went into the falls."

Kylie's first instinct, being a ghost whisperer, was to feel a bit insulted that her gift was viewed as retribution; her second instinct was to remember that in the beginning that's exactly how she'd felt. As if she'd been punished.

"What?" he asked, as if sensing she had something to say.

Put on the spot, she said exactly what came across her mind. "To channel Holiday here, it's a gift, not a punishment."

"It's a punishment to me. Frigging hell!" he muttered.

Kylie still didn't understand how it could happen. Because even Holiday had said that very few vampires had the gift of ghost-whispering. "Seriously, your parents are full-blooded vampires, right?"

He stared at her as if the question required some thought. Looking away, he gazed silently at the sky. After several long seconds he looked back at her. "Okay . . . let's forget about my issues with all this." He ran his palm over his face again as if trying to wipe away his confusion. "Why didn't you want Holiday knowing her sister's spirit was here?"

Kylie bit down on the edge of her bottom lip again, then released it when she found it sore. "I don't think Holiday knows. I wanted to figure out exactly—"

"Wait. You don't think Holiday knows what?" he asked, impatient.

"That her sister's dead."

His eyes widened. "She doesn't know? Shit!" He exhaled. "How did her sister die? How long ago?"

Even before she answered, Kylie suspected his reaction. He wasn't going to like this. "She was murdered. She and two other girls."

Discontent filled his gaze and his posture hardened. Two points for guessing his reaction, Kylie thought, and tried not to be intimidated by his fury.

"Murdered?" he bit out. "How freaking long have you known this, and why in God's name are you just now telling me?"

"I . . . I've been trying to figure it out. Hannah's just now able to tell me things. And I'm still trying to put it all together." A small part of her wondered if maybe he was right, and that she'd been wrong to try to deal with this herself. But she hadn't been doing this alone. She had Derek. Then again, perhaps she should have taken it to Burnett instead of Derek.

Her doubt started to rise and then eased. The calm that lingered from the falls swelled in her chest and somehow she knew she'd been right to follow her instinct. And wasn't that what Holiday told her to always do?

"Damn it. You should have come to me so I could help do the figuring."

Kylie held his gaze. "As if you were receptive to hearing about my ghost issues. Besides, I was following what I felt needed to be done."

Burnett's stance relaxed as if he'd seen reason in her words. "But if it's about Holiday, I'm always receptive."

Kylie saw it in his eyes again. His loyalty to Holiday. Because he loved her, Kylie realized. That realization led her to think about Derek and his willingness to help her with ghosts when no one else would.

Thinking of Derek led her heart back to Lucas. The trip to the falls had lessened her animosity toward him, but not completely. Sooner or later, the two of them needed to talk. She just didn't know how that talk would end. Or even how it would begin. Was she right to feel angry at him for keeping his distance when she knew why he did it—to prevent issues with his dad so he could get voted on the were Council? Shouldn't she be more accepting and understanding?

Burnett reached back and squeezed his neck as if to relieve his tension. "Holiday has to be told."

Kylie dug the toe of her right tennis shoe into the dirt and focused on the problem at hand instead of her Lucas issues. "I know. But I thought maybe if I knew exactly what it was Hannah wanted, then it would be easier."

"You think she wants something?"

Kylie nodded. "They always want something. That's why they haven't crossed over. That's why they come to us."

"Come to you," he said, and then added, "Do you have any idea what she could need?"

Kylie prepared herself for his reaction again. "I'm not completely sure. At first I thought it could be just to get her and the others from the makeshift grave. Maybe to find out who did this to her. But now . . . now I think she feels she has to protect Holiday from something or . . . someone."

His expression darkened, but this time his angst didn't focus on her. His eyes brightened with an instinctual need to protect Holiday.

"Before you ask, I don't know who or exactly what poses a danger to Holiday." Kylie suspected it had to do with a man named Blake, but she wasn't completely sure she should share that with Burnett right now. The last time she shared some personal information about Holiday with Burnett, Holiday had flipped. If Kylie discovered Blake posed a threat, then she'd tell Burnett everything. But she needed more information. Information that neither Holiday nor Hannah seemed willing to give.

He waved his hands out in front of him in frustration. "Then go find Hannah and tell her you need answers."

"It doesn't work that way. You don't go to the ghost. They come to you."

His frown tightened. "I don't like this," he said. "None of it."

On that point, Kylie could agree with him.

He stood there, staring out at the trees as if the answers could be plucked from the limbs. She got the feeling he wasn't accustomed to not being able to get information when he demanded it. If he really was a ghost whisperer, he had a lot to learn about patience. She pitied the poor ghost who showed up first.

Burnett finally looked back at Kylie. "Okay, tell me everything you know. Everything. We'll figure this out."

Even before Kylie started talking she had a distinct feeling that getting Burnett involved was going to be a game changer, and she wasn't sure if that was going to be a good thing . . . or a bad thing.

That afternoon, Kylie stood in front of the open fridge, staring. Listening to the hum of the appliance and savoring the cool air hitting her face while Miranda and Della sat at the table behind her.

Amazing how cool felt so much better when it wasn't coming from death. Not that she wouldn't like Hannah to drop in for a visit just now. She really needed answers. But if she'd learned anything, it was that you couldn't rush ghosts.

Kylie had somehow managed to convince Burnett to give Hannah a little more time before breaking Holiday's heart and telling her that her sister was dead. For some unknown reason, Kylie sensed that knowing exactly what Hannah needed was important. Not that Kylie didn't worry it might be her own desire to postpone hurting Holiday that encouraged this decision.

Burnett also agreed that going to the café to check and see if they could get any information about Cara M. would be a good thing. He was going to arrange for them to go out there Saturday morning with Derek. Burnett wanted Derek to go because when she'd told Burnett about what Derek had uncovered so far, Burnett was impressed at Derek's investigative skills.

Never mind that Lucas was going to have a shit fit when he found out Burnett had asked Derek to join them. But who knew, he might not even find out. With as little face time as she had with Lucas lately, he might never know. Or care.

She closed her eyes. He cared. He just cared more about other things right now.

Nipping at her lip, she remembered she still hadn't answered any of Lucas's texts today. She didn't know how to answer them because she didn't know how she felt anymore. One minute she was mad, the next she was contemplating if being angry with him was fair.

"What's wrong?" Miranda asked.

Kylie opened her eyes, focusing on what was in front of her and not what was going on inside her. "We're out of soda."

"Why don't you just zap us some?"

Kylie looked back at Miranda. "Zap as in . . . ?"

"Zap," Miranda said, and held up her pinky.

"Uh, why don't *you* just zap us some?" Kylie asked, and saw Della's eyes widen.

"Because you need to become a zapper," Miranda said matter-of-factly. "You need to embrace your inner Wiccan spirit."

Kylie had somehow avoided any zapping since the whole paperweight to Burnett's crotch incident. And she'd like to continue avoiding it, but from the look in Miranda's eyes, she knew that wasn't going to be feasible. Well, not without hurting the witch's feelings.

And Kylie hated hurting anyone's feelings. Especially Miranda's.

"Okay . . . how do I do it?" She shut the fridge and inhaled. "Without endangering any of our lives."

Miranda squealed and wiggled her butt in her chair with excitement.

Della shot Kylie a look of approval as if to say she'd done the right thing. "I like the part about not endangering our lives," Della added with a smile.

"Take some very deep breaths," Miranda said. "Relax. Concentrate. Then envision a frosty six-pack and wiggle your pinky."

A frosty six-pack. Kylie inhaled. She held out her pinky, and right then Della chimed in. "We are talking a six-pack of soda and not a cold guy with good-looking abs, right?"

There was a strange kind of sizzle in the air. And suddenly appearing in front of the refrigerator was a shirtless, shivering guy with great abs. His dark hair hung over his brow and his blue eyes studied the three of them in complete bafflement.

"What the . . . !" he muttered.

Kylie gasped.

Miranda giggled.

Della snorted with laughter.

"Go away!" Kylie screamed, her face blood red as she wiggled her pinky at the hot guy. He was gone as quickly as he appeared. Kylie looked back at her two best friends, who were now in fits of laughter. She slapped her hand over her heart, which was racing.

"Don't ever talk me into doing that again!" she screeched.

"Wasn't that . . . oh, what's his name? Zac something?" Della asked. "The actor, I mean."

"Oh my Gawd, it was!" Miranda said.

"I always thought he looks a little like Steve, don't you think?" Della asked.

"Oh, crap!" Kylie buried her face in her hands. "I didn't hurt him, did I? It won't, like, give him cancer or anything?"

"No," Miranda answered, a giggle still sounding in her voice.

"Good," Della said, rubbing her hands together. "Then bring him back. I want to see if he really looks like Steve."

"Are you freaking nuts?" Kylie asked Della. Then she focused on Miranda. "Will he remember this? Will he think he lost his mind?"

"It happened so fast, he'll probably think he imagined it. Besides, it's not your fault." Miranda giggled again. "It's Della's." Miranda pointed at the accused.

"Oh, right. Blame the vampire!" Della bellowed.

Miranda rolled her eyes. "Della put the image in your thoughts and for some reason you just envisioned Zac." Miranda smiled again. "You are obviously attracted to him."

Kylie started to deny it, but couldn't.

"I'm still not taking the hit on this one," Della said.

Miranda looked at Della. "I guess I should have told you to be quiet. Sorry." She covered her mouth when she snickered again. Then she sat up straighter. "But . . . wow. I have to tell you I'm shocked. Only the most powerful witches can transport human beings. Even my mom can't do that."

"Don't you guys think he looks like Steve?" Della asked again.

Kylie dropped into the chair. "I don't care who he looks like. I'm not doing it again. I have no control and no knowledge. I'm sure to screw up."

"That's why you need practice. Besides, nothing bad happened," Miranda said.

"Seriously? I brought a half-naked movie star into our cabin!"

"And what part of that is bad?" Della asked. "I mean . . . I hate to say this, but for the first time I'm seeing that it might be cool to be a witch."

"Thank you!" Miranda sat up straighter.

"I mean, can you just zap yourself anything you want? A hot guy? A cup of O-negative blood? A new pair of jeans?" Della asked.

"Please, you can't do that," Miranda said. "It's totally against the rules."

"But . . ." Kylie stared at Miranda. "You just had me do it."

"Yeah, but you're a newbie. It doesn't count." Miranda looked back at Della. "That's not to say I can't do anything. If it's for a greater good, it'll be okay. If it's for one's own benefit, well, it has to be within reason. If I'm given a tuna sandwich and want turkey, that's not a big deal. It's swapping one meat for another. But if I even do it too much, I'd get called on it."

"By who?" Della asked. "The meat gods?"

Miranda frowned as if to say this was serious and Kylie couldn't agree more. "By the Wicca society."

"Wait," Kylie said. "You mean, they know what I do?"

Della cleared her throat as if in warning, but Kylie didn't understand the warning. She was too concerned about the Wicca society knowing her stupid mistakes to pay attention.

"Yeah," Miranda said. "They're like Santa Claus with their magic crystal balls. They know if you've been naughty or good."

"Great! So someone's looking into a magic ball right now and knows I conjured up a half-naked hot actor? " Kylie asked.

"You did what?" the deep male voice asked from behind Kylie.

Kylie froze, worried that Zac had returned. The fact that she wasn't even the least bit happy about it said a lot about her disposition, too. Then she ran the voice through her head again and recognized the dark tenor.

Crap. She was in trouble now.

Chapter Twenty

Kylie turned in her chair and faced a puzzled-looking Lucas. He wore a pair of black jeans and a solid light blue T-shirt. The shirt fit just tight enough that she knew his abs could compete with Zac's.

He continued to stare. "Did you just say—?"

"It was . . . a spell gone bad. I zapped a guy here for a couple of seconds." Normally, she'd be blushing, but her emotional dilemma with him chased away the embarrassment.

She stood. She felt antsy just sitting there. Her chest swelled with both joy at seeing him, and angst over her unresolved anger toward him. She wanted to kiss him, but she also wanted to let it all out and cry.

"Oh." He looked pointedly at Della and Miranda. Before he put the question into words, they got up—Miranda moved nonchalantly, Della's stance exuded a bad attitude.

"We'll be on the porch." The vamp's tone matched her body language.

"Thanks." While Kylie hadn't confided her most recent misgivings about Lucas to them, she knew they suspected. Just like she knew what went on in their lives. She watched as her two best friends left to give her privacy.

Kylie's gaze stayed fixed on Lucas and his deep blue eyes stayed on her until the door closed. She turned and faced the refrigerator and tried to decide how she felt . . . besides hurt. Just to give herself something to do, she opened the appliance.

"You want something to drink?" she asked, not that there was anything but pickle juice in an otherwise empty jar of pickles and a bottle of Della's blood.

"I texted you three times and e-mailed and you haven't responded." He sounded hurt.

Closing her eyes, she tried to push away the wiggle of guilt tightening her stomach. "I haven't checked my e-mail." She shut the fridge and moved over to the computer desk.

"What are you doing?" he asked.

"Checking my e-mail. You said you e-mailed me." It sounded stupid. Okay, it didn't just sound stupid, it was stupid, but she needed a few minutes to think.

Was she wrong to be angry?

Or right?

She dropped into the chair. With the computer on, it took one mouse click to land on her e-mail. One downward scan of her eyes to see Lucas's name.

The subject on all three of his e-mails was the same: *miss you*.

A knot formed in her throat.

"Are you mad at me for something?" he asked.

"Yes." Her gaze moved back to the screen and it felt as if her heart started swelling—big, then bigger—until it felt as if it was outgrowing her chest. The ache was real and made it hard to breathe.

She swallowed. "No."

"Is it yes or no? Are you mad or not?" He sounded hurt. Or angry. Maybe both.

She closed her eyes and while she didn't hear him, she sensed he'd moved closer. His scent, a wonderfully earthy smell, seemed to take up residence in her cabin.

She inhaled. "Maybe."

"Hmm." He did indeed sound closer. Too close. Right behind her close. Touchable close.

As tempting as it was to turn around, she didn't. She stared at the screen and held her breath.

"Is this what they mean by a woman having the prerogative to change her mind?" A slight sound of humor rang in his voice.

"It could be," she muttered.

"Is this about me not showing up last night? I left a note. You were asleep."

"It's not about that." Her gaze stayed fixed on the computer screen. She spotted three e-mails from her dad. Another emotionally hard thing she needed to deal with. Knowing her mom was dating, knowing that her stepdad and mom probably would never get back together, would make seeing him even harder.

She blinked.

"Then what's it about?" His hand pressed down softly on her shoulder. Warm sensations flowed from his palm. "Because right now, I'd really like to kiss you and I don't know if that's possible. If you really are mad at me, I mean."

Inhaling, her heart raced at the thought of him kissing her. Of feeling his chest against hers.

"It's about you avoiding me," she said. "You're pulling away."

His other hand breezed across her shoulder. "Just until my father gives his approval for me to join the Council. I know it's hard, and yes, being together is going to be even harder with Clara here, but . . . I need his approval. I don't think it will be much longer."

She blinked again, and that's when she saw it. Four . . . no, five e-mails all with the word *fog* in the subject line. Could it be . . . ?

"Oh, shit!" She saw another e-mail from the same address with a subject line that read *talk*.

"Oh, shit what?" he asked.

She opened her mouth to tell him, but shut it at the same time she shut off her e-mail. She hadn't told him her grandfather had been what chased his sister—hadn't told him because it didn't feel right. Telling him now felt even less right.

If she decided to meet her grandfather without Burnett, Lucas wouldn't approve. He'd be overprotective and insist on telling Burnett.

Kylie couldn't let Lucas tell Burnett, because Burnett would not want her to meet her grandfather without his being present. And it appeared as if her grandfather wasn't keen on meeting with Burnett.

She had to meet her grandfather—with or without Burnett. He had answers, and discovering those answers was her quest. How many times had Holiday told her that following your quest was about listening to your heart? And her heart said this was the right thing to do. Lucas would just have to understand.

And just like that, it hit her. Lucas's quest was to get on that Council. And to do that, he had to pretend in front of his pack and Clara that she wasn't that important to him. How could she be angry with him when . . . she had her own agenda that was equally important to her?

Which meant she had to be more understanding. If his quest meant that they couldn't sit together at meals or he had to pretend they weren't boyfriend and girlfriend, she would accept that. Just like she expected him to accept that she had to follow her own quest.

She stood and turned around and faced him. "I'm sorry. I was overreacting." She placed her hands on his chest.

He stared at her, appearing even more puzzled. "You're not mad?"

She offered him a smile that came from deep within. The thought that her grandfather hadn't given up on seeing her filled her chest with a light bubbly feeling. She cut her gaze toward the computer and then met Lucas's gaze. "It hurt to feel that I came second after everyone else, but—"

"You don't come second. When I get on the Council, I'll have the power to put a stop to all this crap. The younger werewolves are clamoring to have someone on the Council to voice their opinion. I'll get their support and the elders won't be able to tell anyone who they should see or share their lives with. They won't hold anyone responsible for the sins of their parents. Please give me a little time."

"I will. And I'm sorry I was a bitch."

"I never said you were a bitch." He pulled her a bit closer. So close that the warmth of his body sent a wave of pleasure through her.

"I know," Kylie said. "And I get it now." She met his gaze and moistened her lips with her tongue. "Didn't you say something about kissing me?"

His brow wrinkled, but with a smile. "I don't think I'll ever understand girls."

"Then stop trying." She lifted up on her tiptoes. She wanted to kiss Lucas senseless, and then she wanted to send him on his way so she could find out what her grandfather said in his e-mails. But the moment Lucas's lips found hers, when his warm chest pressed against her breasts and his hands slipped up under her shirt to fit against the naked curve of her waist, she decided that the e-mails could wait a little longer.

This . . . this was magic. The kind she could do without screwing up.

That night, Kylie lay in her bed with her clothes on, waiting to hear Miranda come in from her nightly outing with Perry. Their evenings were getting later and later. Not that Kylie could blame them. Pulling

away from Lucas after their little make-out session had been hard—
even with her grandfather's e-mail waiting for her.

Lucas had been humming with desire, and she'd been humming
right along with him. The ability that male weres had to seduce their
mate had bitten into her heart and soul. His touch had felt so good,
she hadn't wanted to stop. It was getting harder not to give in. And
yet . . . she did stop.

Maybe because of the e-mails.

Maybe because she didn't want the hint of any unresolved issues
to be involved with her first time. And while she understood that
Lucas was following his quest, deep inside, it still stung.

Then again, probably the biggest reason she hadn't given in was
because Della and Miranda had been sitting outside on the porch.
Yup, that was for certain the biggest reason she'd found the willpower
to stop things from going any farther than they had.

The fact that she and Lucas had ended up lying on the sofa, kissing, while her two best friends were on the porch, had her blushing
when she'd faced the two of them after Lucas had left. Making it
worse was knowing Della could smell the pheromones they'd put out.

However, that blush and those pheromones were, hopefully,
going to help make tonight's plan work. The plan Kylie had come
up with as soon as she'd read her grandfather's e-mail requesting
that she meet him—alone—at Fallen Cemetery.

Had her grandfather learned the truth? That until recently his
wife, Kylie's grandmother, had been buried there in a mismarked
grave?

Her e-mail back to him had been brief: *I'll do everything possible to
be there at 1 AM.* The fact that she hadn't heard back from him bothered her very little. He'd asked. She'd answered. What more was to
be said? But it hadn't stopped her from checking her inbox every fifteen minutes.

The biggest downside to this whole thing was the lie she'd have to tell her roommates. A lie that was only going to work if Della wasn't automatically tuned in to hear Kylie's heart beat fast at the white lie. If Kylie could state the untruth and Della automatically believed it, she might not even check Kylie's heartbeat. Or at least Kylie prayed it would work that way.

A few minutes later, Kylie heard Miranda and Perry on the porch. Kylie got out of bed. Quietly, she moved into the living room, waiting for Miranda to come inside. Kylie knew Della was probably already aware that she'd risen from bed.

The door opened. When Miranda saw her she gasped.

"It's just me," Kylie said.

"What are you doing up?"

Not chancing lying twice, she commenced with her plan. "Did you see him?" Kylie asked.

"See who?" Miranda studied her. "Are you having one of those weird vision things again?"

"No. Did you see Lucas? He's supposed to meet me and we're . . . going somewhere to be alone." Shooting to the window, she glanced out. "I see him," Kylie lied, and felt the guilt. "Gotta go."

Miranda grabbed her elbow. "Are you going to . . . ?"

Perhaps it was Kylie's imagination, but she could swear she heard Della getting out of bed.

"Tell Della for me. Tell her I want to be with Lucas. Tell her I said to please let us have this time." If Della was listening now with her sensitive hearing, she'd recognize that as the truth. Kylie did want to be with Lucas.

Knowing it was imperative she leave before Della arrived, Kylie skirted out into the darkness, leaving Miranda standing there with her mouth slightly agape.

The late August air held a hint of coolness as Kylie bolted off the porch and ran as fast as she could away from the cabin.

Please let this work. Please let me make it. She repeated the words like a litany. Her body tingled with the knowledge that she followed her heart.

With each footfall that took her farther away, her confidence built. Even hearing Burnett's warning of never entering the woods alone, she knew that route offered the quickest escape, and she took it. Moving between the trees, she accepted the risk. Mario, or someone on his side, could be waiting.

But it was a risk worth taking, she told herself, and ignored the sensation of being followed. Ignored the wiggle of guilt she felt for lying to her two best friends.

She had to lie. This was her quest. And the risk should belong to her, not one of her friends who felt compelled to join her. She wouldn't put anyone else in Mario's path.

Suddenly, the phone in her pocket dinged with an incoming text. She slowed down enough to check the message.

Derek.

"Damn," she muttered, her voice whispering in the night air.

No doubt Derek had sensed her emotions and was concerned. But if she told him, like Della or Miranda, he'd think he had to come with her. She pocketed her phone and then pushed herself to move faster.

As she dodged limbs and jumped over thorn bushes, she listened to the night noises—finding peace in knowing that the darkness hadn't fallen silent. If Della had followed, she would have been here by now. Kylie could only surmise that her plan had worked. Della had relented to Kylie's wish to be with Lucas.

Aware of how far she'd gone, she knew she drew near the fence where the Shadow Falls property ended. Her heart knotted with fear that this was where her plan would get upended. Burnett could come running.

However, she'd heard rumors that someone was constantly breaking the rules. Perry, who never liked being limited when he transformed himself into some other creature. Then, Lucas and his pack constantly being called to visit their elders, who didn't respect Shadow Falls's rules.

Maybe, just maybe, Burnett wouldn't guess that the person slipping out of the property was Kylie.

The fence became visible. It loomed in front of her, a good eight feet in height. Kylie's breath hitched. She pushed to move faster, praying she could leap over the metal barrier.

Her body felt weightless as she moved into the air, higher. Higher. Her feet cleared the fence and she came down on the other side, avoiding a bad landing—and serious injuries. She hit hard and rolled a good seven feet.

She picked herself up and brushed her hand over her elbow that had found earth before the rest of her. The pain dulled, coming in second to her sense of success. She was doing it. She was going to make it.

The stickiness of blood met her palm. The berry scent filled her nose. Who knew her own blood could smell this good? She continued moving, fast, then faster, putting distance between her and the fence.

The sounds of the night continued to sing around her. No vampires making the night go silent. She was alone.

She crossed the road and moved into the trees lining the road as she continued onward. If she estimated correctly, she was only a few miles from the cemetery.

She was finally going to meet her grandfather and learn the truth. The mystery of just what she was—of what being a chameleon meant—was about to be solved. A smile widened her mouth.

The sensation of victory filled her chest and gave her speed, agility, and courage.

Or it did until a male voice called out, "Where the hell do you think you're going?"

Blood throbbed in her ears and she didn't recognize the voice at first—except that she knew it wasn't Burnett. It didn't matter. She didn't care who it was, because no one was welcome right now. She had a mission and didn't want company. And that was exactly what she planned on telling the intruder, too.

She came to a sudden stop—or as sudden as she could when traveling at a manic, inhuman speed. Her knees buckled. She wrapped her arms around a tree, catching herself from a bad fall.

Still unsure of the identity of the intruder behind her, still clinging to the tree for dear life, another voice, a different one from the first, spoke up. "I was about to ask the same question."

Chapter Twenty-one

Disappointment shot through her limbs. She had two intruders instead of just one. She wanted to scream, but air locked in her lungs and not one sound came out. Angry, she swung around and confronted the owners of the two voices. She could be proud of one thing: she'd been right. There were no vampires in the woods.

Just a smart-mouthed shape-shifter, in bird form, and a very pissed-off werewolf.

She gulped down a mouthful of air. Still unable to catch her breath, she bent at the waist and with her hands on her knees she waited for her lungs to open up. When oxygen finally flowed to her brain, her thoughts came clearer.

And one thought stood out. She wasn't going to let them stop her.

Straightening, she met Perry's gaze with sheer determination. Then she shifted the same glare to Lucas. "I'm following my quest. Leave and let me do what I have to do."

"Have you lost your frigging mind?" Perry asked.

"What's going on, Kylie?" Lucas demanded.

Kylie stared at the were. "Just what I said. I'm following my quest.

I need for you to leave. It's important and I'm not asking you, I'm telling you. Leave me alone!"

She hoped she sounded more confident than she felt. Any minute now she waited for the night to go silent and Burnett to show up. For some reason, she felt capable of standing up to Lucas and Perry, but bucking authority never came easy for her. And Burnett was authority with a badass attitude.

Before she considered how it would sound, she asked, "Does Burnett know?"

Lucas ground his mouth shut and continued to stare at her with anger, and perhaps shock, at her behavior.

"How did you find me?" she asked the shape-shifter as tiny bubbles of electricity started forming around him.

A second later, Perry appeared in human form. "I was flying around after I left Miranda and saw you jump the property fence."

She glared back at Lucas. "And you?"

His eyes brightened with anger, his frown increased, but he started talking. "Burnett thought I was the one who'd set off the alarm. He called me, and I had a strong feeling that I needed to make sure everything was okay. Then I saw Big Bird here flying—"

"Big Bird?" Perry's voice deepened with frustration.

"Whatever," Lucas continued. "I saw him and thought I'd check and see what he was up to."

"You're checking on *me*?" Perry's eyes turned the same orange as Lucas's.

"Not like that." Lucas's posture became less defensive. "I thought you might have spotted someone breaking in." His gaze shot back to Kylie. "To hurt the very person who broke out." His scowl deepened; his focus and his frustration were now directed at Kylie. "But that's not important. What's important is why you're putting yourself at risk. You know better. So let's get back before Burnett figures it out."

That was exactly why Kylie had to stop yakking with them and get a move on. If Burnett discovered she was missing, there would be hell to pay.

She glanced at her watch. Five minutes till one. Time ran out. She didn't envision her grandfather as being someone who appreciated tardiness.

Remembering she wasn't powerless, she wiggled her right pinky against her ring finger. However, the idea of using it didn't sit well with her.

"Okay," she offered. "Short explanation. I have to meet someone. So we can either do this the easy way or the hard way."

"Meet who?" Lucas and Perry asked at the same time.

"My grandfather. He contacted me and—"

"How?" Lucas asked.

"E-mail," Kylie answered, unsure why she thought telling them the truth would work, but her other option didn't feel right—especially considering she really didn't know what she was doing when it came to casting spells. Just ask poor Zac.

"Don't be stupid," Perry said. "How do you know it was really from him?"

"I know," Kylie said with confidence, and pushed back the knowledge that Perry could be right. All this could be a trick. But every instinct she had said differently. If wrong, she might pay the price with her life. If right, she'd find the answers she'd been seeking since the first day she'd arrived at Shadow Falls.

Risky? Maybe. But a risk she was willing to take. "And here's the thing," Kylie continued. "You two can either agree to let me go, or—"

"No." Lucas's shoulders grew tighter. "You are not—"

She didn't wait any longer. She twitched her pinky and envisioned a big net falling from the sky, snaring the two of them together, and preventing them from following her.

She saw it rushing down from above and barely escaped being caught herself. "Sorry," she called out, and took off running. With every ounce of power she owned, she focused on getting away before they got loose.

Kylie ran. No, that wasn't right. Because she realized at some point she wasn't running, she was flying. If she hadn't been in such a hurry, she'd have taken the time to appreciate the new addition to her gifts. Ah, but no time. She needed to get far enough away that Perry and Lucas couldn't follow her.

Finally, she spotted the rusty cemetery gates jutting out from the earth like sharp weapons that could take a life. The night appeared to grow darker as she drew nearer. Her chest tightened as she remembered Perry's question. *How do you know it was really from him?*

She didn't. She'd come on blind faith. Was that enough?

Slowing down, her feet came back to the ground. She came to an abrupt stop a few feet from the old iron gates. She went to step forward but a sudden movement behind the gate stopped her. Her heart stopped, too. Her last breath felt trapped in her lungs as she took in the view.

Faces, dozens upon dozens of faces, peered at her through the creaky bars. Their lifeless gazes soulfully stared at her with eyes that begged her for help. If only she could help them all. If only one sweep of her hand or wiggle of her pinky could take care of whatever issue kept them chained to this life, when another awaited them.

Then another thought hit. Were any of these ghosts hell-bound spirits? Those who wanted to take her to hell with them in an attempt to soften their own sentence? Great! Why did she have to think about that lovely possibility now?

She forced herself to take a step closer. The idea that she was going to have to step through those gates and move past the hundred or more spirits ripped at her courage. She remembered how it felt last time when she'd come here and had been touched by so many ghosts—the pain was similar to a brain freeze, but one that happened to the entire body.

But it would be worth it if her grandfather waited inside because she'd get some answers. Definitely worth it. Besides, it wasn't as if she hadn't done this before; she'd come here twice. But not in the dark or the dead of night. Something about the blackness, with only the moon's silver glow making the spirits' gazes visible, made the place look so much more . . . haunted.

Which it was. As if to prove the fact, the cold from the spirits surrounded her and made her skin crawl. She looked up and saw a couple of spirits had moved outside the gate and were slowly easing toward her. Stiffening her spine, accepting she had to do it, she took another step closer, planning to just walk inside. Sort of like jumping into the deep end of a freezing pool and getting it over with. Yet as her foot shifted one more time, a voice, a close-to-her voice—too close—whispered in her ear. *"I wouldn't go in there."*

She yelped and jumped back six feet before she recognized the voice. Taking a breath to calm her nerves, she moved up beside Hannah. Then Kylie recalled what what the spirit had said. Did Hannah know something Kylie didn't? Was she wrong and it wasn't her grandfather waiting for her inside?

"Why shouldn't I go in?" Kylie asked, her nerves no longer calm.

Hannah leaned in and whispered again. *"There are ghosts in there."*

Kylie looked at her agape. "But—"

"I know I'm dead," Hannah blurted out, reading Kylie's thoughts. *"Just like my grave buddies. But seeing all of them"*—she motioned to the gate—*"it still scares the crap out of me."*

Kylie looked from the gate to her watch again; she had two minutes. She had to go in. But she needed to get Hannah to talk. "Look, someone's waiting on me, but I need to know. What is it that you need me to do?"

Hannah closed her eyes, but not before Kylie saw panic fill her gaze.

"Don't run off," Kylie said in a hurry when she felt the cold begin to ebb. "I need to know. It's why you're here. I know it's hard to talk about things, but sometimes we have to do things that scare us. Sometimes it helps. Sort of like me walking into the cemetery." She glanced back at the gate and the hundred dead faces peering back at her.

Hannah opened her eyes; the panic made her pupils large and black. *"He's close by."* Her voice weakened.

"Who's close? What did he do?" When Hannah didn't continue, Kylie took a guess. "Is it that Blake guy? The one who called Holiday when she was at the falls?"

Hannah looked down at her hands finger-locked in front of her. *"She loved him. She got everything she wanted. I just wanted to know what it would feel like to be that happy. I'd had too much to drink. He'd had too much to drink. It was wrong."*

Kylie started putting the pieces together, but she wasn't completely sure, so she asked, "Was Blake the man Holiday was supposed to marry?"

Hannah nodded, and when she looked up, tears and shame filled her eyes.

"Is he the one who killed you?" Kylie asked.

Hannah put her hand over her mouth as if the thought sickened her.

"Is he?" Kylie asked again.

When she moved her hands from her lips, they were trembling. *"I . . . I don't know if it was Blake."* Her eyes filled with terror and sadness at the same time. *"I guess it could have been. I don't remember how it happened."* She paused. *"I only recall . . . his aura."* Pain filled her eyes. *"Details I can't remember, I can't put a name on him, or a face, but the evilness of him as he took my life . . . that I can't forget. And I've felt it since. He sometimes comes back to where he buried us. I hear him walking on the floor above. The three of us cling to each other in death and pretend our souls are already gone."*

Hannah hugged herself as if the memory was too much. *"He disguises his aura most of the time. He has the power to appear normal. But when he's not pretending, he's evil and dark."*

"When he's pretending, is his aura the same as Blake's?" Kylie asked.

"I don't know. I'm not sure. I guess it could be. I never paid attention to that aura. It's the other that . . . haunts me." She paused as if in thought. *"There seems to be a small part of me that says I knew the man who did it."* She paused as if her thoughts went in another direction, and from her expression, it wasn't a good direction. *"He thinks killing brings him power—that's why he does it. And the day I was at Shadow Falls, I sensed he was close. I felt him and I knew. I knew I went to Shadow Falls because of him. He's not happy with just killing me. He wants Holiday."* Her words seemed to linger in the night air when she snapped her head back and looked up at the dark sky.

"What is it?" Kylie asked, fearing the killer was close again.

"I think it's that strange shape-shifter from the Shadow Falls camp. The blond kid with eyes that change colors all the time."

The fear Kylie had felt for Hannah and from a murdering evil being faded, and Kylie's own concern rose. If Perry had found her, Lucas wouldn't be far behind. And then probably Burnett. Hoping she'd be less visible, she moved closer to the gate. She looked again at the dead faces appearing as guards of the cemetery. She didn't know if they recognized her from before. She wasn't sure if they even knew she could see them yet. But one thing was clear: if she didn't go in now, she might miss her grandfather.

Kylie looked at Hannah still glancing up at the sky. "Did he see us?" Kylie reached for the gate to open it.

"It's her. I told you it was her," one of the spirits behind the gate said. Then the spirits' arms started reaching through the bars to touch her. Kylie's vision filled with nothing but the arms coming out between the rusty bars of the gate. The cold shot through her skin and stung all the way to the bone. She bit down on her lip, fighting the pain and panic as she pushed open the gate.

"He can't see me. I don't know if he saw you." Hannah's voice echoed from behind her. With the gate open, Kylie pulled her hand free. The ghosts scattered, but the moment she moved a few feet inside the cemetery, they surrounded her. The cold of their spirits crowding around her coated her lips with ice. The pain nearly brought her to her knees. She forced herself to move a few feet away; the reprieve was instant, even if she knew it wouldn't last.

She looked back at Hannah. Fear filled her gaze—a gaze that was just as dead as those from the cemetery, who were now growing closer.

"I can't come in," Hannah said. *"One of them might be a death angel. If they want to send me to hell for my sins, they can. I deserve it, but not until I know Holiday is safe."*

"I don't think they'll send you to . . ." Kylie stopped talking when Hannah started to disappear.

"Save her for me, Kylie. Please save my sister!" Hannah's words rang in the dark.

The cold from the spirits drew closer. "Please," Kylie said, her gaze moving from one ashen face to another. "Give me some space."

They scurried back a few feet. Kylie looked over her shoulder, hoping she might see someone who walked in this world. Her hopes were futile. Everywhere she looked, she saw only death.

But then the darkness cloaking the tombstone terrain limited her vision. Kylie knew from the few times she'd been here that the cemetery was immense. Would her grandfather know she was here? The thought that it might not be her grandfather waiting for her, that it hadn't been him sending the e-mails, stirred deep in her chest, but she pushed it back.

She took a few more steps, then, remembering Hannah's concern over Holiday, Kylie grabbed her phone from her pocket and dialed the one person she knew would help her.

"Are you okay?" Derek answered on the first ring.

"I don't have a lot of time, but I need you to do me a favor. Go check on Holiday. Stay there. Don't wake her up. Don't let her know you're watching her, but don't leave her until I get there."

"Shit! What's happening, Kylie?" Derek asked.

"I can't explain right now. Just please. Do it."

"Where are you?" he asked. "I know you aren't at your cabin."

She bit down on her lip so hard she tasted blood. "Please." The word came out with desperation.

He finally answered. "Holiday is fine. Burnett's watching her place."

"Why? How do you know? Did something happen?"

"No, I felt you were in trouble and I was walking to check on you when I came across Burnett standing outside Holiday's cabin. He said because of what we knew about Hannah and the other girls, he wasn't taking any chances."

"Good." She wondered if that was why Burnett had called Lucas and not left to check the gate when the alarm went off.

"I can feel you're scared out of your wits, Kylie. Tell me—"

"I have to go." She cut the phone off. Then she glanced at the crowd of spirits, shifting from foot to foot, reminding her of hungry zombies waiting for the right moment to move in and feed. Pushing that fear-inducing, insane thought away, she remembered they were just people. Lost souls robbed of life, chained to this world by some unfortunate circumstance.

Looking around again, she asked, "Is someone else here?"

"I'm here," one spirit said.

"I'm here." A barrage of the same words spoken by each of the dead filled Kylie's ears like thunder. They all wanted to be counted. To be acknowledged.

Emotion filled Kylie's chest. "Is there anyone alive here, besides me?"

"No one else is here who can see us," one of the spirits spoke up, sounding desperate.

"But someone else is here?" she asked. Again she wondered why her grandfather had chosen the cemetery as a meeting place.

"In the back of the property," the spirit of a young girl answered, and she pointed toward the darkest area in the cemetery. *"I saw them under the oak trees, hiding in the shadows."*

"Thanks," she said, glancing up one more time, hoping she didn't spot a pissed-off shape-shifter circling in the dark sky. The clouds must have blocked out the moon, because only a few stars stared back at her from the heavens. She started moving. With each step she prayed that in the deepest, darkest part of the graveyard under the trees, she'd find her grandfather. And with him she'd find her answers.

Chapter Twenty-two

The rear of the cemetery stood eerily quiet. Even more statues stood guard over the graves. Most were covered in dead vines. Some were dilapidated, others decapitated by vandals or the passage of time, their heads resting on the ground. Still, they all seemed to watch her as her feet crunched upon the gravel path. Suddenly feeling alone, she looked back and realized that the chill of the dead had subsided. She was truly alone.

The spirits hadn't followed. Why? Fear knotted in her throat. Did they know something she didn't? Even as panic built inside her chest, she kept walking, praying that coming here had been the right thing.

She saw the trees ahead of her; beneath the alcove of gnarled limbs hung shadows—black shadows that could hide anything, or anyone.

Moving closer, she could hear herself breathe, and in the distance a few birds called out as if in warning. She stopped a few feet from the trees. Their heavy limbs seemed to be reaching out for the cracked tombstones nearby.

"Hello?" Her voice seemed to be swallowed by the night.

"You came," answered a voice, deep and serious.

Breath held, she saw a figure move out of the shadows. Malcolm Summers, her grandfather. He looked younger than he'd appeared at her camp; obviously he'd dressed to play the part of Mr. Brighten. She recalled Della telling her that supernaturals didn't age as quickly as humans.

His gaze met hers, and even in the darkness his light blue eyes stood out. Kylie realized they were her exact color. She studied his face and saw the features of her dad, features that she, too, exhibited.

She suddenly felt insecure, unsure how to behave around him. Her chest ached. Should she hug him, not hug him?

"I'm sorry," Kylie blurted out.

"For what?" her grandfather asked.

"For . . . not being able to talk to you that day in the forest."

"It wasn't your fault," someone else said. Kylie's great-aunt eased out of the shadows and stood beside Malcolm. The woman smiled. Before Kylie realized it, she'd been caught in an embrace. The strength and warmth in her aunt's touch surprised Kylie—the woman felt hot.

When the hug ended, Kylie realized that, like her grandfather, the fragileness her aunt had displayed on the the day she'd come to Shadow Falls had disappeared. Kylie did a quick calculation in her head. The woman had to be in her seventies or eighties, but she didn't look older than fifty.

Chameleons must have a long life expectancy. She tucked that info away for future contemplation.

"Look at you," her aunt said. "So beautiful." She glanced back at her grandfather. "What's wrong with you, Malcolm? Give your granddaughter a hug."

He moved in hesitantly. "I'm not much of a hugger, but I guess the moment merits it." He embraced her. And like her aunt, he felt hot to the touch. The embrace was short, but sweet, and reflective of the ones she'd savored from Daniel, and even her stepfather before their relationship had gone bad.

"You're good at it," Kylie said.

"What?" he asked.

"Hugging." Tears stung her eyes when she saw emotion in his expression.

A smile welled up inside her. "You look like my father."

"I noticed that, too, in the pictures."

"I have so many questions," Kylie said.

"I'm sure you do."

"We're chameleons, right?" She held her breath, waiting for him to confirm what her father had told her. Or was Holiday right, that chameleon meant something different? Would Kylie be accepting her role as a witch after tonight?

The look on her grandfather's face shifted from tenderness to concern. "Where did you learn this?"

"My father," Kylie said. Doubt filled her. Had her father been wrong? "He said—"

Malcolm stilled. "But he's dead."

"She's a ghost whisperer." Her aunt clutched the man's arm in excitement. "I told you I sensed a spirit present when we were at the camp." Her gaze shifted to Kylie. "Your great-grandmother had that gift. She would be so proud."

"So it's true? We're chameleons?" Kylie asked again.

"Yes," they said at the same time.

Kylie's chest swelled with victory. She finally knew. Knew for certain. But no sooner had the feeling hit than questions started forming. Deep down, she sensed her real victory would come when they answered those questions.

She stood trying to assess everything they'd said so she could learn more. Her great-grandmother had been a ghost whisperer, but the two of them weren't. So one chameleon didn't have the same gifts as another one. How did that work?

"My father, he was a ghost whisperer as well," Kylie said, realizing she hadn't checked out their patterns. She tightened her brows. Surprise filled her when she saw they were both humans. Then again, she'd also worn the human pattern not too long ago. Exactly what did being a chameleon mean?

"So you've seen him?" Sadness rang in her grandfather's tone.

"And my grandmother." She looked at her grandfather's forehead again. "Can I ask you—?"

"Heidi?" He said the name with such love that Kylie's chest tightened.

"Yes. Actually, she was the one to tell my father that we were chameleons. But no one at Shadow Falls knows what it is."

Her aunt and grandfather gazed at each other. Her aunt nodded. "Tell her."

"I will," he said. "But you must come with us."

Kylie hesitated. "Why can't we talk here?"

"Not just to talk." He rested his hand on her shoulder. The warmth from his touch was familiar. And Kylie recognized it to be similar to Holiday's and Derek's touches. Did that mean . . . Her grandfather continued. "You must come and live with your own kind."

"Live?" *Live? Leave Shadow Falls?* Kylie shook her head. "I can't. I'm going to Shadow Falls boarding school."

"You don't understand the danger you are in, child," he said.

"From . . . Mario?" Kylie asked.

His brow wrinkled. "Is Mario part of the FRU?"

"No." Kylie hesitated to get into a conversation about the FRU. "He's part of a rogue organization."

"The organization you need to fear is the FRU. They are affiliated with your camp, but they are not what they seem. I have reasons to believe they are responsible for your grandmother's death."

Unwilling to lie, Kylie nodded. "I know."

His expression hardened. "You know what?" When she didn't immediately answer, he continued, "Did she tell you something about it?" His tone matched his expression—serious, demanding.

Unsure if confiding in him was best, but sensing it would be wrong to keep it from him, she nodded. "She was paralyzed from the operation. The one they did on both of you. They killed her."

His blue eyes filled with rage and his hands tightened into fists. "Murdering bastards! Only over my dead body will you return to that school!"

Kylie tried not to react to his threat. But yes, she saw it as a threat. She inhaled a breath to calm herself. "I understand how you feel. I was outraged myself. But Burnett assures me—"

"Burnett works for them!" her grandfather roared, and even the trees seemed to cringe at his fury.

Kylie's aunt moved in and rested her hand on his arm. Kylie recalled how the woman's touch had been so warm the day they'd shown up, pretending to be the Brightens. Was the woman fae? Part fae, perhaps?

"Yes," Kylie said. "Burnett works for the FRU, but he assures me that the people who did that are no longer with the organization. And—"

"And you trust them knowing what you know? Trust him, knowing who he answers to?"

"I don't trust the FRU, but I trust Burnett," Kylie said. "He's on our side. And even more, I trust Holiday."

"You are naïve and young. You don't know what's best for you."

She tried not to take offense. "Young yes, but not so naïve," Kylie said. "I'm following my heart."

"Your heart will mislead you," he said. "Mine did. I trusted them. I was blinded to what they really were. Heidi knew . . . or she suspected, but I didn't listen to her."

"I'm sorry," Kylie said, "but I can't—"

"You can," he demanded.

"No, Malcolm! The child must make up her own mind." Her

aunt spoke to Kylie's grandfather, but looked at Kylie. The woman didn't look angry, but disappointment gripped her expression. Kylie's chest tightened at the thought of hurting these people, but giving in wasn't an option.

Her grandfather swung around and stared back at the tree. His sorrow, his anger, his loss filled the darkness like a living, breathing thing. Kylie went to him. Even frightened, she needed to offer comfort.

"The last thing I want to do is to hurt you. You have been hurt too much. I'm sorry that I can't do what you want, but I have to follow the path I believe is right." Some slight movement in the sky caught the corner of Kylie's vision; she didn't look up, but she suspected that speck answered to the name of Perry. He'd obviously found her. Her time was running out.

"And what if you are wrong and I'm forced to face another death in my own family? One whom I didn't even get to know?"

"I don't think that'll happen," Kylie pleaded.

He stared at the ground as if in defeat.

Feeling certain her time ran short, Kylie continued. "I still have so many questions. Please help me understand what I am."

He looked up. The fury faded from his eyes. "It is impossible to teach you what you want to know in a few minutes, hours, or even weeks. It could take years."

"Then I will be coming to you for years with my questions," she said. "But please, answer me this. What does it mean that I'm a chameleon?"

Her aunt came forward. "Like the chameleon lizard, we can change how we appear to the world. And for our own protection, we have had to hide ourselves to avoid persecution."

"Hide from the FRU?" Kylie asked.

"Sadly, from everyone," her aunt said. "The few who did not hide were viewed as outcasts, freaks, and not belonging to any one kind. At first they thought we had brain tumors and then they just assumed we were insane."

Kylie couldn't deny that she related. Though like most prejudices, it had probably been worse in earlier years. While sometimes she felt like a freak, for the most part, she was accepted at Shadow Falls.

"The FRU studied us like lab rats," her grandfather added. "The elders and Councils of all the species viewed us as mutants. Some were forced to work as slaves for other supernaturals."

The truth stung, but she needed to know it, know all of it. "But what are we? A new species?"

"Not really," her aunt answered. "Normally when supernaturals produce offspring, the dominant DNA is passed on. The child will generally have weaker powers than those who were born from parents of the same species. Chameleons maintain the DNA of both parents and those of their forefathers. Chameleons carry a blend from all species."

Her grandfather met her eyes. "My father was vampire and were. My mother fae, witch, and shape-shifter."

"Wait," Kylie said. "Are you saying that I have the gifts of all species?"

"When you wear that pattern you do. Except . . ." His expression showed concern. "If the rule of protector is the same with a chameleon as the others, then you wouldn't be able to use any of these powers to protect yourself."

She shook her head, trying to soak it all in. "But your pattern shows human," Kylie said.

"It is safer to pretend to be one of them," her aunt answered.

"But I'm half-human," Kylie said. "So how could I be that special blend?"

"At first, it didn't make sense," her aunt said. "But when we studied your mother's family history, we found that she came from—"

"An American Indian tribe," Kylie finished for her. And suddenly a thought hit. "Does that mean that my mother's supernatural?"

"Not supernatural, just gifted," her aunt said.

"Like how?" Kylie asked.

"She may be psychic. Or an empath," her grandfather said. "It is believed that those from this tribe can distinguish supernaturals from humans—sometimes they aren't even aware of it, but are simply drawn to them. There are more gifted humans married to supernaturals than regular humans, even though they are much less in the world population."

He tightened his brows and stared at Kylie's pattern. "Your brain has developed quickly. Most chameleons aren't able to bring forth one pattern and utilize those powers until they are in their early twenties."

"I may be developed, but I'm clueless. I don't know how to do it—how to change my pattern or how to control it."

"Which is why you must come with us." He frowned.

"I can't, but I still need to understand." She looked up and this time she knew it was Perry. "A while back, I showed a human pattern and then I'm sending paperweights around a room and . . . Well, it's not good. But maybe I developed early because I'm a protector. Or they think I am. The truth is they don't know what to think of me."

Her aunt smiled. "We heard rumors that you were a protector. That is a huge honor."

"I guess." Kylie wasn't sure how any of this was going to work out.

Her grandfather stared at her forehead again. "If you aren't in control of it, then you must be forming patterns instinctually.

Normally, it's a learned talent that can take years to master. I would assume you needed the power of speed and intuitively you initiated the change."

"Speed?" Kylie asked, confused. "It wasn't about speed. My friend kept messing up her spell and—"

"Spell?" he asked.

"I'm a witch right now." Kylie said the obvious.

"Not anymore you're not," he said.

Chapter Twenty-three

"You're vampire," her grandfather said.

Kylie's first impulse was denial. She couldn't be vampire. But why would he lie? She touched her arm to check for the lack of heat. She didn't feel cold, but if her core temperature had changed, she wouldn't feel it. Then she remembered how hot the two of them had felt.

Then came another realization. She'd literally flown to the cemetery after casting a net onto Perry and Lucas.

Lucas!

Her next breath shuddered as it went into her lungs. What would Lucas say about her new pattern? He hadn't been exactly pleased when he thought she was a witch. If he thought she were a vampire . . .

"Is something wrong, dear?" her aunt asked.

Kylie stood frozen, trying to come to terms with being vampire. Trying to imagine, or rather, trying not to imagine how Lucas would react. Then she wondered if she'd have to start drinking blood.

At just that thought, her mouth started watering. The tangy, ripe, sweet flavor was tattooed in her memory.

"Dear?" her aunt asked again. "Maybe you should sit down. You look pale."

"Am I?" Was that another sign of vampirism? Instantly, she ran her tongue across her teeth and nearly cut her tongue on her sharp canines. Oh, crap! She was vampire!

Even as the fear of change tumbled around inside her like tennis shoes in a dryer, she remembered how cool it had been to fly through the forest. She supposed that kind of power could be addictive. But what good was a power if you couldn't control it? It would be like her sensitive hearing—neat to have, but if you couldn't call upon it when you needed it, it was virtually useless.

She didn't want to be useless.

"How do I control this?" Kylie asked. "Explain it to me."

Her grandfather sighed. "It's not that easy. You have to train your mind. It isn't something I can tell you how to do; it's something that must be learned over time. It could take years. And until then, you could be a danger even to yourself."

"I will be okay at Shadow Falls."

A frown brightened his eyes. He lifted his head into the air as if to catch a scent. He made a sound, a low growl. The growl and even the way he sniffed at the air reminded her of Lucas.

"Someone came with you." He sounded disappointed in her.

"They tried to follow me. I lost them, but it's possible they've found me now."

His expression grew concerned. "Come with us. We'll help you understand everything. You need to learn who and what you are, Kylie. You can't do this alone."

She slowly shook her head. "I can't come with you."

"But you are one of us. We share the same blood. A chameleon alone will not survive. Look at your father. His death was so unnecessary. Do you think your father would not want you to come and know who you are?"

She inhaled. "I think my father would tell me to follow my heart. And right now, my heart says that Shadow Falls is the right place for me."

His frown deepened and he looked at her aunt. "We must go. Someone is coming." He turned to Kylie. "Do not speak of being a chameleon. Let them think what they may. The less we are talked about, the less we are persecuted."

"Wait," Kylie said. "How can I get in touch with you? I still have so many questions."

"I'll contact you," her great-aunt said, and joined hands with Malcolm.

"How?" Kylie asked. "How will you—?"

Her aunt never answered. It was like Perry had said the day he'd followed them. They just went *poof.*

Kylie stood there, in both frustration and in awe. How would her aunt contact her? How had they done the *poof* thing? Could she do that? She heard fast footfalls from behind, someone running toward her. She swung around, expecting to see Burnett. But it was even worse.

Lucas slowed down. He exhibited a tightness to his gait, a sense of anger, and an even greater sense of unease.

When he got closer she noticed his eyes shined bright orange. Of course he would be furious at her for tossing a net over him and Perry. She looked behind him, expecting to see Burnett appear. Expecting to get a tongue-lashing from the vamp.

Then she remembered she was also a vampire. She swung away from Lucas, afraid of what he might say, afraid to see distaste for her in his gaze.

"That was foolish," he ground out.

She knew what he meant. "Not so foolish." She kept her gaze away. "It was my grandfather."

"And?" he asked.

"And I got some of the answers I needed." She started walking. He moved beside her.

"Do you distrust me so much that you couldn't tell me you were coming here?" he asked.

She shrugged but didn't meet his gaze. "I trust that you'd have tried to stop me. And you proved me right."

"You could have reasoned with me, instead of casting a stupid net." His words came out with a light growl.

"I didn't have time to reason."

"Which is why you should have told me earlier. The idea that you didn't trust me infuriates me."

Like he didn't trust her. "I know exactly how you feel," she said, letting him figure out what she meant.

"It's different," he answered, his figuring-things-out ability right on target.

"No, it isn't." A knot rose in her throat. She still refused to look at him, afraid he'd check her pattern and be repulsed by what he found. And God help her, but she didn't think she could deal with that.

"You told me you understood. You said you overreacted yesterday when you were mad, or not mad, or maybe a little mad. Aw, hell, you confuse me!"

"I did tell you that," she admitted. "And I do understand, or I'm trying to, but when you can't seem to offer me the same courtesy, I'm reconsidering my understanding."

"So we're back to you being a woman and having the right to change your mind," he bit out.

"Yeah!" Tears stung her eyes and she moved faster.

They passed a couple of dilapidated statues with missing arms. She saw Lucas glance at them. How much had it cost him to come into the cemetery? He, like ninety percent of all supernaturals, hated cemeteries. Was that why her grandfather had asked to meet her here? He knew very few supernaturals would enter this place.

But Lucas had. He cared about her more than he cared about his fear of spirits. Would he have entered if he knew that she was vampire? Would he still care about her if she turned to him right now and let him see her pattern?

The question, or rather the fear of his answer, drove her to move faster. She wanted to be alone. Alone to contemplate every word her grandfather had said.

Alone to revel in the knowledge that she'd finally gotten the truth.

Alone to figure out what it all meant.

She was a chameleon. However, for now, she was vampire. But for how long? How long before she could control this crazy thing that was happening to her?

The spirits waited for her at the front gate. Lucas grew tenser, as if he sensed them. Slowing down only long enough to push open the creaky gate, she offered the dead reaching out for her one promise: *I'll be back.*

As soon as the icy wind blew the gate closed behind her, she picked up her pace, running. One foot hit the earth and then the other. She moved with purpose. She wanted to be home. She wanted to be at Shadow Falls.

You are one of us. We share the same blood. A chameleon alone will not survive. She heard her grandfather's warning ring in her ears, but she refused to believe it. The mere thought of leaving Shadow Falls sent a wave of pain shooting across her heart. She couldn't leave.

Yet even as she ran to the one place in her life that felt right, the place she felt the safest, she knew that the answers she sought were not at Shadow Falls, but with her grandfather.

The knowledge caused a sharp pain in the very center of her

heart. Tears welled up in her eyes and slipped from her lashes. She felt them hot against her cold vampire skin. Air shuddered in her chest from the emotion when she realized that before she could retreat to her cabin, she'd probably have to face Burnett's fury.

"Slow down," Lucas demanded.

She ran faster. Burnett's wrath was nothing compared to facing Lucas. His prejudice against vampires right now would hurt more than she could stand.

The gate to Shadow Falls loomed just ahead. Her heart thumped in her chest. She prayed Burnett's tongue-lashing wouldn't take too long. While her body didn't feel the least bit tired, her heart did.

"Damn it, Kylie," Lucas muttered again. Everything from his breathless tone to the stomp of his feet hitting the earth told her he was pushing himself to his limits.

"I said stop!" He sounded closer this time.

Just when she was about to take the leap over the fence, she felt him grab her around her waist. They went down. Hard. He wrapped his arms around her to protect her from the fall and they rolled several times.

"What's wrong with you?" he asked.

She ended up on top of him, his hot body reminding her that she was vampire. He stared up at her face. She tried to get up.

He caught her.

"What's the matter?" he asked again.

He rolled her over and landed on top of her. Afraid he'd see her brain pattern, she turned her head and stared at the underbrush. Tears stung her eyes again.

"Hey." His voice came out more tender this time. He'd obviously noticed her tears. "Look at me."

She didn't. She couldn't. "I just want to get this over with," she snapped.

"Get what over with?" His chest moved up and down on top of her as he breathed.

"Facing Burnett."

"He doesn't know, but if you leap over the fence right now, he will."

She looked back him. "He doesn't know?"

"No. I got out without being detected. And if you'll listen to me, I think I can get you in without him knowing, too. Or you can jump over the fence and go head-on with his wrath."

Realizing she was facing Lucas again, she turned her head. The underbrush against her back felt like soft moss, but the emotion in her chest was scratchy.

"Is that what this is all about? Damn it, Kylie. I already know."

She looked back at him, unsure what he meant. "Know what?"

He scowled. "That you're vampire. I . . . smelled you when I first walked into the cemetery."

His insult hit hard. Emotion had her lips trembling. "If I smelled that bad, then why did you bother to come in?"

His expression darkened. "I came in because I thought you were in danger." He exhaled loudly. "I'm not going to lie. I don't like it, and it's going to complicate things with my pack even more, but . . ." He looked into her eyes. "But what's important to me isn't what's up here." He touched her forehead. "It's what's in here." He rested his hand on her chest, on the upper swell of her right breast.

She felt her heart race. His touch hadn't been meant to be intimate, but it felt that way.

"You mesmerized me from the moment I first saw you when we were kids. I didn't know what you were, and yes, I hoped you were werewolf, but it didn't matter. You ensnared me."

The dampness of her tears spilled out on her cheeks. Suddenly, the soft verdant scent filled her nose. She knew it was both Lucas's natural scent and that of the woods.

"I'm still ensnared." He wiped a tear from her cheek. "I don't care if you're part witch and part vampire."

"I'm not just that," she said.

He looked a bit confused. "Okay. Then what are you?"

She smiled through her tears. "I'm a chameleon. Which means I have a little of everything in me." She recalled what her grandfather had told her about not telling anyone. But Lucas wasn't just anyone.

"Even werewolf?" he asked.

She nodded. "I just don't yet know how to control the shifts from one thing to another." She sighed. "Does that make me even more of a freak?"

"It makes you freaking amazing," he said. "Even when you're a vampire." He leaned down and pressed his lips against hers. The kiss tasted of innocence. And odd as it was, she suddenly remembered him kissing her like this before, but way before. Like before she'd ever come to Shadow Falls. She touched his cheek, and when he pulled back, she asked, "Did you ever . . . climb into my window when you lived beside me?"

He looked guilty, but not much. "Just once. I swear, you left the window open. And I didn't . . . I just—"

"Kissed me?" she asked. The idea didn't make her angry; it made her feel cherished.

"You were . . . my first kiss," he said.

She grinned, and then his mouth lowered to hers again. She barely felt the warmth from his lips when he pulled back. "But I'm still pissed at you for throwing that net on me." He exhaled. "Not that I can stay mad at you."

He kissed her again. Only this kiss wasn't so innocent. Not that she complained. He tasted like passion, like raw, sweet passion. His weight came against her in all the right places and she felt differences in what made him male and her female. His vibration, his humming seduction, entered her every place his hard body now touched hers.

She met his kiss with desperation, wanting to feel it, wanting to savor how he made her feel. His hand resting at her waist, warm against her naked skin, slipped farther under her shirt, and his palm cupped her breast. She moaned with the sweetness of his touch and ached for more.

His kiss moved from her lips to her neck. The feel of his warm kisses made her feel liquid inside. Need, want, desire, she felt it all.

When his hand moved to her back to unhook her bra, she rose up to make it easier. When his hand came back around to her bare breast, she trembled with the pleasure.

He slipped the tank top over her head, discarding the bra at the same time, and his eyes shifted downward to what he'd uncovered. She'd thought she'd feel embarrassed. But it wasn't embarrassment stirring inside her. She felt . . .

"You're so beautiful," he said hoarsely.

That was it. That's how he made her feel. Beautiful. Cherished.

He inhaled sharply. "We probably shouldn't—"

She pressed a finger to his lips. "I want this." She moved her hand behind his neck, threaded her fingers in his thick black hair, and brought his mouth back to hers. And in seconds, they were both lost in each other.

Chapter Twenty-four

The kiss went from hot to smoldering in a vampire's heartbeat. She wasn't even aware that he'd removed his shirt until she felt the wonder of his bare chest against her breasts. She shivered with pleasure. His kisses moved down to her neck and then lower. The sensation had her arching her back and saying his name.

And then his phone rang.

His growl, deep and low, came against her bare shoulder. He raised his head. His eyes were bright, the blue irises hot with desire. "I hate . . . *hate* modern technology."

She grinned.

He rolled over to his back and reached into his pocket for his phone. As he studied the little screen, a frown chased away the passion from his expression.

"It's Burnett." He closed his eyes, then opened them. "I should . . . take it." He looked at her with an apology in his eyes.

"I know," she said, and then, suddenly aware of her lack of clothes, she crossed her arms.

His gaze lowered briefly to her covered chest. He reached for her bra and shirt beside him and handed them to her.

She clutched them to her front to cover herself. Their gazes met again. There was a sense of rightness at stopping things before they went any further. And while she accepted that letting it go this far had been risky, she knew she'd savor the memory.

"I don't regret it," she said.

"Good." He looked so darn sexy without a shirt, but wearing a kiss-me grin. "Because I don't, either."

"Thank you," she said.

"For what?" He frowned at the ringing phone.

"For going into the cemetery even when . . . you hate spirits." *For not hating me because I'm vampire.*

A seriousness filled his eyes. "I'd go to hell to keep you safe, Kylie Galen."

She believed him, too.

He answered Burnett's call.

Kylie spent the rest of the night mostly tossing and turning, unable to sleep. The call from Burnett had just been to check if Lucas had found anything suspicious when he'd looked around after the alarm had gone off. Then Lucas and Kylie jumped over the gate holding on to each other so it would appear only one person had entered. How he'd figured it out, Kylie didn't know and hadn't asked. However, the idea that Lucas had tied, and that Perry might also have to lie for her, didn't sit well with her.

Fretting, she stared at the ceiling while mentally juggling everything she'd learned. She was a chameleon. A rare type of supernatural. But at the moment she was a vampire. And that explained why, in spite of how hard she'd tried to dreamscape to Lucas, she'd failed. Vampires couldn't dreamscape. Rolling over again, she thought about everyone seeing her new pattern.

Her great-aunt's words flowed through her head. *The few who did not hide were viewed as outcasts, freaks, and not belonging to any one kind.*

She could already imagine the campers whispering behind her back again. *Look at Kylie. You'll never guess what she is now.*

Not that whispering was going to do them any good. Her sensitive hearing was in tip-top shape. She'd not only heard Miranda and Della each time they'd rolled over in their beds, but she heard some baby birds crying for their mama to hurry up and chew up the worms and regurgitate them back into their mouths. Regurgitating worms was not a pretty sound, either.

Her mind did another U-turn and she remembered her and Lucas's time together. She grabbed her extra pillow and hugged it. A smile worked its way to her lips. Not just because of how sinfully good things had been, but because . . . because now she believed he cared for her. And accepted her. That was huge. It changed things. She just didn't know how yet.

Recalling his touches, she felt her face grow warm. Probably not really warm, considering her core body temperature was extra low, vampire low, but she'd bet her cheeks were red.

Her brain did another veering off the subject and landed on words her grandfather had said. *You are one of us. We share the same blood.*

Her need to get to know her grandfather, to learn everything about her heritage, sat heavy on her heart. But to leave Shadow Falls . . . ?

That wasn't an option. Even with some of the campers not completely accepting her, she belonged here.

As the night continued, she tried to decide what, if anything, she was going to tell Holiday and Burnett, and even Della and Miranda and Derek . . . She couldn't lie to them all. Could she?

A chameleon alone will not survive. His warning stirred in her already heavy chest.

Pulling the pillow tighter, she sat up. She wasn't alone. She had Holiday and Burnett, and everyone here in her circle. And she'd just have to play it by ear on what, if anything, she'd tell the people close to her.

The sound of her stomach rumbling with hunger filled the silent room. She got up and went into the kitchen. Opening the fridge, she reached for the orange juice, but her hand stilled when she saw Della's blood.

Della would kill her, but . . .

"Where's my blood?" Della's voice vibrated through the entire cabin.

Kylie cringed, stepped out of the shower, and debated between the red or the white towel. She chose the white, for purity. If Della killed her, she'd at least be wearing white.

"Did you spill it again?" Della bellowed, no doubt screaming at Miranda.

"I didn't do anything with your blood," came Miranda's offended reply. "I wouldn't touch it with a ten-foot pole."

Kylie tightened the towel around herself.

"Fess up, witch!" Della snapped.

"I told the truth," Miranda shot back. "Clean the stinky vamp wax out of your ears and listen to my heartbeat."

Okay, now their insults were getting to the ugly stage.

Hurrying, Kylie stepped out of the misty warm bathroom right into the middle of the warpath.

"My ears aren't dirty," Della said, snarling. "I'm not the one letting some shape-shifter suck on my earlobe."

"That's enough." Kylie held up her hands

"I'm never telling you anything else." Miranda sounded so hurt.

"Thank Gawd!" Della spewed. "You think I want to hear about you having your earlobes sucked?"

"Bitch!" Miranda seethed.

"Stop!" Kylie yelled.

"I never said he sucked them," Miranda spit out. "I said he nibbled on them." She started walking toward Della, her pinky held out like a weapon.

Della bared her canines and started forward. "Same thing. Equally gross!"

"Cut it out!" Kylie shot between her two best friends.

"She poured out my blood!" Della accused.

"Did not!" Miranda mouthed back.

"She's telling the truth." Kylie looked at Della. "I . . . I did it."

"You poured out my blood?" Della asked.

"No. I . . . drank it. And I'm sorry." Kylie held out her wrist, exposing her vein. "Here, have some of mine."

Della stared at her, her brows creased, and then her mouth dropped open. "Holy shit! You're a vampire!"

"She's a witch," Miranda said proudly, standing at Kylie's back.

"Not anymore," Della said. "Use your eyes, Miss Smarty Pants, and see for yourself. Or did Perry lick them, too?"

Not wanting to draw this out, Kylie faced Miranda. It wasn't as if she could hide it.

"Crap!" Miranda gasped. "What happened? Did having sex with Lucas turn you into a vampire?"

"No," Kylie said.

Della slapped a hand on her hip. "Why would having sex with a werewolf turn someone into a vampire?"

"I don't know," Miranda said. "Maybe it was really bad sex."

Della shot Miranda a bird and then focused on Kylie. "Did you have sex with Lucas?"

"No." Kylie tugged on her drooping towel. "We just . . . made out."

"How far did you get?" Della wiggled her brows.

"Thought you didn't like hearing about it," Miranda said in an angry voice.

"Not about earlobe sucking. That's gross."

"Bitch!" Miranda charged at Della; Della charged back at Miranda.

Kylie caught Miranda by the shirt with one hand and Della by the arm with her other hand. Right then, her towel fell to the floor. Naked as a jaybird, and suddenly furious, she stomped her foot. "I said stop!"

Della and Miranda both giggled. No doubt she looked funny naked and furious.

Kylie released them, and then snatched up her towel. "Look, I have some things to share, but if you don't stop arguing, I'm going to walk away and just let you kill each other."

"You tried that line once before," Della said. "We let you down. We didn't kill each other." She snarled at Miranda. "Of course, it could change this time."

Kylie rolled her eyes. "Are you going to stop arguing or not?"

"Maybe," Miranda said. "Especially if you can explain how the freaking hell you can change your pattern. Oh, and if you give us details about last night with Lucas."

Kylie looked at Della. "Truce?"

"Yeah," Della said. "Besides, it's you I'm pissed at now for drinking my blood. You thieving vamp." She showed her canines, but a smile came with it. "And Miranda's right. We want details on both counts."

An hour later, after Kylie had given all the details—or at least all the details she planned on giving—the three of them walked toward the office. Kylie had confessed about going to the cemetery. She'd known Della would be pissed that she'd been tricked, and

Kylie had been right. But telling them seemed important, and not just to clear her conscience. If she needed to meet her grandfather in the future, she'd need allies. Della and Miranda were her best allies.

As well as her best friends.

And a big part of the reason Kylie couldn't do what her grandfather wanted: to go live with him. A detail Kylie had omitted from the conversation.

"Are you going to tell Burnett and Holiday?" Miranda asked as they neared the office.

"I don't know." Kylie looked up at the porch and listened to someone breathing inside. What if they went berserk and forbid her to see her grandfather and aunt again?

Would Holiday do that?

Probably not. But she could see Burnett doing it. Or trying to do it.

Kylie's heart grew heavy when she remembered she wasn't here to just talk about her grandfather. It was time. Time to tell Holiday about her sister. But first, she hoped to talk to Burnett about what all she'd learned about Hannah. He needed to know so he could look into this Blake character.

But damn, Kylie wasn't looking forward to having either of those chats.

"Shit!" Della caught Kylie's arm. "If you tell Burnett about meeting your grandfather, then I'll get my ass in a sling because I let you go. He won't care that I thought you were going to go get lucky with Lucas."

"He'll blame me, too." Miranda frowned.

"He won't blame you two," Kylie said. "It's all on me."

"Right, like Burnett's reasonable," Della said.

"Well, what do you expect? He's vampire," Miranda smarted off.

Kylie ignored their squabbling this time to stare at the window in Holiday's office. She tuned her ears to see if she could hear Burnett inside.

All Kylie heard was someone punching buttons on Holiday's keyboard.

Kylie moved up on the porch. She hadn't yet gotten to the door when suddenly she recognized the scent and the cadence of breathing coming from Holiday's office. It wasn't Holiday.

Or Burnett.

What was *he* doing in Holiday's office?

She waved at her two friends and moved in to stand by Holiday's door. Derek, completely immersed in whatever it was on the computer screen, hadn't heard her. She studied him and remembered calling him from the cemetery, feeling as if he was the only one she could count on.

Sighing, she also recalled him telling her he loved her. She even remembered when it was with him that she would have shared those hot wonderful kisses. Not anymore.

"Hey." Kylie pushed back her crazy feelings.

He literally jumped out of the chair.

"Damn." He ran a hand over his face. "You . . . startled me." Guilt filled his eyes.

"What were you doing?"

"Something I shouldn't be." A groan spilled from his lips. "Holiday asked me to man the office. When I sat down, her computer woke up. It was on her personal e-mail account, and . . ."

Kylie arched an eyebrow in accusation. "You were reading her personal e-mails?"

"Only because it involved Hannah." He motioned for her to shut the door.

She did and stepped into the room. Suddenly, she felt a little guilty, too, but if the information could help them . . . "What did you find out?"

"The e-mail was from a private investigator. Holiday hired him to find her sister."

"Did he find out anything?" Kylie dropped into the chair facing the desk.

"No. But I didn't know that until I opened it." He pushed a hand over his face again. "Which I shouldn't have done. I saw it and I thought it might answer everything."

"I'd probably have done the same the thing," she said, not sure if it was the truth, but saying it for his benefit. "Where is Holiday?"

"She said something about seeing Burnett."

Kylie heard heavy footsteps, and then the door swung open. "It's not me she's seeing." Burnett's gaze zeroed in on Kylie. "Who's Blake?"

Kylie recalled Hannah saying that it could have been Blake who killed her. Kylie got a bad feeling. "Why?"

"Because that's who Holiday's with."

"That's not good." Kylie popped out of the chair. "Where's she at?"

"Who the hell is Blake?" Burnett asked, blocking Kylie's path.

"He's her ex-fiancé."

Jealously flashed in Burnett's eyes.

"And, he might also be the person who killed her sister and the other girls."

Protectiveness replaced the jealousy in his eyes. His fangs dropped down a quarter of an inch from his top lip. He swung around and in a flash was gone.

It took a fraction of a second before she remembered she could flash just like Burnett. She glanced at Derek, and only when his eyes widened did she realize her own canines were elongated. No time to explain, she lit out of the room and the fizzle that she always felt in her veins when she went into protective mode started to buzz.

Kylie just prayed that the buzz was premature and Holiday wasn't in danger.

Chapter Twenty-five

Kylie caught Burnett's scent and in no time she flew beside him. They didn't stop until they came to a small restaurant on Main Street in downtown Fallen, Texas. Holiday's car was parked in front.

As soon as Burnett had his footing, he twitched his brows to check Kylie's pattern. He didn't say anything, but she saw the shock in his eyes before he turned back to the restaurant.

They rushed to the large front window. "In the back corner," Kylie said, her panic lessening at the sight of Holiday, alive, but not looking happy. Then again, she didn't appear in danger either. The man sitting across from her wore jeans and a light blue shirt. He was tall, dark, and . . .

Kylie almost thought handsome, but stopped herself from going there.

"How did you know she was here?" she asked.

"When I saw she was gone, I called her. She said she was at the café, and when someone walked up, I heard her say his name."

Kylie looked back at the window and tuned her ears to hear Holiday's conversation.

"I just came here to ask you if you've seen her," Holiday said.

"And I came here to try to explain what happened," Blake countered. "I made a mistake. It's been over two years, and I haven't stopped loving you."

Burnett growled and moved for the door. Kylie caught his elbow. Dressed in all black today, he looked fierce.

"Wait," Kylie said.

"For what?" Burnett's nostrils flared.

"We need a plan."

"I've got one." His eyes grew brighter when Blake touched Holiday's arm.

"One that doesn't include murder," Kylie muttered, and then added, "You can't just storm in like a jealous boyfriend."

"I'm not jealous," he said.

Kylie heard his heart skip beats. *Oh, that was so cool.*

"Really?" Kylie arched a knowing brow at him.

"He killed her sister," Burnett defended himself.

"I said he might be the one who killed her."

"That's good enough for me." He reached for the door again. Kylie stopped him again.

"Do you really want this to be the way Holiday finds out her sister is dead? In public?"

He stepped back, his eyes telling her he'd seen reason. "Okay, what's your plan?"

She didn't have one, but said, "We hang back and watch."

He frowned. "He could pull a knife and kill her before I could save her."

"In public?" Kylie asked.

"It's not the smartest move, but this guy screwed up and lost Holiday. That tells me he's an idiot." Burnett never looked away from the window as he spoke. His eyes turned a brighter green. A low growl came from his lips. "He's touching her again."

"That's not why I called you, Blake." Holiday pulled her hand back. Her red hair hung loose and stood out against the pale yellow sundress that she wore. "I just want to find Hannah."

"But she's not letting him touch her," Kylie said. "Let's move before she spots us."

Too late.

Holiday looked up, and her eyes widened at the sight of them standing outside the glass door.

"You got a new plan?" Burnett asked. "Because I'm fresh out of ideas, and she looks pissed."

Kylie almost smiled at the fear she heard in the big, bad vampire's voice. "Don't tell her anything until we get her back to camp," Kylie said quickly.

The door swung open as Holiday stepped out. She looked at Burnett, then Kylie. "What's wrong?"

"I needed to talk to you," Kylie said, improvising.

"About what?" When no one answered, Holiday spoke up again. "What happened?"

Burnett started to answer. Afraid he might tell Holiday the truth, Kylie blurted out, "I happened." She pointed to her forehead.

Holiday tightened her brows and her eyes widened. "Oh, my."

The bell from the restaurant doors chimed behind them and Blake walked out. He stopped beside Holiday. "Is everything okay?" He cut his gaze to Burnett.

Burnett, eyes ablaze, pulled Holiday to his side.

"That depends," said Burnett, "on how quickly you get your ass away from here."

Thankfully, Blake had simply offered Holiday a good-bye nod and left without incident.

Kylie couldn't help but wonder if it was because he was suspicious that they knew the truth. Burnett seemed to share the same thought when he watched Blake walk away. The low growl coming from his chest left no question that Burnett planned on seeing the man again. And probably sooner than later.

Burnett and Kylie rode back with Holiday. Holiday peppered Kylie with questions as she drove. "When did you turn into a vampire? Have you experienced any pain? Have your powers changed?" Then Burnett started in with his line-up of questions about Kylie's newly acquired pattern.

Kylie answered as vaguely as she could, not wanting to talk about her grandfather. She accepted she'd have to come clean, eventually, but considering what other news she had to give Holiday, Kylie didn't want to add anything else for the camp leader to worry about just yet.

Back in the office, Holiday tossed her purse on the sofa and looked at both Burnett and Kylie with her "tell the truth or die" stare. Kylie wondered if her mom hadn't taught it to Holiday, because it sure did look familiar.

"Now, explain to me what's really going on," Holiday snapped. "I can sense there's more."

Kylie bit down on her lip. Burnett took a step forward. He squared his shoulders, empathy filling his eyes. He took a deep, apparently heartfelt breath and looked at Kylie. She nodded at him as if giving him the lead. He looked back at Holiday and, in a deep voice, said, "Kylie has something to tell you."

Kylie's mouth fell open and right then she knew it was official: Men sucked at verbal communication, especially where anything emotional was concerned.

Holiday's gaze shot back to Kylie, and her chest swelled with grief. Grief she knew Holiday was going to feel. An emotion Kylie had personally visited and revisited too often lately. Losing Nana, losing her stepfather—even if it wasn't in death, it still felt that way—losing her real father, Daniel, because his visits had been cut off. Then there was Ellie. Kylie had even found herself grieving over Red, aka Roberto.

Inhaling, Kylie motioned for Holiday to sit down. The camp leader studied Kylie's face and probably read every one of her emotions. Stepping to her desk, she sank in the chair. The cushions sighed from her weight. It seemed to be the only noise in the room.

"What is it?" Holiday asked again.

Emotion lumped in Kylie's throat. "I didn't tell you because you told me that . . . you wouldn't want to know. The whole live for today and tomorrow speech. Because at first I thought it was you."

Holiday leaned forward, gripping the side of her desk. "I don't understand."

"The face of the spirit that I told you I recognized. I thought it was you. But it wasn't . . . you."

Holiday's green eyes filled with tears and Kylie knew that Holiday had already put the pieces together. Burnett, much to his credit, moved behind her and tenderly pressed a hand on her shoulder.

"She's dead?" Holiday's next breath shuddered as she pulled it into her lungs. Tears slipped from her lashes and leaked onto her cheeks. "Why . . . didn't she come to me?"

Kylie wiped her own wet cheeks. "I think because she was ashamed of what happened."

"She told you about . . . that?"

"Yeah." Kylie's voice barely came out as a whisper. Burnett looked at her as if wondering what all she hadn't told him.

Grief filled the room. "What happened?" Holiday finally asked. "Was she mountain climbing? I told her it was dangerous to go alone."

Kylie shook her head. "It wasn't an accident."

Anger tightened Holiday's expression. "She was killed? By whom?"

"We don't know for sure." Burnett sat down on the edge of Holiday's desk. The way he looked at the camp leader warmed Kylie's heart. He cared. She just hoped this whole Blake issue didn't push them farther apart.

"But Blake is the prime suspect," Burnett said.

"Blake?" Holiday breathed in. "No, I don't believe . . ." She stopped as if having second thoughts. She swiped at her face again to clear the tears, and then she looked at Kylie. "Okay, tell me everything you know. And don't leave anything out."

That afternoon, at her cabin, Kylie sat at her kitchen table.

Lunch had been so much fun that day—not—that Kylie had decided to skip dinner. There hadn't been one person who hadn't stared, mouth agape, at her or made some wisecrack about Kylie's new vampire pattern.

Okay, that was a lie. Her close friends hadn't stared—or at least they tried not to. Jonathon and Helen had been taken off guard and before they could stop themselves, they'd done their share of ogling. Of course, then Jonathon had come over and welcomed her to vampire society and suggested she join them at their table.

She had declined. She could tell from a few of the vamps' expressions that she wouldn't be welcomed by all.

When Perry walked into the dining room, he'd checked her out, and then sent her a thumbs-up. Obviously, he'd decided not to be mad at her about the whole net thing. Then Kylie noticed all three of the new teachers eyeballing her. For some reason, she just assumed they'd have better manners, but nope, they found her just as entertaining as the others.

However, there had been one thing that made the whole meal ordeal worthwhile. When a smirking Fredericka pointed her out to Lucas, he'd just shrugged and said, "Yeah, I heard." Then he'd glanced at Kylie, not to stare, but to smile.

That smile, with a devilish twinkle in his eyes, had all sorts of meaning, too. Kylie found herself blushing and caring a little less that she was the freak show while everyone downed their burgers and fries. Of course, that lasted for only a few minutes. Then someone else made some smart-mouthed comment about Kylie's mind being off-the-chart weird.

For all the times she wished her sensitive hearing would stay turned on, she now wished she could cut it off—permanently. One only assumed you wanted to hear what was being whispered behind your back.

Staring at her hands resting on the table, she knew part of her bad mood was due to her hurting for Holiday. Kylie wanted to help her, but Holiday insisted on being alone.

The computer dinged with an incoming e-mail. Kylie rushed over, praying it would be from her grandfather or great-aunt. She'd been checking obsessively, especially since her earlier e-mail had bounced back . . . meaning the address she had for them was no longer active.

She dropped into the desk chair, her breath held, as she opened the screen.

Not from her grandfather or aunt.

She stared at her stepdad's e-mail address and accidentally clicked it open. Then she accidentally read it.

Hey, princess, I'm looking forward to seeing you Saturday. Miss you. Miss your mom.

All the emotions over her mom and dad's divorce came hurtling back. She jumped up so fast the chair slammed against the floor and broke into four different pieces. "Screw it!" she bellowed. Throat tightening with emotion, she stomped over and yanked open the fridge. She waited to feel the cool air hit her face.

It didn't feel cold, because she was too cold. She was a freaking vampire!

She swatted a tear from her cheek and looked back to the

computer. What if her stepdad started asking questions about her mom again? Kylie sure as heck didn't want to be the one to drop the bomb that her mom was dating.

Then again, he was probably going to find out Saturday anyway. She'd already gotten an e-mail from Mom asking Kylie if she minded if Creepy Guy—the one who wanted to take her mom to England and bang her senseless—came to parent day.

Kylie had been a breath away from e-mailing her mom back and saying, *Hell yes, I mind.*

But was it fair to rain on her mom's parade? Shouldn't Kylie be content that her mom was happy? Kylie just wished her mom could be happy back with her stepdad. Wished life could go back to the way things were before.

For a second, she remembered how things had been. Her thinking she was nothing but human, her not knowing things such as vampires and werewolves existed.

Her having never known Derek. Her never reconnecting with Lucas.

Her, without Della or Miranda.

Suddenly, Kylie Galen's world before Shadow Falls didn't seem so desirable. Well, except having her mom and stepdad together.

Kylie heard Della's mattress shift and her footsteps pad against the floor. Kylie did another swipe of her face, hoping to hide the watery evidence. Vampires didn't cry.

"There's some B-positive blood that I brought you behind the milk," Della said.

"Thanks."

"How are you feeling?" Della asked.

"Fine. Why?"

Della moved in some more. "Because usually when someone starts ripping apart furniture, they don't feel so well."

Kylie stared at the broken chair and didn't reply.

"Actually, I'm just surprised that you didn't have any symptoms during the turning stage. I'm glad you didn't, because believe me, it's not fun."

Kylie reached for the blood. "You know, this probably won't last."

"The blood?" Della asked. "I can get more."

"No, me being vampire. I'm not really vampire. I mean, I'm only part vampire."

"You look full-blooded," Della said, and then, "How do you change it?" She moved to the kitchen table.

Kylie opened the bottle and suddenly the idea of drinking the blood turned her stomach. Had she already changed into something else? Oh, great! If so, she couldn't wait until breakfast when everyone would have another field day making fun of her.

Closing the cap, attempting to hide her nausea from Della, she said, "I don't understand how it works. How to make it happen, how to make it *not* happen."

She faced Della. "Am I still vampire?"

Della nodded, and Kylie saw from the girl's expression that she could tell Kylie had been crying.

"Go ahead and say it," Kylie said. "I'm supposed to be a badass now that I'm a vamp."

"I don't care if you're badass," Della said with sincerity.

Frustration welled up inside Kylie because she was being a bitch, because Della was being nice, but mostly because she couldn't go running to Holiday for answers this time.

Holiday didn't have the answers. And the people who did, her grandfather and aunt, didn't want anything to do with Shadow Falls and were now "undeliverable."

A chameleon alone will not survive.

And right now, Kylie felt very alone.

More tears flowed and Kylie swiped at her cheeks. "I hate feeling like a freak," Kylie bellowed out. "I hate feeling as if I have no control over my own body."

Her thoughts went to Hannah. And to Hannah's concern that someone was out to hurt Holiday. *And I'm tired of people dying.*

"Your grandfather didn't tell you how to . . . handle it?"

Kylie let go of a deep sigh. "He said it would take years for me to learn."

"So you're going to go around changing from thing to thing without being able to control it?"

"That's the way he made it sound. I don't know." Kylie dropped into a chair.

After a pregnant pause, Della asked, "What did you think of your grandfather?"

"What do you mean?"

"I mean, did you like him, not like him? Was he some old fart with one foot in the grave?"

"No, he wasn't . . . that old. And he seemed nice. He looked like my dad. But reminded me a little of Burnett, serious and stern."

"But?" Della said, making it sound like a question.

"I didn't say 'but.'"

"Yeah, but you looked like you were thinking it."

Kylie exhaled. "If I tell you something, will you not say anything . . . to anyone?"

"Cross my cold heart," Della said. "And promise not to cry. Especially if I look half as bad as you do when I do it," she said, as if attempting to coax a smile out of Kylie.

Kylie didn't smile. She couldn't. "He wants me to go live with them."

Della's eyes widened and the humor quickly faded. "You're not going to do it, are you?"

"No," Kylie said. "I don't think so."

Right then, she heard her grandfather's voice again. *Come with us. We'll help you understand everything. You need to learn who and what you are, Kylie.*

"Don't think so?" Della repeated Kylie's words. "That sounds like you're considering it."

"No," Kylie said.

And she wasn't, she told herself. She really wasn't.

Although she might not have much of a choice . . .

Chapter Twenty-six

Kylie slipped into bed early that night. Having hardly slept the night before, she'd hoped she'd sleep like the dead. Well, not like the dead, but sleep like a hungry vampire, slightly turned off by the idea of drinking blood, who was mentally frazzled.

No such luck. She lay staring at the ceiling, petting the purring Socks, and worrying about Holiday and wishing Lucas would call. Right then, Socks crawled up on her chest and started giving her kitty kisses on her chin.

Kylie stared at the kitten. "If and when I turn into a werewolf, are you still going to love me? Remember I loved you when you were a skunk."

The kitten meowed with what Kylie hoped was a *yes*.

"Do you think Holiday knows we love her?" Kylie asked.

Talking to Socks did little to ease the worry from her heart. Giving in, she reached for the phone. She wasn't even sure who she was going to call, Lucas or Holiday.

Holiday answered on the third ring. "Hey, is everything okay?"

"Yeah, I'm . . . worried about you, thought maybe I could come over for a while."

The line went silent. "I . . . appreciate it, but I think I need to be alone."

"That's fine," she assured Holiday, although she'd ached to hug Holiday and offer her some comfort.

"Has she come to see you again?" Holiday asked.

"No." Kylie ran her finger under Socks's chin.

"If she does . . . tell her to come see me? Tell her I'm not mad anymore, I just . . . need to see her." There was so much grief in Holiday's voice that tears stung Kylie's eyes.

"I'll do that." Silence, painful silence, filled the line. The only thing Kylie could hear was Holiday's grief. "Holiday . . ."

"Yes?" Holiday's voice shook just a little.

"I love you. I know that sounds sappy, but you and Shadow Falls mean so much to me. I don't know if you understand how much good you do for everyone who comes here."

You are one of us. We share the same blood. A chameleon alone will not survive. Her grandfather's words echoed in her heart again.

"I belong at Shadow Falls," Kylie said, and then flinched when she realized she'd spoken her thought aloud.

"Of course you do." Holiday sounded confused. "Are . . . you okay?"

"Fine," she lied. "Just worried about you."

"Don't worry," Holiday said. "And Kylie, I love you, too. We'll talk tomorrow, okay?"

Holiday hung up. Five minutes later, melancholy still had her in its grips when Burnett called and asked if she'd spoken with Holiday. "I did," Kylie said. "I asked if I could come over, but she said she wanted to be alone."

"She told me the same thing," he muttered.

"Then we should respect her wishes," Kylie said.

Burnett exhaled. "Do you think she still loves him?"

While the question was a complete conversational U-turn, Kylie followed it perfectly. The fact that Burnett trusted her enough to show his vulnerability surprised her. The realization made her feel slightly guilty for keeping things from him. But she didn't have a choice, did she?

"No," she said, certain that Holiday loved Burnett. But it wasn't Kylie's place to say it.

"I'm going to have to bring him in to interview him," Burnett said.

"I know," Kylie said. "But you can't mistreat him or assume he's guilty just because he used to be with Holiday."

"You think I'd do that?" Burnett asked.

"Yeah," she said honestly. "I saw the way you looked at him this morning."

He remained quiet for a second. "Have you spoken with Hannah again?"

"Not yet."

"It would be *helpful* if she could tell us more," he bit out.

As if Kylie didn't realize it. "It's a shame they don't always cooperate."

"If she shows up, ask her to . . . come talk to me."

"Are you sure?" Kylie recalled how he'd reacted to the whole ghost issue.

"Hell, no, but I'll do it if it will help Holiday." The line went silent again. "Before I forget, Derek's going to come to your cabin and walk you to the office at six in the morning. We'll go to the café . . . to see if we can find anything out on Cara M. I've checked and there isn't a Cara M. listed as missing. Do you think maybe you read it wrong?"

"No, I've seen it several times."

"Okay," he said. "We'll go and see what we can find first thing in the morning. Then we'll have to rush back here before the parents start showing up."

Oh, joy, Kylie thought. She had almost forgotten that was tomorrow.

As soon as Kylie hung up with Burnett, she heard a tap at her bedroom window. She expected the blue jay, but was wonderfully surprised when she saw Lucas pushing open her window.

"Why can't you people use a door?" Della called out from the living room.

"'Cause I didn't come to see you," Lucas called out, and smiled at Kylie.

His smile did all kinds of wonderful things to her mood. He moved in, sat on the edge of the bed, and then leaned down and kissed her. It was warm, soft, and, she sensed, purposely short.

"I can't stay long." His gaze lingered on her lips. "No matter how much I want to."

"What's going on?" she asked.

"My dad summoned me again."

She frowned. "I don't like your dad," she said, and then felt bad for having said it. "Sorry, I didn't—"

He put a finger over her lips. "I don't like him very much, either." Then he smiled. "I have to go, but . . . maybe later, you can dream of me." A sexy twinkle filled his eyes.

She frowned. "I tried last night and couldn't. I think it's because I'm vampire."

He frowned. "I knew being a vamp would be the pits."

Kylie rolled her eyes.

"I heard that," Della shouted.

"Can you hear this?" Lucas shot a bird toward the door.

Kylie jerked his hand down. "Don't get her started," she muttered to Lucas, and then called out, "Go to bed, Della."

Lucas exhaled. "I need to go." He leaned down and kissed her again.

The kiss was the last thing Kylie thought about when she drifted off to sleep. She tried again to dreamscape, but nothing happened. So instead, she just dreamed. Dreamed how it could be when she understood everything about who and what she was. Dreamed of when Lucas was free of trying to appease his pack.

Kylie woke up the next morning around 4 AM. The room was cold, so she knew someone else was here, but they never manifested, which was just rude—like playing Peeping Tom. Sitting up, she whispered, "Hannah, is that you?"

No one answered, but the cold somehow felt different.

A shiver ran down Kylie's spine. She pulled the blanket up around her shoulders and sat there, breathing in the cold air. Was this one of the girls buried with Hannah, or was this someone new? It felt new—unfamiliar. Had someone from the graveyard followed her back? As always, when a new spirit appeared, Kylie pretty much went back to feeling anti-ghost.

Kylie listened to her clock mark off two minutes before the cold faded. Socks moved from under the bed and leapt up onto the mattress and curled up into a tight little knot on her lap. "You're a little anti-ghost, too, aren't you?"

The kitten let out a muffled meow that seemed to say, *Hell, yes.*

Kylie pulled Socks closer and then settled back into the pillows, half hoping to fall back asleep, half trying to dreamscape again. No such luck.

Her mind ran from seeing her mom, stepdad, and mom's new boyfriend to Hannah and the trip to the café she'd be making in a few hours. Would they learn who Cara M. was? Would that help them figure out who killed them?

Sitting there, Kylie recalled how Hannah had gone all weird on her when the new teachers had walked into the dining hall yesterday. Did that mean anything? "Hannah, if you can come for a chat, I'd appreciate it. And your sister wants to talk to you and so does Burnett. You're a very popular ghost."

The room remained silent and warm. Realizing if she stayed in bed she'd just let herself get caught up in angst, she tossed back the covers and got up.

Maybe Holiday was already at the office. And hopefully, Della wouldn't bite her head off for wanting to head out early. She'd have to call Derek and let him know she was already at the office.

It was still pitch-dark when Kylie and Della stepped out of the cabin. The temperature was down and there was a fall-like feeling in the black morning air. Della hadn't bitten her head off when she told her she wanted to go see if Holiday was at the office, not literally anyway. But Kylie could tell she wanted to.

No doubt, playing shadow was finally getting to Della. Kylie didn't blame the vamp. Maybe it was time Kylie talked with Burnett about putting a stop to it. Mario hadn't been around in a while. She sensed Mario had backed off and even Miranda said she didn't feel a thing. Kylie could only hope he'd gone forever.

"Too damn early," Della muttered.

"If you don't want to go, I'll be fine."

Della kept walking, but not bitching. "I guess it proves it," Della hissed.

"Proves what?" Kylie asked.

"That you're really not a vampire. I mean, we sleep the best during the AM."

"I told you I wasn't all vampire. I . . ." Kylie went silent when she heard the footfalls coming down the path. Della's eyes widened at the same time, then motioned for them to move into the edge of the woods. They hid behind a bush, waited, and watched—watched as a dark figure moved down the trail.

He wore a dark sweater, one with a hood that partially concealed his face. Kylie didn't recognize his shape or his gait. If it was one of the regular campers, she would have, wouldn't she?

Della sniffed the air. "I don't recognize his scent," she whispered.

"What's the plan?" Kylie asked.

"This?" Della leapt out of the woods, canines showing, eyes a bright green, and landed with a thud in front of the stranger.

Chapter Twenty-seven

Kylie, taken by surprise by Della's aggressive move, stood there a second before she realized Della could be in danger. With the vamp a few feet in front of the man, Kylie bolted out of the woods and stopped about three feet behind him.

Della took a defensive step toward the man. He jumped back and slammed right into Kylie. He swung around, a growl escaping his lips, but the hood still obscured his face and prevented Kylie from knowing who and what she was up against.

"Who are you?" Kylie asked. Feeling the sizzle of protective power, she went to yank off the hood from his head.

He ducked and moved a few feet backward—closer to Della. "Stop this!" he demanded.

"You stop," Della ordered.

He pulled off the hood of his sweater. "Is this the way you treat your teachers?" Hayden Yates asked.

Della, being Della, didn't back down. "If they go sneaking around in the shadows, dressing like some criminal, then yeah, that's the way we treat 'em."

Kylie held up her hand to Della, hoping to calm her, not that

Kylie felt all that calm. Her power was on full alert, her adrenaline set on high.

"Since when is taking a walk sneaking?" He used his teacher's voice.

"Since you sneaked up on us," Della smarted off.

Logic lessened Kylie's adrenaline. "I . . . we . . . You scared us," Kylie said.

"I wasn't scared," Della snapped.

Mr. Yates frowned. "Next time, try saying hello instead of attacking when someone walks up."

"That *was* hello," Della said. "If we'd attacked, you'd be bleeding . . . or dead."

"We overreacted," Kylie intervened, and then remembered that she didn't particularly like this guy. He seemed to be somehow secretive and his dark clothes and concealed face seemed to confirm it. However, Kylie's manners and respect for authority mandated she behave a certain way. "We apologize."

"We do?" Della asked sarcastically.

Kylie motioned for Della to start walking.

Della shot the teacher another frown before turning around. And the moment they were several feet ahead, Della whispered, "I don't like him."

"Me either," Kylie said, yet she couldn't put her finger on why.

"You think he's working with Mario?" Della asked.

"No. I . . . don't know," Kylie said. "Let's not jump to conclusions."

They arrived at the clearing where the office and dining hall stood. Kylie noticed the lights were on in Holiday's office. Then she noticed the dead silence. Not a bird or even the wind dared to make a sound. The fact that Della had stopped walking and her eyes glowed bright green told Kylie she wasn't imagining the sense of danger. Someone was here.

"Everything's fine," a voice, a strange voice, spoke behind them.

Both Kylie and Della swung around. The man, in his early thirties, wore a black suit. A quick check of his pattern told Kylie he was vampire. The way he held out his hands, palms exposed, told her he wasn't looking for trouble. Then again, he was a stranger and on Shadow Falls property. Who the hell was he?

"It's okay." His at-peace stance had little effect on Kylie, and even less on Della.

"I'll be the judge of that." The glow from Della's green eyes spotlighted her extended fangs.

The man pulled his suit coat back and flashed the badge attached to his belt. "I'm Agent Houston, FRU, a friend of Burnett's." The way he said "friend" seemed to mean something, though Kylie wasn't really sure what. "Burnett asked me to stand in for him while he went to pick up a suspect."

"Stand in for him for what? Suspect for what?" Della asked, or more like demanded.

The agent's gaze shifted to Kylie, as if he knew she'd understand. And she did. Burnett had brought his man to watch over Holiday, and obviously he'd gone looking for Blake. But understanding didn't make this stranger her ally. Sure she trusted Burnett, but the badge Agent Houston had just proudly flashed did him more harm than good when it came to her.

"I can't go into details," he said, "but you're going to have to trust me. Kylie knows."

Trust? Not likely, Kylie thought, but when his heartbeat didn't appear to be lying, Kylie looked at Della. "He's telling the truth."

"I know," Della said as if annoyed, but the color change in her eyes said she'd backed down. Or she had until she had Kylie alone, and then no doubt she'd verbally bludgeon Kylie for information. Della didn't like to be in the dark.

"I'm going in to see Holiday." Kylie looked at Della.

"She's popular this morning," Agent Houston said.

Kylie looked to the window and saw a male figure. "Who's in there?"

"One of the new teachers," Agent Houston answered.

Kylie tensed. "Hayden Yates?" She looked at Della. How had he gotten ahead of them? Della's expression matched Kylie's.

"No," the man said. "A Collin Warren. He said he was the new history teacher. Is there a problem with him?" The agent's voice deepened as he took a small step toward the office.

"No," Kylie said. "He's fine." But right then, footsteps echoed from down the path.

"You expecting someone?" the agent asked.

"Not really," Kylie said, but she suspected who it might be.

And she was right.

Hayden Yates, his hood back to covering his head, stepped into the clearing. "Good morning." He lifted his chin, his gaze on the tall FRU agent standing defensively.

"You know him?" the agent asked Kylie.

Mr. Yates squared his shoulders as if insulted.

"He's a new teacher," Della said, but her tone said more. It said she didn't like him, and the agent picked up on it. He took another step toward Mr. Yates.

Mr. Yates didn't back away. He held his ground, and she thought they might come to blows. Then Hayden's gaze shifted to her as if reconsidering his stance. "I mean no harm, just taking a walk," he told the agent in a resigned voice.

Kylie still felt something . . . something not right, something not honest about the man.

Hannah's warning rang in Kylie's ears. *And the day I was at Shadow Falls, I sensed he was close. I felt him and I knew. I knew I went to Shadow Falls because of him.*

Could Hayden Yates be Hannah's killer? Could he have applied for the job here just to get to Holiday? It seemed unlikely, but Kylie wasn't taking any chances. And as soon as Burnett got back, she planned on sharing her concerns.

Kylie waited in the office's entrance for Mr. Warren to finish his conversation with Holiday. In a few minutes, both he and Holiday stepped out. Mr. Warren nodded politely and offered her a soft-spoken "Good morning."

"Morning." Kylie sensed again that he was as shy and unsure of himself as she was. Maybe even more. Sort of a male version of Helen. And yet he'd chosen to teach. No doubt his love of history pushed him down this path. For that, she had to admire him.

When he left, Kylie looked at Holiday and instantly went in for a hug.

They held on to each other for a second longer than normal.

"You okay?" Kylie asked.

"I will be in time," Holiday said.

Kylie heard Mr. Warren speaking to the agent outside. "Is this his first year teaching?" She nodded toward the window.

"How did you guess?" Holiday sighed. "He was recommended by a friend of a friend. He's not so bad when it's one on one. I hope you guys don't chew him up and spit him out."

Kylie grinned. "Perry might consider it."

Holiday frowned. "Promise me you'll not let that happen. He really seems like a nice guy and I think he'll make an excellent teacher. I'd appreciate it if you'd sort of take him under your wing."

Kylie chuckled. "Again, Perry might do that."

Holiday's grin, while a little forced, surfaced. She glanced at the clock on the wall. "You're up way early."

"Couldn't sleep," Kylie said.

"Did Hannah come by?" Grief snuck into Holiday's voice and Kylie's own chest swelled with the emotion.

"No. Sorry." There was a pause. "Is that coffee I smell?"

"Yeah, I . . . normally don't drink it, but this morning I figured I could use it. Grab a cup, and then I want to hear how the whole vampire transformation happened."

Oh, crap, Kylie thought as she went to collect her coffee. It was either time to come clean or to get busy burying herself in lies. She could probably come up with a story that Holiday would believe—a story that didn't include her sneaking out of Shadow Falls to meet her grandfather. But lying to Holiday of all people felt wrong.

"You did what?" Holiday asked, setting her coffee on her desk when Kylie started her explanation a few minutes later. "How many times do I have to explain to you that as a protector, you have no powers—zero—to protect yourself? You didn't even know the e-mail was from him."

"I knew," Kylie said.

"How?" Holiday leaned forward.

Kylie bit into her lip. "He was the fog."

"He was what?"

"My grandfather and my great-aunt, they were the fog. They somehow transformed themselves into fog."

"How . . ." She let go of a deep breath and let the confusion settle around her, and then said, "You still can't just disobey rules."

"I was following the main rule. The one you've told me dozens of times." She paused. "To follow my heart."

Holiday stared at Kylie as if debating the issue. "You could have asked someone to go with you."

"They wouldn't have met me."

"You don't know that," Holiday said.

"Yes, I do. They left when Lucas showed up."

"Wait, Lucas went with you? He knew about this?" There was a reprimand to her voice.

"No. He and Perry followed me, but I . . . detained them and took off. When Lucas caught up with me, my grandfather and aunt disappeared. They don't trust anyone here because of the FRU involvement with the camp. Considering everything that's happened, you can't blame them for that."

"I can blame them if they encourage you to put your life in danger." Holiday fell back into her chair with frustration.

"They don't even know about Mario. And look at me. Nothing happened. I had to go. I had to know the truth."

Holiday closed her eyes and kept them closed. When her lids finally fluttered open, Kylie saw most of her frustration had faded. Her shoulders relaxed. "And what's the truth, Kylie? What did they tell you?"

"My dad was right. I'm a chameleon."

"And what, exactly, is that?" Holiday asked.

"I have a blend of all the supernaturals and I maintain the DNA from all."

Holiday shook her head. "But that's not possible. The dominant parent's is the only DNA that passes to the child."

"That's what makes us different."

Holiday leaned back in her chair, her expression one of bafflement. "That's . . . huge." She tweaked her brows at Kylie's forehead. "So what constitutes the pattern you show?"

"I don't know . . . exactly. He said it usually took years before a chameleon learned to control it. That it takes a while to learn to do it. But then he said something that led me to believe that I can change it according to the powers I need."

"So he changed you into a vampire?"

"No, I . . . he said I must have done it instinctively. When I was trying to get away from Lucas and Perry, I just kept telling myself to move faster. So maybe that's how it happened."

"Have you tried to change it again?" Holiday arched a brow in curiosity.

"No." Kylie shook her head. "The last time you had me try to do something that I wasn't sure how to do, Burnett nearly wound up sterile."

Holiday chuckled. Seeing Holiday smile was so good that Kylie smiled back.

"What else did your grandfather say?" Holiday asked.

Kylie's heart gripped. If Holiday was vampire, she'd hear the lie forming on her lips. Telling Holiday that Kylie's grandfather wanted her to leave Shadow Falls seemed like giving Holiday a reason to dislike him—a reason to insist Kylie stay away from him. And she couldn't stay away.

Taking a breath, she fought the guilt swelling inside her, because Holiday might not hear the lie in her heartbeat, but she could read her emotions. Squaring her shoulders, she met Holiday's eyes. "Not much else. Lucas showed up and . . . they left."

"Who left?" Burnett asked.

Kylie inwardly flinched. She'd been so busy trying not to feel guilty, she hadn't heard him approach.

"Did you find him?" Holiday sat up, tension pulling at her shoulders.

Kylie had suspected Burnett had been looking for Blake, but it surprised her that he'd told Holiday. "Find who?" Kylie asked, to be sure she'd been right.

"Blake," Burnett answered. "And no." He looked at Holiday. "I've left messages at both his work and cell that we need to talk."

"Should I call him?" Holiday asked.

"No," Burnett clipped. Shifting his shoulders as if to push off the stress, he looked back at Kylie. "Who were you speaking of when I walked in? Who left?"

Holiday glanced at Kylie and she could see the message in the camp leader's eyes. She left it up to Kylie whether to tell him . . . or not.

She appreciated that, and when she imagined Burnett's reaction to her disregard for the rules, Kylie almost went with the "not." But realizing the position she was putting Holiday in by lying to Burnett, Kylie reconsidered. She didn't want to be the one to cause even a ripple of discontent between them. Not when her goal was to get them together.

"You're going to be upset," Kylie said.

"How upset?" He frowned.

It turned out Burnett had been quite upset. Kylie had been relieved when, an hour later, Derek showed up and the four of them left for the café to see if they could find out anything about Cara M.

When Burnett and Holiday walked into Cookie's Café, Derek held her back and let the door close. "Is everything okay?"

He'd obviously picked up on Burnett's *cheerful* mood. Although Kylie didn't know if it had everything to do with her, or the fact that he'd been unable to run down Blake.

Looking up at the glass door and seeing Burnett staring back at them, she recalled some of their earlier conversation.

"The FRU is not the enemy," he'd insisted, when Kylie reminded him her grandfather had a reason to distrust Shadow Falls.

"You're not the enemy," Kylie had said. "But I'm still not sure about the FRU. And while I know you don't want to admit it, you wouldn't have hidden my grandmother's body and wouldn't be keeping some facts from them if you completely trusted them."

Burnett hadn't argued with that, but Kylie pointing it out hadn't done much to improve his mood. He was obviously torn between his loyalty to Shadow Falls and his loyalty to the FRU. Not that Kylie worried. She trusted him. Getting her grandfather and aunt to trust him was another matter.

Derek cleared his throat to get her attention. He wore his favorite jeans and dusty green T-shirt. "Did something happen?"

"Not really," Kylie whispered to Derek, slightly bothered by how close he leaned into her, brushing her shoulder with his. Or was she bothered by how aware of his touch she was? Pushing that thought aside, she reached for the glass door.

But she got the craziest feeling that someone was watching her. She swung around, but Derek blocked her view of the street.

"Is something wrong?" he asked.

"No." She still shifted to see around him. But the brief sensation she'd gotten was gone. Were her grandfather and aunt close by? She glanced all around, left and right. The old houses lining the street had been turned into gift shops, and an old red caboose now served as a concession stand. What she didn't see was anyone peering back at her. No one. Nothing.

So she turned back and walked inside the café packed with a chattering crowd.

The smell of bacon flavored the air in the old house that served as a café. She didn't find the smell the least bit tempting. The downside of being a vamp. The room held wall-to-wall tables, filled with hungry people who looked like vacationers. The sound of forks clinking against plates echoed with the voices.

Only one table stood empty and Holiday led the way. A server came out of the back, carrying a tray of food that smelled like cinnamon rolls.

"Is that the same uniform?" Derek asked as they sat down.

"Yeah." Kylie's heart lightened with hope that this would lead them to the killer.

Another waitress, Chris G., according to her name tag, stopped in front of their table.

"You guys ready to order?" Before they spoke, she waved at another table. "One minute."

"Actually," Burnett spoke up, "we're here hoping to get some info on a Cara M., a waitress who—"

"Oh." She walked away.

"Oh, what?" Burnett frowned as she took off. She stuck her head through the door and called out, "Hey, Cara, someone wants to talk to you."

Burnett, Holiday, and Derek all turned and looked at Kylie.

"She can't be alive," Kylie said. "Trust me. She's dead."

Then a pretty blond, with a name tag that read CARA M., walked out of the back. "She looks alive to me," Derek said. "And even kind of hot." He blushed.

Chapter Twenty-eight

Kylie opened her mouth to speak, but didn't have a clue what to say. Or do, for that matter.

"Hi, Cara," Derek spoke up, glancing at Burnett as if making sure it was okay to take the lead. Burnett nodded and Derek continued. "We wanted information on a Cara M."

She pointed to her name tag. "I'm Cara M. M for Muller."

Kylie studied the waitress's face and tried to compare it to the spirit. It wasn't her. Was it? Kylie played emergency recall in her memory but could only envision her long blond hair and blue eyes. Which this girl had, but . . .

"I'm sorry," Derek said. "We were under the impression that Cara M. no longer worked here."

"Well, I'm still here. Been here since I was fifteen, over two years. Why?"

"Is there another Cara M. who worked here?" Kylie tried not to stare, but feeling desperate to discover the truth, she couldn't stop herself.

"No." The girl looked at Kylie. "What's this about?"

Kylie noticed that the waitress's name tag had come unpinned and barely clung on the uniform. "What happens if you lose your name tag?"

Cara cut her eyes toward the back of the restaurant. "The manager has a freaking cow."

"And what would you do to prevent him from having a cow?" Kylie leaned forward.

"What do you mean?" Cara asked.

"She means, do you ever loan your name tag to one of the other girls?" Derek asked.

The waitress leaned closer as if afraid someone might hear. "The boss hardly notices. But I don't understand why you want to know this." She smiled at Derek as if . . . well, as if he was some cute guy and she was some cute blonde. Which she was. Which he was. A frown pulled at Kylie's lips.

Holiday touched the girl's arm. No doubt to send her some calming emotion in hopes of encouraging her to answer. "Have any of your waitresses just . . . disappeared?"

Kylie saw Burnett tilt his head, listening for a lie, and Kylie did it as well.

"They quit all the time. The owner can be a real jerk." Cara spoke the truth.

"Has anyone just left? Never officially quit?" Holiday asked.

Cara paused. "Yeah, there was a girl like that. A Cindy something. Can't remember her last name."

"Did Cindy ever borrow your name tag?" Burnett added his voice to the conversation.

"Was Cindy a blonde?" Kylie tossed out her own question.

"Yes," Cara said to Burnett, and then focused on Kylie. "And yes. Why?"

Between Holiday's casual touches on the girl's wrist and Derek's flirty smiles, the girl answered all their questions about Cindy. Before she walked off, Burnett asked if her manager or the owner of the restaurant was here.

Cara grew nervous. "Did I do something wrong?"

"No," Burnett assured her. "But can you let her know I need to talk to her?" He pulled out his wallet and flashed his badge. Kylie wasn't even sure what the badge meant to humans, but it didn't seem to matter.

Cara's color paled. "Oh, shit. Did something happen to Cindy?"

Yeah, Kylie thought. Something happened. Something really bad, too.

Before leaving, Burnett had the name Cindy Shaffer and a copy of the resume she'd filled out with her emergency contacts. When he sent the info to FRU via his phone and asked for the driver's license, they answered within a few minutes. When he showed Kylie the image of a smiling young blonde, tears filled Kylie's eyes. It was her. And Cindy Shaffer would never smile like that again.

While Burnett spouted orders over the phone for someone at the FRU to contact the Shaffer family, Holiday ordered some cinnamon rolls. They arrived, hot and covered with gooey white icing. Derek ate two, Holiday nibbled on one. Kylie and Burnett picked at their pastries with even less enthusiasm. Even with Kylie's stomach grumbling, she couldn't stomach the taste. That, and she kept seeing the image of the smiling Cindy.

"Are you drinking your meals?" Holiday asked Kylie in a low voice.

"Not regularly, but I'll start." She didn't look forward to it.

Burnett paid for the breakfast. As they walked toward the car, Kylie got the feeling again that someone was watching her. She swung around and saw a male figure disappear inside one of the stores. She'd barely gotten a glimpse of a shoulder and arm, but she recognized those appendages.

Kylie shot across the street.

"What is it?" Burnett's feet ate up the pavement right beside her.

Kylie stopped in front of the store. Her gaze flew to the large carved wooden sign that read PALM READER. She reached for the door. "I thought I saw someone."

Burnett grabbed her, his eyes now green in protective mode. "Who?"

Kylie heard Derek call her name from the other side of the street. "Let me find out." She rushed inside the store.

Burnett rushed in with her.

The first thing Kylie noticed was a voodoo doll hanging from the ceiling with pins in it. The second was a foul odor. She slapped her hand over her mouth and nose. Even while wanting to gag, she searched the room for the man she'd seen enter the building. When the place looked empty, she glanced back at Burnett.

"Garlic." He frowned. "Just breathe it in; the reaction will fade. It doesn't kill us."

"Can I help you?" a voice asked from behind a counter in the corner of the room.

Kylie forced herself to pull her hand from her mouth and looked at the woman dressed in a brightly colored, loose-fitting dress that had con-artist-pretending-to-be-a-clairvoyant written all over it. But just to confirm her assessment, Kylie checked her brain pattern. Human—but shady looking. Definitely a con artist.

Kylie tilted her head to the side to hear if anyone else was in the old house. Not a sound. No one breathed inside these walls but the three of them, and Kylie still wished she didn't have to breathe. The smell crawled down her throat. She focused on the door. Where had the man gone that she'd spotted rushing inside?

Noting that the backdoor stood slightly ajar, she tuned her ears to listen for anything outside. If he'd left out the backdoor, he was gone now.

"Uh . . ." Kylie pushed words around her gag reflex, but before the words spilled out, she noted the hand-painted sign hanging over the register.

NO SHOES, NO SHIRT, NO SERVICE. AND UNDER ANY CIRCUM-STANCES, NO COLD-HEARTED VAMPIRES.

She glanced at Burnett and back at the sign.

He frowned.

"You need a reading?" the woman asked.

"No." Kylie ignored her desire to heave. "A man just walked in. I thought I knew him."

"Yeah. The bell rang, but I was in the back; when I got here the person had vanished. Probably a spirit. I get them all the time."

Kylie put out her feelers for ghosts. No deadly cold filled the space. And who could blame them? The stench of garlic probably scared them off, too. She eyed the woman again, who Kylie now had down as a complete nutcase. A stupid nutcase if she thought a sign and some garlic would actually keep vampires away.

The woman noticed Kylie's attention to the sign. "Don't be too quick to judge. I see them around here all the time. They have a different smell about them."

"Seriously?" Burnett asked in mock disbelief. "You believe in vampires?"

"You aren't the only non-believers," she said. "But I have proof. The Native Americans drew pictures of them on the cave walls on my grandmother's property."

"Interesting stuff for fairy tales." Burnett glanced at Kylie. "You ready?"

As soon as they walked out, he bit out, "Who the hell did you think you saw?"

She didn't consider keeping it from him. She'd been going to tell him, she just hadn't had the time. "What do you know about Hayden Yates?"

"The new teacher?"

She nodded.

"I personally did an extensive check on all the new employees. Why? Do you think I missed something?"

"I think he gives me bad vibes."

"Bad vibes?" Burnett asked.

Kylie nodded. "And this morning before the sun came up, Della walked me to Holiday's office and we caught him following us." She stopped talking, realizing that wasn't altogether true. "Maybe not exactly following us, but he was walking around. And Hannah insists whoever killed her is close to the camp."

"And that's who you think you saw?"

She nodded.

He frowned. "But Blake, Holiday's ex, has been in the area, too. Hannah could have meant him."

Burnett wanted Blake to be guilty, and Kylie wasn't sure he wasn't, but . . . "I know, but I'm just . . . Maybe I'm making more out of it than I should."

"Or not." Burnett snatched his phone from his pocket and dialed. "Della," he said into his phone. "Find Hayden Yates at the camp."

"Can I whup his ass, too?" Della's voice echoed from the phone.

"No, don't let him know you're checking on him. I just want to know if he's there. And do it now!"

"I'm already on my way," she smarted back.

The line went silent for a second. "Okay . . . I'm at his place, peering though his window. He's reading the paper, sitting on the sofa. You sure you don't want me to kick his ass? Did Kylie tell you we think he was following us?"

"Yes."

"Is that an affirmative on whupping his ass?" Della chuckled.

"No," Burnett said, missing the humor. "Thanks." He hung up and met Kylie's gaze.

"I don't think he could have made it back to the camp in that time," Burnett said.

"I know," Kylie said. "So maybe it wasn't him."

Burnett frowned. "But to be safe, I'll do another rundown on him."

Kylie appreciated that.

"Where the hell did you guys go?" Derek stopped beside them.

"I thought I saw someone." Kylie spotted Holiday moving across the street.

"What happened?" she asked.

"Kylie thought she recognized someone." Burnett motioned for them to cross the street. "We should get back to the camp before the parents start showing up."

Oh, great! Now Kylie had the whole parent issue to deal with.

Holiday looked at her watch. "We'd better hurry."

They moved across the street to get in the car. All *five* of them. Yes, five.

Burnett hit the clicker to unlock the doors. Holiday popped in the front seat. Kylie stood by the back door when Hannah leaned in and whispered, *"I call window seat."*

Hannah, Derek, and Kylie climbed in. As soon as Burnett got settled behind the wheel, his shoulders stiffened and he swung around. The look, the sheer panic in his gaze, told Kylie she wasn't the only one hearing and, more than likely, seeing Hannah.

Burnett drove in silence, but kept looking back in the rearview mirror. Kylie shivered from the chill of Hannah's presence.

Have you figured out anything else? Kylie spoke in her mind.

Hannah ignored Kylie's question. Instead, she stared at Derek. *"He's cute."*

"Damn, it's cold in this car." Derek draped his arm around Kylie. The warmth of his arm did feel good, and being this close, close enough to get a good whiff of his natural scent to chase away the scent of garlic, didn't feel so bad, either. And for that reason, she shifted away and cut him a warning look that said, "Don't push your luck."

Sometimes she thought he forgot she wasn't really with him anymore. Not that it wasn't easy for him to forget, with Lucas never hanging around her . . .

"You should definitely choose him." Hannah leaned into Kylie's shoulder. The icy feel of her touch caused Kylie's spine to stiffen. *"And speaking of romance, the bozo in the front seat better watch himself. If he hurts my sister—"*

"I won't," Burnett muttered.

"Won't what?" Holiday and Derek asked at the same time.

"Nothing." Burnett slammed his jaw so tight he had to have cracked a few teeth.

Hannah leaned forward and stared at Burnett in the rearview mirror. The mirror frosted over. *"If you break her heart, I swear, I'll neuter you in your sleep."*

Burnett's jaw tightened some more. Holiday gaped at the rearview mirror and then stared wide-eyed at Burnett. A second later, she swung around and gave Kylie the befuddled look. "Is it her? Is Hannah here?"

Kylie froze, literally from Hannah's icy presence, but also from not knowing what to say.

When Kylie didn't answer, Holiday stared back at Burnett. "Can you see her? Can you see ghosts? How can you do that?"

"We've got a ghost in the car?" Derek's voice rang a bit high-pitched.

"Had a ghost in the car," Hannah said. Her teary-eyed gaze stared at Holiday, and then she vanished, leaving the saddest of sad moods to fill the car like smoke.

The moment Kylie spied her mom and John, her mom's creepy new boyfriend, walking into the dining hall, holding on to each other like a couple of horny teenagers, Kylie found herself envying Hannah's ability to vanish. Why did her mom think bringing John was a good idea? And if she had to bring him, couldn't she keep her hands off his butt while she was here?

Yup, Kylie's mom had her right hand tucked into the back of John's jeans pocket. And frankly, the man didn't even have a nice ass!

Surely her mom wasn't getting serious about him and felt these visits were needed for Kylie to get to know him—before . . . before they did something stupid, like get married.

The thought scared the crap out of Kylie. Inhaling, she told herself she was overreacting; as Nana would have said, she was making a mountain out of a molehill.

Then again, her mom hadn't answered Kylie's question about them having sex. And chances were, her mom wasn't about to answer that inquiry today, either.

Kylie's mom turned around and spotted her on the other side of the dining hall and smiled. Kylie waved, hoping her mom would do the same, freeing her hand from John's ass, but nope.

Taking a deep breath, Kylie faked a smile.

Her mom grinned up at John, and the man swooped down and kissed her. Kissed her . . . with tongue, and right there in front of all of Kylie's campmates.

"Just shoot me," Kylie muttered.

"I think they're cute." Holiday leaned into Kylie as if reading her emotional overload.

"And I think I'm going to puke." Kylie swore she was going to have a sit-down, serious chat with her mom and find out exactly what was going on. When the kiss kept going, Kylie decided again that yup, she'd love to vanish. Just up and disappear.

"Take some deep breaths and calm down," Holiday said. "You're exploding with panic."

Kylie looked at Holiday. "My mom's French-kissing a guy in front of everyone," she muttered. "Of course I'm panicking!"

"Shit!" Holiday snapped.

"Shit, what?" Kylie asked, alarmed at the panic in Holiday's voice.

"Oh, Kylie," Holiday murmured. And then she looked across the room and waved down Burnett, her arm motions serious.

"What is it?" Kylie looked to the door, thinking someone unwanted, possibly Mario, had walked in.

No Mario.

"Damn it to hell and back!" Holiday whispered. "Kylie, where did you go?"

"What do you mean? I'm right here. Standing right next to you." Kylie looked down at her feet, but she saw only the floor. No sneakers, no legs. No Kylie.

"Oh, shit!" she muttered, and while she hadn't thought about it in quite a while, she remembered her dad telling her that they would work things out together. Was this it? Was this what dying felt like?

Chapter Twenty-nine

Wait, Kylie thought. If she was dead, wouldn't she be on the floor in a crumpled, lifeless heap?

"Oh, crap!" Kylie muttered when her mom, a dumbfounded look on her face, walked up to Holiday.

"Where's Kylie?" her mom asked.

"She ran to . . . to the bathroom, I think, but . . . I'm not sure." Holiday's voice sounded an octave too high.

Burnett stopped at her mom's side, his serious gaze trying to read Holiday. "Something wrong?" His calm front almost sounded convincing, but Kylie saw the stress tightening his jawline.

"Uh, Kylie . . . she . . . disappeared. I thought maybe you could find her."

Disappeared? So, she'd just disappeared. She wasn't dead.

"Disappeared?" All sorts of questions filled his eyes.

Holiday nodded and didn't break eye contact as if mentally telling him it was serious.

And hell yeah, it was serious. She was freakin' invisible.

"It's crazy." Her mom sounded confused. "She was here and then . . . she vanished."

Vanished? Kylie suddenly remembered wishing she could vanish. Vanish like a ghost.

Damn! Damn! Damn! If there was ever a lesson in the old adage of be careful for what you wish for, this was it.

Questions flashed across her mind. Was she still a vampire? Had she turned back into a witch and accidentally wiggled her pinky when she made the declaration? Or was this completely connected to her being a chameleon? That's when she recalled that her great-aunt and grandfather had gone *poof*, both from the car the first day they'd shown up at Shadow Falls, and at the cemetery. Was *poof* the same thing as vanishing?

Her grandfather's words echoed in her head. *Come with us. We'll help you understand everything. You need to learn who and what you are.*

More than ever, and maybe not even for the first time, Kylie wondered if he was right.

"You've lost her daughter?" John snapped. "What kind of place loses kids?"

"We haven't lost her," Holiday said, but Kylie saw fresh panic flash in her eyes. "I'm sure she'll show up any minute."

Her mom seemed to relax, but Kylie didn't get a warm fuzzy feeling from Holiday's tone. And when Kylie listened closely, she heard the camp leader's heart beating to the tune of a lie.

Crap! Crap! Crap! Kylie tried to think. She had to get herself out of this because . . . well, apparently she'd gotten herself into it.

"I can do this," she said, needing a little encouragement even if it was as fake as a mall Santa.

She tried to rationalize. If she'd gotten this way by wishing it, maybe she could un-wish it. She started un-wishing, if you could call begging to everything holy in her mind to change her back as un-wishing. She closed her eyes and realized that if it worked, she'd magically appear. That would freak everyone out even more. "Go somewhere else," she muttered to herself. "Somewhere private." She dashed toward the bathrooms.

Hurrying into the room, she heard voices but ignored them, and stormed into an empty stall. Breathing in, then breathing out, she closed her eyes, closed them really tight. "I wish . . . I wish I was visible." She opened her eyes. Her gaze shot to her feet. Or to the space where her feet should have been, but weren't.

A knot formed in her throat; fear bounced around her chest like bumper cars. What if she stayed like this? What if . . . No! She'd been in worse situations. Heck, she'd been kidnapped and chained to a chair and survived. She'd been tossed off a cliff and came through it. All of a sudden, she questioned again if this was Wicca related. She wiggled her pinky. "Turn me visible. Turn me visible."

Nothing happened.

"What the hell have I done?" The knot in her throat doubled in size. She started to cry. "Somebody help me, please?" She leaned against the bathroom stall door. "Daniel." She whispered her father's name, even though she knew the likelihood of him showing up was slim to none. "Can you please, please help me?"

"Think yourself there," a voice said.

Her breath caught when she realized it wasn't just any voice, but Daniel's. She pulled away from the door and saw the vague apparition of him, crowded between the toilet and the stall wall. "Think it. Make it so in your head."

"How?"

"Think it. In your heart. You have the power—" He faded.

"No," she begged, but he was gone.

Wiping her tears, she did what he said. She concentrated on being visible. On being there, physically.

Closing her eyes again, with no faith but desperate enough to try, she concentrated. She opened one eye and peered down. Her feet had never looked so beautiful in all her life.

"Thank you! Thank you!"

"For what?" someone asked in the stall beside her, but Kylie barely listened, too excited that she wasn't invisible anymore.

She walked out of the stall and came to an abrupt stop when she saw Steve and Perry both standing in front of urinals, their jeans hanging low on their butts. The sound of urine hitting ceramic filled her ears. It wasn't a pretty sound.

Her face heated to a nice shade of red.

The stall door behind her swished open. "What are you doing in the boy's restroom?" someone asked.

Steve, pants still down, swung around. Completely around. Kylie slapped her hands over her eyes.

"I didn't see a thing. I swear." Okay, maybe she did, which had her face turning hotter.

"What the hell?" Steve growled. Along with Perry's laughter, she heard the sound of zippers being pulled up.

"I'm sorry." Hands over her eyes, she moved in the direction of the door, but she hit a wall instead.

Perry laughed again. "Our friends are all put up. You can open your eyes now."

She did, but refused to look at anyone. *Their friends!* She darted out, wishing she had a minute to get her head together before . . .

Too late.

Holiday spotted her. And so did her mom and John. All three came hurrying over.

Holiday stared at her wide-eyed with questions flashing in her eyes. Questions Kylie didn't have answers to.

"Was that the boy's bathroom you just walked out of?" her mom asked, sounding a bit annoyed, but mostly worried. John moved in and slipped his hand around her waist. Something about the way he touched her had Kylie envisioning them naked together. Oh, Gawd. They were having sex. She knew it.

Then she saw it. Saw it in her head. And it was not pretty!

"Are you okay?" her mom asked. "You're beet red."

"Yeah." Kylie squeaked. She pushed away the image of them naked before she wanted to vanish again.

"You were right there," her mom said in a mildly scolding voice. "I turned my head and you were gone when I looked back."

Kylie opened her mouth to say something, to apologize, or maybe to say something mundane like *beautiful weather isn't it*, but those weren't the words to leave her lips.

"You didn't turn your head. You were sucking face with that idiot." She inhaled, clamping her mouth shut, but it just flew back open. "You're sleeping with him, aren't you? Have you even read the sex pamphlets you gave me all those years?"

Her mom gasped and her face brightened. So that was where Kylie got her ability to blush. Her mom opened her mouth, obviously to scold Kylie, but nothing came out. Not a word.

John cleared his throat in a scolding tone. What in holy hell gave him the right to clear his throat at her? "Now, Kylie, that wasn't nice."

"You mean the kiss?" Kylie asked. "Because, frankly, I didn't say it was nice. It was actually quite embarrassing."

That's when Holiday cleared her throat. Kylie could handle Holiday's intervention, but not this bozo's, who was doing the dirty with her mom.

"I really think we should go outside," Holiday said.

"I think the girl needs a firm talking-to," John said.

Kylie's spine went ramrod straight. And damn if she didn't feel her canine teeth grow a little longer. She had emotions racing through her so fast she couldn't even begin to define how she felt. Except hungry. For blood. How dare he feel he had the right to correct her?

"I hope you're rich, because that's the only reason I can think my mom might like you."

Her mom gasped, and so did Kylie. Why was she saying these things? Oh, shit, she needed to shut up. What was wrong with her? Had going invisible addled her brain? Or was being vampire making her as ballsy as Della?

"You're being quite rude, young lady." John looked at Kylie's mom.

"She's not being rude!" a deep voice sounded behind Kylie.

The voice rang all kinds of familiar bells, but Kylie couldn't think straight to know who it was, so she turned around to put a face to the voice.

Oh, shit! Could this get any worse?

"I happened to witness it as well. And frankly I agree with my daughter. It was inappropriate." Her stepdad shot her mom a stern look.

Her mom's face turned even redder, but Kylie recognized that red-faced expression, and it wasn't embarrassment. She was pissed!

"How dare you tell me what's appropriate!" her mom snapped.

Shame filled her stepdad's expression. He looked at Kylie. "I didn't know Kylie was there. I wouldn't have done it if I had. I've apologized a hundred times. But two wrongs—"

"Let's all take a walk," Holiday said again. But no one took a step.

It took Kylie about a second to realize what her stepdad meant. She opened her mouth to say something, but what? *Don't worry, Dad, Mom doesn't know that I watched your young skank rub herself all over you and practically give you a handjob in the middle of downtown Fallen?*

Nope, that didn't sound like the right thing to say. So she ceremoniously shut her mouth and started praying for a miracle, because it would take one right now to fix this mess.

"You wouldn't have done what?" her mom asked, and when her stepdad didn't answer, her mom's fury focused on Kylie.

"What did you see?" she asked in her speak-or-be-grounded tone.

And grounded sounded like the best option.

Guilt fluttered in Kylie's chest. But for what? she asked the un-welcome emotion. Not telling her mom had to be the right thing, didn't it?

"Why don't we walk outside," Holiday piped up again, and put a hand on Kylie's mom's shoulder.

Her mom's expression softened. Thank God for Holiday's emotion-altering touch. The panic blossoming in Kylie's gut lessened. Leave it to Holiday to save the day.

But then Kylie saw the way John stared at her stepdad. And when he opened his mouth, Kylie questioned if Holiday could pull off a miracle.

It didn't help matters when Lucas came to a sudden stop beside Kylie, his eyes glowing a shade of pale protective orange. Not that she didn't love that he cared enough to protect her, but the last thing she wanted to have to do was explain his eye color to her stepdad, her mom, and the man who was having sex with her mom. And thinking about that had Kylie's eyes stinging. Shit! Were they glowing now?

"You have no right to judge her after what *you* did." John took a defensive step toward Kylie's stepdad and her own protective in-stincts sparked to life.

"No wonder your daughter lacks respect," John quipped.

Lacks respect? Kylie felt her fangs grow a little longer, and she was so mad, she'd missed Derek joining the crowd, but Lucas hadn't missed it, because he growled.

Holiday moved in, and keeping one hand on Kylie's mom, she rested her other palm on John's shoulder. For a second, the tense energy sucking up oxygen diminished.

Kylie sent up a silent prayer of thanks. Then she noted the expression on her stepdad's face. And she immediately recanted her gratitude.

"Who the hell do you think are? Don't you dare insult my daughter," her stepdad said. Holiday looked from her mom to John and back to her stepdad. Poor Holiday had only two hands. Before anyone could stop it, her stepdad's fist made contact with John's nose. Blood poured. All the vampires in the room, including herself, breathed in the sweet scent.

Lucas tried to move her back, but she wasn't budging. Kylie's mom screamed. John started swinging his fists at her stepdad, missed, but knocked Holiday over in the process.

Burnett flew across the room and tossed John to the floor. And everyone . . . everyone in the room, all the campers, all the campers' parents, all the new teachers, especially Hayden Yates, stared at the foolhardy chaos that was her life.

Refocusing on the mess before her, she felt as if she were the star on some new reality show: *Parents Behaving Badly.* She watched in complete mortification as the scene continued.

John rose to his feet and apologized to Holiday.

Her mom seethed.

Her dad tried to talk to her seething mom.

Holiday tried to touch everyone.

Burnett continued to glare green daggers at John, proving how hard it was for a vampire to accept an apology. Not that she blamed him. Kill him. Kill him. She cheered the vampire on.

Lucas hadn't stopped scowling at Derek and Derek hadn't stopped ignoring Lucas.

Everyone reacted in one manner or another. Everyone except Kylie. She didn't move, not even to breathe. She stood frozen in the same spot, and concentrated . . . concentrated really hard on *not* wishing she could vanish—because down deep, that's exactly what she wanted to do.

Chapter Thirty

Burnett ushered everyone involved in the dispute out of the dining hall. Kylie moved with him like a robot, one foot in front of the other, still not wanting to let her emotions rise to the surface for fear of what might happen. Meaning, she'd either start again with the wiseass comments—channeling Della's attitude—or she'd vanish. Both could cause irreparable damage.

Right as she stepped out the door, followed by Lucas and Derek, she heard someone's parent say, "Wouldn't you know, it's always humans causing shit."

Inhaling the sunshine-filled air, trying not to be insulted for her mom and stepdad, and trying to control the mortification of it all, she watched Holiday guide her mom and John into the office building. Burnett waited a second, then in an unsympathetic voice, he ordered her stepdad to follow him inside—obviously into different rooms. Kylie sensed they were all going to get a stern talking-to. Not that they didn't deserve it, but . . . she felt odd being the one watching her parents getting pulled into the "principal's office" instead of the other way around.

Remembering some of the things she'd said to her mom and

John, Kylie suspected her stern talking-to was probably just around the corner.

Once the office door closed behind Burnett and her stepdad, Kylie swung around with the intention of throwing herself into Lucas's arms. She needed a little TLC—someone to lean on. But Lucas wasn't there. She looked back at the dining hall and saw him moving inside, no doubt heading back to his pack. God forbid his pack believe his assistance in stopping the disruption was anything more than a good deed, or because he actually cared about her.

Right or wrong, her heart broke right then. Derek, however, suddenly appeared beside her. Her eyes stung, her throat knotted, and the next thing she knew she was in his arms. Warm, strong arms that were so good at holding her and offering comfort.

It was wrong. So wrong. She needed to stop this. Stop relying on Derek.

"Quit feeling guilty," Derek whispered in her ear, reading her emotion right on cue. "I'm just a friend, helping out another friend."

No, she thought. He was a friend who used to be more, a friend who'd told her he loved her and wanted to be more again. He was someone that on odd occasions she still thought about having more with, too—someone she knew she could turn to for help. And yet, it wasn't his arms she longed for, it wasn't him she needed to hold her.

A while later, Holiday stepped out onto the office's porch and motioned her over. Great, now it was Kylie's time to get her punishment. Accepting she deserved it, she stiffened her spine and went to face the music.

But the look on Holiday's face wasn't one of reprimand. She immediately embraced Kylie. "Dear Lord, child. Please tell me you're okay."

"I'm okay," Kylie lied.

Holiday exhaled. "You scared the life out of me. What . . . ? What happened?"

When Kylie met the camp leader's green, caring gaze, the air in Kylie's lungs shuddered. "I scared the life out me, too. I . . . just vanished. I could see and hear you, but you didn't know I was there. I . . . I went poof." *Just like my grandfather and aunt had.*

Holiday touched Kylie's forearm to offer calm. "Okay, we need to talk about it, figure it out, but first let's deal with your parents and get them on their way."

Kylie's chest tightened with the realization that as much as Holiday tried, she wouldn't be able to help Kylie figure this out. She needed her grandfather and aunt. *A chameleon alone will not survive. Come with us. You need to learn who and what you are.*

Realizing Holiday was studying her, Kylie blurted out, "I said terrible things. I don't like John."

"Well, if it makes you feel any better, right now, neither do I." Holiday pressed a palm to each of Kylie's shoulders. "Just go talk to them. I think they're all in agreement that they're the ones in the wrong. Your dad's in my office and your mom and John are in the conference room. Can you do this?"

Kylie nodded.

As she walked away, Holiday pulled her back for another hug. "It's going to be fine, okay? There's nothing we can't figure out."

If only that were true.

Kylie stepped into Holiday's office. Her dad, sitting on the sofa, rose and met her face-to-face. And his face showed his emotions. Remorse. Sadness. A lot of sadness.

"I'm so sorry, baby. I behaved like an idiot. It won't happen again, I promise you."

Kylie nodded. "Everything just got out of hand."

He nodded. "But it wasn't all in vain. It forced me to face the truth. I needed that."

Did his voice just shake, or was she imagining it? "What truth?"

"I'm giving your mom her divorce. She wants it; she's got it."

Defeat filled her stepdad's eyes. Defeat, like she could never recall seeing before. One word came to her mind. *Broken.* He was a broken man. Seeing it hurt so damn much!

"Dad, I think Mom's just—"

"No." He held up his hands. "I didn't mean . . . I'm not blaming your mom. I accept I messed up. I don't even understand how I could do it, when I loved her so damn much from the first time I saw her in high school." Tears filled his eyes as he pressed his palm to Kylie's cheek. "Don't ever fall in love, princess. It hurts too damn much."

His words echoed in her head as she recalled the pain she'd felt when she turned for Lucas and he wasn't there. She wondered if her stepdad wasn't too late in offering that piece of advice. But she pushed her own emotions aside to deal with his. He needed her.

He took another deep breath. "Losing her kills me, but I deserve it, and I'll learn to live with it, but what I can't live with is . . . losing you. From the day the doctor dropped you into my arms, I loved you."

Tears filled Kylie's eyes. "You aren't going to lose me."

"Good, because I'm your father and I don't want you to ever forget that."

But he wasn't her father. The words "I won't forget" rested on the tip of her tongue, but she couldn't say them. She looked away. She hadn't meant that cut of her eyes to mean anything.

Yet it had. She heard his sharp intake of air. She glanced back and saw it in his eyes. He knew. He knew that she knew.

"Your mom told you," he said.

Hurt filled his eyes and the same feeling swelled in Kylie's chest.

"No." *My real father came to see me from the grave.* She had to come up with a lie and quick. "I found your original marriage certificate and learned she was already pregnant, and everything else fell into place."

"I couldn't have loved you more if you were mine. I never wanted you to think I didn't love you because of it."

"I know," she said. "And the fact that you loved me when I wasn't yours meant something." She spoke the words to soothe him, because his pain filled the room, but then she realized how true they were. He'd loved her when he didn't have to.

He'd done all the daddy/daughter things with her: sold Girl Scout cookies, helped her build a matchbox car to enter the school race, and gone on all the father/daughter trips. Then there were the hugs, when her mom wasn't good at giving them. She leaned into him, needing a hug now, and thinking he could use one, too.

She savored his embrace. He'd always been good at this. She heard his breath shake, and she cried into his shoulder like she had so many times as a child. That's when she realized she'd forgiven him. He wasn't a bad man; he'd just made some bad mistakes.

He was, after all, just human.

After her dad left, Kylie pulled herself together, and walked into the conference room to face her mom and John. Like it or not, she had some apologizing to do, so the sooner she got it over with, the better.

Kylie's mom shot up from her chair. John followed. "I'm sorry," Kylie said. "I—"

"We're sorry, too. Aren't we, John?" her mom blurted out.

"Yes, I spoke too freely." The apology came from John's lips but didn't appear in his eyes. "It was a mistake that will not repeat itself."

"You're just human," Kylie said, but she didn't say it with all that much confidence. And she studied his face to see if he reacted to the remark. He didn't. She still had to stop herself from checking his brain pattern again.

The scary thought was that if he wasn't human, he was a chameleon. She recalled Red, who'd given his life to save her, telling her that he was the same thing that she was, only not born at midnight. So . . . Mario must be a chameleon, too. And if John was a chameleon, could he be in cahoots with Mario?

She was overreacting, she told herself. Her feelings probably stemmed from the fact that he was the reason her stepdad didn't stand a chance of getting back with her mom. However, she decided to ask Burnett to do a background check on dear ol' John.

Kylie's mom moved closer. "John, can you give Kylie and me some time alone?"

Here comes the scolding. Kylie bit her tongue and told herself she should be happy her mom decided to spare her the embarrassment of scolding her in front of her man toy.

However, the man toy looked unhappy when he turned for the door. Kylie bit her tongue harder. But damn, this guy brought out the worst in her.

The moment John walked out, Kylie blurted out, "I'm sorry. I shouldn't have said those things." And she was sorry, not because she'd said them to John, but because she'd probably hurt her mom. That had never been her intention.

"No, Holiday was right. Showing up here with him wasn't the best idea. I just . . ." She blushed. "He makes me happy, Kylie. I can't even explain it, but it's almost the feeling I got with your real dad."

Kylie recalled something her grandfather said, that the humans who were blessed found themselves attracted to supernaturals. Her suspicions rose about John.

"I wanted you to get to know him, because . . . because he's important to me. And—"

Dear Lord, this was hard to hear. Before she knew what she planned to say, she'd started talking. "Dad's sorry about all this, too, Mom. If you brought John here to make Dad jealous, it worked. I know Dad hurt you, but if you still love him . . . he loves you."

Her mom closed her eyes as if searching for the right words. When she looked up, raw emotion shined in her eyes. "I did want your dad to see me and John, but I can't . . . Your dad and I won't be getting back together." She took Kylie's hand. "I'm sorry, baby. I can't . . ."

Kylie squeezed her mom's palm. "I understand."

Her mom sighed. "Do you?"

Kylie nodded. It still hurt like the devil, but she understood.

Her mom sighed as if she was about to say something difficult. "Please try to see the good in John. He's not the reason your dad and I broke up."

"I know." That was all Kylie managed to say. She wasn't sure she could ever see any good in John.

Her mom bit her lip and made a funny face. "Now, about the question you asked. If John and I were . . . If we . . ."

"Are having sex?" Kylie finished for her, because God knew her mom would be here all day trying to say it.

Her mom blushed. "I'm an adult and I'm capable of making that kind of decision. You're young and . . ." Her eyes widened. "You aren't . . . you haven't . . . ?"

"No, Mom. I haven't," Kylie said. "But I will someday, and I don't want you to have an aneurism when you find out."

Her mom looked horrified. "I won't. As long as you're thirty."

Kylie rolled her eyes. "Mom."

"Okay, twenty-nine." She paused. "You know, it hurts to see you grow up."

"I know; it hurts to see you grow up, too."

Her mom's brow wrinkled with confusion. "What?"

"I could say it hurt to know you're having sex, but I thought you'd prefer the euphemism."

Her mom chuckled at the same time a cold entered the room, a familiar cold. Daniel? A quick glance around the room told her he couldn't manifest. But she knew he'd tried.

Her mom smiled. Then she reached over and hugged her. "I swear, sometimes when I'm with you, I can almost feel your father here."

"Me too," Kylie said, and wondered how much her mom could really feel.

The chill in the room grew colder, but oddly it came with a hint of anger and frustration. Had her dad overheard the conversation and was making his opinion known about the whole sex-with-John issue?

I know, Dad, Kylie spoke in her head. *I don't like him, either.*

Even before her mom and John pulled out of the parking lot, Holiday and Burnett had Kylie by her elbows. "Let's talk," Holiday said.

Kylie gazed back at the dining hall. "Shouldn't ya'll be in there?"

"First things first," Holiday said as Burnett led them to the office.

"How the hell did you disappear like that?" Leave it to Burnett to cut to the chase.

"I don't know." Kylie walked into the office. "I wished I could vanish like a ghost when I saw my mom and John kissing, and then . . . I did."

"You wished yourself invisible?" Holiday asked.

"I guess," Kylie said.

"Then how did you come back?" Burnett closed the door.

"I un-wished it." Knowing how crazy it sounded, she glanced at Holiday and dropped down on Holiday's sofa. "Sort of like how you tried to teach me to shut off a ghost."

"Visualization." Holiday arched her brows as if impressed.

Not that Kylie shared her viewpoint. "It was scarier than hell. I remembered what my dad said about us working things out together and I thought I was dead." She paused. "How am I going to stop it from happening again?"

Holiday looked at Burnett as if expecting some wisdom from him.

"What?" He held up his arms in defeat. "I ain't got shit. I'm just now learning to deal with ghosts."

Holiday rolled her eyes. "You read the reports at the FRU. Did it say anything, or lead you to assume anything, about a chameleon's gifts?"

"No. The only thing it stated was some of the case studies considered themselves chameleons." He frowned. "There could have been more in the other reports, but they conveniently disappeared."

Right then, Kylie couldn't help but remember her grandfather's warning about the FRU.

"We need to read the other files," Holiday said. Her eyes stayed on Burnett. "How can we do that?"

Kylie closed her eyes. She didn't know what they were going to do, but she knew what she was doing. First, she was going to find a way to get back in touch with her grandfather, and then . . .

A wash of pain spilled over her. Could her grandfather be right? Did she have to leave Shadow Falls and go with him in order to get the information she needed?

After a few minutes of both Burnett and Holiday trying to come up with a solution, they finally concluded that Kylie should be careful about what she wished for.

Right! As if she hadn't come up with that one by herself.

Burnett's phone rang. He answered the call. "Yeah," he said. "How long has she been missing?" Both Holiday and Kylie tried to pretend they weren't listening, but how could they not when the call was obviously about Cindy, the waitress at the diner, the once-smiling young woman in her driver's license who was now in the grave with Holiday's sister?

"Okay," Burnett said. "Get me the file. Did you get anything back on the other matter?" Burnett's eyes shifted to Kylie, telling her that the "other matter" involved her, as well.

Burnett listened and suddenly that's when it hit Kylie. She couldn't hear the conversation on the line. What happen to her . . . "Hey," Kylie screeched at Holiday. "Am I still vampire?"

Holiday tightened her brows. Shock filled her eyes. "No."

"What am I now?" Kylie asked.

"Welcome to my world," Holiday said.

"I'm fae?" Oh, great. More "Kylie's a freak" moments from the other campers were predicted to arrive soon. As if the parental chaos wasn't enough to get them talking about her.

Her aunt's words echoed in her mind. *The few who did not hide were viewed as outcasts, freaks, and not belonging to any one kind.*

Holiday nodded and smiled a smile that came with a lot of empathy. And Kylie not only saw it, but felt it.

Burnett must have heard the conversation, because as soon as he pulled the phone from his ear, he stared at her forehead and said, "Damn."

"What did you learn?" Holiday asked, as if sensing Kylie didn't want to discuss her ever-evolving brain pattern.

"Cindy Shaffer disappeared about six months ago."

"So after Hannah disappeared," Holiday said.

"Do we know for sure that Hannah didn't just leave for a while and then . . . ." He paused and sympathy flowed out of him in waves.

"And then was killed," Holiday said, and the words no more left her lips than the grief floated off her and filled Kylie's chest. Kylie had always been empathetic to others, but this was so much more intense.

Not a cakewalk, Kylie thought. Being fae would take some getting used to, but at least she could go back to eating food again. Then she thought about Derek and how he'd said her emotions had felt supersized. That must have been so hard on him.

Burnett moved in. "The police are investigating her disappearance. They have a suspect—old boyfriend—but they couldn't prove anything. I'll go over their files, but considering what we know, I don't think this is tied to her personally."

"What else did you learn?" Kylie asked, remembering Burnett's glance at her during the call.

"I had another check done on Hayden Yates."

"And?" Kylie asked, but even before he spoke she felt his discontent at having to tell her.

"He's clean. There's nothing in his background that points to him being anything other than what he says he is."

Kylie exhaled, not sure she believed it. She'd been so sure there was something hinky about him. Then she remembered . . . "Can you check out my mom's boyfriend?"

"You think *he's* behind Hannah's murder?" Burnett asked, confused.

"No, nothing to do with Hannah. I just . . . don't like him."

"I don't, either," Burnett clipped, "but that doesn't mean he's a criminal. There's a lot of people out there that I don't like."

Kylie frowned. "He gives me the creeps and I'd feel better if—"

"I'll do it," Burnett said, but she felt his emotions and knew he believed it was a waste of time.

"There's something else I want to talk about," Kylie said.

"Why do I have the feeling I'm not going to like this?" Burnett asked.

Kylie glanced at Holiday, who looked equally concerned. "I think it's time to call a halt to the whole shadow thing," Kylie said.

"No!" Burnett's expression grew grim.

Kylie sat up straighter and felt her backbone stiffen. "I'm tired of never being alone."

"You're alone in your room when you go to your cabin," he countered.

"Della's listening to every move I make. I can't do it anymore. I want my life back. Mario hasn't tried anything else for weeks now. Miranda said she doesn't feel any unwelcomed presence. I don't feel his presence. Maybe he's given up."

"People like him don't give up. He's waiting for the opportunity to strike."

"I promise to be careful, and if I feel anything, you'll be the first person I tell."

"No!" he said again.

Kylie felt an odd kind of energy building in her gut. Everything inside her said she was right, that they couldn't force this on her. She didn't understand the ball of vigor, or her lack of fear at standing up to them right now. If she wasn't so mad at his out-and-out refusal, she might have been more afraid that something else weird was happening to her.

"I'm not a prisoner here," she said. "I have a say in this."

"A say in if you get yourself killed or not?" he asked in anger.

"I'm not going to get killed." She tilted her chin back and looked at Holiday, hoping she'd see reason in the camp leader's eyes.

"This is because you want to see your grandfather again, isn't it?" Holiday asked, and while she saw Holiday's disapproval, Kylie also felt Holiday's compassion.

"Partly." Kylie didn't even consider lying. There was just a sense of rightness to her request. "But that's not all it's about. I'm tired of being babysat."

Burnett went to speak again, but Holiday intervened. "Would you promise to stay out of the woods?"

"She's already broken that promise," Burnett said.

"I promise." Kylie ignored Burnett.

Holiday leaned forward. "Will you promise to confirm with us when you meet your grandfather?"

"Will you promise not to stop me?" Kylie asked.

"I promise we will assess the situation and only stop you if we feel your life's in jeopardy."

"By whose judgment?" Kylie asked. "Some people's idea of safety is not reasonable." She didn't even flinch when she looked at Burnett—who, by the way, looked even more furious. And she felt every bit of his anger.

"This is insane. My job is to protect you," Burnett snarled.

"No," Holiday corrected him. "Our job as school administrators is to teach Kylie how to survive in the human world. Like it or not"—she glanced at Kylie—"she has the right to leave. And that is the last thing we want to happen right now."

Somehow, Kylie knew that the ball of energy in her gut had been about projecting how serious she was on this issue. Was that a fae talent, or was that from her chameleon abilities? Kylie didn't know. But it was pretty damn cool, even if it scared her.

"Do I have a choice in the matter?" Burnett bit out.

"No," both Kylie and Holiday said at the same time.

Burnett's phone beeped in an odd kind of way. He grabbed his device and pushed a few buttons. "Someone just jumped the front gate." He turned to leave, but stopped when a figure flashed in the doorway.

Blake, Holiday's ex-fiancé and the suspected murderer, stood there. "I heard you were looking for me."

Kylie jumped to her feet and stood beside Burnett, ready to defend Holiday.

But Holiday acted as though she didn't need protecting. She jumped up and met Blake's glare. "Did you do it?" she asked, fury pouring out of her.

"Did I do what?" he asked.

"Did you kill Hannah?"

Chapter Thirty-one

"What?" His gaze cut to Burnett and Kylie and then back to Holiday. Disbelief filled his eyes and rolled off of him in waves. "Hannah's dead?"

Kylie tried to listen to his heartbeat, but not being vampire anymore, all she could do was read his emotions. They came off sincere, but could she trust that?

"Answer me, damn it!" Holiday slammed her palms down on his chest. Her emotions were a whole bag of raw pain, betrayal at its worst.

Burnett moved to Holiday's side and gently pulled her back, but his eyes were bright green and on Blake with warning.

Blake exhaled, his frustration sounding in the released air. "You are so biting on the wrong vampire! This is meritless."

"Not so meritless," Holiday said. "She told me you were furious with her when she told you that she planned on telling me the truth."

"Of course I was furious. We were getting married. I loved you. She told me if I showed up at my own wedding, she'd stop the ceremony."

"Did you kill her?" Holiday demanded, her anguish filling the air Kylie breathed.

Blake stared at Holiday, hurt radiating from him. "Of all the people in the world, you know me better than that. Do you really think I could murder Hannah?"

"What I think doesn't mean shit," Holiday seethed. "I didn't think you'd sleep with my sister, but you did."

"We were drunk and . . . I'd just started dating you. It was a damn mistake. And then the next thing I know, I'm in love with you. I'm still in love with you. And yes, I wanted to tell you then, but I was scared. At first, Hannah acted as if it never happened, so I convinced myself—"

"That you could get away with it?" Tears pooled in Holiday's eyes.

"No, I convinced myself that one mistake wasn't enough to stop two people who loved each other from finding happiness."

"That's enough." Burnett walked over and grabbed Blake by the arm. "You're coming with me."

Blake pulled away and the two men stared each other right in the eyes.

"Not yet." Holiday looked at Burnett. "I want to talk to him."

"You did," Burnett countered.

"Alone. I want to talk to him alone," she said.

Burnett's body turned into one knotted muscle. Jealousy oozed from his pores. "He's a suspected serial killer, Holiday, who illegally entered Shadow Falls. I need to get him to the FRU office."

"Serial killer?" Blake's eyes turned defensive. "I didn't harm Hannah or anyone else."

"That's what they all say," Burnett clipped, and reached for Blake again. The man moved back, his eyes growing hot.

"What's wrong?" Blake baited Burnett. "Worried she might still feel something for me?"

Holiday moved in and rested her hand on Burnett's arm and spoke with honesty. "Burnett has no reason to worry. I want the truth from you, Blake, that's all. And then I want you to climb right back under whatever rock you've been hiding under." She motioned with a firm hand for Burnett and Kylie to leave.

Burnett's body language and emotions said what he thought of that idea. But something told Kylie that Holiday needed this time alone with Blake, and Burnett needed to give it to her.

Kylie touched Burnett's arm, felt the warmth flow from her touch, and saw his expression soften. He looked back at Holiday right before he walked out. Kylie looked at Blake. And right then, her gut told her that he wasn't Hannah's killer.

But if it wasn't him, who was it? Then Kylie again remembered Hannah saying the killer was here. Here at Shadow Falls. Kylie couldn't help but think again of Hayden Yates. It didn't even matter that Burnett's check had come back clean; she didn't trust that guy. And by God, she wasn't going to lower her guard where he was concerned, either.

Burnett didn't move more than a foot away from the door. Kylie figured he was listening to every word spoken in the other room. For Holiday's safety, of course, so it wasn't really an evasion of privacy. At least that's what Kylie wanted to believe.

She couldn't hear the conversation, and as slightly uncomfortable as it made her listening in on private conversations, her own need to protect Holiday had her wishing she could.

"Was Blake telling the truth?" Kylie asked, wondering if the emotions she'd read from Blake were as telling as his heartbeat.

Burnett glanced over at her. "About what?"

"About not killing Hannah?"

"It doesn't matter," he said gruffly, and looked back at the door.

"Doesn't it?" she asked.

He shook his head. "The heart can lie. People, evil people with no conscience, have no problem lying."

Kylie remembered Della telling her that in the beginning. But as much as Kylie wanted to believe Blake was their man, what she'd felt from him wasn't evil. "For what it's worth, his emotions felt real."

"You mean when he said he still loved her?" Burnett's jealousy practically bounded out of him and bounced off the walls.

Kylie swallowed. "I meant his shock about Hannah being dead, but . ... that, too."

Burnett closed his eyes and pressed a hand against the door.

"But just as real were Holiday's sentiments when she said *all* she wanted from him was the truth. She doesn't love him, Burnett."

He looked back at Kylie, sadness radiating from his eyes. "She used to."

"Is that important?"

"It is when that's what stopping her from letting anyone else get close," he said. There was a pause, and then as if to change the subject, he said, "I don't agree with Holiday's decision on removing your shadows."

"I know," Kylie said. "But tell me this—how would you take having someone shadow you all the time?"

She heard him swallow and felt his emotional answer. He wouldn't have accepted being shadowed for a single day.

All of a sudden, the room turned cold. Ghost-visiting cold. Then Hannah appeared beside Burnett; her presence came with a thick swarm of panic. *"He's here! He's here! You've gotta stop him! He's going to try to kill her,"* she screamed at Burnett.

"Who's here?" Kylie asked.

Burnett didn't wait for an answer. He bolted through Holiday's door, without bothering to open it. Ripped off the hinges, the door landed with a loud thud on the floor. He walked across the splintered wood and faced Blake.

Door removed, Kylie watched the scene from the outer room.

Blake, already on his feet, stared at Burnett with fury.

Holiday, still sitting at her desk, wore an expression of shock. She shot up from her desk chair, showing how slow fae reaction time was to that of a vampire.

Burnett, both his hands fisted at his sides, spoke to Blake. "Either you come the easy way, or the hard way." His threat rang with honesty. "I don't care which."

Kylie's gaze shifted to the spirit. Hannah stood frozen, gaping at the scene playing out. An ugly brown aura surrounded her. While deceased, there was plenty of emotion lingering beneath the icy chill of death. Kylie picked up one emotion loud and clear. Shame—big, heaping mounds of shame. Then she felt the spirit's surprise. Oddly, Hannah's initial panic and fear had faded.

Something didn't feel right. It was almost as if Hannah hadn't known Blake was here, and if she hadn't known Blake was here, how could *he* be the one causing her panic? "Did Blake do this?" Kylie asked Hannah in a hurried breath. No answer. "Hannah?" Kylie said her name again. Then the ghost faded.

"What's going on?" Holiday asked Burnett again, and Kylie's gaze locked on the three people in the room.

Blake looked back at Holiday. "I didn't do this. I probably don't deserve another chance with you, but I don't deserve this." He turned to Burnett. "I'll go with you, I'll answer your questions, but if you lay a hand on me, I'll kill you."

And from the man's emotions clouding the air, his threat rang with as much sincerity as Burnett's.

It had been a lazy Sunday afternoon with a lot of frustration floating in the air. Miranda was frustrated because there was a new shapeshifter ogling Perry. Holiday was frustrated because . . . well, as if losing her sister the first time hadn't been bad enough, now her spirit hadn't shown back up. Burnett was frustrated because he couldn't find one thread of evidence against Blake. Therefore he couldn't hold him.

Kylie was frustrated over the whole disaster that was her life.

The only one not in a pissy mood was Della, and Kylie, even being an emotion-reading fae, wasn't sure what mood Della was in, but it felt wrong. The girl was following Kylie around like a lost puppy.

Even now, pulling up her e-mail, Kylie felt Della standing over her shoulder. Kylie turned around and frowned. "What?"

"What, what?" Della asked.

"You're reading over my shoulder. You're not even my shadow now."

"I'm not shadowing you. And I didn't know your e-mail was so private," Della said.

Right then, Kylie got a huge sense of anxiety, coupled with a sense of sadness, and then anger from the vamp. Della's emotions were dancing all over the place.

"What's up with you?" Kylie asked.

"Not a damn thing." Della dropped into a kitchen chair.

Kylie shifted her gaze back to her e-mail and clicked to check mail. No new e-mails. Nothing from . . .

"You're hoping to get something from your grandfather, aren't you?" Della asked.

Kylie looked back again. "Maybe. Why?"

Della frowned. "You're going to go live with him, aren't you? You're gonna leave Shadow Falls."

The question cut like a knife in Kylie's chest. How could she explain to Della that leaving was the last thing she wanted to do? Yet, there was a part of her that said it might be the only way she could learn about who and what she was.

And after seeing the shock on everyone's faces at the camp when her new fae pattern emerged, there was a part of Kylie that longed to be with people who didn't judge her. And the sooner she learned to control this changing-pattern game and the powers that came with it, the sooner she could come back to Shadow Falls and really fit in.

"That's what this is about?" Kylie asked.

"Yeah, that's what it's about. And don't think I didn't notice you didn't deny it, either."

Kylie chose her words carefully. "I don't have plans to do that." That was the truth. She was still praying that it wouldn't prove the only way.

"But your fae ass has thought about it, haven't you?" she asked.

"Yeah, my fae ass has thought about it, but—"

"But nothing! I'm not letting you go, Kylie." Tears filled the vamp's eyes. "I lost Lee, I lost my parents and my sister and all my friends back home. You and Miranda are all I have, and Miss Witch is so obsessed with a certain shape-shifter right now, I hardly even have time to argue with her anymore."

Della stood up and swiped at her cheeks. "I'm freaking tired of losing people I care about."

Kylie stood up. "You're not losing me." Her own eyes stung. Even if she had to go away, she'd be back. She belonged here. Surely Della realized that.

Della huffed. "I'm leaving next weekend to go . . . to go do what I gotta do for Burnett. And all I can think about is that you won't be here when I get back."

"I'll . . ." Kylie finally heard what Della said. "Where are you going?"

Della frowned. "I can't tell you."

"Shit." Kylie shook her head, recalling the anxiety she'd read from Della. Was Della scared? Of course she was scared, Kylie realized, but Della would never admit it. Kylie went and hugged the vamp. Della didn't like it, but she didn't fight it too hard. "Whatever you're doing for Burnett, it damn well better not be too dangerous."

"Group hug! Group hug!" Miranda said, bolting through the door.

"No." Della lurched back. "That one was just for Kylie," she said, trying to sound badass, but Kylie read her embarrassment loud and clear. "Go hug Perry." Della stormed into her bedroom and slammed the door.

"What crawled up her butt and put her in such a sunny disposition?" Miranda asked.

Kylie rolled her eyes. Then the computer dinged with a new e-mail, and she scurried over to see who it was from. Her mom.

The thought crossed Kylie's mind like sandpaper. If she did have to leave Shadow Falls, what in the hell would she tell her parents?

Kylie glanced back at Miranda. "Maybe you should go pick a fight with Della so she'll know you still care."

Dinner that night was supposed to be a celebration to kick off the new school year. Books and class schedules were passed out. Kylie and Della had all the same classes. Miranda was in two of Kylie's five classes. Kylie couldn't help but wonder if this wasn't Burnett's idea of shadowing her without calling it shadowing.

Not that she was going to let that thought ruin her night. Sitting at a table with Della, Miranda, Perry, Jonathon, and Helen, Kylie downed her second piece of pizza. It was good to enjoy food again. Not that her improved mood had anything to do with the thin-crust pepperoni. It wasn't even the party atmosphere, or the party itself; it was what was happening after the party.

She eyed the clock—only two hours to go.

Right then Steve came over to their table and dropped down in an empty chair beside Della. Kylie almost grinned when Della literally blushed.

"What's up?" Steve asked.

"Hi, Steve," Kylie said, wanting him to feel welcome. Before coming to the dinner, Della had confessed that Steve was also supposed to go with her on the mission for the FRU. Della, of course, was pissed. Ahh, but she hadn't been able to hide the excitement in her stream of emotions.

Jonathon and Steve started chatting about some classes. Della seemed to relax and so did Kylie. Miranda nudged Kylie with her elbow and leaned in. "I think he likes her," she whispered in a very low voice. But Della, not missing a word with her sensitive hearing, shot Miranda a scowl.

"Here's to a great year." Someone made a toast across the room. Everyone seemed to be in a festive mood, and for the time being, everyone had stopped staring at Kylie's pattern. Probably another reason Kylie was in a better mood.

But no sooner did she appreciate not being stared at than the hairs on the back of her neck started doing a two-step. When she swerved around, Hayden Yates turned his head. Her heart gripped when she saw Holiday standing next to him in the crowd. Not talking with him, but talking to the shy teacher Collin Warren.

Kylie still didn't like Hayden being that close to Holiday. She zeroed her gaze on him and when he glanced back, obviously feeling his neck hair dancing, their gazes met. *I swear if you hurt her, you'll pay for it.*

He looked away; Kylie kept her gaze locked on him for several moments, and she hoped like hell he understood her message, because it wasn't a threat. It was a promise.

Just thinking about the possibility of anyone hurting Holiday made Kylie's blood thicken and start to fizz—a sure sign that while her pattern might have changed, she was still a protector.

Someday she hoped to be able to say that with a total sense of pride, but right now it seemed to be just one more thing making her different from everyone else.

Kylie had no sooner turned back when she felt another pair of eyes on her, only a different kind of feeling tiptoed up her spine. Even from fifty feet away, Lucas's gaze felt like a caress. He winked. He glanced at the clock and she knew that like her he was counting down the time until they met.

"Damn!" Jonathon yelled, pulling Kylie's gaze from Lucas. "You cut yourself." Jonathon was holding Helen's hand; blood oozed from his grip.

Helen, looking a bit squeamish, had a bloody apple in her other hand and a bloody knife sitting in her lap. "It's okay." Her words lacked confidence. "It's not bad. Is it?"

Jonathon released his hold on her hand to look at it. His eyes grew bright, no doubt because of the blood, but even more apparent was his concern for Helen. "You need stitches," he said.

Helen looked up at Kylie. "Can you just fix it?"

Kylie's breath caught. It had been a while since she'd thought about her healing powers. And the few times she'd thought about them, she remembered those powers had failed Ellie. Kylie had failed Ellie.

"I . . . don't know if I can." She looked into Helen's eyes, saw her pain, but a lump of fear formed in Kylie's stomach right alongside the two slices of pizza. "I couldn't dreamscape when I was vampire; I probably can't heal as a fae."

"But faes are known for their healing," Helen reminded her.

"Oh, yeah." Kylie let go of a breath that shuddered on its escape from her lips. "What if I mess up?" She could still recall how devastated she'd been when she hadn't been able to bring Ellie back from the dead. Looking at her hands, she remembered how her palms had been coated with the girl's blood.

"You won't," Helen said with complete confidence.

Looking up, Kylie remembered how Helen had helped her by checking out her brain to see if she had a tumor the first week she'd been at camp. Helen had helped Kylie, and she couldn't say no.

She stood and moved over to the chair next to Helen. The shy and trusting girl held out her bleeding palm. Breathing in, Kylie recalled that she had to think healing thoughts. Amazingly, her hands suddenly felt hot. She gently ran her fingertip over the wound. Her touch created a tiny wake around the pooled blood on Helen's palm.

Fearing failure, Kylie put her whole palm over the wound. Hesitating to check to see if she'd done it, she suddenly realized that the entire lunch room had gone silent. Not a sound echoed in the large room.

Cutting her eyes up briefly, she realized everyone stared. Everyone! *Freaking great!*

Helen lifted her hand away and brought it in front of her face. Wiping the blood away with her other hand, a shy smile lifted her lips.

"You did it," Helen whispered, sounding as self-conscious as Kylie at all the unwanted attention.

Kylie leaned in. "Why is everyone staring?"

Helen made a funny face and came closer. "Because you're glowing."

"Glowing?" Kylie asked.

Helen nodded.

Kylie noticed that light did seem to emanate from her skin. "Shit!"

"No shit!" said Della. "You look like a firefly. This is so freaking cool!"

More like *not* cool! Kylie thought.

Holiday walked over, eyes rounded, and bafflement coming off her in waves.

Kylie stared up at her, mortified. "Make it stop. Please. Pleeeassse."

Chapter Thirty-two

"Where are you going?" Della asked when Kylie stepped out of her bedroom an hour later with her hair and teeth brushed, and—thank God—no longer glowing.

She almost told Della she didn't have to report to her anymore, but decided she'd probably ask Della the same thing if she were leaving the cabin.

"I'm going to meet Lucas," Kylie said.

Della titled her head to listen to her heartbeat.

"I'm not lying," Kylie said.

"I know. I heard," Della said. "Have fun. And don't do anything I wouldn't do."

"Gosh," Kylie teased, trying not to be grumpy. "That leaves my options wide open."

Della grinned. "But if you come home glowing, I'll know what you did."

"Not funny," Kylie said, and meant it. Then she took off.

Thankfully, she'd stopped glowing about ten minutes after she'd healed Helen. Out of sheer desperation, she'd asked Holiday, "Why did that happen? It never happened before when I healed someone."

Holiday's shrug and "I don't know" didn't surprise Kylie. But it was just one more thing that had Kylie taking her grandfather's warning more seriously. What if these crazy things continued? Right now, it was just the supernaturals who considered her a freak of nature. What would happen if she did something like this in front of regular humans?

Running down the path, hoping the feel of the wind in her hair would take the edge off her mood, she made it to the office in no time. The sound of a few people still lingering in the dining hall filled the night. Before anyone saw her, she cut around to the back of the office. The second she saw Lucas waiting for her by the tree, her frustration vanished.

She ran toward him and he snagged her up and pulled her to him. His arms wrapped around her waist. His thumbs slipped under the hem of her tank top to touch her bare skin. The kiss was sweet and warm. When he pulled back and smiled, she knew what he was thinking.

"Don't mention it," she said, feeling another "glowing" joke coming on.

"I'm just jealous."

"Jealous?" she asked, thinking she'd been wrong. "Of what?"

"I want to be the only thing that makes you glow."

She thumped her hand on his wide chest. "I'm telling you just like I told Della and Miranda. It's not funny."

"You looked beautiful." Honesty flowed from his comment. "Like an angel."

She frowned. "I don't want to be an angel. I want to be a regular supernatural."

"Okay, I won't talk about it anymore. I'll just kiss you instead."

And what a kiss it was. Hotter, sweeter, and more mind-numbing than ever. When he pulled back, she heard his pulse humming, a natural seduction mechanism for weres, and she wasn't above being seduced by it. She was lost in the sound.

"It must be close to the full moon again." She smiled up at the heat in his eyes, knowing her eyes held the same.

"Yeah." He inhaled as if trying to get oxygen into his brain. "You are driving me crazy. Sometimes, I just want . . ." He took a step back. "Let's try talking for a while."

She grinned. "I kind of like driving you crazy."

"That's mean." He pointed a finger in her face, but his tone rang humorous.

Not really mean, Kylie thought. It wasn't as if she'd planned anything to happen tonight. But if it did . . . Right then, she recalled Holiday's words of wisdom about boys, or rather sex. *When you do make that decision, it's a decision you make rationally and not one you just let happen. You understand the difference?*

Kylie did understand the difference. Problem was, it was easier to let it happen than to plan it. Planning it meant talking about it. And that would be embarrassing.

She inhaled sharply with a sudden realization. If she couldn't talk about it, she shouldn't do it—because unless she wanted to go through what Sara did with her pregnancy scare, it was essential that they talk about it.

"What is it?" Lucas asked.

She opened her mouth to answer—to talk about it—but closed her lips just as quickly. They could talk about it later. Later, but, for certain, before anything happened.

"Nothing." Her voice sounded like a frog ready to croak.

He studied her face. "You're almost glowing again."

"Crap!" She held out her arms and studied them in a panic.

He chuckled. "No, you're just blushing. Where did you slip off to in your head?" He tapped a finger to her temple and with her fae gifts, she felt the passion ooze from him.

"Nowhere," she lied. "Let's just . . . talk." *But not about sex.* Because obviously, she wasn't ready to have that conversation.

He studied her as if he didn't believe her, then reached for her hand and laced his fingers into hers. His palm felt warm, but not nearly as warm as it had when she'd been a vampire.

"Okay. Let's talk." They sat down on the soft ground, under the alcove of the tree. "Why don't you tell me how you got out of being shadowed? It doesn't sound like Burnett just to ease up on something like that."

"He didn't want to. But I . . ." She recalled the strange feeling she'd gotten when she'd stood up to Burnett and Holiday. As if the power of persuasion was . . . a real power. Then again, maybe it was. "I persuaded him."

"How? He's not easy to persuade."

"I . . . sort of threatened I might leave."

"Leave?" Concern filled his blue eyes. "You were just bullshitting him, right?"

Mostly, but I'm beginning to worry. She almost told him that, but decided she didn't want to get into that particular conversation with Lucas, not when they had so little time together, so she just nodded. "I agreed not to go into the woods, and to tell them before I went to see my grandfather again."

"What?" His super-charged werewolf protectiveness spilled out of him. "Burnett's going to let you go see your grandfather again? Alone?"

She nodded. "As long as it doesn't appear too dangerous."

"How are you going to know if it's dangerous?" He shook his head, his dark hair scattered across his brow. "Don't go until I come back." He cupped her chin in his hand. "Promise me."

"Come back from where?" she asked.

His frown tightened. "My dad again. This time I'm going to have to spend some time there. A week or more."

She tried to wrap her head around what he said. "But school starts tomorrow."

"Yeah." Sarcasm flowed from him. "But my dad doesn't see getting an education as being important."

"Can't you just tell him no? That you'll come to see him during parent weekend?"

"I wish," he said.

"But why for so long?" Suddenly she couldn't help but wonder if Fredericka planned on going with him.

He touched her cheek. "He's being insistent, Kylie. He gets something in his head and he won't let it go. I'm sorry."

The sincerity in his apology filled her chest. Sincerity and . . . guilt. For what?

He brushed her hair behind her ear. "You know I have to do this to get on the Council. I wouldn't do any of this if it wasn't for that. And . . . when it's over, it's over."

"What's over? What does he want you to do?"

"He just . . . He's crazy and I have to go along with him for now. Please . . . just understand for a little longer. In less than a month, the Council will make their choice. A month is all I need and then I don't have to go along with his plans."

"What plans?" She felt a touch of resentment swell inside her. "I hate your secrets."

"I know," he said. "I hate them, too. But you have to trust me on this."

For some crazy reason, when he said *trust,* she sensed he meant something . . . more. More as in . . . "Is Fredericka going?"

"No," he said. "Just me."

"Not even Clara?" she asked, still confused about the emotions she read in him.

"No. She might come for a while but not stay." He pulled her against him and they just sat there for the longest time not talking. Her heart hurt for him because she sensed how much he really didn't want to go, didn't want to do whatever it was his father had planned.

But he was going and was probably doing it—whatever it was. And he felt guilty about doing it, too. Why?

"Will you call me?" she finally asked.

"I'll try, but if he's monitoring my calls, I can't be caught . . ."

"Talking to me," she finished for him.

He exhaled and she knew it was the truth before he answered. "I don't like it."

Neither did she. Not even a little bit.

A second passed and then he said, "You didn't promise me that you won't go see your grandfather until I get back."

"I can't promise," she said, aggravated that he wanted promises and answers from her, but still held so much back. "I'll do what I have to do." And he'd just have accept it, as she was trying to accept what he'd told her, or rather what he hadn't told her.

Monday morning, the first-day-of-school jitters at Shadow Falls didn't feel any different from all Kylie's first-day jitters. She was both excited and anxious about being forced into a room full of people who seemed to know some secret to life, a secret she didn't have.

In spite of knowing what she was, and being surrounded by other supernaturals, she still felt like the outsider—the floater, floating to one group and then another, and not really belonging anywhere.

No doubt she'd follow Della and Miranda and socialize with whoever they hung out with, and their friends wouldn't reject Kylie, but she wouldn't get that sense of belonging. Just as it had been in her old school. Only difference was that she would have been with Sara, another misfit.

While putting on her makeup, Kylie thought about Sara. They hadn't talked in weeks but Kylie would change that later. While she accepted they had changed and probably didn't have nearly as much in common as they once had, Sara was still . . . Sara. And today, Kylie missed her more than ever.

The morning air had a touch of fall to it. Deciding what to wear, and how to wear her hair, had taken way more time than it should have. She hadn't thought she'd even care, since Lucas wasn't here, but the vibe had been contagious as Miranda and Della had worked to get themselves picture perfect.

Kylie hadn't dressed up for anyone. Yet when Derek looked over from the fae breakfast table, his eyes told her she looked pretty. She found herself smiling and then that smile vanished and she started missing Lucas.

After breakfast, they had Meet Your Campmate hour. Kylie drew Nikki's name, the new shape-shifter, the girl Miranda accused of having a crush on Perry. Kylie had worried that the new camper would pepper her with questions about the glowing episode, but nope. All Nikki wanted to talk about was Perry. Miranda had been right. The girl had a serious thing for Perry. Not that Kylie suspected Perry would play along. Nevertheless, before the hour ended, Kylie had nicely mentioned that Perry was already otherwise committed.

The girl had nicely ignored her, too.

The hour hadn't ended when Kylie debated what, if anything, she'd tell Miranda. Jealousy was an ugly emotion. Kylie was lucky that Fredericka hadn't gone with Lucas to his dad's place, or she'd have been battling the green-eyed emotion herself.

Kylie's first class was English with Della, Miranda, and Derek. Although absent, Lucas was in the class as well. Ava Kane, the new teacher, had an easy teaching style, not that any of the guys noticed anything other than her body. Not a male in the room wasn't mesmerized. Even Derek. Chances were, if Lucas had been there, he'd have been just as taken.

While the boys only had eyes for the teacher, the teacher only had eyes for Kylie's forehead. Was her pattern doing something new? She actually turned to Della and asked. Della assured her that she was still just a regular boring-ass fae.

When the class ended, Miss Kane stood by the door. And when Kylie walked past, Miss Kane leaned down and whispered, "Sorry. I shouldn't have stared, I'm just fascinated by . . . you."

Kylie felt her sincerity. "It's okay," Kylie offered, even though she wished it weren't. At least the woman apologized, which was more than what ninety percent of the campers would do.

History class—next in line—was difficult to sit through. As hard as Collin Warren tried to hide his jitters about teaching, they rang loud and clear. His nervousness filled the room like smoke, yet unlike Miss Kane, not once did the man look Kylie in the eyes. Frankly, she wasn't sure he looked anyone in the eyes.

Yet, because of Holiday's request that Kylie take the nervous teacher under her wing, when the class ended, Kylie hung back to offer a word of support. The students all left the room, except for her. She hoped the man would acknowledge her, but he sat at his desk, head down, shuffling his own papers.

She moved to stand in front of his desk. He still didn't look up. Okay . . . this was weird. She got being shy, but this was over the top—the kind of shyness for which a person might require medicine.

"Hello," she said.

He exhaled as if unhappy, but looked up. "Can I help you?"

Emotions flowed from him—something more than just extreme shyness. Almost fear, mingled with frustration.

"I wanted to say welcome to Shadow Falls. It can be hard—"

"I . . . I need practice." He glanced away. "I'll get better at it."

"I wasn't going to criticize." She sympathized with how he must feel, knowing he'd sucked his first day at teaching. "Practice makes perfect, my Nana used to say."

He looked up. "Do you see her?"

"See who?" Kylie asked.

"Your Nana. Isn't she passed? I hear you have the gift of speaking with the dead."

The question caught Kylie off guard. "Yeah. I mean, she died about four months ago, but I haven't spoken with her."

"But you talk to others, right? The dead?"

Kylie nodded. "Yeah." Unable to read him at the moment, she added, "I know it sounds pretty freaky."

"Not at all. I'd love to be able to ask the dead questions."

Kylie tried to digest what he'd said.

He diverted his eyes. "I mean . . . with my love of history. How great would it be to talk to those who lived before us?"

"That makes sense," Kylie said. And it did, but it was still odd. Most supernaturals would never have wanted to deal with the dead, not even for the love of history. She looked to the door. "I should go before I'm late."

As Kylie walked away, she felt him watching her. Okay, Collin Warren was even stranger than she'd first assumed. She really hoped Holiday knew what she was doing when she hired him.

Kylie had just left that cabin and started down the path to her next class when her phone rang. Glancing at the number, a wave of nostalgia hit.

"I was going to call you, too." Kylie sighed.

"The first day of school doesn't feel right with you not here," Sara said.

"I know." Kylie bit down on her lip.

"How are things?" Sara asked. "You still got two cute boys after you?"

"I pretty much decided on one."

"Derek," Sara said.

"No," Kylie corrected. "Lucas."

"Hmm, for some reason, I thought you'd go with Derek, but Lucas is yummy."

Why did you think that? "How are you doing?" Kylie asked, deciding she didn't want to know Sara's answer to the other question.

"Still cancer free," Sara said. "As you well know."

Kylie ignored the comment. "I'm glad."

"When are you coming home next?" Sara asked.

"I think there's a parent weekend in two or three weeks." If she wasn't still pulling stunts like glowing and vanishing, that was.

"Good, because I need a Kylie fix. Agh, there's the bell. I gotta run. I'll call you in a week or so."

A week? There was a time not so long ago when not a day would go by without them talking.

Kylie pushed away the melancholy at how her life had changed. Then, pocketing her phone, she hurried to class. The thought that it was Hayden Yates's class sent a shiver of dread skittering up and down her backbone.

The second she walked up to the door of Hayden Yates' classroom, Kylie decided that the awkward vibes Collin Warren gave off weren't nearly as unsettling as Mr. Yates's.

The man hadn't even looked at Kylie, yet somehow she knew he'd been keeping tabs on her—that he not only knew she was standing at the door, but he'd been waiting for her.

The question that had weighed on her mind grew heavier. Was he behind Hannah's and the other girls' deaths? If so, did he know Kylie suspected him?

Stepping farther into the classroom, she noticed that everyone was already in their seats. Only one seat remained. Kylie's gut turned into a pretzel.

Fredericka sat right behind the empty seat. The girl smiled, or rather smirked.

Kylie hadn't thought about having to deal with the she-wolf in her classes. Trying not to look at Fredericka, Kylie went and sat down.

As she slipped into the seat, she heard the were say, "Oh, boy. Extra light now the glowworm has shown up."

Kylie gritted her teeth and stared at the book on her desktop.

"Bitch," Della muttered from across the room.

Kylie, suddenly angry with herself for letting Della fight her battles, swung around and faced her nemesis. "In addition to glowing, I've discovered other new talents. Here's one you're going to love—giving smart-ass weres the mange. Especially ones that still slightly reek of skunk."

Chuckles escaped from several of the nearby students. Fredericka rose defensively from her seat, her eyes glowing a shade of pissed-off orange.

Seeing the fury in the wolf-crazed gaze, Kylie questioned the wisdom of spouting off her mouth. No doubt about it, she was about to get her ass whupped by a were—and on the first day of school. How special was that?

Chapter Thirty-three

"Sit down!" Mr. Yates's order echoed through the room. "Kill each other on your own time, not mine."

Kylie turned around, surprised the suspicious teacher hadn't let the she-wolf take her out.

The tension still hung thick when he started teaching. Facing forward, Kylie debated if she would get a pencil stabbed in her back from Fredericka.

But nothing happened. Mr. Yates started talking about how adrenaline can create strength in humans, and how it partly explained how supernaturals received their powers. His teaching skills were above average, and he had everyone hanging onto his every word. Even Kylie found it hard not to be enthralled. Yet everything in Kylie's gut told her he hadn't come here to teach. And considering Hannah's warning that the killer was here, Kylie wasn't about to let down her guard.

Her need to stay on guard shot up a notch when the class ended and she was half out the door and she heard him clear his throat.

"Kylie, stay a few minutes."

Kylie froze, her back still to him. Della, equally wary of the man, leaned in and whispered, "I'll be right outside the door."

Pulling her books closer to her chest, remembering she suspected the tall thirty-something teacher of being a serial killer, she moved back into the room with caution.

"Did I do something wrong?" An image of the three girls, their decomposed bodies in that grave, filled her mind. What kind of evil person did that?

"No—well, yes. As a protector, you shouldn't pick a fight with a were."

"She started it," Kylie said, and frowned at how juvenile that sounded. But this man gave her the creeps and brought out the worst in her.

His concern was touching—not—but she suspected there was more to this little chat. "Is that all?"

"I feel as if we got off on the wrong foot." Sincerity, a heavy dose of it, seemed to flow from him, but Kylie didn't buy it for a second. If an evil person without a conscience could lie to a vampire, he could also fake his emotions.

He continued, "I'd like to believe you would trust me."

Had he told Hannah and the other two girls the same thing? Did he get them to trust him and then wrap his hands around their necks and choke the life out of them? She could swear he looked at her throat.

Chills spread down her spine. She heard the sound of the other campers leaving the area. Was Della still outside the door? If she screamed, would Della be able to get here in time to save her?

"I don't trust very easily," Kylie said.

"I got that feeling." He took a step toward her.

She took a step back, his presence making it hard to breathe. "You know what else I don't do?" Her heartbeat played to the tune of fear, but she fought not to let it show.

He laced his fingers together. She couldn't help wondering if he was remembering how it had felt to use his hands as weapons.

"What's that?" he asked.

"Let anyone hurt someone I love." Kylie listened again, and there wasn't a sound coming from outside. The only noise bouncing off the freshly painted walls was the whishing noise of the ceiling fan.

Had Della left?

He tilted his head to the side. "What are you accusing me of doing?"

"What have you done?" Kylie fed her lungs a mouthful of air and held it.

"Nothing," he said.

Liar! She could feel it, feel him hiding the truth. "Like I said, I don't trust very easily." She turned her back on him, and with each step, she expected to feel him snatch her back, to feel his hands wrap around her throat, choking the life out of her the way he'd done the others.

Three days later, after suffering through yet another Hayden Yates class, unable to think of anything except the threat this man posed to Holiday, Kylie stormed into the office. Burnett and Holiday were arguing again; she heard them before she reached the porch, but she didn't care.

Well, she did care, just not enough to quiet the alarm blaring inside her. Hayden Yates was hiding something. That something was probably murder. And until Kylie could make Burnett and Holiday see this, Holiday's life was in jeopardy.

Walking right into Holiday's office, Kylie slammed the door behind her. "I don't like him."

"Me either," Burnett roared.

Holiday cut her eyes from Kylie to Burnett. "You two aren't even talking about the same person."

Kylie looked at Holiday for an explanation. Holiday obliged.

"Blake has offered to help look into Hannah's disappearance. He was the last person to see her alive, so I think we should accept his help."

"A suspect helping with the investigation, that makes about as much sense as fried ice cream."

Holiday leaned her elbows on her desk. "You can't find one thing that points to his guilt."

"He slept with your sister!" Burnett roared.

"Guilty of murder, not of being a piece of shit."

"And I'm telling both of you," Kylie said, "Hayden is guilty."

"There's no proof of that," they said at the same time.

"He wears a glove over his emotions. Every time he opens his mouth to speak, half truths come out. I feel it."

Burnett shook his head. "I've dug so deep into his background, I can practically tell you when he stopped wearing diapers."

Holiday's chair squeaked. "Kylie, if Hayden was out to hurt me, he's had plenty of opportunity. I interviewed him the first time when I was away taking care of my aunt's funeral. It was just him and me."

Kylie frowned. "I don't care. I still—"

"Both of you are wrong," Holiday insisted. "Blake didn't do this, and neither did Hayden. And if we don't stop focusing on them, we'll never find the killer. And we might never find Hannah's and the other two girls' bodies."

Burnett's eyes brightened and Kylie could read his mind. It wasn't finding the bodies that worried him so much; it was protecting Holiday. Hannah's warning felt imminent and Burnett felt that, too.

"Where the hell is Hannah when we need her?" Burnett bit out. He looked at Kylie. "You haven't seen her, felt her? Nothing?"

Kylie dropped on the sofa. "The last time was when she saw Blake here in the office."

"See," Burnett bellowed. "She probably figures we caught the bastard."

"I don't think so." Kylie almost feared disagreeing with Burnett when he was in this kind of mood, but getting them to see her point felt crucial. "She didn't look as if she thought it was over when she left."

He folded his arms over his wide chest. "Can we have a séance? Hold hands and call her back?"

"A séance?" Holiday rolled her eyes. "You have so much to learn about spirits."

"I don't give a damn about learning about spirits. I just need Hannah to come and tell me once and for all who she thinks is trying to hurt you."

On Friday morning, Kylie had skipped breakfast and Meet Your Campmate hour. She barely made it to English on time.

Obviously, Burnett wasn't the only one who needed to learn more about spirits. Kylie didn't know enough, either, because while she had felt Hannah's presence in the last few days, and again this morning, the spirit wouldn't manifest. Kylie had tried to appeal to her the way Holiday suggested. No luck. Kylie had even resorted to begging. Nothing.

Sitting at her desk, she reached down to make sure she'd brought her phone. The slight bulge in her pocket was reassuring. Maybe she was dreaming, but she hoped Lucas would either call or at least text her. But so far, nothing. That stung.

Looking up at the front of class, Miss Kane started talking about famous authors and the books they would be reading for the first six weeks. Who knew Jane Austen and so many others were supernatural? Kylie sure as hell didn't.

Intrigued by the conversation, Kylie barely noticed the noise when it started. Just a slight knock, as if someone were tapping on a door. The tap became a loud knock. Confused, she looked around, and oddly, no one else reacted.

Inhaling a strange vibe, she stared straight ahead again. As the noise grew louder, a slight movement to the right of the teacher caught Kylie's attention. The closet door behind Miss Kane rattled on its hinges, telling her where the banging originated.

Cutting her eyes left and right, she prayed she'd see someone, anyone, reacting to the obvious disruption.

Nope.

Then the cold of a spirit sent goose bumps racing up her arms. A trail of steam floated up from her lips, impairing her vision. Miss Kane said something, but Kylie couldn't hear over the ear-piercing hammering.

"Kylie? Kylie?" Someone called her name.

Who? Kylie couldn't think.

Forcing herself to look up, she saw the teacher staring at her as if waiting for a response. Kylie tried to talk, just a muttered, "Huh?" but not a word would leave her shivering lips. Then she saw it. Steam, lots of steam, billowing out from under the closet door.

Damn! Damn! This wasn't a normal spirit's visit. It felt more like the beginning of a vision.

That thought had hives popping out all over her chilled skin. Not because visions were scarier than hell, but because visions generally ended up with Kylie unconscious, or even worse, babbling incoherently.

Not here, Kylie pleaded. Not in front of twenty-five other campers.

An icy touch whispered across her shoulder. She looked back. A woman, her skin a pale ashen color, with dark purple circles under her gray eyes, stared at Kylie.

"She needs to see you." The spirit wore a white nightgown and her long brown hair hung around her shoulders. She raised her hand and pointed to the closet in front of the class.

"Who are you?" Kylie asked, and realized she'd forgotten to talk in her head.

All the students were now staring. Kylie could hardly think. So cold. She could barely feel her own skin anymore.

"Who's in there?" she asked.

In the distance, like static noise, Kylie heard others talking. Someone else called her name, maybe it was Della, and then she thought she heard Derek, but nothing sounded right, or felt right.

"She needs to talk to you."

Suddenly, realizing it could be Hannah behind that door, Kylie forced herself to stand up and walk to the closet. Even determined to do it, she hated doing it in front of people. But what choice did she have? Her knees wobbled as she neared the closet door.

She saw Miss Kane backing across the room, fear turning her complexion pale.

Kylie completely understood. She was pretty damn scared herself.

She reached for the closet's doorknob. Before she touched it, a hand ripped through the wood. Bony fingers latched onto the front of her shirt and yanked her through the splintered wood of the closet door. And yet it wasn't the closet.

The dark, dank place smelled of dirt, herbs, and death.

She screamed. Hard. Loud.

"Kylie? Kylie?" The voices echoed in the distance and then faded. Now, the only sound she heard over her own screams was the clanking sound of metal hitting metal.

She lay flat on her back. Gritty dirt rained down on her cheeks from above. The desire to brush it away hit, but her arms were locked at her sides. Even before she opened her eyes, she knew where she was.

The grave—she was in the grave with Hannah and the other girls.

And something told her she might never escape.

Chapter Thirty-four

Buried alive.

Panic scraped across Kylie's mind and clawed at her chest. Opening her eyes, she saw only darkness, but felt more particles of dirt sift down. She went to blink and each speck of grit scraped across the top of her lids.

Please, I don't want to be here, she screamed in her mind. Her eyes adjusted to the dark and tears stung her sinuses, but the watery weakness helped wash away some of the grit.

She went to breathe, but her mouth wouldn't open; something held it shut. Her lungs demanded oxygen, so she drew air in through her nose. Her throat knotted at the smell, the smell of death and then a heavy herb scent. She forced herself to turn her head to confirm what she suspected: that this vision had landed her in the grave.

A long strand of red hair rested against the side of her face. As had happened in the other vision, she was the spirit. She was Hannah—only unlike the woman whose body she inhibited, she breathed. The thought that she was in the corpse brought on another wave of nausea. Then another followed when she saw a large black beetle move across her lashes. Its prickly legs inched over her cheek and poked its head up into her left nostril.

She started snorting and struggling to free herself, but nothing worked.

Turning her cheek a little farther to the right, her gaze came upon the face of Cindy Shaffer. A scream rose in Kylie's throat, but stayed bubbled in her mouth that was still forced closed. Her heart thumped against her breastbone at the sight. The girl's facial skin hung loose, exposing some cheekbone. But the girl's mouth was covered with duct tape. Staring down past her own nose, Kylie saw she bore the same tape. And the decomposing body she was in was shackled with chains. Was this supposed to mean something? Or had the killer really done this?

Another loud clank came from above. Kylie's gaze shot up toward the noise. She saw a long iron spike being pushed through a hole in the slats that appeared to be decaying wood flooring. The piece of iron dropped on top of her, and the cold of it sizzled against her forearm, which was pinned at her side. On one end of the metal bar was some kind of ornament, a cross. Kylie recognized the emblem as being like the rusty fence and gate at the cemetery.

Footsteps sounded on the floor above as if someone was walking away, but then he returned, and another piece of rusty fencing was pushed through the hole. This time, Kylie saw the hand of the person shoving the iron inside. As the arm moved almost in front of her face, the cuff of the shirt rose slightly upward, exposing the edge of a silver watchband.

What am I supposed to learn from this? Kylie asked with her mind, and looked at the dead girl at her side. Another wave of panic filled her lungs when a fat snake at least two feet long slithered up her chest and then higher. The cold, damp feel of its underbelly muscles inching across her cheek had a scream building in her throat.

She had to get out of here.

• • •

"You're fine." The calm sound of Holiday's voice had Kylie opening her eyes seconds later. She took a quick look around. She was in Holiday's office. But why was she . . . ?

The vision played in her head like a horror movie in fast forward. Panic flooded her chest. She jackknifed up, jumped off the sofa, and slapped at her arms, legs, and face, hoping to chase away the feel of death and underground creatures moving against her skin.

"It's okay," Holiday said again.

No, it wasn't. She'd been dead and had a snake crawling over her face and a bug playing peekaboo inside her nose. That was so not okay.

Kylie took a deep breath, then bent over and barfed—once, then twice. Barfed all over someone's dark pair of shoes.

"Oh, damn!" a deep voice said.

Kylie recognized the voice and the shoes.

She looked up at the disgusted expression on the badass vampire and started to apologize, but instead barfed again. She missed Burnett's shoes this time, but made a direct hit to the front of his shirt.

"Oh, fu—," Burnett muttered, but never finished the word.

Holiday wrapped her arm around Kylie. "Breathe. Just breathe. It's going to be okay." She guided Kylie back to the sofa. Burnett, holding his arms away from his shirt front, handed Holiday a damp cloth, which was quickly pressed to Kylie's forehead.

Kylie reached for it and wiped her mouth, and then looked at Burnett. "I think you need it worse than me." Tears filled her eyes and her whole body trembled. "Sorry."

He looked down at his shirt and back up at her. "I'm not mad."

She focused on Holiday's face, felt the calm flowing from her touch, and tried to remember exactly what had happened. How had she gotten . . . Her memory started to fall into place one piece at a time.

But it only took a few pieces for her to start panicking again. "Please tell me I didn't go wacko in English class."

Holiday's gaze filled with empathy. "It's not your fault. And Della brought you here as soon as she got you out of the closet."

Kylie flopped back on the sofa and started to wish she could vanish, but stopped herself before it came true. "I hate this. I really, really hate this."

Kylie stared at the ceiling. Burnett left the room, but returned in record time wearing a different shirt. Obviously he didn't keep a new pair of shoes handy in his office because he now stood in his socks.

After a few minutes, Holiday asked Kylie, "Can you talk about it?"

"I was Hannah. But . . . most of the time when I have these types of visions and I'm the spirit, the spirit isn't dead and . . . in a grave with bugs and snakes." Kylie's breath shuddered.

"Hannah's trying to show you something. That's what visions are all about," Holiday said. "Tell me what happened."

Kylie swallowed a tight knot down her throat. "I don't know what she wants me to see. We were in the grave. There were snakes and bugs. I saw plenty of those." She wiped her face, remembering the snake slithering across her cheek.

"Tell me everything," Holiday said. "Everything."

Kylie started recounting it, from the footsteps sounding on top of the rotting wooden planks above her, to the herb smell and the scrap pieces of iron that looked like they came from the cemetery. When Kylie finished, Holiday's expression went white.

"What is it?" Burnett asked, not missing the look on her face.

"Someone knows Hannah is reaching out from the grave."

"How do you know that?" Kylie asked.

"The tape over their mouths and the chains. You said you smelled herbs and that you saw someone adding iron from the graveyard. In the past, it was called cold iron. It's basically iron, but some of it was blessed by practicing Wiccans. It was used to keep spirits from escaping, and . . . the herbs, there are several that are used to silence spirits. That's what she was trying to tell you. That someone is trying to stop her from communicating with us."

"And Blake knows you are a ghost whisperer," Burnett said. "It's logical that Hannah would come to you."

"But if that's the case, why is he just now trying to silence them? He would have done that in the beginning."

"She's right," Kylie said. "It's someone here. Hannah told us that much. And excuse me for sounding like a broken record, but Hayden Yates is bound to have heard I'm a ghost whisperer. *Everyone* here has." And if they hadn't, today sealed the deal.

Holiday twisted her hair in a tight rope and then met Kylie's gaze. "I don't want to suspect someone here," she said, and then met Burnett's gaze. "But Kylie's right. It could be someone from Shadow Falls. And if it was the iron from Fallen Cemetery, then Hannah's and the other's bodies are close by."

"Fine," Burnett growled. "I'll go back and run Hayden Yates through every damn database I can find. Until then, you don't let the man within two feet of you."

"I still don't think it's Hayden," Holiday said.

"And I still do," Kylie insisted.

"Who else could it be?" Burnett asked.

"One of the new students or teachers," Holiday said, "but . . ."

"Most serial killers are men. And I don't see a teen being able to pull this off."

"And Hannah keeps calling the killer a he," Kylie said.

Burnett huffed. "I'm not sure Collin Warren could look at someone long enough to kill them."

"But he's strange," Kylie said. However, Kylie's gut just knew that Hayden Yates was up to no good.

"Being extremely shy doesn't make him a killer," Holiday pointed out. "It just makes him socially awkward."

Burnett shook his head. "But just to be sure, I'll check him out again, too. You stay away from both of them."

Holiday rolled her eyes. "How am I going to run a school and not talk to any of the teachers?"

"I could always lock you in my cabin," Burnett said.

"You wish," Holiday said.

Burnett's eyes brightened and a smile barely tilted his lips up slightly. "That I do."

Kylie smiled for a second, too, completely getting Burnett's underlying message. Then for some reason, Kylie thought about Lucas, and started missing him, wishing he could be here to help her cope. *Don't ever fall in love, princess. It just hurts too much.*

Her stepfather's words echoed in Kylie's head and right then, she knew. She loved Lucas.

As if the epiphany gave her heart and mind a reboot, she suddenly recalled being in Miss Kane's closet and screaming at the top of her lungs. She closed her eyes as embarrassment flooded through her. If any of the other campers hadn't quite made up their minds about whether she was or wasn't a freak, she'd made it easy for them.

Kylie felt Holiday slip her soft hand against her wrist, as if reading some of her emotional angst. The touch had little effect this time. Kylie was in love with Lucas, a guy who couldn't even be seen in public with her, and she'd made a complete idiot out of herself with one of her ghost visions.

"Burnett," Holiday spoke softly, "why don't you go find some shoes and give Kylie and me a few minutes alone."

Something about being alone with Holiday had Kylie letting go and allowing herself to fall apart. She fell against the camp leader's shoulder and started sobbing.

Holiday held her, held her so tight that Kylie cried harder. After a few minutes, Holiday spoke. "I'm so damn sorry. Hannah shouldn't have come to you. You're too young to have to deal with this."

The words brought a sudden halt to Kylie's pity party.

She pulled out of the embrace. "No. I mean, sure, it's hard, but this is what I do. I'd do it for a stranger. And I'd do it for your sister again and again." *And if it meant stopping someone from hurting Holiday, I would do that and more.*

Kylie wiped her face to clear the tears and knew she was all red and blotchy. Not that she cared. This was Holiday. Her mentor, her big sister. Her friend.

"Besides," Kylie added, "it's not just the vision. It's Lucas. I think I love him. No, I'm pretty sure I love him. Oh, shit! I'm in love with a boy who can't love me back."

Holiday brushed her hand over Kylie's cheek. "Oh, hon, he might not supposed to be in love with you, but that doesn't mean he can't, or that he doesn't."

Kylie inhaled deeply, trying not to let herself cry again. "He hasn't told me he loves me. I mean, I haven't told him either, but . . . Derek told me he loved me. And . . ." She closed her eyes, trying to figure out how to put it. "And sometimes I'm confused about what I feel for him, but just now, seeing what you and Burnett have, or what you could have, it made me realize I want that. I'm tired of hiding what I feel and being afraid of it."

The tears Kylie had stopped shedding filled Holiday's eyes. "Love's always scary."

Kylie felt Holiday's emotions blend with her own. "It shouldn't be scary," Kylie said. "Burnett loves you. Even I can see it. And I know you love him. Don't lose out on something wonderful because you're scared."

"I just need some time," Holiday said.

"Time we might not have. Life's fragile. Look at Hannah, and Cindy and the other girl. They don't get the opportunity to love again. We have the chance and we're not doing it. I should have told Lucas how I feel. I should have forced him to be honest with me about what's happening with him. You should tell Burnett how you feel."

Holiday bit down on her lower lip. "I thought I was the one offering advice here."

"Yeah, well, the tables turned," Kylie said. *Things change*. Kylie just hoped with all the things changing, the one constant in her life would be Shadow Falls. The thought of losing Holiday and everyone here, even the ones who considered her a nutcase, was too much. They were her family.

That night, Kylie had tried to dreamscape with Lucas, but it wasn't working. She texted him, called him, and even e-mailed. No answer came back. Then at two in the morning, staring at the ceiling, her phone rang. She grabbed it without checking the caller ID.

"Lucas?" she said his name at the same time she hit the light switch. The cold in the room came on faster than the light.

"Sorry," the voice on the line said. "Just me."

Kylie shivered then frowned when she recognized the voice. "I just tried—"

"It's okay," Derek said, but his tone said it wasn't really okay. "I just woke up and felt you worrying. I tried to call you earlier to see how you were after the vision, but you didn't call me back."

Kylie pulled the blanket up around her neck. The spirit standing by the bed faded, but before she did, Kylie recognized her as the woman from earlier that day. Remembering who was on the phone, Kylie's chest swelled with emotion.

"I . . . It's been crazy." She'd gotten his messages. She just hadn't wanted to talk to him because of the emotional storm she felt about

Lucas right now. It wasn't fair to Derek, because even though she wasn't doing anything wrong, she knew their friendship offered him hope that she would change her mind, and she didn't think that hope had a hell of a lot of merit.

"You're pulling away again," he said.

"Derek, it's—"

"Kylie, you don't have to explain. I know." He paused. "It's okay. And someday I'll even be able to say that and mean it."

"You're a special guy," Kylie said, hurting for him.

"I know," he said, and chuckled. "And that's why I'm not completely giving up. But I'm working on it. I just called to check on you."

"I'm okay," Kylie said.

"Then I'll say good night." Rejection sounded in his voice.

"Derek, I'm really—"

"Just say good night, Kylie," he insisted.

"Good night," she whispered, and nothing was sadder than the sound of that dead line.

Putting her phone down, Kylie looked around. The cold from the spirit had lessened but she could tell she lingered nearby.

"Who are you?" Kylie asked.

The woman didn't answer. And why should she? They never made it easy.

But then, neither did the living.

"Kylie! Kylie!" The voice jolted Kylie from a deep sleep before the sun rose the next morning. She shot up, chills crawling up and down her spine like spiders. Without even knowing why, her blood sizzled with the need to protect. Protect someone.

Still half asleep, she pushed her hair from face and stood in the middle of the room, breathing in and breathing out. Her pulse raced, and panic filled her chest, crowding her lungs. Something was happening. She felt it.

Someone needed her. Someone needed Kylie's protection.

Who?

Her mind raced as she tried to make sense of what she felt. Then Kylie remembered the voice. She let it play in her mind, again and again, until finally she recognized it.

"No!" She grabbed her jeans and T-shirt.

Holiday was in trouble.

Chapter Thirty-five

Right before Kylie lit out of her room, she glanced at the clock on her nightstand. Five AM. Holiday would be at the office already.

Kylie stormed into Della's room, but the girl wasn't there. Probably at an early vampire ceremony. Kylie didn't wait a second longer; she bolted out of the cabin and flew like the wind to the office. The only thing that felt heavy about her was her heart. As if her heart knew Holiday's situation was bad. Really, really bad.

When Kylie got to the office, she found the door ajar. Not a good sign. Even worse, there was glass shattered all over the wet floor of the entrance. The broken handle of the coffee pot lay in the corner, another sign that a struggle had taken place.

"Where are you, Holiday?" Kylie's voice trembled. Tears filled her eyes and she tried to think.

Burnett. She needed to contact Burnett.

She reached into her pocket for her phone, only to realize she hadn't brought it. She ran into Holiday's office. The room looked undisturbed. Whoever had gotten Holiday had done it in the entrance area. He'd probably been waiting for her when she came in this morning, or maybe walked in when she'd been making coffee.

Hands shaking, Kylie grabbed Holiday's office phone. She couldn't remember Burnett's cell number. But damn, she could get to his cabin quicker than find his number.

She tore out, her feet barely touching the ground. She didn't know if she'd morphed into a vampire or if in protective mode she simply had more power. She didn't really care. Only one thing mattered, one thought echoed in her mind. Save Holiday. She had to save Holiday.

She made it to Burnett's cabin, and didn't even knock. She screamed his name when she entered, but no one answered. No one.

She went into his bedroom. The bed stood empty.

Recalling the vampire ritual, she tore out again. Della had told her once where they held it. She shot through the woods, not caring about her promise to not enter. If she ran into trouble, being in protective mode, she could kick ass and ask questions later.

She exited through the line of trees into a clearing. The wind whizzed past as she moved. Coming to a jolting stop, she found herself circled by a half-dozen angry vamps, their eyes glowing at the idea of an intruder disturbing their ceremony.

Lucky for her, the Shadow Falls vamps weren't likely to attack. A good thing, because even in protective mode, she didn't know if she could take on all six of them.

"Where's Burnett?" Kylie snapped. "Or Della?"

"What is it?" Burnett came to a stop beside her.

Kylie never answered. She didn't have to. He saw it in her eyes.

"Holiday?" The sound in his voice had Kylie's chest aching. Her blood pumped faster.

Kylie's breath caught. "He's got her."

"Who?" he demanded as Della stopped at his side.

"I still don't know," Kylie answered, and her eyes spiked with more tears. But they had better find out, and soon, before it was too late.

• • •

Three minutes later, after Kylie had explained everything, Burnett had spouted out orders for all the vamps and her to go search the Shadow Falls property. If Holiday was still here, they'd find her. Burnett headed back to the office to see if he could find clues and to check to see if the alarm was functioning.

Kylie headed to the west side of the property. But when she passed the trail that led to the cabin where Hayden Yates lived, she did a complete U-turn.

She slammed down on his porch. Heard him moving around inside. Heard him talking to someone.

She stormed in without knocking and oops, forgot to open the door. It landed with a loud crack on the floor. Hayden stood by the sofa, his hooded sweater in one hand as if he'd just removed it, and his phone in the other. His dark hair appeared darker, wet with sweat. His skin looked flushed, as if he'd been running. But from what?

Or better yet, from where?

"Where is she?" Her tone came out deep, filled with fury and warning.

He cut off the phone. "Where is who?" he asked in innocence.

"Don't play games with me." Her blood now fizzed in her veins. Her patience, if she'd had any at all, was now gone.

He tossed the hoodie and his phone on the sofa. Beside those two items was a watch. A black-banded watch.

"You're vampire now. Try listening to my heart for the truth."

Kylie had already listened to his heart, but it didn't matter. Didn't matter that he had a different watch from the one she'd seen in the vision. He could have two watches. "That only works with people who have a conscience."

"And you're assuming I don't."

"You've been hiding something ever since you got here." She took a step closer. Her intent was to get answers, and she didn't care how.

He apparently read her mood, because he held out his hands, palms up. "Perhaps, but it isn't what you think. I haven't hurt your precious camp leader."

"I didn't tell you who it was! So how the hell—"

"I'm no fool. Burnett stakes out at her house most nights."

"If you've hurt her, I'll kill you." She didn't flinch at hearing the words. They were true. For Holiday, Kylie would kill.

But what if she'd failed Holiday and it was too late? Anger, fear, and love burned in Kylie's chest. Her hands shook.

"I don't doubt you could kill me," Hayden said, holding his submissive pose. "Your strength right now appears . . . palpable." He inhaled and she could swear he looked sincere, even respectful. "It isn't my place to"—he hesitated again—"speak up." He ran a hand through his hair. "It would probably be beneficial for me to just keep my mouth shut. But unfortunately, unlike you believe, I do have a conscience."

He closed his eyes again and when he opened them, she saw complete honesty. And she saw something else, but she wasn't sure what it was. Something about him that looked . . . familiar in a weird way. "I saw Collin Warren out and about this morning. Something told me he was up to no good."

Kylie listened to Hayden's heart speak the truth. She continued to study his eyes, which held no dishonesty. "Who are you?" she asked.

He brought both hands up and brushed his hair from his brow. "See for yourself."

Kylie did see. His pattern was the same as her father's. Hayden was . . . a chameleon.

Her breath caught. He had all sorts of information she needed, but not now. Because more important than even the answers he held was Holiday's life. Then her gaze shifted back to his sofa, and she realized he did have one thing she needed.

She snagged his phone and lit out as she heard him protest.

· · ·

Kylie flew off his porch. The sunrise had painted the horizon a bright color, not that she took the time to enjoy the view. She held the phone up and realized the problem. She still couldn't remember Burnett's number. So she dialed Della.

Della didn't answer, damn it.

Kylie left a message. She told her what she suspected—that Collin Warren had Holiday and that she was looking for him now. She didn't slow down, didn't stop until she stood in front of Collin's cabin. She listened. Not a sound echoed from inside. She had to see for herself. She started up the porch steps when she heard quiet footfalls sound behind her.

Heart stopping, Kylie swung around, expecting Collin, but found Fredericka instead.

"What are you doing sneaking around?" the were asked.

Kylie didn't have time to chat, so she turned around and went to check out Collin's cabin. The door was locked, so she simply crashed it in. She'd done it at Hayden's cabin, what was one more?

Fredericka's gasp sounded behind her. Kylie ignored it.

She went into Collin's bedroom, looking for anything that might help her find Holiday.

"What's going on?" Fredericka asked, following her into the room.

"Just leave. I don't have time for pettiness." She opened the drawer and yanked everything out.

"What's going on?" Fredericka asked again.

Kylie sighed. "Holiday's missing and I think this creep took her."

"Shit!" Fredericka said. "I knew he was weird."

Kylie went to leave.

"Wait," Fredericka said. "I followed him a couple of days ago. He went to some old cabin in that park next door."

"Where?" Kylie roared; every instinct in her seemed to be turned on.

"I'll . . . show you." She held up her hands as if half frightened.

They ran into the woods. Kylie's patience was pushed when she had to slow down for Fredericka, but Kylie held her tongue. Normally, she wouldn't have trusted the were to spit on her if she was on fire, but her gut said the girl wasn't pulling any tricks now. No doubt Fredericka knew Holiday had gone to extra lengths to get her to Shadow Falls, and to keep her here.

They came upon the property gate. Kylie jumped without even trying. Fredericka barely made it and landed hard on the other side.

Kylie hesitated and looked back.

"I'm fine," the were growled, and bounced onto her feet.

I didn't ask. Kylie bit her tongue. They started to bolt again when Hayden's phone rang. Kylie pulled it out of her pocket and saw Burnett's name. Obviously, Della had given him this number.

"Where the hell are you?" Burnett barked. "And why do you have Hayden Yates's phone?"

Kylie and Fredericka arrived at the cabin before Burnett. But he'd said he was on his way, which meant he would be there soon. Weeds and young trees grew around the structure as if someone had forgotten it existed. The sounds of the night suddenly went silent. Burnett must be close by.

He'd ordered them to wait before moving into the cabin. But Kylie heard someone inside. She listened; God help her, she only heard one person breathing. Fear stole her next breath. Her blood fizzed so strong, it almost burned.

Protect Holiday. Protect Holiday. The words echoed in her head like a litany.

She motioned for Fredericka to stand back. The girl's eyes filled with rebellion. Kylie didn't have time to argue. She stormed into the building; the door splintered, the walls wobbled.

Collin Warren jumped up from the floor. At his feet lay Holiday. A very still, very dead Holiday.

Chapter Thirty-six

Fear filled Collin's eyes when he saw Kylie, while pure evil seemed to surround him.

Kylie picked up Collin Warren and tossed him across the cabin. She heard his body hit the log walls with a loud, cracking thud. The air gushing out of his lungs sounded in the room, but she didn't see him land.

She heard a scuffle happening behind her. Fredericka screamed. Kylie ignored it.

On her knees beside Holiday, Kylie removed the rope from around her throat.

"Is she dead?" Kylie heard Fredericka ask. The question floated in the room—unanswered.

Kylie's gaze stayed locked on Holiday. Kylie's heart stayed locked on the fact that she'd tried to save Ellie and failed—tried to save Roberto and failed then, too.

Burnett's footsteps sounded in the cabin; she heard him let out a sound of pure anguish. He knew. He knew Holiday was dead.

Kylie still didn't look up. Everything she had—everything she wanted to believe in—stayed focused on Holiday. This couldn't be happening. Not Holiday.

"No!" Kylie screamed.

Not Holiday, who had always been there for Kylie, always listened, always cared. Memories of them together filled her mind. Memories of them laughing, sitting side by side at the falls, even eating ice cream while talking about heartaches and boys. How many times had Holiday offered Kylie a warm, comforting touch?

"You can't go," Kylie said with a half sob. Tears rolled down her cheeks and landed on Holiday's pale face. Kylie ran her hands over Holiday's swollen, bruised throat.

When Kylie didn't feel her hands heat up, she closed her eyes and prayed. *Let me save her. You gave me this power, now let me use it. I'll pay whatever price it takes, even if it's my own life. Do you hear me? My life for hers!*

A ball of warmth formed in her chest and then slowly spread to her hands. Her hands tingled and then turned hot and then hotter still. Holiday's body felt so cold, so lifeless under Kylie's palms, but she didn't stop. She couldn't.

"She's glowing again," Fredericka's voice sounded in the distance.

But even as Kylie's light filled the small room, Holiday didn't respond. Another somber, grieving sound came from Burnett. It was the last sound Kylie heard before her vision went black.

Darkness surrounded Kylie. Exhaustion pulled at her mind. Where was she? Why did she feel so depleted? So dead?

She tried to open her eyes, but the effort felt too much. *Wake up! Wake up!* a part of her brain demanded. The feeling of urgency filled her chest and she fought to push the cobwebs from her mind.

As the last few clouds of confusion and exhaustion were cleared, she came to. She was in someone's arms, someone who ran. Kylie's body jolted up and down with the footfalls. She forced her eyes open and looked up at . . . Fredericka?

What was . . . ?

"Put me down," Kylie demanded.

"Burnett said to carry you," Fredericka bit out. "Believe me, I don't like it, either."

"Put me down!" Kylie demanded, and the she-wolf came to a sudden stop and dropped her none too gently on the ground. The feel of her butt hitting the hard ground brought it all back.

Collin Warren had Holiday.

Holiday . . . dead.

Pain filled Kylie's chest.

Bolting to her feet, she saw Burnett, holding a lifeless Holiday in his arms.

Kylie rushed over. "Let me try again!" she begged.

"You already did," Burnett bit out.

"But maybe this time—".

"Kylie! You already saved her," Burnett said. "She's weak, but she's breathing. Now, let Fredericka carry you back to camp so we can get both of you help."

"I'm fine," Kylie insisted.

"You're still glowing, Kylie," Burnett snapped. "And I don't know what that means."

Kylie didn't know either. But she didn't care. She stared at Holiday's chest, waiting to see it shift upward, bringing in oxygen. She held her own breath.

Only when Holiday breathed did Kylie draw air into her hungry lungs.

"Let's go," Burnett muttered. "I have a doctor meeting us at the camp."

Kylie pushed herself to run, but it wasn't nearly as fast as before, and damn if she didn't feel every muscle burn. Not that she was complaining. Holiday was alive and so was she. Nothing else mattered.

Kylie sat in Holiday's living room, silent and still glowing, while the doctor checked Holiday out in the bedroom. Burnett, on his feet, kept a listening ear turned to the door.

All the other students gathered in the dining hall. School had been canceled while everyone waited for news. Kylie wondered if Holiday knew how loved she was. That everyone, even Fredericka, cared.

Everyone except . . . Collin Warren. Questions start flipping through her mind. Kylie looked at Burnett. "What happened to Collin?"

Burnett shook his head.

Kylie's gut knotted. She recalled tossing the man across the small shack, recalled hearing the sound of his lungs give up air. Had his soul given up as well?

She'd said she would kill for Holiday, and she would, but now the thought that she might have taken a life made her want to puke. "Did I . . . ?"

Burnett shook his head. "Fredericka. She said he came at you with a knife. She attacked. They fought. He lost."

Kylie now recalled hearing the struggle, but the idea left her stunned. "Fredericka saved my life?" *Oh, hell.* She didn't want to be indebted to someone who hated her. Then she couldn't help but wonder why she'd done it. She could have let Collin kill her.

Burnett stared at Kylie as if reading her mind. "She comes off as a real bitch, but I don't think she's as bad as she lets people believe." He hesitated. "That happens when you have a rough upbringing. People think the worst of you and it just gets easier to let them think it than to try to prove them differently." He looked back at the bedroom door. "Holiday believed she was salvageable."

So did Lucas. Kylie sat there and chewed on her feelings. About Fredericka, then about Lucas. She missed him. Wished he was here.

Then she reheard Burnett's words and picked up on the personal reference in his tone. *That happens when you have a rough upbringing.* A piece of the puzzle of who Burnett was suddenly fell into place. She didn't know why it felt important but it did. She looked up at him. "You were raised in a foster home with Perry, weren't you?"

Burnett's gaze stayed fixed on the door. "She's going to be okay." A smile brightened his eyes. "The doctor, he just said she was going to be okay." He reached back with both hands and laced his fingers behind his neck. When he glanced at Kylie, he was still smiling. "Yeah. I was raised in foster care. Why? You thinking that's why I'm a mean bastard? Because of my rough upbringing?"

Hearing the humor and relief in his voice, she smiled. She knew if he weren't so relieved by the doctor's news, he'd probably be pissed that Kylie figured it out. Then the opportunity occurred to her. "No, but I'm thinking that's why it might be so hard for you to tell Holiday how you feel. To admit that you love her. And I think she really needs to hear that."

His eyebrows arched. "I'm not the one who's been pushing the other away."

"But you haven't told her how you feel, either. And you gotta trust me on this. A woman needs to hear that."

A few minutes passed in silence; she knew Burnett was thinking about what she said, and that felt good. But then the vamp looked back at her with questions in his eyes. "How did Hayden Yates know about Collin Warren?"

Kylie chose her words carefully. She hadn't told Burnett that Hayden was a chameleon and wasn't sure if she should.

"When I went to his cabin, he'd been out running. I accused him of being involved. He denied it. He said he'd seen Collin out and the man looked suspicious."

Burnett digested what she'd said. "Supposedly, Collin's always been socially flawed but no one saw the evilness in him until now." Burnett paused again. "How did you end up with Hayden's phone?"

"I'd forgotten mine when I left. So I . . . confiscated his." She shrugged.

"Did you know he left a message with me, saying he had a family emergency and had to leave for a few days?"

Kylie tried not to let her disappointment show. "No, I didn't know that."

"Do you still think he's involved?" Burnett asked. "If you do, I'll bring his ass back here now."

"No," Kylie answered honestly. "I was wrong. He didn't have anything to do with Holiday. If anything . . . he helped save her."

Burnett studied her. "And you don't see it as suspicious his leaving right now?"

"Maybe a little," Kylie said, so she wouldn't get caught in a lie. "But I'm sure he didn't have anything to do with Holiday's abduction."

"I'm still questioning him when he gets back," Burnett said.

Me too. Kylie shook her head. *If he comes back.* Her heart sank.

Then she recalled the phone again, still tucked in her pocket. Hayden Yates had to be working for her grandfather. And if so, he was probably in contact with Hayden. That meant she might have her grandfather's number in the phone.

If her grandfather hadn't changed his number again.

Thirty minutes later, after Burnett had visited Holiday, Kylie moved into the bedroom. Holiday, her red hair looking redder against the white sheets, looked pale, but alive. The bruise on her throat hadn't gone away.

She touched her throat and motioned for Kylie to hand her the water on her bedside table.

"You brought me back." Holiday's voice sounded raw, painfully raw.

"But I didn't heal you all the way." Kylie's throat hurt hearing Holiday talk. "Do you want me to see if I can—?"

Holiday shook her head. "I think you've done enough. You look worn out."

Kylie felt worn out, but not so much that she couldn't try. "I could—"

"No. I'll heal." Holiday looked concerned. "You haven't stopped glowing."

"I know," Kylie said. "But it'll go away, right?"

Holiday nodded but didn't look confident. Then she motioned for Kylie to sit in the chair beside the bed. "I got to see Hannah before she passed over. Right as I was dying, everything slowed down and she came to me. We talked. We made amends." Tears brightened Holiday's green eyes. "None of this would have happened if not for you. Thank you. I know the cost you have to pay, and I promise to live my life so it won't cost you even the tiniest piece of your soul."

Kylie took her hand and squeezed. "I don't think you've ever lived it any other way."

"I can be better." Holiday swallowed. "Nothing like dying to show you how to live."

Kylie smiled. "I hope in that message, you're talking about Burnett."

Holiday grinned. "The stupid vamp just asked me to marry him. Here, now? As if looking like I just died is how I wanted to be proposed to."

Joy did a lap around Kylie's heart. "And you said?"

Holiday took a sip of water. "I asked him if we couldn't just live together in sin."

Kylie frowned, but then she saw something in Holiday's eyes. "And?"

"He told me it wouldn't be a good example to our students. So . . . I agreed to marry him." She pushed a hand against her forehead. "Dear God, what am I getting myself into? He's not an easy man to deal with."

"I can hear you," Burnett called out from the other room, a chuckle sounding in his voice.

Holiday rolled her eyes.

Kylie squeezed Holiday's hand tighter. "He loves you," she whispered.

"Yeah, that's what he said." She sank deeper into her pillow, looking exhausted, but she also looked happy.

A sense of rightness filled Kylie's chest. She'd done it. Or at least, she'd helped do it. Burnett and Holiday were getting together.

She couldn't help but wonder if she and Lucas would have the same luck.

Holiday stared up at the ceiling for a second. "I also saw your grandmother, Kylie."

"Nana?" Kylie asked. "What did she say?"

"No, not Nana, the other one. Heidi."

Kylie saw something almost sad in Holiday's eyes. "What did she say?"

"Just to say hello." Holiday sighed.

Something told Kylie there was more. What was it that Holiday didn't want to tell? Kylie almost asked, but when Holiday's eyes fluttered closed, Kylie realized now wasn't the time to push. Later, she thought, and reached down and touched Hayden's phone in her pocket. Later.

. . .

It was after lunch before Kylie could sneak away to her bedroom. She pulled out Hayden's phone and searched for her grandfather's number. Unfortunately, there were no names listed. Just numbers. Three had been called the most. Kylie sat down on the edge of her bed and called the first.

She held her breath while it rang.

A woman answered. "About time you called," the voice said.

"Who is this?" Kylie asked, unsure how to approach the call.

"This is . . . Casey. Who are you?"

"I . . ."

"What are you doing with Hayden's phone?"

"I . . ."

"Damn that bastard! He said he wasn't seeing anyone else. Tell him I said to go to hell! He wasn't that good in bed anyway, as I'm sure you probably know." The line went dead.

"Uh-oh." Kylie considered calling back and trying to explain, but what would she say? *I'm not his girlfriend, just someone who stole his phone after accusing him of being a serial killer.* That might complicate matters even worse. Best to let him handle it on his own.

"Sorry, Hayden," Kylie muttered.

Before Kylie called the next number, the phone dinged with an incoming text. She debated over reading it, thinking it might be from his pissed-off girlfriend. Then she saw it wasn't from that number. She might be invading his privacy, but after stealing his phone, what was one more sin?

It took a second to figure out the phone's features to display the message.

But she was so damn glad she did.

Chapter Thirty-seven

The message wasn't for Hayden. It was from him.

You're answering my messages? Hayden

Kylie typed back. *Only because I hoped it was either you or my . . .*
She paused. Should she let him know she assumed he was with her
grandfather? She didn't see any advantage to playing dumb. . . . *my
grandfather.* She tapped her fingers on the phone waiting for a reply.

The phone dinged. *What did you tell the others?*

She decided to be honest. *Only that you helped save Holiday's life.
You can come back.*

She waited for him to respond. When he didn't do it quickly,
she wrote, *Sorry I suspected you.*

He replied: *If you did the right thing and came to live where you
belonged, I wouldn't have to return.*

Kylie considered her answer.

I belong at Shadow Falls.

She no sooner finished typing the words than her reflection in
the dresser mirror caught her attention. She hadn't stopped glowing
yet. How long could she continue to believe she belonged here when
everything pointed to the fact that she was different? Different even
from all the other supernaturals.

Her chest swelled again at the thought of leaving. She rejected it. But what was going to happen in two weeks when her mom was expecting to pick her up for parents' weekend? How would she explain the fact that she was freaking brighter than a fifty-watt bulb?

The phone pinged again. *It's not safe for you to stay there.*

Holiday and Burnett won't let the FRU do anything.

It's not just the FRU. You were right in what you told your grandfather. There's an underground rogue gang after you.

Swallowing a knot in her throat, she texted, *Is my grandfather's number in the phone?*

It took a few minutes for him to get back. But he did. *Yes.*

She typed in. *Thank you.* And hit send. Then remembering, she sent one more message. *Call your girlfriend. I might have upset her.*

Her grandfather answered the next number she dialed. And he didn't bother with formalities. Hayden had obviously told him to expect her call.

"I sent him because I was concerned for your safety," her grandfather said, his voice just an octave lower than her father's.

"I'm not upset," Kylie said. "Although I wish someone would have told me."

"You need to come with us, Kylie. It's not safe. You were right about the underground rogue. I don't trust the FRU not to harm you. How can I trust them to keep you safe from others?"

"Please," Kylie said. "You don't understand what you're asking." Tears filled her eyes. "I . . . This is home to me. Burnett's not like the FRU you remember. And Holiday . . . she took me in. Both of them have protected me." Her throat grew tight. "People have died here saving my life. These people you don't trust are my family." Her voice shook and she swiped the tears from her cheeks.

"*We* are your family."

"I can't leave," Kylie said.

There was a long pause. "I will send Hayden back if you offer your word that you have not told the others."

"I haven't told anyone." Silence fell again, then she blurted out, "I'm glowing. How do I stop it?"

"Glowing?" he asked, and paused as if in thought. "You have the gift of healing?"

"Yes," she answered.

"I'm assuming you used it."

"I . . . brought someone back to life."

He didn't speak for a few seconds. "Your gifts are indeed amazing."

"But how do I stop it?" She hadn't been fishing for compliments.

"You must release the energy you drew inside you to complete the healing."

"How?" Kylie asked.

"Meditate."

"I'm not good at meditation." She bit down on her lip.

"Then you'd better learn. And fast." He exhaled. "Kylie, if other gangs learn just how gifted you really are, you'll be a commodity. They will either want you working for them, or they'll want you dead. It won't be just one gang coming after you."

His warning rang in her ears. *Great. That's all she needed.*

"I will send Hayden back," he went on, "but think carefully on this, my child. I deserve to get to know my only grandchild."

Monday morning Kylie sat in the dining hall while everyone stared. She wasn't glowing anymore. Her internal bulb had blown sometime during the night.

She'd stayed in her room all weekend and meditated, and slept.

Obviously, bringing someone back to life took it out of you. Holiday and Burnett had dropped by with food, TLC, and news that all the bodies of the girls has been turned over to their families. Both Burnett and Holiday were now glowing, but it was a natural glow. They were in love.

That only made Kylie miss Lucas even more.

Derek had called twice just to say he was thinking about her. Lucas hadn't. She didn't even know if he was aware of what had happened. Still, his silence was hard to take.

Helen and Jonathon had dropped by. And Miranda, Perry, and Della had checked on her almost every hour. Even during the night, they'd crack open the door and peer at her. Of course, that could be because she looked really cool glowing in the dark. Hell, they could have sold tickets to the other campers for a dollar a peek. Not that they would. They were her friends.

Kylie stared down at her runny eggs and frowned as she felt all eyes in the dining hall on her.

Nope, right now, glowing wasn't the problem. It was her pattern. She'd changed again. She was finally a werewolf and Lucas wasn't around to enjoy it. And neither was Socks. Her cat hadn't come out from under the bed all morning. He made his prejudices known. Just as clear as the other werewolves here at the camp. Not one of them had come to say hello, or go to hell.

"You hanging in there?" Della asked.

"Like a pro," Kylie answered, and looked up to see Hayden Yates walk into the dining hall. Her heart did a little dance. He was back. Relief at knowing she wasn't completely alone washed over her.

We are your family. Her grandfather's words sliced through her.

"You still can't lie worth a damn," Della said.

Kylie looked away from Hayden before anyone guessed they shared secrets.

Della was right. She'd lied. She wasn't hanging in there like a pro. More like by a thread. She was confused, scared, and worried. She might have stopped glowing, but what was next? What freaky thing would she be calling her grandfather or running to Hayden to help her fix? And if she really belonged at Shadow Falls, why did Hayden's presence bring her so much comfort?

"Let's get this show on the road," Chris, the Meet Your Campmate leader, announced after breakfast. Kylie stood outside beside Della. She fought the need to fan herself. Her sudden increase in her body temperature would take getting used to.

"And first on our list of names is none other than our brand-new were." Chris's gaze shot to Kylie.

Kylie's breath caught. The first people announced were generally the ones someone had paid in blood for Chris to arrange. Swallowing, her gaze shot to Derek. But he stared at Chris in concern.

"Kylie, you get the pleasure of Fredericka's company."

Oh, great. The were had saved her life only to kill her later.

"I can follow you if you want," Della whispered, her eyes bright.

Kylie shook her head, tired of always being under someone else's protection. "No."

Fredericka walked up. "You wanna walk to the lake?"

"Sure," Kylie answered. *Why not? The lake would be a nice place to die.*

"I'll see you later." Della's tone came with all kinds of warnings for Fredericka.

As they started walking, neither Kylie nor Fredericka talked. Kylie listened, but amazingly, she barely heard their footsteps. The ability to move in silence must be part of being were. Her mind chewed on what Fredericka really wanted.

Or it did until her friendly blue jay showed up and did a song and dance right in front of them.

Fredericka frowned. Kylie shooed the bird away. "Go!"

As they continued on, Kylie did some thinking. She didn't believe the she-wolf really wanted to kill her. Then again, hadn't she already tried once? Putting a lion in Kylie's bedroom several months back hadn't been an act of kindness. But if the girl really planned on murder, would she have let the whole camp know they were together?

Then another thought suddenly hit. Was Fredericka pissed that Kylie hadn't said thank you for saving her life?

She'd planned on doing it. She really had. But she'd spent all her energy on stopping herself from glowing this weekend. Nevertheless, she should have done it first thing this morning. Was it too late?

Better late than never.

"Burnett told me you saved my life," Kylie said. "I should say thank you."

Fredericka's dark black hair swung loose around her shoulders. She was at least three inches taller than Kylie, and probably outweighed her by twenty pounds. Not that Kylie was seriously frightened anymore.

"I probably did it more for Holiday than you," the were said.

Probably? "I figured that," Kylie said, "but thanks anyway."

Fredericka nodded and remained quiet for the next few minutes. Kylie hated the tense silence. "Did you pay blood to get Chris to match us up?"

The were nodded. "Three pints. He said since he might get in trouble for pairing up enemies, I had to pay more."

"That's a lot of blood," Kylie said, when she couldn't think of anything else to say. Then the thought of blood had her remembering how she'd felt when she thought she'd killed Collin Warren. Fredericka had to feel the same, didn't she? Kylie's gratitude suddenly grew. "I'm sorry that . . . you had to . . . ki—Do it."

"It was nothing." She glanced at Kylie. "I've killed before."

Kylie couldn't swear on it, but something told her that if she'd been able to hear the girl's heartbeat, it would have told a different story.

"It still can't be easy," Kylie said.

"I'm over it," she snapped, but her tone said she wasn't.

And I'm still sorry.

More silence hung in the air. Fredericka finally spoke again. "You were wrong to sic your skunk on me."

"I didn't sic him on you," Kylie said, being honest. "You attacked him."

"It still wasn't nice," she said, and growled.

"Neither was putting a lion in my room." There, Kylie had thrown that bone out for them to chew on.

"I guess so." Fredericka looked away, but not quick enough.

Kylie saw the truth. "You didn't do it." She shook her head. "Why did you lie and say you did?"

She didn't answer for a long time. "I heard rumors that you thought I did it. I figured, why not let you believe it? I didn't like you."

"And now?" Kylie asked, still wondering why the were had paid three pints of blood to have an hour with her.

"Still don't like you," she said matter-of-factly. "But after I saw what you did for Holiday, I don't hate you as much."

"Well, there's a compliment I'll savor," Kylie said, letting a little humor slip into her voice. Fredericka didn't respond.

They arrived at the lake, and the girl stood there and looked out at the water. "I love Lucas," she confessed.

Kylie inhaled and tried to figure out how to play her cards now. Honesty seemed the only way. "So do I."

The were looked at Kylie, anguish filling the girl's eyes. "I know. That's why I wanted to talk to you. While I don't like you, I like *her* even less. And at least I know he cares about you. Even before you showed up here, he'd mentioned you to me. I was jealous of you even then."

Kylie shook her head, trying to play catch-up with Fredericka's conversation. "I'm not following you."

"I'm talking about Monique. I know he's told you that he can get out of it. But I'm not sure he can. I don't think you should let him do it."

"I'm still not following you," Kylie said, but she already had a feeling she didn't like what Fredericka had to say.

Fredericka just stared. "Shit. He didn't tell you? He said he did and you understood. That damn dog lied to me."

Frustration welled up inside Kylie. "Lied about what?"

"Lucas's betrothal ceremony is tonight."

Fredericka's words bounced around Kylie's head. "His what? He's . . . getting married?"

"Engaged, but with weres when you get betrothed, it's written in stone. He thinks he can get out of it, but I don't buy it. You don't just change your mind. And she's a complete bitch. If he goes through with this, he'll be stuck with her for the rest of his life."

"No!" Denial shot through Kylie and anger welled up inside her. "You're lying. You just want to start trouble. You'll do anything to break Lucas and me up."

"You bitch." Fredericka growled. "I'm trying to help and this is what I get? Yes, I've tried everything to break you up. It didn't work. But I'm not lying." She pulled an envelope from her pocket. A small envelope, like an invitation. "If you don't believe me, go see for yourself." She stepped away, and then turned back. "Just make sure you keep your were pattern on, or someone will rip your heart out before they ask questions."

· · ·

Kylie didn't want to believe Fredericka. More than anything in the world, Kylie wanted this to be just another one of the were's tricks to come between her and Lucas. Yet the girl was right about one thing: Kylie had to see it for herself.

The ceremony was taking place at another state park around five miles from there. As a were, Kylie could make that run fairly quickly. All day, she considered whether or not to tell Holiday and Burnett, but decided she'd rather ask for forgiveness than for permission. And speaking of forgiveness . . . She swore if Fredericka was lying, she'd never forgive her, never trust her again.

But if she wasn't lying . . . Kylie wasn't sure she'd ever forgive Lucas.

The ceremony was supposedly happening at midnight. Which made it easy to get away.

Kylie tiptoed out of her room. Della yanked open her bedroom door.

Easier to get away, but not easy.

"Where are you going?" Della snapped, her gaze moving up and down on Kylie. "And all dressed up?"

Kylie didn't know what one was supposed to wear to a betrothal, but her black dress and low black pumps would have to do.

"I need to go somewhere," Kylie said, stating the vague truth. She hadn't told Della or Miranda about this. At first, Kylie thought it was because it just hurt too much. Then she thought it was because they'd try to talk her out of going. Right now, she realized it was because she was worried they might say, "I told you so."

They hadn't been pro-Lucas lately.

Not that Kylie totally believed it yet. But she obviously believed it enough to sneak out of Shadow Falls to find out. But how could she not be suspicious? Lucas never told her anything. And damn, that hurt.

"You're meeting your grandfather?" Della asked, studying Kylie with suspicion.

"No," Kylie said.

Della frowned. "You've been acting weird since you walked off with Fredericka."

"I need to go," Kylie said.

"I'll come with you."

"No," Kylie pleaded. She needed to do this alone.

Della's chest puffed out. "Then tell me where you're going."

"You're not my shadow anymore," Kylie countered.

Della's scowled. "No, I'm your friend."

The honest emotion in Della's voice pulled at Kylie's heart. "Look, I'm going to try to meet up with Lucas." It was the truth—or a form of it.

"I thought you hadn't heard from him," Della said.

"Fredericka told me where he was."

Della made a face. "You trust her wolf ass?"

"Not really," Kylie said. "But I'm going anyway, and as your friend, I'm asking you not to stand in my way."

"I don't like it," Della said.

Kylie paused in thought, trying to find a way to get Della to understand. "I don't like that you're doing work for the FRU, but I respect your wishes."

Della frowned. "But I'm not doing it alone."

Yeah, Della was going with Steve, not that she was thrilled with it, but that wasn't the point. Convincing Della to let Kylie go was what mattered. Right or wrong, finding out the truth about Lucas once and for all felt crucial. She had admitted to loving him; now she needed to know if she'd given her heart away foolishly.

It took some time, but Della backed down.

And ten minutes later, when Kylie jumped over the fence leaving Shadow Falls property, she knew Burnett might come running.

It was another chance she took. However, since she suspected that several of the weres might be attending the ceremony—if there really was a ceremony—she hoped Burnett would assume she was one of them. Then again, she *was* one of them, she reminded herself.

As Kylie ran, she felt an odd kind of power flow through her. Different than the strength that came with being vampire. The way her limbs moved seemed less human. The power of a wolf, she supposed.

Her chest tightened, remembering Lucas telling her how he wanted to run with her as a wolf. *Please, please let Fredericka be wrong.*

Trying not to break all her promises to Burnett, Kylie avoided the woods whenever possible. But as she drew near the park, she wasn't going to have any other option. As she moved in a lithe run, her gaze kept shifting to the moon. She felt it calling her, like water to a person left in the sun too long.

When she entered the line of trees, the darkness grew blacker. The moon was no longer visible through thick foliage. The night air was warm, almost too warm. She felt a sense of danger sting her skin.

Ignoring it, she kept running. She didn't stop. Not even when she realized she wasn't alone.

Chapter Thirty-eight

The cold finally started to impair Kylie's speed and she glanced over to see who the spirit was keeping pace at her side.

The ghost, a woman, the one who appeared in the classroom right before the vision, moved with powerful strokes. Her white gown flowed around her, and her long brown hair danced in the wind.

With Kylie's attention on the spirit, her foot caught on a root and she tumbled down onto the earth—hard—landing facedown.

Pushing up with her arms, breathing in the scent of moist dirt below her, she stared at the spirit looming over her. "Who are you?"

"I'm not important. You are." She held out her hands and instantly a long, bloody sword appeared. *"You must kill him."*

Kylie got to her feet and stared at the spirit's bloody hands; red liquid flowed onto the sword, then dripped to the ground. One slow drop at a time.

For the first time, Kylie understood a symbol connected with the spirit world. This ghost had blood on her hands. And now she wanted Kylie to do her bidding.

Drawing herself to her full height, Kylie spoke in her mind, *I don't know what you heard, but I don't . . . I haven't killed anyone, and I'd kind of like to keep it that way.*

She stared at Kylie with gray, dead eyes that held no emotion, no soul. Fear raced up Kylie's spine. Something about this spirit was different from the others. Something scary.

"Then you, too, will die," the ghost said as if it didn't really matter. Without warning, the spirit faded. But the spot where she'd stood was coated with ice. Dark, black ice.

"Couldn't you have told me that first?" Kylie muttered, and then inhaled. "No!" She fisted her hands. "I'm not going to think about this now."

Her heart pounded in her chest and she commenced running, running to Lucas, or rather, to the truth about Lucas.

She remembered the last time he'd kissed her, the way he'd held her, the way she'd felt so loved. Fredericka was lying. She had to be lying.

A few minutes later, Kylie sensed others around her.

Other wolves.

She wasn't sure how she knew, she just did. Not wanting to draw attention to herself, she stopped running and started walking. Hoping to hide the windblown look, she pulled the band from around her wrist and put up her hair.

As she moved closer to the park, she heard voices. Happy voices. She thought she recognized Will's voice. She stopped beside a tree so as not to cross paths with him or any other of the Shadow Falls campers. The last thing she wanted was to be recognized.

Only when Kylie couldn't hear anyone moving around her did she continue on. When she left the line of trees, she saw the crowd, standing in rows. A hundred or more wolves gathered together. A few in the back line turned and looked at her. Thank goodness they weren't from Shadow Falls.

Fredericka's warning rang in her ears. *Just make sure you keep your were pattern on or someone will rip your heart out before they ask questions.*

She felt a few of the bystanders checking her pattern and she prayed it was still were. Her breath hitched in her lungs until they turned around as if content she was one of them.

But Kylie didn't feel as if she belonged. Her heart ached at knowing Fredericka hadn't been lying. She almost left, but stopped herself. Maybe this wasn't even about Lucas. Maybe Fredericka sent her here hoping she'd see the crowd and believe the lie.

Stiffening her spine, she moved in and stood in the last row. Obviously weres didn't need to sit down, because no seats were provided. Her view of the front was blocked, but that meant people up front couldn't see her, either.

A voice suddenly started speaking, welcoming everyone here. Kylie's chest ached when she recognized the deep tenor.

Not Lucas, but his dad.

Her chest started to burn with the idea of Lucas getting engaged to someone else.

"Tonight I present to you my son and his bride-to-be," Lucas's father said. "You will witness their vows, their promise to each other."

Kylie closed her eyes. As betrayal filled her chest, music filled the dark night. The slow bell-like music was unlike anything Kylie had ever heard.

A young woman, dark hair pinned up with flowers, wearing a long black evening gown, walked down the aisle. The attendees oohed and ahhed over her beauty. Even Kylie couldn't deny it.

The crowd in front of her shifted, and Kylie saw Lucas's father. Standing beside him was . . . Lucas. The air in her lungs shuddered. He wore a dark gray tux that fit his hard frame just perfectly. Tears stung her eyes when she saw him reach out and take his future bride's hands.

The crowd shifted again, and she lost the view, but she could still hear. Words were spoken.

Vows.

Promises.

Lucas Parker gave his soul to Monique. *His soul.*

The sound of Lucas's voice cut into Kylie like a dull knife. She wanted to run, to escape, but to leave now would draw attention.

She waited. Her breath held, and she kept staring directly in front of her. The crowd shifted, and the view opened up again. Not a sound filled the night as Lucas pulled the girl into his arms and kissed her. Kissed her like he'd kissed Kylie.

Her breath caught. Anger and betrayal filled her.

She swung around to escape; not realizing another line had formed behind her, she slammed into someone.

"Sorry," she muttered.

"Kylie?" She heard someone say her name behind her.

She tried to dart around, but suddenly the crowd seemed to close in as everyone started applauding, cheering on the kiss.

"Excuse me," she said, pushing through another line of weres.

"Kylie?"

She heard her name again. And this time, she glanced back and saw Clara moving in.

She darted though the crowd, only to land in the midst of another close-knit group of weres. She looked back one more time. Lucas had his arms around the woman. He looked happy. Genuinely happy.

More than anything, Kylie wanted to disappear, to vanish. Then she realized she could disappear. She wished it, wished it with all her heart. Clara charged through the crowd, stopping beside Kylie. The girl looked around . . . and looked right through Kylie.

"Did you see the blonde that was here just a second ago?" Clara asked.

Kylie inhaled and left. Now, merely a wisp in the air, she took off running.

She didn't look back again. She couldn't.

She was crying when she entered the woods, crying when she left them.

Perhaps this was fate, she told herself. Because now she knew the right thing to do.

When she jumped the fence back into Shadow Falls, she didn't go to her cabin, she went to Hayden's. She didn't know if she was visible until he opened the door and stared at her. At her, not through her.

"What happened?" he asked, sounding urgent.

"Tomorrow." She forced the words through her tight throat. "Tomorrow I'll leave."

He ran a hand a through his mussed hair, sleep still filling his eyes. "We could go now. It would be easier."

"No." She shook her head. "I have to say good-bye."

He frowned. "They won't let you go."

She inhaled a breath of resolve. "They can't stop me."

When she got to her cabin and saw who waited on the front porch, her heart stopped.

She started to run away, but realized running wouldn't accomplish anything.

He still wore the tux, but he'd unbuttoned his shirt and the bow tie was gone. When his blue gaze met hers, regret filled his eyes.

She moved up the steps, and he studied her every move. He could probably tell she'd been crying, but she refused to cry in front of him now.

"Go back, Lucas," she said. "You're missing your own party."

"Don't do this," he growled. "I told you I was doing what I had to, that it didn't mean anything. It doesn't mean anything."

It sure looked as if it meant something. "Well, it should have meant something." *You gave her your soul.* She waved him away from the door. "I'm tired, do you mind?"

"Damn it, Kylie. As soon as I'm on the Council, I'll call off the engagement. I had to do this before my dad would give me his approval for the position. You said you understood."

She bit down on her lip. "How long have you been seeing her?"

He closed his eyes. "Dad's had it planned for a few months. He's been bringing her around, but I haven't—"

"Stop!" She shook her head. "Of all the things I considered you were hiding from me, I never imagined this."

"Try to see this from my point of view," he pleaded.

"I do see it," she said, and God help her, but there was some truth to her words. "You did what you had to do. As hard as it is, I understand that." *Lucas belonged with his pack, his people.*

And so did she.

He reached for her. She stepped back. She couldn't let him touch her. It would hurt too much. She held out her hand. "No."

He shook his head. "Please, don't do this. Damn it!" He swung his fist, closed his eyes and when he opened them, he looked at her. Right at her. "I love you."

Now he told her. Now! She lifted her chin. "I think you vowed your love and soul to Monique tonight."

She darted around him, entered the cabin, and shut him out. Then, leaning against the cold door, she wrapped her arms around herself. Her heart felt swollen, inflamed.

Don't ever fall in love, princess. It hurts too much. Her stepfather's words whispered through her broken heart. He'd been so damn right.

When she heard Lucas leaving, her breath caught.

"He's a piece of wolf shit," Della roared. Kylie looked up. Miranda stood beside Della in the kitchen. Had they heard everything? More tears filled her eyes.

"Sit down." Miranda pulled a chair out. "I'll get you some ice cream."

"No . . . not now." Kylie didn't have any strength to explain or to even talk.

"Tomorrow." She went into her room. Socks looked out at her from under the bed, and then disappeared. Even her cat betrayed her. It was the last straw. Kylie dropped on the bed and cried herself to sleep.

Not that she stayed asleep for long. At four in the morning, Kylie knocked on Miranda's door. "I need to talk to you."

Della had already gotten up and stood by the kitchen table, staring sleepy-eyed and suspicious at Kylie.

When Miranda came out, wearing her duck slippers, she pushed a curtain of hair from her face. "What time is it?"

"Early," Kylie said. "I'm sorry, but . . . I have to talk to both of you." *Make it short and sweet. Short and sweet.* She'd told herself all morning.

She'd tried talking herself out of this, but she couldn't. Leaving Shadow Falls was the right thing to do. But the right thing didn't always feel right. Coming to Shadow Falls had felt wrong, yet it had turned out to be a step toward finding the truth. This was just another step—a needed step.

Someday, Kylie hoped her choices could be made by what she wanted, and not by what she needed. But that time hadn't arrived yet.

"No," Della said.

"No, what?" Miranda asked.

"She's going to tell us she's leaving." Della's eyes filled with emotion.

"No, she's not," Miranda smarted back.

Short and sweet, Kylie thought again. "Della's right. I need to go live with my grandfather for a while. Not forever. I'll be back." God, she hoped so.

Miranda stared, her expression one of disbelief. "You can't do that. What will your mother say?"

"I haven't figured that out. But I will. I just need you guys to understand, and not be mad. And . . ." Tears filled her eyes. "And take care of Socks because he doesn't want to . . . go with me."

"You're leaving us," Miranda said. "You can't leave us. We're roommates, we're best friends."

Della stood there, stoic, tears glistening in her dark eyes, and she swiped away every drip of moisture that slipped from her lashes.

Kylie went to hug Miranda first. The witch started crying and Kylie's heart hurt so much she couldn't breathe. When Kylie turned to Della, the girl held up one hand. Anger flashed in her eyes.

"Oh, hell no," Della screamed. "You're freaking leaving us. I don't hug people who walk out on me." The vamp stormed back into her bedroom. Kylie felt the door slam all the way to her soul and it hurt so damn bad.

She walked into her room, picked up her suitcase, and left, before it got harder. Inside, Kylie felt raw. Sooner or later, it would stop hurting, she told herself.

Derek stood outside her cabin. He looked as if he'd woken up, pulled clothes on without thinking, and came running. His jeans weren't snapped, his shirt unbuttoned.

She wasn't sure how he knew, but he did. She saw it in his green eyes.

"Why?" he asked when she walked up to him.

"Because I have to figure things out."

"But you've already figured a lot out while you've been here."

"I know," Kylie said. "But it's time to take the next step."

He didn't try to talk her out of it. He didn't speak on the walk to the office. But she felt him reading her every emotion. When they arrived at the office, she looked back at him. For some reason she recalled the first time she'd seen him—sitting in the back of the bus, not very happy to be there.

She dropped the suitcase and hugged him. Tight. They had something special. She wasn't sure what it was, or if it should have been more, but she knew she cared about him. Probably always would.

He touched her cheek. He didn't say anything, but that touch said so much. He still loved her.

She picked up her suitcase and walked up on the porch. She left her suitcase by the door, then looked out toward the exit. She'd called Hayden earlier and told him to meet her at four thirty. She suspected he was already here. He didn't seem like the kind of guy who'd be late.

"Holiday." Kylie called out her name when she walked in.

"In the office," Holiday called back. "I just poured you a cup of coffee."

Kylie moved to the door. Holiday sat at her desk, her red hair hanging loose. She looked . . . happy. She wore her love for Burnett very well.

"You're up early . . . again," Holiday said.

Two cups of coffee waited on the desk. Had Holiday known she'd be here? Kylie went and sat in the chair. "How—?"

"Lucas came by late last night," the camp leader confessed.

Kylie swallowed. *Short and sweet.* She didn't want to talk about Lucas right now. "I have to go live with my grandfather for a while. Just until I figure out who I am."

Desperation entered Holiday's gaze. "You can't . . ."

Emotion lumped in Kylie's throat. "I need to figure this out."

"We can figure it out together," Holiday said, but her expression was one of sad acceptance. And it wasn't like Holiday not to fight harder. Unless . . .

Kylie remembered that when Holiday died, she'd spoken with Heidi, Kylie's grandmother. "She told you I had to go, didn't she?" When confusion filled Holiday's eyes, Kylie explained, "Heidi, she told you about this."

"No, not . . ." She paused. "She said I shouldn't stop you from making your own choices."

"And this is my choice." *Damn, it hurt to say that.* "I'll be back. You know that."

Holiday pressed her open palms on the desk. "What am I going to tell your parents?"

Kylie paused. "I'll figure it out and call you."

Holiday exhaled. "Burnett is going to be so furious."

"I know. That's why I was hoping you'd just tell him about this. I don't think I could face him right now."

"I don't like this." Holiday's voice sound so tight.

Tears filled Kylie's eyes and she stood up. "Della wouldn't hug me good-bye. Please don't say you won't."

Holiday bolted up. "I'll hug you for me and Della. And Burnett."

The embrace lasted for several long seconds. "I love you," Holiday said. "And I expect a phone call from you this evening. And every day. Every morning and night."

Kylie nodded. "Thank you for not fighting me on this."

Holiday put a hand on each side of Kylie's face. "Don't think I don't want to."

"But you know it's the right thing?" Kylie asked, hating that she needed a little more confirmation. But damn, should doing the right thing feel so wrong?

Holiday inhaled. "I don't know if it's right. I won't stop you." She frowned. "But I will say this. If this is about what happened with Lucas—"

Kylie inhaled. "This isn't just about him." And it wasn't. He was just the proverbial straw that brought the camel to its knotty knees.

Holiday sighed. "Sometimes, when we're hurting, we make choices we wouldn't normally make."

Kylie shook her head. "Remember how my dad told me that we would work out these things together? I think by 'we' he meant chameleons."

Holiday frowned. "You don't know that's what he meant. You thought he was telling you that you were going to die. Maybe if we went to the falls you might—"

"No, this is right," Kylie said, and there was a part of her that believed it.

Holiday exhaled, her breath shaky. "Then I have to let you go, even if I don't agree."

They hugged again. *Short and sweet.* Kylie walked out.

The dad-blasted blue jay swooped in. More tears filled Kylie's eyes. "Go," she told the bird. "It's time to leave the nest. For both of us."

Turning, she spotted Hayden waiting by the gate. She picked up her suitcase, the same one she'd brought with her to Shadow Falls last June. She started walking and got a few feet from the gate when a sudden whisk of wind, a familiar whisk, flashed past, then stopped.

Della's arms embraced her. "Promise me you'll get your wolf ass back here soon. Promise me, damn it!"

Tears filled Kylie's eyes and she held on to Della extra tight, the way only really good friends do. "I promise," Kylie said. "I promise."

It was a promise Kylie intended to keep, too. Della, obviously another believer in short and sweet, flashed away. Kylie looked back one more time. She saw a crying Miranda with Perry running up from the path into the main clearing; she stopped and just waved. Kylie knew that Miranda had helped convince Della to come. Dear God, she was going to miss her roommates.

Then Kylie's gaze shifted to the office porch. Holiday stood there. But not alone. Burnett stood by her side. Even from this distance, she saw his disapproval, but she also saw how his arm tenderly circled Holiday's waist. A warmth filled Kylie's chest; she'd played a small part in helping that happen. And somehow she sensed that had been part of her destiny.

Suddenly she saw Derek standing to the side of the office. He met her gaze and smiled.

If she wasn't hurting so much, she would have smiled back. Right before she went to turn away, she felt another presence. Felt it, didn't see. Somewhere behind the first line of trees, a certain blue-eyed were watched. He was hurting, but so was she.

She turned toward the gate. Hayden had come closer. "You ready?" he asked.

No, her heart said, but her head said yes. She didn't know what awaited her at her grandfather's, but nothing, nothing would take the place of Shadow Falls.

"It's hard to say good-bye," Hayden said.

"I'll be back," Kylie said. "I swear I will."

And she wanted to believe that more than anything, too.